I0563279

For D.B.

Editor, mentor and friend
Brilliant at all three

LIGHT & SHADOW AT PEMBERLEY

A Sequel to Pride and Prejudice

Lee F. Elliott

PART I

CHAPTER 1

*L*ady Catherine de Bourgh was rich, highborn, and mistress of the fine country seat of Rosings in Kent but in spite of these blessings of fortune, she was known to all her friends as a disappointed woman. Her favorite nephew, a man of wealth and excellent abilities, had disobliged her by his marriage to a most unsuitable young lady. This was the more distressing as Lady Catherine had for many years looked forward to Mr. Darcy's alliance with her own daughter, the heiress to Rosings. That her Anne, the delicately nurtured child of a distinguished and ancient family, should be overlooked in favor of a Miss Elizabeth Bennet without birth or fortune to recommend her, filled her ladyship with unremitting grief.

On a day in early June, she said to her friend and confidant Lady Metcalf, "I do not know how to endure this unkindness and ingratitude on the part of my nephew. He was always my favorite and now I shall never see him again!"

"Dear Lady Catherine, is the young lady so very unacceptable? I have heard that her father is a gentleman and very learned, although on the mother's side there is an uncle engaged in trade."

"In trade and resides in Cheapside!" said her ladyship with bitter disgust, "All the world must know by now that Darcy has married beneath himself. Yes, the father may be considered a gentleman, but the family has no true distinction. And how could a girl with no special claim to beauty or accomplishment ensnare a man so far above her? It is incomprehensible!"

Lady Metcalf could not resist asking, "How is your dear child, Miss de Bourgh? I suppose that she must feel this desertion most acutely. Were they not engaged these many years?"

"The marriage was expected, of course, and it was the dearest wish of all the family. When Darcy was born, his mother and I stood by his cradle and I pledged that should I ever be blessed with a daughter, the two would be destined to marry. Then, when my Anne was born four years later the understanding was renewed."

"This must be a sad time indeed for Miss de Bourgh," said Lady Metcalf sympathetically.

"Well, my daughter is not so weak-minded and sentimental as to give way to lamentations and regrets," said Lady Catherine, "She has maintained an air of complete indifference to Darcy's marriage, which is just what one would expect from one of her noble descent."

Since the failure of Lady Catherine's matrimonial plans for her daughter, there had been much speculation in that small corner of Kent. Would her ladyship search out another suitor for Anne de Bourgh, or would the young lady remain a spinster for the rest of her days? True, she was a great heiress, but so very plain, so dull, so completely without wit or conversation that even wealth might not secure an eligible match. And what gentleman would be inclined to take a wife who was always in delicate health and prone to serious indisposition? When there were no more interesting topics to hand, this question was often canvassed among Lady Catherine's friends and neighbors.

Had Lady Catherine found solace in the commiseration of her relations she might have endured her disappointment with greater stoicism. They, however, proved to be traitors, and far from echoing her disapprobation were loud in their praise of her ladyship's new niece. The young Mrs. Darcy had become the favorite of London society upon the couple's return from their wedding trip. To Lady Catherine's annoyance, not a day passed without a letter from some unfeeling correspondent, full of accounts of Elizabeth's wit and beauty and of Darcy's happiness. The grandeur of Rosings had taken on a melancholy aspect as its mistress brooded on the death of her dearest hopes, with only her daughter, always in uncertain health, and Anne's governess Mrs. Jenkinson for company.

It should not be imagined that the Darcys, in the first full bloom of their domestic felicity, had forgotten what was due to their aunt. Several letters arrived at Rosings from both Darcy and Elizabeth filled with a respectful and sincere desire for reconciliation. Would Lady Catherine honor them with a visit to Pemberley whenever it might suit her convenience? All Mr. Darcy's plans for autumn shooting in Scotland were put in abeyance until she should name a date. This overture met with only a cold reply, citing the demands on Lady Catherine's time and the fragile state of Anne's health. Return post brought a proposal from Darcy that he and his wife should wait upon his aunt at any time that she might name. The answer to this suggestion strained the bounds of the most ordinary courtesy. Lady Catherine did not put herself to the trouble of responding to her nephew's request, confining herself to commonplace remarks on the state of the weather and the roads, and forbearing even to mention Elizabeth's name. The correspondence devolved into a mostly one-sided affair with an occasional letter arriving from London.

With its mistress in her present state of mind, it may be imagined that Rosings was not an agreeable place, even for the more regular visitors to the house. Lady Catherine depended on a steady flow of friends and relations in order to exercise her genius, which extended into many unexpected directions. There was no field of endeavor in which the lady was not willing to venture an opinion, from the mastery of the piano, which she had never had time to learn, to the cultivation of gooseberries. Her friends usually bore with her often ill-judged and determined advice on every aspect of their lives because of the superb hospitality at Rosings. An hour's lecture on the design of closet shelves or the proper maintenance of carriage wheels was not too much to endure for such comforts, such excellent dinners and claret, as were to be found there. So famous had Lady Catherine's state of gloomy resentment become, however, that regrets poured in as the usual annual visits were cancelled.

On that June day, after Lady Metcalf's carriage vanished around a curve of the long drive of Rosings, Lady Catherine retired to her bedchamber to spend an hour reading the latest novel, as was her custom. She sighed heavily as she settled herself on her chaise longue, reflecting on the death of her most treasured idea, of seeing her daughter well and richly married to Fitzwilliam Darcy. Then she shrugged and opened her book, and after a while fell asleep.

Her ladyship, so confident that she *knew all*, could not have imagined that under her very roof, in another wing of the house, a revolution of the most shocking nature was underway.

Anne de Bourgh, supposed by her mother to be resting in bed like a proper invalid, was at that moment lacing a pair of stout half boots, with quick and practiced motions. Her bedchamber was almost as splendid as her ladyship's, with elegant furnishings and a bookcase overflowing with hundreds of books. In one corner was a fine Cheval glass, generally ignored by Anne who disliked looking at herself in a mirror.

Her task completed, the young lady jumped up from her armchair and began to pace around the room, looking at the door frequently as if expecting someone. Anne was of middle height, but so slender as to appear smaller than she really was, and almost fragile. Most of the time she walked with slumped shoulders and an air of timidity that confirmed her insignificance to those who bothered to notice her. Now, however, she moved with an active grace, her shoulders thrown back as if ready for any challenge. Her delicate face, usually so pale and expressionless, was full of animation and her large gray eyes were brilliant. Her mother would hardly have recognized her.

The door opened and a lady of about forty with a gentle, refined countenance entered in some haste. "Oh, Miss Anne, Mary has just made certain that your mama is in her bedchamber taking her ease as usual at this hour. I suppose that you may risk going out of doors for a brief time, but I do so worry while you are gone. I fear every moment that Lady Catherine may ask for you."

"That's hardly likely, Mrs. Jenkinson," replied Anne, with an ironic smile, "As you know, my mother has very little interest in seeking out my company. She tolerates my presence at meals but otherwise is quite content to ignore me."

She went over to the older woman and kissed her affectionately on the cheek, saying, "In any case, I'll return within the hour. Do not distress yourself."

As the young lady dashed out the door, she turned and added, "Besides, as you know, I must get out of the house or *go mad*."

Rosings was a large, rambling mansion with several staircases and it was by the most inconspicuous of these that Anne made her escape. This route took her through a back door and across the stable yard, from which it was a short distance to the woods by way of an extensive shrubbery. She encountered a few of the servants as she rushed towards the sanctuary of the trees, but they were her old friends and would not betray her to Lady Catherine.

The park was famous for its ancient oak grove, which had become Anne's favorite haunt. She felt safe there, knowing that she could not be found unless she wished to be. There was a footpath that led to the river, edged with ferns and wildflowers that shimmered in the dappled afternoon light. When Anne reached this point she quickened her pace, and as she did so, impatiently pulled the hairpins from her tightly wound hair, which then fell in thick waves across her back, very beautiful and the color of ripe wheat shining in autumn sunlight. Her mother, of course, disliked Anne's hair and always insisted that it be confined in the most unbecoming style.

Anne glanced at the small watch at her waist and then, with considerable agility began to run, not as though pressed for time but with an air of joyful exuberance, jumping over the various tree roots and rocks that characterized sections of the pathway. After about five minutes, she arrived at the riverbank and sat down on a large boulder in the sun that served as a convenient seat. An hour passed during which Anne was perfectly quiet, listening and observing, hearing every bird, looking down at the surface of the water for the insects and fish and amphibians that fascinated her. A pilgrim in a great cathedral could not have displayed more reverent attention than did Anne in her sacred realm of woods and river.

The light began to change and her seat was abruptly in the shade.

She was so familiar with the way the sunlight traversed the river as the day grew long that she did not need to look at her watch; it was past time to hurry back to Rosings and her captivity. Had she not been of a stoical disposition, Anne would have left her beloved retreat with tears, but as it was she squared her shoulders and walked resolutely in the direction of her mother's house.

~

ONE WEEK LATER, Lady Catherine was to be found in the handsome drawing room at Rosings with the only beneficiaries of her wisdom, Mr. Collins, rector of Hunsford, and his wife, the former Miss Charlotte Lucas. The young couple always accepted her ladyship's invitations with humble gratitude. As dependents on Lady Catherine's patronage, they were awarded the least degree of consideration compatible with good breeding by their hostess, who considered their presence as *faute de mieux* in the absence of her social equals. There was consolation in the fact, however, that Mrs. Collins had only four months earlier been delivered of a son, opening up new possibilities for the display of Lady Catherine's sagacity.

"My dear Mrs. Collins, it is imperative that you confine the child's evening meal to a little porridge in warm milk, after which you must send him away with his nurse for the night, however much he may scream. Early discipline in this way will avoid the weakness and self-indulgence in later life that is so much to be deplored."

Mrs. Collins, who had no intention of allowing her darling to know a moment's want, murmured her acquiescence. Having rooted out Lady Catherine's spies from her household during the previous year, she now enjoyed the pursuit of her own method of domestic economy, even venturing to purchase an entire leg of lamb for Sunday dinner on occasion.

Having completed Mrs. Collin's tuition for the day, Lady Catherine turned to a more important topic.

"Mr. Collins, you will be pleased to learn that my nephew, Colonel Fitzwilliam, will arrive Tuesday next and will no doubt stay for a least a fortnight. It is a misfortune that my other guests have been prevented, but I must do what I can for his entertainment with what poor means are at my disposal. Of course you and Mrs. Collins will come for dinner Wednesday next."

Mr. Collins' pleasure at this gracious invitation was evident in his stammered thanks, after which he found the presence of mind to inquire after Miss de Bourgh.

"I had hoped, your ladyship, that Mrs. Collins and I would have the infinite honor of Miss de Bourgh's company at tea this afternoon."

"Alas, Mr. Collins," replied Lady Catherine, "My daughter came downstairs earlier today and even expressed a desire to walk in the garden with Mrs. Jenkinson. She wished to observe some unusual type of butterfly that is common at this time in the summer. She is so clever that I doubt she has her equal in the entire country. She strongly resembles me in this way, as in many others. If only my child enjoyed my excellent health! I had to forbid her excursion out of doors as I noticed that she was somewhat pale."

This subject having been so quickly exhausted, the company fell silent for a moment. Presently, Lady Catherine, sounding most unlike her usual overbearing self, said in a low, bitter tone of voice, "Of course, Darcy should have been here this month and is no doubt sadly disappointed to be prevented. He must now regret falling prey to a young woman of no breeding who has separated him from his family."

It was hardly appropriate that Lady Catherine had formed the habit of speaking so freely of a family contretemps to a young couple who were her social inferiors and dependent on her largess. But Elizabeth's supposed treachery had become her monomania and she was unable to resist any opportunity to express her sense of outrage.

Mrs. Collins flushed and looked down at her hands in an agony of indecision. Elizabeth Darcy was her oldest and dearest friend. How many times had she wished to defend her and object to lady Catherine's abusive remarks. Almost daily fate provided an opening for her to prove her loyalty to Elizabeth, and every opportunity found her courage unequal to the task. The moment passed and she said nothing. The conversation turned to parish matters and Lady Catherine displayed an exact knowledge of the personal affairs of all the inhabitants for several miles around – and a perfect willingness to set these affairs to rights, if only her advice were followed.

The weather being fine, the Collinses walked home through the park, following a pleasant route through the grove of oaks. Mr. Collins droned on in his usual fashion about her ladyship's kind condescension, which by now Charlotte could intersperse with appropriate murmurs of agreement, while paying her husband not the slightest attention. She was vexed with herself for not challenging Lady Catherine's calumnies against her friend. But, as she had told herself on similar occasions, such a patroness would be essential to the success of her darling little Henry, now at home asleep in his crib. This was a convenient reflection, but the truth was that Charlotte was afraid of Lady Catherine and had gradually assumed her husband's air of servility.

Mr. Collins' eloquence was soon exhausted and his wife ventured a question on a new subject.

"How strange it is that we see so little of Miss de Bourgh. It must be very dull for a young person to be always at home without any society other than that of her mother and Mrs. Jenkinson. Tell me, Mr. Collins, have you ever heard what the nature of Miss de Bourgh's infirmity might be? Is there a serious illness or mere general delicacy of health?"

"Why as to that, my dear, Lady Catherine was so condescending as to confide in me that her daughter has no particular ailment, nothing so much as a susceptibility to ill health against which her ladyship has made it her life's work to guard the young lady. And she has been so successful in this endeavor that she is able to note with pride that Miss de Bourgh has never been afflicted by a significant illness."

"Of course," he continued, "Society has suffered an irredeemable loss by the necessity of preventing the young lady's entry into the world at large."

This was old ground and Mrs. Collins sighed. While acknowledging to herself the futility of introducing a new idea to the familiar discourse, she asked, "I have often heard you say as much, William, but how have you become convinced of Miss de Bourgh's amiability and accomplishments? For myself, I have hardly ever known her to open her mouth, and she has certainly never taken part in conversation, in my experience at least."

Mr. Collins stopped dead in the middle of the path, aghast at his wife's irreverence. He looked about as if expecting the gods of the oak grove to rain down wrathful thunderbolts at such heretical remarks.

"Good heavens, Mrs. Collins! Who would have thought you to have so little discernment and understanding of true refinement! Certainly the young lady does not rattle on like so many of her sex. Her demeanor is at all times the model of quiet dignity befitting her high station in life. She adds to the pleasure of any gathering by her mere presence. I am shocked to hear you express such absurd ideas."

Charlotte had to admit to herself that she had been absurd. To attempt a rational conversation with her husband, with whose limitations she was by now so familiar, was to be foolish indeed. She said no more but wondered if Miss de Bourgh could really be so dull and spiritless as she appeared in company. The young lady honored the parsonage with a brief visit now and then, but never stayed for more than a few minutes and had nothing to offer beyond the most commonplace remarks. Occasionally Charlotte had made forays in the direction of engaging Anne's interest with some topic, and once or twice she had seemed to respond. Unfortunately Lady Catherine had been present and had interrupted them almost immediately, calling Mrs. Collins' attention away in her usual imperious manner. Charlotte had given up, although she still observed the silent girl at times with a mixture of pity and curiosity. But the enigma of Miss de Bourgh did not engage her mind for long today, as the parsonage, containing the world's only truly important inhabitant, came into view and she hurried to return to the nursery.

CHAPTER 2

$\mathcal{T}$he morning of the following Tuesday found Anne at work on a watercolor of a bouquet of wildflowers that she had picked that morning, going out at dawn to avoid her mother's observation. A library table had been placed next to a large window of the bedchamber and here Anne spent many hours reading, writing or drawing. There were many piles of books both on the table and overflowing onto the turkey carpet and these volumes represented diverse subjects, most prominently natural philosophy.

Anne had just mixed the very color of the flower she was depicting when Mrs. Jenkinson entered the room. The older lady came over to regard the painting in progress and said, "Why Anne, that is lovely! You do so very well. And are not those Forget-me-Nots?"

Anne smiled up at her friend and replied, "They are 'Forget-me-Nots' or at least my sad attempt at *Myrtensia avensis*." The young lady studied her watercolor and said, "I suppose that for one self-taught, it might be worse."

Mrs. Jenkinson sat down in a chair at Anne's side, saying, "How I wish I had been able to teach you – and the piano as well." She shook her head and added, "Your mama should have engaged a more accomplished governess all those years ago."

"Oh, never say that!" cried Anne, "You have been my best teacher and dearest friend all these fifteen years. I could not have endured my life without your kindness and understanding. You know me better than anyone, and as far as I can tell, care for me much more than anyone in my family."

They were silent for a moment and then Mrs. Jenkinson said, "Your cousin the colonel should be here by early afternoon. You will, I hope, greet him when he arrives. I'm sure he is very fond of you."

Anne shrugged and replied, "I see no reason to do so. I'll send word to Mama that I am indisposed. As for Fitzwilliam being fond of me, I don't think he has remembered my existence for years. I am only the pathetic invalid in the corner as far as he is concerned."

Mrs. Jenkinson hesitated and then said, 'Could you not confide in him? He seems such a good young man."

Anne's expression was disdainful as she answered, "How can I trust him – or anyone but you and the servants. He would tell mama and then I would be a prisoner indeed."

ON THE FOLLOWING Tuesday the village of Hunsford was favored with the sight of Colonel Fitzwilliam making his way to Rosings on a fine black horse. The day was fair and he had instructed his servant to follow with his carriage. As the second son of an earl, Fitzwilliam considered himself a poor man with his way to make in the world, but he was never without the appurtenances of a gentleman of rank and was the very epitome of an admirable young officer. He was a credit to his family and his regiment, always doing his duty with great energy and ability. He had seen much of the world and had made good use of his opportunities. Though not a scholar, he was well read and could talk sensibly on many subjects. His taste in the arts was particularly fine, and he was often consulted by his friends on such matters. He was brave, an excellent horseman and had even had the foresight to be moderately handsome. But his best quality was the one that became known to others only after closer acquaintance: he had a kind and understanding heart. It was this last that made him the beloved friend of his cousin Darcy.

The colonel entered his aunt's house with all the freedom of an old resident. The butler, delighted to see his mistress' good-natured nephew bring some life into the now dreary house, directed him to the formal gardens where her ladyship was explaining some finer points of cultivation to the head gardener. As he went in search of his aunt, Fitzwilliam wondered if he would encounter his cousin Anne that day. On many of his visits he barely saw her, as she would be confined to her room for some unspecified illness.

A short walk in the brilliant June sunshine brought him the sight of his aunt engaged in earnest conference with Edwards, her head gardener of many years. Even from some distance, Fitzwilliam could see that Lady Catherine seemed a bit agitated. Edwards, however, exhibited his usual sang-froid: he was one of the few people not in awe of Lady Catherine and he preserved an impenetrable dignity in the face of her worst attacks.

The cause of the present unpleasantness was the gardener's failure to prune certain shrubs to her ladyship's satisfaction. The question of pruning often prompted their most serious disagreements. Lady Catherine believed that shrubs of all kinds were incipient revolution-aries, kept from insurrection only by the most severe measures. She had been lecturing Edwards for several minutes when Fitzwilliam joined them.

"How dare you ignore my explicit instructions regarding that line of hydrangeas," cried the lady, flushed with rage, "I told you last week that I would not tolerate such an undisciplined, wild display of foliage."

Edwards stood blinking in the sunlight, apparently quite unper-turbed. His minions, engaged in some major reworking of a flowerbed nearby, were pretending not to hear the altercation.

The man replied with an air of resigned patience that any pruning undertaken at this juncture would remove the buds that would be flowering in a few weeks' time.

"Well, then you should have done it before. Who was ever driven to distraction by a stubborn mule like you!"

This was Edward's cue to bring out his heavy artillery, "As I was never one to stay where I was not wanted, I'll be glad to relieve your ladyship of my presence and go down the road to Lord Dumbello's. He's that eager to have me. Just the other week he said as how there was no one like me for roses, and that I could name my own terms too."

"Go then, you miserable man," cried Lady Catherine, quite beside herself, "Go and shorten Lord Dumbello's life with the aggravation you always cause."

Fitzwilliam was not at all surprised to witness this contentious scene. He had watched this sort of feud with Edwards for some twenty years and thought that his aunt secretly rather enjoyed such exchanges as adding some dramatic interest to the otherwise routine existence at Rosings. Now Fitzwilliam saw that Lady Catherine's anger was all too genuine; since her disappointment in Darcy's marriage she had lost pleasure in everything.

The lady finally became aware of the colonel, now standing at her side and regarding her with an expression of great concern. He had never seen her looking so unwell and so much her actual age.

"My dear aunt," Fitzwilliam began, "How glad I am to see you, but I am distressed to find you in such a state of agitation. It cannot be good for you to be here in this hot sun."

Lady Catherine was overjoyed to see Fitzwilliam, both for his own sake, and as a reminder of the happier days when he had come to Rosings with Darcy, as recently as a year ago. She accepted his arm and they returned to the house, where the colonel was insistent upon her taking a cool drink and resting for a while on the shaded terrace where there was a pleasant breeze.

Fitzwilliam was a lively, agreeable and interesting young man who was in demand at many country houses where there were more amusing occupations and company than could now be found at Rosings, but he still found time to visit his opinionated and difficult aunt. He was genuinely fond of Lady Catherine and valued the better qualities of her character that were commonly overlooked by those who feared her or who only saw her as overbearing and imperious. He had observed that her tendency to interfere in the affairs of others was motivated by a real if misguided desire to do good and that she was capable of true generosity. He even had the capacity to be grateful for her many kindnesses to him when he was a boy.

He soon persuaded his aunt to retire to her chamber to rest for the remainder of the afternoon. Even after he had settled into his familiar quarters, it was still a beautiful summer day with several hours before he had to dress for dinner, and the colonel decided to walk in the park.

Anne was already at large in her favorite woods. She had seen Fitzwilliam riding up to the front door of Rosings from the window of her bedchamber and had felt a strange mixture of joy and unhappiness. Her cousin was here at last after so many long months. She admired his tall, lithe figure and his countenance that was so distinguished by a lively intelligence and a genuine kindness. How well he rode! What a fine bearing he had on horseback. Even Darcy was not his equal. It had been her impulse to go downstairs to see her cousin, but that would never do. He would greet her kindly enough but then barely speak to her the rest of his stay. Dwelling on this probability made Anne so restless and wretched that she at once ran off into the woods after making sure that the way was clear.

Fitzwilliam's favorite path led to the grove of oaks which lay in the direction of the parsonage, and here he shortly found himself after a ramble through a meadow filled with wildflowers. He smiled to himself as he remembered how his cousin Darcy had spent many hours haunting the grove in the hope of encountering Miss Elizabeth Bennet. Only Fitzwilliam had been acute enough to perceive his friend's passionate attachment to the lady. Only he had been aware of the distress Darcy had felt at her refusal of his first proposal, and had observed the gradual change for the better that this disappointment had initiated in his cousin. And after so many months of uncertainty and unhappiness, how felicitous was the outcome of all of Darcy's struggles! Fitzwilliam fervently hoped that he would find the same joy in marriage that his cousin now enjoyed.

He was deep in these reflections, leaning against a huge oak and gazing out at the distant hills that were suffused with the golden light of a late summer afternoon, when, in the corner of his eye, he caught sight of a flash of color that did not properly belong to the green shade of the grove. Turning he saw a slight figure in blue dashing along with startling agility over the moss covered ground. To his astonishment he recognized his cousin Anne. For a moment he doubted his senses, but even at some distance, there was no mistaking the small, almost childlike figure with the familiar dark gold hair. Fitzwilliam stood as if fixed to the spot, attempting to comprehend this astonishing vision of his invalid cousin. Then curiosity brought him back to active life and he determined to follow her.

He traced the path that she had appeared to take towards higher ground. The largest, most venerable oaks lay in that direction and he wandered for some time without finding any sign of Anne. The branches of the trees bent very near to the floor of the grove and curved in massive shapes, making it difficult to see any great distance. So it was that Fitzwilliam came across his cousin with an abruptness that startled them both. Anne was sitting in the crook of one of the longer branches, perched a good six feet above the ground. She was deeply absorbed in a book and did not hear his approach across the soft moss. She became aware of him, lost her balance, and fell from her retreat with a cry of surprise. It was just enough of a height that a fall might have caused at least slight injuries, but with the quick reflexes of a military man, he was able to catch her and place her safely on the ground.

Anne took only a moment to recover from her sudden descent from the tree and then looked up at Fitzwilliam with an expression of mingled confusion and pleasure.

"Oh, you are out walking! I never thought to see you here – surely you are fatigued from your journey." She paused not knowing what to say further and then continued shyly, "I am so happy to see you, cousin. How long it has been since your last visit. Why, it was before Darcy's wedding."

Fitzwilliam could hardly credit that this really was Anne de Bourgh, so different were her appearance and manner from the last time he had seen her. He was also feeling confused, a rare state for the poised young officer. The year before his cousin had been a silent and melancholy figure who was deemed too frail to undertake more than an occasional short ride in her pony cart. "Well, I don't really get fatigued, if you remember, Anne, and I was eager to see the woods again," was all that he could think of to say.

He was about to ask for an explanation for the young lady's seemingly unbelievable alteration, when Anne cried, "Oh heavens, what o'clock is it, Fitzwilliam?"

"It's nearly half past four," he replied after taking out his pocket watch.

"So late! I must hurry," and Anne began to run off with as much alacrity as she had shown earlier, but after a few steps she turned and said, "Please do not let anyone know you have seen me out-of-doors. It would be dreadful if Mama should find out!"

Without waiting for a reply she left in a great hurry and Fitzwilliam was left alone in the grove. He bent to pick up the volume that had fallen out of the tree with Anne. It was *"The Natural History and Antiquities of Selborne."* He had expected to find *"Cecilia"* or *"The Mysteries of Udolfo"*, and her choice of reading matter added further to his surprise. The colonel walked back to the house and readied himself for dinner with a new enthusiasm for what he had thought would be a rather dull visit to Rosings.

When Anne regained her bedchamber she found Mrs. Jenkinson there, working at her embroidery. That lady was alarmed when the Anne threw herself into an armchair and cried, "Oh, something most terrible has occurred! What a disaster!"

When the account had been given, Mrs. Jenkinson said, "Well, the colonel is an honorable gentleman and if you asked him not to tell Lady Catherine that you were in the woods, he will keep your confidence. That is my opinion, at any rate, so do not distress yourself, my dear. However I do think that you owe him an explanation at some point."

Anne was still shaken by her encounter with her cousin. Her mother could be a terror and it was dreadful to imagine the parental reaction to her child's disobedience. "I won't go down to dinner tonight, dear Mrs. Jenkinson, if you will make my excuse as to ill health. I am afraid that I would give everything away if I had to see Fitzwilliam this evening and try to pretend it's for the first time.

FITZWILLIAM ENTERED the drawing room hoping for a conversation with Anne and was disappointed to find that only Lady Catherine was present.

"My dear Anne is not well this evening, and is forced to sup in her room. She is quite fatigued as she so often is. She sends her apologies to you, Fitzwilliam, and hopes that she will be better able to greet you tomorrow."

The young man reflected that Anne had looked very well indeed just a few hours ago, but he kept silent on that subject. Nothing would have induced him to betray his cousin's secret.

Dinner was not a lively affair. Fitzwilliam was unable to remember an occasion when he had dined alone with his aunt at Rosings. The house was often full of guests, drawn there by the generous hospitality that Lady Catherine's wealth could supply. The colonel tried to engage his aunt's interest in several topics, with some degree of success, as he enjoyed the gift of pleasing his company, wherever he might be. By the time they returned to the drawing room, her mood was greatly improved. Fitzwilliam disliked undoing the good effects of a pleasant meal by introducing an unwelcome subject, but now he had a duty to perform and nothing could shake his determination to fulfill it. He had seen Darcy and Elizabeth before leaving town and had been requested to bring their wishes for reconciliation to Lady Catherine. Of course, Fitzwilliam knew quite well how this communication would be received, but was resolved to try the role of peacemaker in any case.

His aunt's features, which had softened into more agreeable lines over the course of the evening, assumed their former rigidity as soon as the names of the miscreants were mentioned. A man with less courage than the colonel would have abandoned the project, but he soldiered on, even daring to describe the happiness of the young couple and their desire that the breach in the family be healed. His reward for these efforts was a torrent of abuse against his friends and a command that their names never be heard again in her presence.

"Indeed, Aunt, I cannot promise to do that," replied Fitzwilliam, "I cannot see such an unfortunate rift in my family without trying to bring about a *rapprochement*."

To this Lady Catherine made no reply, but rose and left the room with the air of frigid disdain that she was so well able to assume. After a moment she seemed to reconsider, for to Fitzwilliam's surprise, she returned and taking his hand said, "I know your good heart, dear nephew, and know that you mean well. Never think that I do not value you at your true worth."

Then Fitzwilliam was left alone to stroll on the terrace in the twilight, where the view of the meadows, touched with a rising mist, was lovely. He would never have imagined that his first day at Rosings would offer so much interest. More than anything the colonel loved a mystery but that his cousin Anne should provide him with one was a surprise indeed.

CHAPTER 3

*I*t is a misfortune that some of our most profound philosophers confine themselves to living quietly in the more obscure corners of the kingdom, their valuable insights into the human condition never brought to the notice of a world so sadly in want of such wisdom. An example of such a deep but unheralded thinker was Mrs. Collins of Hunsford parsonage. Having married for a comfortable establishment and an assured income rather than out of love or respect for her husband, she had made the best of her bargain with a truly stoical resignation and a determination to be unaffected by what was disagreeable in her situation. To the foolishness of Mr. Collins and the officious interference of Lady Catherine, she paid as little attention as she did to changes in the weather. And now she had the reward for all her patience in her darling child, a consolation for the absence of any sympathetic friend, such as Elizabeth Bennet had been.

When Colonel Fitzwilliam came to call upon the Collinses on the morning after his arrival, he found the lady in her favorite small sitting room overlooking the garden at the back of the parsonage. The infant Henry lay in his crib in the morning sunlight, and his soft cooing mingled with the humming of the bees in Mr. Collins' flowerbeds. Fitzwilliam had to admit to himself that it was a pleasure to find the intelligent, well-bred Mrs. Collins alone, and to be spared the vicar's effusive complements.

The colonel, knowing what was expected of him, said all that was proper in praise of the little boy. Taking Henry in his arms and holding him aloft, he declared, "What a fine fellow! Upon my word, Mrs. Collins, he is the handsomest child I've ever beheld. And what a look of extraordinary intelligence there is about him!"

Charlotte had always found Colonel Fitzwilliam to be a kind and agreeable gentleman, but now she realized that she had never before appreciated the extent of his good judgment and perspicacity. She was happy to furnish him with all the particulars as to Henry's many accomplishments during his first four months. When this subject was temporarily exhausted, she asked the colonel to take a chair and tell her the news of London.

"Our dear friends send you their love, of course, and wish me to say how they long to see you and to meet little Henry. They would certainly be here now, if it were possible, but I need not explain what it is that prevents them."

"I have not seen Elizabeth since her marriage," said Charlotte, with a sigh, "You can imagine what a loss it is to me, Colonel Fitzwilliam. Do you foresee any change in the present state of affairs?"

"Perhaps I am too sanguine, but I do believe that there will be a reconciliation. My aunt, for all her anger and resentment, has enough sense to see that she must accept a marriage that is acclaimed by all her friends to be a source of joy rather than regret. Also, I am sure that she is curious to see her nephew and her new niece and observe Mrs. Darcy in her role as an ornament of the fashionable world. This curiosity alone will persuade her eventually to forsake her present animus."

"You give me hope that my friend will be restored to me," cried Charlotte, "I pray that it will not be long before this joyous event takes place."

"I will mention one concern," continued the colonel, "I am afraid that my aunt's health is being affected by her self-imposed isolation. I have never seen her anything but vigorous and active, but on this visit to Rosings, I find a much older woman, more frail in mind and body. I will take this opportunity to ask you, Mrs. Collins, to send word to me if you observe any worsening of her health."

Charlotte replied that she had seen the same changes in her ladyship, and promised to do as Fitzwilliam requested.

The colonel took his leave, expressing his satisfaction at the prospect of seeing Mr. and Mrs. Collins at dinner that evening. He had come to the parsonage with half a mind to ask Mrs. Collins about Anne, not revealing what he had discovered the day before, but hoping to learn whether the lady who was Anne's nearest neighbor had made any progress in knowing his cousin better. On reflection, however, he thought it best to trust to his own observation.

After her guest's departure, Charlotte was gratified by the arrival of a letter from Elizabeth, who had continued to correspond faithfully with her old friend. Mr. Collins did not show much interest in these communications, as they proceeded from the pen of one who had had the temerity to offend his patroness. This was just as well, thought Charlotte.

My dearest Charlotte,

I hope that you are well and that darling Henry is as happy and blooming as you described him in your last letter. How we long to see him, for I am sure that there is not his equal in the whole country! But, as you know, we are exiles from the neighborhood of Rosings. I look forward to the day when Henry can travel and you can come to us at Pemberley.

Although we had planned to stay in London another month, Darcy and I were impatient to return to the country, and we are now at home! So you must write to me here at Pemberley. I was so happy to see this beautiful place again. The only thing I miss about London is the pleasure of attending concerts, something that we enjoyed almost every evening. You know that I have always been fond of music, and now that I've been so fortunate as to attend the best performances, it has become a passion. On our last night in town we heard the most wonderful concerto by Hummel – so glorious that I cannot stop thinking about it. Was it not clever of me, dear Charlotte, to fall in love with a man with the means to indulge my excellent taste in the arts? Mr. Darcy is standing at my shoulder, watching me write this, and so I must provoke him if I can.

When we arrived here, almost the first thing we did was go into the music room and there was a magnificent pianoforte, in addition to the one my darling husband gave to Georgiana last year. Darcy says that he expects to have the pleasure of hearing us play duets when she returns to us in the autumn. As you will recall, Georgiana is paying a long visit to her dearest friend, with whom she attended school for some years.

By now you must have seen our good friend Colonel Fitzwilliam. Darcy was unkind enough to ask the poor man to intervene on our behalf with Lady Catherine. I think that if my dear husband wished to see Fitzwilliam come to a violent end, he would have done better to send him on an expedition to pacify the South Sea islanders. At least he would have had the satisfaction of dying for the glory of his country instead of ignominiously in Kent. But the colonel is a courageous man and went off on his mission with such a brave spirit. Lady Catherine, as you know, wrote a remarkably abusive letter to Darcy at the time of our marriage. He has never allowed me to see it, and I believe he actually burned it, which is no doubt best for the continuance of family feeling.

That is all my news. We will go to Scotland in August, to Lord Munford's castle in the western Highlands for the shooting. Such a long journey! But we will break up our trip into stages, staying with Darcy's relations on the way. We are particularly looking forward to seeing one of his old school friends, a Mr. Grey, who has been out of the country for some years. Of course Colonel Fitzwilliam will be at his father's, as will other friends whose company we have enjoyed here in London.

Please kiss little Henry for me. I send my dearest love, and hope for an early reunion with my Charlotte.

Yours as ever,

Lizzie

Mrs. Collins read this letter without the slightest degree of envy for her friend's rich and fashionable life. She had only to look over at her child to feel that she had all that she could wish for.

In a moment she heard her husband enter the house with the usual amount of noise and confusion. He hurried into the sitting room still attired for trout fishing, which had become his favorite occupation when he was not taken up with parish business. Lady Catherine had recommended the pastime as a remedy for the nervous exhaustion to which he might be in danger of succumbing due to the heavy demands of his profession. On this day at least, he had managed to be as clever as the trout. Opening his creel, he produced a handsome fish, thrusting it towards Mrs. Collins for her closer admiration. Predictably, it slipped from his grasp and the couple were soon on the floor, trying to retrieve the trout from under the table. Charlotte eventually emerged, fish in hand, as her husband cried, "Oh, Mrs. Collins, Mrs. Collins, how can you be so clumsy!"

CHAPTER 4

*C*olonel Fitzwilliam was a keen observer of human nature, and could find some degree of interest in any gathering, however unpromising it might seem. With the social circle now so limited at Rosings, he did not anticipate a very lively evening, but he was eager to see his cousin Anne again. Lady Catherine had assured him that her daughter was much improved and would be present.

He entered the drawing room to find the rest of the company already assembled. Apparently Mr. Collins, in his eagerness to show his respect for her ladyship, was often early. Fitzwilliam greeted all those present with his usual good- natured affability and was particularly attentive to his cousin, who, while perfectly polite, barely looked at him.

The colonel had little expectation of brilliant conversation and therefore was not disappointed by the rather spiritless company in which he found himself. He made several attempts to draw out Mrs. Collins and eventually discovered that they shared an interest in poetry. Charlotte expressed great admiration for Cowper's work and Fitzwilliam was quick to echo her enthusiasm. The colonel all this time was watching Anne acutely, something he had seldom troubled himself to do for many years. At the mention of poetry her color was heightened and her large grey eyes seemed to shine with unusual interest, but she did not venture an opinion.

"Cousin Anne," said Fitzwilliam, 'Have you read Cowper? Do you enjoy his poetry?"

Anne blushed as the company turned its attention towards her, and said in a barely audible voice, "Why, yes, I have always loved poetry and Cowper is one of…"

But she was unable to continue as Lady Catherine broke in with, "Oh, Anne is well read in all the major poets. I have seen to it that her education is well above that which is ordinarily afforded young ladies. You remember her tutor, Mr. Grenville, Fitzwilliam? A brilliant scholar, and full of praise for Anne's abilities. 'Her understanding is far above that of most young ladies and most gentlemen for that matter,' as he often said to me. I have always supervised a plan of study for her, have I not, Mrs. Jenkinson?"

"Indeed, your ladyship…" began Mrs. Jenkinson, but her attempt to enter the conversation was no more successful than Anne's.

"Anne has so many talents, but of course her indifferent health has not allowed her to pursue them. I was sorry to have to dismiss her music and drawing masters years ago, but it would have been a danger for her to continue such exhausting studies." Turning to her daughter, Lady Catherine continued, "My dear, do you recollect how well you began with riding when you were a child? I do believe, Fitzwilliam, that she would have been as excellent a horsewoman as I was in my youth, had it not been necessary to discontinue her instruction."

"And why was that, Aunt? Pray, do remind me as I would have imagined being out-of-doors to be beneficial for a young lady." said Fitzwilliam innocently.

"Surely you are aware of the dangers of too much outdoor activity for a girl with Anne's delicate constitution. For an ordinary young lady, there is probably no harm in moderate exercise, but I have always known that Anne is in no way ordinary."

"Oh, I am certainly of your opinion," said her nephew, turning to smile at Anne, "But, Cousin, I have still not heard your thoughts on Cowper."

But Anne merely blushed and looked down at the floor. He was unable to elicit another word from her for the rest of the evening.

Anne had lived such a life for the past fifteen years that she might almost be compared to the heroine of that charming fairy tale, *Sleeping Beauty*. Her mind had been awake but her affections and inclinations had slumbered. Mrs. Jenkinson, widowed when very young and forced by poverty to become a governess, had been Anne's only friend and confidant but the older lady was almost as ignorant of the larger world as was her pupil.

As usual, Anne had been silenced and made to appear a fool by her mother the evening before, but now a brave idea had occurred to the young lady. While sharing a pot of coffee with Mrs. Jenkinson the next morning Anne said, "I'm going in search of my cousin and am resolved to tell him everything. He will no doubt be fishing at his favorite spot on the river."

Her governess replied, "I have been hoping you would confide in the colonel. You cannot continue as you have all these years, my dear. Perhaps he can help you, reason with your mama and convince her to give up this delusion that you are an invalid."

"I very much doubt that," said Anne, " and I cannot believe that he cares anything about me. Who does, except for you? But at least it will relieve my feelings somewhat." Anne looked in the mirror for once before she took her secret route out of the house. How she despised her own plain and insignificant appearance. Who could care about such an unprepossessing spinster?

FITZWILLIAM HAD HOPED to find his cousin at breakfast, but according to Lady Catherine the young lady was in need of rest and might not appear at all that day. The young man was disappointed. Now that he was aware of a hidden side of Anne's character and pursuits he wished to learn more.

Rosings was blessed with an excellent trout stream, which formed the boundary of one side of the park. Mr. Collins was not the only enthusiast to be found on its banks. Fitzwilliam kept the necessary accoutrements of the fly fisherman in the gunroom of his aunt's house so that he should always have the means of satisfying his passion for the sport whenever he visited Kent. It was a particularly lovely morning, and after breakfast he made his way to a stretch of water that had never disappointed him. He had found a promising spot and chosen a fly that seemed to bear some resemblance to the insects gliding tranquilly over the surface of the water, when Anne appeared on the bank just above him. Fitzwilliam was surprised but greeted her cheerfully, and after a moment's hesitation she made her way down to his side.

"I have come to thank you, Fitzwilliam," she began hesitantly, "many people would have told my mother that I spend my afternoons exploring the woods when she thinks I am resting quietly in my room. They would no doubt do so with the idea of preventing an invalid from foolishly endangering an already weakened constitution." Then Anne looked up with a shy and rather mischievous smile.

"How glad I am that you have come to talk with me, Anne," said Fitzwilliam, smiling too, "My curiosity has been painful indeed and even kept me awake last night. From what I have witnessed, your ill health has been greatly exaggerated all these years. It is very odd and I feel that some dryad has taken the place of my cousin. Pray convince me that you really are Anne de Bourgh."

"You mean Anne, the pale, dull girl in the corner, never allowed to exert herself, or speak, or even breathe without the permission of her mama. Oh, yes, I am that same shadow by the hearth, rarely noticed by anyone until now."

"Until I saw you yesterday?"

"Yes, now only you and Mrs. Jenkinson, and the servants who are so kind and loyal, know that I have staged a revolt, if merely a secret one."

They were walking along the stream and came to a bench that had been placed to take advantage of the view of the hills.

"Let us sit here a while," suggested Fitzwilliam, "for I want you to tell me how this all came about."

"It began about one year ago when I came across 'The Antiquities of Selbourne' in the library," said Anne. "I read it with such interest that soon I was possessed by the longing to go out of doors and discover all I could about the birds and tortoises and other creatures described in the book. Very soon I was leaving the house in the early morning to spend hours in the woods and meadows. It was such a delight to me that I never thought about my health and I gradually became stronger, until one day I realized that there was really nothing at all wrong with me, that it was all my mother's fancy."

"But how have you done all this without Lady Catherine discovering your activities?"

Anne laughed, and Fitzwilliam realized that he had not heard her do so for years. "My mama is so much a slave to habit that there is nothing easier than to escape her observation," she explained, "For example, at this time of the morning she is always with her steward going over accounts. Also, Mrs. Jenkinson helps me evade detection since she knows that my life is hardly tolerable otherwise. From being my governess, she has become my friend."

They sat in silence for a moment, and then Fitzwilliam said, "I feel like a veritable callous fool, not to have had more thought for you all these years, and never to have imagined what you have suffered. As your older cousin I should have been more attentive. When my aunt first began to speak of your ill health when you were about twelve, I did protest and ask for an explanation, but did not receive one. How blind I have been! Perhaps I should speak to my aunt, not revealing your secret, but advising her to give you more freedom."

"No, pray do not, as it will do no good. It is her *idée fixe* that I am an invalid and nothing will change her. I have known my mother for six and twenty years and I can assure you that it is so."

Fitzwilliam nodded as he knew very well that his cousin was correct about Lady Catherine. "I remember coming to Rosings and hoping that we would go riding together," he recollected, "When I was informed that you were confined to your room, I went to speak to my aunt and protested with some audacity that you surely would do better to be out-of-doors. My aunt scolded me for wishing to endanger your life. It seems so outrageous now, but she convinced me that several physicians had concurred as to your fragility."

"Oh, physicians have always told Mama whatever she wished to hear," said Anne with a shrug. "It began when she decided to think of me as 'delicate.' By the time I was sixteen my mother was convinced that I was an invalid. I have to say that I believed it myself for all these years, after being examined by so many grave and eminent physicians brought especially from London. And of course, both my father and brother really did suffer from a weakness of the heart that eventually caused their deaths."

After a moment's reflection, Anne continued, "The only good I can find in my long imprisonment is that I have had a great deal of time to read. I have almost exhausted the library here at Rosings. Very soon I shall have to beg you to send me books. No novels, however, as that is my mother's only form of censorship. I suppose that she fears that I would learn too much about the world. How dreadful *that* would be," she concluded with a laugh.

Fitzwilliam promised to send her books whenever she might require them.

"But now it is ten o'clock," Anne said, with a glance at the watch that hung at her waist, "I have two hours before mama leaves her chamber where she will now have gone to read the latest novel, as is her usual practice from the hours of ten to noon, once she has completed the business of the estate. For that time, do please teach me something about fishing. It does look so amusing. Do you remember that you began to instruct me when we were children?"

"Yes," replied Fitzwilliam, "We were good friends then, were we not?"

"You were my *best* friend," said Anne, "How hard it was to lose your company and see you forget me over all this time."

For some time they were silent as Anne watched Fitzwilliam cast onto the swiftly moving stream. He caught three trout and placed them into his creel.

"Tell me, cousin," she said as she watched him change to a different fly, "Do ladies ever fish?"

"Well, I don't know any ladies who fish, but as the sport is more dependent on skill than strength, I do not know any reason why they should not excel at it. Indeed, a learned friend of mine at Cambridge tells me that the first book on fishing was written by a lady, the abbess of a convent, many centuries ago."

"Really! How remarkable," cried Anne with a smile of delight, "then you will be able to teach me! I will meet you here every morning."

Fitzwilliam was at first quite taken aback and reluctant to undertake Anne's tuition without her mother's knowledge, but he found to his surprise that his cousin's will was as strong as Lady Catherine's.

"You know that she will never allow me to do anything if we ask her permission," was an argument to which he could find no rejoinder. At last he agreed, saying, "Very well, I will let you try, but the rod may be too heavy for you. If you can lift it, we will see how you do, but remember, if your mother finds out that I am instructing you in such a dangerous activity as angling, my death will be on your conscience."

Anne laughed and ran off towards the house, saying "Tomorrow morning, this will be our rendezvous point!" and leaving Fitzwilliam with the complete refutation of every notion he had ever had about his cousin.

CHAPTER 5

*M*r. Fitzwilliam Darcy of Pemberley in Derbyshire was not a man of whom anyone would have ever expected unconventionality. He valued the traditions of his family and of his country. However, after his marriage to Miss Elizabeth Bennet, some degree of unorthodoxy might have been detected in his domestic arrangements. For generations the ladies of Pemberley had retired to a pleasant morning room after breakfast to complete their correspondence and meet with the housekeeper to oversee the organization of the great house. This custom was now overthrown by Mr. Darcy, who could see no occasion for being separated from his Elizabeth for one moment more than necessary. He had arranged that an *escritoire* be placed in the library near his own desk. Here, as he met with his steward, Mr. Fisk, and his tenants, he could look across at his wife where she sat beneath the tall windows with the morning sunlight on her dark hair. At first Mr. Darcy's visitors were rather surprised to see the lady of Pemberley so near the center of estate business, quietly attentive at times, although never entering the conversation, or engaged in writing to her many friends. All soon decided, however, that the presence of such beauty could only be a welcome influence on the day's concerns.

After the matters at hand had been dealt with, and Mr. Darcy's tenants had been answered as to their requests or complaints, the young couple would walk in the park or venture out on horseback to admire the splendid scenery of Derbyshire, for Mrs. Darcy, never before her marriage a horsewoman, had begun to delight in the activity.

When the Darcys had first returned to Pemberley after staying in town, Elizabeth had been touched by the attention with which her husband had caused every aspect of the house to reflect his love for his bride. A suite of rooms had been newly fitted up with exquisite taste and a fine disregard for expense or difficulty. The windows of Mrs. Darcy's bedchamber faced southwest and overlooked the lake, with a view of hills and a winding river. Below was the spot where she and Darcy had first met again after her refusal of his proposal of marriage. Now they often sat on the window seat together and recalled their mutual discomfiture at seeing each other.

"We had just been in the long gallery admiring your portrait and my aunt had asked if you were really so very handsome. It was the shock of my life to see the subject of the painting approaching across the lawn."

"And for me, as well," her husband replied, "You were in my thoughts at that very moment, just before I looked up and saw you. It had been a long ride to Pemberley, full of sad reflections, for I realized that through my pride and arrogance, I had lost all hope of winning the only woman I could ever love."

They spent many happy hours, going over all the small details of the story of their courtship, never tiring of its repetition, for to lovers no other subject has such charm. They often recalled their double wedding with Jane and Bingley and how, when the vows had been completed and "man and wife" pronounced, Mrs. Bennet's sobs of joy had been audible throughout the church. "Well, at least she did not faint from happiness," said Elizabeth, laughing, when they spoke of it one morning. "And I remember that papa kept you in his library for an hour the afternoon before the wedding. Now, do tell me what he said to you."

"Well, he was very stern and said that you were the rarest and most precious jewel on this earth and that if I did not make you the happiest of wives I would have him to answer to. He was quite terrifying."

"No doubt he said the same to Bingley," said Elizabeth, much amused.

"And then there was the carriage ride after we escaped and were on our way at last, just the two of us," continued Darcy, "At first we were silent and could think of nothing to say. I could hardly believe that you were my wife at last and I felt so overwhelmed with joy that I could not speak. Then you smiled and said 'Well, I suppose that we both really *are* of a taciturn disposition after all,' and we began to laugh, and we talked and laughed for the rest of the journey. And do you remember how bitterly cold it was and how I had the privilege of putting my arms around you to keep you warm? What an exultant bridegroom I was! And then at the inn that evening, you were quiet and almost shy at dinner. I had never seen you like that."

Elizabeth smiled at the recollection, and said, "Well, I did not know exactly what to expect and it occupied my thoughts."

"Do you remember what you said the next morning?" asked Darcy, taking her in his arms.

"Oh, yes. I said that I'd not known that marriage could be so delightful," Elizabeth replied, resting her head on his shoulder.

"And then everything was perfect," said Darcy kissing her, "and will be forever."

Their honeymoon journey had taken them into Devon where Elizabeth was to discover that she had married a true romantic. When she had asked Darcy about their destination he had replied vaguely, "Oh the typical seaside watering place, since I cannot take you to Italy as I would like." How great was her surprise when they arrived at a wonderfully picturesque cottage in a remote and beautiful spot a few miles from Sidmouth. Here their luggage was carried in and then Darcy dismissed his equipage and servants to the nearby village. Elizabeth had walked into a charming sitting room that had large windows overlooking a wild coastline that stretched into the far distance. There was a fire in a great stone fireplace and a table was set for dinner nearby.

"What is this place? How did you ever find it?" said Elizabeth, "You have been keeping this secret and I had not a suspicion. And I thought that you only liked grand houses. How much there is to learn about my new husband."

Darcy replied, "I have owned this cottage for ten years, having found it for sale when I was on a walking tour of the coast. I had just finished at Cambridge and wanted some time alone to think about my future. When I saw this place I had to have it. I hope you like it and are not disappointed. It is not luxurious and there are only Mr. and Mrs. Barton, the housekeeper and her husband. What do you think?"

In answer Elizabeth went to him and without words convinced him of her complete happiness. After dinner they sat on the sofa by the fire and he told her more about himself and the things he loved. "I have always been attracted to the sea and this is my idea of heaven. Perhaps I would have been a sailor – entered the Navy, had it not been for Pemberley."

"Then I would never have known you!" cried Elizabeth, "I am so glad that you stayed ashore." Then she remembered a question that she had wished to ask earlier. "You told me that you were on a journey to think about your future when you discovered this cottage. Did you come to any decisions then, almost ten long years ago?"

"I did," replied Darcy, caressing her hair and then kissing her cheek, "I decided that I wished to be an honorable man like my father and to do good in the world like both my parents, and that I would take on the responsibilities of Pemberley whenever my father should die."

"Was there ever any question that you would remain at Pemberley?"

"No, not really, but I will tell you something that seems absurd now. I wanted to be an explorer, to go to South America and discover lost worlds. What a foolish youth I was."

Elizabeth protested that there was nothing foolish in such a wish. "I am happy though, that you are here and not in the Andes, but had I been a young man I would have done just that myself."

"Another way in which we are alike," said Darcy, "and how many others? It will be a pleasure to find it all out. But there was another thing I realized on that coastal walk; that more than anything else I wanted to find a woman to love with all my heart. It took a long time but now my wish has been fulfilled. I knew it from the moment I first saw you, although my mind stupidly refused to recognize the truth for a while, and then I made such a muddle of everything that I almost lost you." He gently turned her face towards his and said, "Kiss me, my love, and I'll tell you the rest."

After she did so, Darcy went on, "For years I searched for you, but it was a fruitless effort. There were a few flirtations, since as heir to Pemberley I knew that I had to marry, and should do so while still fairly young, but, thank God, I was always saved from a terrible mistake. There's been no one but you, loveliest Elizabeth, no other woman has ever touched my heart."

After a while, Darcy said, "You know, you can hear the sea very well from our bedchamber. I love the sound of the waves crashing onto the rocks, and in the morning the sea birds will awaken us with their cries. Would you like to hear all this for yourself? It's getting late, my beloved."

They stayed at the cottage for two months and learned to know each other more intimately every day. The housekeeper and her husband were very quiet and discreet. Delicious meals appeared as if by magic but the newly wedded couple enjoyed a perfect solitude. The weather was unseasonably mild and they walked the paths along the cliffs for hours. Elizabeth was astonished by the wild beauty of the landscape and never tired of it. "How happy it makes me that you are such a great walker, my darling," said Darcy, "We love to do the same things. How fortunate, and how much we will enjoy the next fifty years together."

Some days, when the weather was less favorable, Darcy would send for the carriage and they would explore all that part of Devonshire. Elizabeth thought it the most superb country she had ever seen. They laughed a great deal on these jaunts and she was delighted to find that Darcy could be very light-hearted and amusing. Darcy had some very agreeable married friends who lived nearby and occasionally there was a evening party and twice there was a a ball in Sidmouth, but most of the time the newly married couple wished only to be alone together. That there was never a moment's disagreement or a cross word was a miracle to Elizabeth who had only witnessed her parents' marriage at close hand.

She was sad to leave the cottage and start for London and said as much to Darcy the day before their departure. "Can we ever again know such bliss? Please tell me that we will come back here and that it will be just the same."

"We'll come back for our first anniversary and it will be even *more so*," replied Darcy.

Elizabeth's reaction to their London Season was more ambiguous. There were so many concerts, receptions, dinners, excursions and other diversions that she had much less time alone with Darcy. At the same time she enjoyed her entré into London society as a challenge for an untried young woman of narrow experience from the country. Her wit, beauty and innate elegance made her a favorite of everyone who came to know her and she was greatly sought after by all the foremost hostesses. She found a *modiste* who dressed her to perfection and soon she was setting the style for that season. Darcy was immensely proud of his lovely wife and had great pleasure in giving her the magnificent family jewels that had been secure in a bank vault for many years.

After three months, Elizabeth observed a change in her husband. While he was as affectionate as ever, she noticed that he seemed remote and sad at times and she had increasing difficulty in teasing him out of his darker moods. At last, one day at breakfast, she said, "You know, my dearest, I love London and our house here and my new friends, but what I really want is to be alone with you again. I was so happy when it was just the two of us. Would you mind terribly if we leave for Pemberley instead of remaining here for the rest of the season?"

Elizabeth was surprised to see her Darcy break into exclamations of delight and jump up at once to make arrangements for their departure. How stupid of me not to understand before this, she thought, and if I never see London again it will be fine, if that makes my Darcy a happy man. I had no idea that he disliked it here and I believe he has been enduring our stay in London just to please me.

At Pemberley, their joy at being together was more remarkable each day and Elizabeth began to think that the place was enchanted and that they lived under a happy spell cast by some benevolent spirit. Darcy would generally awake a bit earlier than his bride, to enjoy kissing her into consciousness and then, after a while, leaving her to sleep somewhat longer. Then there was breakfast together in the lovely small dining chamber overlooking the lake, after which Elizabeth would meet with the housekeeper for half an hour. When that was completed, Darcy was always to be found in the library, and Elizabeth would enter the room and run into his arms, feeling that they had been apart for hours.

Their blissful encounter would often be interrupted after a few minutes by the advent of the estate's steward, Mr. Fisk, and various tenants. Always, when Elizabeth went to her writing desk, she would find a small piece of notepaper mostly concealed in a corner of the blotting pad. It was a love letter, and there was one every morning in the same spot. Darcy, even in the middle of his business meetings, would glance over at his wife as she opened the missive, with a look that was just for her. These notes were invariably so passionate that Elizabeth could not restrain her blushes. She would read them briefly and then lock them in her desk to peruse again later. At one point she said, "I will keep your letters forever as my most greatest treasures. But what if our descendants should come across them in a hundred years? What will they think of us?" Darcy laughed and replied, "Why, as to that, they will be terribly envious." What she had observed of her parents' marriage had not prepared her for the possibility of such profound love and so close a connection with her husband. She hated to be separated from him, even for a moment.

On a morning soon after their return home, Darcy had led Elizabeth out-of-doors, arousing her curiosity by saying, "I have a gift for you, my darling, the best that I have ever given you." His countenance was alight with happy anticipation as he put his arm about her waist and kissed her. Elizabeth laughed and said, "You have given me so much, my love, what else could there possibly be?"

"Wait until you see," was Darcy's only reply.

They walked to the stables of Pemberley, a commodious stone structure, fitted up with every possible attention to equine comfort.

They were greeted by Wilkins, the head groom, who led the way to a paddock where a beautiful little chestnut mare was grazing. When she saw Darcy she gave a friendly whinny and trotted over, having been encouraged in this behavior by many sugar lumps.

"Oh, what a lovely creature!" cried Elizabeth, stroking the soft neck, which had been brushed to a fine gloss that morning.

"This is Eilis, my love, and she has been waiting for some time to make the acquaintance of her mistress. Her sire was Irish, hence her name, and she is the gentlest horse one could ever find for a lady." Then turning to Wilkins, Darcy inquired, "Has James been taking her out every day?"

"Oh, yes, sir. He takes her up on the hills every morning, and says that she is the quietest, most willing and agreeable mare he's ever ridden."

"And is she really to be mine?" asked Elizabeth, "I'm afraid that it will take some time for my skills as a horsewoman to be worthy of her."

"We have all the time in the world," said Darcy with a smile, "and you will learn at whatever pace suits you best."

"Has Eilis seemed happy in her new home?" Elizabeth asked Wilkins, "I hope that she does not miss any of her old friends from her last stable."

"Why, no, my lady," said Wilkins, looking somewhat puzzled, "she has taken to the place and seems quite contented, but she has been here almost a year now, since last summer."

Elizabeth looked thoughtful at this intelligence but said nothing more until she and Darcy were walking across the lawn towards the house.

"Here is a mystery indeed, my love," she said, smiling up at her husband, "By my recollection of events, you must have obtained Eilis *after* my very ungracious refusal of your offer of marriage at Hunsford. I am quite perplexed, I confess."

"There is no mystery, my Elizabeth," said Darcy, "I had already seen Eilis. She belonged to the daughter of my neighbor Lord Faulconer and was often in the hunting field. The lady had decided that an animal more dashing, that is more likely to break its rider's neck, was required. I returned to Pemberley, deep in despair at your refusal, but on some impulse bought the mare anyway. I had no hope that you would ever change your opinion of me, but in some obscure corner of my mind I could not entirely give up my dream of seeing you here someday. Eilis has been the recipient of many confidences when I have encountered her at the paddock fence during my evening walk."

This was an explanation that could not fail to delight Elizabeth. She soon improved enough as a horsewoman to be able to ride with Darcy over the wild and splendid country that has made Derbyshire so appealing to romantic sensibilities. Their first weeks at Pemberley proved to be a period of blessed tranquility, with no one to please but themselves. The autumn seemed likely to be more exacting, with many visitors expected after the Darcys' return from Scotland.

ON A RAINY MORNING that seemed to promise no possibility of venturing out of doors, the young couple were attending to the day's correspondence. Elizabeth looked up to see an expression of concern on her husband's countenance as he read a letter that had just arrived.

He met her questioning look and said, "Here is some disappointing news, my love. My friend Grey writes that he may not make one of the party in Scotland. He gives no details but cites 'family concerns' as most probably preventing him. As I have told you, I have not seen him for several years, since he went abroad after completing his degree at Cambridge."

"Mr. Grey seems a rather mysterious person," said Elizabeth, "What has kept him away for so long? Does he not miss his family and friends?"

"It is a sad story," Darcy replied, "Grey is the son of Lord Harwith, who has a great estate in Surrey. His mother died when he was about eight years old, with the birth of a stillborn younger brother. Poor Grey has known a great deal of tragedy for he also lost his older brother at an early age. He has, therefore, only his father, and the two men could not be more unlike. I believe that it is in part to avoid the unceasing disagreements with the earl that Grey has spent so much of his life abroad."

"Why did they quarrel?" asked Elizabeth, "One would expect them to value each other all the more after having suffered so much bereavement."

"Unfortunately, Lord Harwith is a despicable reprobate who has spent his life in the unbridled pursuit of pleasure. He has managed to do considerable damage to one of the finest inheritances in England through his devotion to gambling and the racetrack. Grey has been so disgusted by his father's mismanagement and his abusive treatment of his tenants, that he decided to stay away altogether. I recall that it was over the matter of the enclosure of some marginal land that they had their final falling out. Since then Grey has spent his time wandering about in obscure parts of the continent, following, as I understand it, scientific studies of the most advanced kind. I know that he has presented papers to the Royal Society, and that his prolonged absence has been lamented by many prominent members of that body."

"Studies in what branch of knowledge?" inquired his wife

"I was afraid that you would ask me that very pertinent question," said Darcy with a smile, "As far as I can understand it, Grey is interested in examining the rocks and minerals that make up the earth's structure, to determine how they came to be and to reach a conclusion as to their age. On all our expeditions when we were boys, he would carry a small hammer with which to chip off small bits of rock for study. He is a rather dignified fellow, but he can go into ecstasies over an odd boulder or an unusual depression in the ground. We even spent some time exploring some of the caverns in the neighborhood when he visited me here years ago."

"You make me shudder, my darling," cried Elizabeth, "I shall not be able to like Mr. Grey at all if he leads you into caverns. What a dreadful idea!"

Darcy laughed, "Somehow, my love, crawling about in the cold and damp of an underground passage in the dark does not seem so appealing as it did when I was fourteen. Heavens! If my father had known to what dangers we exposed ourselves. Once we had penetrated deep into a cavern only to lose our candles in a waterfall into which we blundered unexpectedly. Fortunately I found a bit of candle and dry tinder in my pocket."

This was too much for Elizabeth, and she begged him to tell her no more tales of such peril lest she have nightmares for weeks.

~

SINCE MOST OF their acquaintances were still in London enjoying the Season, Elizabeth had been quite free from social obligations, but that afternoon she felt the necessity of visiting a neighbor whom she had met soon after arriving at Pemberley. This was Lady Templeton, a baronet's widow who had been a friend of Darcy's mother and who, having suffered some reversal of fortune, lived in a rather neglected mansion near Lambton. Despite her lack of wealth, Lady Templeton had preserved her position as an arbiter of fashion in her small circle. She lived for card playing and gossip, and it would have been difficult to decide which was more dear to her heart. Her family was an ancient one, having been settled in the county for generations, as she never failed to inform any new acquaintance within the first five minutes after they were introduced.

"She enjoys the position of having been a friend of my mother's," Darcy had explained, "but in truth, my mother was so good hearted that I believe she tolerated Lady Templeton out of kindness, rather than from any natural sympathy with the lady. She is one of those people who somehow, without any great claim to rank or the ability to charm, are invited everywhere and become fixtures. You will see her at every gathering at all the houses of the county families and you will wonder why, especially after you know her better. She does have a talent for gossip and for discovering the weakness of others, so I suppose that she is feared by many."

For Darcy this was a rather ill natured speech and Elizabeth surmised that Lady Templeton must be a true dragon. Thus she set out for her visit without any anticipation of pleasure.

She found the lady alone in her somewhat gloomy drawing room, decorated in the style of thirty years before. Lady Templeton welcomed her visitor effusively, as Mrs. Darcy was one of the most important ladies in the county and could expect a gracious reception wherever she went, in spite of having been an insignificant Miss Bennet, with an uncle who was in trade and lived in Cheapside.

"So delighted to see you, my dear Mrs. Darcy. How is your charming husband? My goodness, if you knew how many hearts were broken hereabout when news of his marriage reached us! And what news of Miss Darcy? Will she be returning to Pemberley soon?"

Elizabeth replied that Georgiana was spending a few months with a school friend and would not be rejoining them until the autumn.

Tea was brought, and after the servant had departed, Lady Templeton began her self-appointed task of introducing Elizabeth to the foibles of all their neighbors.

"My dear Mrs. Darcy, you will no doubt have noticed Mrs. Devereaux's attire at church Sunday last? Did you ever see anything so outré as her bonnet? She is really not quite the thing as the wife of our rector, although I am sure she is a good sort of woman. You may not know that her father was in trade in York."

Elizabeth had heard this, but was unable to share Lady Templeton's horror at the fact.

"Yes, an old Mr. Jones was her father and he must have done quite well for himself, as his daughter was able to marry so far above her station and bring her husband a comfortable fortune. Still, for a man of Mr. Devereaux's breeding it must be a trial at times."

Elizabeth said that she had found Mrs. Devereaux to be kind and agreeable and that she rejoiced that the rector had such an amiable wife. At least in her own case, she thought to herself, no one could accuse Darcy of having married her for her money.

Her response did not prevent her hostess from making similar observations about all their mutual acquaintance.

"But, of course you have not had the opportunity to meet your neighbors at Castle Faulconer. Lord Faulconer and his daughter Lady Margaret, who is so, shall we say, *famous* in the county, are still in Bath for another week or two, I believe."

"I presume," said Elizabeth, "that you mean famous for her virtue or good works, as otherwise it is hardly complimentary to so describe a lady."

"How I do wish that such was the source of her renown," said Lady Templeton, leaning forward confidentially, "but to tell the truth, Lady Margaret is known for her wild, ungovernable behavior which has been the scandal of the county and a sad trial for her poor father. It is a perfect example of what may be the result of a girl losing her mother at an early age."

Elizabeth had to admit to herself that her curiosity was aroused, and she asked what the young lady could have done to cause such consternation.

"You will be astonished to hear, Mrs. Darcy, that she disobeyed her father's wishes and actually followed the hounds last winter, taking the most terrible risks and pushing her mount over the most dreadful fences, just like the rest of the field! But that is not the worst of it. On many occasions she has been seen out riding *alone* with young gentlemen of her acquaintance. And it is common knowledge that she goes about Bath and even London *by herself,* without even her maid! And there is something about her manner, so free, almost improper, without any of that softness of demeanor so appropriate in a highly born young lady. I myself have heard her express the most shocking opinions."

Well, thought Elizabeth, there is at least one interesting character in the district.

"I must admit, however," continued Lady Templeton, "that she is a great beauty, and no doubt that explains why she has her own way in so many things. I pity Lord Faulconer from the bottom of my heart." Then, with a significant look, "But Mr. Darcy knows Lady Margaret *very* well. No doubt he has told you all about her and her, shall we say, *eccentricities.*"

"Oh yes," replied Elizabeth, "I am aware of the existence of Lady Margaret," as she thought to herself that there could hardly be a more malicious old woman in the whole county than her interlocutor.

Soon after Mrs. Darcy took her leave, rejoicing that she had done her duty for the present and would not have to suffer Lady Templeton's company again for a while. As she returned home she tried to remember what Darcy had told her about their closet neighbors. He had mentioned Lady Margaret as an old friend, "a bit too much for her father to manage," but that he thought that she would amuse Elizabeth and that she was the "best-hearted girl in the world."

When she arrived home, Elizabeth told her husband about her visit in detail, not neglecting to mention the lady's sly remarks on the subject of Lady Margaret.

"Lady Templeton is truly perfect," said Darcy, laughing, "She never misses an opportunity to imply something unpleasant about anyone, even those who have been kind to her. I have indeed known Lady Margaret all my life. I suppose that many have thought it would be logical for our two estates to be joined by marriage. Those who take such a dynastic view of what should be an affair of the heart, found it strange, no doubt, that we never regarded each other with the slightest interest, except as friends. She lacks the qualities I value most highly in a wife, especially the good sense and gentle spirit that I have found in you, my beloved."

Elizabeth could not resist asking Darcy what he had thought of her sound judgment after her refusal of his first offer of marriage, considering the gentle way in which she had done so. Then they took their evening walk in the park.

CHAPTER 6

hree weeks are hardly sufficient for a visit to a pleasant country house, at least in the opinion of Colonel Fitzwilliam as he prepared to leave Rosings and return to his regiment. His aunt had been very glad of his presence and made him sensible that after his departure all sublunary happiness would cease. More than on any other occasion, she had made an effort to be agreeable and had seemed to appreciate his company. This was not the chief reason for Fitzwilliam's regret at the end of his sojourn in his aunt's house. He was not a vain man or one likely to dwell on every accomplishment, but he felt that he had done something remarkable in winning the confidence and friendship of his cousin Anne.

He had hardly noticed her existence for some years, and he felt truly remorseful for having overlooked her in his assumption that she was only a pitiable invalid. As children they had been great friends, but after Anne had been immured in a sick room as being constantly in danger of succumbing to some unspecified illness, Fitzwilliam had rarely spent any time in her company. At first he had questioned his aunt's decree that Anne should be kept indoors and asked to know the nature of his cousin's ill health. He never received a satisfactory explanation and was forced to accept that Anne could no longer live a normal life. Fitzwilliam had been sixteen at the time and unhappy to lose the company of the little cousin who worshipped him as an older brother and always wished to accompany him wherever he went.

Now, every morning, except when the weather was very unfavorable, he met Anne by the stream. He was surprised by her determination to master the principles of angling and by her ability to lift the fishing rod, which he had imagined would be too heavy for so slight a girl. First he had her cast in an open meadow, aiming for a rock, after which he introduced her to the various ways of placing a fly on the water without startling the trout. His cousin was able to accomplish this objective with some degree of regularity after a few days, but without that delicacy of touch needed to deceive the fish into taking the hook.

Anne bore with the difficulties involved, never making any complaint, so that her cousin was surprised one day, when after losing a third fly in the branches of a large elm tree, she suddenly threw down the rod and began to weep with vexation. This display of temperament was so unexpected that Fitzwilliam was at a loss for some minutes, but then he sat down beside her and tried to find some words of comfort.

"Please do not be so downhearted, dear cousin. I not only lost innumerable flies when I was learning, but I even managed to fall over my brother's best rod and break it into several pieces."

This image of the dignified Fitzwilliam must have presented an irresistibly amusing picture to Anne's mind, for after a brief moment of reflection she could not suppress a smile and then she began to laugh.

"I wish that my brother had found the incident so entertaining," muttered Fitzwilliam.

"Please forgive my display of bad temper," said Anne, glancing at the rod that she had flung into some shrubbery, "You must think me very spoilt and ill-natured."

"Why, not at all, Anne," replied Fitzwilliam, "but I am surprised that such a little matter should cause you such distress. After all, we engage in this pastime for our amusement. We may still be sure of a good dinner even if we have no success at all."

Anne had to smile at the idea of fishing to keep body and soul together, no doubt a hopeless undertaking in her own case. Then, after a moment's thought, she said, "You excel at so many things that you cannot imagine the feelings of one who has no accomplishments at all. I play no musical instrument and I have never learnt to draw. I have not been allowed to ride all these years because of my 'delicate health.' I have never done *anything*, as my mother has always insisted that my strength was unequal to the task."

Fitzwilliam, who now had daily evidence of Anne's strength, could only shake his head at his aunt's attitude. That it had been the guiding principle by which Lady Catherine had ordered her daughter's existence, he well knew by his own observation.

Anne continued, "The worst failing of my education has been that I have never learnt to be at ease in company. I am too frightened to say one word, even if I could think of one. I am sure that I must seem either stupid or intolerably proud. I am afraid that I will spend my life here at Rosings, without friends and without the courage to venture out into the world." To Fitzwilliam's dismay, he again saw tears in Anne's eyes.

"Do listen carefully," he replied, "Very few of us do anything well without practice and application. You have the intelligence to excel at whatever you wish, including attracting the interest and friendship of superior people, by which I mean superior in character and understanding. You lack only opportunity."

"But if I am always silent and can think of nothing to say, how will they find me worth knowing," asked Anne doubtfully.

"It is difficult to be shy and it will take some determination to overcome it, but I am sure that you can. Why I myself was shy when young." This was not entirely true, but Fitzwilliam's intentions were good. "What you must do is think less of your own feelings and more of the sensibilities of others. When you apply all your effort to discovering the interests and talents of those with whom you converse, you will soon forget about being afraid to speak."

Anne listened respectfully to this advice, for there was no one she regarded more highly than Fitzwilliam.

He continued, "I have been thinking for some time that it would be well for you to know Mrs. Collins better. She is a very kind lady and understands the world to a degree that is surprising in one who leads a rather narrow existence here in Kent."

"But Cousin, I believe that she does not like me," said Anne.

"Nonsense. She does not know you, and I am sure that she would be happy to have such an intelligent, well-informed young lady for a friend. Promise that you will try to know her better."

Anne, who felt gratified to hear her cousin so describe her, said that she would make a sincere effort to become friends with Mrs. Collins.

"Very good," said Fitzwilliam, "Now let me see if I can untangle your line.

ON THE EVENING but one before his departure, Fitzwilliam was taking a turn about the park with his aunt. Lady Catherine was truly sad at the thought of parting with her nephew, and wished to give him the benefit of as much of her advice as possible in the time left to her.

"Do you return directly to your regiment, dear Fitzwilliam," she inquired, "or do you have any engagements on the way?"

"I must first venture into Hampshire to visit Mr. Thornton, the father of my old friend Stanley Thornton who was killed in a fleet action several years ago. I always try to spend a few days with him once or twice a year."

"That is admirable, nephew, but it must be rather dull. Has Mr. Thornton a large family?"

"No, Aunt, that is the sad thing. Mr. Thornton lives entirely alone, having lost his wife and two sons. I believe that he has no close relations and few visitors."

"And is he a gentleman of large property?" asked Lady Catherine, coming to the question that she always found the most pertinent.

"I hardly think so. In fact, he lives in a venerable old manor house that is quite dilapidated, and with few comforts. But I am afraid that I sound ungrateful for his hospitality, which is no doubt the best that he can afford. I think that being able to converse with me about his son is one of the few pleasures in his life."

His aunt was caught between appreciation for Fitzwilliam's kindness in sacrificing his time and comfort to visit the unfortunate Mr. Thornton, and a strong inclination to advise him not to waste his effort in doing so. However, she had something of more significance to discuss with him.

"Fitzwilliam, I must claim the privilege of being one of your nearest relations to mention a subject of utmost importance to your future."

A preamble like this was always enough to induce a feeling of apprehension in any member of Lady Catherine's family, but the young man did not lack courage and looked at his aunt attentively.

"My dear boy, it is time you were married." She paused a moment to let her nephew comprehend the momentous nature of what she had said, and then continued, "You have no fortune of your own, except, as I know, a trifling six hundred a year, plus your officer's pay. Hardly enough to live on in a manner befitting your rank and family connections." Somehow Lady Catherine always seemed to know the incomes of her relations and friends down to the last shilling.

"You must marry, and marry well, to a young lady of distinguished family who can bring you a large fortune. A fortune such as you would have had if your father had arranged things better." At this criticism of his father, Fitzwilliam's face grew stern, and even Lady Catherine knew not to pursue that line of thought.

"I am acquainted with two or three ladies who would be more than acceptable, and I would like to arrange for you to know them, perhaps by holding a gathering here this summer. You have already met them, I am sure." And she named three young women whom Fitzwilliam had indeed encountered at various balls in London. He groaned inwardly, and had to make an effort not to resent his aunt's interference, but answered her with civility.

"Aunt, you have given me something to think about. I must say that marriage is not a subject to which I have given any serious attention. But please allow me to consider the matter before you undertake any activity on my behalf."

He then had to listen to a fairly long monologue on the advantages of marriage with a rich and well-born lady, but in the end his aunt agreed to his request that she delay engaging in any matchmaking activities.

～

EARLY ON THE morning of his departure, Fitzwilliam met Anne at their favorite section of the trout stream. The young man had brought his cousin a parting gift, wrapped in oiled linen and enclosed in a leather tube and Anne colored with pleasure when she had opened it. It was a beautifully made fly rod, perfect in scale and weight for a lady. Fitzwilliam had sent to his rod maker in London and driven the man to distraction with his demand that this rare present be ready in time. It had been brought from town by special messenger only the night before.

Anne was deeply affected and almost in tears. "Cousin, you are the first person who has ever done something so dear and thoughtful for me. I am only sad that you will not be here to afford me further instruction."

"As for that, Anne, I will be here in the fall, and although the fishing may not be ideal then, we will continue to practice. In fact, I expect to find evidence of continued effort when I return. I have instructed Stevens to keep all your tackle in order for you."

With heightened color and eyes bright with unshed tears, Anne thanked him for his kindness and was said how happy she was that they were now friends again after so many years.

As he rode off that day, after the usual farewells had been said to his aunt at the front door of Rosings, it occurred to Fitzwilliam that Anne was becoming a rather pretty young woman. She is, in truth, not plain at all, he thought, remembering how she had looked earlier that morning when she had stood in the green shade of the elm trees and thanked him for his gift with a shy smile. Fitzwilliam determined that he would henceforth take an older brother's interest in Anne's happiness and progress.

Anne had not gone to say goodbye to her cousin at the door, wishing to avoid her mother's company, and instead to have solitude in which to think of all the happy times she had spent with

Fitzwilliam during his stay at Rosings. As she watched the dashing young officer canter off down the drive, she had difficulty restraining her tears. It would be so many months until she would see him again. Mrs. Jenkinson came to stand at her side and said, "I do believe that Colonel Fitzwilliam is the finest young man I have ever met, and in his own way just as handsome as Mr. Darcy. There is such distinction and nobility in his face and bearing and such kindness in his manner and address. And clearly he is very fond of you, dear Anne."

Anne shrugged and turned away to hide her emotion, "Oh, I daresay he'll not give me another thought until he finds time to visit us again. Why should he?"

CHAPTER 7

*M*r. Edward Thornton lived alone at Thornton Abbey, a large and decaying mansion at the edge of the New Forest in Hampshire. Colonel Fitzwilliam turned his horse down the long, narrow lane to the house at about one o'clock, two days following his departure from Rosings. A more striking contrast with the beautifully maintained grounds of his aunt's estate would have been difficult to imagine. Thickets of coarse shrubbery almost barred his progress, and his first view of the Abbey revealed it to be even more dilapidated than Fitzwilliam had found it eight months before. He found one ragged groom to take charge of his horse and then made his way up the broken steps to the massive front door. After a few minutes of knocking on the hard oak with the head of his riding crop, he was able to attract the attention of Alford, the old butler.

Mr. Thornton was in the library and the butler led Fitzwilliam there immediately. It was a cold and depressing house, but a sensitive eye such as the colonel's could see that it had once been beautiful. The Abbey had come into the Thornton family during the time of Elizabeth, and the well-proportioned rooms, elegant plasterwork, and splendid mullioned windows represented the finest aspects of the builder's art of that period. The decline of the house echoed that of the family itself, for Mr. Thornton was the last of his race, having lost his wife and all of his children.

When the old gentleman heard Fitzwilliam announced, he rose to his feet with some effort and greeted the young officer with obvious pleasure. Though the day was warm, there was a fire in the enormous fireplace, and Mr. Thornton insisted on his guest's taking a seat in its immediate vicinity with as much solicitude as if there had been a howling blizzard without. Mr. Thornton had not been well for several years, but on this occasion the colonel saw a very marked deterioration in his appearance, finding him thinner and very pale. But if Mr. Thornton suffered from increasing frailty, he seemed to forget his ill health in his delight at the arrival of his friend.

"My dear Colonel, how much I have been looking forward to your visit, and how kind you are to come out of your way to see a dull old man in such an obscure corner of the country."

"Oh no, my dear sir. Never in life could I experience dullness of any kind here in your lovely part of Hampshire. Some of the most interesting conversations I can recall have been here in this very room with you."

This was not flattery as Mr. Thornton was an exceptionally well read and intelligent man and he and Fitzwilliam had much in common. He also contrived to be informed on the important concerns of the day, and his guest had observed that in spite of the obvious poverty of the house, there were always to be found a few recent books and periodicals and a comfortable fire in the library.

There followed the usual exchange on the state of the roads and the weather that had characterized Fitzwilliam's journey to the Abbey. Mr. Thornton inquired after the colonel's family with much kind interest and it saddened his guest to be unable to return the courtesy. Soon the old gentleman rang for the butler, suggesting that rest after such a long ride must be welcome and expressing the happiness he would find in seeing his young friend at dinner. Fitzwilliam, who could spend eight or nine hours in the saddle without much ill-effect, saw that his host was fatigued from even this short interview, so he followed Alford to the bedchamber that was familiar from other visits.

This room had a pleasing view of the remnants of a once elegant garden, beyond which was the forest where Fitzwilliam and Stanley Thornton had played as boys. Fitzwilliam had visited frequently when the two were at school together. Stanley had not gone to sea until rather late, at the age of fifteen, when he had finally obtained his father's permission to do so. Mr. Thornton's reluctance arose from the fact that his older son had died in a riding accident and he had a great fear of losing his younger child as well. In the event, his trepidation had been only too well justified. Many years before, the unfortunate old man had also lost his wife and two younger children to a virulent fever. As far as Fitzwilliam was aware, Mr. Thornton saw few other visitors and had no surviving relations, although he did correspond with some old friends who like the master of the Abbey were too infirm to travel.

Being at Thornton Abbey brought back many memories of Stanley to Fitzwilliam. They had seen little of each other after taking up their respective professions, but had maintained a fairly regular correspondence. The colonel spent the afternoon walking about the grounds and thinking of his lost comrade, whom he had considered one of the most admirable and talented men of his acquaintance.

Like many elderly people with no one to please but themselves, Mr. Thornton was in the habit of dining rather early. He apologized to his guest for this unfashionable practice, saying that his few servants were too set in their ways for any change not to throw the house into complete confusion. As always, Fitzwilliam expressed his happy acquiescence with all of his host's customs. The food, although simple, was well prepared and the claret excellent. Fitzwilliam suspected that the wine was the last of a once great cellar, put up in a more affluent time, and he appreciated Mr. Thornton's generosity in sharing what he could probably not afford to replace.

After dinner they retired from the spacious dining chamber, chilly even on a summer evening, and took their Port in the library, which was the only really comfortable room in the house. As it always did, conversation turned to Stanley Thornton, his bravery and skill as a naval officer and his many amiable qualities as a son and friend.

"You know, my dear Colonel," said Mr. Thornton, "while going through some papers I found a treasure which I do not remember ever having shared with you. It is a letter from one of my son's fellow officers who was present on the day of the fleet action that claimed Stanley's life."

So saying, he produced a couple of pages, much read and creased, from a cloisonné box that he kept on his chair-side table. "I so valued the letter that I put it away too carefully and could never find it until the other day. I believe that it is safer to keep it by me here."

He handed the letter to Fitzwilliam. 'It is from a Lieutenant Aubrey who distinguished himself in the same battle."

In a style that was not graceful but clearly motivated by the desire to give whatever comfort might be possible to a grieving father, Lieutenant Aubrey explained that he took the liberty of expressing his sympathy and wished as well to relate some particulars as to the brave part played by Stanley in the battle, by which he had saved many of his shipmates. The letter had described how the rudder of the ship had become entangled in some floating spars and rigging brought down during the engagement, leaving the ship without the ability to steer, and in danger of being raked by the broadside of a French man-of-war that was closing rapidly. Stanley, under heavy fire, went over the rail, and suspended from a line was able to free the rudder, allowing the vessel to come about. As he regained the quarterdeck he was hit by a sniper's bullet and dreadfully wounded.

"He lived long enough to speak of you, sir," continued the letter, "and to regret that you should be left alone in the world. He asked me to send you his dearest love. I have never served with a braver officer, and indeed, during the last few weeks of his life he was so fierce in his desire to take on any hazardous duty that the rest of us hardly dared to compete with him for the honor." Lieutenant Aubrey ended with respectful condolences and promised to call upon Mr. Thornton when next on shore leave.

"And he did in fact pay me a brief visit, flying through in a great rush on his way to Plymouth. A big, kind, agreeable young man. I have followed his career ever since and was glad to see in the Navy lists that he was made Post-Captain." Mr. Thornton carefully folded his precious letter and replaced it in its repository. "It saddens me to think that my son left on his last commission weighed down with disappointment and sorrow. You read how he was eager to undertake the most dangerous duty. I am afraid that he had little care to preserve his life. Do you remember the unfortunate turn that events had taken for Stanley just before he returned to sea?"

"I know that he had become engaged to a young lady, for he wrote to me at length describing his happiness. Then just before he joined his ship he wrote again to say that the match was broken off. It was the letter of a man in despair, but he gave no particulars."

"I know very little myself," said Mr. Thornton, "The lady was a Miss Delaford, of excellent family, whom he had met in Bath, where he had gone to visit a fellow officer. There was an immediate sympathy between the two young people, which rapidly deepened into mutual affection. In the tradition of naval officers, my son lost no time in securing her promise to marry as soon as possible, preferably before he returned to sea. I had sent the usual letters expressing gratification at the match to Miss Delaford and her parents, and was stirring myself to journey to Bath, when I received word from Stanley that all was at an end. The lady had parted from him in such a way as to give him no hope of reconciliation. The last time I saw him, on his way to join his ship, I wished to press for more details, but seeing his distress did not have the heart to do so."

"I'm afraid that I can add nothing to your comprehension of the matter," said Fitzwilliam, "I received word of the engagement, then about three weeks later the news of its dissolution. Stanley wrote that he would give me further particulars the next time he saw me, but alas, that day never came."

As there seemed no way to untangle the mystery the conversation turned to other subjects, and the moon was rising in the clear night sky before the two men went to their beds.

CHAPTER 8

The last weeks of July found Mr. and Mrs. Darcy deep in preparation for their journey to Scotland. Elizabeth soon learned that departure for an extended absence from a great country house was almost as demanding a proposition as the governance of the household. An infinite number of details had to be discussed with the housekeeper, especially as the arrival of a number of guests would follow hard upon the Darcys' return home. Darcy saw that the responsibility for all these arrangements was rather wearisome for his young wife and he did what he could to set her mind at ease.

"I'm afraid that this is all very tedious for you, my darling" he said one afternoon, "My mother used to say that preparing to leave Pemberley for a month was like climbing out of quicksand, although I doubt that she spoke from personal experience."

"How I wish that I had known your mother," said Elizabeth, who liked the stories she had heard of that lady.

"It is unfair that allowances are made for the households of bachelors," continued Darcy, "No one thinks much of it if the hot water is a little late arriving in the morning. But, my angel, you need not make yourself uneasy. With such a housekeeper as Mrs. Reynolds everything always goes smoothly at Pemberley. The greatest difficulty is in making plans for our expedition to Scotland, but there is still time to order anything you need from London." Then Darcy sat down next to Elizabeth to go over a series of lists with her and they reviewed every possible necessity for a visit to a remote Highland castle.

"Will the ladies be invited to accompany the shooting party?" asked Elizabeth.

"Generally not," replied her husband, who could not help but smile at the idea of the feminine contingent of the gathering hiking for miles across the rough moorland in the cold wind and intermittent rain, "But you may see us off in the morning, walking as far as you wish, and unless the weather is very bad, the ladies are driven out to join us for lunch. You will also be able to ride, as my aunt is a very accomplished horsewoman and will be glad of your company."

When it was certain that all eventualities had been provided for, Darcy proposed that they enjoy the fine day with a canter on the hills above Pemberley. They had been out for about an hour and a mist of fine rain had begun to make them think of returning home, when a solitary rider appeared, moving at a reckless pace across the rocky ground.

"That looks like Lady Margaret Faulconer," said Darcy, "I know no one else who rides like that over this rugged country. No regard for her own safety or that of her mount." He led Elizabeth toward the newcomer at a sedate trot, carefully picking their way through the outcroppings of limestone.

Lady Margaret, for it was indeed she, rode to meet them at a less judicious pace, and pulled up, controlling her spirited bay horse with no apparent effort, checking his restless movements with the almost invisible action of her strong hands on the damp reins. Elizabeth found herself staring in complete astonishment, for the lady was riding astride.

Darcy, who did not seem in the least surprised by this unconventionality said, "So Lady Meg, you are back from Bath. We did not expect to see you for another week, but I am glad of the opportunity to make you acquainted with my wife."

During this speech Lady Margaret had been regarding Elizabeth in a frank, appraising manner. The results of her survey must have been favorable, for she suddenly smiled at the new Mrs. Darcy with a most winning, open expression.

"I had heard that your wife was a beauty, and in this case the report was not an exaggeration. And may I congratulate you, Mrs. Darcy, on how well you sit your horse. You are no doubt aware that Eilis was mine before your husband so obligingly bought her for you, and I'm glad to see that she has a worthy rider who will not pull at her mouth."

Indeed, Elizabeth did look very well on horseback, having a natural grace as a rider, which made her appear more accomplished than she really was. She said all that was proper as to her great pleasure in meeting Lady Margaret, while feeling somewhat in awe of the dashing figure before her. Her new acquaintance was herself beautiful, with a fiery, almost daunting loveliness that once seen could not be soon forgotten. She was somewhat taller than Elizabeth and more strongly built, having a look of intense activity, even in repose. Her features, beneath a head of abundant chestnut hair, were perfectly regular, but it was the constant change of expression in her exquisite face and dark eyes that made her fascinating. Her countenance would shift from quiet abstraction to dazzling animation as if lit by some inner flame. Elizabeth could only wonder that this enchanting creature had not won Darcy's heart, but he greeted her much as he would have his old friend Bingley or his cousin Fitzwilliam. They were soon deep in discussion of the problems of their respective stables and the prospects for that year's hunting.

Soon, however, the rain became too heavy to be ignored, and Darcy was anxious to see Elizabeth safely home and established in front of a warm fire.

"Lady Margaret," said Elizabeth, "Will you give us the pleasure of your company and come to Pemberley for tea. You are closer to our house than to your own, and we could send you home in our carriage later. I am so looking forward to knowing you better."

The lady seemed glad of this offer of hospitality and within half an hour the two women were comfortably seated in front of the library fire. Darcy had left them to become better acquainted and was attending to some estate business. Lady Margaret had let down her long hair to dry, and as they talked Elizabeth soon felt that they were old friends. She had rarely had the experience of such immediate sympathy, without the effort and hesitancy that generally characterize the first steps in forming a friendship.

"I so admire the practicality and elegance of your riding costume," ventured Elizabeth, "and how much more sensible to ride astride as the men do."

"And how much safer," agreed Lady Margaret, who would never have seemed to any observer to make safety a matter of the least concern. "But even I, as outrageous as I am in the opinion of the county, only dare to do so when I am unlikely to meet anyone. But Mr. Darcy has known me too long to be surprised at anything I do. Has he told you how I used to steal his apricots?"

Seeing Elizabeth's puzzled look, Lady Margaret began to laugh, "Well, they were really his father's apricots. You see, I was a rather lonely child and spent much of my time exploring out of doors, often venturing as far as Pemberley. One time I came across the orchard when the apricots were ripe, and thinking that no one would miss a few, I managed to eat more than was quite wise. By the time Darcy and Wickham came across me, I was feeling very unwell. Mrs. Darcy was summoned and was so very kind. After that I spent many happy hours visiting here. Darcy was eight years older and so infinitely my superior, but he was so condescending as to ride with me and even allowed me to accompany him on many of his rambles in the hills."

Elizabeth was unable to resist asking if Lady Margaret had known Wickham well.

"Oh, fairly well. At first I thought him more amiable than Darcy, but Wickham does not improve with further acquaintance. He could see no advantage in being kind to a small girl, and soon ignored me completely. But I was forgetting that he is a relation of yours, your sister's husband. Please forgive me. I am so stupid sometimes that I really should be barred from civilized society." Then Margaret looked very wretched indeed.

Elizabeth hastened to explain that Wickham was not a favorite of hers either, although she was now obliged to think as well of him as possible.

At this moment Darcy appeared and took some tea with the ladies.

"As soon as we returned I sent word to Lord Faulconer that you were safe here with us, Lady Margaret, and I requested that you stay with us for dinner and remain for the night if that plan suits you. Your father has been so gracious as to send his consent, as well as your maid and whatever things you may require,' said Darcy, taking a seat by the fire.

"How delightful!" cried Elizabeth, "You are our first dinner guest since we arrived at Pemberley."

Lady Margaret looked truly pleased but said, "Thank you for wishing me to stay. I suppose that my father will be able to spare me for one evening, although I do worry somewhat about his tendency to melancholy."

"I promised that you would return by mid-morning tomorrow and I believe that he will do very well until then. I asked him to join us, but he must not have wished to venture out in this weather."

After a few minutes Darcy left them again and the two ladies sat in an agreeable silence for a time. Lady Margaret spoke first, "Now I have seen for myself the blessings that marriage may confer when the two parties are in truth suited to one another by temperament as well as from love. If you will allow me to say so, you have wrought the most remarkable change in my old friend Mr. Darcy. He was always a man of evident goodness and many talents, but tended to appear stiff and proud in company. I perceive that you have transformed him into a very different sort of being. I do not even think that anyone will be afraid of him anymore."

Elizabeth had to smile, for her new friend's words brought back to her recollection her first impression of Darcy at the assembly ball at Meryton, when his cold, forbidding demeanor had ensured him the dislike of the entire assembly. She could see for herself that he was now quite changed, to a degree that had impressed all his old acquaintance in London that spring.

The Darcys spent a very pleasant evening with their guest, and after all had retired to rest, Elizabeth could not resist praising the practicality of Lady Margaret's riding attire to her husband and inquiring archly if he did not wish his wife to imitate her. Darcy, who observed her barely repressed smile, replied, "Although I would not be very happy were you to do so, I do not feel that I was placed on this earth to tyrannize over my fellow creatures, especially the one I love best in the world. Therefore, my darling, you must follow your own judgment in the matter." This wise reply led to a most delightful eagerness on Elizabeth's part to assure him of her desire to please him in this as in all things.

~

THE NEXT MORNING was warm and sunny, and the Darcys and Lady Margaret were taking breakfast on the terrace when the butler hurried in with a letter.

"Oh, sir! This has just come by express from Kent. The man is waiting for a reply."

Elizabeth was alarmed to see Darcy look very grave after he had broken the seal and given the letter a rapid perusal.

"This is from my cousin Anne. My aunt has had some sort of apoplectic attack and is quite ill."

Even as he spoke, he rose from the table, "I will send an answer that we will reach Rosings as soon as possible, departing at once. Lady Meg," he continued with a bow to his guest, "I hope that you will forgive me if I take leave of you now."

Lady Margaret, who was always quite decided in her actions when the circumstances seemed to demand it, expressed her wish that Lady Catherine should recover quickly from her illness, told Elizabeth again how happy she was to have gained a new friend, and left at once to return to Castle Faulconer. Elizabeth was no less diligent, and within the hour the Darcys were on the road to Kent.

CHAPTER 9

he third morning after their departure from Pemberley found the Darcys entering the village of Hunsford. Elizabeth never failed to be impressed by the extraordinary difference that the possession of great wealth made in the business of moving about from one place to another. Although their journey had been made as rapidly as possible, a luxurious carriage and the best inns had made it reasonably comfortable.

As they approached the parsonage Darcy turned to his wife and taking her hand said, "My darling, I have a mind to leave you with Mrs. Collins until I see how things stand at Rosings. If my aunt has recovered and if she should insult you, I could never forgive her or enter her house again. Do you mind staying here for a few hours until I am sure that you will meet with a proper reception?"

Elizabeth thought this a sound plan and told her husband that she would be happy to stay with her old friend until Darcy should see fit to come for her. They found Mrs. Collins at home and overjoyed to see Mrs. Darcy for the first time since the latter's wedding. The rector had left for Rosings just moments before to see if he could be of any assistance to his patroness, Lady Catherine.

"How is my aunt, Mrs. Collins?" Asked Darcy. "Have you had a report of her today?"

"I am glad to be able to tell you, Mr. Darcy, that she is somewhat better. I was with her this morning, and the weakness of her left side that had so alarmed us is all but gone. She was sitting up and seemed much recovered. Dr. Crawford, who came from London two days ago, is very encouraging."

"And how are her spirits, Mrs. Collins?" asked Darcy. "You know that she has never been ill before in her life."

"I am afraid that in that regard I cannot give you such a favorable report. She is very quiet and subdued. Not at all her usual self."

Darcy then hurried to Rosings, leaving his wife at the parsonage.

Elizabeth's first words after his departure showed that she well understood her duty to her friend, "I am concerned about Lady Catherine, of course, but as you say she is out of danger so we may proceed to the most important subject at hand. Is your darling son asleep or may I have the delight of making his acquaintance at once?"

The ladies spent the next half hour in the nursery, and Elizabeth's appreciation of little Henry's perfection was almost equal to his mother's.

The two friends then retired to a sunny window seat and Mrs. Collins began a narrative of the events of the past few days.

"I must first explain a circumstance which will very much astonish you, Elizabeth," she said. "Over the past weeks I have come to know Miss de Bourgh quite well. In fact, I do not think I am exaggerating when I say that we have formed a friendship."

Elizabeth did express her amazement at this news. "I would not know how to make a friend of someone who never speaks and who seems quite indifferent to everyone around her. How did you accomplish this prodigious feat?"

"We must give that good man Colonel Fitzwilliam the credit," replied Charlotte. "Before he went away, he came to see me and asked that I exert myself to know his cousin better. He said that she was a young lady of unusual sweetness and intelligence, but sadly shy of company. He pointed out that his aunt's temperament was hardly well calculated to bring out the best qualities of such a timid girl. I then remembered a hundred instances when Lady Catherine had interrupted her daughter's tentative efforts at joining in conversation. Do you remember how Miss de Bourgh has occasionally stopped outside the parsonage gates when out in her carriage?"

"Indeed," replied Elizabeth, "And I thought it an exceptionally rude thing to do. I recall her keeping you standing out in a cold wind one day."

"Well, I know it seemed a very strange way to pay a visit," said Charlotte, "but I now understand. The poor girl is so shy that she had not the courage to descend and enter the house. After my conversation with the colonel, the next time I saw her stop I overcame my own diffidence enough to ask her to come in and take tea. I was rewarded with a really lovely smile. It made her quite pretty. We spent a very pleasant hour together and I discovered that she is a well-read and thoughtful person, anxious to learn more about the world, but frustrated in her attempts to do so by her mother's excessive solicitude. I would not have you think that she openly criticized Lady Catherine, but one would have to be very dull not to see what an oppressive life the poor young lady has had in that household. Since that day we have met at least three times a week and have had many conversations of exceptional interest. She has a particular fondness for natural philosophy and loves to ramble around the countryside. Unfortunately, she is only able to do so by deceiving her mother, who thinks her too delicate for such activities. While I cannot approve such a course of action, I can certainly see how Miss de Bourgh has been driven to it."

"You mean that she is not sickly, as we have so often been told that she is by Lady Catherine?" cried Elizabeth in surprise.

"Very far from it my dear. That is purely a peculiar notion of her ladyship's. Miss de Bourgh's pale and sad appearance, to which we have become accustomed in our past acquaintance with her, has, I believe, been due more to depression of spirits than to any bodily frailty."

Elizabeth merely shook her head in silent dismay at the unhappiness of the young lady's situation. She also had to admit to herself a feeling of shame at her own failure to perceive anything more in Anne. On her previous visit to Rosings she had dismissed her as uninteresting, proud and probably stupid. "I should have made an effort to know her," she said, "How quick I am to judge on such slight information."

At times it was a cause of worry to Elizabeth that those she loved gave her so much credit for excellence of character and temperament. To her husband she was an angel and the source of all joy on earth, with only one or two minor but charming faults, so as to make it possible for her to associate with lesser beings. Her beloved sister Jane and her friend Charlotte gave her credit for all the important virtues, while perhaps not seeing in her quite so much perfection as did Darcy. In her heart she sometimes thought herself unworthy of their high opinion, and often wondered how she could improve her very imperfect nature before they might perceive the truth and suffer the disillusionment that would follow. She now resolved to take a very different approach to Miss de Bourgh and to try to win her friendship.

"And now, my dear Lizzie," said Charlotte, interrupting her reflections, "I must tell you about the drama which took place on the morning of Lady Catherine's falling ill."

A drama at Rosings was a difficult thing to imagine and Elizabeth regarded her friend with curiosity.

"We had just finished breakfast and Mr. Collins was about to start on his usual rounds, when one of the servants from the great house arrived in a state of terrified haste and confusion. The poor man finally managed to relay the information that her ladyship had succumbed to a violent fit of apoplexy and had been carried unconscious to her chamber. My husband's response to this news was such as to make me fear that he would fall victim to a similar fate. Fortunately I was able to calm him enough to allow us to leave immediately for Rosings in our pony cart. Somehow we survived the drive, which was completed at a dead gallop with our conveyance threatening to overturn at every moment."

Elizabeth could well imagine that Mr. Collins would be rather worse than useless in any emergency and was grateful that her friend had lived to tell her tale.

"The physician from Hunsford, Dr. Williams, was already with Lady Catherine," continued Charlotte, "and for the first hour, while he completed his examination, there was nothing for us to do but wait in a state of painful anxiety. I asked for Miss de Bourgh and was told that she was in the library. There I found her in a pitiable state, weeping all alone in a corner of that vast room. When I tried to comfort her, she burst out with the most anguished imprecations against herself, saying that she had caused her mother's illness. It took some time for me to understand what had occurred, but I finally was able to conclude that the girl had on that morning defied Lady Catherine's oppression for the first time."

Elizabeth wondered how Anne could have lived under such tyranny for so many years without doing so before.

"For some time," continued Charlotte, "it has been Miss de Bourgh's habit to rise quite early in order to avoid being observed by her mother, as Lady Catherine is rarely abroad out of doors before noon. The young lady had gone for a walk and had been so fortunate as to come across an unusual tortoise that held some considerable interest for her. She had knelt upon the ground to better observe it, when her mother, contrary to her ordinary regimen, appeared around the shrubbery and let out a cry of utmost horror. Well, my dear, I know that you have had occasion to see Lady Catherine in a passion. At first she threatened to dismiss Mrs. Jenkinson for allowing Miss de Bourgh to encounter the dangers of the morning dew. The young lady, in her anxiety to defend her friend, made it clear that not only was the control of her governess at an end, but that even her mother's authority was no longer to be absolute. She could, she informed her ladyship, decide for herself how best to preserve her own health. Lady Catherine's rage at this unprecedented rebellion ended with her falling to the ground in an apoplectic fit, and by the time her daughter had returned with assistance, her ladyship was unconscious."

"Heavens, Charlotte!" cried Elizabeth, "How dreadful for Miss de Bourgh! Her first attempt at independence to end in such a disaster. Has she seen her mother since Lady Catherine regained her faculties?"

"I think not," replied Mrs. Collins, "and I know that the poor girl has been suffering terribly."

The sound of the carriage announced the return of Mr. Darcy, who entered the room accompanied by Mr. Collins. The two gentlemen had left Rosings together and the rector had been pleased to accept Darcy's offer of a ride home. Elizabeth remembered her husband's cold disdain when Mr. Collins had approached him at a ball and sought the honor of his acquaintance. The incident had occurred before Elizabeth had ever imagined that Darcy would become her suitor. Now she could see that he tolerated the rather annoying clergyman because of her own friendship with Charlotte, and she inwardly blessed him for his forbearance.

Elizabeth could see the relief in her husband's countenance as he informed them of the excellent report that he had received from the London physician who had arrived two days before. "Dr. Crawford seems certain that my aunt will recover completely and I feel great confidence in his opinion. He is one of the most eminent physicians in London, recommended by Lord Dumbello when word reached him of my aunt's illness. Crawford does caution that an extended period of rest will be necessary to avoid any repetition of the apoplexy, which he says could be fatal another time. I will discuss with him how best to manage Lady Catherine's convalescence before he returns to town in a few days."

Everyone expressed their gratification at this news, and Darcy, turning to his wife, added, "I saw my aunt for a few minutes and she immediately rebuked me for not bringing you to her at once, saying 'I'm glad enough to see you, nephew, but where is my new niece? Where is Elizabeth?' So, Mrs. Collins, thank you for your hospitality. How happy we are to have such a friend, that is, friends," and he included Mr. Collins in the compliment with a somewhat reserved bow.

The Collinses saw their visitors to their carriage and promised to call the following morning. As the Darcys traveled the short distance to Rosings, Elizabeth learned that Lady Catherine was indeed making a remarkable recovery.

"She was sitting up with no sign of weakness although she has not yet been permitted to walk. She seems very much her old self," related Darcy, "Her manner was as imperious as ever but I think that she is touched by our coming to her side without delay. I believe that her plan is to save face by pretending that there has never been any kind of estrangement as a result of our marriage."

"She is certainly unpredictable," replied Elizabeth, "but I am glad of this change of attitude. I know that you are fond of your aunt and I will be happy to be her friend if she will allow it."

On their arrival at Rosings the Darcys were shown to the finest guest chamber of the house and every attention was paid to their comfort. "My goodness, what a different reception from what I anticipated," commented Elizabeth as she stood with Darcy, looking down at the splendid gardens of Rosings from one of the great windows. "What a lovely room this is. I wonder who arranged the flowers so beautifully."

Darcy bent to kiss her and said, "My love, you are so good to come to Rosings with me and express a willingness to forgive my aunt's past insults. Heaven knows, she does not deserve it."

Elizabeth smiled and replied, "My dearest one, I am not at all good, or if I have any virtues they arise from my love for you. I would face much worse trials then putting up with Lady Catherine in order to make you happy."

Soon Elizabeth received a summons to Lady Catherine's bedside. Dr. Crawford met her at the door and gave his approval for the interview, with the warning that the invalid must rest after a brief visit was paid.

Elizabeth found her ladyship reclining on a chaise in the handsomely appointed room. The older lady was somewhat thinner and her complexion had lost its usual fine, high color, but otherwise she appeared unchanged. She indicated a chair placed immediately at her side and Elizabeth sat down obediently.

"How well you look, my dear," said Lady Catherine, "I always thought you pretty but you have become quite a beauty." Elizabeth had not expected such a compliment and murmured her thanks.

"I have had excellent reports of you from my friends in London. Although I no longer spend time there myself, I rely on my many correspondents to keep me informed. I admit that I was uncertain as to how you would fare in the highest ranks of society, used as you were to a circumscribed life in a small country village. I'm happy to say that by all accounts you have done very well and have won the esteem of people whose good opinion is worth having. I have recently received a letter from my old friend Lady Carlyle, in which she praises you as most elegant and amiable and admired by all who have had the pleasure of meeting you."

Elizabeth heard some of Lady Catherine's former condescension in this speech but she had the impression that the older lady was making an effort to modify her usual arrogant manner. Therefore she expressed her thanks for these favorable comments in what she hoped was the tone of a grateful niece.

"Much more important than these reports, however, " continued Lady Catherine, "was the assurance of my nephew Fitzwilliam of the great happiness that Darcy has found with you. In the course of his last visit he spoke to me of reconciliation, although at the time I rebuffed him unkindly, I am afraid. He gave me much to think on, however, and even before my illness I had resolved to write and try to restore communication with you both. Therefore, my dear, let me now welcome you as my niece. I can see the transformation you have wrought in Darcy. He is clearly a man with every source of joy in his wife."

With great solemnity Lady Catherine offered Elizabeth her hand and turned her cheek to be kissed. Elizabeth felt tears come into her eyes. She knew how much the restoration of family peace would mean to her husband, although he had never uttered a word of complaint. Lady Catherine also seemed much moved and the two ladies parted on better terms than either would have imagined possible.

CHAPTER 1c

*L*ady Catherine's physician ordered complete rest and solitude for his patient for the balance of the day, and the Darcys were left with an afternoon to reacquaint themselves with Rosings, now that their banishment was at an end. The day seemed to threaten rain but Elizabeth was anxious to see the rose garden in its summer beauty, as she had the ambition to create something of equal splendor at Pemberley.

"Is it not odd, my love," she said to Darcy as they traversed the terrace leading to the flower gardens, "that we have not yet seen your cousin Miss de Bourgh? Did she greet you when you arrived?"

"She met me when I entered the house and clearly had made careful arrangements for our comfort, as you have observed. But before I could ask her more than the most preliminary questions about her mother, she took her leave on some pretext. Of course I was soon preoccupied with discussing my aunt's condition with her physician and with paying a brief visit to the sickroom."

"She almost seems to be avoiding us, but I hope that I am wrong about that. I would so much like to be her friend if it is possible." And she told Darcy about her conversation with Charlotte. He was not as surprised as she had expected him to be to learn that his cousin was not the dull and feeble person she appeared to be.

"When she was a child of ten or eleven years old, she was very lively and inquisitive," explained Darcy, "but soon thereafter my aunt began to believe that her health was at risk and that her activities must be greatly curtailed. This was soon after my uncle's death, whereupon Anne became the center of my aunt's attention. By the time she was sixteen her life had become a very narrow one and Fitzwilliam and I knew less and less of her. It is remarkable that my cousin's spirits should have survived such an excess of maternal solicitude."

They had reached the top of the stone steps that led down to the rose garden when Darcy became concerned that a sudden downpour might interrupt their walk. Seeing Elizabeth's reluctance to return to the house, he quickly left her to fetch oilskin capes.

The view from this point was lovely, the gardens below giving way to meadows and the oak grove beyond. Elizabeth was enjoying the cool air and the beauty of the scene before her, when Miss de Bourgh appeared on a garden path, having emerged from behind a boxwood hedge. The young lady was walking listlessly and even at a little distance Elizabeth could see that she was weeping. After standing indecisively for a moment, Anne sat down on a stone bench and seemed to be making an effort to compose herself.

Elizabeth was uncertain of how to proceed. She could imagine how Miss de Bourgh might feel at having her distress observed by someone she barely knew, but it was unthinkable to simply walk away. This dilemma was of short duration however for Anne looked up and saw her.

At first it seemed that the girl would flee back into the shrubbery, for her initial movements seemed to suggest such a course of action. Then, with an evident determination to overcome this impulse, Anne came forward to greet her guest, who was now descending the steps.

Elizabeth expressed her happiness at seeing her new relation. "I am so looking forward to knowing you better, Miss de Bourgh. Mrs. Collins has been telling me how much she enjoys your society and how greatly she values your friendship. I consider myself very fortunate in our close family connection and hope that you will think of me as a friend as well." She went on to say how much she and Darcy appreciated all the attention to their comfort, the lovely bedchamber filled with flowers and every kind of carefully chosen appointment.

Anne's face still bore the evidence of her tears, but she murmured her thanks for these remarks. She looked at the lovely Mrs. Darcy with a mixture of admiration and diffidence. Elizabeth did not comprehend how great was the change in her own appearance since her last visit to Rosings, when she had been a pretty and lively young lady but without the least pretense to fashion and only one outmoded gown for evening parties. Now, in the months since her marriage, it had become evident that she possessed a great natural elegance, and her perfect taste in dress was widely admired. Happiness in her marriage and her ever -growing confidence had transformed her into a striking beauty. Elizabeth was alone in not being aware of this. She had some natural degree of vanity but, while she took pleasure in exquisite clothes, her greatest desire was to give Darcy reason to be proud of his wife. He had become the center of her existence and any pains she took were for the reward of pleasing him.

"Come, let us sit upon this bench for a few minutes, if you have leisure to do so, Miss de Bourgh," said Elizabeth, "I believe that we are now safe from the threat of rain." The sun had indeed appeared and the garden was an inviting spot, with the intoxicating fragrance of Lady Catherine's roses.

Anne nodded assent shyly and they took their seat. Elizabeth asked a few questions about the cultivation of roses and was impressed by the depth of Anne's knowledge, which was both practical and scientific. There were some books in the library at Rosings on this and related matters and she had read them all, as Elizabeth discovered after some gentle questioning.

"I have much to learn as I am afraid that I paid but little attention to our garden when I was growing up at Longbourn. My sister Jane made better use of her opportunities. I hope that you will be so kind as to visit us at Pemberley and advise me, for I have many questions."

Anne, who was feeling better able to converse with Mrs. Darcy, replied that she would be very glad to be of assistance.

Darcy had returned from his mission and had reached the steps, but seeing the two ladies decided not to interrupt their conversation, as he no longer felt any anxiety about his Elizabeth encountering a drop of rain.

~

ANNE HAD SENT an invitation for dinner to Mr. and Mrs. Collins. It had occurred to her that Elizabeth would be eager to spend as much time as possible in the company of her dear friend Charlotte after the long separation that they had endured. Dr. Crawford, a most gentleman-like man of an old Kentish family, was also of the company. It was a small gathering but Anne had never before done the honors of the house and found herself almost ill with anxiety as she waited for her guests in the drawing room that evening. She had long made every effort to shrink from attention and the thought that she must be brought before everyone's notice made her wish to run away and hide like a small child. She considered herself to be plain and uninteresting, and the necessity of conversing with her guests filled her with despair.

Mrs. Collins had imagined the feelings of her young friend on this occasion and had managed to arrive early. She was the first to enter the room and found Anne in a sad state of nerves. Before Charlotte could offer any reassurance, Dr. Crawford entered the room with Mr. Collins. The clergyman hurried along beside the eminent physician, pressing him to repeat for the tenth time the encouraging report of Lady Catherine's continued improvement.

Dr. Crawford was saying, "Please set your mind at ease, Mr. Collins. As I assured you a moment ago, Lady Catherine is out of danger and we may look forward to her complete recovery." This was said with the gentlemanly forbearance of one all too well acquainted with the foolishness of the Mr. Collinses of the world.

The physician came up to the two ladies to make his bow and had a smile of particular kindness for Anne. During his stay in the house he had observed much and deduced even more. He had seen the books that Anne had left out on the table in the library and had surmised that she was an unusually intelligent girl, very timid and much oppressed by her mother. He had taken the trouble to prepare some topics of conversation to put her at her ease, and in a few minutes Anne was surprised to find that she was not as anxious as she had expected to be.

A few minutes later Darcy and Elizabeth entered the room. All were struck by the beauty of the couple and their overflowing happiness. Anyone who had known Darcy before his marriage would hardly have recognized him in the cheerful, animated man who seemed glad for all the world to know of his felicity. Anne, who had been acquainted with him all her life, was particularly struck by the change in her cousin. If only, she thought, some force could transform *me* into a different sort of being. She was very glad for Darcy and had no feeling of jealousy. Her mother's wishes for the cousins to marry had always seemed absurd to Anne as there had been no attachment on either side, and she had been humiliated by Lady Catherine's attempts to promote the match.

The group was soon engaged in general conversation without the need for any effort on the part of their hostess. Dr. Crawford managed to draw Anne out somewhat by the simple expedient of asking her opinion on several topics of current interest in the county. He was surprised to find her well informed on the prospects for the year's harvest, the need for a better bridge across a local river and the fashion for importing a new breed of sheep from Belgium. She was also able to describe the characteristics and architecture of some of the ancient churches in the neighborhood. Darcy soon joined their conversation and Anne spoke with some degree of confidence and spirit under the kind influence of the two gentlemen.

A half hour had passed very agreeably and Anne had begun to feel some concern about the proper way in which to seat her guests at the dinner table, when sounds of someone arriving in the front hall were heard. Full of curiosity, Anne left the room found that Colonel Fitzwilliam had just entered the house. She went up to him, full of joy and gratitude. He took her hand and said, "Dear Anne, I have come here as quickly as ever I could to be with you. Are you well?"

They went into the drawing room and all were delighted to see Fitzwilliam, particularly as it had seemed unlikely that he would be able to reach Rosings for several more days. The colonel was given the news of Lady Catherine's improvement and his relief was evident.

Anne, standing quietly beside Fitzwilliam, felt great happiness at the presence of her greatest support and ally. She had always had perfect confidence in her cousin and now that he was here, she would fear nothing.

Fitzwilliam left to pay a brief visit to his aunt and to dress for dinner, which was delayed on his behalf. On his return he was pleased to see how well Anne did her duty as hostess. With the patience of a well-bred woman, she was listening attentively to Mr. Collins' rambling account of his difficulties keeping honeybees.

"After the hundredth sting, Miss de Bourgh, one wonders if it is altogether a worthwhile endeavor. Despite my taking the greatest care, the creatures seem to bear me unrelenting ill will. I'm sure I've done nothing to deserve such malice."

Anne murmured some words of sympathy, thinking to herself that if Mr. Collins bore himself about the apiary as clumsily as he did in the drawing room, she could not wonder at the animosity of the bees.

"And your new sheep, Mr. Collins. How do they come along?"

"Oh, very much better, thank you. Except for the incident when they got into the garden two weeks ago and destroyed the lettuces. You are *so* kind to inquire, Miss de Bourgh." Mr. Collins was enchanted by the young lady's interest in the small affairs of the rectory.

All this time Anne was now and then under subtle scrutiny. Someone who had kept herself so very shut off from the world could not fail to be an object of curiosity. All those present wished her well, but it was natural to wonder whether she had any talents or brilliant qualities that had hitherto been concealed. Elizabeth, now that she had decided to be of service to the young lady if it were possible, made a careful study of Miss de Bourgh from where she sat at the other side of the room. What she saw at first was not encouraging as Anne appeared rather unprepossessing to the casual observer.

What can her mother be thinking, thought Elizabeth, to allow a girl with such delicate coloring to appear in that dreadfully unbecoming shade of cerise? She has a lovely complexion, I see now, but looks quite sallow in that color. Her dress, although of the most expensive fabric, is several years behind the fashion and much too old for her. Lady Catherine seeks to make her daughter a copy of herself, but two women were never more unlike, at least in looks and manner. Had I but the dressing of this unfortunate young lady, she would present a very different aspect to the world. Mrs. Darcy was not averse to the notion of taking on Anne's amelioration as a worthwhile project, if only the opportunity should present itself.

Anne, with a look of encouragement from Fitzwilliam, somehow got through the daunting task of sending everyone into dinner in proper form, and soon the party was happily engaged in a most pleasant meal. Darcy and Fitzwilliam, who had not seen each other for several weeks, were full of conversation, which they took care to make of general interest. Dr. Crawford, intelligent and well informed, was an agreeable addition to the company. Mr. Collins, fortunately for all concerned, was too much in awe of Darcy to make any but the briefest remarks. The ladies were able to join in occasionally during the brief moments of silence that the gentlemen left them as points of entry.

At the conclusion of dinner Anne became aware of her guests' attention turned towards her expectantly. It took her a moment's reflection to remember that it was now her duty to lead the ladies to the drawing room. She rose with a blush and Elizabeth and Charlotte followed her example with a good-natured alacrity intended to make her awkwardness less apparent. Anne was quickly made more at ease by the coordinated efforts of the two old friends, who introduced topics designed to allow their young hostess to appear in the best light. By the time the gentlemen joined them, Anne found that she was actually enjoying herself.

Darcy and Fitzwilliam soon persuaded Elizabeth to take her place at the piano, and all listened to her performance with delight. During her time in London she had studied with one of the best masters, and at Pemberley she had been practicing daily. She had always had a lovely voice but now began to show some degree of mastery on the pianoforte. Darcy looked on with an understandable pride in his wife, whom he had won against what had seemed to him almost insurmountable obstacles. He could not resist going to her as she rested her voice and reminding her of their first conversation at that spot.

"Although you did so in a light and satirical tone, you accused me of being a hopelessly unsocial being, arrogant and unfeeling towards my fellow creatures. And never, my darling, was such a characterization so well deserved."

"How outrageously I treated you and how well you bore it," laughed Elizabeth. She turned to Fitzwilliam who had walked across the room to join them. "Were you not dismayed to see your cousin so abused?"

"Frankly, I could not have been more delighted to see Darcy jolted out of his complacency. His very genuine superiority to the great majority of humanity had made circumstances too easy for him. Some challenge was needed to make him more tolerant," replied Fitzwilliam with a teasing smile at Darcy, who responded with an amused laugh.

The change in him is truly remarkable, thought Fitzwilliam, To realize it, I have only to remember how he would once have responded to being the object of even the most harmless jest.

Fitzwilliam then continued, "How odd society would be if your example were followed more often. Most young men are at pains to present their best qualities to the world, while you seemed determined to conceal yours, Darcy. Perhaps that is the only way to attract the interest of the more angelic sort of lady. They take pity on such imperfection."

"Well, then there is little hope for you, Fitzwilliam," retorted Darcy, "since you have no faults."

From across the room, Anne watched the three friends at the piano wistfully. She could see how irresistible Elizabeth was, and how quickly she became the focus of any company fortunate enough to enjoy her presence. So this is to be my fate, no doubt, she thought, and I will always be only an observer, never a participant in this great game of words and laughter, of which I understand neither the rules nor the theory. Anne tried to resign herself to this view of her future with a stoicism rare in a young woman of twenty-six. Dr. Crawford, who was sitting with his hostess, noted her momentary abstraction and following her glance could imagine what her feelings were. He too had felt an impulse to join the gentlemen paying court to the fascinating Mrs. Darcy, but had resisted the inclination in order to make quiet conversation with Anne. He pitied the lonely girl with all his heart and had devoted some time to thinking of a stratagem to free her from the rule of Lady Catherine. On the morrow he planned to discuss his idea with Darcy and Fitzwilliam and he hoped that they shared his concern for Anne.

At the insistence of the company, Elizabeth began to sing again. This time she was joined by her husband, who had a fine baritone voice and they made a very charming tableau to the delight of all present. There was no conscious design in this, however, for they were aware only of each other.

Feeling himself to be *de trop*, Fitzwilliam had made his way to Anne's side and asked if he might join her conversation with Dr. Crawford and Mr. and Mrs. Collins. His cousin greeted him with a slight smile, motioning for him to sit with them. Even a very acute observer would not have guessed how Fitzwilliam's crossing the room to her had changed Anne's mood into one of quiet happiness. How modestly he asks to join us, she thought, as though the sun asked permission to shine upon the dull earth.

Conversation now centered on the habits of the various hawk-like birds of the region and it was discovered that Dr. Crawford was an amateur ornithologist. Fitzwilliam, who knew little of the characteristics of birds of any kind, made himself agreeable by asking pertinent questions and listening carefully to the answers. Occasionally he glanced in the direction of Darcy and Elizabeth, who were now standing by the open door to the moonlit terrace and talking softly. Fitzwilliam had greatly admired the young lady who had become Mrs. Darcy when she had first visited Rosings. hardly more than a year before. At times it was only with difficulty that he repressed an unworthy pang of envy at Darcy's good fortune.

At length the Collinses departed for the parsonage and all were glad to retire to rest. Anne was very fatigued. She had known few demands on her fortitude, having always been encouraged to regard herself as weak, requiring protection, and incapable of the slightest exertion. She hoped that she not acquitted herself too badly that evening, but was unable to form any conclusion, as the entire experience was too new to her. She was aware that everyone had made an effort to help her through her trial and while she was grateful, she felt that it was somewhat humiliating to need such assistance.

She would have been left with these unsatisfactory reflections if her cousin Fitzwilliam had not come up to bid her goodnight, with a mirthful warmth in his eyes. He made a solemn bow and thanked her quite formally for "a most extraordinarily delightful evening." Then, smiling, he said, "Well done, dear Cousin. I see that you have the gift for putting others at their ease and making all things tend to the enjoyment of your guests. What a great lady you are destined to be."

CHAPTER 11

The next day it rained, but the second morning was particularly fine and Fitzwilliam rose early with the intention of enjoying an hour's fishing before breakfast. He wondered if his cousin Anne would think of joining him at their old meeting place. He had had little opportunity to speak with her the evening before, although he had observed her first tentative steps into the realm of social intercourse with extreme interest and an anxious solicitude. How valiantly the butterfly struggles against the most stubborn and constrictive of cocoons, he thought.

After catching and throwing back two small trout, he was contemplating returning to the house to see if any of his friends were about, when he saw Darcy and Elizabeth walking down the hill toward him, accompanied by Dr. Crawford. There was something of the solemnity of a delegation in their demeanor as they approached him, and Fitzwilliam went to greet them with some curiosity.

"I told Elizabeth and Dr. Crawford that finding you on a summer morning was a simple matter," said Darcy, "Any sport?"

"Little enough that this interruption is not unwelcome."

"This seemed like an excellent opportunity for a family conference," said Darcy. "Dr. Crawford has told us of his conversation with you yesterday and suggested that we confer on the best plan for ensuring our aunt's complete recovery."

"Yes, Colonel Fitzwilliam," began Dr. Crawford, "I have been telling Mr. and Mrs. Darcy what I told you; that I am convinced that Lady Catherine must have a complete change from her usual pattern of life and leave Rosings until she is completely well. If she stays here, the sources of irritation that brought on her first attack may induce a second, possibly fatal illness. I believe that she can do no better than to go to Bath for a prolonged stay. There is enough to interest her there that she will not be dull, while at the same time she will find no cause for aggravation."

"The second idea the colonel and I discussed relates to Miss de Bourgh," continued the physician, "We do not feel that she should accompany her mother to Bath. There has been some conflict of wills between mother and daughter. Forgive me if I speak frankly, but in my profession it is often necessary. I believe we have all heard something of the disagreement that lead to her ladyship's collapse. Lady Catherine gave me a detailed account of it – from *her* point of view."

Darcy had given Fitzwilliam some idea of what had occurred, based on what Mrs. Collins had related to Elizabeth. Charlotte may perhaps be forgiven for repeating what Anne had told her of the dreadful contretemps with Lady Catherine. There is always some pressing reason to be found for breaking such confidences and the more confidential the information the more quickly does it seem to become general knowledge. Anne, who was at that moment nervously going over the proposed menu for that day's dinner with the housekeeper, would have been mortified had she known that the absurd and painful scene with her mother was known to everyone at Rosings and at the parsonage.

"Elizabeth and I want Anne to come with us, first back to Pemberley and from there on to Scotland," said Darcy. "It is time she saw something of the world beyond Rosings and Hunsford. I do not believe that she has ever been out of Kent."

"I should add that there is no reason for apprehension in regard to Miss de Bourgh's health," said Dr. Crawford. "The young lady has allowed me to perform an examination and I have found her to be quite strong and without any symptoms of chronic illness. The idea that she is an invalid has been entirely an unfortunate conception of her mother's, seconded by the opinions of incompetent or sycophantic physicians. It is tragic that she should have led so confined an existence, but now we have the opportunity to release her from her imprisonment."

Fitzwilliam looked thoughtful and after a moment during which his companions looked at him as if he were a source of particular wisdom, he said, "How happy I was to hear your reassurances, Dr. Crawford, when we spoke yesterday. It certainly confirmed my own impression." Turning to Darcy and Elizabeth he continued, "I had been forming my own plan to take her to my parents in Yorkshire and from there she could go with them to Scotland. They would be overjoyed for the opportunity to see her after so many years, but I suppose that the estrangement that has existed for so long due to my aunt's inexplicable attitude towards my father might make it impracticable. It would be best for her to go with you to Pemberley and from there to Scotland. My aunt is less likely to object. But perhaps that is not convenient for you?"

Darcy and Elizabeth said that they would be delighted to take Anne with them to Pemberley. It would be a great thing to rescue her from the circumscribed life she was leading at Rosings.

"The only thing that remains to be decided is this," said Fitzwilliam, "Who will go to Bath with my aunt? You know that she will never go alone."

A few more minutes in conference provided an answer. Anne clearly no longer needed a governess, so Mrs. Jenkinson would accompany Lady Catherine. There was also the idea that Mrs. Collins and little Henry might benefit from taking the waters. The devoted Mr. Collins would surely be willing to part from his wife and child for a time in order to assist his patroness. In short, all contingencies had been provided for and it only remained to persuade Lady Catherine. Fitzwilliam understood at once that this duty was to fall primarily to himself.

"What does my cousin Anne think of your idea?" he asked.

There was a brief silence, then Darcy spoke, "We have not yet mentioned this to her although both Dr. Crawford and I have broached the subject with Lady Catherine."

Fitzwilliam flushed with irritation, very annoyed with his friends. "I see no reason to exclude Anne from this discussion," he said sharply. "Though she seems very young because of the life she has led, she is twenty-six years old. She has sense and intelligence and should be allowed to have a say in such important deliberations. Perhaps we should consult her feelings before we pursue this further."

His three companions could see that he was annoyed and they felt somewhat ashamed that it had never occurred to them to consult Anne. Fitzwilliam was the best natured of men, but once decided on a proper course of action he was immovable. They all walked back to the house having agreed that a conference with Anne was to be arranged as soon as possible.

The party reassembled in the breakfast room where Anne awaited them, having summoned up the usual splendid morning's repast for her guests. Everything at Rosings was predicated on Lady Catherine's conception of what was due to herself and to those fortunate enough to be counted among her friends and relations. Her ladyship liked to advise lesser beings such as Mrs. Collins on the minute details of living on a small income, but her own wealth was vast and the luxury of her house reflected this happy state of affairs.

The company was in good spirits and breakfast was a cheerful affair. Dr. Crawford had been able to give a very reassuring report on his patient. She might even be carried down for dinner the next day if her improvement continued.

Anne was beginning to feel more at ease as hostess and on this occasion asked Elizabeth many questions about London. Much was said about museums and shops, but Elizabeth was most enthusiastic about the concerts that had given her such pleasure during her first season in the capitol. "But perhaps, cousin Anne, I will soon have the delight of introducing you to some of these diversions," she added somewhat hesitantly. This was an opening for the introduction of the plan that Anne's friends had been at pains to invent for her. Darcy had been elected as their spokesman and he began an explanation in the calm and reasonable manner that rarely failed to persuade his listeners. He tactfully made no mention of the disagreement between his cousin and her mother.

"Dr. Crawford believes that my aunt must have as much rest as possible, taking only the most limited advantage of the activities which Bath has to offer. There will be society enough there that she need not be bored, but at the same time she will not be tempted to overexert herself as she would here at Rosings."

Anne listened attentively and agreed that her mother always had some matter that seemed to urgently engage her attention. "Until this illness I have never known her to endure a moment's repose. She is not contemplative by nature."

This was such a delicate understatement that Anne's friends had difficulty repressing their smiles.

"Perhaps you will agree then that Bath would be a rational choice for her convalescence?" Anne nodded and Darcy continued, "This brings us to the second part of the plan I have in mind. If you accompany your mother to such a fashionable watering place, I fear that Lady Catherine will concern herself with your *entré* into Bath society and neglect the measures necessary for her recovery. Every evening will bring some ball or other *fête*, which she. being a fond mother and anxious for your amusement, will insist on attending with you." At this Anne was unable to suppress an ironic smile of her own. Was Darcy speaking of *her* mother?

"Elizabeth and I would like to propose that instead you spend the next few months with us, first joining us for our journey to Scotland and then returning to Pemberley. We would be delighted to have you with us for as long as possible, certainly through Christmas. Perhaps your mother will be able to join our family party by then."

This was a distinct surprise to Anne. She had not imagined that she would be invited to stay with her newly married relations and she was immediately certain that she could only be an encumbrance to them. Her next sensation was one of dismay at the idea of leaving her home for the first time and being thrust into the fashionable world of the Darcys.

Elizabeth was quick to add her own affectionate wish for Anne's company, "I would be so very happy, cousin Anne. What a splendid time we will have together."

Anne listened quietly, her color rising slightly, but her face was unreadable. She looked at Fitzwilliam and saw his expression of fond concern. It was apparent that he approved of the proposed arrangement. There was a moment's silence before she spoke, "It is clear that you have all given much thought to the best interests of my mother and myself. As you know I have led a very retired life and the thought of leaving Rosings cannot help but be daunting to me. I thank you for your care and ask that you give me some time to consider what you have said. Forgive me if I leave you for now."

She rose and left the room abruptly. Fitzwilliam followed her almost at once with a murmured apology to his companions. The Darcys and Dr. Crawford were left to finish their breakfast.

"My love," said Elizabeth, turning to her husband, "would it be possible to spend a few days in London on our way back to Pemberley?"

"I think that it might be arranged," replied Darcy, "but I thought that you were tired of London."

"Oh, I am, a little," she said, including Dr. Crawford in a conspiratorial smile, "but there is the important business of new gowns for Miss de Bourgh – a great *many* new gowns."

By the time Fitzwilliam left the breakfast room Anne had disappeared. He would have thought it a simple matter to find her, as he was familiar with most of her favorite haunts. After looking in the library, the rose garden, and their usual fishing spot, he thought of the oak grove. As he made his way there he tried to dismiss some feeling of annoyance with Anne, but could not avoid the feeling that she should have waited to talk with him instead of vanishing. Perhaps I should have been the one to present her with the plan, he thought, but since she is to stay with Darcy and Elizabeth it was important that the suggestion come from them first.

It was a warm day and the colonel was somewhat overheated and his usual good humor rather overstrained by the time he entered the cool green shade of the oaks. After wandering about for a few minutes he caught sight of Anne pacing back and forth under one of her beloved trees. She saw him at the same moment and walked towards him. Her face was troubled but he could see no trace of tears.

"I am very sorry, Fitzwilliam," she began "to have put you to the trouble of coming here in this heat to find me. It was absurd of me to rush off like a frightened child but it is very disconcerting for someone who has always been so insignificant to be the focus of attention."

Fitzwilliam's irritation faded away at this speech. "You have never been insignificant," he replied, "It is just that it has never before fallen to your lot to be at the center of a family drama."

Anne smiled slightly at this explanation, "No, my mother holds that position, as she ever has. I am merely an inconvenience. Are Mr. and Mrs. Darcy, married not one year, to be burdened with the constant presence of a tiresome, spinsterish relation? How could you wish such a fate upon your friends?"

"Your description of yourself is too ridiculous to deserve refutation. As for your belief that newly married people should be left to themselves, it may have some merit, except in the case of Darcy and Elizabeth. There is already such a perfect understanding and sympathy between them, as if they had been together for a lifetime, that you could not be the source of any disharmony."

They began to walk in the direction of the house and Fitzwilliam went on to describe the many advantages to be gained by a period of residence with the Darcys. He mentioned balls, visiting, concerts and diversions of all kinds, in short all the amusements likely to appeal to a young lady's imagination.

Anne, in spite of her recent distress, had to smile at her companion's idea of a persuasive argument. "Surely you of all people know me well enough to understand that everything you mention makes me quake with terror," she said, "To be thrust into the midst of society, to be forced to converse with strangers, to be at a ball where I will either be compelled to dance or even worse to be the object of pity and scorn as one not asked to dance – this is the worst misery I can imagine. I very much hope that my mother will allow me to stay here at Rosings while she goes to Bath."

Fitzwilliam looked thoughtful for a moment, and then tried a different tactic. "You know very well that Lady Catherine will never let you stay here. You will be required in Bath and it will be even more difficult than it is for you at Rosings. But of course no one can compel you to stir from your mother's side. You may prefer to continue to spend the remainder of your youth attending upon my aunt's whims and living securely in her shadow. No doubt there would be less to cause you apprehension in such an existence."

He saw at once that his words had hit the mark. Anne's color rose as she said, "You have made this into a challenge, but surely you see that I am not sufficiently courageous to encounter what I most fear."

Her cousin knew that he had won the game but took care not to reveal any hint of triumph. "And you forget that I am a soldier and an officer, used to judging who has courage and who does not. You are like the new recruit who fears his first taste of action, half certain that he will turn and flee at sight of battle. But I have seen enough of you, Anne, to be sure that you will not falter, but will engage the enemy, whoever they may be, with resolution and tenacity."

The idea of the fashionable world as a battlefield amused Anne very much and for a moment she almost forgot her trepidation. Then she asked, "And if I fight well for the next few months, may I expect to be honored with some sort of decoration for bravery?"

"Oh, there will be time enough to judge what kind of medals you deserve at the end of your first campaign. Barring some crisis, I will join you in Scotland for the latter part of your visit there."

This made the sojourn at Castle Munford appear in a more attractive light and by the time they had regained the house Anne was almost resigned to being placed under the protection of Darcy and Elizabeth.

Fitzwilliam stopped near the steps that led to the terrace. "Anne, this may be the most important decision of your life. Do not let fear keep you a prisoner. You were not meant to waste away here at Rosings, but to be part of the great world. Trust me to know what is right for you and I will not fail you."

By the time that everyone at Rosings had gathered for dinner that evening, Anne had regained her composure. She went up to Darcy and Elizabeth when they entered the drawing room and thanked them for their kind invitation to join them at Pemberley and to accompany them to Scotland.

"I never thought that I would have the opportunity to see so much of the world," said Anne, "Derbyshire and the Highlands! I long to see the beauty of which I have read so much. This afternoon I began to read a history of Scotland so I will be better informed when we reach far Caledonia."

The evening passed very pleasantly and Anne seemed more at ease than anyone could remember. Elizabeth told her of the proposed sojourn in London and the many interesting things that they would do there for two or three days. The prospect of shopping did not seem particularly exciting to Anne but she did ask to be taken to visit Westminster if there were sufficient time.

"We shall find the time to do so," said Darcy, "most definitely. And I hope that we may attend a concert as well."

AFTER THE OTHERS had retired for the night, Fitzwilliam took his usual stroll in the garden and looked at stars that were particularly brilliant with a half moon in the dark sky. The garden was fragrant with the white roses that were in full bloom. As he made his second circuit of the path through the rose garden, he saw that Anne was standing before him. He had not heard her approach across the lawn and was startled to see her slight form in the moonlight.

"I have come to see the stars, Fitzwilliam," she began, "for I knew that you would be here and would teach me something about them, just as you have taught me about so many other things."

"Are you not cold in the night air?" he answered, coming up to her and looking down into her face.

Anne laughed and shook her head, "Not at all. I solemnly promise not to die from exposure to moonlight and this very pleasant light breeze. Now please do show me where to find Hercules."

Fitzwilliam had a rather good knowledge of the constellations and they spent an hour looking up into the sky. "Do you see the Plough? That is Ursa Major" he said, "and there is Orion's Belt. Those are both simple to find, but now I will show you some others."

Anne was an attentive student and Fitzwilliam had never enjoyed the role of teacher so much. "You learn quickly, Anne," he said, "you are very clever at everything as far as I can see."

"I never thought to hear that," she replied, "but if it is so, you are the only one to have found it out."

"Others will do so very soon, and you will be valued as you deserve." Fitzwilliam observed that the moonlight was very becoming to Anne and that she was prettier than he had ever seen her before.

"And now, we must go in," he said, "for you really might catch a chill and I want nothing to interfere with your departure for London."

This was not the only night on which Fitzwilliam instructed Anne on the constellations. For the next week they met almost every night, just as she met him in the early morning to fish on the riverbank. No one else knew of these meetings for neither wished for others to join them and spoil the perfect tranquility of those hours, and their friendship became as close as what they had known as children so many years before. As they watched the sky darken and the stars appear, Fitzwilliam wondered aloud where they might both be at that time the following year.

"As long as I am not once again here at Rosings, I shall be glad," said Anne, "If only some circumstance will save me from that fate. I love my mother but would be pleased never to live with her again."

"We shall see," replied Fitzwilliam, "Whatever happens I will do all that I can to promote your happiness. You lost your brother many years ago but I promise that you will never lose *me*."

CHAPTER 12

The following days found the colonel and Darcy in the library, planning the dispersal of the inhabitants of Rosings to different parts of the kingdom with the skill of chess players moving pawns around a board.

"Elizabeth and I will depart for London with Anne in three day's time. We will remain there for two or three nights only before leaving for Pemberley. Then we will begin the journey to Scotland as soon as may be, perhaps within ten days."

"Why go to London at all?" asked Fitzwilliam, "Surely it is inconvenient to open your house for such a short visit."

"True enough," replied Darcy with a smile, "but convenience does not enter into the discussion when there is the matter of new frocks for my cousin Anne. Elizabeth declares that she cannot go into society with her present wardrobe and there is nothing for it but a day at the dressmakers in town. In fact, we will remain at Pemberley only long enough to receive Anne's new raiment, after which we set off for your father's castle at once."

The gentlemen found the subject of ladies' finery too complex for further contemplation, and Fitzwilliam merely nodded before saying, "I will accompany my aunt and Mrs. Jenkinson to Bath one week from today. Dr. Crawford has offered to attend Lady Catherine on her journey as well and I am very glad of it. He has a sister there and often visits her. As you know, I received word this morning that our arrangements are complete and that one of the finest houses in the town is being made ready for my aunt's accommodation. Mr. Collins will follow our party in about a week and leave Mrs. Collins and their son with Lady Catherine for some extended period."

"That will be pleasant for my aunt," said Darcy, "but how is Mr. Collins to manage without his wife? I fear that there will be absolute chaos in the parish."

"Your concern is only too well justified," replied Fitzwilliam with a laugh, "but fortunately the good rector has a new curate, an intelligent, able man with a kind wife. They will take care of Mr. Collins and avert any real disasters."

"And will you come to Scotland? It will be rather late to start but we will be disappointed if you do not."

"I will make every effort to do so and should not be prevented if my aunt continues to do well and my regiment can spare me," continued the colonel, thinking of Anne. Fitzwilliam had promised to do all in his power to join them in the Highlands.

At this point they were interrupted by a summons from Lady Catherine. On this day she had at last been given permission by Dr. Crawford to come down to the drawing room, where she was now comfortably enthroned on a chaise. Elizabeth and Mrs. Jenkinson were with her, but at a nod from her ladyship the latter hurried out of the room. With much of her old imperious dignity, the invalid motioned the gentlemen to sit near her.

"Nephews, I have yielded to the advice that you and Dr. Crawford have given me and agreed to repair to Bath, although how I shall endure the life of idleness to be found there I do not know. I have also resigned myself to relinquishing the care of my daughter, trusting that no harm will come to her away from the protection of her home and her mother. However, I cannot do so without emphasizing once again that my child is not like other girls, and that serious consequences will attend on any stress to her constitution."

Her ladyship paused for effect, looking solemnly at her companions, especially Darcy.

"As you know, I was married when still very young to a man much older than myself, your uncle Sir Lewis de Bourgh. That he was the best of men, you are well aware," she said nodding towards Fitzwilliam and Darcy, "but for your benefit, Elizabeth, I will merely say that there was never a better husband. He taught me all I know. He directed my education, which had been quite inadequate, and knowing that he could not expect to live to an old age, he taught me how to maintain and improve this estate."

And Lady Catherine, with an expressive gesture of one pale hand that seemed to take in the splendid room, continued "We lost our two sons, as you remember one in infancy and one at the age of seven. Sir Lewis, afflicted with a weakness of the heart for most of his life, followed them when Anne was only eleven years old. On his deathbed he enjoined me to always protect his only surviving child. 'My dear wife,' he said, 'I fear that Anne has the constitutional infirmity of the de Bourghs. Keep her safe so that at least one of our children may live on.' And so I have done to the best of my ability."

Elizabeth had heard this family history from Darcy but was still moved almost to tears and felt true sympathy for Lady Catherine.

"So you see how difficult it is for me to allow you to take my daughter out into the world, and what a great charge is laid upon you to keep her from all harm." Darcy and Elizabeth exchanged a glance, both wondering if they had been unwise to take on this weighty responsibility. After a moment Darcy again assured his aunt that Anne's welfare would be their chief concern.

If Lady Catherine had looked into her own heart she would have had to admit that the prospect of being rid of her daughter for some months was not entirely unwelcome. Her ladyship loved Anne of course, as all mothers must, but in truth she did not particularly like her child. They did not enjoy each other's company and there seemed to be some degree of essential antipathy between the two. Whether it was because they were too different or too much alike, it was as yet impossible to tell. Anne's character was still too unformed and would assume more definition only when she was exposed to the vicissitudes of life away from Rosings. For many years Lady Catherine had subjected Anne to the same discipline she exerted in her flower gardens: any exuberant new growth was to be mercilessly cut back to conform to her ladyship's idea of order and harmony.

By the conclusion of the family conference, Lady Catherine was somewhat reassured and trusted that her daughter would not be led into any serious danger, either at Pemberley or in Scotland. "But she must have at least one cloak heavily lined with fur if she is to venture so far north," said her ladyship to Elizabeth, after the gentlemen had been allowed to depart, "and she must not be suffered to walk out of doors unless the weather is very fine." The two ladies discussed at length what clothing should be ordered for Anne during the two days to be spent in London. Naturally Elizabeth did not mention her own ideas, which involved a very different style of dress for the young lady.

Dr. Crawford came in during this important conversation and urged Lady Catherine to rest for the balance of the day. "I will obey you, doctor, as soon as I have spoken with my daughter Anne. You must admit that I have been an admirable patient, following your advice to the letter, but I will be unable to take my ease until I have concluded all the family business which has been preying on my mind." The physician may have had a rather different opinion of his patient's tractability, but he knew that it was useless to protest. Anne was summoned and left alone with her mother.

Anne had seen Lady Catherine every day since her mother had fallen ill, but always in the company of Dr. Crawford or some members of her family. This was an interview that the young lady had been dreading. But surprisingly her ladyship said nothing about the altercation that had had such unfortunate consequences. Instead she spent considerable time giving Anne advice on how to conduct herself in the new milieu that she would encounter during her time with the Darcys.

"I must admit," she began, "that in spite of my initial misgivings about Darcy's marriage, I have formed a most favorable impression of his Elizabeth and feel that you may safely be entrusted to her care. I have explained to her at length that your health must be her constant concern and she has promised to protect you from all harm." Anne was still astonished at her mother's *volte- face* in regard to Elizabeth, as she had never before known Lady Catherine to admit to having been in error.

"You will enjoy your time at Pemberley, a house that almost rivals Rosings for elegance and comfort. However, I am less certain that your uncle's castle in Scotland will be found to be so agreeable. Oh, it is luxurious enough. Your uncle has spent endless amounts on his favorite projects, both here and in Yorkshire. Dear Fitzwilliam would be a rich man, with an income of at least four thousand a year, if not for his father's extravagance." At this point Anne, who could not fail to be interested in anything concerning Fitzwilliam, began to pay close attention.

"Your uncle's wife brought him a great fortune on their marriage, some portion of which should rightly have been secured to provide for a younger son. But your uncle, and it pains me to say this of my own brother, is hopelessly foolish about money. I trust that Edward, the heir, whom you will soon meet, is a wiser man than his father, for he will have much to do to restore the Munford estate to its former prosperity."

Then Lady Catherine looked even more solemn, as she leaned forward confidentially to say, "My dear, you see the results of a marriage contracted without the proper settlements. Part of his mother's fortune should have been safeguarded for Fitzwilliam before he was even born. What were the solicitors for his mother's family thinking of?" Lady Catherine was quite indignant. "The daughter of a great family, with a large fortune, cannot marry as if she were a kitchen maid!"

Anne, who had heard her mother on this topic before, knew enough to merely look thoughtful and nod agreement.

"Now," continued her ladyship, "I will give you some advice, to which I am sure you will pay strict attention. You know that your happiness is the first object of my life."

Anne replied meekly that she would, of course, value her mother's council in all things. Anything, at this point, to avoid further discord and part on good terms, she thought.

"The reason that you may not find Castle Munford to your taste is that there may be people there of less distinction and breeding than those with whom you have always been associated here at Rosings. Your uncle is not so careful as I would wish about whom he invites to his Highland retreat. I speak from personal experience, as I went there with your father on a few occasions many years ago. That was soon after he began to make the ancient pile habitable by the expenditure of huge sums. I do not accuse him of entertaining anyone disreputable exactly, but simply not of that social eminence worthy of being so honored. Therefore you must be on your guard. Although you have spent your life quietly here in Kent, it is well known in society that you are a great heiress. Many people may pay court to you, seemingly eager for your friendship. All such overtures should be suspect!"

This was a new idea to Anne, who could not imagine that anyone outside of her small circle at Rosings would ever have heard of her.

"My dear child," continued her mother, "I do not wish to wound you by what I am about to say. You must believe that I only have your best interest at heart." Anne had enough knowledge of her mother to realize that this last expression always preceded something very wounding indeed.

"You are superior in every way to other young ladies in your delicacy and nobility of mind, your intelligence and sweetness of disposition. However, your charms are not of the kind to recommend you to the disinterested and enthusiastic attention of young men. They are attracted to the more common kind of girl, those said to be pretty by the vulgar herd. You may pride yourself on possessing distinction rather than beauty. The latter soon fades, leaving behind only disappointment and regret."

Anne had never thought of herself as pretty, but to be told that she was not by her own mother in such bald terms was more painful than she would have thought possible.

"So beware, my child. Worthless men may court you with flattering words, hoping to obtain a rich wife who will rescue them from the consequences of their misspent lives. Women may pretend the most affectionate interest in you because of what they hope to gain from having a rich friend. Receive with suspicion all such friendly overtures, as it is unlikely that they proceed purely from a true regard for you."

Even Lady Catherine had the penetration to see that her daughter was distressed by these admonitions, and she continued, "I only mean to protect you, my dear Anne. Who else will tell you the truth, if not your mother? Go now and think on what I have said. You will appreciate the wisdom of my advice after you have seen something of the world."

And her ladyship turned her cheek for her daughter to kiss. She watched Anne leave the room and felt some regret for having introduced such painful ideas to her child's innocent mind. But it was necessary, she told herself, Otherwise she will be an easy prey for every fortune hunter and opportunist in England. Heaven knows that my poor Anne has no other obvious source of attraction except her fortune.

Lady Catherine congratulated herself on having performed an unpleasant but unavoidable duty in order to protect her daughter. However, she had a deeper motive for letting Anne accompany the Darcys than she might have been credited with by any of her family, none of whom suspected the more subtle workings of her mind. If, she reasoned, Anne had a wretched experience in the course of her journey with her cousins, as seemed more than probable, then the girl would return to her mother's side with a much more pliable disposition. Any rebellious tendencies would be effectively quelled when Anne realized that she was not capable of meeting the difficulties of life beyond the confines of Rosings, and Lady Catherine would have an obedient child to command once more.

AFTER LEAVING her mother's presence, Anne fled to her bedchamber where she was able to give way to the tears that had been restrained with only the greatest difficulty during her interview with Lady Catherine. She had never felt more painful sensations or such mortification and despair. I must be a very repulsive object, incapable of inspiring affection in anyone, she thought, for otherwise my own mother would not say such things to me.

She sat before her looking glass and wondered how she must

appear to the world, for her mother to feel obliged to issue the kind of warnings that she had just been given. Anne looked with increasing distress at her own slight figure and woeful pale countenance, stained with tears. She did not see that her face was distinguished by fine grey eyes and perfect features. No one had ever noticed that Anne had everything necessary for beauty except animation and confidence. Now Lady Catherine's words penetrated Anne's heart and mind, poisoning all her hope for the future. A wish came to her that she might confide in Fitzwilliam. He would tell her if her mother's opinion were true. But she rejected this idea immediately, reasoning that Fitzwilliam, like everyone else, must feel only pity for her.

After an hour of the most painful reflections, Anne managed to regain her composure and recollect her duty to see that her guests were provided with tea, it being late afternoon. She bathed her face to remove any trace of her distress and left her chamber, much older in suffering and resignation that she had been only a short time before.

FOR THE NEXT two days Anne was determined that no one should become aware of the wretched state of her mind. Before her conversation with her mother she had begun to think with some degree of enthusiasm of seeing so many unfamiliar places and of embarking on what was, for her, a great adventure. Now she tried to conceal her unhappiness by asking Darcy and Elizabeth many questions about Pemberley and Scotland. With them she was fairly successful in concealing her misery. Fitzwilliam, however, was not deceived and saw that his cousin had suffered a serious injury to her spirits. He observed with what effort she tried to smile and match Elizabeth's light-hearted anticipation of the delights that awaited them. Only he noticed the profound sadness that marked her countenance in the moments when she thought herself unobserved. He attempted to speak with her about the alteration in her spirits on several occasions, but Anne always managed to change the subject.

On the morning of the Darcys' departure for London, Fitzwilliam at last found his opportunity. It was still very early when some impulse led him to the rose garden. There he encountered Anne taking leave of the scene of many of her private reflections and daydreams. There was a fine mist of rain falling but she was walking with the hood of her cloak thrown back and seemed oblivious to the chill, damp air. When she became aware of Fitzwilliam she looked uncertain and bade him a half audible "good morning." On this morning of departure she felt unable to hide her lack of spirits and could only hope to hold back her tears.

Her cousin came up to her slowly as if she were some wild forest creature that might be frightened into flight by any untoward movement. Returning her greeting, he gently raised the hood of her cloak, arranging the folds to shelter her face from the rain.

"You might take cold out here in this weather. And I see that you have worn light shoes to walk about in the wet grass." He shook his head and added with a faint smile, "I thought you more sensible, Anne."

She was moved by the tenderness of his concern for her and turned away lest he should see her emotion. After a moment she regained some composure and turned back to face him. Fitzwilliam was watching her with an expression of kind solicitude and after a brief silence offered her his hand. She blushed at the touch of his strong fingers, roughened by long hours on horseback.

Fitzwilliam had resolved to protect Anne with all the affection of an older brother. He noticed her rising color but he was not a vain man and it would never have occurred to him to see her confusion as a compliment to himself. She is very understandably apprehensive about leaving her home and everything familiar for the first time, he thought. It had seemed a natural thing to take her hand, but after a moment something that he could not define made it necessary to release his gentle hold. Dismissing this odd awkwardness from his mind, he began the speech he had planned to deliver should the opportunity present itself.

"I can see that you do not wish to talk about what is distressing you and I have not pressed you to do so. I know that my aunt has said something to cause you pain and undo all the good effect of your recent association with friends who wish you happiness and esteem you greatly." At this Anne turned away, once again in danger of giving way to tears.

"I can imagine something of what Lady Catherine would say to an inexperienced daughter entering society for the first time. She thinks to protect you, but instead has harmed you in some way. You know me to be your friend, do you not?" Anne was just able to nod but did not reply. "Then I ask you to try to forget whatever she has said to change your happy anticipation back to trepidation. Ascribe any words that gave you pain to an excess of maternal solicitude. Remember that people will for the most part behave as you expect them to and that with some exceptions it is better to be determined to think well of those you meet. They will feel it and act accordingly. Anyone whom you allow to know you cannot help but feel a true affection for you and a regard for your many excellent qualities."

Fitzwilliam, in his desire to spare Anne embarrassment, spoke these words in a rather formal manner. She knew that he meant to be kind and she tried to smile, while doubting everything he said. He offered her his arm and they returned to the house where serious preparations for departure were now in progress.

PART II

CHAPTER 13

*I*n later years Anne was able to recollect very little of the progress from Rosings to London, although the journey came to represent for her the true beginning of her life. The weather, which had been so unfavorable that morning, did not improve, and they traveled in a heavy downpour for almost the entire distance. Darcy and Elizabeth were at some pains to entertain their young guest, whose air of sad abstraction they had noted with concern. This melancholy they saw as a natural response to a first separation from her mother and her home. Darcy would have spent some of the time pointing out sights of interest to his cousin had not the passing scenery been almost entirely obscured by rain and fog. Elizabeth, however, could always find some source of amusement for her companions and began to tell Anne tales of her own *entré* into London society.

"When we returned from our wedding trip the season had just begun in earnest and we were buried under a mountain of invitations as soon as we were known to be in town. I was, I admit, a bit apprehensive at the idea of making my first appearance as Mrs. Darcy, knowing that I would be the object of a certain amount of curiosity." She smiled at Darcy, "You, my love, seemed to feel no misgivings at all."

"My only concern was that having had you to myself for more than two months, I would have to share you with an undeserving world." At this a look of perfect understanding and affection passed between them.

Elizabeth continued, "I had visions of being devoured by the dragons of the fashionable world. Although they may *appear* to be ladies of the highest standing, Anne, they are actually mythical beasts, who with one exhalation of their fiery breath can make an end of anyone unfortunate to offend them."

This presented such a droll image that Anne had to smile, even in her despondent mood.

"I quickly found, however, that by standing my ground and concealing any hint of fear, I could repel their most ferocious attacks. In fact, in the face of my seeming intrepidity they were reduced to almost fawning attempts to ingratiate themselves with me. So, you see I am adept at withstanding the more alarming inhabitants of London society and will protect you at all times if the need should arise. And my dear husband is the best dragon slayer since St. George, so you must not be anxious about anything with two such devoted and well-armed friends."

Anne thought to herself that it might really be possible for her to come to love Elizabeth. If only, she thought, I can forgive her for being so very beautiful and perfect at everything.

After a moment's reflection, Darcy added playfully, "I think that there is more danger to be apprehended from the snakes than from the dragons of the *beau monde*. The former are more subtle, and just when you are alert for more obvious hazards you are likely to tread upon one." And Darcy and Elizabeth amused Anne by examining their experience of London society to determine whether there were other kinds of wild beasts to be observed there.

They stopped at an inn for a mid-day repast and when the journey was resumed everyone fell silent. Elizabeth soon slept after Darcy had arranged cushions and lap rugs to make her slumber a restful one. Anne had not had very much experience of observing a couple deep in love and it was a revelation to her. Darcy clearly had no other thought beyond what would give his Elizabeth happiness and comfort. That she was the center of his existence was evident in every look and action. Elizabeth in turn was a being transfigured by her adoration for Darcy, which illuminated her beautiful face whenever she looked at her husband. And this is something I will never know, thought Anne, who always a realist, could imagine no other fate than that of a dreary spinster.

As they completed that last half of the journey, Anne was glad to be left to her own thoughts, and she gazed out of the window at what little was visible of the countryside. She did not think of Rosings or of her mother or of any of the familiar things she was leaving behind. Instead her mind was drawn to memories of her childhood and her early friendship with her cousin Fitzwilliam.

She remembered how as a boy he would come to Rosings with Darcy in the summer. They would spend most of the day on horseback or exploring about the countryside on foot. Naturally she was not allowed to accompany them; not only was she a young girl but she was even then held by her mother to be sickly and in need of constant supervision. One day when she was about eleven years old Fitzwilliam had been riding near the oak grove and had seen his little cousin Anne watching him from her perch on the branch of a large tree. He trotted over to her and said, "Would you like to come with me, Anne? I have something to show you."

She nodded shyly and he lifted her into the saddle in front of him. Anne remembered being both fearful and delighted as they cantered off. After a long ascent to the summit of a high range of hills Fitzwilliam reined in his horse. Before them was an endless view of the distant fields and forests that lay far below them. Anne even thought she could perceive the sea as a thin line of silver away to the south. "Have you never been here before?" asked her cousin. She shook her head, wondering how he thought she could have reached such a remote place on her own.

"I didn't think that you had," he said. "I thought that you might like to see this view so that you would know how much more there is beyond Rosings and the park and the village. It is very beautiful, is it not?"

They rode back and forth along the ridge, looking in every

direction as he tried to identify a few far off towns, barely visible far away. The fast moving clouds cast shadows across the land followed by radiant bands of sunlight that illumined the green hills. Finally, as the light had begun to fade somewhat, they started back down the slope and met Darcy halfway. He had been sent in search of them by his aunt, who was in a state of the most painful anxiety. The house had been in an uproar after Anne had been missed. Darcy had seen Fitzwilliam ride off with her but had been unable to convince Lady Catherine that her daughter would be safe. Fitzwilliam's interview with her ladyship on his return was very unpleasant and he had not dared to take Anne riding again as the incident had precipitated an intensification of Lady Catherine's mania for protecting her child. Fitzwilliam had never accepted the idea that his young cousin was too frail for any of the ordinary activities of life but his aunt's rule had been absolute until her own illness.

It was late afternoon and the sky had begun to clear when they entered the outskirts of London. Elizabeth and Darcy began to point out things that might interest Anne. Their young companion was both fascinated and repelled by what she saw. Having lived all her life in peaceful retirement in the country, she was astonished that such noise and crowding could be tolerated by rational beings. Their arrival in a fashionable and somewhat more tranquil part of town reassured her however, and dusk found them drawing up in front of Darcy's handsome house in Grosvenor Square.

Anne was extremely fatigued from the first long journey of her life and Elizabeth, alarmed by her exhausted appearance, sent her off to bed at once. She later came up to sit with Anne as she ate her supper by the fire that had been lit against the evening chill.

"I am afraid that I am a great nuisance to you," said Anne, "I don't know why I am so tired from a journey in the most comfortable and well-equipped of carriages. And I really do not require a fire at this time of year."

"Nonsense," replied Elizabeth, "It is delightful to have you with us and you could never be a burden. You will get used to traveling and it will not fatigue you so much, although you saw that I myself could not stay awake this afternoon. I hope that you did not think me rude for allowing myself to sleep."

Anne assured her that on the contrary she had considered it the sensible thing to do, and would have followed her example had she been able to do so.

"Oh, yes," said Elizabeth, "I have always been blessed with the gift of being able to sleep wherever I may happen to be. I remember that when we were returning from our wedding trip I once fell so soundly asleep that Darcy carried me like a child from the carriage and I knew nothing until I found myself in our chamber at the inn with my dear husband beside me waiting patiently for me to awaken." Then she smiled and then blushed at the recollection.

The next morning found Anne almost completely recovered from her fatigue of the night before. She entered the breakfast room to find that Darcy and Elizabeth were not yet about, and spent a few moments of solitude with a particularly fine cup of coffee. She was rather surprised at her own eagerness to see something of London. How odd, she thought, that the misery I felt on leaving Rosings seems less overpowering this morning. I suppose that even I have some of the resilience of youth.

Darcy and Elizabeth soon appeared and Anne had to admit that it would be impossible to imagine more agreeable and considerate companions and hosts. After breakfast the carriage was ordered and they set out for the important appointment with Elizabeth's dress-maker, escorted by Darcy, who having seen them safely to their destination, set out for his club.

Madame Delavant, who was the most popular *modiste* in London, greeted Mrs. Darcy with joy. Elizabeth was her favorite client, having brought Madame even more acclaim by wearing her gowns with unequalled elegance during the London season just past. She welcomed Anne with the greatest respect, concealing the dismay of an artist of couture at the young lady's unbecoming and outmoded attire. Soon the ladies found themselves deep in drifts of fabric, all of the most exquisite colors, chosen with an expert eye to flatter Miss de Bourgh's fair complexion.

If Elizabeth had anticipated treating Anne as some sort of life-sized doll who could be measured and dressed without being consulted in any way, she was doomed to disappointment. Anne was found to have very decided opinions of her own, which had never before been expressed. She did not at all care for any quantity of bows and lace, preferring a more simple style of dress. This did not at all accord with Elizabeth's initial idea of what would suit Anne's delicate fairy-like proportions, and this led to something of an impasse, until Madame Delavent, who was not afraid to speak her mind, intervened.

"I must agree with Miss de Bourgh, my dear Mrs. Darcy, although at first I was of your opinion. A more unadorned style of dress will be most becoming to Mademoiselle."

After further consideration Elizabeth had to agree. She had then to contend with Anne's reluctance to order as many gowns as were required for her entrance into society. "How can I possibly need all this?" asked Anne, who was beginning to feel very tired, "It seems an absurd extravagance." Elizabeth, who knew that Lady Catherine had arranged an allowance for her daughter that would not have disgraced a princess, began to feel somewhat exasperated. At last, however, the process was completed and everything ordered to be ready as soon as possible and sent on to Pemberley.

Darcy, who had returned and had been waiting for them patiently, saw that they were both fatigued and more than a little cross when they eventually appeared. He, however, was in high spirits. He had found his club sparsely occupied, as almost everyone had retired to the country, but he had gained word during his tour around town of a concert that night that was sure to please Elizabeth and Anne.

"Boccherini, Haydn and Mozart! And a celebrated violinist from Venice whose name I cannot at the moment recall. Let us return home so that you both can rest from your labors and be ready for the evening that I have planned for your amusement." The ladies, who were by now thoroughly sick of sartorial concerns, agreed readily to this proposal.

Despite the fact that there was "no one in town," the concert hall was found to be quite well furnished with human forms of one kind or another. From this, thought Anne, it might be surmised that music lovers were not necessarily part of the fashionable world and vice-versa. She felt somewhat indifferent to her surroundings, however, in her anticipation of hearing really first rate musicians, something which had never fallen to her lot in Kent. Elizabeth, who had not known that Anne felt any enthusiasm for music, was delighted to find a subject that they could discuss with enjoyment and the slight restraint that had resulted from their differing opinions at the dressmaker's was soon forgotten.

"You have so much knowledge, Elizabeth," said Anne when they had taken their seats, "and I hope that you will take pity on my ignorance and begin to educate me. What would I not give to have learnt to play and sing when I was young! I suppose that it is too late for me to do so now."

This was an unusually animated and unguarded speech for Anne and Elizabeth was surprised for a moment, then she replied, "You quite over-rate my attainments, and I fear that you will be disappointed when you discover by how much you have exaggerated my talents. But I must disagree with your assumption that you are too old to study music. One of the most accomplished ladies of my acquaintance here in London took up the pianoforte when she was your age. Now, at nine and twenty, she is very proficient."

Anne, who had considered herself too antiquated at six and twenty to attempt to learn anything new, was delighted with this information. At this moment Darcy, who had been greeting a few acquaintances, returned with two gentlemen who had wished to pay homage to the ladies. One was familiar; Sir Frederick Lindsay was well known in London society, a well-bred elderly man with a large estate in Hertfordshire who knew Elizabeth's father and never failed to inquire civilly after the Bennet family at Longbourn. He now expressed his pleasure at meeting Miss de Bourgh and hoped that she was enjoying London sufficiently to consider honoring the capitol more frequently.

Anne made a polite response, surprised that Sir Frederick seemed to know who she was and to be making an effort to be particularly agreeable to a shy young lady from the country. She had no way of knowing that the baronet had an elder son as yet unmarried and with expensive habits, and that the appearance of a great heiress had to be of some considerable interest.

Attention then turned to a younger gentleman who had waited patiently at Sir Frederick's side to be included in the introductions. Anne and Elizabeth caught the name "Lord Holland" as he made a bow with singular grace and a modest air. As he stepped forward, Anne was struck by the extraordinary beauty of his person. He was nearly as tall as Darcy and his countenance and figure were of almost too great a perfection. She noticed that he was very simply dressed and moved about unobtrusively as if somewhat abashed by his own good looks. His most striking feature was his arresting dark eyes, which expressed a most amiable gentleness. He seemed to be meeting Darcy for the first time, but they soon found that they had several mutual friends and had in fact met briefly on one or two occasions. The concert being about to begin, Sir Frederick and Lord Holland retired to their seats, which happened to be directly across from those of Anne and her friends.

With the first strains of a Mozart violin concerto, Anne lost interest in everything but the sublime music, which revealed to her a hitherto undiscovered source of perfect felicity. During a brief pause between movements however, she experienced the sensation of being observed. She turned her head slightly and met the luminous eyes of Lord Holland whose attention seemed to be fixed on their party. He acknowledged her glance with a courteous bow before redirecting his gaze towards the orchestra. Anne had never before found herself the object of such intense scrutiny, and to her annoyance she felt herself blush with confusion. She felt his eyes upon her on several other occasions during the concert and resisted with some difficulty the impulse to look again in the gentleman's direction. She was not flattered, but merely annoyed at being distracted from the glorious music, which had awakened feelings she had not imagined before this evening.

Lord Holland did not fail to return to say a few more words during the intermission, conversing mainly with Darcy in an easy, agreeable manner. It soon developed that he was to be one of the party at Castle Munford. "Lord Munford's older son is my friend," he explained, "and may I say how very delighted I am that I will encounter you and Mrs. Darcy and Miss de Bourgh there." Elizabeth responded to this compliment with her ravishing smile, and went on to speak of her eagerness to see the Highlands for the first time. This led to a conversation in which all the delights of Scotland in autumn were enumerated. Anne, who had trouble enough talking to strangers about subjects of which she had some knowledge, did not participate in their discourse. Instead she listened carefully, while thinking that she must appear to be rather stupid and plain to the alert observation of Lord Holland.

She was spared any further interaction with their new acquaintance by the crush of activity that marked the end of the evening's entertainment. Darcy had seen the two ladies into the carriage when he was arrested in his progress to join them by a gentleman who appeared at his side and laid a friendly hand on his arm.

"Darcy, my good old friend, how happy I am to see you!" cried the young man joyfully, "I came in for the second half of the concert and did not see you until just this minute."

Darcy returned the greeting with equal delight, "Grey, my dear fellow, I did not know that you were in town! What a fortunate chance that you are here tonight." Turning to Elizabeth he said, "My dearest, this is my friend John Grey, about whom you have heard so much."

The necessary introductions were made and Darcy insisted that Grey must come for dinner the following evening. "We were to leave for Pemberley tomorrow afternoon but it can easily be put off for another day. You have no objection I hope, my dear," he asked Elizabeth.

"By no means," she replied, "Mr. Grey, after all I have heard from my husband in your praise, I would be most delighted if you would join us for dinner."

Mr. Grey replied that he would be more than pleased, even though it meant disillusioning Mrs. Darcy, who would soon discern that he could not live up to Darcy's overly kind account of him. Then, after all the compliments that politeness required, Mr. Grey turned and disappeared into the night.

During the drive home to Grosvenor Square, Darcy made the ladies familiar with all the important information regarding his friend: how the two of them had been at school and at university together and how they had not seen each other for several years, since Grey's departure for the continent.

"But Grey is an excellent correspondent," added Darcy, "unlike so many of our sex. He has written to me from innumerable parts of Europe where he has pursued studies in the natural sciences. I've kept all of his letters. They are most interesting and written in a very entertaining style."

"There is one thing that puzzles me, cousin," said Anne, "As the eldest son of an earl should he not be addressed with some honorific instead of plain 'Mr. Grey?'"

"You are correct, of course," replied Darcy, "At school he was known as Lord Conarvan, but after his last quarrel with his father he abandoned the title, preferring to be known by his mother's family name. It is eccentric of him but if you knew the earl you would understand Grey's sentiments."

Then they were at the door of the house and Anne was grateful to retire for the night as she was quite fatigued from all the new impressions that the day had offered. She had expected to fall asleep at once, but found that her mind would not let her rest until she had reviewed in detail all that had occurred, from her tedious hours at the dressmaker's to the delight of her first London concert. Somehow the image of Lord Holland's face and intense gaze returned to her mind's eye repeatedly, and although she could not be sure whether she found the recollection a welcome one, it was the last thing she saw before sleep claimed her.

CHAPTER 14

The next morning passed very pleasantly. Darcy and Elizabeth took Anne for a brief tour of the capital, and she found much of interest. The only shop they felt required to visit was that of a well-known furrier in Bond Street, where a fur-lined cloak was purchased. This had been strongly recommended by Lady Catherine as absolutely necessary for her daughter's survival in the Scottish wilderness. Anne was beginning to feel at ease in the company of the Darcys who were clearly solicitous for her every comfort and enjoyment. They, in turn, were surprised to find that the young lady could be playful and even amusing.

"Cousin Elizabeth, I see now that you have been less than candid about our destination," said Anne as she tried on various cloaks at the furrier's shop. "You and Darcy have insisted all along that we will be visiting Lord Munford's castle in the Highlands. But I am no longer deceived, as it is clear that we are to travel much farther north, at least as far as Lapland, no doubt by sleigh across vast ice fields. Otherwise I would have no need of such a cloak. I can barely stand upright in this garment."

Anne did indeed look very small enveloped in its folds. Elizabeth could not restrain her laughter and both ladies were instantly overcome by mirth. When she regained her composure Elizabeth replied,

"Your mother allowed us to bring you with us only on condition that you be protected from every draft of cold air. I think that I will have done my duty when you are wrapped in this rather voluminous mantle, although perhaps a bear skin would be preferable."

"I can make no objection," replied Anne, "as long as you promise me that I shall see a reindeer."

After the adventure of the fur-lined cloak, Anne surprised her friends by announcing that she must acquire a riding habit before leaving London. "But I cannot remember when I last knew you to ride," said Darcy with some degree of alarm, "surely your mother would object."

"I have not been on horseback since I was eleven years of age," said Anne, "so it is time that I took it up again." Then, with a conspiratorial smile at her friends, she added, "I cannot recall my mother enjoining me *not* to ride before we left Rosings, can you?"

No, they had to admit the truth of this statement, but of course it would never have occurred to Lady Catherine that such an admonition would be necessary. It soon became obvious to Darcy and Elizabeth that Anne was determined to have her way, and a visit to another fashionable shop provided the young lady with a very elegant riding habit.

Mr. Grey appeared punctually for dinner, and Elizabeth and Anne soon found much to like and admire in Darcy's old friend. He was handsome and had the perfectly amiable manners of a truly well bred man. He had, in addition to these recommendations, an air of quiet confidence gained during his many years of travel in every part of Europe. The ladies at first thought him a serious sort of person from his initial air of studious gravity, but they realized in the course of the evening that he was a most delightful companion, with a lively and original wit. He told them entertaining stories of his journeys, often adding details that made them stare in disbelief, until his slight smile made it clear that he was enjoying spinning a wild tale for their amusement. He kept his company either in a state of rapt attention or helpless with laughter throughout dinner and Anne forgot to be shy with this new acquaintance.

Grey had spent some time in the Pyrenees, searching the wild mountainous region between France and Spain for caverns. He described the beauty of the landscape in some detail, having found it even more glorious than the Alps.

"It must be a dangerous place to travel, however, Mr. Grey," said Anne, "I have always heard of the banditti and brigands of all kinds who haunt mountain passes, waiting to fall upon the unwary traveler. Did you not fear to encounter them?"

Grey looked thoughtful for a moment, and then answered in a very solemn tone, "The tales of robbers have been much exaggerated, Miss de Bourgh, and I was fortunate to have no experience of them. The people of the region are, for the most part, honest and hospitable." Then looking even more serious, he added, "There is a more significant threat, one which you would never suspect, a wild animal of a most ferocious aspect that in England only assumes the most harmless form. I speak not of the wolf or the bear, but of that most inconspicuous rodent, the squirrel."

Seeing the incredulous expressions of his listeners, he continued with an air of the utmost gravity, "I see that you find it difficult to believe that such a diminutive animal could be a threat but I can tell you that it is so. Imagine, if you will, large packs of these little beasts, at large and desperate for food in an area with few acorn-bearing trees. They forsake their usual habits and begin to prey on creatures much larger than themselves. Woe be to the ignorant wayfarer who ventures alone on the mountain paths at night, liable to be dragged off to a horrible fate unless he is on his guard and heavily armed. The danger to be apprehended from an attack of several score of rogue squirrels is only too real, I assure you."

And he went on to describe the squirrel hunts in which he had assisted his friends among certain of the villages nearest the mountain passes, going into some detail as to the appearance and natural history of the small mammals, not neglecting tales and local folklore surrounding this hazard to travelers.

So convincing was this narrative that the ladies listened with perfect attention and the better part of belief to what Grey was telling them. It was Darcy who put an end to his friend's deception by being unable to restrain his laughter any longer. Elizabeth and Anne, though somewhat indignant at having been imposed upon, could not help but join him in his mirth.

After a moment Elizabeth rose and said to Anne, "Come my dear, let us leave them to their port. Gentlemen, you will find us in the drawing room plotting our revenge." Then the two ladies swept gracefully from the room.

Grey was silent for a moment as Darcy poured out some of the best Port his cellar could offer in honor of this reunion with his friend. Then he said thoughtfully, "Darcy, you are a happy man. With such a wife as that, you can defy the gods to bestow any higher felicity, unless it be children who resemble *her* in every respect." Then he added with a wicked smile, "Let us hope that they will not take you for a model. You are certainly more fortunate than you deserve."

"How I have missed your delicate compliments, dear old Grey," replied Darcy laughing, "but you may insult me as much as you like for it only reinforces my complacency and my pity for all the other men in the world who can never hope for such a wife as mine."

The two men spent an enjoyable half hour exchanging information on all the particulars of their lives for the past few years. Grey had presented a paper at the Royal Society the week before, and he outlined its contents for Darcy, who listened with interest even though his bent was more for the arts and literature than for science.

At last Darcy saw his friend look more serious, and Grey said, "I am particularly grateful for this evening as I expect to leave London very shortly and I do not know when I may return." He went on to explain that having almost exhausted his small income, which normally would have sustained him for the next few months, he was obliged to seek some sort of employment. A post as secretary to the new envoy being sent to St Petersburg had just been offered to him and he saw the necessity of accepting it.

"It may turn out well enough," added Grey, "I have never been to Russia. Perhaps it is just the place to continue some of my studies. The envoy will no doubt give me some leisure to pursue them."

Darcy expressed his disappointment that Grey would be forsaking his native land again so soon for a place so distant. At the same time his mind worked rapidly, trying to find a solution to his friend's difficulties that would allow him to stay in England. Darcy knew that Grey had a young half brother whom he supported at school, and that the expenses involved had probably left Grey without adequate funds himself. It was like Grey's generous nature to make such a sacrifice. At the same time Darcy knew better than to offer money to help his friend, who was much too proud to even consider such a thing. At last an idea presented itself which might be acceptable, and Darcy's face brightened as he proposed it.

"I have an idea which may perhaps be more appealing to you than a sojourn in St. Petersburg. You will not, I trust, accuse me of unjustified pride when I say that Pemberley has one of the finest private libraries in the kingdom."

Grey, who had spent some happy hours there when he had visited as a schoolboy, was quick to agree with this assessment.

"Since the death of my father I have not given this great treasure, my library, the attention it deserves. No catalog of its contents has been made for at least thirty years, and many of the bindings are in need of repair. Also, I would like to make appropriate additions to the collection, but with all the responsibilities of the estate have not had time to turn my mind to the task. Grey, would you consider spending the next few months at Pemberley and undertaking this daunting project? It would be extremely helpful to me, and it would be splendid to have you there as our guest after all these years of not seeing you."

Grey did not answer at once, but sat for a moment considering the idea. Finally he replied, "Old fellow, I can imagine no greater pleasure than spending some time in the library at Pemberley. Knowing you, I have no doubt that it needs attention, as you probably just pull off the shelves whatever interests you at the moment, taking no account of the suffering of the less entertaining volumes."

Darcy had to smile at this reproach, which was perfectly accurate. Grey went on, "I can even rebind the damaged books for you. When I was in Florence a few years ago, I had an old bookseller teach me the technique, thinking it might be useful for a bookworm like myself. And of course Derbyshire is one of the most interesting counties in England for anyone with an interest in geology."

Darcy was delighted to perceive that his friend felt a very real enthusiasm at the prospect of a prolonged visit to Pemberley, and he began to rejoice in the success of his proposal. Then, however, Grey added in a very serious tone, "Before we settle on this very agreeable plan, I must insist that you discuss it with Mrs. Darcy, who may have other feelings about my addition to the domestic scene. She is obviously the most good-natured of women or she could not put up with you, but we should not demand too much of her forbearance."

Darcy replied that he knew that his Elizabeth would be delighted at the prospect of Grey's visit, but finally agreed to consult her wishes and to repeat the offer on the morrow with a letter directed to Grey at his club. "But, you see," added Darcy, "my wife very much enjoys having guests about the house whom she can indulge almost as much as she does me. My cousin Anne is to be with us all the rest of the year."

"But your cousin Miss de Bourgh is a charming and intelligent young lady. What a pleasant companion she must be for Mrs. Darcy! Her questions about my research were most well informed. In any case, it is another matter to have a dull, pedantic character like me about the house all the time."

Anne would have been amazed if she had heard herself praised in this way. Mr. Grey's conversation was so interesting and amusing that Anne had for once forgotten to be shy.

After Grey had taken his departure and Anne had retired for the night, Darcy told Elizabeth about the invitation he had issued to his friend. She was quick to express her delight at the prospect.

"He is very thoughtful to request that you consult my wishes, but of course I could not be more pleased. How splendid to have several months with the company of one of your best friends. I have never met a more agreeable gentleman. His good humor even overcame Anne's usual reticence."

"It is better that Grey remain in England for a number of reasons, not the least of which is that his father's state of health is known to be uncertain," said Darcy after a moment's reflection, "and although the two have not seen each other for years, I know that Grey would go to the earl should the old man's illness become serious."

They sat in happy silence for a while, contented to be together in the warmth and comfort of their drawing room. A heavy rain had begun to beat against the long windows that overlooked the square and Darcy was glad that he had insisted on sending Grey home in the carriage.

"There is one other thing that I should mention, my angel," he said, kissing the head with its dark curls that lay against his shoulder. "Grey requests that he not be known to the neighborhood of Pemberley as the heir of Lord Harwith, but merely as a private gentleman who is obliging me by assisting me with my library. He takes no pride in his noble connections, I am afraid. Since he has been out of England for many years, I have no doubt that he will be able to maintain his anonymity."

Elizabeth turned to look into her husband's face and replied, "It is an odd fancy of Mr. Grey's but harmless enough, I suppose. We must do whatever we can to make his time with us enjoyable. I think that he must have need of a long rest in the peace and retirement of the country. What an adventurous life he has led!" She rose, and going at once to her writing desk, she wrote a most graceful and kind invitation to Mr. Grey, begging him to come to them at Pemberley for as long a visit as possible.

CHAPTER 15

Once Mr. Grey was certain that his presence at Pemberley would be welcomed by all of its inhabitants, he lost no time in gathering together his few possessions and writing a letter of thanks and regret to Sir Jocelyn Gill, His Majesty's new envoy to the court at St. Petersburg. The enticements of a Russian winter seemed well lost to Grey when compared with the good company, magnificent library and innumerable caverns he would find in Derbyshire. So much alacrity did he display in settling all of his business in London that he was able to join the Darcys and Miss de Bourgh in their carriage for the journey north that very afternoon.

His friends found him a most entertaining addition to their party and the time passed very pleasantly for all. The two ladies listened with amusement to the good-natured banter of the gentlemen as they recalled their youthful escapades. Grey described a prank at school involving a ripe peach and the headmaster's hat that had almost led to their expulsion, and at the conclusion of the tale Elizabeth thanked him for introducing her to a hitherto unsuspected side of her husband's character. Also, it was a fine thing to have a natural philosopher as one of the party who could point out and interpret aspects of the passing landscape and identify every species of bird seen from the carriage windows.

Mrs. Darcy had little time for rest when they reached Pemberley for a mere ten days were to elapse before the departure for Scotland. After seeing Mr. Grey put into possession of one of the most comfortable guest chambers, she had to leave Darcy in charge of making his friend at home. Darcy had been at some pains to persuade Grey to come to Scotland with them but without success. This was understandable, for to go to such a fashionable house party in his current state of poverty and to have to rely on Darcy for guns and other necessities could not be acceptable to the young man. Hence, Grey was to spend some weeks alone at Pemberley. Darcy knew him well enough to have no fear that he would be unhappy in such solitude but he did ask one favor of his guest.

"Please make me this promise, Grey. I request most earnestly that you stay above ground while I am away. Do not undertake any explorations of the caverns here about until I return and can organize a rescue party should you run into difficulties."

Grey found this proposal most unwelcome as the activity was a passion with him. He protested that he was a cautious man and would take no risks. In any case, it was absurd to talk of rescue parties when there was no one in the vicinity to participate in one.

"You are incorrect in your assumption," replied Darcy, "There are two or three other madmen like yourself in this part of Derbyshire and when I return from Scotland I will seek them out for you." In this way Darcy finally gained his point, and Grey agreed to honor his request, although with no very good grace.

"Since you are still here, however, I will go look at a spot I remember from my last visit here when we were boys," and he described a cavern that was to be found at no very great distance with a precision that was remarkable after an absence of more than ten years. Darcy remembered this as a fairly innocuous passageway into a hillside on the estate and made no objection.

"But if you have not returned for tea we will begin to worry," he said at last, as Grey went grumbling off, muttering that he had never expected his friend Darcy to turn into such an old woman.

~

THAT AFTERNOON LADY MARGARET FAULCONER rode towards Pemberley in a light rain. She had received a letter from Mrs. Darcy inviting her to join them for tea that day, with the added inducement of meeting Miss de Bourgh and of seeing all the wonders of new gowns just arrived from London. Such finery held little interest for Lady Margaret, but she was happy at the thought of seeing the Darcys again and had some curiosity to meet their young cousin. It was tiresome that they had returned home only to leave so soon for Scotland, but at least she could look forward to their company in September. It had been a rather lonely summer for Lady Margaret, self sufficient as she usually was. Her father had been in such low spirits that it had been deemed impossible to invite guests and a prolonged trip to London had been unthinkable. This was no disappointment, however, for the she disliked the city, but even so, her solitude had begun to pall.

Any other young lady would have ordered her carriage to go out on such a day, as it had threatened rain since early morning, but Lady Margaret scorned such frailty. The weather had to be very dreadful indeed to keep her from her daily ride, but on this occasion she had at least worn an oilskin cape, and she was now very glad of this uncharacteristic forethought. It was, she admitted to herself, becoming very wet indeed, although she was more concerned for the preservation of her fine new saddle than for herself.

She was making her way up a long open hillside, holding her bay horse to a trot over the stony, uneven ground, when something caught her eye at the edge of a copse of huge old trees just to one side of her path. It proved to be the figure of a man toiling up the hill in the same direction that she was taking herself. Lady Margaret was now very close to Pemberley, which would be visible from the top of the rise, and at first she assumed that the man must be one of the workers on the estate. When she came along side of him, however, she saw a creature that could have no proper business on the property of her friend Mr. Darcy.

No one had ever accused Margaret Faulconer of lacking courage, but she was appalled by the appearance of the wretch before her and her first impulse was to spur her horse to a gallop and seek refuge at Pemberley. She quickly rejected such a cowardly course of action and instead stopped to challenge the man. He was a loathsome sight, dressed in the tattered rags of what looked like a gentleman's old clothes. "Stolen no doubt," she thought to herself. More remarkable was the fact that he was covered from head to foot with a layer of mud, making his face unreadable under the grime. He had a large coil of rope over one shoulder and she noted that he had an odd hat with the remains of a candle stuck into its band.

Reining in her horse, which was understandably alarmed at this strange apparition, she asked the man what he was doing on Pemberley land. After a moment's hesitation he removed his hat and asked humbly in a strong north- country accent if she were the mistress of the great house.

"Not that it's any of your business," she replied, "I am a friend of the Darcys and know that they would not like to see such a rough fellow loitering about the place. With that rope over your arm, I have no doubt that you are a housebreaker. If you wish to preserve your life I advise you to be off as soon as possible, for when I reach Pemberley I will inform Mr. Darcy of your presence."

"Oh, no, my lady," replied the man in his almost incomprehensible accent, "I am no housebreaker. I am a mudman, collecting some very fine mud from the woods nearby," and he began to open a canvas sack that he had taken off his other shoulder. "Here, I'll show you the rare mud that I have found this day."

At this Lady Margaret decided that she was dealing with a lunatic and thought it the better part of valor to be off. A 'mudman' indeed, she muttered to herself as she cantered away.

A few minutes later the lady entered the drawing room at Pemberley to find her friends sitting peacefully around the blazing fire that kept the chill damp of the afternoon at bay. As soon they saw their guest Darcy and Elizabeth hurried her to a chair by the hearth and rang for fresh tea, all the while scolding her for coming by horseback in the rain. It took a moment for them to notice that Lady Margaret was very perturbed and to allow her an opportunity to speak.

"For heaven's sake, I am fine. I was wearing a waterproof cape and do not even feel cold," she managed to say at last. "But Mr. Darcy, you must send some of your people at once to expel a most detestable wretch from your property. I came across the creature, who is probably a housebreaker, not a quarter of a mile distant from here." And she went on to describe her encounter with the peculiar being, saying that he must be either a criminal or a madman. "I have ridden around this country all my life and never once had the misfortune to come across such a repellent object."

Her host and hostess hastened to soothe and reassure her, and she soon regained her composure enough to notice Anne regarding her shyly from the depths of a large armchair. "Oh, you must be Miss de Bourgh," said Lady Margaret, rising quickly and crossing the room to greet her as Elizabeth made the formal introduction.

"I am so sorry to have failed to acknowledge your presence as soon as I entered the room, but I was so distressed by this matter of a trespasser on Mr. Darcy's estate that I was rather distracted." Anne, who was all too used to going unnoticed, said that she understood and sympathized with Lady Margaret's discomfiture.

The three ladies were rather puzzled to see that Mr. Darcy, far from summoning his servants to investigate the disturbing news of an intruder, was standing thoughtfully at the range of windows that gave a view of the western aspect of the park. Suddenly he turned and left the room abruptly, and in a moment could be heard issuing orders in a somewhat urgent voice. Elizabeth wished to join her husband and find out what he was about, but felt it her duty to stay with Lady Margaret to ensure that she was comfortably situated by the fire and provided with tea. Conversation, however, was at a standstill as the occupants of the drawing room waited for Darcy's return.

After a few minutes they heard his voice again, but now he seemed to be in earnest debate with a newcomer to the front hall, who could be detected both protesting and occasionally laughing. As the ladies looked at each other in bewilderment, Darcy entered the room almost dragging another figure with him.

"Stop arguing with me, Grey. You must come in here to get warm until your bedchamber has been provided with a good fire and hot water. I don't want you taking a chill and dying just when we are trying to leave for Scotland. Otherwise I would let you have your own way, as stupid as it might be." So saying Darcy positioned his soaked and dripping friend on the hearth, motioning for him to surrender his tattered greatcoat to the servant who had followed them into the room.

Lady Margaret, who had been observing all this with a look of disbelief, now leapt to her feet, nearly overturning the small table that held her teacup.

"But this is the miscreant I told you about, Mr. Darcy! I'd like an explanation at once, if it is not too much trouble," she cried indignantly.

The two men turned to her with the most irritating composure imaginable. The rain had been falling quite heavily for the past fifteen minutes and most of the mud that had coated Grey had been washed away by the torrent. He was still very far from being a fit object for a drawing room, however, and he still held his battered hat with the candle. Darcy at once undertook his friend's introduction as an "old schoolmate," and explaining that Grey had been exploring caverns that day, an occupation that was generally incompatible with a correct and gentlemanly appearance.

Grey made a low bow that seemed to Lady Margaret to be imbued with more than a suggestion of irony. "My friend Darcy is the most gracious of hosts," he said in a voice that held not a trace of a north-country accent, "but I am here as a consulting librarian to rescue the neglected treasures of Pemberley." Darcy began to protest this statement as giving a misleading idea of Grey's position, but he was silenced by a glance from the other man.

Lady Margaret reacted to this information with rising anger and contempt. Her heightened color made her beauty even more striking as she said, "I am glad to know that alarming helpless women in lonely spots is not your only occupation." She turned to Anne and Elizabeth and said, "Miss de Bourgh, I would be so delighted if you would show me some of your gowns that have just arrived from London. In the matter of the latest fashions I am not at all *au courant*, and you would oblige me by sharing your insights into the subject."

Anne had been watching everything that had passed with barely concealed amusement. She had never witnessed such an entertaining scene in her mother's drawing room. Now, doing her best to look serious, she said that she would be delighted to satisfy Lady Margaret's curiosity, and the three ladies departed. Grey, who had intended to make some kind of apology to Lady Margaret, thus lost his opportunity.

"Well done," said Darcy, handing him a cup of tea. "I am glad to see that you have already made a friend in the neighborhood."

CHAPTER 16

The next day was Sunday and Mr. and Mrs. Darcy were glad of the opportunity to see all their neighbors before the departure for Scotland. The weather was extremely fine and the party from Pemberley decided to walk the last half- mile to the village, sending the carriage on ahead. As they drew near the church Darcy and Elizabeth were greeted by friends and tenants, all of whom were eager to pay their respects to the new Mrs. Darcy. Anne and Grey walked on, deep in conversation, and as at ease as if they had known each other for ten years instead of one week. The gift of making friends quickly was all on the young man's side and Anne found it remarkable that she could talk so readily to a new acquaintance. This was partly due to the fact that Mr. Grey had never seen her in the role of the dull spinster daughter of Lady Catherine. Here, away from Rosings, she could attempt to take on a different character, especially in the company of a gentleman who was clearly disposed to find her clever and interesting.

Anne had been asking her companion about the caverns in the district, her curiosity having been stimulated by what she had heard of his excursion of the day before. She wished to know how the underground chambers were formed and how long they had existed.

"The rock in this part of England, Miss de Bourgh, which seems so substantial, is actually very much subject to the action of water. Over many eons underground streams find their way through fractures in the rock, gradually forming caverns. As for the exact time when these wonders of nature were formed, why you can imagine the difficulty of assigning a date to something that is no longer there, distinguished by a void rather than substance."

Anne asked more questions on the subject of Grey's explorations into the caverns of England and Europe, and both of them were surprised to find that they had reached the church, having been unconsciously led along by the sound of the bells and the groups of village residents hastening to the service. Darcy and Elizabeth joined them and they were ushered into the cool, vaulted interior of the ancient building.

Darcys had worshipped in this church for more generations than anyone had ever attempted to count, but it was known that their ancestor had been granted lands in the county by the conqueror and that there was not a more distinguished old family in England. Mr. Darcy could attend holy services in the company of his forebears who were ranged in tombs throughout the church. As Anne made her way to the family pew with her cousins and Mr. Grey she observed that Lady Margaret and her father were already seated in their place of eminence. Darcy had explained that the Faulconers preferred this church, as most conveniently near their demesne, and attended here fairly often. The young ladies caught sight of each other at the same moment and exchanged friendly smiles. Then Lady Margaret's lovely face took on an expression of cold dislike and she returned to the perusal of her prayer book. Anne realized that she had seen Mr. Grey, who had brought up the rear of the party from Pemberley.

I suppose that she will hate him forever, thought Anne, and she felt real regret for she thought Mr. Grey such an excellent young man.

Lady Margaret had made a rapid departure on the previous afternoon after viewing Anne's gowns. While the three ladies were closeted in Anne's bedchamber admiring the piles of dresses that lay everywhere, as the distraught maids tried to bring order out of chaos, there had been nothing but good-natured laughter and conversation. As soon as they had returned to the drawing room, however, Lady

Margaret's demeanor changed to cold reserve and she had insisted that her horse be brought round so that she could return at once to Castle Faulconer. All the appeals of Darcy and Elizabeth that she stay to dine, or at least allow herself to be taken home by carriage, met with refusals that were just short of uncivil. It was no longer raining and she must be off at once as her father was expecting her.

John Grey, with a most remarkable alacrity, had made good his transformation into a being fit for the usages of proper society, and had returned to the drawing room. He had spent all the intervening time rehearsing a most abject apology for the way in which he had imposed on the young lady. It was effort in vain, however, for she would not allow him to finish his speech. Instead, she turned away to Elizabeth saying, "It was delightful to see you again, Mrs. Darcy, and to have the pleasure of meeting Miss de Bourgh. For the rest, I suppose that I may congratulate myself on having been the means of providing entertainment for your *other* new resident at Pemberley." Then she was off, cantering her horse down the drive with such dash and spirit that the company could only look after her with admiration.

During the church service, Anne found herself reviewing the events of the previous afternoon and it was only with difficulty that she could attend to Mr. Devereaux's intelligent and well-reasoned sermon. Her thoughts were soon distracted by the wonderful old building with its ancient monuments and carvings. She then reflected on all the interesting experiences that had marked the past two weeks. She had begun to feel quite at ease with Darcy and Elizabeth, and believed that she had found a friend in Mr. Grey.

After the service Anne found that she had to undergo a bewildering number of introductions to many of the parishioners who were standing about in front of the church. She liked the kindly and dignified rector, Mr. Devereaux; what a contrast he was to Mr. Collins, whose sermons usually reduced her to stupefied boredom or barely concealed mirth. She also liked the amiable Mrs. Devereaux. This lady seemed happily unaware of the judgment of some of the less charitable parishioners that the rector had married beneath himself to the daughter of a carriage maker. She lived in perfect contentment with her husband and three children, and her only occupation from early morning to the moment she fell asleep on her guiltless pillow at night, was contributing to the felicity of all those within the range of her benevolence. Anne could not help but reflect that her mother Lady Catherine would probably find Mrs. Devereaux beneath her notice as "not quite a gentlewoman."

After complimenting the rector's wife on the beauty of the gardens visible beyond the rectory gates, Anne spent a few minutes with the lady discussing the cultivation of roses. When Mrs. Devereaux was called away to greet parishioners who still milled about the church door, Anne found that her friends had migrated to the far side of the churchyard where they stood talking with Lord Faulconer and Lady Margaret. All of Anne's timidity returned when she saw the necessity of crossing the distance under the curious eyes of so many strangers. Indeed, she was an object of some interest to the denizens of the village, all of whom had heard that she was a great heiress from Kent, news that was bound to arouse almost as much speculation as the arrival of a young unmarried gentleman of wealth and position would have done. Anne began to make her way towards the spot where the Darcys were engaged in animated conversation with their friends, and since she was too shy to meet anyone's eyes, she was immediately set down in popular opinion as insufferably haughty.

When she was halfway to her destination she saw Lady Margaret come to meet her with a quick step and a good- natured smile. She took Anne's arm, saying, "How thoughtless of us to leave you stranded, Miss de Bourgh, when you are new to the neighborhood and must encounter all these unfamiliar faces. But come and meet my father, who is anxious for the honor of welcoming you to the district." Anne thought that Lady Margaret was a more sensitive person than she had at first supposed, to come and rescue her in such an obliging manner.

"I am quite out of humor," continued the lady in a confidential tone, pausing for a moment in their progress toward the little group by the churchyard gate. "My father and the odious Mr. Grey are getting on like a house-afire," and she turned her eyes heavenward with an amusing expression of mock despair. "First they discovered a common passion for chess. How the subject arose I cannot imagine. Then my father discovered that Mr. Grey has some knowledge of geology, and immediately invited him to dinner and to see the endless cabinets of dusty rocks that fill our library. I foresee many a dreary evening burdened with the presence of that person while you are away in Scotland." Lady Margaret looked genuinely put out at the prospect.

Anne would have liked to defend Mr. Grey but had not the opportunity to do so before they joined the others and she had the pleasure of meeting Lord Faulconer. He was a tall, imposing man with sad, kind eyes and an air of attentive gravity. He expressed his pleasure in the anticipation of Anne's extended visit to Pemberley after the excursion to Scotland and hoped that he and his daughter would often have the honor of seeing her at Castle Faulconer. Anne thanked him and said how much she looked forward to spending some months in such a beautiful part of England. Conversation then turned to the wonders of Scotland that she and Elizabeth would be seeing for the first time but which were well known to Lord Faulconer from his youth. After a few minutes Elizabeth claimed Anne's attention in order to introduce her to an elderly lady who had appeared while Anne was concentrating on the effort of conversing with someone so much taller than herself as Lady Margaret's father.

This was Lady Templeton, who as arbiter of local fashion was determined to be among the first to meet a young lady of such eminent family and fortune as Miss de Bourgh. She said many gracious things, welcoming Anne to the neighborhood with the kindest wishes for her happiness amongst them. Anne was rather struck by the coldness of the lady's eyes, which were as dark and shiny as two black currants, and she did not feel much desire to know Lady Templeton better. Fortunately, attention soon turned to Mr. Grey, who was presented by Darcy as "an old school friend," to which Grey immediately added with a respectful bow, "the new librarian at Pemberley."

Lady Templeton looked a bit thoughtful for a moment, and then said, "A school friend of Mr. Darcy's? Then very likely you are related to the Greys of Somerset, of Creedmore Hall? I went to school with a Miss Grey, a dear friend who is now Lady Belthorpe."

Darcy happened to know that Lady Belthorpe was his friend's aunt and he was appalled to hear Grey reply that it was indeed likely that some relationship existed, but that he had made very little study of such matters.

Lady Templeton looked somewhat taken aback for an instant but then resumed her interrogation. Her expression took on what Anne imagined to be the cold determination of a tigress that has spotted its prey across a wild savannah. Then the lady remembered to add what she believed to be a pleasant smile, but which often had, in fact, a disturbing effect on sensitive individuals.

"And your parents? Perhaps I know them. Where do they reside?"

Grey said that his mother had died some years before and that it seemed unlikely that Lady Templeton would know his father, who resided in a wilderness to the southeast of London.

"I did not know that such a wilderness existed," replied the lady, "But I begin to think that you are not an entirely serious young man. And what does your father do in this remote part of the kingdom?"

"Oh, " said Grey, without a moment's hesitation, "he is a farmer."

Lady Templeton was at a loss for words at this, but presently said, "Well, he must be a worthy person to have afforded you an education that has given you such advantages as the friendship of Mr. Darcy."

Grey answered that opinion was rather divided on that subject and that any good qualities he could claim for himself were almost entirely owing to the excellent influence of Mr. Darcy.

At that point Darcy could bear no more and said that as much as he regretted it, an immediate return to Pemberley was necessary so that preparations for the journey to Scotland might be completed. All in the company were surprised to discover how much time had been idled away in the delightful freshness of the morning air, and after many expressions of friendship and farewell the Darcys, along with Anne and Mr. Grey, returned home.

CHAPTER 17

The following Sunday found the Darcys within a few miles of Lord Munford's castle in the Highlands, along with numerous servants, innumerable trunks and other forms of impedimenta, all arranged in two handsome carriages of the latest design, that were drawn by horses that would have done credit to a Duke's equipage. When Mr. Darcy had first appeared in the social sphere in which he was to encounter his future wife, Miss Bennet, rumor had reported his income to be ten thousand pounds per annum. In such cases rumor is usually guilty of exaggeration, but in this instance, as it turned out, the sum enjoyed by the Darcys was more than twice that amount. So, Mr. Darcy could well afford such luxuries, and he was a man who liked to travel in comfort whenever possible.

This inclination had, however, exposed him to the merciless raillery of Mr. Grey, who had watched the preparations for departure with much amusement. Grey, who had explored the mountains of Europe with nothing more than a rucksack on his back, asked Darcy how many years they planned to be gone, and whether they should not take some furniture as well, since the assumption seemed to be that no civilized amenities were likely to be found at Castle Munford. At last they were ready to depart and began at a stately pace down the drive, until Mrs. Darcy's maid remembered a small but important dressing case and everything came to a standstill while one of the footmen hurried to retrieve it.

"I do believe we are affording Mr. Grey a good deal of amusement," said Anne, turning to look back at the house through the carriage window. Leaning against a column of the portico and holding an ailing volume protectively in his arms, Grey seemed barely able to contain his mirth at the drama of one more item being wedged into the already bursting carriages. Mrs. Reynolds, the housekeeper, Mr. Fisk, the steward, and several of the servants stood watching the procedure in respectful silence, feeling no doubt that the honor of Pemberley necessitated traveling in such great style. When at last the house disappeared from view and the horses' pace began to increase, Darcy sighed with relief.

En route they had stayed with various relations who lived obligingly near the road to Scotland. Anne met for the first time several cousins of whose existence she had been almost unaware. These offshoots of the noble houses of Munford and de Bourgh seemed to have been waiting patiently for years only for the opportunity to overwhelm their relations with the most gracious hospitality and speed them on their journey in the most agreeable fashion. It was an unusual circumstance for these kind hosts to be able to show their appreciation for many visits made to Pemberley over the years. By the last day of the journey Anne felt quite weary with the effort of meeting so many new people, and she wondered how she would manage for weeks as one of a large house party. *I hope that no one will notice if I disappear for a few hours each day,* she thought as she watched the wild, open country passing by. *Surely in such a large company I will go unobserved.*

She looked across at her companions, who seemed to possess the ability to enjoy both the journey and its conclusion equally well. Elizabeth was looking very beautiful that morning, her face slightly flushed with the excitement of being so near Castle Munford at last. It was difficult for Anne not to envy her. Elizabeth seemed to know nothing of anxiety at the prospect of meeting strangers. A house full of unfamiliar people, an aunt and uncle she had not seen since she was a child; this was enough to fill Anne with something close to terror.

136

Even more frightening was the thought of the numerous guests they would encounter at the castle, some of them her own age, who were sure to consider her a fool when she was unable to think of anything to say to them. So anxious had Anne become that she began to wonder how she could have been so idiotic as to consent to come with the Darcys. So painful was her trepidation that she had been unable to eat breakfast that morning and her friends were concerned to see her so pale and quiet.

Darcy attempted to entertain her with stories and legends of the rugged countryside, which was so different from anything in Anne's experience, and he was rewarded with an occasional smile or question from his young cousin. "What I find so remarkable," she said at last, "is what seems to be the almost complete absence of human activity in this landscape. We have hardly seen a living creature all morning, except for a few birds in the distance. There is, however, something intoxicating about these great, unobstructed views of a country so indifferent to the small concerns of mankind." At this Darcy had to smile, for he had not been able to detect any sign of enthusiasm for the landscape or anything else in Anne's demeanor that day.

A moment later a rather violent lurching of the carriage to one side interrupted their conversation, as one of the wheels was wrenched partly off its axle by a concealed depression near the edge of the roadway. The coachman brought them to a halt with minimal damage to their conveyance, and everyone felt glad to have escaped being overturned. Darcy leapt out immediately to survey the damage and to confer with his entourage. For some time the uneven track they had been traveling had hardly deserved to be called a highway, and their path had become quite steep. Fortunately the weather had been fine. Anne had asked Darcy at one point what they would have done had heavy rain reduced the road to mud. Her cousin had only laughed and shrugged and replied that they would then have had to deal with a major inconvenience.

Anne and Elizabeth soon descended from the carriage as well, happy of the opportunity to walk about for a few minutes. The head coachman now suggested that the ladies and their more important belongings be transferred to the second carriage, which would then proceed to Castle Munford while repairs were being made. This seemed like a reasonable plan, although Elizabeth was concerned that it would disturb the repose of her maid Marguerite who had been feeling unwell and who was taking up a great deal of room in the second conveyance. There was also some concern that there might be an inadequate amount of space for such a large coach to maneuver around another.

While this important discussion was underway, the group became aware of an elegant barouche making its way up the hill, headed in the direction of the castle. A young man of striking appearance was driving two splendid horses with obvious skill and good judgment, for he was able to pull up beside the disabled carriage with a minimal amount of fuss and dust. He was accompanied by four servants, including a driver and two outriders, and a more perfect example of unaffected elegance could not have been imagined.

Anne recognized the newcomer as Lord Holland, the young man whom they had met at the concert in London only three weeks before. Darcy greeted him by name, and Holland turned over the reins to his servant and descended to come over to them with the greatest alacrity. He bowed to the ladies and thanked Mr. Darcy for his good-ness in remembering their brief meeting in town. Then he turned to look at the damaged wheel with the air of an expert in such matters, and offered to render whatever assistance might be in his power.

"Perhaps you will recall, Mr. Darcy, from previous visits to this area, that there is a small village just two miles before you reach the park gates of Castle Munford. There is a perfectly competent black-smith there and I would be glad to see that he repairs the wheel at once if you wish to remain here. There is plenty of room for me to take my barouche around your two carriages. I would also be delighted to convey Mrs. Darcy and Miss de Bourgh the rest of the way to Lord Munford's."

Darcy considered this proposal for a moment; he had confidence in his servants, but thought that he would prefer to stay with the two carriages and oversee repairs. At the same time he was eager to deliver Elizabeth and Anne to the comfort of his uncle's house. A cold wind had begun to make itself felt, and there was a hint of rain in the air. He had heard nothing but favorable reports of Lord Holland and the young man's suggestion had been made with such good sense that Darcy could find no fault with this solution to his dilemma. Elizabeth at first made some objection to leaving her husband's side, but a glance at Anne's exhausted countenance made her change her mind. In a few minutes the damaged wheel was removed and secured to the back of Lord Holland's barouche and the two ladies were on their way.

Their rescuer had turned over control of his horses to his coachman, and joined Anne and Elizabeth in admiring the glorious scenery, which became more remarkable with every mile. "The castle, as you will soon see for yourselves, has one of the most magnificent prospects imaginable, overlooking a loch that seems to extend into the distance forever," said the young man.

"Then this is not your first visit?" asked Elizabeth.

"Oh, I have had the honor of being Lord Munford's guest on several occasions," replied Lord Holland. "I am an old friend of his elder son, and we have had many a fine day's shooting hereabout. There is no better sport anywhere. I have stayed at the castle before so many modern comforts were added; it would not have been a very agreeable place for the ladies in those days. There was a cold and damp even on the warmest afternoon that only the most robust constitution could tolerate."

Anne asked if Lord Holland were acquainted with Colonel Fitzwilliam.

"I have met the colonel on two or three occasions, but for the past few years he has rarely found the opportunity to join the party that gathers here each autumn. I regret that I do not have the good fortune to know him well as he is known to be such an admirable officer and much loved by all who enjoy his friendship."

These sentiments served to raise Anne's opinion of Lord Holland. He continued, "I am surprised that I have not had the pleasure of seeing Mr. Darcy here before. Has it been many years since his last visit?"

Elizabeth replied that the illness that had afflicted Darcy's father during the latter part of his life and the necessity of taking on the responsibilities of the Pemberley estate, had made it difficult for her husband to undertake prolonged journeys for several years.

"And did you first become acquainted with Mr. Darcy in London?" asked Lord Holland, then added, "but I believe it was in the country, was it not?"

Elizabeth was somewhat taken aback at this rather personal question, but answered that she had first met Mr. Darcy in Hertfordshire where he had been visiting his friend Mr. Bingley.

"Ah, yes," exclaimed the gentleman, " I believe that Mr. Bingley has the good fortune to be married to your sister."

Surprised, Elizabeth said, "Why, Sir, I find it remarkable that you should have so much knowledge of my family."

Lord Holland looked abashed. "I beg your pardon, Mrs. Darcy. I hope that you do not think me impertinent. Sir Frederick Lindsay, who was so kind as to introduce me to your party at the concert, is the source of my information. He speaks of your family with the greatest respect and mentioned that your father is a distinguished scholar."

Elizabeth enjoyed the opportunity to speak of Mr. Bennet's accomplishments, and then the conversation turned to books and music. It was evident that Lord Holland was a man of considerable education and taste and they found that they admired many of the same authors. Several attempts were made to draw Anne into the discussion, but either from fatigue or diffidence, she made only the briefest responses. She did, however, take the opportunity to observe Lord Holland rather closely as he talked enthusiastically with Elizabeth about their common interests.

Anne considered his extraordinarily handsome face and figure more against him than otherwise, as she found it difficult to imagine that a man so well favored could be anything but vain. She had to admit, however, that he gave no hint of such a failing. Nothing could be simpler, but at the same time so appropriate as his style of dress, and there was certainly no hint of conceit in his manner. She still found that the brilliance of his eyes made her feel ill at ease, but could not understand why this was so, as their expression was of the most perfect gentleness.

They stopped briefly in the village, if a collection of a dozen or so simple stone buildings may be so called, and left the wheel in the care of the blacksmith. Anne found the man's speech almost impossible to understand, but it seemed that all possible haste would be taken to restore mobility to the Darcys' carriage. After leaving one of his servants to oversee the project, Lord Holland gave the order to continue on to Castle Munford, which lay only two miles distant.

The road now led them up a steep grade and through a narrow pass, bordered on either side by walls of bare rock that seemed to rise above them to vertiginous heights. A dark, rushing stream paralleled their route through this defile as they began to descend, and Anne could not help thinking how easily a mishap might send their carriage down onto the half submerged boulders fifteen feet below the roadway. Elizabeth, who was not cursed with the kind of imagination that envisions every possibility of disaster, was leaning forward in happy anticipation, her lovely face alight with excitement.

They rounded a curve that was bounded on each side by a thick stand of fir trees, and immediately saw the castle far below at the end of a winding and precipitous track. It was a massive grey building situated on a prominence overlooking a great loch, the more distant shores of which were obscured by a rapidly thickening fog. Anne had never dreamt that there could be such an endless expanse of wild, empty country as that which she saw extending on every side to meet the darkening sky. The bleak monotone of the landscape was broken only by the subdued green of scattered plantations of evergreens. Although the scene could hardly have seemed less hospitable, Anne, far from being dismayed, was filled with an exhilaration that was completely new in her experience. The bracing air, the untamed beauty of the land before her seemed to Anne more splendid and liberating than anything she could have imagined in the pastoral confines of Kent.

Lord Holland was quick to see the ladies supplied with lap rugs to protect them from the increasing cold. It was impossible to hurry their descent towards the castle because of the challenging configuration of the road, and he suggested pausing to close the carriage, but with one voice Anne and Elizabeth protested against losing the wonderful view. Surely the rain would hold off until they had reached their destination. Finally they came to the last, level approach to the towers and battlements that marked the end of their journey. Anne found it a romantic sight, although the building lacked anything of the symmetry or grace that she had thought necessary for an edifice to be considered beautiful. One wing, on the side of the castle most distant from the loch, looked so ancient that she half expected to see warriors in chain mail walking on its parapets, but even this section looked newly roofed and repointed. She knew little of such matters but could imagine that only great expenditure and effort could have restored this venerable structure so far from civilization to such perfect condition. It is all a bit too flawless, she thought, perhaps a small residue of decay would be more in keeping with the spirit of the place.

They passed through an imposing stone gate which seemed to have escaped the close attention paid to the rest of the castle for there was a coat of arms that was so badly eroded by time as to be almost indecipherable. A huge door opened directly onto a paved courtyard, without the added dignity of a portico or steps, and before this they came to a halt. Almost instantly the door was thrown open and it seemed that a fair sized whirlwind rushed forth and engulfed the travelers. This force of nature was Lady Alicia, closely followed by her husband Lord Munford and a retinue of servants. Before Anne could draw another breath she found herself embraced by her aunt and ushered into an immense and tenebrous hall that extended far into the distance before culminating with the sweep of a ponderous oak staircase. Nothing could have been kinder than the reception given them by Anne's aunt and uncle. Elizabeth they had met earlier that year, and they seemed to have already formed a genuine affection for her. The cordial greeting given Lord Holland made Anne believe that he must be a favorite guest. It was for their niece, whom they had not seen for several years, that Lord and Lady Munford extended their most animated welcome. That the young lady who had always been represented as a forlorn invalid never likely to leave Kent should have come all the way to Scotland seemed almost miraculous.

Everything about the noble couple was large and impressive. Both were tall and handsome, and Lady Alicia had preserved much of the beauty for which she had been famous in her youth. So well did the Munfords agree that they considered any separation a hardship, and their friends could only shake their heads in disbelief at the spectacle of such a happy marriage. That they had achieved this felicity was perhaps not so very extraordinary as they were both blessed with good dispositions and the inability to dwell on any source of discord for more than ten minutes.

"My dear child," said Lady Alicia, taking Anne's hand, "this is happiness for which we would never have dared hope. To have you with us is a great joy and we have been awaiting your arrival with such anticipation." Her uncle also expressed his own gratification at seeing his niece, but was almost immediately off to lead a rescue party to bring Darcy and his equipage and servants to the castle, as a storm seemed likely to break very soon. Lord Holland tried to assure the earl that everything was being done, but Lord Munford was always delighted to have a pretext for rushing off on horseback. Lord Holland, far from seeming fatigued from his journey, insisted on accompanying his host, and the two gentlemen disappeared almost at once.

"Well, that will keep them amused for a while," said her ladyship, "Come, my dears, and I will show you to your bedchambers."

Anne and Elizabeth were led up the stairs, which were lit by a beautiful expanse of mullioned windows. The day had grown so dark, however, that the impression was one of unrelieved gloom, and candles in sconces were already lit along the hallways. After passing through several dim corridors, they reached Elizabeth's room. Lady Alicia, who had been talking cheerfully about the difficulties of roads and weather, threw open the heavy door saying, "I hope that this room will be to your taste. I'm afraid it may be a bit simple compared to Pemberley."

Her guests could not have been more surprised at the delightful bedchamber, furnished in the most comfortable and modern style. They had both expected to find only cold stone floors and dark heavy furnishings. Elizabeth expressed her pleasure at being given such charming accommodation and Lady Alicia was clearly pleased.

"This is the first year that we have been able to entertain ladies in anything approaching a truly civilized manner here. If you only knew, my dear ones, what privation I have endured in this castle from my determination not to be apart from my husband. But now all the effort seems worthwhile since you are here."

Mrs. Darcy was left alone to rest and Anne and her aunt proceeded along another series of hallways. "I hope, Aunt," said Anne," that I will be able to find my way back to the center of the house this evening."

"Oh, that would be very difficult," replied Lady Alicia, "I will send a servant to guide you until you are familiar with this labyrinth. It will be easier when there is more daylight. I'm afraid that we will have a bad storm tonight."

Anne's bedchamber was located in the uppermost floor of one of the towers that stood at each corner of the main body of the castle. The round chamber was enchanting, with windows overlooking the loch which was now almost lost to sight in the heavy fog. One of the servants had lit a good fire, and everything was in readiness to protect the delicate Miss de Bourgh from taking a chill.

"It is a lovely view on a brighter day," said her aunt, "I think that you will be comfortable here, and your maid will have a closet just through there, so you will not find yourself too solitary in this part of the house. I hope that you will feel like a princess in this tower."

Then Lady Alicia left her niece to rest, only adding that she herself would return in two hours to guide Anne to the drawing room where she would meet her fellow guests, "for I know, my dear, that you are not very used to being in company, especially with so many strangers. Have no fear, for I will be there with you, and they are all agreeable people." Anne really began to love her aunt, and could not help but reflect how very different she was from Lady Catherine.

Anne's maid, Celestine, a young Frenchwoman engaged in London, soon appeared and was busily at work in the dressing room arranging all of her mistress' exquisite new clothes. Anne sighed, for she would have welcomed some time to herself in her tower. She sat by the fire and felt too fatigued to do more than stare at the flames. After a few minutes she got up and found her writing desk and retrieved a letter that she had already read several times.

Lady Catherine had written at some length of her activities in Bath; she was generally pleased with the society to be found there. Mrs. Collins had joined her as her companion, and her little boy was a very charming infant. Most children were troublesome but he was quite good tempered and amusing. Anne was surprised that her mother could enjoy the presence of a baby, but stranger things had happened.

The letter continued:

I am happy to report that your cousin Fitzwilliam seemed to like his visit to Bath very much and was quite sorry to leave. Of course he is very fond of me, but I suspect that he has begun to form an attachment to a most eligible young lady who moves in the first circles here. I have known her family, a noble one, for many years, and was glad to see the two young people furthering their acquaintance at every opportunity. You are aware of how much I wish to see Fitzwilliam well settled in life, with a good income and an amiable wife. Lady Emma Foxworth has every grace and accomplishment possible, is heiress to a large fortune, and is considered the greatest beauty in Bath. I was delighted to see that my dear nephew found her charming and took every chance to enjoy her company. Of course nothing is settled, but I feel certain that when they are next brought together, and I will arrange that they are as soon as possible, that there will be a happy outcome for all concerned. Since I know that you share my high regard for your cousin, I am sure that you will be pleased to learn of this development.

There were several more pages full of long descriptions of Bath assemblies, where the notice of Lady Catherine had been sought assiduously by all the best people in the place. The letter closed with the usual admonitions to dress warmly and not to venture out of doors except in very fine weather. Anne did not bother to read further, but resumed her contemplation of the fire. Her most dear Fitzwilliam would of course marry and she would lose her best friend, the only person who had ever shown an interest in her as a person worth knowing. He would have no further time for her once a wife claimed his attention. She found herself in tears as she contemplated the future without him.

CHAPTER 18

"How very pretty you look, my dear," said Lady Alicia when she came to fetch her niece. Anne, always skeptical when offered a compliment, imagined that there was a note of surprise in her aunt's voice. Any approach to prettiness was the outcome of a rather drawn-out dispute with Celestine. Anne had thought to wear one of her old familiar dresses, only to be told that everything had been left at Pemberley, except what had been acquired in London. This made Anne so angry that she had stamped her foot and thrown a small book of poetry across the room. Celestine, who had been brought up in France where her mother had once been personal maid to a duchess, merely shrugged. "Perhaps I misunderstood my lady. Surely she did not intend to wear those *other* dresses here." Then she made a grimace of distaste at the thought of the attire that had been so carefully chosen by Lady Catherine for her daughter.

Anne had finally been driven to wear a gown of a light, silvery blue, but she utterly rebelled at having her hair dressed in anything but her usual simple and unbecoming style. Celestine, who knew how to choose her battles, gave in for the moment, but she secretly determined that if she were doomed to live in such a barbaric country she would at least have the satisfaction of transforming her new mistress into a paragon of fashion.

As Lady Alicia led Anne through the corridors towards the great staircase, she tried to give her niece some idea of the other guests she would encounter in the drawing room. There were several young people who were friends of her son Edward, the most important of whom was Lady Clarissa to whom the heir had become engaged only the month before. "A lovely girl," said Lady Alicia, "we are so pleased. And her parents, Lord and Lady Popenjoy, are here as well." There were also some old friends of Lord Munford who had made their way to the castle for the shooting many times before, but now brought their wives with them for the first time. "It will be so pleasant for me to have other ladies here," said Lady Munford, "and to have some amusement besides the stories of each day's sport."

As they descended to the hall Anne saw that it had been brightly lit, which quite dispelled the earlier impression of gloom. Large fires roared in cavernous fireplaces on either side of the wide stone floor, but contributed little in the way of warmth. A footman, who had been well concealed in the shadow of a suit of armor, sprang forward to fling open the doors of the drawing room for his mistress and her guest. Anne saw that all within was brilliance and light, and she was greeted by the sounds of laughter and conversation. The large room, which had been decorated in the most pleasant and elegant style, seemed filled with people and she had the uncomfortable sense that she was the last to make an appearance that evening. Indeed, there was a brief moment of silence as everyone turned to take note of the new arrival. Lady Alicia tucked Anne's arm within her own and led her forward. The unfamiliar faces and names passed by in a blur for Anne; as usual she was so self-conscious that she was unable to take note of the information being imparted as introductions were made. She saw that the party consisted of the fashionable and exquisitely dressed of both sexes, all of whom seemed quite at their ease, as though they had known each other for years. The greetings she received were courteous and friendly but Anne imagined herself to be the object of some degree of curiosity and critical examination.

"And here, Anne dear, is your cousin Edward, whom I do not believe you have seen since you were children."

Edward was a tall, athletic man of thirty-four with an agreeable countenance and a cheerful manner. He resembled his younger brother, but to Anne's eye did not possess Fitzwilliam's noble demeanor or look of lively intelligence. The heir stood near the fire with the young lady who was to become his wife in a few months' time. Lady Clarissa was delicate, pretty and ready to laugh at every attempt at wit that fell from the lips of her betrothed. They seemed completely absorbed in each other's company, and Lady Alicia, wishing to find a safe haven for Anne in that room full of strangers, led her away to the spot where Darcy and Elizabeth were standing together.

They had just seen Anne and came forward to greet her, Elizabeth feeling rather guilty that she had not been keeping a closer watch for the reticent young lady. "You see Anne," said her aunt, "Here is Darcy, none the worse for a couple of hours delay in the mist." Assured that her niece was under the protection of her cousins for the moment, Lady Alicia went off to see to her other guests, but as everyone knows, the fluidity of such a gathering is beyond the control of the best-intentioned guardians of the timid. For a few minutes Darcy and Elizabeth stayed by Anne's side, talking of the day's events, but soon their attention was claimed by new and old acquaintance. Anne felt very conspicuous there by herself but tried to look at her ease, as if she did not at all mind standing alone in an unfamiliar setting. Not knowing where to cast her eyes, she turned and gazed out of the window at the rain and fog that shrouded the loch. She wished that someone would come to talk with her but dreaded it at the same time.

After a few minutes, a young man who identified himself as Mr. Germain appeared at her elbow. He was a somewhat rotund gentleman whose hair seemed to have been cut with assistance of a large bowl. His locks closed about his round head like the halves of an oyster shell and his dress was rather foppish. Anne thought him a bit absurd and wondered how he happened to be a guest at Castle Munford. It was soon revealed that he was an old school friend of Edwards's. Mr. Germain made several attempts to engage Anne in conversation by asking her the usual questions about her opinion of the weather, and her previous experience, if any, of Scotland. Even this mundane exchange was a challenge for someone cursed with extreme shyness and she could produce nothing but monosyllabic, barely audible replies. Although she was one of the most intelligent people in the room and could have discussed any number of scholarly topics with someone capable of putting her at her ease, she was without an idea of how to talk about trivial subjects. Her mind went blank and she felt cold with discomfiture.

Mr. Germain, who was not clever, could think of nothing to counteract this incommunicativeness on the part of the young lady and he soon withdrew with a bow and some excuse of paying his compliments to his hostess. He was discouraged at his initial failure but determined not to give up on the possibility of making himself agreeable to so great an heiress as Miss de Bourgh. Anne was glad to see him leave but was humiliated at her own timidity and she turned back towards the window with barely suppressed tears. Inwardly she berated herself as a fool, incapable of the most ordinary social interaction. In London and at Pemberley she had begun to experience some increase in self-assurance, but now she felt herself to be as awkward as she had been at home with her mother.

She was just beginning to think that she could not very well continue to stare out at a blank landscape without appearing even more ridiculous, when a gentle, low voice spoke close by her side. "Miss de Bourgh, you give me hope that I have found another being who enjoys a rainy day."

She turned and saw Lord Holland, who had apparently entered the room after her own arrival there. He was quite simply dressed as usual and she thought how well he contrasted with some of the other gentlemen in their excessive finery. He looked into her face attentively and seemed to be waiting patiently for a serious reply to his remark.

After a moment's hesitation she said, "I must confess that I often find satisfaction in liking things that are unappreciated by the great majority of humanity, but I am fond of the rain for its own sake. Colors frequently seem more brilliant and the clouds in their infinite variety are more interesting to me than the clearest blue sky."

He seemed to consider her words, then said, "This day reminds me of a few years ago when I was here for the shooting. There was a great deal of rain and we frequently came back drenched and would shiver before that very fire. Understandably there was a fairly constant flow of complaint from my companions, but I must say that I rather enjoyed it. There is something so exhilarating about fighting one's way across such wild country during a cloudburst, with the wind in one's face."

Anne nodded appreciatively; she could imagine how it must be and wished that she could venture out onto the high moorland.

"And if it were not for the inclemency of the weather, I would not have seen one of the most beautiful sights in my experience," he continued.

She looked up at him with interest and he went on, "At the end of a long day we were walking back to the castle in a driving rain. We had just reached the summit of that hill over there." Lord Holland gestured toward the far side of the now obscure loch.

"Just then the deluge ceased and the most extraordinary rainbow appeared over the loch and the distant castle. It was a triple rainbow, Miss de Bourgh, of the most remarkable definition and clarity."

Anne, who had an excellent ability to see things in her mind's eye, could well envision how glorious the sight must have been. Her eyes shone with the thought and her face became animated. She looked very pretty at that moment but of course, she had no knowledge of it.

"How fortunate I was to see something so remarkable," added the gentleman, "But tell me, have you ever made a study of rainbows?"

Anne had to admit that she had not, and immediately Lord Holland began to explain something of what was known of the optics of rainbows. He seemed to know a good deal about the natural sciences and could convey information without the least appearance of conceit or self- importance. It came as a surprise to Anne when dinner was announced and she realized that she had quite forgotten her timidity and unhappiness of half an hour before.

She was sent in to dine with Lord Popenjoy, a distinguished peer of about sixty who Lady Alicia was sure would be able to engage her niece in conversation for an hour or so. On Anne's other side was a young man who could talk of nothing but shooting, and whose name she never did quite comprehend. She felt more at ease now and discovered that prompted by a very few brief questions this sportsman would rattle on happily about his obsession. The exchange had the advantage of giving her some idea of how the gentlemen spent their time each day. Anne found Lord Popenjoy's conversation more interesting as they found that they admired some of the same authors. All of the guests at dinner seemed well bred and well behaved and Anne wondered at her mother's parting warning that Lord Munford's friends might not be quite of the best society.

The ladies now withdrew to the music room where Lady Alicia asked her niece if she would like to sit next to the fire, "for the dining chamber is always cold, my child, and there does not seem to be any way to improve it. I do not wish for you to take a chill."

In vain did Anne protest that she was quite well and required no special attention; a screen was carefully placed by her chair to shield her complexion from the heat of the fire and her aunt occasionally took her hand to monitor its return to warmth. It was disagreeable to be the object of so much solicitude and have the other ladies think her some kind of invalid. Anne could not but be resentful of her mother for always ensuring that her daughter would be regarded as frail and sickly.

Elizabeth came to sit by Anne as well and seemed to feel ashamed that she had not taken better care of her young friend earlier that evening, but very soon the gentlemen joined them and the lovely Mrs. Darcy was called away to the pianoforte. The entire company was delighted with her playing, which had greatly improved in skill and expression since her marriage to Darcy. He had recognized that she had true ability and had encouraged its development, never letting anything interfere with her practice each day and securing the best masters. Now he stood near her, his entire being suffused with love and pride at what his wife had accomplished in a few month's time.

Elizabeth was at last allowed to rest for a while and another lady, whose playing was in no way to be despised but who was not the equal of Mrs. Darcy, undertook to entertain the group. During the pause that followed this performance, Lord Munford called everyone's attention to the presence of another talented musician. "Holland," he cried, "where is your fiddle? Do not try to tell me that you do not have it with you, for I saw it carried in when you arrived."

All eyes turned to Lord Holland, who had been standing near Darcy and had listened to both ladies with obvious appreciation. In vain did he protest that he was unworthy to follow such accomplished performers. Lady Alicia seconded her husband, adding, "I will not be content until we have heard you play with Mrs. Darcy this evening." This proposal met with universal enthusiasm and Lord Holland's instrument was sent for.

There was an immense pile of sheet music and it took Mrs. Darcy and Lord Holland a few minutes to look through it.

"What would you say to this, Mrs. Darcy?" asked the gentleman.

"Oh, the D major?" she replied, "Do you not think it a little modern for our friends? Although you are kind to choose something I studied recently."

"Let us rouse them from their after-dinner torpor," whispered Lord Holland with a smile.

The audience was indeed enlivened by the music that followed. One would have thought that the two performers had played together many times, so well did their instruments answer and echo each other. Intent on the score, they only exchanged occasional glances but were able to communicate a high level of musical understanding.

Few of those present had any real insight into the piece that was being performed but even the least informed were struck with the beauty of the two young people before them. At other times Elizabeth generally gave the impression of being light-hearted and playful. She could discuss many subjects in a sensible and well-informed manner, but a smile or laugh was never far away, and her wit could resist few opportunities for a drôle or amusing remark. At the pianoforte, however, she could at times seem transformed into a different being; her lovely face became serious and intent and it appeared that she had entered a realm of the mind far distant from her surroundings. To Darcy she always looked like a beautiful seraph gazing on the divine, with the locks of her dark hair falling forward, and her lips slightly parted.

Anne had managed to escape her prescribed place by the fire, and had made her way to a spot near the pianoforte. Darcy saw her and quietly found her a favorable position to Elizabeth's left. Here she remained, so struck by the power and fervor of the music that she felt her heart expand with what was both a transcendent delight and something close to pain. At one point during the rondo Lord Holland looked across to her and smiled slightly. The glance did not last as long as one beat of her pulse, but with it he seemed to say that he knew that she felt the glory of the piece as he did.

At the conclusion of the sonata, everyone overwhelmed Mrs. Darcy and Lord Holland with praise. Even those who had the misfortune to be almost deaf to the beauty of the music sensed that they had been present at something very fine indeed. "One would have thought that you had been born to play together," said one lady, "You both just took up that score as if the difficulty were nothing."

Elizabeth laughed and thanked her admirers for their compliments; she herself felt that she had never played so well before, and she stated that any competence on her part was the effect of collaboration with a musician of Lord Holland's genius. Of course the gentleman averred that just the opposite was the case, and this might have gone on for some little time, had not Darcy expressed an opinion that his wife had need of rest, which prompted all to retire for the night.

⌇

The Darcys' bedchamber overlooked the loch and they stood together by the arched window, admiring the splendid view, since the rain had ceased and the moon had emerged to cast a silver light over the quiet landscape of mountains and glistening water.

"Tell me, my love, have you ever stayed in a castle before?" asked Darcy drawing close to his wife.

"Not a *real* castle like this one," Elizabeth replied, "with battlements and towers and even the remnant of a moat! It is like a dream."

"And do you think that you will like it here?"

"Oh, yes, I am so delighted with everything, but I have to add that I would be happy anywhere as long as I am with you, beloved."

They remained by the window, close in each other's arms for some time, until Darcy said, "My darling, you must be very tired and in need of rest."

"No, my love," replied Elizabeth, "I am never in the least fatigued – when I am near you."

CHAPTER 19

*A*s was her habit, Anne awoke very early the next morning. It was unusual for servants to be abroad before Miss de Bourgh had been out-of-doors to assess the weather and listen to the birds. On this day, however, she lay abed for a while, thinking about the previous evening and all of the dramatis personae gathered at Castle Munford. There could hardly be a more respectable and well-bred group of guests, so evidently Lady Catherine had been incorrect as to the kind of society to be encountered at her brother's house. Perhaps her mother was misinformed in other ways as well. As for the castle itself, Anne thought that it must meet all the requirements for a gothic romance, although she had never had the opportunity to read such books. Lady Catherine did not approve of young ladies reading fantastical stories. For herself, she never failed to have the latest novels at her disposal but kept such dangerous volumes in her own locked bookcase so that Anne could not read them.

The most vivid experience from her first hours at the castle had been the delight of hearing Elizabeth and Lord Holland play together. She then remembered something curious about her cousin Darcy. During the last movement of the sonata when she had been standing by his side, she had been surprised to see his face become pale and tense. His manner in taking his wife away from the pianoforte had been rather abrupt and almost discourteous, more like the old Darcy than the amiable man who had become familiar since his marriage.

These thoughts allowed her to avoid for a time reflecting on the way in which she had acquitted herself on the previous evening. Then she recollected with shame her display of temper with Celestine. How many times had she seen her mother become angry over the most trivial things; heaven forbid that she should ever behave like Lady Catherine! Just as disheartening was the memory of how overcome by shyness she had been on meeting the other guests at the castle, in spite of her resolution to smile and appear at her ease. It would have been agreeable to blame Darcy and Elizabeth for not keeping better watch over her, but she had, in truth, to acquit them. No doubt if she had not seemed cold and proud, more of the company would have approached her. Lord Holland had saved her from complete misery and she could not but consider him a very kind and tactful gentleman. Then all her mother's warnings came back to her, and she wondered what could have actuated such consideration toward the most uninteresting young lady in the room.

Her bedchamber, which faced southwest, was still fairly dark, but the light that was beginning to illuminate the distant hills prompted her to dress quickly and with little sound so as not to awaken Celestine who slept in the dressing room next door. Anne hoped to have an opportunity to walk on the wild uplands near the castle before anyone else should be awake. She found her way slowly along the passageway from her tower to the main corridor, for everything was quite obscure. She had begun to think that she should have brought a candle when a light appeared just a few feet ahead at the junction with another hallway. In another moment she was brought face to face with Lord Holland.

"Why, Miss de Bourgh!" he exclaimed, "I see that I am not unique in being an early riser."

Not knowing what to reply, she merely nodded. It was annoying to have her morning outing interrupted in such a way. I suppose that I will have to be up before dawn now, she thought to herself. In the dim light she saw that Lord Holland was dressed in shooting attire, which became him very well.

"You will think me fanciful," he said, "but you put me in mind of Persephone, making her way through the darkness to bring light and springtime to the world. Perhaps you will permit me to illumine the rest of your path through this stygian gloom."

Anne looked at him solemnly for a moment. Compliments were usually distasteful to her because she assumed that they were insincere and thus an insult to her intelligence. But this seemed an odd sort of compliment, and she could perceive amusement in his eyes.

"I have no objection to such classical references," she said at last, "although I believe that it was Persephone's mama who was responsible for rescuing her from the underworld. You do not at all resemble my mother."

"But no doubt she would deliver you as Demeter liberated her own daughter, should the need arise," said Lord Holland.

"Oh, it is clear that you do not know my mother," said Anne with a faint laugh as they reached the staircase.

As they walked on in the gloom, Lord Holland said, "Miss de Bourgh, from our conversations thus far I can tell that Lady Catherine has seen to your education with great care. Is she very learned? Has she read Milton, for example?"

Anne had to laugh at the idea and replied, "No, mama prefers the lightest sort of novels. She looks disapproving when she sees me reading *Paradise Lost*."

"Indeed? For myself, I greatly admire ladies who read serious books."

When they had descended to the hall Anne paused for a moment, not wishing that Lord Holland should discover her intention to walk outdoors. She was afraid that he might suggest accompanying her, something that she was not sure to be quite proper.

Instead he said, "I will leave you here Miss de Bourgh, for I perceive that this is the time of day at which you take pleasure in some quiet and solitude. If you wish to walk in the hills nearby, allow me to suggest that you depart by the front door here and after walking through the courtyard gate you will see a convenient path on the far side of the garden." So saying Lord Holland opened the heavy door and bowed to Anne courteously.

AFTER AN HOUR'S ramble on the nearby hills, Anne made her way back to the castle. She found Lady Alicia standing on an elevated terrace overlooking the loch, watching Anne descend the steep path. "My dear, I was almost thinking of sending one of the servants to look for you, but as it turns out you are in good time for breakfast. Most of the ladies have just come down."

"I must say that for a hopeless invalid you are very agile at making your way over rocky ground, my child," continued her aunt, "When I awoke this morning and found that you had gone out, I was concerned, but after some reflection decided that an intelligent young woman should be able to take a walk without the entire household going into an uproar."

Anne thanked her aunt for this mark of confidence and the two ladies walked back to the house together. They made their way around the imposing mass of turreted walls and reached the western aspect of the building where a newly constructed addition formed a rather startling contrast with the ancient structure. "I fear that we will be unable to go out riding today," observed Lady Alicia, "It will begin to rain very shortly. You see those threatening clouds in the west. Such a pity. But I am so delighted that you wish to join me in my favorite activity. Heavens! I hope that your mama does not send a thunderbolt in our direction when she learns of it."

They found the breakfast room full of ladies, some talking animatedly and others who seemed barely awake. Anne chose some food from the long sideboard, which was supplied with every imaginable dish, and then sat down next to a short, round figure in a black gown who was vaguely familiar to her from the evening before.

"Miss de Bourgh," began the lady, turning to reveal bright eyes in an amiable pink-cheeked face, "you met so many new people last night that I will introduce myself again. I am Elizabeth Grinspoon, a cousin of your uncle's and thus a distant relation of yours as well, but in some way much too remote and complicated for either of us to comprehend it."

"Lady Grinspoon's mother was your uncle's second cousin," said Lady Alicia, who was standing nearby, overseeing the replenishment of the breakfast dishes by a troop of servants who had just entered the room. "I am glad that you are sitting together as you share an interest in books. I will tell you, Anne, since she is too modest to mention it herself, that Lady Grinspoon is a well-known author. But I see that there is no coffee here for you, my child," and their hostess left them to admonish the butler for this grave oversight.

"Oh, I doubt that you are familiar with any of my books, Miss de Bourgh," said Lady Grinspoon, "perhaps you have heard of the novels of Charles Ellcroft? That is my *nom de plume.*"

Anne said that she believed that she had seen the name in a periodical at some point, but that few novels came her way at home as her mother did not approve of them for young ladies.

"Well, I cannot say that I agree with your mother. Who else could be better suited to the reading of romances? Although I am sure that quite a few gentlemen read my books without acknowledging it."

At Anne's request Lady Grinspoon mentioned some of the titles of her works: *The Secret of the Tower*, *The Last Farewell*, and *Agnes Blandford.*

"I find thinking of titles more difficult than the actual writing. Often my publisher has to invent them for me." Anne asked how long she had been producing novels.

"For about ten years, and I attempt to finish one each twelve-month. You see, I have the honor to belong to one of the poorer branches of the family and I had to take to my profession after my husband died. Novel writing, you must understand, is the last refuge of the educated pauper," and the lady laughed merrily at this reflection. "I have a slender talent, but it has enabled me to live quite well and to carry my two daughters to London every season where they both made good matches."

Anne said that she would very much like to read her new acquaintance's work, and Lady Grinspoon replied that she believed that the library at Castle Munford was well stocked with all of them.

"Your aunt has the goodness to be one of my most faithful readers. But I have heard, Miss de Bourgh, that you are a scholar and a natural philosopher. That was my information from Mr. Darcy when I dined with him yesterday evening. He was full of praise for your erudition."

Anne was quick to say that her cousin had exaggerated in regard to any accomplishments she might possess, but she was delighted to find during the conversation that followed that Lady Grinspoon shared many of her interests and was very fond of walking. The prospect of such an agreeable companion on some of her rambles in the hills was not unwelcome, although Anne had always thought of herself as a solitary being.

The rest of her first day at the castle, however, provided no further opportunity for venturing out-of-doors as a settled rain began to fall soon after breakfast. "Will the gentlemen return early from their shooting?" Anne asked her aunt.

"Oh goodness no, my dear," replied Lady Alicia, "for no one among them will admit to disliking being out in the wet and mist for hours. Men, you know, are such odd creatures, and would rather be soaked through than express a preference for dry clothes and a warm fire."

The day passed very pleasantly for the ladies at any rate. Anne enjoyed conversing with Lady Grinspoon, who was remarkably good-natured and had a drôle wit and refreshingly blunt approach to the subjects that came under discussion. She told her new young friend something of the story of her life.

"I grew up in Devon in my family's ancient manor house, a romantic if inconvenient sort of place. My father was very rich and there was never any concern about money. My two brothers and I were thoroughly spoilt, although my only extravagance was books. My parents were dear, light-hearted people whose only fixed idea was that I was a delicate creature who might die if exposed to the slightest draft of air. So I spent my time reading and they, knowing nothing of such things, let me have whatever books I wanted."

"Of course I read many novels in addition to everything else imaginable, and thus I learned much about the real world, perhaps more than was quite good for me." She caught Anne's quizzical look at this last statement, and continued with an amused smile, "But surely, Miss de Bourgh, you are not under the impression that the novel is merely a clever invention with no relation to what we will encounter when we venture out into the realm of men and works?"

Anne admitted that such had been her impression, although she certainly respected the skills required of the novelist.

"Well, it is a common and understandable error to think so," continued Lady Grinspoon, "But the truth is that nothing necessitates a more acute observation of one's fellow creatures than the writing of a believable novel. Oh yes, Miss de Bourgh, if you would understand the real world, do not neglect the dedicated reading of fiction."

After this digression, Lady Grinspoon continued, "My father had the misfortune to be led into some questionable investments by an old friend, and when I was eighteen we suddenly found ourselves rather poor. So it was a matter of some relief to my parents when I began to be courted by the baronet whose estate lay close to ours. Of course, since I had read so many novels I knew that one should marry only for love. But it was a matter of a commission to be purchased for one brother, and a church living for the other that my husband-to-be had in his gift."

"But you are shocked by my frankness," said the lady with a laugh, seeing that Anne was rather taken aback by such candor, "but one should always be frank and open on all subjects with young ladies, for who has so much need of information as they? Instead the poor lambs are let out into a pasture full of wolves with no way to protect themselves."

"In any case, I married Sir Harry Grinspoon, who was another dear, good man, much like my father, and almost of the same age. Alas, he was also given to speculation, and when he was killed in a hunting accident I found that I was left with almost nothing to support my daughters and myself."

Anne repressed a shudder; she knew little of poverty, but it seemed a dreadful thing.

"Of course we had to leave Grinspoon Hall to the heir, and we sought refuge with an aunt who lived a retired life in Truro. It was there that in desperation, rather than from any passion for literary pursuits, that I wrote my first novel. With the help of a friend of my late husband's I was able to get a publisher to look at this first attempt, and my pen has been my means of support ever since."

Apparently it had been a satisfactory source of income, for Lady Grinspoon was richly, if simply dressed, and seemed to have the enviable ability to do what she pleased. The other ladies at the castle seemed delighted to meet the famous "Charles Ellcroft" and frequently asked when her next book might be expected to appear.

"I had heard over the years that you were a frail, delicate child," said the lady at one point, "much given to sickness and unable to stir out into society. But this report seems to have been incorrect, so I suppose you have a mother who fancies you to be in need of constant protection in spite of all evidence to the contrary. My mother was prone to such absurd ideas as I told you, and you may only look at me to see how ridiculous they were." And Lady Grinspoon, plump and robust, laughed merrily.

In the afternoon, Anne found a comfortable spot in a window seat of the library and began to read "The Lover's Revenge" by Charles Ellcroft, which was full of ruined abbeys and mysterious cloaked figures that appeared on moonlit nights with dire but incomprehensible warnings for the courageous heroine. Anne had hitherto read no novel published later than twenty years before, for that was all that the permitted collection at Rosings had afforded. The experience of reading purely for amusement, with the pleasure of losing herself in a world of romance and invention, was so delightful that Anne was amazed to look up and find that the gloomy day was beginning to fade and to perceive that the sounds of the returning hunting party were to be heard in the hall.

After a few moments Anne was startled to see two of the older gentlemen she had met the evening before enter the library, still in their hunting attire.

"Here is a fire, Richardson," said one, "Let us warm ourselves here for a moment, for my hands are half frozen. We will not disturb the ladies in this room." Anne, mostly hidden by a heavy curtain, was unobserved, and thought of revealing herself, but seeing them so quickly established in front of the fire, with many sighs of gratification, she delayed too long in doing so. Feeling a fool, she remained in her retreat and hoped that they would leave soon.

"What a noble pile this is, Carlton," said the other, "Every luxury out here in the most remote part of the Highlands. It is remarkable."

"You should have seen it some years ago," replied Carlton, "It was little better than a ruin, with rooks flying in and out of holes in the roof, and crumbling battlements." After a pause he continued, "Yes, you will be amazed, but I have it on the best authority that our host has spent every bit of twenty-five thousand pounds on the place."

Richardson received this information with appropriate exclamations of astonishment, "Incredible! But Lord Munford has a splendid estate in Yorkshire as well, does he not?"

"Oh, yes," replied Carlton with the complaisant tone of an old family friend whose knowledge is indisputable, "but he loves this spot and would be here all the time if possible. Never fear, he can well afford the expense. A very clever, forward-looking man is our host."

"But there is a second son, is there not? It must be galling for him to see so great a fortune poured into a hunting lodge."

"Colonel Fitzwilliam, the best young fellow you are ever likely to meet, and an excellent shot. I hope that he will join us here if his duties allow it. No, he loves this place as much as his father does, and I am sure he does not begrudge every penny spent upon it. He is a keen sportsman, and the salmon fishing here is a passion with him. But there will be no cause for him to repine, I am sure. Munford told me that when the lad turns thirty-five he will come into a princely sum. 'My younger boy has proven his worth,' he said to me one time, 'he is no idle puppy, and I mean to do everything handsomely by him.'"

"Is the young man aware of his good fortune?" asked Richardson.

"Why, I think not, for Munford has told me that he always wanted Fitzwilliam to form a strong character by making his own way in the world, although, of course, his commission was purchased for him some years ago."

There was silence for a moment as the two gentlemen enjoyed the warmth of the fire. It was beginning to be very cold in the window seat, and Anne was torn between interest in the conversation and impatience that they might take themselves off so that she could move about.

"It is hard for a young man to believe that his prospects are so limited, however," continued Carlton. "He has an unusual delicacy of feeling, as I should know, for I've watched him these thirty years. Thinking himself poor, he might hesitate to approach a lady if he should find one to his liking. I mentioned this problem to his father once, but after seeming to consider my point, Munford said that there would be time enough later for his son to look for a wife."

There was another pause, then Carlton added, "One never knows about young people though. When I was in Bath just before coming here, I heard a rumor that he is in a way to offer for a lady of great wealth and fashion there."

"Well, that will please his family," replied Richardson, "The Munford star will long remain in ascendancy with such judicious marriages. But Carlton, we had best go dress for dinner. It is getting late."

The gentlemen stirred themselves and left the comfort of the hearth with some regret. When the door had closed behind them Anne emerged from the window seat and went to stand before the fire, feeling chilled to the bone. She found herself in a state of great agitation, but could not at first determine the source of her emotion, and she paced back and forth on the little oriental carpet that marked the area of warmth provided by the now dying embers.

Surely my uncle does not discuss his financial and family concerns with a loquacious person like Mr. Carlton, Anne thought, for she now remembered meeting her uncle's apparent confidant the evening before. He seemed a bluff, red-faced man with no interest besides hunting, but who knew what confidences were forthcoming when the gentlemen enjoyed their sacred after-dinner ritual of passing around the Port decanter. She thought that Mr. Carlton must have some good qualities of mind that were not immediately obvious, or that he must be an exceptionable shot. Sir Wilfred Richardson had seemed a pleasant and intelligent gentleman from a brief conversation with him before dinner.

Anne wondered if Mr. Carlton's revelations were true. If so, Lady

Catherine must be quite misinformed as to the degree of Lord Munford's wealth. She had no real idea of what twenty thousand pounds might mean, but it seemed a prodigious sum.

Anne was a young woman with a natural bent for self examination, and after a moment had to admit to herself that merely overhearing masculine gossip could not have caused the heavy pain that seemed to oppress her heart and the onset of a throbbing in her temples. The discomfort in her breast was very real, and she sat down in a chair by the hearth. Was she dying of some hitherto undiagnosed cardiac disease? Had her mother been correct about the frailty of her constitution all these years? Anne immediately rejected this idea with scorn, and with her innate courage turned her mind to the real source of her distress. It could only be the further evidence of her cousin Fitzwilliam's regard for and serious intentions towards the celebrated Lady Emma Foxworth.

Although she had been distressed by her mother's letter, Anne had not taken it to be reliable. Lady Catherine frequently proclaimed the existence of romantic attachments and probable matches among her friends and acquaintances, and she was more often mistaken than otherwise in her predictions. Anne had often had to smile at her mother's ill-conceived pairings of the most unlikely people and her unsuccessful attempts at match making. What could have been more ridiculous than her mother's untiring determination to promote Anne's marriage with Darcy, despite the obvious indifference of both parties? But now it seemed that there was in existence some general opinion that Fitzwilliam was likely to be soon engaged to the young lady in Bath. That he would only marry for love she did not doubt for a minute; he must be sincerely attached to this paragon of beauty and accomplishment.

Anne had just spent several hours reading a novel of the most romantic type, which described with some degree of subtlety the finer shades of love in all its stages of development. It had been Lady Grinspoon's first work and Anne could not help but wonder if there were anything autobiographical in the tale of a young lady forced to abandon the man she loved in order to save her family from ruin by making an advantageous marriage. The story had continued with the loss of the heroine's wealth and position after her husband's death but ended happily when her beloved returned from foreign lands having gained a fortune, and the two were married at last. Many layers of mystery and strange and sinister happenings had been folded into the plot to ensure the book's popular success, but of the feelings of the heroine the author had written with great understanding. A passage in which she had reflected on her love seemed to Anne to speak with the very soul's truth.

In only a few hours the power of the novel had been effectual in changing Anne's perception of her own inner life. Until today she had comprehended that she loved her cousin, but that love was a vague, half-formed thing comprised of unacknowledged hope and longing. Now she experienced the completely developed emotion in all its force, while at the same time she saw how vain and foolish it was to nurture such feelings for Fitzwilliam. She pressed her hand over her heart as if the pressure could lessen her pain, but her despair was too great for tears.

The library door opened and her aunt appeared, a paisley shawl over her arm, with which she immediately covered Anne's shoulders.

"As I suspected, dear child. You have been sitting too long in this huge, chilly room. You should have rung for one of the servants to build up the fire. But come along, for it is time to dress for dinner."

To Lady Alicia's credit, she noted Anne's look of woe before she had even completed these remarks.

"Why, Anne, whatever has distressed you? I never saw a sadder countenance," she cried, looking into her niece's face with real concern.

With some effort Anne answered, "Dear Aunt, I am quite well, just perhaps overtired. It was a long journey here and I have not yet recovered from its effects."

She expected that this speech would prompt a suggestion that she retire to her chamber for the rest of the evening and not attempt to take dinner with the other guests at the castle. Such would certainly have been Lady Catherine's response. But Lady Alicia surprised her by saying, "Well, Anne, then go at once and spend the next hour lying down, and I will come and fetch you. You will feel better after a brief period of repose."

So assured was her aunt's manner that Anne found herself agreeing to this plan, and making her way through the dim passageway to her tower before she could think of any objection.

At the appointed time she was surprised to see Elizabeth at her door instead of her aunt.

"I asked to be allowed to come for you in Lady Alicia's place," said Mrs. Darcy, entering the room with a rustle of silk. Casting an appreciative eye on Anne's elegant gown, she added, "How very pretty you look, Anne." It was true that Anne was in very good looks despite her misery. The early stages of unhappiness in love will sometimes add some degree of interest to a young lady's features by disturbing that placidity which is the expression of an untroubled mind.

After a moment's hesitation Elizabeth continued, "I wanted to say how sorry I am for not taking greater care of you. I know that all this is new to you, and you must have felt yourself to be quite deserted among all those strangers yesterday evening. I am such a thoughtless creature, but I do hope that you will forgive me."

Anne saw tears fill Elizabeth's eyes and hastened to say, "Please, do not distress yourself. Dear Elizabeth, you and Darcy have shown only the most perfect kindness and solicitude towards me. I am ill at ease, I admit, and conversation is difficult for me at first, but I shall do well in time. You should not have to feel responsible for a grown woman of six and twenty."

Elizabeth was impressed with the spirit of this reply and felt a new respect for the girl who stood before her. For her own part, Anne thought that to resent Mrs. Darcy would be as unreasonable as for a cart horse to resent the speed and beauty of a passing thoroughbred. The two ladies went down to the drawing room with more sincere feelings of friendship than they had experienced hitherto.

CHAPTER 20

*A*nne's second evening at the castle gave her fewer moments of distress than had her first. At least she was not compelled to stand gazing out of the windows pretending interest in a fog-enveloped landscape. Elizabeth was careful to stay at her side and to bring her into conversation with the other guests of her own age. This was not a simple matter, as Anne found great difficulty in thinking of anything to say when confronted with their light-hearted banter. The more gay the party became, the more silent she became. In spite of this diffidence she was treated with kindness and respect. Some of the young ladies seemed eager to know her better and did not seem discouraged by her reserve. With the young gentlemen she felt herself to be hopelessly stupid, unable to reply to their efforts to engage her interest with mundane observations or less than successful attempts at wit. After a few moments' encounter with her silence, her pale face and downcast eyes, they would retreat in confusion.

Had our heroine been from a poor and obscure family instead of the heiress of an ancient and noble line, she would have known the true suffering of those who have no skill in the usages of society, and no power of attraction or wit to compensate for other deficiencies. Even so, she was only partly shielded from the consequences of her timidity, for Anne's character was such a mixture of extreme sensitivity and nervous pride that she could hardly have experienced worse chagrin had she been the unprepossessing daughter of the most impoverished parson in the land.

The most enjoyable moments of the evening were spent in conversation with her new friend Lady Grinspoon, who seemed to have the happy ability of being amusing without a trace of malice. She had made it her mission to educate Anne in the ways of the world, especially as she had observed the young lady's lack of ease with her fellow guests. She herself had once been as shy as Anne, although no one could have seemed more fearless and outspoken than the woman she had become.

"The greatest advantage one may have in making one's way in society is indifference to its opinion," advised Lady Grinspoon as she and Anne sat in a quiet corner after dinner. "Of course, it is an attitude more easily cultivated when one is rich. The less you care for the opinion of the world, the more it will roll at your feet like an obedient dog before its mistress."

"But there are those for whose opinion I must always be anxious," Anne protested, "and surely one must never fail in courtesy, even to those whose company holds little interest."

"You are correct on both counts, my dear. The opinion of those we love must always be of greatest importance. But as for the rest of humanity, the advantage of being well brought up, as you have been, is that you are not capable of failing in courtesy to anyone, and therefore need give the matter no further thought."

Anne had to smile at this last comment, for few people could be less concerned with courtesy than Lady Catherine de Bourgh when she was in a passion. The spectacle of her mother in a rage had always been so dreadful to Anne that she had made great effort to control a similar tendency in herself. When she had been a child, the best model of good manners had been her cousin Fitzwilliam, who had been naturally kind and polite to all around him.

Lord Holland did not fail in attention to Miss de Bourgh, although he seemed to take care that his conversation with her not be of such exclusivity as to arouse comment and speculation. Twice during the evening he approached her with an air of quiet gravity to engage her in discussion of some topic of serious interest. At the same time, an amused light in his dark eyes seemed to suggest that the two of them had the best of a private joke at the expense of the rest of the company.

Lord Holland's skill as a musician, in addition to that of Mrs. Darcy, was soon demanded by all those present as the culmination of the evening's entertainment, and their playing seemed even more superior than at their first collaboration. Once again, Mr. Darcy exhibited some degree of asperity in his insistence that his wife not be prevailed upon to exhaust herself by the entreaties of her admirers. The guests soon hurried to their chambers through the drafty corridors of the castle for, as Lord Munford had remarked at dinner, it would be necessary for the gentlemen to make an even earlier start the next morning in order to find the best day's shooting.

ANNE WAS UP AT DAWN, and wrapping her cloak close about her made her way up the path to the hills as the first light appeared in the east. She reached the nearest crest just as the mist over the loch became suffused with color. Anne recalled the beautiful description, "Now rosy Morn ascends the court of Jove, lifts up her light, and opens day above," wishing that she had been allowed to learn Ancient Greek. How well it must sound in Homer's original words. Alas, her tutor Mr. Grenville had been sent away when she was thirteen and her mother had decided that a formal course of study was too enervating for her invalid child. Anne looked back towards the castle to see if the shooting party were in evidence. On the previous morning she had watched the gentlemen, along with a large entourage of attendants and ponies, making their way to the moorland that lay to the northeast. Today no one was yet abroad, although she could imagine that her uncle would soon be harrying his guests into motion with the urgency of an officer mobilizing his troops for battle.

She decided to descend the hill and investigate the small river that cascaded steeply to the loch about a half- mile further on. She could hear the roar of the stream even from this distance, although its banks were concealed in a continuous line of ancient fir trees. As she approached her goal, she saw a rustic bridge across the torrent that should, she thought, afford a fine view of the loch. Anne was so intent on attaining her object, and the sound of the water rushing over the rocks was so loud, that she was quite startled when she was overtaken by another person on the path. It was Lord Holland, and he had actually been compelled to touch Anne's shoulder to gain her notice. The unexpected contact and the surprise of finding him at her side made her heart leap violently, and she might have lost her balance on the rough ground had he not supported her by taking her arm.

Anne recovered her self-command in an instant and drew her arm away with annoyance. "Good heavens, sir," she said with indignation, "you have given me a very unpleasant turn by your abrupt appearance."

Lord Holland, she saw, was somewhat out of breath, as if he had been in some haste to overtake her. It took him a moment to reply but when he did so it was in a tone of sincere apology.

"Miss de Bourgh, I pray that you will be so good as to forgive this ill-mannered interruption of your solitude. My excuse is a well-justified concern for your safety which led me to follow you in great haste as soon as I observed you take this path."

The young man went on to explain that he had been standing on the terrace that marked the boundary of the castle gardens when he had seen Anne begin to descend the hill towards the river. "As you are aware, Miss de Bourgh, I have acquired a thorough knowledge of all the walks around the castle for some miles in every direction. The bridge over the river is an attractive object for a morning excursion but it can be an extremely treacherous one. After such rain as we have had, the surface is often quite precarious, and on one occasion I came close to finding myself thrown into the stream. Such an event could easily be fatal, as the danger of such heavy water and sharp rocks must make clear. I know that your uncle has plans to replace the bridge and I hope that he will do so before some accident occurs. You can imagine my alarm when I realized that you might venture out to see the view."

Anne studied Lord Holland with an expression of some annoyance, although her vexation had begun to dissipate. "You must have very excellent vision to have observed me from so far away in an indistinct morning light," she said thoughtfully after a moment, "and I must compliment you on the ability to overtake me over such a distance."

To her surprise he began to laugh. "I begin to think that you have an uncommonly suspicious mind, Miss de Bourgh. You suspect me of having followed you on your walk like a hunter stalking his prey, and waiting for an excuse to swoop down upon you with my unwelcome presence. What a dark view you take of your fellow creatures."

Now Anne was truly mortified, and she protested that she had never had such an idea, but he only looked amused.

"Please, do not distress yourself. I sometimes wish that I had a mind capable of such a clever ruse for ingratiating myself with a young lady. But I can see that I will have to be at some pains to win your trust. May I begin by escorting you onto the bridge so that you may admire the prospect of the river and loch in safety?"

In her embarrassment, Anne could think of no way to refuse Lord Holland's company and they continued on together as the path penetrated a line of dark trees. At the bridge her companion ventured out to ascertain the advisability of going any further. Anne had to admit to herself that it was easy to imagine coming to grief there as the surface of the bridge was uneven and the railing inadequate. The river surged over rough boulders some twenty feet below.

Lord Holland returned to her side and offered to be her protector should she wish to go forward, but that he must insist that she take his arm. Anne, still feeling some guilt at her distrust of the gentleman's motives, assented and they moved cautiously to the center of the bridge. As she looked towards the loch, Anne's foot slipped but she regained her balance at once without much difficulty. To her astonishment she felt Lord Holland's arm go around her waist as he took possession of her arm with his other hand. Her immediate response was to make a wild effort to escape him, but he held her in a circle of immovable strength that she could sense even through the heavy folds of her cloak.

"For God's sake, let me get you off this bridge in safety before you pitch us both into the void!" he cried with real alarm in his voice. At this Anne let him assume control of her movements, while she continued to feel the most extreme perturbation at being held so close to his side, crushed against the rough wool of his greatcoat. When they reached the security of the riverbank he released her at once. She found herself shaking with an ill-defined fury, but before she could form some angry rebuke at the liberty he had taken, Lord Holland forestalled her. "It was bad judgment on my part to put you in such peril, Miss de Bourgh. Pray forgive me, and excuse the means by which I found it necessary to protect you."

This was said with such humble contrition that Anne felt her resentment subside. Without a word she turned away and began to walk back to the castle. He accompanied her as if the little drama on the bridge had never taken place, and talked so amusingly of his previous visits to the Highlands and of the odd local customs and superstitions of the district, that she soon found herself suppressing a smile. In a few minutes they had reached the summit of the hill that overlooked the castle. To the northeast, the thin line of the assembled shooting party could be seen ascending to the moorland above the loch.

"But Lord Holland!" exclaimed Anne, "You have been left behind and surely will be at some inconvenience to join your fellow huntsmen."

Lord Holland looked unperturbed and replied, "There is no difficulty in that regard, as I plan to take my leave of Munford Castle this morning."

"I see," said Anne, "but it seems rather a long way to come for a two night's visit. Do you always tire of a place so quickly?"

"Hardly," replied the young man with a smile,. "And never before have I left this delightful retreat with such reluctance," he added with a slight bow. "However, I will return in about ten day's time after I have attended to some family business."

They walked on and Anne had to admit to herself that she was glad that Lord Holland was not leaving for good. She had yet to form a definite opinion of the gentleman but she would have been sorry to lose the opportunity to observe him further.

"In explanation, Miss de Bourgh, I must give some account of my situation, if it is not asking too much of your patience."

Anne merely looked at him attentively, and he continued, "I will travel northward today some thirty miles on behalf of my brother who has a large demesne there. I will meet with the steward and my brother's solicitor from Glasgow, and we will spend several days going over all the concerns that arise when such a property has not seen its master for so long a time."

"Your brother must be grateful to you for taking so much trouble to assist him," said Anne.

"My brother, alas, is an invalid, much afflicted by a long and distressing illness which has robbed him of his youth and spirits. He has been for some months at Bath at the insistence of his physician, but thus far has received little benefit from the waters."

They walked on in silence for a moment, then Lord Holland began again, "So precipitous has been the recent decline in my brother's health that last year I was compelled to resign my commission in order to be of assistance to him.'

"Your commission!" exclaimed Anne with surprise.

"Why, yes," he replied, "But of course, you did not know. I was an officer in His Majesty's navy with the rank of post-captain."

"Heavens! What a sacrifice to make for your brother! To give up a career in which you must have distinguished yourself to return to the monotony of an ordinary existence," cried Anne, who had a very romantic idea of naval life.

"It was, I admit, very difficult," her companion agreed. "I miss my old life and my friends in the service. I went to sea at the age of thirteen, so you can imagine that I sometimes feel out of place ashore."

After a moment he went on with a laugh, "The only thing I do not regret is the experience of being almost prostrate with my sensitivity to the movement of the ship for the first week of every voyage. Now *that* is true suffering."

"I believe that you are in good company in that respect," said Anne. "Did not our dear Lord Nelson suffer from the *mal de mer*?"

Lord Holland replied that he thought that such had indeed been the case. At Anne's prompting he went on to mention some of the actions that he had seen and the naval heroes he had known. The last half-mile passed quickly and they soon found themselves at the castle. Her aunt appeared as they reached the terrace and it was clear that she had been keeping watch for them. Anne felt some confusion at having been observed walking alone with Lord Holland at this early hour, but her aunt greeted them with no sign of disapproval and merely hurried them along to breakfast.

Within the hour Lord Holland had taken his departure, leaving in a fine mist of rain that had begun to fall. Soon the fog rose off the loch and surrounded the castle in a soft grey cloud. The ladies spent most of the day before the drawing room fire and amused themselves with cards and conversation. Elizabeth took advantage of the opportunity to spend some hours of practice at the pianoforte, and Anne was glad to find a pleasant corner where she could begin reading another of Lady Grinspoon's novels. Within the span of only a few days sojourn at the castle, the guests had fallen into a routine of sorts. Lady Alicia had the happy facility of being able to influence the habits and moods of her visitors, in effect to train them to behave and react as she wished, while remaining the most tranquil of hostesses.

CHAPTER 21

he next morning brought the first really fine weather, and at breakfast Anne was assured by her aunt that they would finally set off on horseback, as had been promised.

"Colonel Perrin will be here by ten o'clock, my dear, and we will show you some more of our splendid scenery," said Lady Alicia. This gentleman was a near neighbor, near at least as distance is calculated in the Highlands. He was Lady Alicia's faithful knight and always ready to accompany the ladies on such excursions. An old war injury had made it necessary for him to give up shooting, but he still rode perfectly and was always an agreeable companion.

Darcy, who had anticipated his aunt's plans, had been down to his uncle's stables early that morning to ascertain that the proper mounts had been chosen for Elizabeth and Anne. Indeed, he had exchanged detailed correspondence with Lord Munford to be sure that no untrained, skittish brutes would endanger his wife or cousin. Accordingly, two of the most tractable and placid animals imaginable were brought round for Mrs. Darcy and Miss de Bourgh. It was a strong contrast with Lady Alicia's fire-breathing chestnut mare, which came dancing into the courtyard throwing its head about and generally making life a misery for the groom who led it. Nothing could have been more beautiful than the way in which her ladyship brought her horse under perfect control with the quiet assurance of an expert rider.

Elizabeth was disappointed in her somnolent mount, for having never experienced anything unpleasant on horseback she believed herself to be more competent than she really was, but she accepted the horse that had been chosen for her with a good grace. Anne felt only relief at the sight of her quiet gelding, for she approached the prospect of riding with a mixture of determination and timidity. Her aunt had spent some time the evening before acquainting her with the principles of horsemanship, which only made her niece more anxious.

"My child, you look very well indeed, as if you had been born to ride," said Lady Alicia once Anne was safely mounted and was being led around the courtyard by a groom, "Some people simply have a naturally good bearing on horseback. It is something they are born with."

After another ten minutes of milling about and waiting for another lady who had decided to join the excursion, they set off. Anne was put into the care of the head groom who kept her horse on a lead, which made her feel rather foolish, but which was reassuring at the same time. After a few minutes she found Colonel Perrin at her other side. She had noticed that he walked with what seemed to be a painful limp, but once on horseback he was the picture of graceful strength. He talked to her as they rode along instructing and correcting the young lady with the most gentle tact, and Anne soon forgot her fear. Elizabeth rode forward with Lady Alicia, which could not have been particularly comfortable for either lady due to the very different pace of their animals. It was clear that the young Mrs. Darcy could not bear to be anywhere but in the front of the group in any situation in which she found herself.

They soon reached a glorious view of the loch, having made their way up a fairly steep rise. Anne thought that riding must be the most delightful pastime imaginable as she admired the scene before her. She thought her horse the dearest creature in the world and her companions remarkably kind and agreeable. The cool, pure air off the moors brought color to her cheeks and she found herself full of an exultant joy.

Lady Alicia happened to look over at her niece who was at a little distance, and remarked to Elizabeth, who was still close by, "Why Anne is really a very pretty girl, do you not agree, my dear? It was dull of me not to see it before this moment."

"Oh, I have always thought that she could be quite lovely," replied Elizabeth somewhat inaccurately, "Her features are delicate and perfect and her figure well-made. Her complexion is exquisite, as you can see. It is only a lack of self-assurance that causes her to be overlooked."

Anne would have been surprised indeed if she could have heard herself so praised. At that moment she was excitedly asking questions of Colonel Perrin about every aspect of the wonderful prospect before them. Her eyes were bright and her color high with the effects of exercise and she had forgotten to be concerned about how she appeared to the rest of the company. Colonel Perrin looked at her with evident admiration and wondered how it was that he had not heard that Miss de Bourgh was such a beauty.

The group rode home along a ridge that afforded a continuation of the same fine view for about an hour more. The more experienced riders cantered ahead but Anne had the continued protection of the groom and the attentive colonel who seemed content with a sedate pace. When they had come within a quarter of a mile of the castle, the young lady's companions felt that she had done so well that she was allowed to go at a slow canter under their careful supervision. The sensation was so exhilarating that Anne wished that the ride would never come to an end.

The weather continued very fine for the next few days and Anne made rapid progress as a horsewoman. It became evident that she possessed a good deal of natural ability, and her aunt and Colonel Perrin were delighted. They spent hours instructing her, and their devotion was well rewarded by the unflagging efforts of their pupil. Some evenings found Anne almost overcome with fatigue, but she always ignored such weakness and joined the party assembled in the drawing room at the appointed time.

"How well you look, my dear niece," said her aunt as Anne entered the drawing room about a week after their first time out riding, "You did so beautifully today and it has brought the roses to your cheeks." Lady Alicia and Lady Grinspoon were seated by a long window where they could enjoy the late afternoon sun. Anne joined them as the other guests gradually made an appearance.

Presently Lady Alicia said to Lady Grinspoon with a tolerant smile, "I see that Darcy and Elizabeth are late again." Then with a laugh she added, "Oh the delight of being young and in love," and she left Anne and Lady Grinspoon in order to see to her other guests.

"I have observed that my cousins are often late in joining the company in the evening," said Anne to her friend, "It does not seem very courteous, but my aunt only seems to be amused by this lack of attention. Why is this so?"

"If you wish, I will be happy to explain this and a number of other things that it would be well for you to understand," replied the older lady, "but we will wait for a more private time and place."

At that moment they were interrupted by the persistent Mr. Germain, who was still determined to be agreeable to the young heiress, and bored her with some inconsequential discourse almost every day at about this time.

"Ah, Miss de Bourgh," he began, "You must be looking forward to the ball on Thursday next. I understand that our numbers will be increased by the addition of many fashionable young people who will be coming some distance to join us. All the ladies are in an ecstasy of anticipation, no doubt." And Mr. Germain rubbed his hands together in what was one of his more unattractive mannerisms.

Anne's uncle had just entered the room and came over to greet the trio by the window. "Heaven knows where we shall put them all," said Lord Munford, "I suppose they will be hanging from the rafters in the attic. Germain, you will not mind, I am sure, giving up your room for a couple of nights and moving into a crofter's cottage?"

Then Lord Munford laughed heartily at Mr. Germain's horrified countenance. "I am only joking. We have plenty of room for yet another crowd of the size we already have here." Turning to Anne he continued, "Well, my dear niece, you have had little experience of balls, I believe."

"Less than that, uncle," replied Anne, "I have had none whatsoever."

"This will be an informal sort of affair," said Lord Munford, "Nothing so elegant as a London ball. Your aunt says that we may be as rustic as we like here, and for my part I prefer to be rather *décontracté*."

In a few minutes the two gentlemen wandered off and Anne turned to Lady Grinspoon with some distress. "What ball, Lady Grinspoon?" she cried, "I do not remember any mention of a ball."

"My dear child, it has been the favorite topic of discussion every day for the past week. Have you not heard the other young ladies on the subject of gowns here in this very room each afternoon?"

Anne felt very much a fool and replied, "I suppose that I thought they were only speaking of such things in a general way, and I am afraid that I did not pay much attention."

"I am certainly flattered that you have been so wrapped up in reading my novels that you have been unaware of everything going on around you. An author could ask for no higher praise. But why should the prospect of a ball distress you so. You have surely brought some appropriate gown with you?"

"Oh, yes," replied Anne absently, "That is not a problem."

When Anne retired to her chamber that night, she asked Celestine if there were anything in the overflowing armoire suitable for the forthcoming Highland revel. The young Frenchwoman rolled her eyes heavenward in exasperation and replied with a heavy sigh, "Does my lady not remember that I asked her to choose a gown last week and that she said that it did not matter and that I might decide for her?"

"Oh, I suppose I thought that you were referring to dressing for dinner that evening," said Anne.

"*Mais c'est incroyable*," muttered Celestine to herself with a shrug as she turned away to her duties. Surely there had never been such a young lady, indifferent to balls and likely to run out of her chamber in the morning without even a glance in the mirror. If Miss de Bourg had been more docile it would not have mattered, but all Celestine's efforts to dress her mistress' hair prettily and add those subtle feminine touches that only Frenchwomen can master had been stubbornly resisted. With an expression of hurt pride she said, "Naturally all is in

180

readiness for the ball, my lady, and I have chosen the lavender silk, as I told you this morning before you went riding."

"Oh, yes, I remember now" replied Anne abstractedly as she climbed into the enormous canopied bed, although in fact she recalled nothing at all of the conversation.

It was almost always a lengthy procedure for Anne to fall asleep at night. Her mind was reluctant to surrender to oblivion, and she lay awake particularly long on this occasion, musing over her own eccentricities.

There is, no doubt, an odd self-conceit in believing oneself different from one's fellow creatures, she thought, but surely I am a rather strange being, at least in the society in which fate has placed me. Here was an entire household in a state of furious anticipation over a ball, and she could not summon the slightest enthusiasm at the idea. Instead she felt only a sickening anxiety that she would acquit herself badly and seem an absurd and pathetic figure. How could she have been so completely unaware of the forthcoming fête? The other young ladies had made some effort to engage her in their conversation each day, but had been discouraged when she had met their attempts in the manner of one encountering a foreign language for the first time. Anne wished that she could seem light and silly like the other girls; she saw that the ability to produce a credible imitation of their frivolity would have been a useful skill.

Also, she realized, much of the force of her mind was occupied with thoughts of her cousin Fitzwilliam and she often descended into such daydreams so deep as to make her unaware of the world around her. It is quite hopeless, Anne concluded as she finally felt herself falling asleep, for I will never be like them. I have begun too late.

∾

"WELL, my dear, are you resigned to the prospect of the ball now that you have had some hours to consider it?" asked Lady Grinspoon the next afternoon as she and Anne walked in the windblown shrubbery that served as a garden at Castle Murford.

"Alas, Lady Grinspoon," replied Anne, "By my foolish inattention, I have lost a valuable opportunity to torment myself into an appropriate state of terror. I have only a brief time to distress myself as to the possibility of being without partners or of forgetting the forms of the dances that I was taught so long ago. At least when I first came here I had several days en route in which to reduce my nerves to the breaking point with the thought of meeting new acquaintances. No, in the time remaining I cannot do justice to this dire situation."

Lady Grinspoon, who was by now accustomed to her young friend's sense of the absurd, had to smile, but then she said with a look of sympathy, "Dear little soul, how you remind me of myself at your age. If you find that the opposite of a compliment then you must bear it as well as you can. I too was cursed with shyness, but I promise you that you will survive the affliction and someday even laugh at the recollection."

Anne had difficulty believing in her friend's prophetic powers, but she thanked her for the comparison.

"It is unfortunate that Lord Holland has not returned," continued Lady Grinspoon with a sidelong glance at her companion, "He is really one of the finest dancers I have ever seen. I have been at a ball in London where I was able to confirm this fact. And I have no doubt that he would have been delighted to have the chance of seeking you out as a partner."

Anne did not reply for a moment, then stopped and looked thoughtfully into the distance. "Lady Grinspoon, I understand what you mean to say. Lord Holland has been very agreeable and it might be assumed that he has some interest in obtaining my good opinion, but I assure you that there is nothing in it. I think that he is just the sort of young man who likes to make himself pleasant to all around him, even the more unprepossessing of the ladies."

"I disagree with you on every point, my dear, especially that absurdity about being unprepossessing. It is clear that he enjoys your company."

Anne began to be disconcerted at the thought that others at the castle might be imagining that Lord Holland had romantic intentions towards her. She knew it could not be possible.

After a few minutes silence, she inquired, "Do you know much about Lord Holland's character and history. Lady Grinspoon? I will admit, trusting that you will not misunderstand me, that I find him an interesting and singular person."

"As you have probably noticed, I make it a point to know a good deal about everyone," replied her friend. "I find the study of people amusing and it provides ideas for my novels. In the case of Lord Holland I have heard a little of his family's situation, although I do not claim to know the young man himself very well."

The two ladies found a seat that was somewhat sheltered from the wind off the loch, and Lady Grinspoon continued, "His older brother is the Marquess of Roscree, and has long been considered a paragon among young noblemen. He has always been well known for his virtues and talents and for being the favorite of his father before the latter's death. I have heard that the old marquess had not the least interest in his younger son, seeing him as but a pale reflection of the heir. Since there is a family tradition of naval glory, Lord Holland was sent off to sea at the earliest possible age. His father never expressed any wish to see him again and the boy spent his rare time ashore with various relations."

"How very sad," said Anne, "The father must have been a very heartless person."

"It does appear so, but Lord Holland does not seem to have suffered any irremediable harm from his upbringing."

"He must have been fortunate in his senior officers," said Anne, "Certainly he is a well-educated man."

"Indeed," said Lady Grinspoon, "At any event, two years ago the older brother began to exhibit symptoms of a dangerous weakness of the chest. The present marquess had been in the habit, I have been told, of swimming in all kinds of intemperate weather, and having taken a chill, developed the illness that has persisted to this time and is almost certain to take his life. He is now in Bath but there has been no improvement in his condition. The latest intelligence is that there is no hope of recovery and that Lord Holland will soon accede to the title."

"I wonder if there is any affection between the two brothers. They cannot have spent much time in each other's company."

"It is unlikely, I suppose, that there is a great deal of family feeling when the young men have been separated for so much of their lives, but I have always heard Lord Holland praised as most kind and helpful to his brother. As you know, he gave up his commission to be useful in the management of the estate."

"Perhaps that is not out of brotherly duty, but simply in anticipation of his almost certain inheritance of the title. Why continue in the dangers and privations of a naval captain's life when he will soon be rich and independent?" suggested Anne.

Lady Grinspoon laughed, "No one could accuse you of taking an overly trustful view of your fellow creatures, my dear. But let us give the young man credit for virtue until we have reason to think otherwise. What harm can there be in such a charitable attitude?"

Anne could say nothing against her friend's benevolence and the two ladies continued their walk.

CHAPTER 22

*A*nne made her appearance rather early on the evening of the ball. Indeed, she was enough in advance of the other guests to find her aunt alone in the Great Hall, except for the servants who were making last minute preparations. In this way Anne had thought to escape coming into much notice, whereas a later arrival might have made it necessary to descend the staircase before the eyes of the assembled company. How very different were her expectations from those of the other young ladies at the castle, who were still in their chambers, each one full of the anticipation of triumph and delight, and each calculating how to make her entrance with the greatest degree of éclat.

"How very lovely you look, my dear child," said Lady Alicia, "Your gown could not be more charming. That shade of lavender is perfect for you."

The gown, from the best *modiste* in London, suited Anne very well indeed. There was a becoming color in her cheeks, the result not of high spirits, but of a vexing scene with her maid, Celestine, over the contentious issue of the arrangement of Miss de Bourgh's hair for the ball.

"My lady," the young Frenchwoman had insisted, "there is little advantage in a beautiful gown if you will not allow me to complete the ensemble with a few soft curls and ribbons. The present style is much too severe for a young lady." Celestine could express herself very well in English when she had something important to say.

The suggestion was made as if it were a new idea, but in fact represented the battlefield over which many skirmishes had been fought between the two women. Anne was heartily sick of the subject and exclaimed with some heat, "What is this tiresome preoccupation with my hair? You wish to make me look like some insipid doll!"

Celestine shrugged and replied softly, "I believe that is what most young gentlemen like best."

"Then they are even greater fools than most young ladies," retorted Anne with disgust.

"Ah, my lady," replied the Frenchwoman with a sly smile, "there we are in complete agreement."

The contretemps ended with Anne victorious, although she made a concession by agreeing to wear some fine pearls given to her by her mother when she left Rosings. Thus attired she went forth to meet all the terrors that a first ball may hold for a highly-strung and self-conscious girl. She remembered what Fitzwilliam had said, comparing her to a soldier on his first campaign who must learn to face the enemy without flinching. The unfortunate result was that she appeared at the fête with the stoical countenance of one fearing possible annihilation, rather than the smiling face of pleasurable anticipation.

Her kind aunt would have loved to see Anne looking happier and thought, "If only she could look as she does when we are out riding, with those lovely grey eyes so full of joy, why she would be the most sought after young lady at any ball." She was too wise to voice this opinion to her niece and instead kept the girl close by and attempted to distract her from her fears by telling her about the new guests who had arrived that day.

Anne ventured to ask if there were any likelihood that Fitzwilliam would reach the castle that evening, for there had been talk of such a possibility.

"Alas, no" replied Lady Alicia, "A letter arrived to tell us that my son will not be here for another week because of his regimental duties. I am so disappointed."

Anne had known that it was not probable that her cousin would be able to join them, but she had cherished some hope until this moment. She had avoided coming into the drawing room that afternoon because she dreaded the word that he would be delayed still longer by his duties. Or was it the young lady of Bath who kept him from joining his family? She wished that she could ask for further intelligence, but could not have endured that anyone should suspect how attached she was to Fitzwilliam.

"And I regret to say," continued her aunt, "that our friend Lord Holland will not be with us. A messenger brought word that he is compelled to finish up some important business for his brother before he can return. What a pity, for he is an excellent dancer." And Lady Alicia sighed, feeling the heavy burden of a responsible hostess that all the young ladies should be provided with good partners.

A moment later Lord Munford appeared, his handsome features alight with good humor and his tall well-made figure remarkably impressive in the Munford tartan. He had a compliment for both ladies, and stooped to say a soft word close to his wife's ear. Whatever it was must have pleased her, for she looked up at her husband with a smile full of affection. They stood together hand in hand while they awaited their guests, clearly finding perfect contentment in each other's company.

There can be no happier couple in all of England, thought Anne, and how rare a thing a marriage like this one seems to be. Then she reflected on how unlikely it was that she should ever enjoy such bliss as she saw before her.

Her thoughts were interrupted by the entrance of a brilliant throng of excited guests, and the musicians in the minstrels' gallery began to play at a slight nod from Lord Munford. Very rapidly the room filled with people, and in a moment she heard someone close by whisper, "There is the beautiful Mrs. Darcy," and a murmur went round the company.

Elizabeth was descending the stairs on Darcy's arm, and all who saw her were enchanted; it was simply natural to her to be the center of interest wherever she might be. She delighted others as much by her animation and the expression of her beautiful eyes as by her loveliness.

The ball began with the strains of a bagpipe played by one of Lord Munford's retainers. Anne's uncle leaned down to whisper to her, "My dear niece, as chance would have it, your first ball is like nothing you will find in London. Welcome, Anne, to our *ceilidh!*"

Elizabeth was to open the ball with Lord Munford, who was clearly pleased to lead his new niece to the center of the Great Hall. Anne heard all around her exclaiming at the distinguished and handsome pair. Nothing could have been more graceful than Elizabeth's bearing, while at the same time every movement expressed lively enjoyment.

Anne was so entranced by the tableau before her that she at first did not hear a polite voice asking for the honor of being her partner. It was Sir Wilfred Richardson, whose *tête à tête* with Mr. Carlton she had inadvertently overheard in the library, and which had seemed to confirm Fitzwilliam's attachment to a fashionable young lady in Bath. There had been a few vague remarks about such a possibility since then, which she had heard in Lady Alicia's drawing room as the ladies chatted during the afternoon. Anne, being naturally pessimistic, had concluded that the rumors must be true. It was unfair to harbor ill will towards Sir Wilfred for having been the part of that unwelcome conversation in the library, but she had no very friendly feelings when he spoke to her.

There was, however, no good way to extricate herself from the necessity of dancing with him and she tried to smile and be gracious to the elderly man. He was, in fact, about sixty years of age, hearty and very agreeable, a rich widower with a fine estate near Salisbury. After a few minutes she found it impossible not to like Sir Wilfred. The gentleman had a sweetness of manner combined with a lack of self-importance, which appealed to Anne, who was finding how much she detested pretension in any form.

"I am glad of the chance to speak with you, Miss de Bourgh," he said, "I have hesitated to bore you and the other young ladies with too much of my conversation. Heaven knows, there are plenty of amusing young men here at the castle. Who needs tiresome old fellows underfoot?"

Anne had to smile at this, which was said with a twinkle in Sir Wilfred's eye, as if he secretly thought himself at least a match for the "young men." He was not at all decrepit, in spite of his self-deprecation, seeming as ready for a twelve-mile walk across the moors as any man in the room.

"I have not had the opportunity of telling you that I had the honor of knowing your mother when she was no older than you are now."

Anne looked up at him with interest, and he continued, "Oh, yes, I remember when she first made her appearance in London, along with her sisters. They were known as the 'three graces,' but your mother was by far the most beautiful. She outshone all the other young ladies that season, and I may say with authority, broke many a heart."

Then he hesitated for a moment and continued, "Not that such a kind-hearted lady intended to break hearts. Oh, no. It was just inevitable, as splendid as she was. I saw her riding in Rotten Row one time; a finer horsewoman I never beheld. I was just a poor second son then, almost too afraid to speak to her. Before any of her admirers knew what happened, Sir Lewis de Bourgh carried off the great prize." Then, as if remembering to whom he was speaking, he added, "Of course, your father was the best and most distinguished of men."

Anne found this conversation extremely interesting. She had never imagined her mother to have been a great beauty, although Lady Catherine was still acclaimed a very handsome woman.

Sir Wilfred soon revealed that he was to leave for Bath in two day's time, and would be pleased to carry letters to her ladyship, or perform any other service for Miss de Bourgh. Anne was not always very quick to discern the motives of those around her, but even she could perceive her partner's eagerness to have an excuse to call on Lady Catherine.

"Why, yes, Sir Wilfred, "Anne replied, "I would be most obliged if you would carry a letter and some books to my mother."

Her response brought the happiest of smiles to her partner's face, just as the dance was ending. At her request, he returned her to her aunt's side, but Anne was in that safe place for only a moment before her hand was solicited for the next dance. It was one of the young men who had arrived at the castle that day, and Lady Alicia introduced him. Anne was not to lack partners that evening if her aunt could help it. A few delicate hints from their hostess' lips had made it seem imperative to many of the gentlemen present to secure Miss de Bourgh's hand for a dance at some point during the ball. Anne had no idea that her seeming popularity was largely due to her aunt's care of her.

This new partner was a rather empty-headed young man of fashion who was the very type to make Anne ill at ease. With older, sensible people she could converse without too much diffidence, but the inconsequential banter she encountered with those of her own age left her tongue-tied and awkward. Mr. Tillbridge, for such was the gentleman's name, was anxious to impress Anne with his expertise as a whip, and the extraordinary celerity with which he had traversed the twenty miles between his father's house and Castle Munford.

"It is little short of a miracle that I am here tonight, Miss de Bourgh, for as I was coming around Clicburn Mountain at a dead gallop, there was a bit of rubble in the road, which almost caused us to be pitched into the river 100 feet below. Only the most excellent driving, I can assure you, could have saved us from disaster." The young man paused, expecting Anne to make some remark full of wonder and admiration for his boldness and skill.

Anne wished to ask why he had been driving at such a pace on a dangerous road in the first place, but knew that this was not the desired response. Unable to think of anything to say, she was silent except for a murmured "Yes, how interesting."

Mr. Tillbridge was disappointed at this lack of enthusiasm for his exploits but went on to mention his superiority as a shot, and the certain humiliation of the other sportsmen when he made his appearance in the field.

This subject was no more successful in eliciting the feminine admiration that the young man had come to assume was his due, and after a few more essays of the same kind, he said with an irritated laugh, "Well, Miss de Bourgh, I am afraid that I am a most confoundedly dull fellow, at least in your eyes." Both were relieved when the dance was over.

Anne asked her partner to take her over to a corner where she had seen her cousin Darcy, who was leaning against a column and watching the dancers. He looked very much as he had used to before his marriage, when he had struck most observers as proud and cold. However, he brightened as soon as he saw his cousin, and smiled kindly.

"Let me get you some refreshment, Anne," he said, "You must be in need of it, as you have danced every dance so far. By the by, you dance very well."

When Darcy returned, they stood together for a while. Anne had refused his offer to find her a chair; she was not fatigued, but was wondering how she would ever learn to converse with frivolous people such as Mr. Tillbridge. She thought of asking Darcy for advice on the matter, but his attention was clearly fixed on his wife, who was dancing at some distance from them, at the other extremity of the room. His gaze was intense, and his countenance bore a sadness that was not at all suitable for a happy bridegroom. Anne kept silent but tried to remember if she had seen her cousin look like this at any other time recently.

Darcy had forgotten Anne's presence as he struggled with feelings that he had believed were conquered. He was a man almost helpless in the grip of jealousy, that most painful and degrading emotion. He despised himself for it, and had labored with every ounce of his strength to overcome it, hoping that Elizabeth should never suspect his weakness. It was an insult to the purity of the loveliest being in creation that he should feel such a cold and gnawing misery whenever he saw her in the company of other men. He was like a man who had found a priceless treasure where no one else had ever thought to look. Having placed his jewel in a fine setting where it might be admired as it deserved, he now began to regret having to share what he most loved with the world. How he would have preferred to stay forever at Pemberley, lost in the bliss of being alone with his beloved, contented to ignore the rest of humanity. But he knew that Elizabeth was not meant for such solitude, and Darcy did not hesitate to sacrifice any inclination of his own to ensure her happiness.

After a moment, he recollected that his cousin was there at his side, and said with a smile, "Well, Anne, I suppose that I have been standing here long enough, and I would be most delighted if you would do me the honor of dancing with me." For the rest of the evening Darcy was as cheerful and pleased with everything as anyone could remember seeing him.

"Who ever saw such a change in anyone?" said Lady Alicia to her husband later that evening, "since his marriage to Elizabeth, he has become the most good-natured and sociable of men." Lord Munford, of course, agreed with his wife, as was his strict policy at all times, which may be one explanation for the perfect felicity of their marriage.

Anne had been gaining some little confidence during the course of the ball. While she could not congratulate herself on any great success in her conversations with the other young people present, at least she did not think that she had completely disgraced herself, and she had remembered the necessary forms of the dances fairly well. Unfortunately, as the ball progressed, she was an irresistible object of resentment to some of the young ladies who had been at the castle with her for these last weeks. They were envious of her wealth, her fine clothes and what they considered to be her haughtiness and reserve.

Miss Faircroft and Miss Belmore had been watching Miss de Bourgh for some time, and amusing themselves with many unflattering remarks about what they saw as her deficiencies of style and grace, when they decided to undertake more aggressive maneuvers against her. Neither girl had attracted a partner for the last dance, and they approached Anne during a brief moment when their victim was unoccupied.

Anne had been attempting to find a chance to sit with her friend Lady Grinspoon all evening, but had been arrested in her progress towards that part of the room every time she had started in that direction. This time she found herself accosted by the two young ladies, one on either side, apparently eager for her company. Although she had spent almost every afternoon in the same drawing room, Anne had found very little to say to them, and in truth thought them foolish and empty-headed.

"Why, Miss de Bourgh," began Miss Belmore, "What a great success you are having tonight. You must be quite exhausted from so much dancing."

"But you have been rather unkind to some of the young gentlemen," added Miss Faircroft, "for I have been talking with Mr. Tillbridge and one or two others, and they say that nothing can win your smiles or conversation. Why, Mr. Tillbridge said to me, 'Does Miss de Bourgh never smile? She is as cold as a statue.' See, there is a group of the poor creatures you have put to shame for their attempts to please you." And Miss Faircroft nodded in the direction of a troop of young men, who seemed to be looking in Anne's direction and laughing among themselves.

Miss Belmore took up the offensive and said, "How I wish I had an affectionate aunt to ensure me amusing partners for every dance. Alas, we have to manage on our own and cannot hope for the kind intervention of Lady Alicia."

Anne, looking across the room, saw her aunt speak to a well-dressed gentleman who immediately began to make his way towards the group of young ladies, his attention clearly fixed on Miss de Bourgh.

Everything became clear to her at once; that she had partners only at the instigation of Lady Alicia, and that dancing with her was a tiresome duty. Once this idea had occurred to Anne, nothing could have dissuaded her from believing it. She turned pale, and her two companions had the satisfaction of knowing that their barbs had hit home. They were to be denied the pleasure of tormenting her any further, however, because without a word Anne turned and left the ball, finding her way up the stairs in spite of the tears that had begun to sting her eyelids. The gentleman who had been dispatched to ask Anne to dance wondered at her sudden departure and returning to his hostess, commented that he feared that Miss de Bourgh might be indisposed.

CHAPTER 23

*L*ady Alicia looked across the lines of dancers and saw her niece run quickly up the staircase, but there was no opportunity to follow Anne and learn the reason for her flight from the ball. Lord Munford had signaled to his wife that the important event of the evening was at hand; the company was to learn of the engagement of his eldest son to Lady Clarissa. Already the musicians had fallen silent, and the guests were called to attention, as the young couple, with their parents, assembled in a handsome group for the announcement. Lord Munford was in excellent form, and was clearly delighted with the match. He was equaled in his enthusiasm by the father of the young lady, for there was distinction of birth and fortune on both sides. After the usual speeches had been completed, congratulations poured in from every side, and it was fully two hours before her ladyship had leisure to think of her niece.

After several attempts to break away from the compliments and good wishes of her friends, Lady Alicia at last made her way to Anne's chamber. A gentle knock brought no response, and after a moment she opened the door as silently as possible. She was not very surprised to see that Anne had gone to bed, and was to all appearances asleep. The lovely ball gown she had worn lay in a heap on the floor. Anne's maid had certainly not expected her mistress to retire so early, and in

Celestine's absence some violence had been done to the garment in its removal. Lady Alicia picked it up absently, and shook her head at the sight of several torn seams. She went across the room to stand at the young girl's bedside for a moment, but Anne did not awake, and it seemed sensible to wait until the next day for an explanation.

~

THE NEXT MORNING anyone in the southwest tower wing of the castle might have been puzzled by a rather loud cry of dismay, followed by an agitated outpouring of rapid French. Celestine could have been seen to dash from her mistress' chamber in evident panic, and tear along to the breakfast room where she found Lady Alicia enjoying a solitary cup of tea. Fortunately it was still quite early, and there had been no one sufficiently awake to hear any of the manifestations of Celestine's distress.

"Oh, my lady, you must come at once, I beg you! Ah, it is really too bad! Who ever saw the like?"

The countess looked up alarmed for a moment, then said calmly, "Do not make such a fuss, Celestine. It is not your fault about the gown. I saw it last night, and there will be no difficulty in mending it. My niece was simply fatigued last night, and I daresay was too good-natured to call you away from the festivities in the servants' hall to assist her."

To her ladyship's surprise, the young maid began to weep, "Oh, it is not that, my lady. Please come at once and see what she has done!"

Lady Alicia leapt from her chair, her face ashen with fear. She was not an imaginative woman, but all kinds of vague and terrifying ideas took hold of her mind at that moment. She tried to solicit an explanation from Celestine, but the girl had lapsed into an incomprehensible stream of French, and it seemed most sensible to simply hasten to Anne's room.

Anne was found to be still abed, with a pillow over her head, and did not respond when they came in. Lady Alicia looked around the room with some degree of puzzlement; she saw no evidence of torn garments or other disasters. In a moment, however, as she moved around the foot of Anne's bed, her eye was caught by a mass of shimmering gold silk lying on the floor by the dressing table. As she bent to examine it, Lady Alicia gasped, then looked around at the weeping Celestine in dismay.

"You see, your ladyship," cried the girl, "She has cut off all her lovely hair, her only beauty! Oh, why do such a terrible thing?"

"Don't be a fool, girl! No more of your hysterics," said the fond aunt, bending to pick up a long tress. Anne continued to bury her head under the pillows, and Lady Alicia fervently hoped that the situation was less dire than it appeared.

"Celestine," she commanded, after a moment's reflection, "Go at once and find toast and coffee for your mistress, and do not forget to bring cream."

When the two ladies were alone, it took some degree of patience for Lady Alicia to persuade Anne to emerge from her hiding place.

"Well, it is not very bad," said her ladyship, holding the tear stained face gently and running her fingers through the cropped locks, "At least you have cut it fairly even. But, my dear child, whatever possessed you to do such a thing?"

The question produced such a violent fit of weeping that Lady Alicia had to spend some time soothing her niece before she could expect any reply. Finally the story was told, although in a very disconnected and halting fashion, and punctuated with more bursts of tears.

Anne had returned to her room, full of the conviction that except for the intervention of her aunt, she would not have had a single partner the entire evening, with the possible exception of the odious Mr. Germain, who seemed to have been put on the earth solely to plague her. After managing to remove her gown with difficulty in the absence of Celestine, she had retreated to her bed to indulge in the most desolate reflections. Surprisingly, she had fallen asleep fairly quickly, no doubt from exhaustion and an excess of emotion.

At about four in the morning the moonlight had fallen across her bed and awakened her, and Anne had gotten up to wander fitfully about her chamber. She had lit a candle, and sat down at her dressing table, wondering how she would spend the rest of the dreary night. The sight of her countenance in the mirror, wretched as it was, and to her own eyes plain and insignificant, inspired a violent self-disgust. Her embroidery scissors were at hand, and she began to trim off long strands of hair, almost without understanding what she was about. In a few minutes the operation was completed, and Anne saw with the greatest dismay that she had managed to infinitely increase her misery. She had retreated to her bed, and prayed to awaken to find that this was only a terrible dream, "but alas it is not. Oh Aunt, I shall have to hide myself here forever."

"No, my dearest, we shall make it come out well enough, but why did you have such foolish ideas about the ball? I did only what any mother would do to ensure that her child enjoyed her first ball, for you are like a daughter to me. You have entirely mistaken the matter, and I can assure you that without the intervention of aunts and mamas, no young man would ever have the courage to ask a young lady to dance."

Anne regarded her aunt sadly, and did not believe a word of this reassurance.

"But however did you come to entertain such gloomy thoughts?" asked her ladyship handing her niece a handkerchief, and smoothing her hair. "But of course, your mother was always thus, a prey to every sad reflection. I do not say a word against her, for I do not think she can help being as she is, but Anne, you were made for happiness, if you will but try for it."

At that moment Celestine returned with nourishment for the sufferer, who was persuaded to sit up, and take some coffee. The maid had regained her composure, and studied her mistress speculatively.

"Now, Celestine," began Lady Alicia, "You are a clever young Frenchwoman."

To the evident truth of this assertion the girl could only nod her agreement with grave dignity.

"As all the world knows," continued her ladyship, " a clever Frenchwoman can make what might have been thought a serious error in judgment appear to be the most elegant and original sort of innovation. You will reshape Miss de Bourgh's hair in such a way that all the other young ladies at the castle will be dying of envy."

Celestine seemed to warm to the idea of such a challenge at once and pointed out that several ladies of the highest fashion had been pleased to adopt very short-cropped tresses during the most recent season in London.

"And you, my dear," continued Lady Alicia, turning to her niece, "will accompany me to the drawing room this afternoon."

When Anne began to protest, her aunt said, "You are descended from a race of warriors, not one of whom ever shirked his duty or displayed fear. I know that you are incapable of cowering in your room - not the daughter of Sir Lewis de Bourgh."

LATE THAT AFTERNOON three gentlemen stood near the great windows of the drawing room, where a hard rain could be heard beating on the panes. They were Sir Wilfred Richardson, with his friends Mr. Carlton, and Lord Graylock, and they were rather tired and chilled. All the gentlemen had been out early that morning as usual for the shooting, for who among them would have dared admit fatigue, after only two or three hours repose the night before? The trio looked longingly across the expanse of polished floor and turkey carpets, to where a great fire burned on the hearth, but not one of them would have ventured to take up space in that sacred precinct where the ladies had begun to gather and warm themselves.

They had fallen silent after an exhaustive analysis of the day's sport, when a footman opened the heavy oak doors with more than the usual degree of solemnity.

"Ah, here is our hostess, " said Sir Wilfred, "How much she must have to do, and how well it is all accomplished. I'm sure she has been up since daybreak, while all the other ladies did not begin to stir until noon or one o'clock."

"And Miss de Bourgh accompanies her aunt," observed Carlton, "How very well she looks! There is something different in her appearance, but I cannot tell what it may be. A very handsome young lady of the delicate type."

"Well, the family is known for the beauty of its women," said Sir Wilfred sagely, "You should have seen her mama thirty years ago."

Then he added, "I had the honor of dancing with Miss de Bourgh last night; she has a most gentle and pleasing manner, all quiet dignity. Some of our modern females would do well to take her as a model."

The aunt and niece had indeed made their entrance with some degree of *éclat*. As they moved toward the group of ladies near the fireplace, Mrs. Darcy and Lady Grinspoon rose to greet them. Elizabeth had been informed earlier in the day of the *crise de coiffure*, and had been to Anne's room several times to offer advice and comfort. She had also enlisted Lady Grinspoon in a plan to protect Anne from unkind remarks. Should any of the young ladies approach with evident ill-will, there was to be a flanking action to cut off the attack, and two lionesses could not have been more alert or fierce than were Anne's friends in her defense.

Surprisingly no such defense was necessary, and in one of those odd reversals seen both on the battlefield and in the drawing room, everything seemed to be in Anne's favor. She had managed with a strength of will that she had not known she had possessed to assume a look of cheerful unconcern. Some happy fate had blessed her with hair that freed of its former weight, curled naturally about her lovely face in the most charming manner. Many of those present asked themselves how it was that they had never observed before that Miss de Bourgh had bewitching grey eyes, full of intelligent light, and fringed with dark lashes, or that her features were so well formed and her complexion so refined.

Beneath her brave pretense Anne was still a timid girl, and only the remembrance of how her ancestors had fought bravely at Agincourt had made it possible for her to enter the drawing room. Like a new-made frigate weighing anchor for the first time, and entering the open sea, she knew not whether she would encounter storms or fair winds. As an act of courage, she could not have done more that evening had she faced a line of cannon fire. Cutting off most of one's hair in the middle of the night as an act of despair may seem ridiculous to those with a less passionate nature than Anne's had proved to be, but it was the first thing she had ever done that proceeded from the depth of her own heart.

The two young ladies who had treated her so unkindly at the ball now approached Miss de Bourgh with some trepidation; they had been alarmed at seeing how badly they had wounded their victim. It had even occurred to their very unimaginative minds that Anne was shy rather than proud, and they had been thinking for at least the past half-hour how they might make amends.

"How very charming you look today, Miss de Bourgh, " said Miss Belmore with a tone of subdued sincerity. She had encountered a frightening glance of barely concealed warning and menace from Mrs. Darcy, who had never before seemed anything but gay and friendly. "How I admire your *toute enesmble.*"

"You are too kind, Miss Belmore," replied Anne, who had been preparing what she would say for several hours, "I was intolerably bored with spending all my time enduring my maid's attentions to my hair, the endless brushing and plaiting. Since she is a Frenchwoman who grew up during the Terror, who better to understand the coiffure *à la guillotine?*"

The other ladies were rather taken aback by this reference to the *dérniere mode* of the French aristocracy, but Miss Faircroft, who also was anxious to show her contrition said, "Oh, Miss de Bourgh, what a bold idea you had. I would never have the courage to do such a thing, and I'm sure I could not look so well if I did."

"You are right, no doubt, Miss Faircroft," broke in Mrs. Darcy, "I'm quite sure you could not. Not every girl can have the style and dash of my cousin."

For the first time in that company, Anne was seen to laugh in amusement; never had she expected to hear such adjectives applied to herself. It was absurd, but delightful, and in a moment when they were left alone she found a chance to press Mrs. Darcy's hand affectionately, "Cousin Elizabeth, how good a friend you are to me. I could almost believe what you say, for it is spoken with such conviction."

"It is only the truth, did you but know it," replied Elizabeth emphatically, "You will put us all in the shade someday, and I am unselfish enough that I will rejoice to see it."

Anne was left alone for a moment when Mrs. Darcy saw her husband enter the room, and hastened to greet him. One would think that they had been separated for days rather than hours, thought Anne, and made her way over to the piano to look idly through some new sheet music that had arrived at the castle. She felt strangely at ease, and at least for now the burden of caring how she appeared to other people seemed to have been lifted from her shoulders. Indifference must be the most under-rated state of mind, she mused, and how I wish I could maintain it towards all but those who command my love and esteem.

She became aware of a tall figure at her side, and turning she saw Lord Holland. His color was high from a long ride in the cold wind and his eyes were bright with pleasure.

"How glad I am to see you again, Miss de Bourgh," he said animatedly, "I have just met Mr. and Mrs. Darcy, and have heard something of the ball. It went off very well, I understand."

"Why, yes, Lord Holland, it was, I believe, considered a great success. And of course, my cousin's engagement to Lady Clarissa was announced."

"How sorry I was not to be here for that," rejoined the young man, " but I knew that it was to take place. What a happy event for both families."

He studied her for a minute, and she was certain he was taking in every detail of her altered appearance; the admiration in his eyes made it evident that he approved the change.

He was too well-bred to mention anything specific, but said, "You make the other ladies look rather old-fashioned, Miss de Bourgh, if you do not mind my making the observation." After a thoughtful pause, he added with a smile, "Yes, you have taken the wind, and none will catch you now. The ladies will have to trim their sails directly, or they will be *hors de combat.*"

For the second time that evening Anne laughed without self-consciousness, and she thought Lord Holland both charming and clever.

Encouraged, he continued, "But you will have to spend the season in London next year, if you will permit me to say so. In that assembly of ladies, who combine all the accomplishments of wit and originality, you will be quite at home."

"Beware, Lord Holland," said Anne, "or I will think you guilty of flattery."

"You could not think so, Miss de Bourgh. You could not be so unkind to me, or so unjust to yourself." After a pause, he began again, "I have spent little time in town, but when I have it seems that the fair sex begins to outstrip their self-appointed masters in every respect."

"What an astonishing idea," said Anne, "and if it were true, what would be the point? More romantic novels or finer embroidery stiches? There would be little scope for the exercise of greater powers."

It was his turn to laugh, but then he continued with a half serious air, "It is my theory, Miss de Bourgh, that in one hundred years the ladies will rule, and we men will take our place as their humble minions. Ships will have lady officers, and the men will be allowed to sit in the forecastle and mend sails. Ladies will sit in parliament, and their husbands will stay patiently at home, and await the results of their deliberations."

"And do you think the gentlemen will enjoy such a state of affairs?" asked Anne, willing to enter into the spirit of his caprice.

"Oh, if their wives remember to take notice of them, and pet them, and make much of them occasionally they will like it very well. After all, it is a wearisome business making the world go round." Then his eyes brightened and he said, "But, I recall now that the ancient Greek Aristophanes, wrote a play in which the ladies of Athens wrest from their husbands the control of the city. It was a long time ago, but now I recollect the satire, which I read as a boy."

"And how did they accomplish this prodigious feat," Anne inquired, wishing that she had had a better classical education.

Lord Holland thought for a moment, then Anne was amused to see him blush deeply, and look chagrinned, something she had hardly ever seen a gentleman do.

"Why you know," he said, almost stammering, " I have really forgotten. How bad my memory is, but I am just another ignorant sailor."

"No matter," replied Anne, "My old tutor comes to visit us at Rosings fairly often, I will ask him the next time he visits."

"Oh, Miss de Bourgh," said Lord Holland, with a look of horror, "I beg you, pray, pray do not."

Anne was highly amused, but refused to give him any reassurance. *I will ask Lady Grinspoon if she has heard of Aristophanes*, she thought, *his plays must be very shocking indeed.* She reflected that she liked Lord Holland better than she had thought possible; he had always seemed too sure of himself, too self-possessed. To see him blunder in some way made him seem younger and more pleasing.

Her uncle joined them, and expressed regret that the young man had found it necessary to absent himself from the ball, "And I observed when you entered the room that you return here with a rather pronounced limp. So I suppose you would not have been much use to the ladies last night anyway. Did you take a fall from your horse?"

"Oh, no," replied Holland, "I was walking across a field with my brother's steward, and turned my foot in a badger hole. Ridiculous is it not, after all the endless miles we have walked on the moors while I have been here with you? But I should be able to rejoin the shooting in another day or two."

"Well," said Lord Munford, "Why not join the ladies for their ride tomorrow? Colonel Perrin has a cold, and will not be able to accompany them, and I do not like to see them set out with only a groom or two as entourage."

Lord Holland was delighted at the prospect, "It would be an honor, Miss de Bourgh," he said turning to Anne.

"But, Holland," added his host, "We have missed your music making. If you had to sprain something I'm glad it was not your hands. Why, we must hear you and Mrs. Darcy play together again tonight."

CHAPTER 24

*T*he next morning was very fine, and the riders were even more full of enthusiasm than was the shooting party. The little group included just Lady Alicia, Elizabeth, Anne, and one of the grooms, so that Lord Holland's agreeable companionship was more than welcome. The other ladies in the house party had decided long before that they preferred rising late in the morning and sitting by the fire in the drawing room, to going out into the bracing Highland wind.

Mrs. Darcy was rather vexed to learn that the well-behaved mare she had been riding almost every day had come up lame that morning and that she would have to change to another mount. One of the stablemen led forth an old hunter with the unflattering appellation of Aggitator. This animal was known for having a quiet and tractable, if somewhat taciturn disposition. The youthful exploits that had earned him his somewhat alarming name were long past and no one at Castle Munford had ever known him to give trouble. Elizabeth looked so well on horseback that she was given credit for being much more expert than she really was. Although he was always disinclined to leave his comfortable stall, it was assumed that Aggitator would probably keep up with the other horses, and Mrs. Darcy would have a tolerable outing.

Lord Holland was on a fine black gelding, with manners as good as his master's, and Anne was impressed with the peaceful, sagacious way in which the gentleman managed his horse; there was no show or drama intended to impress the ladies with his fine horsemanship. Lady Alicia's mare put on a bit of a performance for those assembled in the courtyard, and then the little group set out in the best of spirits.

Since the day was so favorable they decided to take a trail that led to a superb view, high over the loch. Anne was delighted for she had not seen the prospect before, and had heard much of the beauty of the scene.

"We could not go there, my dear," said her aunt, "until your riding had improved to this point, because the way we must take is quite narrow, and we must go single file for some distance."

For the moment, however, the group was still on open ground, and they rode in a loose formation with Elizabeth and Anne somewhat behind Lady Alicia and Lord Holland, but close enough that a general conversation about the ball was possible. The sun, for once, made a prolonged appearance, and the breeze felt delightfully mild, in comparison to the usual conditions of such excursions in the Highlands. The little group could not have been in better spirits.

All this time Aggitator was meditating evil in his wicked old head; the pleasant weather made him feel young again, and in any case, he very much resented being removed from his paddock where he had planned to spend the day grazing and gossiping with his friends. He sensed the inattention and inexperience of his rider, and when an excuse presented itself the result was disastrous.

They were making their way through some gorse bushes, when a flock of partridge flew up to their left with a great rush, and much cheeping. For Aggitator, who had not seen such a thing above a thousand times, it was a perfect opportunity to bolt.

And bolt he did, with a tremendous leap forward which would have unseated Elizabeth, had she not had some natural ability as a rider. Before anyone could react, he had taken off at a dead gallop, shooting ahead through the low shrubs and briars. For an instant everyone looked after Elizabeth in dismay. Anne's horse began to wheel about in excitement, until the groom took hold of its bridle, and brought it under control. Lady Alicia had all she could do to control her own mare, and shouted, "Go after her Holland; the trail narrows just ahead, and then it will be too late!"

But Lord Holland was already gone in a great burst of speed, flying across the rough ground, and leaping his horse over rocks and gullies.

Elizabeth was making valiant efforts to regain control of her mount; she hauled back on the reins, but Aggitator's tough old mouth was proof against such attempts, and he soon had the bit in his teeth. In vain did she remember Darcy's advice to try to turn a run-away, for there was no space in which to do so. Her situation became even more terrible when the beast stumbled slightly, and she lost her grip on the reins, which came to rest behind Aggitator's ears. In such terror as she had never known, Elizabeth clung to the pommel of her saddle.

Lord Holland meanwhile, had come up behind her. He knew that the situation was a desperate one, for he had ridden this way before, and realized that only a few seconds remained in which he could rescue Mrs. Darcy. In another two hundred feet the path continued up the mountainside with a sheer drop off to the right, and width enough for only one horse to pass. A rider who lost her seat along this section of the trail would probably be killed, and most certainly terribly injured.

With this horrible possibility present to his mind, Holland gave his horse one fierce cut with his whip and pulled alongside Elizabeth. He saw that she had lost the reins, and calculated that an attempt to pull the animal up by retrieving them could easily fail. She looked round at him with a face that was deathly pale, but determined. There was not a moment to be lost, and he shouted, "Mrs. Darcy, you must come to me! Trust yourself to my arm!"

Almost at the same instant that he said these words Holland leaned towards her, and in a single motion he grasped her around the waist and pulled her onto the saddle in front of him. He pulled up at once, and they both watched Aggitator gallop up the mountainside, with the reins flying about his forelegs.

Only now did Elizabeth see the full extent of the danger she had faced, and she began to tremble violently, and almost fainted in the arms of her rescuer. He held her firmly, and spoke gentle reassuring words, as if she were a child. "There, you are quite safe, and nothing shall harm you while I am here," but in her half swoon, Elizabeth did not hear him.

In a moment they were joined by the rest of their party. Lady Alicia was beside herself with joy at Elizabeth's deliverance, for she had quite expected to see her niece dashed to death on the rocks.

"Never have I seen such a brave piece of horsemanship, Lord Holland," she cried, "We are forever in your debt."

Lord Holland did not reply, but got quietly down from his horse, and assisted Mrs. Darcy to dismount. The others also leapt down and Elizabeth was soon seated on a boulder with her friends grouped around her. A flask of brandy was produced from Lord Holland's saddle and she was persuaded to take a small amount. After a few minutes the color began to return to her face, and she turned to her preserver.

"You have saved my life, Lord Holland," and without allowing him time to reply, she continued, "Oh, do not deny that you have done so, for it is clear to all here that I should have met with destruction had you not shown such skill and courage. No, you must endure being our hero, although I know that your modesty will resist the appellation."

Lady Alicia and Anne added their praise to this speech of Elizabeth's, and Lord Holland looked somewhat abashed. He replied that the honor of preserving Mrs. Darcy from harm was one that he would always recall with the greatest happiness. Then, with some urgency, he added, "But we must return to the castle at once. You have displayed remarkable fortitude, but after such a shock, rest and care are essential to avoid some adverse reaction."

He called the groom to him and said, "McDonald, you shall give Mrs. Darcy your horse, so that we may escort her home. You will follow that wretched animal, Aggitator, on foot, and I will send you assistance as soon as may be." Then in a voice shaking with anger, Lord Holland added, "And I hope that once that devil is retrieved, he may be shot! I may do it myself."

Everyone looked at him in surprise, as Lord Holland had heretofore shown nothing but the greatest calm. But nothing more was said;

Elizabeth was helped into the saddle, and was led back to the castle by Lord Holland.

Once there, Elizabeth had to endure being put to bed and fussed over by her aunt, who feared that some kind of nervous fit might be the result of the day's events. Only with the greatest difficulty was Lady Alicia dissuaded from sending for a physician. After an hour Elizabeth insisted on getting up and going down to the drawing room. Against all her objections Darcy had been sent for, and she did not want to have him subjected to further alarm by finding his wife treated as an invalid, when she was uninjured and recovering well from her shock.

She was sitting before the fire, with Anne and Lady Alicia, when the doors of the chamber were flung open violently, and Darcy burst in, his face white and his eyes ablaze with emotion. Taking no notice of his aunt and his cousin, he fell on his knees before Elizabeth, and without a word took her in his arms. The other ladies, feeling themselves *de trop*, rose quickly and left the two alone.

"Direct any of the company who may come down for tea to the library, Armstrong," said Lady Alicia to her butler, who was standing nearby, " Mr. and Mrs. Darcy are not to be disturbed."

As she walked across the Great Hall with Anne, she continued in a confidential tone, "I have never seen a man so madly in love as your cousin is with his bride. I am happy for them, of course, but there can be danger in such strength of emotion; it almost frightens me sometimes."

Anne, who was just beginning to have some idea of how love might transform the most tranquil of lives into a sea of storms, wondered at her aunt's words; surely marriage was a safe haven for such passion, and once vows had been taken before God, all doubt and anxiety must be past.

~

DARCY, once he was alone with Elizabeth, held her closely and repeated several times, "I might have lost you!" He looked into her face, kissed and held her for some time, as though unable to let her go, and Elizabeth felt that the force of his emotion was beyond anything she had yet seen in her husband. She tried to reassure him and even managed to laugh, saying, "My darling, you see that I am fine. Nothing has harmed me. Let us be joyful this evening, and thank God that such an exceptional horseman as Lord Holland was there to pull me off of that terrifying animal."

Finally Darcy became more composed and was able to hear Elizabeth's account of her peril and how her life had been preserved. As she rested in his arms, she thought of her first impressions of Darcy and how he had seemed cold and haughty and the last man to be capable of a passionate attachment. The night before her wedding, her father had taken Elizabeth aside and said, "I have been observing your Darcy and have concluded that he is the very opposite of the cool, restrained fellow that he appears to be at first. How fortunate he is to have you, my dear child, with your level head and ability to see the rational side of everything. My little Stoic philosopher!"

THAT EVENING all the guests were reassembled in the drawing room, and Mrs. Darcy's narrow escape, and Lord Holland's dashing rescue were the topic of much excited conversation. The hero of the moment entered somewhat late, and all eyes followed him with interest as he crossed the room to bow before Mrs. Darcy, and say how much he hoped that she was completely recovered from the strain of the day's events. Elizabeth assured him that she was perfectly well, and thanked him again for preserving her life.

Darcy, who was standing at his wife's side, added, "There is no way I can express all my thanks, Holland. All that friendship and the sincerest gratitude may do are at your service for as long as I live. For, as I am sure you are aware, you have preserved not just one, but two lives today." And Darcy offered Lord Holland his hand, which the other gentleman received with every expression of modesty and goodwill.

The rest of the company were gratified to witness this interesting scene; as a house party the time at Castle Munford had been pleasant for all the guests, but to have an adventure to discuss certainly made things more interesting. The preservation of the beautiful Mrs. Darcy from certain death by the dashing Lord Holland would still be a topic worth discussing in town next season. The only person who was unhappy that evening was Lord Munford, who was terribly distressed that a horse from his stable had put his lovely niece in peril. That afternoon Aggitator had been sent off to a remote spot, where he could break no heads, unless an occasional farm boy were to make the mistake of riding him.

CHAPTER 25

$\mathcal{D}$arcy remained at the castle the next morning, as nothing could have induced him to be separated from his Elizabeth. Just before falling into an exhausted sleep the night before, she had made the request that they go out riding as soon as possible; the following afternoon if he did not object to giving up shooting for the day, "For I do not wish to have time to become afraid. The sooner I go out again on horseback, the better." Darcy knew that this was true, and agreed that if her reliable mare were recovered from its lameness, they would do as she wished.

And so it chanced that he was sitting at the breakfast table with his aunt, when his cousin Fitzwilliam came striding into the room. Lady Alicia was out of her chair instantly, and threw her arms around her son. "Oh my dearest boy, you are finally here. How long we have been awaiting this moment." Darcy's pleasure at seeing his cousin was almost equal to that of his aunt; he had feared that he would have to return to Pemberley without having seen Fitzwilliam.

Lady Alicia insisted that her son must be hungry, although the young man claimed that he had already breakfasted before setting out that morning. "But that was hours ago," said his mother. Soon Fitzwilliam was seated before a vast array of dishes, and trying as best he could to answer his mother's innumerable questions.

Lady Catherine, he was happy to inform them, was very well indeed, and had regained her former strength. Everyone in Bath was afraid of her, and she quite ruled society there. Mrs. Collins was still in attendance with her little boy; Lady Catherine had become very much attached to them, and the vicar must shift for himself as best he could. Mrs. Collins, for her part, seemed to be able to endure the separation from her husband with a good deal of fortitude. Fitzwilliam had recently spent three days in Bath with his aunt, driving the ladies about, and escorting them everywhere with his usual good humor.

There was a brief silence after Fitzwilliam had finished his narration. Both his mother and his cousin Darcy would have liked to ask if there were any truth in the rumors of an attachment to Lady Emma Foxworth, which had been reported to them by several sources. But somehow it was impossible to ask the young man such a direct question; there was that about Fitzwilliam that made even his most intimate friends reluctant to inquire into his personal affairs before he was prepared to offer such information of his own accord. For all his engaging manners, and excellent disposition, there was reserve that it was difficult to overcome. If Fitzwilliam had a defect of character, it was that he liked to appear mysterious, and to do the unexpected. In truth, he had no great secrets to conceal, unless acts of simple kindness such as his visits to the unfortunate old Mr. Thornton could be so considered. It had pleased him to start out at dawn that day so that he might surprise his mother at the breakfast table. It amused him to travel great distances, and appear when no one had thought to see him. Fortunately, wherever he went, he was welcomed with delight by his friends, for there was no better companion than Fitzwilliam. Any close inquiry into his activities or intentions, however, would be met with a non-committal response, and a change of subject. The young man was at heart a romantic, but as in the dull modern world there was little scope for knightly deeds, he contented himself with being enigmatic.

His mother could not help but ask why he had been so long delayed in joining the family party at the castle, "For, my dear, Darcy and Elizabeth will have to return to Pemberley in a week's time, and in fact everyone is leaving soon. You will have no one but your dull old parents for company. Could you not have come to us sooner?"

Fitzwilliam would only say that he had found it necessary to visit a friend before commencing his journey to Castle Munford, and then he changed the subject. His mother and cousin should be forgiven for assuming that his visit must have been to meet the family of Lady Foxworth. They had both received letters from Lady Catherine prophesizing that the betrothal of the two young people must very soon bring joy to all their friends. In fact, Fitzwilliam had been staying with the reclusive Mr. Thornton in Hampshire; the old gentleman's health had recently shown symptoms of further decline, and the colonel had done what he could to bring him comfort.

It was with a bit of unworthy envy that he heard the story of Elizabeth's danger and Lord Holland's gallant courage the day before. How much *he* would have liked to rescue a lady from some great hazard. However, he said all that was proper in praise of such an act of bravery and fine horsemanship. Then he required a complete report on the progress of his young cousin, and listened carefully to all they could say on the subject. Then Fitzwilliam's eyes brightened, and he asked eagerly, "But where is Anne? She is usually about by now. You have said she is well and has learned to ride, and to converse with strangers, and to at least tolerate the demands of social intercourse. I would like to see the result of all these developments myself."

"Oh, she is out on her morning walk," replied his mother, " and will soon make her appearance for breakfast. You have only to remain here for a few minutes, and you will see her."

"Why, Darcy and I will walk out to meet her," cried Fitzwilliam, rising from his chair with even more than his usual energy, and in an instant the two young men were off by way of the French doors that opened to the nearby hills. By the time they had reached the first rise, they caught sight of Anne walking along the loch with Lord Holland some distance away, obviously deep in conversation.

"Let us encounter them when they return to the house, Fitz," said Darcy, "Holland is leaving today as he is unexpectedly called away to Glasgow on business, and I am sure he is glad to have a last interview with Anne."

"What do you mean?" asked Fitzwilliam, "Do you approve of our cousin walking alone with the man like this? Is it a common occurrence?"

"I never knew you were so strict in your views; my aunt does not object, and that she is the best judge of what is proper you must allow."

The two young men turned back towards the castle, and in a moment Darcy said, "I should tell you that Holland shows every sign of being attached to our cousin. In fact I have no doubt that he means to propose marriage, although possibly not at once. His attentions have been quite marked since they first met - in the most respectful and delicate way, of course."

Fitzwilliam stopped walking abruptly, and turned to face Darcy, with a countenance hard with displeasure, "And who is Lord Holland to presume to address Anne? Here is a fellow who has given up his commission, and loiters about, amusing himself at the country houses of his friends and acquaintances. I have not seen him for some years, but I do not remember anything very special about him."

Darcy was quick to defend the savior of his wife, "You are unfair, Fitz. He seems to me to spend most of his time preserving the interests of his invalid brother in a very dutiful manner. In addition he has everything to recommend him to a girl like Anne; he is well read, an accomplished musician, and certainly showed himself a gallant man in his actions yesterday. And as you know, he comes of an ancient and distinguished family."

The two were silent for a moment, then Darcy added, "And from all I have heard, he will almost certainly be Marquess of Roscree, as his brother sounds unlikely to live through the winter."

Fitzwilliam had seen the marquess in Bath ten days before, and admitted that the young man had looked as though the first gust of wind might blow him away. Then he asked, "But do you have any reason to believe that Anne returns his regard?"

"Yes, I have indeed. She gives him a great deal of her time and conversation, and seems always willing to be pleased by what he has to say. She smiles frequently, and seems to have lost her shyness in his company. With another girl it might not mean much, but with Anne, you must admit, it is significant."

Fitzwilliam did not seem very willing to accept the truth of these observations, but said, "Lady Catherine may not like it. She would like to see Anne a duchess, or not married at all."

"I think I can persuade her. After all," said Darcy with a smile, "I am a great proponent of marrying for love. Why should Anne not have the man, if she likes him. Her fortune is one of the largest in England, and surely should allow her to marry where she wishes. And by all I can discover Holland has a good income of his own"

"Has Holland said anything to you about his intentions," asked Fitzwilliam presently.

"We had a few minute's private conversation after dinner last night. I had repeated an invitation to join us at Pemberley next month. He replied that he would be delighted to accept, but that I should know that he had become very much attached to Anne and that he hoped to win her affection. He would not, he said, like to enter my house without my being aware of his intentions. He expressed himself in the handsomest way, saying that he knew that as yet he could not dare to address himself to her. There could be no hope of winning the love of such a young lady in so short a time as they had known each other here at the castle, but that if I did not disapprove, he would value the opportunity to continue to try to recommend himself to her."

Fitzwilliam looked very thoughtful for the rest of their walk and then when they had almost reached the house, he said, "So, he is to install himself at Pemberley, is he? Darcy, I can assure you that I mean to find out everything there is to know about Lord Holland. I doubt very much that he is worthy of Anne."

"Well," said Darcy after a moment, "Let us walk down and join them by the loch, for I see that they are still there, and you may begin to form your own impression of the man."

"No, I will see Anne later, after Holland has left," replied Fitzwilliam rather crossly, "I think I will ride out and find my father and brother, if you can tell me in what direction they have gone today."

THE RELIABLE MARE was still lame, and Elizabeth and Anne spent much of the afternoon by the drawing room fire, as it turned out to be a cold, grey day with a hint of winter in the air. Along with Lord Holland, most of the other guests had departed; Anne had been particularly sorry to lose the company of Lady Grinspoon, who had become a dear friend during the past weeks. She had learned a great deal from reading the lady's novels, and from the many private conversations that they had had while walking about the castle grounds and over the surrounding hills. Perhaps Anne would have been happier without such knowledge as she had acquired from her friend; Lady Grinspoon's observations on human nature, and the nature of gentlemen in particular could hardly dispel the young girl's native cynicism. Her narrations of the great world frequently included examples of the inconstancy of the male heart, and the necessity for a sensible woman to be always on her guard, lest her affections be too easily engaged.

"We will see Lady Grinspoon again soon, Anne," said Elizabeth, "for as you know, she has promised to come to Pemberley for Christmas. I do agree with you that she is excellent company, and I plan to read all her novels during the winter."

"Dear cousin," replied Anne with an affectionate smile, " I am afraid that you will have little time for reading. From all that I can tell, you will have a continuous house party for the rest of this year."

"Yes, if only we can put the house to rights," sighed Elizabeth, "You have heard about the problems with the drawing room fireplace, and the plaster in the library. As soon as we left everything began to fall apart. Thank goodness for our excellent steward and for Mr. Grey, whose advice has been so helpful." Darcy and Elizabeth's sojourn in Scotland had been punctuated with lively and rather alarming letters from Mr. Grey, one example of which Elizabeth now produced for Anne to read.

Dear Darcy,

You will be glad to know that all is peace and contentment here in the heavenly precinct of Pemberley. I have been spending my time usefully, cataloging your books and exercising your horses, and out of respect for your (very unreasonable) request I have not ventured into a single cavern.

There have been one or two very minor problems. I hesitate to mention them, but know that it is your nature to always be worrying about something, so I might as well supply you with some fresh material.

I had just begun sorting through some volumes on the top shelf to the left of the fireplace, when I noticed that a half dozen or so books were damp and showed signs of long-term water damage. One of these, I regret to inform you, was a copy of Allot's second folio. Darcy, I don't mind telling you, I could have wept like a woman when that beautiful binding crumbled in my hand. Of course, I sent for your steward, the good Mr. Fisk, and when we had removed a number of books we found that there was evidence of leakage all along that side of the fireplace. With the help of the servants we removed all of the volumes in that part of the library to the gallery. The upshot of it all is that the paneling and shelves had to be all pulled out, revealing a leak from the roof two stories above, with damage to the chimney and the related plaster in the library and the adjacent music room. You will be glad to hear that an excellent team of masons is now rebuilding the center of your house, and the plasterers and cabinetmakers are expected from London next week. All your books and musical instruments are safely placed in the long gallery. As I said, just a few minor problems, and I should have forborn to even mention them, except that I knew that Mr. Fisk was writing to you as well. You need not thank me, old friend, even though my investigations have prevented Pemberley from eventually falling down around your ears.

All in all, the last few weeks have been very agreeable; I have been to Castle Faulconer for dinner, and what charming people they are. I have rarely met with so kind a reception.

Try not to concern yourself too much about the little inconveniences we have had here. By the time you have returned most of the dust should have settled. My best compliments to Mrs. Darcy and Miss de Bourgh, and I wish that you may have an uneventful journey home.

Yours, JG

"Good heavens!" exclaimed Anne, "Could the house have really fallen down? How will you be able to receive your guests with everything in disarray?"

"My husband says that Mr. Grey very likely does exaggerate somewhat, but that it is a blessing that the problem was discovered. It is very distressing, of course, but as we do not expect visitors for several weeks, it may all turn out well." Then Elizabeth produced a second letter. "I have also received a communication from Lady Margaret which may amuse you, as it presents a very different account of Mr. Grey's intercourse with our neighbors."

My dear Mrs. Darcy,

Even though I have not had the pleasure of knowing you for very long, I take the liberty of writing to you as to an old friend. My father and I do so look forward to your return, since having you nearby gives us the promise of many delightful months to come. And I do so wish to be better acquainted with Miss de Bourgh as well.

It has been very dull here, and the only variation in the normal routine has been a source of annoyance rather than a pleasant diversion. I do not, of course, dream of criticizing a friend of Mr. Darcy, but I must say that the scholarly Mr. Grey has been very much under-foot, and I regret that my first unfavorable impression of him has not in any way been altered on further acquaintance. He and my father have become inseparable, and it seems as though Mr. Grey is here for dinner almost every night. They spend hours in the library going through the endless drawers of dusty rocks that my father has ignored for the past thirty years, and I am usually compelled to remain in their company. As if this martyrdom were not enough, I am constantly encountering Mr. Grey when I am out riding. I was crossing the little bridge over Tenbrook Run the other day, and on looking up, whom should I see but the ubiquitous Mr. Grey on Mr. Darcy's bay hunter. I could not shake off his unwelcome company, for he insisted on escorting me back to Castle Faulconer, and boring me with an interminable discourse on the subject of the approaching hunting season, and all that he is doing to prepare Mr. Darcy's horses for it.

Do hurry your return, my dear Mrs. Darcy. If you knew how much the dreary social circle in our corner of Derbyshire stands in need of your happy influence, you would start out for Pemberley at once.

Looking forward to seeing you again soon, I am your newly acquired but faithful friend,

Margaret F.

Anne was rather puzzled by the second letter. "I am surprised that Lady Margaret writes at such length about someone whom she dislikes so much. Does it not strike you as odd, cousin?"

"Yes," replied Elizabeth, "It makes me think that Lady Margaret must either truly dislike Mr. Grey, or that she must like him very much indeed without realizing it." She looked thoughtful for a while, and then added, "I have known an instance of an initial strong disapprobation which ended in love."

Anne sensed that an intriguing story lay behind this remark, but Elizabeth was spared further explanation by the entrance of her husband. Darcy was delighted to bring them word of Fitzwilliam's arrival, as he knew that the colonel was a favorite of both ladies. Anne, who had not observed him with Darcy earlier in the day, almost jumped up from her seat to go in search of him, but remembering discretion and dignity in time managed to ask calmly, "But why have we not seen him? Is he here in the house?"

"No, not at the moment," replied Darcy, "He went off to find my uncle almost immediately, and I suppose he will return with the shooting party later."

Anne felt a cold discomfort about her heart, and wondered that Fitzwilliam could not make the effort to have come to find her before leaving to spend the whole day on the moors. And she and the Darcys were to leave in just a few days! Clearly her cousin did not consider seeing her very important.

Elizabeth did her the service of asking the question that Anne could not for fear of betraying her emotion, "How is it that Colonel Fitzwilliam has delayed joining us here for so long? You did, I believe, inform him of the day on which we would begin our journey back to Pemberley?"

"Now that is an interesting subject," said Darcy, looking very wise, "You know how Fitzwilliam must always be so mysterious. It is one of his more annoying traits. In reply to the same question from his mother, he would only say that it had been necessary for him to visit a friend's house on the way here. But my aunt and I are convinced that he has been to visit the family of the beautiful Lady Emma Foxworth near Wells."

"It certainly seems a most reasonable explanation," agreed Elizabeth, "for even the colonel would hardly be so secretive except about a romance whose happy conclusion was not yet completely certain."

"Oh, I am sure we shall hear good news in the near future," said Darcy jovially, "Why, he has all the symptoms of a man in love, separated from the object of his adoration. I never saw him in a worse humor than he was this morning."

"And is not general incivility the very essence of love?" said Elizabeth with a laugh, "If your cousin is rude and inattentive to us all this evening, we will accept the truth of your surmise."

This conversation was so painful to Anne that she rose hastily and walked over to the long windows that overlooked the loch.

"I wonder if it is likely to rain this evening," she said, keeping her face turned away from Darcy and Elizabeth, and pretending to take great interest in the sky. Her friends exchanged puzzled looks, for it had been a fine day and the late afternoon sunlight was streaming in, without a single cloud visible.

In the next instant Fitzwilliam entered the room, with a countenance alight with the good humor so natural to him. He greeted Elizabeth with brotherly affection, saying how much he rejoiced that she was safe and unhurt. His eyes, however sought about the room until they found his cousin Anne, and then remained fixed upon her for some moments.

She had turned to face her friends, but remained standing before the windows. She was wearing a dress of pale yellow silk, and the fading light outlined her slender figure, and made an aureole of the short loose curls that clustered about her delicate face. Fitzwilliam could not move or speak for what seemed like a very long pause; the being before him seemed at once familiar and altogether different from the Anne he remembered from only a few weeks before.

He had to make an effort of will to break the silence that seemed to hold him prisoner, then walked over to her with a convincing attempt at his usually cousinly manner.

"Well, Anne," he said, "I hear from Darcy that you have become quite an able horsewoman in a very short time, but that no one has taken you salmon fishing. Why anyone would waste time shooting when they could be fishing, I cannot imagine." As he said this Fitzwilliam took in all the changes in Anne's appearance, and his eyes lit up with the animation and warmth that always made him fascinating to those around him.

She glanced up at him only briefly, offering him her hand in a manner that seemed cold and formal between two old friends. To smile and look at her ease was completely beyond her power after what she had heard of his forthcoming engagement. Fitzwilliam was dismayed and hurt, but continued, "But I have brought you a light salmon rod, most ingeniously designed to suit your height and strength. I hope we will have the opportunity to go out on the loch tomorrow, if the weather permits it."

Anne still declined to look directly at her cousin, and in a dry, flat tone replied, "I am sorry that you went to so much trouble, especially as we will be so occupied in preparing for our return to Pemberley that I fear that there will be little time for such an outing."

Fitzwilliam was so taken aback at this ungracious reply that he could say nothing more for several minutes. Darcy and Elizabeth were startled by this reappearance of the distant, unresponsive Anne that they had believed gone forever, but had no idea at all as to the origin of this transformation.

"Please, let us go sit by the fire," said Elizabeth, "There is a chill in the room, or perhaps I am not quite recovered from my experience of yesterday."

Conversation was far from lively; there was a constraint that could not be overcome, although everyone but Anne made valiant attempts. The state of the roads, the weather, and Lady Catherine's health were topics that served for a while. Several times Fitzwilliam tried to engage Anne's attention. Once their eyes met, but she quickly looked away, flushing with what seemed to him to be irritation. Suddenly he could bear no more, rose abruptly and left the room without a word.

Elizabeth looked after him in consternation, "Has everyone gone mad this evening? Anne, how could you be so unkind to your best friend in the world?"

Darcy went after his cousin at once, and the two ladies were left alone. "Anne, what is amiss?" asked Elizabeth, "You were cold and unfeeling towards poor Fitzwilliam."

Anne could bear no more, and the tears began to flow. Soon she was sobbing onto the shoulder of Elizabeth's cashmere shawl, saying indistinctly, "Indeed, I am sorry, but I do not feel at all well tonight."

"Perhaps," ventured Elizabeth, producing a handkerchief, and trying to comfort Anne, "it is because a certain person had to take his departure today. But, my dear, you will soon see him again. Do try to compose yourself, and be kind to your cousin; he has all the affection and care of an elder brother for you."

This stung Anne to the quick. She wondered how Elizabeth could be so blind as to where her real attachment lay, but could only be grateful that no one had penetrated the secret of her heart.

DARCY FOUND FITZWILLLIAM ALMOST IMMEDIATELY; he was standing in a doorway of the hall that opened onto the courtyard, and did not appear to know what to do with himself.

Seeing his friend's face, Darcy exclaimed, "Fitz, the last time I saw you look like this, we were nine year's old and you had just fallen off the stable roof into a rain barrel."

Fitzwilliam had to smile faintly at this, but then shrugged and turned away.

"I am surprised that you allowed Anne's behavior to upset you. You know how she can be as well as anyone. Of course, we certainly hoped that she was beyond such childish sulking. I suppose the departure of Holland may have upset her, but that is no excuse. I am really very angry with her."

After a brief silence Fitzwilliam was able to say with some conviction, "Oh, do not be angry. I am sure Anne did not intend to appear unkind. You must be correct that she is very attached to this Holland.

The first experience of love can be painful enough to make anyone uncivil. If I am not myself it has nothing to do with Anne." Then, to cover the confusion he felt, he added with some degree of vehemence, "I only hope this peace will not last long. What kind of life is this for a soldier?"

"I, on the contrary, hope it lasts forever. I do not like to think of you facing cannon fire ever again, even if it is your profession."

"You are a good friend, Darcy," said Fitzwilliam, "I am sorry for my irritable mood this evening."

Darcy tried to persuade him to return to the drawing room, but without success.

"No, I will see you later. My horse cast a shoe just as I returned here this afternoon, and I must see that the oaf of a blacksmith my father has here does not go too far wrong."

Darcy returned to the two ladies, thinking that there might have been a serious quarrel with Lady Emma and that perhaps Fitzwilliam's marriage might not be so certain a thing as his aunt had led them to believe.

CHAPTER 26

The next morning brought a heavy rain that lasted the entire day and made it impossible to venture out-of-doors. This was particularly disappointing to Anne. There had been little opportunity to speak to Fitzwilliam again during the evening before, although she had passionately wished for the chance to apologize to him. As she had dressed for dinner, she could think of nothing but his expression of pained surprise at her apparent coldness. Even though he does not love me, she reflected, how am I to live without his friendship?

Fitzwilliam had been unusually quiet all evening, and made only the briefest replies to the efforts his family made to draw him into the conversation. This was so completely unlike his normally cheerful manner that everyone was struck by the change in the young man. They were all convinced that this was the effect of his separation from a young lady in far-off Bath. He did manage to summon some enthusiasm on the subject of his brother's engagement, and asked all the appropriate questions about the forthcoming wedding.

All the while, Fitzwillliam was suffering most acutely from a source that had never troubled him very much before in his thirty years; his heart, which had remained so impervious throughout several rather prolonged flirtations in the past, was now dealt a severe wound from a totally unexpected quarter. The shock of the blow was so recent that as yet he had only a vague idea of his own feelings; he had felt certain of Anne's friendship and could not imagine why she had changed towards him. As he sat in the midst of his family, pretending to take some interest in the general conversation, he frequently stole glances at Anne, who was sitting opposite to him. Where was his shy little cousin who had seemed so in need of his kindness? He realized now how much she had been in his thoughts during the weeks since their last meeting.

Once, in spite of his caution, her eyes met his for a moment. Anne tried to smile, but the effect was far from successful, and Fitzwilliam told himself that what he thought he had seen in her face for one instant was nothing more than his imagination.

Just as everyone arose to retire for the night, Anne found a moment to go up to her cousin and say, "Oh, how I hope that we may go out on the loch in the morning." He had only a moment to reply that of course they would do so, that nothing would give him greater pleasure.

But the rain put an end to all the wonderful possibilities of several hours in each other's company in a boat in the middle of the loch, where all misunderstandings between the two young people might have been dispelled.

Lord Munford always liked to ride out in disagreeable weather, however, and informed his two sons that there was no reason why the three of them should not go to inspect a small hunting lodge that he owned about ten miles away. "For the ladies do not need us to entertain them when the day is so inclement and they are busy packing for their departure."

Darcy was invited to join their excursion, and the four gentlemen set out. Fitzwilliam had only the chance to say to Anne that he felt the disappointment very much, "For you are the best of fishing companions, and now I shall not be able to teach you anything about salmon this year."

Elizabeth was standing by Anne, when this remark was made, and said later, "How glad I am that you and Fitzwilliam are on good terms again. He is so very fond of you, and could not be more kind if you were his sister." Anne could only sigh at this familiar remark, and go off to oversee Celestine's arrangement of her trunks, and drive the poor Frenchwoman to distraction in the process.

By late afternoon, she had wandered into the library, and was seated at a massive table reading a volume on salmon fishing. The rain pounded on the mullioned windows, but a good fire made the room fairly pleasant and warm. Anne had read the same page several times, without understanding a word of it, when the heavy doors opened, and Fitzwilliam came in. He was still dressed for riding, and his face was flushed from the cold wind.

"Oh, Anne," he said, with a rather hesitant smile, "Of course, this is where I would expect to find you, out of all the rooms in the castle."

"Were you looking for me, Cousin?" asked Anne, trying to keep the eagerness out of her voice.

"Why, I know there is always a fire here this time of day," replied Fitzwilliam, "and I am glad you are here."

He sat down in a chair on the other side of the table, and looked pleased when he saw what Anne was reading. "You should ask my uncle if you can take that with you, to study and be prepared for next year's sport."

His cousin only looked sadly into the fire, reflecting that by the following year he would probably be married, and that they would never again go fishing together.

Fitzwilliam was discouraged by this lack of enthusiasm, and changed the subject.

"I must tell you what my very kind father has done this day. Do you recall hearing about Brunefenn Lodge, which lies west of here at the edge of the estate?"

"Yes," replied Anne, "I have heard that it is a very charming place, with a wonderful prospect of the loch and mountains. I had hoped to ride there, but we never went so far in that direction."

"Well, it is beautiful. The house is not grand in any way, but the setting is so magnificent that one thinks of nothing else. And there is a fine stretch of salmon water that runs through the property."

"How I should like to see it," said Anne, "I think a simple house

226

would be the best thing to have here in the Highlands, as much as I admire this great castle."

Fitzwilliam agreed, and went on, "My father, the best and most generous of parents, has made me a gift of the place, along with some thousands of acres. He said that he wanted me to have something all my own, now that my brother was to be married, and would be increasingly taking an interest in the family property. Anne, I never expected such a thing, and such a mark of my father's regard makes me so very glad. And my brother is delighted for me."

Anne's face lit up with real joy, for her cousin's happiness was dearer to her than anything else in life. "Ah, how many happy times you will spend there, cousin. I know how you enjoy being here. I love and esteem my uncle even more than before."

When he saw her face so full of delight at his good fortune, Fitzwilliam was silent for a moment. He had a pair of yellow riding gloves in his hands, and began to pull at the fingers of one in a way that quite threatened to tear the leather.

He flushed slightly, and continued, "You are so good to be interested in my concerns. And I would like to think that you would find the place to your liking," and he broke off uncertainly, "Your opinion is very important to me."

"Oh, I should so love to visit there. Perhaps some day I shall," said Anne politely, while reflecting that to visit Fitzwilliam and his wife would probably be more painful than she could imagine.

"Visit? Well, certainly, I hope that of all things," said the colonel, who had been thinking of his cousin during the long ride home, as she was the first person with whom he wished to share his joyful news. Looking very intent, the young man tried to continue but he got no further for Lord Munford came bursting into the room.

"Ah, here you are, my dear boy. Good evening to you, Anne. Has Fitzwilliam told you the news? Well, I have a plat of the whole property I want to show you, Fitz. Let us find it." The two gentlemen left the room, and Anne was left to wonder what her cousin had meant to say.

Fitzwilliam had thrust his gloves into his pockets as he had left the library, but one had fallen to the floor near the hearth. Anne saw it lying there and gazed at it uncomprehendingly for a long moment. Then she rose and retrieved the glove, carried it back to her seat, and studied it as if she had never seen such an object before. The leather was worn, and discolored, with a partly ripped seam, and seemed to have spent many hours in the rain. She smoothed the fingers, then slipped it on; her small hand did little more than fill the palm. The glove was still damp, and creased from the motion of his fingers. She lifted her hand and rested it against her cheek, falling into the kind of reverie that had occupied her mind for so many weeks.

She heard someone approach the library door, and without thinking, she quickly concealed the glove in the folds of her gown. Fitzwilliam entered, accompanied by his brother Edward.

"Why, Anne," he said, "Are you still here? It is getting dark. I will send for candles."

Anne looked at the old clock on the mantle, and saw to her astonishment that an hour had elapsed since her cousin and her uncle had left the room.

Before she could reply, Fitzwilliam added, "I have lost a glove somewhere and thought I must have left it here. I don't suppose you have seen it?"

As though from a distance Anne heard herself say that she had not seen a glove.

"No matter," said her cousin, smiling at her and appearing to be in rather better spirits, "It was worn out anyway." He remained by the door, looking across at Anne, as though he had something more to say, when Edward broke the silence.

"Come along, Fitz. We must go dress for dinner. You know how father hates for anyone to be late."

FITZWILLIAM WAS DETERMINED to find another opportunity to speak to Anne. His cousin had not been out of his thoughts for a moment since he had seen her by the drawing room window, so different and to his eyes lovelier than he could have imagined. It was an image that had possessed his mind and heart during the long ride in the wind and rain. When his father had announced his intention to give his younger son the old hunting lodge, Fitzwilliam's first thought had been of Anne, and of how she would love the spot. What Darcy had said about Anne's possible attachment to Lord Holland had very much disturbed him, and when he had found himself sitting across the library table from her that day, she had seemed so beautiful to him with her luminous grey eyes shining in the firelight, that he had found himself unable to be cautious. He had to know if she had indeed formed an attachment to Holland. If it had not been for Lord Munford's inopportune entrance all their mutual incomprehension might have been at an end.

At dinner that evening Lady Alicia expressed a wish to visit Brunefenn as she had not seen the place for some years. "Perhaps we should go tomorrow if you do not mind making the excursion again so soon," she said.

"Why not?" replied Lord Munford. "Anne, you should come too, if a few hours on horseback will not be too fatiguing for you."

Anne protested somewhat indignantly against the idea that she would have any difficulty riding so far. "I am on horseback almost that long every day and am never tired."

Lord Munford smiled and said, "I apologize for even suggesting that the excursion might be beyond your abilities, my dear niece. You are becoming the equal of any of us on horseback."

"Well, then" said Lady Alicia, "Let us all go tomorrow. My dear Elizabeth, will you be one of the party?"

"I would not miss it for worlds!" replied Elizabeth gaily, "I am so anxious to see the colonel's demesne."

As they retired for the night Darcy asked his wife if she were sure that she wished to accompany the group to Brunefenn. "My darling, you had a very dreadful experience the last time you were on horseback. I would understand if you never wished to ride again. Please do not feel that you are obliged to come with us."

"I do feel some trepidation, my love, and I cannot hide it from you," replied Elizabeth, taking her husband's hands in her own. "But I do not wish to be afraid and will fight the tendency with all my strength. And in any case, I know that I will be perfectly safe as long as you are with me."

"My brave Elizabeth," replied Darcy, taking her in his arms, "Every day I spend with you makes me love and admire you even more."

The family party left at mid-morning for the eight-mile ride to Brunefenn. They rode at a leisurely pace, occasionally breaking into a trot or a slow canter depending on the terrain. The route was more of a track than a true road, and Lord Munford announced his intention to improve the situation the following year. "It will be a much more convenient thing to make this little journey after my workman complete the road project. Of course, my dear Fitz, I hope that you will spend much of your time at the castle as you always have, but I know that a young fellow enjoys being in his very own place part of the time."

Darcy was delighted to see that Elizabeth seemed quite at ease on the gentle mare that had now recovered from its lameness. "How magnificent this country is," she exclaimed to her husband as they reached the summit of a hill with a long view of moorland and loch, "and how fortunate I am to see it. You have given me so much, my love, including a wider world in which to live."

Lady Alicia, Lord Munford and Fitzwilliam stayed close to Anne, telling her all the romantic legends of that area, where ancestors of the Munfords had lived for hundreds of years.

"Brunefenn is an unusual name, is it not?" asked Anne."

"Brunefenn was the name of a Norman lady who married one of our Highland forebears, Sir Lionel Munford," explained Fitzwilliam. "She was a great heroine, for she defended the castle from a horde of raiders while her husband was off at war in the Borders."

"Is there a castle? I have only heard you mention a hunting lodge."

"There are only the ruins of the castle, very near to the lodge. It is said that on stormy nights the ghost of Brunefenn can be heard calling the people to arms," said Lord Munford.

"Oh, how very romantic!" cried Anne, "You must bring Lady Grinspoon here sometime. It sounds just like one of her novels."

Soon they had their first sight of Brunefenn Lodge, a large stone house that stood in the hollow of a wooded hillside and had a splendid view of distant hills and the loch. Lord Munford explained that he had built the lodge some five years before and that it was well supplied with modern comforts. "When you assisted me with the plan of the house, you did not imagine that it was intended for *you*, did you Fitz?" he said to his son.

"It certainly never occurred to me, Father." replied the young man, "I thought that you were planning it as auxiliary accommodation for hunting parties should the castle ever run out of space."

"I do enjoy having a few little secrets," said Lord Munford laughing.

When they arrived at the door of the house they were met by the caretaker and his wife who said how honored they were to receive a second visit to the Lodge. Lord Munford had sent word ahead and a midday repast had been made ready in the dining chamber. This was a handsome paneled room containing some tapestries and fine old furniture that had been in the Munford family for generations. Anne thought the house very lovely with its well-proportioned rooms and large windows overlooking the loch. It was not designed to impress, but to charm and delight with the warmth and comfort of its appointments.

Everyone was in good spirits; the caretaker's wife was a fine cook and the meal was excellent. "There is the beginning of a fine wine cellar here," said Lord Munford as he ordered a second bottle of claret "We will need to augment it by and by."

Fitzwilliam led the tour of the rest of the house. He frequently asked Anne's opinion of the building and it's situation and the surrounding landscape. "I cannot imagine a more wonderful habitation, cousin. How happy I am for you," was her only reply. She wondered to herself how Fitzwilliam's wife would like the place someday. Perhaps Lady Emma could learn to appreciate living part of the year in the remote Highlands even after the elegant pastimes of Bath.

The last object of the visit was the ruined castle that lay just a short distance from the Lodge. There was one turret that was fairly intact and Anne wished to ascend the circular staircase but she was told that it must first be repaired. This may be my only opportunity, she thought, as I doubt I will ever come here again.

"Come, Anne," said Fitzwilliam, motioning to her, "I want to show you the best preserved section of the castle." They made their way up some rough steps to a walkway that once would have marked the periphery of the central courtyard of the keep, and went through an arched doorway. This was the entrance to a chapel that had a roof that was almost intact and was supported by Romanesque vaulting. The fenestration of the outer walls was Gothic in style with delicate stone tracery.

"You can see that it is very ancient, probably eleventh century, and that the Gothic windows were added to a building of the Romanesque period." They walked about looking in every corner as Fitzwilliam spoke of the transition from Romanesque to the Gothic style.

"It is an exquisite chapel and seems to me to retain something of the sacredness of its original purpose," said Anne, "Would you restore it to its former beauty?"

They were standing in the apse where the light was rather dim. Fitzwilliam looked down into Anne's face and did not speak at once. "That would be a matter for the châtelaine of the castle to decide and it would require much thought," he said at last, "What would you do if this were *your* ruined castle, Anne?"

So serious was her cousin's expression that Anne was taken aback for a moment. Fitzwilliam seemed very different from her usually mild and light- hearted cousin, almost a stranger as he looked to her for an answer as if the question had great significance for him. She was attempting to find her voice and make an intelligent reply when the rest of the party entered the chapel.

"Why, there you two are, here in the dark," cried Lady Alicia, "I remember that this spot made such an impression on me when I first visited Brunefenn years ago. There is, I believe, something uncanny about this chapel. It must be the dim light that makes one's companions look very unlike themselves when they stand here in the apse."

"Well, Lady Grinspoon really must see this wonderfully romantic place next year when she returns to Scotland," said Elizabeth, "for surely she could find enough inspiration for two or three books here."

Lord Munford observed at this point that it was three o'clock and time to return home. They all walked back to the house and were soon on horseback and headed eastward. The mood of the group seemed to incline them to keep more or less together, but after the first half hour Fitzwilliam called Anne's attention to a stone circle that stood on a hillside near the track. They turned off the path to look briefly at the ancient monument and so found themselves a hundred yards behind the others.

Fitzwilliam had been hoping for an opportunity to speak to Anne privately and had been glad of the chance to fall behind the rest of the company. Now he found it difficult to begin, but after a moment asked, "Anne, I understand that Lord Holland has been very marked in his attentions to you these last weeks."

This was certainly an unwelcome subject and Anne replied, "I see that you are *au courant* with the family gossip, but this is not really a matter worth discussing."

Fitzwilliam was somewhat dismayed; he would never have thought that his little cousin could look at him with such a remote and cold expression.

"It seems very well worth discussing to me," he continued hesitantly, "At least tell me if there is some likelihood that he will be successful in his courtship."

Anne was annoyed to be questioned by Fitzwilliam when he had said nothing of his own circumstances. If the so-called family gossip were to be believed, her cousin was as good as engaged to Lady Emma Foxworth. Finally she replied, "Let us abandon this conversation, if you please."

"I only enquire, Anne because your happiness is very dear to me. Do you feel that Lord Holland is a trustworthy person? Does he truly value you as you deserve? I do not know him very well and I need to be reassured on this point."

Anne seemed to consider his words and then answered angrily, "I suppose you mean to ask if he is really just after my fortune, as no gentleman could *possibly* be in love with someone as plain and uninteresting as the pathetic Anne de Bourgh."

Fitzwilliam protested at once that he had no such idea, but Anne would not listen. "Of course that is what you mean! You are just like my mother, always ready to think me the last person who could ever attract the affection of *anyone*, much less a worthy and accomplished man. Well, I can tell you that Lord Holland is a rich man in his own right. Darcy, of course, has investigated the matter thoroughly."

"You are completely wrong, Anne" said Fitzwilliam, when he found an opportunity to speak, "You should know me better than to think such things."

"You forgot that I even existed for years!" she replied, "It is clear that you have never thought of me as anything but a tiresome burden – when you bothered to think of me at all." At that Anne touched her horse with her crop and cantered off to join the rest of her companions. She even rode a bit ahead so that they would not see her tears.

Fitzwilliam reached the castle in a very bleak state of mind; he felt that he had never been so inept, and was wretched at the idea that he had wounded Anne's feelings. His only idea was to find the chance to speak to her again.

Securing another interview was more difficult that he would have thought possible; everything seemed to conspire to prevent the two young people from being alone. All the guests had left, even Edward's fiancé and her parents, but Lady Alicia took the idea of a family party very seriously indeed, and herded the entire group from drawing room to dining table and back again with the alacrity of a sheep dog with its flock. Of course she had no idea what was passing in the mind of her son; all would have been made easy for him had she known. Fitzwilliam had to content himself with looking at his cousin whenever he had the chance, and when their eyes met he was saddened not to see an answering smile.

At the end of the evening, he loitered in the great hall as everyone said goodnight, with the intention of trying to separate Anne from the company. He might have succeeded for, from a glance that they exchanged, he believed that she understood that he wished to speak to her. But Lady Alicia put her arm about her niece's shoulder's and led her upstairs saying, "My dear child, I will come with you to your chamber and make sure that Celestine has all in readiness for your departure in the morning. I do not quite trust her knowledge of the proper way to pack hats."

The morning found him up at dawn; he knew Anne's early habits, and thought that with any luck at all he would find her by the loch, taking a last look at the prospect that had become so familiar to her. He was bitterly disappointed to meet not Anne, but Darcy.

"Well, Fitz," said Darcy, "This is a sad thing. Only a few days in your company, and we must take our leave. I am very disappointed."

"The last time that I heard from you," replied Fitzwilliam, with some degree of irritation, "you gave the date of your departure as a week hence."

Darcy was dismayed, "Are you certain? I thought I wrote to you that we had to return early because of the problems with my house." After a moment's reflection he said, "Why, I believe you are correct. I informed Lady Catherine, but she must not have thought to tell you."

"By then I had left Bath, no doubt," said Fitzwillliam, with some disgust.

Darcy was very sorry for the confusion, but hoped that they would see his cousin very soon.

"Yes, you will see me, probably much sooner than you expect," replied Fitzwilliam, who had determined to follow Anne to Pemberley as soon as his respect for his parent's feelings would allow it.

After a pause, Darcy ventured on another subject, "If you are planning to subject Lord Holland to an extensive investigation, Fitz, I suggest you get on with it as soon as possible," he said with a smile, as though he considered such an inquiry more than a little ridiculous. Seeing Fitzwilliam's black look, Darcy continued, "Oh, I know you dislike him, although how you can do so when you barely know the man, I cannot understand."

"I remember that he has sly ways, and that basilisk gaze with which he contrives to fascinate the ladies. I remember his fine dark clothes that he thinks so much about, while he pretends to be so unaffected. He is not the sort of man for my cousin."

"Well, I hope you learn to look upon him more favorably, because he seems likely to become part of the family. Elizabeth told me yesterday that he had spoken with her before his departure, and had confided that he was very encouraged by his last conversation with Anne, that she was kinder than he had dared hope. Naturally, he wished to further recommend himself to my wife as her approval may assist in furthering the match."

"And what does Anne say?" asked Fitzwilliam, with an even darker brow and an air of extreme displeasure.

"Why, as to that, I do not think that Elizabeth has had a favorable opening for such an inquiry. But a modest young lady like Anne would not be likely to reveal her true feelings."

"Nonsense!" replied Fitzwilliam with vehemence. All the while he was watching for Anne, hoping that she would appear on the path. He would ask her himself and determine the truth of the matter.

But fate seemed inexorable in frustrating all of his plans that morning. For once he was annoyed with the mother he loved so well, for she did not leave Anne's side for a moment, until the Darcy's carriages were rolling out of the castle gates. Fitzwilliam had his horse saddled and rode along side them for a few miles, but finally had no excuse for continuing further. With a last nod to Anne, he turned and rode back towards his father's house.

CHAPTER 27

*N*ow it is necessary to take the reader back to the time of the Darcy's departure from Pemberley and relate what occurred there while Anne and her friends were in Scotland. As it happened, John Grey's next few weeks were equally full of interest.

As Grey and Mr. Fisk stood looking after the Darcy's carriages in the early morning light, Grey reflected that his stay at Pemberley would be the first time he had enjoyed anything like rest or repose for many years. He had travelled almost constantly since leaving university, anxious to avoid any communication with his father, Lord Harwith, although he often heard news of him from other members of the family. During Grey's last interview with the earl, the latter had attacked his son with a horsewhip, only to have it quickly taken away from him. The young man had taken his departure at once, vowing never to see his father again, and the past eight years had been spent abroad. Now Grey was faced with a dilemma, for a relation had written to inform him that Lord Harwith's health was failing, and that after a life of such dissipation he could not be expected to live long. Perhaps it would be necessary to return to Harwith Hall, to see the wicked old man before he died but Grey loathed the idea. In any case, Lord Harwith had often seemed to be seriously ill before and had always recovered and resumed his former habits.

For the present, he meant to enjoy this peaceful interlude at Pemberley, cataloging and repairing books, riding, studying the countryside, and looking for caverns.

"Well, Mr. Fisk," said John Grey to the steward, "I suppose you are used to having Mr. Darcy gone for long periods of time."

Mr. Fisk was an intelligent well-educated man, somewhat like the Mr. Wickham who had been at Pemberley for so many years when Darcy's father was alive.

"Yes, sir," he replied, "the household is quite accustomed to being without its master for extended periods, although we hope that may change now that there is a Mrs. Darcy. But I trust that you will enjoy your time here, Mr. Grey, and will let me know how I may ensure that you do so."

"Why, thank you, Mr. Fisk. I will probably go walking in the morning first thing, then work in the library for several hours, and in the afternoon take out one of Mr. Darcy's hunters for some exercise, if you think such a schedule will be convenient for the staff in the house and the stables."

Mr. Fisk, who was pleased to have his or anyone else's convenience consulted, answered in the affirmative, and hurried off to attend to his duties. Grey looked out across the valley, saw that it promised to be a fine day, and without further delay set off on his morning walk.

About two hours later, Lady Margaret Faulconer was trotting her bay horse along a little frequented lane that ran near a small stream between some meadows. She was riding astride and posting along in the best cavalry fashion. As she rounded a curve, she was surprised to see a man standing behind a tree in the corner of a fenced pasture. Puzzled, she reined in, and in a moment understood the situation. A large bull stood menacingly on the other side of the tree, as if daring the intruder to venture out into the open. The man looked in her direction as he heard her horse approach, and she saw that it was Mr. John Grey.

He bowed, while keeping a wary eye on the bull, saying, "Lady Margaret, I did not expect to have the pleasure of meeting you in this rather remote spot."

Lady Margaret merely nodded in acknowledgement of this greeting, but was almost unable to contain her delight at finding Grey in such a predicament. Now she should have her revenge for the trick he had played on her when they had first met.

"Why, Mr. Grey, you do seem to be in some difficulty. That is the most dangerous bull anywhere in this part of the country. He has a fearsome reputation, and your life would certainly have been in jeopardy had you not reached your present retreat. But why do you not simply climb over the wall?"

"There are some particularly obnoxious nettles on this side, Lady Margaret, and I was hoping that the beast would go away soon so I would not have to scramble through them" replied Grey, somewhat testily, "I don't suppose you could go to find the farmer who owns this monster."

She looked thoughtful for a moment and then said, "No, I don't believe I could, for as you see, I am not properly dressed to pay visits, even to a farmhouse. I am afraid I must leave you to your fate. Perhaps in three or four hours the animal will become bored, and you can escape." With this she began to move down the lane, but Grey called after her.

"At least let me take advantage of this meeting to apologize to you, Lady Margaret."

She turned back then, and replied, "Why, whatever for, Mr. Grey?"

"For pretending to be a vagrant madman when we first met near Darcy's house, when you were riding over to see them and I was coming back from a cavern, covered with mud."

"Oh, that," she said, dismounting and coming over to the pasture gate that fronted the lane, "I had quite forgotten about it. You overestimate your importance if you think I care about your childish games."

With these words she approached the gate, and before Grey could react had opened it and entered the pasture. Taking hold of a low branch, she shook it at the enormous bull and shouted, "Shoo!" It gave her a look of alarm, and in the next second had turned and was tearing off into the distance.

Grey hurried to her side, and when she saw the expression on his face she almost collapsed in helpless laughter.

"Are you quite mad, Lady Margaret?" said Grey, "You could have been killed."

It took a few moments before she could control her mirth sufficiently to answer him.

"Mr. Grey, that is Mr. Simpkin's dun-colored bull, famous as the most cowardly animal in Derbyshire. If you but glare at him he will run in terror."

Then she laughed again, while Grey could only look after the bull in disgust.

"Well, he certainly acted fierce enough when I entered this pasture. In any case, a sensible person should always assume that a bull is a dangerous animal."

Lady Margaret had regained her composure but had no intention of letting Grey off easily, "So the man who has spent his life traveling in the most remote and hazardous corners of Europe returns to England only to be terrorized by Mr. Simpkin's bull. Oh, if you could have seen your face when I frightened him off." The young lady began to laugh again, leaning against her horse's side for support.

"Very well, Lady Margaret, you have had your revenge two or three times over, I would say," said Grey, who had hardly ever been put out of countenance to such a degree before.

"Yes, revenge is sweet," she said, leading her horse over to the stone wall, in preparation to remount and be on her way, "But what are you doing here? It is not a particularly attractive place to walk, or perhaps you are lost as well as terrified."

"Thank you for inquiring," he replied coldly, "but I know exactly where I am. However I am having difficulty finding a cavern called 'Gaping Pillbox' that is supposed to be approximately in this area."

"Oh, I see. Well fortunately for you, I know precisely where it may be found. As much as I hate to oblige you in any way, let me tie up my horse and I will lead you to it."

"You are too gracious, Lady Margaret," said Grey. They left the lane and were soon walking along the small stream that bordered it. After a few minutes, they found themselves before a great opening in the side of a steep hill, where the water came rushing out from underground.

240

"Well, here it is, Mr. Grey, the 'Gaping Pillbox'. Do you mean to explore it at once? I only ask so that when you do not return to Pemberley the household may be spared a prolonged search."

"No, thank you," he replied stiffly, "I only wished to locate the entrance today. As you see, I am not wearing the proper sort of clothes for such an undertaking."

"Ah, yes," said the lady thoughtfully, "as with any other endeavor, one must have the proper attire." Then she added, "Mr. Grey, since there is no one else to do so, and since you may have family who are eager for your continued existence, as unlikely as that seems, I would like to point out a few simple facts, that would be obvious to a normal person, but in your case, appear to require enumeration."

"You have all my attention, Lady Margaret," replied Grey.

"There are several reasons why anyone of sense avoids going into a cavern. For one thing it is exceedingly dark, and even with the illumination provided by a candle, it is unlikely that you will be able to see very much. And were you to provide yourself with hundreds of candles, it is not probable that you would see anything very striking. It is also cold, dank and generally unhealthy, as well as slippery, and unpredictable. You know the difficulties of walking along a streambed above ground. How much more hazardous to clamber over slick rocks in almost total darkness. And, lastly, judging from your appearance when I first saw you that day at Pemberley, a cave must be the dirtiest and most disagreeable place imaginable. It would certainly be unnecessary to mention these considerations to anyone else, Mr. Grey, but perhaps you have overlooked them."

"How I can I thank you enough, Lady Margaret, for taking the trouble to enlighten me on this subject. I have been going into caverns for sixteen years, but never have I heard such a succinct description of the attractions of the pastime."

The lady merely nodded, as Grey continued, "But there is an aspect of the thing of which you may be unaware."

"And what is that?" she asked cautiously.

"Why it is the rapturous delight one feels when one finally emerges from underground. It makes all the uncomfortable circumstances you describe worth enduring."

Lady Margaret stared at him for a moment, before saying, "You are an excessively odd person, Mr. Grey, and I will leave you to your fate."

He escorted her back to where her horse was tethered, and started to assist her to remount.

"No, thank you. I am perfectly capable of managing for myself," said the lady, bounding into the saddle, and gathering up the reins, "By the by, you will find an invitation to dinner from my father when you return to Pemberley. Pray, do not imagine that such a courtesy comes from me, but I am willing to put up with much that is disagreeable in order that my father may be amused and in a more cheerful state of mind."

Then she cantered off before Grey could make any reply.

THE WEATHER HELD for the rest of the day, and Grey decided to ride over to Castle Faulconer, in spite of Mr. Fisk's suggestion that a carriage be put at his disposal, for "You do not know the road well, sir, and the moon is not yet half full."

"Oh, thank you, Mr. Fisk" replied Grey, "I shall do very well. I have eyes like a cat."

It was about four miles to the edge of Lord Faulconer's demesne, which bordered Pemberley to the east. The road led through a small, neat hamlet that stood near the castle gates, and Grey was struck by the prettiness and evident prosperity of the place. Lord Faulconer, he thought, must be an excellent landlord. How very unlike his own father, who would as soon let his estate fall into ruin as be bothered to order repairs.

Another quarter of an hour brought him his first sight of the castle; it looked ancient, and wonderfully romantic, on a hill above a fast moving stream where willows grew, and fat cattle grazed. The building was uncompromisingly martial in appearance, quite plain with few modern touches. In contrast, magnificent gardens could be seen stretching off at either side of the stone forecourt. Lord Faulconer himself appeared in the doorway to greet his guest, followed by several servants. The old gentleman was sincerely delighted to see Grey again.

"Why, my dear sir, you have found your way here without difficulty, I trust. It is a pleasant ride over from Pemberley, is it not? I used to enjoy it when Mr. Darcy's father was alive, and I was in better health."

Grey said that the ride had been very agreeable and then mentioned how much he had admired the group of neat cottages that flanked the castle gates.

"Oh, you must give my daughter credit for that," said Lord Faulconer, "Two years ago she oversaw the renovation of all the dwellings on the estate after extensive research on modern design, and consultation with a London architect who was here for some months. At first I was concerned about the expense, but it has turned out to be an excellent investment."

They started to enter the house, but Grey's host stopped, and asked, "Would you like to see something of the gardens while it is still full daylight? I believe we are likely to find Margaret there; she must not know that you have arrived."

They entered a series of formal terraces that overlooked the rushing water far below. The effect reminded Grey of gardens he had seen in Italy, and he thought that nothing could have been better suited to the austere stone building with its massive ramparts and towers.

He expressed his admiration, and was told, "Oh, Margaret will be pleased to hear such praise, for all that you see before you is the result of her study and effort. She became interested in renovating the gardens after a trip to the continent years ago."

Grey thought to himself that evidently there was a great deal more to Lady Margaret than just a beautiful face and a quick temper.

In another moment they found her cutting roses, and placing them in a large basket that was held for her by a footman. She was wearing a simple white gown, and there was nothing in her appearance to suggest that she had taken any special pains to dress for the occasion of Mr. Grey's visit.

"Ah, there you both are," she said, looking up briefly, but going on with what she had been doing, "So, you found your way here without mishap, Mr. Grey?"

Then without waiting for him to reply, she added, "I met our guest earlier today, father, as he was walking in Simpkins Dell, and helped him find the cavern there. He would probably still be wandering about, had I not happened along."

"No doubt I would be," said Grey, "It was kind of you to assist me, Lady Margaret." He expected her to begin a narrative of his adventure with the bull, but she said nothing about it, contenting herself with looking at him with a mocking smile.

They returned to the castle, and were soon seated in a great drawing room, which might have been cold and grim had it not been for comfortable furnishings, a fire burning on the hearth, and the magnificent tapestries that covered the walls.

Lord Faulconer once again gave his daughter credit for all that was beautiful and elegant in their surroundings, "Why, remember my dear, the difficulty you had finding someone who could repair the old tapestries? She found them in the attic, Mr. Grey, where they had been neglected for years, and you can see how much they improve the room. It was a dreary place before Margaret took things in hand, I can assure you."

The young lady merely said, "I enjoy these little projects; one must have some kind of occupation." Then she added, "Papa, I know that you are most eager to show Mr. Grey your collection of minerals and your library. Why do you not begin to do so now, while I attend to a few things, for I am sure that you will require many hours in which to pour over your collection together."

Lord Faulconer agreed readily to this suggestion, and led his guest to the library. Grey thought with some amusement that Lady Margaret seemed to be more the parent in the household than was her father, and evidently arranged everything to suit herself. He found that he was disappointed to be deprived of her company and wished that she had accompanied them.

The two gentlemen spent a pleasant hour looking over Lord Falconer's collection of volumes on natural philosophy, several of which were newly arrived from a London bookseller. His lordship clearly spared no expense to keep his library up to date, and he was eager to hear Grey's suggestions as to further acquisitions. One entire wall of the room was lined with cabinets containing mineral specimens, but it was decided that they should wait until after dinner to begin pulling out drawers.

They joined Lady Margaret, not in some vast, cold hall, but in a small, pleasing room, where a table was placed near the window for the three of them.

"I hope you do not object to such a degree of informality, Mr. Grey," said his hostess, "but when we have small parties I like to sit in here where we can be warm and comfortable. It seems absurd to me to be in a drafty great chamber at a table that can seat forty people."

Grey thought the arrangement delightful, and said so.

"Of course, we do not entertain friends very often, do we my dear?" said Lord Faulconer, "I have become almost a recluse since my health has gotten worse these last few years. Why I believe that Mr. Grey is our first dinner guest for two or three months."

Lady Margaret agreed that such was the case, and then added, "Yes, Mr. Grey, my father and I are most unsociable beings and try as best we can to avoid our fellow creatures. Of course that is almost impossible, especially once hunting begins."

"My dear child, do not tell me that you mean to put yourself in such peril again this year," exclaimed her father, "If you only knew what I suffer every time you are out with the hunt."

"Well, Papa," she replied, "I must do something, or I might well die of *ennui*, for as you know I cannot bear to sit at home doing embroidery or some other trivial thing."

"Do you dislike those feminine pursuits which contribute to much to a civilized society, Lady Margaret?" asked Grey.

"Not necessarily," she replied, "but anything becomes tiresome when it is forced upon one by the expectations of a society which seems designed to send women to an early grave out of sheer boredom, failing some worse eventuality."

"Why, that is a very gloomy view of things," exclaimed Grey, "I would have said that you do very much as you please, Lady Margaret, from my limited acquaintance with you."

"That is only because I have the best father in the world," said the young lady with a smile for Lord Faulconer.

"I would never dare oppose my daughter," said her father with a laugh, "nor would any other man who valued his life. And it has been thus since she was two years old."

Grey then observed that it was really the ladies who ruled the world, kindly allowing men to keep their illusions of power. Lord Faulconer agreed, and his daughter vehemently disagreed, and this led to a somewhat prolonged debate, which fortunately ended in laughter, rather than ill feeling, and Grey was pleased to find that Lady Margaret could see humor even in a subject that was clearly of some importance to her.

The balance of the evening was spent very pleasantly, going over Lord Faulconer's collection while Lady Margaret looked on with a mild degree of interest. Grey's host proposed a game of chess, and the two men found they were quite evenly matched. After each had won a game, Lord Faulconer said, "You will have to play with my daughter next time, Mr. Grey, although she is likely to beat you. I hardly ever win when I play with her."

"You exaggerate, Papa," said the young lady, 'but I should be happy to oblige Mr. Grey whenever he likes, for he does not play too badly."

"That is something to look forward to, Lady Margaret," said Grey.

"Then you do not shrink from the idea of being defeated by a lady? What a dreadful humiliation that would be!"

"Oh, no," replied the young man, "I particularly like the company of ladies who are cleverer than I am, so much so that I am willing to put up with any related inconveniences."

"How very unusual," said Lady Margaret, "Why so, when most of your sex prefer relative stupidity?"

"Why, because with clever ladies, I can be more at my ease. I find myself relieved from the burden of appearing to be intelligent, and have only to listen and admire."

"Very well reasoned, Mr. Grey," said his hostess, "I had not given you credit for so much sense."

Lord Faulconer mildly remonstrated with his daughter at this point for what he considered a discourteous remark, but the young lady only laughed.

When Grey rose to take leave, his host very kindly urged that a carriage be sent for to convey him back to Pemberley, but nothing he could say would change the young man's resolve to return home on horseback.

As their guest rode off, Lord Faulconer remarked to his daughter that he had rarely met anyone so intelligent or agreeable as Mr. Grey.

"Well, he is not quite so objectionable as I thought him to be," replied Lady Margaret, "but is it good to be on such friendly terms with someone who is, after all, only Mr. Darcy's librarian?"

"You surprise me, Margaret. Mr. Grey is obviously a gentleman whom Darcy treats as an equal, even if he is here assisting with the library at Pemberley. Why, they were at school together!" After a moment, he added, "And you are the one who always expresses such scorn for the distinctions of rank. Anyone who heard you on the subject might think you some kind of revolutionary! Thank goodness that I have been the only audience for some of your more radical ideas."

"Yes, Papa, I know that I am a very shocking character. But I would advise you not to become too fond of Mr. Grey's company, for I think that he may disappear underground one day, never to be seen again."

CHAPTER 28

$\mathcal{T}$he next afternoon found Mr. Grey riding in another direction from Pemberley, following Mr. Fisk's careful directions. "It's four miles over the moors to Gilmore Grange, sir. If you follow Wildfell Run down from Cragmore Knob, you'll see the place off to the north."

The big hunter Grey was riding was fresh and eager for a gallop, and the distance passed away in a blur of windswept speed, until they pulled up at the view of the Grange on its exposed and bleak hilltop. This was the home of Dr. Gilmore-Jones, an old friend whom Grey had not seen in many years, or had even suspected to be living in Derbyshire.

Before Darcy had left for Scotland, he had mentioned this neighbor, whom they had both known at Cambridge.

"You remember Gilmore-Jones, do you not, who was a Fellow at Cambridge when we were there? Well, he lives just a short distance from here, and, I am sure, would be delighted to renew your acquaintance."

"What, Dr. Gilmore-Jones has left Cambridge!" said Grey in astonishment, "How is this possible, for I never knew a man better suited to the academic life?"

"Love, my friend," replied Darcy, "What else but love can make a man so completely alter his circumstances and rejoice in doing so. He met a young lady, whose society made all else seem dry as dust by comparison. At about the same time, his father died and left him a comfortable fortune and the Grange, where the family has been established for generations. So they were able to marry without delay, and live there as happily as any two people in the country."

"Well this is excellent news," said Grey, "You will recall that Dr. Gilmore- Jones was my mentor in all my pursuits in natural philosophy."

"Yes," replied his friend, "And he also shares your obsession with cave exploration. But if you are expecting him to help you get into trouble wandering along some underground river any time soon, then I must disappoint you. He is confined at home with a broken knee."

The Grange was an ancient and uncompromisingly plain building, which seemed to have been situated by some ancestor of Dr. Gilmore-Jones in total defiance of the wind and weather. This must be a bitterly cold place in the middle of the winter, thought Grey as he handed over his horse to a groom who had come running out from the stable yard.

To his surprise, however, the interior of the house could not have have been more cheerful and welcoming. A neatly dressed servant showed him into a large and handsome room, lined with books, where Dr. Gilmore-Jones was sitting before the fire. In spite of Grey's protestations, he rose from his chair with the aid of a cane and greeted his visitor.

"How I have looked forward to this meeting," said Dr. Gilmore-Jones, "Mr. Darcy wrote to me a few days ago and told me that you were at Pemberley. Nothing could have pleased me so well as the thought of seeing my favorite pupil again."

At Grey's insistence, Dr. Gilmore-Jones sat down again, and they were soon conversing as easily as if they had been separated for only a few days rather than eight years. The older man was about fifty years of age, but had the manner and endurance of someone much younger. He gestured with disgust to his right knee which he had propped up on a footstool.

"I did not break it, but only dislocated it in a very annoying accident. But Mr. Anderson, the surgeon says it is almost as serious as a fracture. It has been three weeks now, and I would defy him and throw away this cane, but it would distress my wife. So it will be another month before I can show you around this remarkably interesting country as I would like to."

At that moment Mrs. Gilmore-Jones entered the room, followed by a servant bearing a tea tray. The lady was remarkably pretty, with a quiet, graceful manner, and expressed her great happiness at Mr. Grey's residence in the neighborhood, "For I have heard my husband speak fondly of you so often, and nothing could be more timely than the arrival of a friend who will help to amuse him during this period of inactivity."

There followed a pleasant hour of conversation, during which Grey gave Dr. and Mrs. Gilmore-Jones some idea of his travels during the past few years.

"I have greatly enjoyed your letters, but of course was never able to reply, as you did not stay in any place long enough," said his host, "but I have often feared for your safety. Grey would never let a trivial thing like a war prevent him from traveling to some remote place he wished to see," added Dr. Gilmore Jones to his wife.

"Sometime I will tell you the story of how I was captured by the French and almost shot as a spy."

"Good heavens! How did you escape?" exclaimed Mrs. Gilmore-Jones.

"There was an officer whom I had met at a scientific assembly in Paris, and he was kind enough to save me from a firing squad. But other than that incident I have been remarkably fortunate."

Grey was persuaded to give all the particulars of this adventure, as well as his impressions of Italy and the Levant. When these subjects were temporarily exhausted, he mentioned that he had dined at Castle Faulconer the evening before. Dr. and Mrs. Gilmore-Jones were full of praise for the earl and Lady Margaret.

"Why they are the kindest and best of friends, and we have the pleasure of seeing them now and then, although not so often as we would like. They did us the honor of dining at the Grange two months ago. Nothing could be more gracious and unaffected than Lady

Margaret's manner to everyone, and she has done so much to assist the poor of the district."

After a moment the lady added, "How dreadful that such tragedy should have befallen them."

Seeing Grey's inquisitive look, Mrs. Gilmore-Jones continued, "You could not know, of course that Lady Margaret's mother died in Italy some years ago, when the family was in Rome. A fever took her from her husband and twelve year old daughter in only a few days. Poor Lord Faulconer has never recovered, is that not so?"

"Yes, my love," said Dr. Gilmore-Jones, "He was a very different sort of man before that sad event, always out of doors and an active kind of person. Now he spends almost all of his time at the castle and leaves most of the estate business to his daughter. Although I must say that she certainly deserves his confidence."

Grey would have liked to hear more, but felt he had stayed long enough for a first visit. Mrs. Gilmore-Jones kindly pressed him to return as often as possible, "for it has done my husband more good than you can imagine to see you today. And perhaps you can persuade him not to go into a cavern by himself again."

"Oh, yes, my dear," laughed Dr. Gilmore-Jones, "Grey is the very soul of caution, as you can perceive from the stories he has been telling us."

Grey had been too polite to ask how his friend had happened to be injured, but now his curiosity was satisfied.

"I was making my way down a stream passage, and turned my foot in a submerged depression in the rock," said Dr. Gilmore-Jones, "My kneecap had the bad judgment to go in the opposite direction, but I was fortunate enough to be able to drag myself out and get to my horse which was tethered nearby."

"Did you ever hear of such a thing, Mr. Grey?" asked the lady, "I am sure that you would not be so reckless?"

Grey somehow avoided a direct answer to this appeal, and rose to go, promising to return quite soon. As he did so, he turned rather hesitantly to Dr. Gilmore- Jones saying, "I would ask you a great favor, one which you must deny me if you find it at all distasteful to your sense of honor."

Dr. Gilmore-Jones was somewhat surprised, but answered at once, "Why, you know I will do anything in my power to oblige you, my friend."

"Thanks to the cooperation of Mr. and Mrs. Darcy, I have been able to pass in the neighborhood as plain Mr. Grey, librarian, a gentleman without any claim to distinguished birth or fortune. As you recall, I began to use the name 'Grey' while at Cambridge. You, sir, will understand why I have no wish that my true identity become known, and I ask only that you not mention my real circumstances if you can avoid doing so." Then, turning to the lady, he added, "I will leave it to Dr. Gilmore-Jones to explain the dreary story behind my request, and can only hope that what he has to relate will not prejudice you against me, Mrs. Gilmore-Jones."

And then with a bow and repeated thanks, Grey was gone.

It may be imagined that the door had no sooner closed behind their visitor than Mrs. Gilmore-Jones pulled her chair near her husband's and eagerly demanded an explanation for Grey's odd petition.

"It is really very simple, my love," replied her husband, with a sigh. "John Grey's father happens to be one of the worst men in the kingdom, whose reputation could besmirch even this most virtuous young man who has the misfortune to be his son."

Of course, Mrs. Gilmore-Jones was hardly likely to be satisfied with this parsimonious reply, and she had soon learned that Mr. Grey was the son of the infamous Lord Harwith, whose life of wild dissipation had earned him the soubriquet of "the wickedest peer in England."

"Why, I have heard of him!" cried the lady, "He must be a dreadful person, but can you tell me more particularly of his crimes against propriety? I know that he is a gambler, but little else."

Dr. Gilmore-Jones looked grave, and said firmly, "Most definitely, he is guilty of other transgressions, but these are not things of which a man can speak to his wife."

And to Mrs. Gilmore-Jones' great disappointment, she could obtain no further information. She was a kind-hearted woman, and felt sympathy for the poor young man, driven across the world to escape from the influence of such a father, and pledged that she would befriend him with a compassion equal to her husband's.

As Grey rode back to Pemberley his thoughts returned to what he had been told about Lady Faulconer's death. It was, of course always a terrible thing to lose one's mother, as Grey well knew, but apparently this loss had been very sudden and unexpected and particularly dreadful for Lady Margaret. He had sensed that there was sadness at the castle, and that the earl, though very agreeable, suffered from a depression of the spirit which his daughter constantly strove to relieve. Grey now very much regretted that he had made such an unfavorable impression on the young lady at their first meeting, for everything he had seen of Lady Margaret increased his admiration. It would be much to gain her friendship, and he hoped that hers was not a character that would forever remember an affront to her dignity.

CHAPTER 29

The next few weeks could hardly have passed more pleasantly for John Grey. He dined six more times at Castle Faulconer, and passed several enjoyable evenings with his friends at Gilmore Grange. The rector, Mr. Devereaux, had also been found to be an excellent companion, and he had twice been to the parsonage, where he had been welcomed with great kindness by the clergyman and his wife. Grey was a disciplined man, and rose at dawn each morning to begin his work in the library, but by mid-afternoon he was glad to set off on excursions and visits. The discovery of the water damage behind the library wall, and the consequent necessity to remove books and furniture and arrange for repairs had called a halt to these more agreeable pursuits for a few days, but after all was in train and Mr. Fisk put in charge, Grey did not hesitate to venture out again.

His friendship with Lord Faulconer had rapidly increased in intimacy and confidence, as it sometimes happens when men have many interests in common, and enough difference in age and situation that there is no cause for rivalry of any kind. The earl had been quite desolate after the death of Darcy's father, who had been his closest friend, and Grey's appearance was an unexpected blessing for the older man.

Lord Faulconer began to take more interest in many things and was even persuaded by Grey to venture out on horseback, something he had not done for years.

Lady Margaret, by contrast, did not seem to feel any increase of friendliness towards the young man. She always received him politely enough, and was willing to talk to him on various subjects. They would often walk in the gardens of the castle, while she listened with great attention as he described the rare plants and the agricultural practices he had seen in his travels. They played chess together in the evenings while the earl looked on pensively, and found that they were well matched. Grey won the first game but was defeated in the next two contests. As he rode homeward one night, he wondered whether he was not at some disadvantage in this form of competition, for it was increasingly difficult for him to remain attentive to chess when in the presence of his hostess. Grey hardly saw the board while such an exquisite hand and arm were to be observed moving the pieces, and the firelight illumined Lady Margaret's lovely face and turned her auburn tresses to gold. It occurred to him that there might be serious danger to his peace of mind if he were to continue to visit the castle so frequently, but he quickly dismissed the idea. That Lady Margaret appeared to find his company merely tolerable, and treated him with a very formal courtesy at best, and amused scorn at worst, surely should protect his heart from the power of this beautiful, willful girl. Such were the reflections of a clever man who had seen much of the world and learned many things, but who knew almost nothing about the power of love.

The two young people were out on horseback almost every afternoon, and it was not surprising that they encountered each other on more than one occasion. On one cool, blustery day Lady Margaret found Mr. Grey in the middle of the narrow bridge across Claybourne Run. Her mind was clearly preoccupied, for she did not see him until Grey hailed her from just a few yards away. The young lady was startled, and her horse, sensing this, shied slightly and side-stepped, until she calmed him, saying, "Gently, gently, Buccie! It is not the ogre from under the bridge, all appearances to the contrary."

Then, looking up at Grey, she added, "Really, sir, you are a most inconvenient obstacle. One of us will have to back off this bridge, and you are certainly the logical choice for the honor. "

"My apologies, Lady Margaret," said Grey, unable to suppress an amused smile, "I thought you would see me here and allow me to finish crossing. Are you always so inattentive to the road ahead when you are moving along at such a blistering fast trot?"

"Until you entered the county, Mr. Grey," retorted the young lady, "there was no reason to apprehend the presence of large, insensate objects in the middle of one's path. Now, with your permission, I would like to get on my way."

"Perhaps you will permit me the honor of accompanying you," said Grey, after he had maneuvered his horse out of the way, and Lady Margaret had begun to move along at a brisk pace.

"That would be quite unnecessary and inappropriate," replied the lady.

When Grey continued to ride along at her side, she gave him a sidelong glance and said, "Since this is a public highway, I suppose that there is nothing I can do to divest myself of your presence."

"Why, of course, I will be gone at once if you wish it, Lady Margaret," replied the young man, making as if to turn his horse, "but I hoped you would show me something of this neighborhood so that I would know better where to exercise my friend's hunters."

Lady Margaret looked thoughtful for a moment and then said, "Very well Mr. Grey, I will show you a pleasant little route to Ferndean Hall, which happens to be my destination today."

In the next instant the lady had left the road and was crossing an adjacent field at a gallop. Grey was surprised, but was quick to follow and narrow the lead Lady Margaret had taken. They proceeded over rough and stony country, and Grey was torn between admiration for his companion's skill, and alarm at her recklessness. Over hedges and stonewalls they flew, Grey following her lead as closely as possible since the ground was entirely new to him. He was a fine horseman but was always inclined to take the safer line where one was in evidence. On this occasion, however, his only thought was to keep within a few lengths of the young lady. At last there was a particularly treacherous downhill jump across a stream, and Grey, having successfully negotiated it, saw Lady Margaret pull up at the edge of a wood.

When he trotted up to her, she greeted him with, "Still here, Mr. Grey? I really thought to have left you a mile or two behind."

"An agreeable, if unchallenging little run, Lady Margaret," replied Grey, "Tell me, have you ever hunted in Ireland?"

"No," answered the lady, "I have not had the opportunity."

"Well there they have *real* walls, and *real* hedges, not these insignificant little things you hardly notice jumping."

"I see," replied the young lady shortly, disliking to hear of a place where there might be horsewomen whose skill could rival her own. "Well, Mr. Grey, I have no more time to waste in your company. I am on my way to the Hall on important business."

Grey did not reply, as he had suddenly become lost in admiration of Lady Margaret's beauty. How perfect, how elegant she looked on her great bay horse, so slender and straight, her eyes bright, and her auburn locks half escaping the dashing little hat she wore.

After a moment of silence, during which the lady made no move to leave, despite her words, she added, "But perhaps you might be useful, Mr. Grey. I have observed that you are rather knowledgeable in some unexpected ways. Do you know anything of hounds?"

"Ill-favored canines, unintelligent, noisesome olfactoriums, expensive, inconvenient, and unrewarding to maintain," replied Grey, in a most serious voice.

Lady Margaret looked astonished for a moment, then began to laugh, "Why Mr. Grey, you *have* been out of England for a long time. Thank goodness no one else heard you make such a blasphemous remark. You would make yourself very unpopular indeed!" and then she attempted to look severe, but only went off again in a fit of laughter, and added, "You do have a talent for reducing things to essentials. But you may as well come along, as we are almost there now."

The lady explained that the venerable Colonel Dalrymple having died last summer, the hounds were for now in the care of Squire Redfern of Ferndean Hall, a well-meaning gentleman but probably not up to the demands of such a great responsibility. Lady Margaret was on her way to give him some much needed advice.

The Hall was a fine, modern house, built on the site of an ancient building that had burned some ten years before. Grey thought that the squire must be a wealthy man, judging from the number of windows and marble adornments to be seen. The effect was somewhat spoilt by the old, rambling farm structures close by and the absence of garden or shrubbery. The squire seemed to have been watching for them and ran out to meet them, followed by several minions. He was a young man, strong and handsome, in a well-cut coat that Grey surmised was new and worn only for the special occasion of Lady Margaret's visit. The squire hurried forward to assist the lady to dismount, but she was too quick for him. He only seemed to notice Grey when forced to do so by Lady Margaret's introduction, and was clearly disappointed that she had not come alone. Grey was amused to observe that his new acquaintance could not look in the young lady's direction without a blush, and that a slight stammer began every remark he ventured to make.

They were soon surveying the accommodations that had been made for the hounds behind the stables. Grey thought a very good job had been made of the arrangements, but Lady Margaret still found much that could be improved upon and did not hesitate to offer her suggestions. The howling and barking that had begun as soon as they had appeared was almost intolerably loud, and the lady had to make a great effort to be heard, addressing herself more to a grizzled old huntsman who respectfully followed the group, than to the squire himself. It was perhaps as well, as the young man did nothing but stare at his guest with an evident longing that was almost painful to see.

Why, this poor fellow is very far gone indeed, thought Grey, and Lady Margaret does not appear to have the slightest idea of his adoration.

After every question had been settled to the lady's satisfaction, she announced her intention of returning home, in spite of the Squire Redfern's eager entreaties that she take some refreshment before starting out. When this was refused, as well as the honor of accompanying her back to the castle, her admirer could only bid them farewell with a last passionate glance for the object of his adulation, and a cold bow for Grey, for whom he had conceived a violent dislike in the space of the past hour.

Lady Margaret seemed content to ride along at a fairly decorous pace, and made no demand that she be left alone, much to her companion's surprise. She even asked his opinion on a few subtle questions that had arisen during their visit to the kennels. Grey was gratified to be enjoying a conversation with the lady during which he was not a target for her scorn or her barbed wit.

They were nearing the pretty hamlet that stood at the castle gates, when they saw a carriage approaching at a sedate pace. It proved to belong to Mrs. Dalrymple, widow of the late Master, and a prominent person in the neighborhood. With her was Lady Templeton, widely known for her malicious ability to detect and spread scandal, so that most of her acquaintance lived in dread of her. Seeing Lady Margaret and Grey together caused slightly raised eyebrows and quizzical looks on the part of both the occupants of the carriage.

There was no way to avoid a meeting and Lady Margaret and Grey rode over to greet the two ladies. Mrs. Dalrymple was glad to hear news of the hounds, which had been the chief interest of her deceased husband's life for many years. This occupied a few minutes conversion, during which Lady Templeton was observing the young people with a cold intensity that made Grey ill at ease, not for himself but for his companion.

Finally, when the subject of hounds and hunting had been adequately canvassed, the inimical old lady interposed a question, "Why, Mr. Grey, what news from your good father, the farmer, who toils away in that remote part of England you have mentioned? Does he expect a good harvest?"

"It is so kind of you to inquire, Lady Templeton," replied Grey politely, "but I am afraid that I have had no communication with my father. Not every farmer, you know, can read and write."

"Heavens, Mr. Grey," exclaimed Mrs. Dalrymple, "surely that cannot be true in the case of your own father?"

The young man looked thoughtful for a moment, and then replied,

"Well, Mrs. Dalrymple, I can only say that I should be astonished to receive a letter from him."

Even Lady Templeton was speechless at this statement, and in a moment the carriage moved on.

"How very disagreeable," said Lady Margaret, in a moment, "That tiresome Lady Templeton would make it her life's work to ruin my reputation if she could. Now it will be all over the county that I was out riding with you. The old dragon thinks it disgraceful that I go out on horseback alone, but to be seen in the company of a gentleman is even worse."

Grey was dismayed, and expressed his regret that he might be the cause of any unpleasantness for the young lady.

"Oh, no. You misunderstand me," replied the young lady, "I care nothing for Lady Templeton and the stupid gossip she tries to spread. My position and the respect I command make it beyond her ability to injure me. My indifference to the opinions of ignorant, narrow minds, and the fact that I enjoy good will of all the worthwhile people in the neighborhood has always protected me. It is merely an annoyance."

Grey said nothing, but thought to himself that reputation was a much more fragile thing than Lady Margaret seemed to comprehend.

They rode the rest of the way to the castle in silence, until the lady remarked, "You know it is one thing for me to incur the enmity of Lady Templeton, but it is quite another matter for a newcomer like you. I can see that she has taken a dislike to you for some reason. Beware, Mr. Grey! The consequences could be most unpleasant. I know that you like to be mysterious, and I would never gratify your vanity by asking you anything about your family or circumstances, but if you have a weakness our local dragon will find it out."

Grey at that moment very much wished to confide in Lady Margaret, and might have done so, had they not been hailed by Lord Faulconer, who had been sitting on a bench at the edge of the garden and watching for his daughter's return. And so, unfortunately, the opportunity passed, and Grey had time to consider how very disagreeable it would be to explain all that he had kept hidden for the past few weeks. What if they were to recoil from him when it was known that his father was the notorious Lord Harwith? He had felt

260

the effect of such prejudice in the past when new friends suddenly became wary on learning of his parentage. Grey felt that today had been the first occasion of Lady Margaret's giving some indication of friendliness towards him, and how difficult it would have been to risk losing such hard-won good will. She had passed more than an hour in his company without subjecting him to any of her usual mocking remarks. It was so much more satisfactory to pass himself off as an obscure gentleman and scholar.

Lord Faulconer was delighted to see Grey, and appeared to find no impropriety in his having accompanied Lady Margaret on her errand. He would not allow the young man to depart without a promise to return for dinner the following day.

The father and daughter sat together for a while in the garden after Grey had ridden off, and after a few moment's thought Lord Faulconer began, "My dear child, do you not think that is a very agreeable young man, with all the qualities most certain to deserve the lasting esteem and affection of his friends? Why, he is intelligent, well bred, kind and attentive, with a brilliant mind, and an active disposition. Surely, with the exception of Mr. Darcy, he is the most exceptional young man ever to make an appearance in our little universe here in Derbyshire?"

Seeing her father's eager and hopeful expression, Lady Margaret could not help but smile. She merely replied that in her life and travels she had, on occasion, seen worse young men than Mr. Grey.

Lord Faulconer's countenance, which was rarely very cheerful, now fell into lines of disappointment and sadness. "You will never be serious, Margaret, and I fear for your future happiness. Anyone can see how much Mr. Grey admires you, and you are barely civil to him. I am amazed at how well he tolerates your sarcasm and cutting remarks, when any other man would have been driven off very quickly."

Lady Margaret looked thoughtful for several minutes, before turning to her father with a grave expression on her lovely face, "Dear Papa, what a great and generous heart you have, and what a romantic idea of the world you still maintain in spite of everything."

Lord Faulconer turned his face away at this, and seemed very much moved by his daughter's words. She continued, "Here is a young man without fortune or connections, and unlike every other father in England, this presents no disadvantage to your mind. I know that you have been thinking that a great romance will be the end of my acquaintance with Mr. Grey, and you have been imagining a future in which the three of us will live together in an Elysium of perfect harmony, with endless chess games before the fire in the evening, and strolls in the garden, and perhaps even a flock of grandchildren playing about your feet."

Lord Faulconer colored slightly, and replied, "I am not sure it is altogether a pleasant thing to have a daughter who knows me so well. I admit that it has crossed my mind that Mr. Grey would be a good match for you, especially as he is the only young man who has ever stood up to you. His lack of fortune does not matter, not when our family has been blessed with such great wealth. The requirement that your first-born son take the name of Faulconer would almost certainly not matter to him. I am aware that my attitude in this regard would seem eccentric, or even irresponsible to most fathers in my position." After a pause he added, "but I have learned to have little interest in what may be the prevailing opinion in this or any other matter."

They were silent for a while and then Lady Margaret began again, "Papa, I believe that you wish more than anything else for my happiness, but you know already what I am going to say. I will never leave you and I will never marry. You have heard me say so before, but perhaps you have never understood how serious is my resolve. I need not explain my aversion to matrimony and to the idea of trusting my tranquility and honor to the mercy of another person in that way. After all that we have endured there is no necessity to say any more about it."

Lord Faulconer seemed unable to reply for some time, but then he said with a voice almost choked with emotion, "You break my heart, dear child, but I do understand you, and can only pray that someday you will come to feel differently."

But Lady Margaret rose and seemed to be determined to bring an end to the subject, "Now, Papa, have you ever known me to change my mind about anything? Well, perhaps I have altered my opinion about such things as the proper mash to feed my hunters, or some aspects of rose cultivation, but you must admit that even these are rare events."

Her father agreed with a heavy sigh, and was only with some difficulty distracted from his sad reflections.

CHAPTER 30

When Mr. Grey arrived at Castle Faulconer the following evening he was delighted to see that Mr. And Mrs. Devereaux were also of the party. He had been to the rectory several times for dinner, and very much enjoyed the company of the intelligent, scholarly clergyman, and his kind, good-natured wife. A few moments later Dr. and Mrs. Gilmore-Jones entered the drawing room, and greeted Grey in a manner that was friendly, but not indicative of the fact that the two gentlemen had known each other so well at Cambridge. Grey's secret was clearly safe with his old mentor. The young man's only regret at being in such a pleasant company was that he had intended to reveal the truth about himself to Lord Faulconer and his daughter that evening, and now such a course of action seemed impossible.

Lady Margaret's greeting was almost gracious, and she seemed glad of the opportunity of speaking a few private words to Grey as they stood by the fire together.

"Mr. Grey, I must tell you that this is the closest thing to an evening party here at the castle that we have attempted for several years. My father's spirits are so improved that he was willing to let me invite our friends tonight. In fairness, I am obliged to give you the credit for this transformation and say that I am very grateful to you for your happy influence."

Grey was surprised, and was only able to bow and murmur his thanks for this unusually kind speech from Lady Margaret. He would have liked to explain to her how much the friendship with her father meant to him as well, as he had grown up rather worse off than if he had actually been an orphan, with the worst reprobate in England for a parent. The mutual regard and confidence that had sprung up so quickly between Grey and Lord Faulconer was something the young man had come to value more than he could say.

On this night, dinner was served in the Great Hall which formed the center of the most ancient part of the castle. An enormous fire on a vast hearth served to dispel the evening chill, and candles had been lit everywhere to make the room cheerful. Everyone was in the happy frame of mind which makes all one's companions seem charming and amusing, and laughter frequently filled the circle of warmth and light defined by the massive dining table.

To Grey's surprise, Lady Margaret told the story of their first meeting, when she had encountered him walking near Pemberley, recently emerged from a cavern and covered with mud.

"It amused Mr. Grey to let me think him a madman of some sort. Certainly his appearance was both alarming and extraordinary. When he entered the drawing room at Pemberley with Mr. Darcy it was quite a shock, I can assure you." Turning to Grey, she continued, "You were very wrong indeed, to play such a trick, and it will take a long time for me to forgive you."

"But it is just like him," said Dr. Gilmore-Jones, laughing, "Grey could never resist such an opportunity." Then looking rather conscious, he added very quickly, "Well you don't have to know our young friend for very long to perceive that he cannot resist a good jest, so you should not take it personally, Lady Margaret."

"I believe you are correct, Dr. Gilmore-Jones," replied the lady, "but Mr. Grey's droll sense of humor will lead him into serious trouble someday, I am sure."

Grey looked very grave, and said, "This proves that none of you understands my character. No one could possess a more serious cast of mind, or be less given to frivolity than myself."

"Oh, we all know better by now," said Mr. Devereaux, "I remember the story you told about the elusive alpine white tiger that only you and a handful of other people had ever beheld. Why you were so convincing that I quite believed you at first. My children certainly found the tale amusing."

"As a matter of fact, "replied Grey, "some very reliable people claim to have seen that tiger. I must admit that in my case, the concurrent blizzard and violent winds may have played tricks on my perception of the creature."

Later, when everyone had returned to the drawing room, Lady Margaret begged her guests to excuse her for a few moments, "For my favorite horse seemed to be a bit lame this afternoon and I cannot be easy until I am certain that all is well."

She left the room after declining the offers of the gentleman to accompany her. When she returned her friends saw with dismay that she was in great distress and unable to repress tears of grief.

"Oh, Papa!" she cried, "It is Buccie. He is in terrible pain, and Cranbrook says he fears it is the colic. They have just begun trying to keep him walking in the stable yard, but he is so weak, and you know what will happen if they fail."

"My dear child," exclaimed Lord Faulconer, hastening to his daughter's side, and taking her hands in his, "Poor Bucephalus!" Then he added, "Has Mr. Brown been sent for?" This was a famous local expert on all equine ailments.

"He is away, visiting a sister who is ill," replied Lady Margaret, " and there is no one else who knows anymore than Cranbrook."

Grey, who had been listening intently, said, "I believe that I may be able to help. At least I would like to try to do so."

"Do you have some experience in the treatment of colic?" asked Lady Margaret, looking up at the young man, with some dawning of hope in her tear-stained face.

"I once spent a few months at a famous horse farm near Lipica, east of Trieste. I was fortunate enough to learn many things from my time there."

266

"Please do whatever you can, my dear Grey," cried Lord Faulconer, "You cannot imagine how attached my child is to Bucephalus."

"Very well. We shall see what can be done. Lady Margaret, please be so good as to have your housekeeper and cook join us in the stable yard, as I will need to ask them to prepare a mixture of certain herbs. Let us go at once and examine the animal."

The other guests had sense enough to see that they were *de trop*, and made haste to take their departure, so that little time was lost before Grey was able to ascertain that Bucephalus did indeed exhibit all the alarming symptoms of colic. Several grooms were struggling to keep the horse moving, but the wretched animal was evidently in great pain, and wanted nothing more than to fall to the ground. Lady Margaret had by now regained some of her self-command, but stood trembling in the cool night air as her father tried to comfort her.

Cranbrook, who had commanded the stables at Castle Faulconer for many years, was brought to despair by this catastrophe, and was pitifully grateful for Grey's appearance on the scene.

"Oh, sir, we have tried everything I know to do without improvement and if he goes down it is all over."

"Does this horse have any special friend among his stable mates?" asked Grey calmly, as he went over the wild -eyed, shaking horse with the unmistakable air of an expert.

"There is an old gelding he always passes the time with out in the meadow, from whom he hates to be parted," replied the man.

"Then go at once and fetch him. He will bear Bucephalus company this long night." His order was obeyed immediately, and the presence of the old hunter seemed to make a difference in the sick animal's willingness to continue to circle the yard, especially as Lady Margaret walked on his other side.

After Grey had given exact orders to the cook as to the preparation of the herbs, the whole castle was thrown into a whirlwind of activity, and very quickly the remedy was brought down from the kitchen.

All this time Lady Margaret had been watching Grey with increasing respect and admiration. His quiet but commanding presence seemed to reassure everyone, while they hastened to obey him.

She was thinking how very glad she was that he was there, when Grey came up to her, and said, "It would be better for you to leave when I administer this remedy. Your horse is not going to like it, and it will only distress you to see it."

"Surely you know me well enough by now to be aware that I will do no such thing."

"Very well," replied Grey, turning away, "There is certainly no time to dispute the matter with you."

Lord Faulconer also attempted to persuade his daughter to return to the house, but she refused, and instead went to stand near the poor animal to reassure it as best she could. Grey's handling of the horse was at once kind and masterful and the unpleasant business was soon completed.

"We must continue to keep him walking for the next several hours, and there is nothing more to be done, Lady Margaret," said the young man, " Please go and rest, and I promise that you will be called at once should anything new occur."

Lord Faulconer seconded this suggestion so forcefully that at last the lady agreed, and soon Grey was left to continue his vigil in the stable yard while the exhausted grooms walked the two horses back and forth.

Lady Margaret was awakened at about two o'clock in the morning by the moonlight across her bed, and felt a sudden alarm as she remembered all that had transpired that evening. A great fear took hold of her, although she told herself that she would have certainly been called had any disaster occurred, and she dressed quickly and made her way through the quiet house and down a back staircase to the stable yard.

It was an extraordinarily clear autumn night, and it was almost as bright as day, with the brilliant moon just beginning its descent. For a terrified moment she thought that the yard was empty, but immediately perceived the two horses at the far end near a great oak tree and turning to come towards her. When she saw that they were led by Mr. Grey she went to meet him.

Even at some distance she could see the transformation in her beloved horse. Bucephalus ambled along without any evidence of distress, favoring Mr. Grey with an occasional gentle nudge against his shoulder. The young man seemed half asleep, but became alert as soon as he was aware of Lady Margaret's presence.

She ran her hand over the smooth neck of her horse, exclaiming with delight at the wonderful improvement that just a few hours had effected.

"Yes, we have had good results from our treatment," said Grey, "he will do very well now, and I think that soon we may end our perambulations. But you have come out without a cloak, Lady Margaret, and the night air is cold."

When the lady showed no inclination to return to the house, Grey removed his coat and laid it over her shoulders, in spite of her denials that she felt the chill.

After a few moments during which she talked to Bucephalus and caressed him, Lady Margaret turned to Grey and asked, "How does it happen that you are so knowledgeable? You said something about a horse farm, but I was too distracted to comprehend it at the time."

"At one time," he replied, "I found myself in Trieste, very short of funds, and determined to travel on into Greece. A nobleman who had a magnificent and renowned horse farm to the east of the city invited me to stay with him there as his tutor, with the understanding that I would help him to perfect his English. In the course of several months I also learned all that the head of his stables could teach me about the treatment of equine disease. Also, there are some remarkable caverns in the vicinity. And so you see that it was time well spent."

They walked on in silence for a while, but then the lady stopped and looked at Grey with a serious expression, the moonlight illuminating her face so that her companion had to catch his breath at her beauty.

"Mr. Grey, I now regret how ungracious I have been to you all these weeks. I am not a good judge of character, and I have completely mistaken yours. The great esteem in which my father holds you is clearly justified. Will you excuse the prejudice I have shown against you?"

Grey looked thoughtful, but then he smiled and replied, "So, at last, are we to be friends, Lady Margaret?" The young lady nodded in answer, and the two young people stood regarding each other for a moment.

"Will you give me your hand as pledge of this new friendship?" asked Grey. She was startled, but after an instant's reflection extended her hand, which he took into his much larger one very solemnly. They seemed to stand thus for a long time, in the strange, cold light of the moon, and Lady Margaret found that she felt little inclination to pull away from the warmth of his gentle hold. Then abruptly she broke away, and taking off Grey's coat said briskly, "Well, I must go, but I am sorry to leave you here without any assistance. Where are the grooms?"

"Oh, I sent them to bed some time ago. I am quite able to manage by myself, and now you may go to sleep knowing that all is well." Lady Margaret was persuaded to return to the castle, but found it difficult to stop thinking about her interview with Grey, although why this was so she did not understand.

She slept briefly at last, but awoke at dawn as was her habit. Again she felt a great anxiety about Bucephalus, and hastened to return to the stables. The yard was empty, and Lady Margaret went at once to the stall where, to her joy, her horse was to be found standing calmly in a fresh bedding of straw, clearly wholly recovered from his illness of the evening before. Just outside the stall Mr. Grey slept wrapped in an old blanket on a pile of hay. The lady looked down at him for a while; there was no denying that he was handsome, and she felt that she had never found a man to be so before. It seemed very important that she not awaken him and she crept off as quietly as possible.

CHAPTER 31

*L*ate in the afternoon of the same day Mr. Grey might have been observed making his way across the pastures that lay between Pemberley and the village. It had rained briefly and the grass was wet, but somehow the young man found walking most conducive to serious thought. He had left Castle Faulconer rather abruptly that morning, not even agreeing to stay for breakfast, to the surprise of his friends. They were eager to express their thanks for all that he had done, and were disappointed to see him ride off in such haste.

His excuse was that the cabinet makers just arrived from London were to begin their work in the library that morning and that he wished to be on hand to ensure that all went well. This was true, and he did in fact spend much of the day watching them work and making plans for a new arrangement of Mr. Darcy's books when the room should be completed. The actual reason for his haste to leave the castle that morning was that he needed solitude in which to think of all that had happened the night before.

The rector, Mr. Devereaux, was delighted to see Mr. Grey appear at the gate of his back garden, although he was surprised that he had not come on horseback.

"Why, who would have thought to see you walk this far!" he

exclaimed, "but your feet are wet, my dear Grey. Come and sit by the fire, and we shall have some tea."

The agreeable Mrs. Devereaux was also clearly pleased to see their visitor, and insisted that he stay for supper as well, "It's just a simple meal, Mr. Grey, but I know that you will not mind, and we will send to Pemberley to let them know that you will not be back for dinner."

Grey protested that he had never meant to put Mrs. Devereaux to any trouble by arriving at that time of day, but she only laughed and said how much pleasure it would give them to have his company that evening, when they had anticipated nothing but the dull family routine. No one could have been more gentlemanly than Grey, but in all his travels he had demonstrated a talent for appearing close to dinner time and looking famished, so that ladies found it imperative that he be fed as expeditiously as possible. The Devereauxs were alarmed to hear the details of the near fatal illness of Lady Margaret's adored horse, and relieved to know of the happy outcome of the emergency.

There were three small boys at the rectory, and with them Grey was already very much a favorite because of the wonderful stories he could tell, some of which were true and many invented. The meal was a lively one with their eager questions, which came rapid fire, two or three at a time, until at last their father had to intervene.

"Now, now, Edgar, Christopher, John. Let us try to return to some semblance of decorum! Mr. Grey cannot eat a bite of his dinner because of you. It is time for you to maintain a well-behaved silence and let the grown-ups talk."

They were good children and tried to do as their father bade them, but in a few minutes Edgar forgot himself so far as to ask an important question about the pirates that prowled the Barbary Coast, and the barrage began again.

"Well, Grey", said the rector, "You can see what strict discipline prevails in this house. There is little peace to be had at any time except in my library. We will retreat to that sanctuary shortly, and leave my poor wife to deal with these young ruffians."

When the two men found themselves seated comfortably by the library fire with some good Port at hand, Mr. Devereaux looked over at the young man rather thoughtfully and said, "We all of us, I suppose, have our little points of vanity, and I am prone to some degree of self-satisfaction on my ability to see into the motives of my fellow men. Something tells me that your visit tonight has a deeper purpose than the desire of being besieged by my offspring and eating a mutton chop with us."

"You are right, sir, and I am not surprised at your perspicacity. One need not have had the privilege of knowing you for long to expect such a degree of penetration to be combined with an equal kindness. I only hope that what I am going to tell you does not lessen me in your estimation."

The rector poured himself a little more Port, and settled himself more comfortably in his chair, "Well, another of my bits of complacency is to see myself as an excellent judge of character, and I seriously doubt that anything you may tell me will diminish my opinion of you. You have all my attention and interest, and I will be honored to be your confidant, both as a clergyman and as your friend."

This was sufficient encouragement for the young man, and he began his narrative with the revelation of his true identity, followed by a justification of his having hidden it from all his new friends in Derbyshire. At this information the rector sat up very straight in his chair, and any after dinner languor was dispelled.

"The son of Lord Harwith, and his heir!" exclaimed the clergyman, "Good heavens, my young friend, you do astonish me."

Grey looked embarrassed and continued rapidly in an attempt to justify himself, "You have heard something of my father perhaps? You know his reputation? If so you will, I hope, understand my motive in what I have done?"

Mr. Devereaux leaned back in his chair with the air of a man preparing to hear a long narrative. He found the port bottle at his side, and poured himself another glass, after silently offering it to Grey, who declined. Finally he fixed Grey with an intense and appraising look for a long moment.

"Yes, I am afraid I do know of your father, for he was, for a time, at my college at Cambridge, many years before my time of course. The stories about him were still common gossip, because of his absolute

_____." Then the rector paused, at a loss for words, "But how can I discuss such tales with his own son? These things, I will admit, went far beyond mere youthful foolishness and high spirits, if the reports are to be believed. There were things I do not like to dwell upon, and could never bring myself to repeat."

Grey bowed his head, for even so many years of separation from his father had not diminished the shame he felt at having such a parent, "Unfortunately they are true," he said after a long silence, "I know that they are, because he used to tell me about his life at the university before he was sent down."

The older man perceptibly drew back in horror, "To talk of such things with his son! And I thought I was too old to be shocked by anything."

"And he only became worse with the passage of time," continued Grey, "All England knows of his crimes against every principle of decency, and only his rank and wealth protect him. But I do not wish to sully the peace and goodness of your home by talking of him any further."

Grey's face was cold and distant for some time, and Mr. Devereaux pitied the young man for the dreadful memories that must haunt his mind.

Then Grey looked up, and asked almost appealingly, "Do you blame me, sir, for taking my mother's name and separating myself from my father? You are aware that his infamy is universally known, and I would likely be shunned for simply being his son."

Mr. Devereaux seemed to consider his answer for a while, then said, "I do not blame you, my young friend, and, in fact, I admire you, for you have rejected the base life into which your family circumstances might have led you and become a scholar and a man of excellent character. I hope that I would have displayed such courage and good judgment in your circumstances. And I will further admit that the prejudice against you for the misfortune of being the son of the notorious Lord Harwith would have been extreme."

"Thank you," said Grey, "You cannot imagine what a comfort your words are to me, and how it relieves my heart to reveal my secret, which has been known until now only by my friends at Pemberley and by Dr. Gilmore-Jones, who was at Cambridge when I was there. But sir, could I impose on your kindness this evening to advise me on another subject which is of the greatest importance to me?"

Mr. Devereaux asserted that nothing could give him greater pleasure, but he was astonished at the young man's next revelation.

"You wish to take orders! But it would be highly unusual when you will be inheriting such a great title and estate. But I know you well enough by now to be sure that you have given the idea very serious thought."

"I have, sir, for a long time, and now I feel certain that it is what I wish to do. Despite his occasional bouts of serious illness, my father may live another twenty years. By taking orders I would be following the dictates of both my mind and my heart."

"But have you thought of returning to Cambridge, where you would be welcomed as a distinguished scholar? Mr. Darcy has told me of some of your accomplishments in the area of natural philosophy."

"I have considered it, but I believe that the life of a clergyman in a rural district would suit me better. Perhaps I would even be fortunate enough to secure a living, however poor, not too far from my friends here in this neighborhood."

Mr. Devereaux's blue eyes, usually so calm and soft, became bright and penetrating, and he said quietly, "Yes, I have observed that not only have you close ties with Mr. Darcy and his family, but that you have in even such a short period of time, formed a real attachment to your new friends at Castle Faulconer. I could not but observe the genuine affection in which you are held there when we all had the pleasure of dining together last night, and if I am not mistaken, your wish to remain in the area may have something to do with at least one inhabitant there."

Grey's composure deserted him for a moment, and he said with emotion, "Ah, nothing can escape you, Mr. Devereaux, but of course I know that there is no hope. I am not such a fool as that, but all the same, it would be something just to be near her. But I trust that my feelings are not so obvious to everyone else."

"No, no. Do not trouble yourself about that, but in my profession one must necessarily become observant," said the rector kindly. He paused for a moment as if inviting further confidences, but when Grey only continued to stare into the fire he added, "As for your taking orders, I am sure your vocation is genuine, or you would not be considering it. Let me think of your situation for a week, and then we will talk again."

The two men sat in silence for some time, then Mr. Devereaux added, "But there is one thing you must do without delay, and that is to inform Lord Faulconer and Lady Margaret of your true identity."

Grey nodded and agreed to the truth of this assertion, and said that he would soon go to his new friends on that difficult mission.

"No, my dear Grey, it must be done at once, tomorrow! What if they should learn it from another source? I will go with you, if you have no objection, and explain that I understand and sympathize with the unhappy circumstances that led to such a stratagem."

"How kind you are, sir," replied Grey with an attempt at a smile, "especially to call what I have done a 'stratagem' instead of a 'deception.' I will gratefully accept any help you can give me."

It was finally arranged that the two men would go to Castle Faulconer the next afternoon after church. "Do not lose sleep in worrying tonight," said Mr. Devereaux, as he said goodbye to Grey, "Between us we shall explain things very well."

That the rector was an exceptional man may be ascertained by the fact that he did not immediately awaken his wife that night to tell her the romantic and extraordinary story of Mr. Grey. No, he would keep his own counsel for now, he thought, watching the young man start out across the meadows toward Pemberley.

CHAPTER 32

*W*hen Grey arrived at church the next morning he was glad to see Lord Faulconer and Lady Margaret just ahead of him, making their way to the door of the building while replying to the greetings of their neighbors and tenants. He made an effort to join them and succeeded just as they reached their pew. Lord Faulconer motioned to Grey that he should sit with them and his daughter favored him with a welcoming smile. He would have been delighted with this evidence of their regard for him had he not been full of apprehension at the prospect of revealing the truth about himself. How he upbraided himself now for practicing what had seemed to be a harmless deception! He had thought to spend a few months at Pemberley restoring the library to its former glory, and then to be off again and resume his travels. To fall in love had been no part of his plan, but he could not deny that it had happened, and that to stand next to Lady Margaret in the little church and to share the support of the prayer book with her so that his hand almost touched hers, seemed to him the greatest happiness life could offer. Since he had looked into her face in the moonlit stableyard Grey's heart had been completely hers.

It is to be feared that neither young person heard much of Mr. Devereaux's edifying sermon. Lady Margaret, whose heart had never been in any danger before, began to feel that there might be a man in the world who could make her reconsider some of the principles which were the basis of her aversion to wedlock. Mr. Grey had hardly been out of her thoughts since the previous morning when she had found him asleep in the stable. How intelligent and capable and kind he was! She glanced at him cautiously during one of the hymns to see if he were really as handsome as she remembered, and blushed with confusion when his eyes met hers. She had never felt shy or self-conscious in her life and had certainly never blushed before, but these new feelings were mingled with an equally novel flow of happiness.

When the service was ended and they made their way out of the church, Lady Margaret was unusually silent while her father talked with Grey and a few other friends who joined them in a little group around the rector. For once she could think of nothing to say to anyone, and would have been happy to go home to her garden where she could be alone and think.

She was lost in her reflections when she heard the sharp voice of the dreaded Lady Templeton saying in loud tones, "Why, it is Lord Conarvan! How good of you to attend our simple little church, my lord. I am sure we are all very honored."

Looking up in confusion Lady Margaret saw that this speech was directed at Mr. Grey, and that he had turned pale and seemed unable to answer.

"I am sorry to correct you, Lady Templeton, but this is Mr. Grey, who is a guest at Pemberley," said Lord Faulconer politely.

"Indeed it is not," replied the old lady with something approaching a sneer, "This young man, who likes to amuse himself at our expense, is Lord Conarvan, the only son of that distinguished peer, Lord Harwith of Harwith Hall in Surrey. Let him deny it if he can!"

Everyone looked at Grey, who was the picture of misery and despair. Mr. Devereaux, who had been observing this turn of events with dismay, began to speak in defense of his friend, but the young man said, "Thank you, sir, but even your benevolence cannot aid me now. What Lady Templeton has revealed is true, and I cannot explain further except to ask you all to believe that a man may be driven to such a deception by circumstances that are none of his own doing. I have only the greatest respect for everyone I have been privileged to know while I have been at Pemberley."

"One does not lie to those one respects," said Lady Templeton, who had no intention of being robbed of her triumph, "and we might never known the truth had I not written to my old friend Lady Belthorpe with my suspicions. Your aunt was surprised to hear that you were back in England and begs me to remind you of the family connection since you claimed to be uncertain of it."

"I can only beg the forgiveness of so many of you who have been so kind to me during the past few weeks," said Grey wretchedly, to the small group who had gathered to witness this remarkable scene.

There was silence for a moment, and even Lady Templeton could think of nothing further to say to add to the young man's humiliation. Then Lord Faulconer spoke, a bit stiffly as if it were with some effort, "Well, now Grey, or rather Conarvan," he corrected himself with an embarrassed air, "Anyone who knows you must be certain that you had a good reason for what you did." Looking at the others he added, "I am sure a satisfactory explanation will be forthcoming, but for now let us leave this young man in peace."

Lord Faulconer's words always had the force of law, and people began to wander off.

"With your permission, Mr. Grey, for such is the name he prefers, and I will call upon you and Lady Margaret in two or three hours time," said Mr. Devereaux as soon as the opportunity presented itself, "I have some things to say in Grey's defense, although when you have heard all I think you will hold him blameless."

"No doubt, no doubt," replied Lord Faulconer, although his face was sad and grave, "We shall be glad to see you whenever it pleases you to come, will we not, Margaret?"

Lady Margaret had been standing with downcast eyes and appeared almost to be unaware of what had been transpiring, but now she raised her head, and her companions could see that her face was flushed and her eyes brilliant.

"Papa, you must do as you think best, but for myself I have no interest in being the dupe of this person ever again." Then with a look of scorn for Grey she turned and went to her carriage to wait for Lord Faulconer.

$$\sim$$

GREY FINALLY RETURNED to Pemberley that afternoon a weary and dejected man. He had parted with Mr. Devereaux at the gates of Castle Faulconer after their visit there.

"Well, Grey, I must leave you here," said the rector, "I need to visit a sick parishioner who lives nearby and have just time before evensong."

"How can I thank you for your kindness in accompanying me, and helping me to make my explanation. It was an act of true friendship that I will never forget," replied Grey.

"Oh, it was nothing, my dear fellow, and I was glad to be of assistance. And it is clear that Lord Faulconer holds you in as high esteem as ever and sympathized with your situation. Why, he said that he would have done the same thing; what good fortune that he was at Cambridge at the same time as your father and knew all about him."

"Yes, fortunate indeed," said Grey in a bitter tone, "Would that Lady Margaret were so understanding."

"I must admit that she seemed quite angry, and that some of her words before she left us must have wounded you deeply. However, no doubt she will change her attitude eventually and reconsider. Lady Margaret has a temper, as anyone can see, but I know that she has a kind heart."

"I hope you are correct, sir," replied Grey, "but at the moment the matter seems altogether without hope, and you are the only person who knows what that means to me."

"Oh, do not despair, my young friend," said Mr. Devereaux, turning his horse and calling back as he trotted off, "Come for dinner on Wednesday and we shall talk it all over. Farewell for now."

Grey's ride back to Pemberley gave him plenty of time for gloomy reflections. He did not think that Lady Margaret would ever forgive him. He knew that the scene in the drawing room of the castle that day would stay burned into his memory forever. Lord Faulconer had been kindness itself, and willing to believe only the best of Grey, but his daughter had left the room before the interview had even begun. Her eyes had been bright with anger, and she had seemed too beside herself with rage and disgust to speak at first. It was clear that she was present only at her father's earnest request. Grey had just begun to speak when she jumped up from her seat and said, "Father, if you are willing to hear any more lies from this duplicitous person, it is your affair, but it is more than I can stand. You must excuse me." She swept from the room, and was not seen again.

As he neared the house Grey's misery was so deep that at first he did not notice the noise and commotion that filled the courtyard of Pemberley. Finally he looked up and it penetrated his tired mind that his friends had returned from Scotlland.

End of Part Two

PART III

CHAPTER 33

"Good heavens! Poor Fitzwilliam," exclaimed Mr. Darcy, upon opening the first of a pile of letters he had just received. It had been ten days since the return to Pemberley, and repairs had been so far completed that he could now sit in his library again without becoming coated with plaster dust. Elizabeth and Anne sat by the fire reading, while Grey examined the bindings of books and replaced them on the newly built shelves.

Anne started violently at these words, dropping her book, and Elizabeth cried, "What on earth has happened!"

"Oh, I am sorry to have alarmed you, my love," said Darcy, scanning the rest of the letter quickly, "He will be fine, but my aunt reports that he will be confined to bed for the next few weeks."

Anne, who was beside herself with anxiety, rose from her chair and in another moment would have snatched the letter from her cousin's hand, but Darcy began to read its contents aloud, and with some difficulty she managed to sit down again and listen.

Dearest Nephew,

I am sorry to have some distressing news. My son is confined here with a broken leg. He and his father were out riding and his horse slipped on some loose stones as they were galloping along in their usual breakneck fashion.

Thank goodness it is the smaller bone in the lower leg that is broken; the fibula the physician called it. Your uncle sent for the best doctor in Edinburgh who gave us strict orders that Fitzwilliam was not to be moved for several weeks, but that he should heal perfectly well if all is done properly. As if this were not enough there was also a dislocation of the right shoulder and my unfortunate child has his arm in a sling to add to his discomfort.

You can imagine the difficulty of keeping my son quiet and amused, and I would wish you were all still here to assist me, except that it is now so cold and wintery here that you are better off back at Pemberley. We have never been here so late in the year and I never appreciated how harsh the wind can be. Fitzwilliam, who is always so calm and sweet-tempered, is quite agitated at being confined as he is, and I have never seen him so out of sorts. Of course he cannot write, but sends his love to you all, and wishes me to tell Anne to not neglect the fishing there, and that you, Darcy, are not a bad teacher should she wish to improve, until he can be there himself.

Your visit here gave us the greatest joy. How I love your Elizabeth, and am grateful for the happiness she has brought you. And it is such a gift to have had my darling niece with us. I am writing to them both, but wanted to get this news to you immediately. Think of us here, shivering in this bitter weather, and know that we send you our dearest love.

Your affectionate aunt,

Alicia Munford

"Oh, how dreadful for Fitzwilliam," cried Elizabeth, "He, especially, would be miserable condemned to such inactivity. But at least it seems that his injuries will heal completely."

"It must be very dreary for them all. You know that my uncle is fond of adhering to his plans; he is always in Yorkshire this time of year preparing for the hunting, and will be fretting about his hounds," said Darcy.

Anne had by now recovered somewhat from her shock and had managed to sit back in her chair with some degree of composure. Mr. Grey, however, had seen her turn pale, and read in the expression of her eyes, now bright with emotion, what her friends had been unable to detect during so many weeks in her company. She happened to look up and meet his gaze and when she saw the kindness and understanding there, found herself in danger of tears once again.

"Miss de Bourgh, I wonder if you would be so kind as to assist me in the long gallery for a few minutes," said Grey, "There are several dozen volumes of natural history to be brought down and replaced on the shelves, and I would like to have your opinion as to how they should be arranged."

"Why, certainly, Mr. Grey. I would be pleased to assist you in any way that I can," answered Anne in a faint voice. Elizabeth was reading Lady Alicia's letter for herself and Darcy was going through the rest of the day's correspondence, so that Anne was able to leave the room without any danger of her distress being noticed.

Half of the volumes belonging to the library were still in the gallery, spread out on tables so that Mr. Grey could enter the titles into the catalog he had been working on, and assess the need for any repair to the bindings. For some time he and Anne went over the collection and she was able to make some excellent suggestions, particularly with regard to those volumes that dealt with botany. She also made a list of several important books on the subject that should be acquired.

When Grey could see that she was now quite calm, he ventured, "Miss de Bourgh, perhaps you will allow me to add to the reassurance you have already received that your cousin will recover completely."

Anne looked up at him gravely for a moment, and then replied, "Oh, are you sure, Mr. Grey? Will he still be able to walk long distances and ride and hunt as well as ever? He would be so unhappy if he could not do so."

"Why yes, he will be as fit as ever in a couple of months. I speak with authority, for I have suffered both of your cousin's injuries, although not at the same time. And you see that I am quite well, although a bit more cautious than I once was."

They looked over the books on another table for a while, then Grey said, "It is unfortunate that Colonel Fitzwilliam's shoulder was dislocated, for otherwise I am sure he would write to you himself to let you know how he does."

"Why should you think so, Mr. Grey?" asked Anne somewhat suspiciously.

"Because you must be a great favorite with your cousin. That much is obvious."

"Indeed?"

"Indeed, yes," replied Grey, "A man does not teach a young lady to fish unless she is a great favorite. I can assure you of that."

Anne was beginning to smile, "And did you ever teach a young lady to fish, Mr. Grey."

"Why, yes I did, Miss de Bourgh. It was a lovely spot in the Pyrenees, the water just churning with trout."

"And did your lessons go well?"

"I cannot say that they did. In fact my rod ended up in the river." Grey began to laugh, and Anne could not help but join him in his mirth. Then he told a tale of salmon fishing in the west of Ireland and described the countryside and curious superstitions and customs there so entertainingly that Anne's mood lightened considerably.

Soon they were again searching through the piles of books that were strewn about the hall, all the time talking and laughing, so at ease were they in each other's company. Grey had been in so much haste to remove all the volumes from the library after he had discovered the leak, that little order had been preserved in their arrangement. Anne had enough knowledge to be of considerable assistance, and they accomplished a great deal in half an hour. Grey had just asked her to look for Herbert's *A Treatise on Tree Bark*, when they heard Elizabeth's light step on the stairs. She entered the gallery and with a sigh gazed about at the disorder of books heaped in every corner of the great chamber, but was still able to smile at her friends.

"Do not despair, Mrs. Darcy," said Grey, "By the end of the week all will be put to rights, as difficult as it may be to believe at the moment. With Miss de Bourgh's assistance I will soon be ready to direct the servants in replacing all these volumes on the shelves."

"Oh, I have every confidence that it will be so, Mr. Grey. You are so very kind to go to so much trouble and I am afraid that you are exhausting yourself. And *you*, my dear Anne, how good you are to spend this lovely morning among these dusty piles of books."

Anne replied that there were hardly any activities that could please her more, unless it were hunting for interesting beetles in the woods.

"But I am here to tell you that my husband has proposed an outing for this afternoon, since the weather is so unusually fine," continued Elizabeth, "There are some wonderful views he wishes to show you which are not far from here, and he promises that there will be no shortage of interesting rocks, Mr. Grey. We shall set out in the barouche after lunch, and end our excursion at Castle Faulconer, as they have sent to ask us to visit them this afternoon."

Grey looked up eagerly, but at once his face became grave as he said, "Perhaps it would be better if I were to remain here. There is so much to be done that I do not wish to lose a single hour."

"Oh no, Mr. Grey!" cried Elizabeth gaily, "You shall not escape. You have spent almost every moment working in this room ever since we returned from Scotland. No, you must tolerate an afternoon in our company as best you can. In any event, Lord Faulconer mentioned you particularly in his note, and says that he has missed seeing you at the castle recently."

"The note was from Lord Faulconer then? Not from Lady Margaret?" asked Grey, looking even more dejected. Elizabeth replied in the affirmative and the young man made another attempt to avoid the proposed excursion, but found that it was impossible to withstand the enthusiasm of his hostess. All the while Anne was studying him with sympathetic interest.

Why he really *is* in love with Lady Margaret, she thought, It is clear from his despairing look every time her name is mentioned and I should have seen it before. Anne wished that there were some way in which she could help her new friend, for whom her esteem had grown with every passing day.

Elizabeth returned to the library where Darcy was discussing a new method for pasture drainage with one of his tenants. The farmer soon departed, and Darcy left his desk to sit by the fire with his wife.

"Well, my love," began Elizabeth, "Everything is in train for our little expedition today, although I must say that Mr. Grey tried his best to avoid accompanying us."

"I can understand that he is hesitant to go to Castle Faulconer. You saw how Lady Margaret treated him when she and her father called on us last week. Why, she did not even acknowledge his presence other than by a frigid nod in his direction. I have never seen her treat anyone thus, and it shocks me for I have always thought her so good-natured. Her father, as usual, was gracious and kind."

"Yes, his friendship for Mr. Grey is unchanged at least. But do you think that the neighborhood will ever forgive him for concealing his identity? At church last Sunday I thought everyone very unfriendly and cold to him."

"Certainly, dearest," replied Darcy, "Mr. Devereaux's evident respect and liking for Grey will go a long way to ensure that any difficulties in that regard will soon be overcome. "

"It will be a bitter disappointment for Lady Templeton. What a malicious old woman!"

"You know what a difficult time I had persuading Grey not to leave us," said Darcy, "Why, I found him almost packed and prepared to be on his way the evening we returned from Scotland. If you had not added your earnest plea that he remain, I do not think that I would have prevailed."

They sat quietly together for a while, and then Elizabeth said softly, "You know, my love, I suspect that Mr. Grey may have a *tendresse* for Lady Margaret. Do you think me very fanciful?"

Darcy smiled, and then raising his wife's hand to his lips, replied, "No, my angel. As always I am of your opinion. *And* I believe this visit to the Faulconers may have been at your instigation. I observed your little *tête à tête* with Lord Faulconer in front of the church on Sunday."

"Well, we did agree that any estrangement was a great misfortune that must not be allowed to continue. That dear Lord Faulconer is so very good and so firm a friend of Mr. Grey. Are we really to continue to call him Mr. Grey?"

"Yes, for he is quite adamant that he will be known by his mother's family name. He is distressed to have offended his aunt, Lady Belthorpe, who was unhappy to have to learn from Lady Templeton that her nephew had returned from abroad. Grey has written to apologize and plans to go to Bath in a few weeks to see her and make amends."

"And is Lady Belthorpe his mother's sister?"

"Yes, and Grey says that she is the only one of his relations to whom he is attached. He lived with her for a year or so after his mother's death, and would have remained there until he was old enough to go to school, but unfortunately Lord Harwith remembered that he had a son and insisted that the boy be returned to him. What sort of wretched life Grey must have had with such a father can hardly be imagined."

Elizabeth looked thoughtful for a while, and then said, "We must all admire Mr. Grey, for he is a fine man in spite of having such a parent. How fortunate we both have been to have had fathers whom we could esteem."

"Yes, fortunate indeed," agreed Darcy, "Why, think of poor Anne. It was such a dreadful thing for her to lose her father."

"And was he a very superior sort of man?" inquired Elizabeth.

"Oh, the best, and sensible as well. He would never have treated his daughter like an invalid and kept her from every form of enjoyment in life. My aunt was a very agreeable woman before his death, but since then she has become more difficult with every year that passes."

"Well, my love, you and I will rescue Anne. I would like to see her well married and never to live at Rosings again. If I am not mistaken, Lord Holland is a very determined man"

"After some reflection, then, you still believe that he might do as a match for our cousin? That he would make her happy?" asked Darcy.

"Yes, I do think so, for he is so very intelligent and shares so many of her interests. And he will be here in less than a month," replied Elizabeth, and then added, "You do think well of him do you not?" for Darcy's face had become very serious as soon as the young man's name had been pronounced.

With what seemed to be something of an effort, Darcy smiled, and then said, "Of course. How could I not like the man who saved your life! He will be very welcome. In view of his attentions to Anne, I have, however, made inquiries of friends in London as to his fortune and character, and before he arrives I should know a great deal more about Lord Holland."

CHAPTER 34

$\mathcal{T}$he weather was not quite as favorable that afternoon as had been hoped, for although the rain had held off, there was a chill wind, and the ladies admired the countryside from the shelter of the various blankets and shawls with which Darcy insisted in enveloping them.

Anne was enraptured with the magnificence of the rugged peaks and the lovely vales of ancient trees through which they passed. She was so at ease with her friends by now that she did not hesitate to express her enthusiastic delight in what lay before them.

"I believe that I find this country even more beautiful than Scotland," she said, as the carriage turned back to take the road towards Castle Faulconer, "There is so much contrast between the wild moorland and the verdant dales that one could never tire of this landscape."

"I am of your opinion, Miss de Bourgh," said Mr. Grey, "as much as I love Scotland. And Derbyshire has the further attraction of being well supplied with caverns."

"You and your caverns!" cried Darcy, looking at his friend with affection and exasperation, "I suppose that now you will be exploring every burrow for miles around."

"Indeed I will," replied Grey, "and I hope that Dr. Gilmore-Jones will soon be able to accompany me, if his doctor will allow him to throw away his cane."

"It is his wife who will decide that question, you may be sure, and I think it will be some weeks before you enjoy the pleasure of your old mentor's company."

"Well, so be it," answered Grey unconcernedly, "I would do nothing to distress the lady, and in any case, I am quite used to going into caverns by myself. I have done so all over Europe."

Anne had many questions about caverns at this point, and Mr. Grey's learned disquisition on the subject lasted for the rest of the journey to Castle Faulconer. Although the young man was evidently very much out of spirits in comparison with his usual liveliness, he had made every effort to be a pleasant companion and not to burden his friends with a consciousness of his unhappiness.

"And so, Miss de Bourgh," he concluded, as the carriage came within sight of the castle, "You have no doubt perceived, after this lengthy monologue of mine, that we in fact know almost nothing of how these interesting natural features in the landscape came to be, but if I live long enough I hope to throw some light on the subject, so to speak."

This last remark was punctuated by an exclamation of delight from Elizabeth, whose first visit to Castle Faulconer this was.

"What a splendid and romantic building!" she cried, "It is my very idea of a fairy tale castle, even to the moat and battlements."

"I knew it would please you, my love," said Darcy, "It is unusual in having been so well preserved and very little altered or added onto. Not like my uncle's castle, which was almost a ruin when he began work on it."

As they crossed an ancient bridge over the willow-lined river, Lady Margaret's gardens could be seen ascending the long slope up to the venerable building whose stones were a soft golden color in the afternoon sunlight.

"What a magnificent garden!" said Anne, "I seem to remember hearing that Lady Margaret designed it all herself."

"Indeed, yes," said Grey in an animated tone, "Her taste and originality are extraordinary, do you not agree?"

Something in his tone made them all turn to look at him and at once Grey's face became solemn again.

Lord Faulconer was to be seen standing just within the great stone gates of the front courtyard. He greeted his guests with evident pleasure, gallantly handing the ladies down from the carriage in his sweetly old fashioned and courtly manner.

"Well, well, here you are at last. Mrs. Darcy, Miss de Bourgh, I bid you welcome and hope that this will be the first of many, many visits to Castle Faulconer. Your presence here today confers the greatest pleasure and honor upon our house. Darcy, Grey, I am delighted to see you."

His guests expressed their thanks for this amiable reception, and soon they were all seated in the drawing room, where Lady Margaret had met them with her usual vivacious charm.

"My dear friends, how happy it makes me to see you here. And of course, you are to stay to dine with us. Papa did not specify it in his note, did he? But it goes without saying."

In vain did her company protest that they were not dressed for dinner as they had been driving about the countryside, but Lady Margaret laughed and said, "No matter, for we are *en famille,* as it should be with our nearest neighbors and best of friends!"

Poor Grey received no benefit from the kindness of their hostess, for she pointedly ignored him except for a cold motion of greeting in his direction.

Soon they were all seated and taking tea, and Lady Margaret began the conversation by inquiring about the visitors who were expected at Pemberley.

"Mrs. Darcy, you are to have quite a full house within the next month, are you not?" she asked, "It is a great deal of trouble for you, I am afraid."

"I made every effort to dissuade my wife from attempting so much, and I admit I would prefer to live a reclusive existence this first year of our marriage," said Darcy, "but it seems we are to have guests continually through Christmas."

"Lady Grinspoon is to arrive in two weeks time from London, and is to bring dear Georgiana with her," said Elizabeth, "As you know, my new sister has been spending the last few months in Devonshire in the family of a school friend. I have been longing for her to come to us, as we have not seen her since the spring. And in a little more than a month we expect Lord Holland, a very agreeable young man, who was so good as to save my life when we were in Scotland."

Nothing would do at this point but for Elizabeth to narrate the story of her narrow escape from death and Lord Holland's bravery and excellent horsemanship. Lord Faulconer and his daughter were duly impressed, and said that they would look forward to meeting such a paragon of a young man. Darcy and Grey were silent, each reflecting, no doubt, that he could have effected such a rescue of a lady in danger with at least equal dash and gallantry had he been given the opportunity.

"We have some expectation of seeing Lady Catherine, Anne's mother, here at some point during the next month or so. And my parents, and my aunt and uncle will be with us for Christmas, along with my younger sisters and my nephews and nieces," continued Elizabeth, "but perhaps most delightfully, my sister Jane and Mr. Bingley are to be with us in only a fortnight's time."

"Ah, yes," said Lord Faulconer, " and how pleased we will be to meet them. We do know Mr. Bingley, as you have brought him here several times in years past, my dear Darcy, but now we look forward with great anticipation to becoming acquainted with his bride."

"As you all know, " said Darcy, "we have some hope that they may settle here in the vicinity, for if anything could increase our happiness it would be to have the Bingleys near us."

"Indeed, I have something particular to say in that regard," said Lord Faulconer, "I have been in correspondence with Lady Blanchard about Thrushfold Hall, and after much deliberation she has decided to sell the place. It is a beautiful spot, as you know, and not more than twelve miles from Pemberley. The house is a distinguished building dating from the time of Queen Anne, and the park has many delightful natural attractions, including one of the finest stands of oak I have ever seen. Much needs to be done, for the Hall is in some disrepair, but I do not think that will deter Mr. and Mrs. Bingley."

"No, in fact I think they will enjoy making it all their own by the process of restoration and improvement. You are very good, sir, to have taken so much trouble to inquire about it," said Darcy.

"Not at all, not at all," said his host, "It will add greatly to our happiness if they like the place and decide to stay here among us, will it not my dear," he concluded turning to his daughter.

"Yes, what joy for us all," cried Lady Margaret, "I have an idea! When your sister and her husband arrive, Mrs. Darcy, perhaps we can all go together to see Thrushfold Hall, and make a very pleasant outing of it."

"Perhaps we should secure the services of an architect from London to accompany us and give some notion of what needs to be done," suggested Lord Faulconer, and everyone agreed that this was an excellent idea.

Anne, who had said little up to this point said, "What a pity my cousin Fitzwilliam cannot be here, for I think that he knows as much about houses as any architect."

This led to an explanation of Fitzwilliam's misfortune in being thrown from his horse, and the description of his injuries and expected recovery. "But we hope that he may be here in a few week's time, if his duties permit it, for I am sure he will return to his regiment as soon as possible," said Darcy.

"How very shocking it is to be injured!" exclaimed Lady Margaret, "Even the best of horsemen are subject such accidents. I suppose I have been very fortunate."

"Considering the way you tear about the countryside, Lady Margaret, I would say that an angel must ride at your side every minute," said Mr. Grey, who had been mostly silent until now.

This led to some good natured raillery at Lady Margaret's expense on the part of her old friend Mr. Darcy, and a repetition of her father's entreaties that she give up any idea of hunting that year. She took it all in good part, but was clearly not to be influenced by anyone in her determination to follow her own inclination and be as reckless as she wished.

At last Elizabeth changed the subject, saying, "Lady Margaret, would you be so good as to show us about your gardens while it is still full daylight? I have heard so much of your rose beds and would be grateful for any advice as to how to improve the ones we have at Pemberley."

No request could have pleased Lady Margaret so well, and she led the company out of doors with the caution that, "Of course, nothing looks very well this late in the season, but there are still a few fine blooms to be seen in a sheltered spot near a south facing wall."

The sun had come out and the wind had died down, so that it was now a perfect autumn afternoon. As the group wandered about the gardens, Lady Margaret became animated and gay with such an attentive and appreciative audience, explaining how she had come to see that a series of terraces ascending from the river was most suitable for the austere setting of the castle.

"No doubt everything I have done here is against the current fashion, and I am sure would not meet with the approval of Mr. Gilpin and his followers. However, I do not mind saying that I believe that the result is somewhat successful and suits the place fairly well."

"Your gardens always put me in mind of Italy, Lady Margaret," ventured Grey, "Were you not influenced by your time there in the overall scheme?"

She turned to look at him with a mocking smile, "It is possible, Mr. Grey, but it is not very agreeable of you to make the observation. How pleasant it would have been to let my friends believe that it has all been my own genius at work."

"We are still convinced of your brilliance, Lady Meg," said Darcy, "and if you did borrow some of your ideas from Roman gardens, I have no doubt you have greatly improved upon them."

They continued to walk about, and Elizabeth, who knew the way to a gardener's heart, asked many questions. Upon reaching the roses she exclaimed with delight at the many rare and exquisite varieties to be seen.

"I will cut some for the dinner table this evening," said her hostess, " and then you shall take them home with you." So saying she took up a basket and a pair of scissors that sat upon a wall, and began to search out the finest blooms for Mrs. Darcy.

While his daughter was so engaged, Lord Faulconer, with a degree of guile highly uncharacteristic of him, managed to lead Anne and the

Darcys to a spot at a little distance on the excuse of showing them a fine prospect. Grey was quick to see his opportunity and went to speak to Lady Margaret.

"Will you give me permission to call upon you tomorrow, and give some fuller explanation of my circumstances, Lady Margaret? If you understood what led to the misrepresentation of which I admit to have been guilty, perhaps I could regain your confidence."

"I have heard it all, Mr. Grey. Do you not suppose that my father has repeated your justifications to me? He has defended you most faithfully, but I confess that I do not have his kind and forgiving nature. My good opinion, once forfeited, is not likely to be regained."

"If you knew what my life has been!" said the young man despairingly, "But I see that you have no interest in understanding me."

At that moment Lady Margaret dropped the rose she had just cut with a little cry of dismay, and a few bright drops of blood fell on her white muslin gown.

"Oh, you are wounded!" cried Grey, "Allow me to help you."

He took hold of her hand, and producing a linen handkerchief from his pocket wrapped it gently around the afflicted finger, keeping some pressure to stop the bleeding.

The lady resisted at first, but then allowed his attentions quietly.

"No rose without a thorn, Lady Margaret, " said Grey very softly, holding her gaze with his own.

For a moment he thought that he saw not anger but sadness in her eyes, and his heart leapt with an almost painful joy, but at once she pulled her hand away violently.

"That may be true, Mr. Grey, but, I still do my best to avoid the thorns. Only a fool would do otherwise."

She turned away and hastened to rejoin the rest of her guests, who had by now descended towards the river, and were walking among the old willows on its banks. Grey stood watching her for a minute, then stooped down to retrieve the fallen rose.

There was no further possibility of any private conversation, even had the young man had the heart to attempt it, for he had all he could do to appear to be in good spirits. After dinner everyone had the rare pleasure of hearing Lady Margaret play the harp, which she did with great skill and perfect taste. As many times as Grey had dined at the castle his hostess had never condescended to display this accomplishment before.

How very defenseless is the person who plays before company, thought Grey, for I can study that beautiful countenance at length without being considered impertinent. How like an angel she is, and how I wish she would look up at me if only for a moment!

As if in answer to his thought, Lady Margaret did look up and her eyes met Grey's, but he could not read their expression. Her fingers stumbled over the next few notes and she tossed her head with a gesture of annoyance. One more song, ancient and sad, completed the evening, for she would play no more, and the party soon broke up.

CHAPTER 35

*A*lthough Anne spent much of her time thinking anxiously of Fitzwilliam and waiting impatiently for another letter from her aunt, the next few weeks were in some ways the most agreeable she had ever known. Her friends, and especially Mr. Grey, with the utmost kindness and delicacy of feeling did everything possible to nurture her growing self-assurance. It was an extraordinary thing for Anne to have her opinion sought and to be listened to with sincere interest when she ventured to take part in the general conversation. This was very different from her experience in Scotland, where there had been so many people and the subject matter under discussion had been of a more frivolous nature and quite foreign to Anne's thoughtful cast of mind. At the dinner table at Pemberley there was a great deal of laughter, as well as lively discussion of literature, natural philosophy and history, all the things most interesting to her. Anne was pleased to discover that her lonely childhood at Rosings had at least afforded her a reasonable grounding in the many topics that arose. Always, when she began to speak, she would become aware of Mr. Grey listening with great attention, and the esteem and liking she saw in his bright, kind eyes gave her courage.

When they spoke of novels, Darcy, who had read nothing more

recent then *Evelina*, was a bit at sea, while his wife and friends knew the latest books that were all the rage in London.

"In a few days you will have the famous 'Charles Ellcroft' as your guest, my love," said Elizabeth to her husband one evening when they were all at dinner. "Perhaps you should read one of Lady Grinspoon's books before she arrives, so that you will have some knowledge of her work."

"Oh, the renowned Charles Ellcroft!," cried Grey, "How I look forward to meeting her. I have read everything Lady Grinspoon has written with the greatest of pleasure."

"You see, Darcy," he continued, "you make a great mistake by not reading novels. How else can we men learn the proper way to behave? It has been my salvation, I can tell you. Otherwise my only idea of good conduct would have been what I learned from being cudgeled by the amiable masters at our old school."

"You may be correct, Grey, but *not* reading novels does not seem to have injured me in any material way," replied Darcy, smiling at Elizabeth.

"Well, there you have been luckier than you deserve," said his friend, "but what do you think, Miss de Bourgh? Does fiction add to our understanding of society?"

"Why, I suppose that I could just say that it depends on the novelist," replied Anne, "but I know that you will not let me off with such a simple response, Mr. Grey."

"You are correct," said the young man gleefully, "No simple responses will do at this table. We must all be as verbose and recondite as possible. Is that not your rule, Darcy?"

"Certainly, it must be so when you are here, old friend," replied his host.

"It is a pity that Lady Grinspoon is not with us yet," said Anne, "for she has certainly given this question a great deal of consideration. But I will venture to assert that I think most novels are at fault in making the characters either too virtuous or altogether too bad. Surely most people are neither so perfectly one or the other?"

"You are right, Miss de Bourgh," said Grey, after a moment's reflection, "but from my own experience I can state that while the perfectly good man may be an impossibility in this imperfect world, the perfectly villainous one is not."

His friends, knowing what experience Grey had of villainy in his own father, did not press him to elaborate. The disadvantage of such a parent seemed to pursue the young man even in Derbyshire, for the local people had still not forgiven him for his having assumed a false identity when he first came among them. There was coolness towards Grey in the neighborhood, although he was now included in every invitation that was sent to Pemberley. This state of affairs might have continued for a while longer had it not been for an incident that turned the tide of popular opinion.

THE WEATHER HAD BEEN VERY pleasant and Anne had been out riding every day with Grey and Darcy. Elizabeth, pleading the necessity of preparing for so many guests, had not accompanied them, instead insisting that Anne ride her mare, Eilis. If Darcy suspected that his wife's near escape in Scotland had affected her pleasure in riding, he said nothing but was pleased to encourage Anne's progress as a horsewoman.

Eilis, sensible and sure-footed, was the perfect mount for Anne whose riding improved rapidly. Soon she was confident enough to gallop and to take small jumps under the careful tutelage of her friends.

One day they were riding along a ridge top and making their way to a rather distant farm where Darcy wished to call upon one of his tenants.

"I must tell you, Miss de Bourgh," said Grey, "that it is remarkable that you have been riding for less than three months, for anyone seeing you would think that you had been brought up to it."

"Thank you, Mr. Grey," replied Anne, smiling happily, "certainly nothing has ever given me greater pleasure. What delight to be out here in all this beauty and to have the freedom to go wherever one wishes!"

"Oh, my cousin's aptitude for riding does not surprise me," said

Darcy, "It is in the blood. Anne's father was a superb horseman, and my aunt in her day was a fearless and expert rider."

"How I wish I could have known her then!" cried Anne, "I cannot imagine my mother doing anything but what duty and prudence demand. She must have been so very different when she was a young woman."

"Indeed, she was," said her cousin, "She changed a great deal after your father and brother died. When I was a young boy she was always gay and happy, alert for any possibility of amusement and pleasure, and ready to play games with us or take us riding."

"I was too young then to have anything but a very indistinct recollection of those days. How very sad it is," said Anne.

Her reflections were interrupted by Mr. Grey, who said in an urgent voice, "Do you see all that smoke rising on the other side of the next hilltop, Darcy?"

"Good heavens!" cried Darcy in alarm, "It is coming from the farm of my tenant, Mr. Smith."

They cantered over to the brow of the hill, where the view across the valley below afforded them the sight of a well-built farmhouse, now in flames, with the evidence of frantic efforts by the inhabitants of the place to save the building. Darcy led his friends along a steep path down the slope and in a few minutes they had reached the farmyard.

Mr. Smith came running over to them at once, followed by his two sturdy sons, who looked exhausted and fearful.

"It just started a few mintues ago," cried the poor farmer, "We tried to beat it out, but had to get my wife and the younger ones outside." And he pointed to Mrs. Smith who stood nearby with two small children who were weeping pitiably.

In a moment Darcy and Grey were off their horses and organizing a line of men from the nearby stream to the burning house. Several laborers had seen the smoke and had run to help, and buckets were passed along rapidly. For the space of half an hour they worked desperately, but it soon became clear that the fire had advanced too quickly, and that the best that could be hoped was that the other farm buildings might be saved.

Grey broke away from the line for a moment to see how Anne was managing, and found that she had moved away to a little distance with the horses. She had tethered them to a fence and was speaking gently to Mrs. Smith and her children, who seemed to look to the young lady for comfort.

"Are you doing well enough with the horses, Miss de Bourgh? How very good you are at managing them. But I will send one of the farm lads to take them from you in a few minutes."

"Oh, we are all right here, Mr. Grey. Please, do not be concerned," said Anne calmly, "but I am afraid that poor Mrs. Smith is terribly distressed."

"I shall be right enough soon, my lady," said the unfortunate woman through her tears, " Your ladyship had been so kind."

As Grey began to walk back to the farmyard, he heard one of the children, a little girl about five years old, crying for her puppy and saw her struggle to get away from her mother's strong grasp.

He turned back and bending down to the child asked her, "Why, where is your puppy, my dear?"

"Oh, sir, her small dog that her father just brought to her last week was in its basket in the parlor," said Mrs. Smith, "only six weeks old, the poor little thing."

Grey quickly asked a question about the interior of the house, and then ran to the stream where he took off his coat and soaked it through. Covering his head and shoulders with the garment, he made his way to the front door of the flaming house and disappeared inside. Anne was astonished at his bravery, although that end of the building was not yet engulfed in flames. Darcy and the other men paused for a moment in amazement, unable to imagine what Grey could be about.

Before anyone had sufficient time to react, Grey reappeared with the puppy in his arms. The young man was covered with soot, but was unharmed, and he hastened over to the little girl who received her pet with rapturous delight.

"There, child, I believe he is quite unhurt. I had no difficulty finding him as he was crying with fright."

"I've always known that you were a bit mad, Grey," said Darcy, "and now I suppose that everyone will be aware of the fact."

Anne had handed over the horses to a farm boy, and was standing nearby, her face full of admiration for her friend, "Oh, Mr. Grey, that was a splendid thing to do!"

The house had been given up for lost by now, and the exhausted men soon formed a circle around Grey and Darcy. In a moment Darcy turned his attention to his unhappy tenants, who were staring in dejection at their smoking house.

"It is my own fault, sir," said Mr. Smith, "Three times this year you wanted to send your mason to rebuild that chimney, but I always put it off because we did not want the house in disorder. What a price to pay for my bad judgment!"

"Do not distress yourself, for we shall put it all to rights," said Darcy, "Why, Lady Margaret has given me some ideas which will allow us to rebuild the place to be better than before." Turning to Mrs. Smith he assured her that a cart would come at once to fetch the family and whatever possessions they had managed to save, "for as you know I have a vacant house near the village, and you will be comfortable there while we rebuild."

Finally all was arranged, and plans set in motion for the reconstruction to begin immediately, and Darcy was able to return home with Anne and Grey.

They were much later than had been expected, and Elizabeth, who had been watching for them, came to greet them eagerly.

"I was beginning to worry," she began, but then was speechless at the sight of Grey with his face covered with soot and his ruined coat. Being a sensible woman she did not waste time in exclamations, but gave them an opportunity to explain what had happened.

"How very kind of you to rescue that poor child's pet, Mr. Grey, "said Elizabeth later when they were all at dinner," but you could have been killed! What if the roof had fallen?"

"Perhaps it was not a rational act, Mrs. Darcy," replied the young man, " but I can remember a time when a small dog was my only friend, just when I was the same age as the little girl."

Grey's action that day had the good effect of bringing about a reversal of the opinion held of him in the neighborhood. Many thought him to have been absurd to risk his life to save a dog, but none could deny that it was an indication of a tender heart. The ladies were touched and declared that Mr. Grey was clearly nothing like his disreputable father. The gentlemen smiled and shook their heads at the idea of such a foolish deed, but decided that he must be a good sort of fellow. In truth, everyone was delighted to have a young nobleman to ask to dinner, especially one who was so conveniently unattached, and Grey suddenly became the favorite of all the mothers with households of unmarried daughters.

CHAPTER 36

*A*fter some weeks of serious effort Elizabeth was at last able to take some rest from her labors and to feel that Pemberley was well prepared for the arrival of their guests, even should they all appear in the same hour. She and the housekeeper, Mrs. Reynolds, had come to understand each other very well, and the household was beginning to run more smoothly than at any time since the death of Darcy's mother. The servants, who had not known what to expect of their master's bride, now regarded her as seasoned troops look to a new officer who shows every sign of possessing a genius for leadership. Elizabeth had no experience of the running of a great house but she had a rational mind and a good- natured but unequivocal way of issuing orders that led everyone to obey with cheerful alacrity.

What she had not thought to find in her marriage was the kind of thoughtful and reliable friend that her husband was proving to be. From her own observation of her parents she had been afraid that after the initial months of conjugal felicity had passed that Darcy might begin to drift towards that sort of benevolent indifference that marked her father's disposition. But even Elizabeth, with her determination to comprehend the truth of any situation even if it should cause discomfiture, had to see that her husband was more in love with her than ever and that his devotion became more evident with every passing day.

One night as they sat together on their favorite window seat, from which the starlit park and lake were visible, Elizabeth made some remark about the ephemeral nature of love and happiness.

"Is there not a universal tendency to learn indifference to even the greatest beauty of nature and landscape if it is there to be admired every day? Will there ever come a time when we look out of this window with less than rapture at such perfection? And I am afraid, from what I have observed of life, that time and habit may have the same influence over love."

Darcy looked thoughtful for a moment, then smiled and drew her to him, "No, my angel, that will never happen to us though we live together for sixty years and end as two ancients sitting by our hearth. I waited for so long to find you, then to win you, and now you are my first thought morning and evening and all the hours in between. I would no more let our love die than I would let Pemberley fall into ruins."

If any man were likely to keep such a promise it was Darcy, who seemed to order his life in such a way that he never forgot what was most important to him. No one at Pemberley had ever seen him in a temper, and although he could be stern on occasion this was almost never necessary as something about the young man made instant obedience to his wishes seem the only possibility.

"Yes, my lady, the master is so much like his father," said Mrs. Reynolds one day, "There is never any question that his way is the best way."

Elizabeth was delighted to be able to agree with this statement and her admiration and respect for her husband continued to grow as she watched him deal with his tenants and all the complexities of a large estate. But perhaps the greatest source of her happiness proceeded from her consciousness that he considered her his friend as well as his beloved. Darcy discussed all that passed at Pemberley with his wife, teaching her about the details of its management with an evident appreciation for her intelligence and judgment. Elizabeth, who had never known her parents to have a serious conversation, was gratified and delighted to feel that she was important to her husband in this way.

Far from leaving Elizabeth alone to contend with all the difficulties of preparing for so many guests, Darcy spent time with her every day going over the plans for accommodating and entertaining their friends. He was often present at her sessions with Mrs. Reynolds and was able to make useful suggestions. "Who would ever have thought that a gentleman could understand so much about housekeeping," remarked that good woman one day in astonishment.

Each afternoon Darcy would come in search of his wife and insist that she take a walk with him; they had formed the habit of following a different direction each day, either through the beautiful woods towards the hills behind Pemberley or along the stream. Sometimes they would encounter Anne, who had not neglected to begin fishing with the rod Fitzwilliam had given her. She had begun to find all the best spots with the help of Darcy's elderly gamekeeper who usually followed along behind her at a respectful distance carrying her creel, although she often threw her catch back. Occasionally Grey would be out fishing as well, and advising Anne on the selection of dry flies.

One day shortly before the arrival of Lady Grinspoon, who was the harbinger of all their guests, Darcy produced a letter from his pocket as he and Elizabeth walked along a familiar path.

"I have received a letter from Dr. Crawford, dearest, but could not very well discuss it at breakfast, as you will see. You remember that he is always in Bath this time of year, and that I had written to him with some questions?"

"Oh, yes," replied Elizabeth. "Let us sit here for a moment, for I am anxious to read it."

After they were seated on a bench by the path, she read as follows:

My dear Sir,

I thank you for your recent letter, and I am pleased to be able to reply with favorable news of Lady Catherine. As you know, I had not seen her for two months, as I had been obliged to return to London, but I had left her care in the hands of the excellent Dr. Winslow. He has sent me reports of her progress, but when I saw her on my arrival here her evident improvement in health and spirits exceeded my fondest hopes. Your aunt may not only be said to have recovered from her illness, but I believe that she is actually more vigorous and cheerful than I have ever seen her. I certainly give some credit for this transformation to the salutary effects of taking the waters here, but believe that the agreeable social intercourse and constant variety to be found at Bath has been an equally efficacious treatment. Lady Catherine has expressed a wish to come to you at Pemberley at some point before Christmas, and I was pleased to be able to give my permission for her to undertake the journey.

As to your second point of inquiry, my response must be less exact, but I hope that I can be of some assistance to you at least. I am not personally acquainted with the Marquess of Roscree, but know something of the family, which has long been held in the highest respect. Of a long and noble line there now remain only the elder brother, the current marquess, and Lord Holland. I have seen the young marquess in the pump room several times in the last week, and have observed him as closely as I could in an unobtrusive manner. He is always conveyed in a Bath chair and appears to be extremely weak, as he has difficulty even sitting upright. I cannot be certain whether he can walk, but it seems unlikely. From his extreme pallor, and frequent cough, I am afraid that the young man may have a serious affliction of the lungs. Were I his physician, I would be in some doubt of his surviving the winter. As you will comprehend, dear sir, for me to inquire more fully of his own physician and relay the information thus obtained to you would fall outside the ethical boundaries of my profession.

You also asked for any intelligence that might be attainable as to the reputation of the Marquess of Roscree's younger brother, Lord Holland. I can only say that I have heard nothing to his discredit, although he has spent little time in Bath. There seems to be a general feeling that he made something of a noble sacrifice by leaving the Royal Navy to be of assistance to his brother.

I hope that this communication is of some use to you, and that you will not hesitate to inform me of any way in which I may serve you in the future.

I have the honor to be, etc. etc.,

Reginald Crawford

"Ah, our good Dr. Crawford," said Darcy with a smile, "He is always direct and to the point."

"Well, he has been very prompt in answering your letter," said Elizabeth, "Did you inform him as to the reason for your interest in Lord Holland and his brother?"

"I did say that Holland had been quite attentive to Anne in Scotland, and that it seemed prudent to know more of his family and situation."

"The poor marquess! How sad to have lost one's health at such an early age. Was it not due to some sort of misadventure?"

"Yes, he almost drowned while swimming in the loch at his estate in Scotland, and has never been well since. I disliked having to inquire as to his health, but as it affects Holland's prospects in such a material way I felt bound to do so, although from other sources I have learned that Holland has a considerable fortune of his own."

"Well, at least we can feel that he is not an ineligible young man, and that we have not made an error in inviting him here," said Elizabeth, "If she does like him, then there should be no great obstacles in their path."

"You mean my aunt, of course. I'm afraid that she will press Anne to accept Holland, which will make my cousin learn to dislike the match. I'm certain that Anne will not be pleased to hear that her mother is planning a visit."

Anne had received a letter of her own that day, in which her mother informed her that she would soon enjoy the superior care and protection that only Lady Catherine could provide. This was far from welcome news, and other aspects of the letter caused her even more distress, especially the closing paragraphs:

After Christmas we will return to Rosings, where I am sure that the quieter pace of life will be beneficial to you, my dear child. As you have been at pains to reassure me, I have no doubt that my nephew and his bride have made every effort to look after you properly, but with your delicate constitution you must be in great need of rest and repose. Now that my own health has improved, we can return to our old way of life at home and I am sure that you will be grateful to do so. Perhaps, if you are sufficiently strong, we will make a brief visit to Bath in eight or nine month's time. Elizabeth has written that she and Darcy are eager to have you with them in London for the season next year, but I do not believe that this is advisable. The frenzied whirl of social activities in the cold damp so common there could have serious consequences for one so fragile.

I was distressed to learn of Fitzwilliam's injuries, and sympathize with the poor boy for having to lie there for weeks in that gloomy place with only his parents for company. But I must admit that I have been a bit put out with your cousin. He neglected to bring his courtship of Lady Emma Foxworth to a happy conclusion before he left Bath to go to Scotland, and now the affair will drag on for heaven knows how many months. I cannot imagine why he has not made his addresses to her, for they always seemed to be talking together earnestly in some corner of the Assembly Rooms or wherever they might happen to be. And since Fitzwilliam has been gone the poor young lady has become quite pale and spiritless. I cannot but think that your cousin is in love with her, for she is remarkably beautiful and known for her accomplishments and sweet temper. No doubt there is some silly lover's quarrel at work here and as soon as he is able your cousin will return and propose. It should be so, for the young lady's mother and I have gone to considerable trouble to forward the match.

Lady Catherine, could hardly have composed a letter that was so well designed to distress her daughter had she expended hours of effort over the production with malicious intent. That it was no doubt written with sincere maternal solicitude and a perfect ignorance of Anne's feelings was of no consolation, of course. Elizabeth found the young lady wandering about the library in an aimless and disconsolate fashion, still holding the letter.

"Well, my dear Anne, here you are," cried Elizabeth, "I am surprised, as Darcy and I expected to find you fishing with Mr. Grey as the weather is so fine. We have just returned from our walk by the stream."

"Oh, yes, cousin," replied Anne, trying to smile, "Perhaps I will go out in a little while."

Elizabeth could see the effort that the girl was making to appear cheerful, but decided not to allow the pretense to continue.

"Come sit with me, Anne," she said, "and we will talk for a while.

You have had a letter from your mother, and I can see that it has distressed you greatly."

By now Anne had every confidence in Elizabeth's kindness and affection for her, and by way of reply simply handed the letter over for her friend's perusal.

After she had finished reading Lady Catherine's missive, Elizabeth gave it back to Anne, saying, "I understand it all, my dear."

For a moment Anne thought that Mrs. Darcy might have guessed the truth of her feelings for Fitzwilliam, but it was soon apparent that she only referred to the prospect of Anne's being immured at Rosings once again.

"But we shall not allow it to happen!" cried Elizabeth with determination, "When your mother is here we shall persuade her to let us take you to London with us in March. At the worst you will be at Rosings for only a few weeks."

"Oh, yes, we know how persuadable my mother is," said Anne with a bitter smile, "No, once I am there it will be almost impossible to leave again."

"You must have more faith in me and in my husband," said Elizabeth with determination, "Why I have stood up to your mother on more than one occasion, and I am quite capable of doing so again."

"How dear you are to me, how true a friend," said Anne taking Elizabeth's hand, "and if anyone can change my mother's mind I am sure it will be you. I will not give up hope while you are with me."

Elizabeth was happy at this evidence of affection and embraced the girl fondly, saying, "You have become like a sister to me, dearest Anne, and you may be certain that I will find a way to help you."

They were silent for a moment, after which Elizabeth added, "Besides, a great deal may happen in the next month or two. It may very well be that you will never live with your mother again."

Anne knew very well that her friend was thinking of Lord Holland, and how convenient a means of escape from Lady Catherine's despotism marriage could be. But Elizabeth was disappointed, for this opening failed to elicit any revelation of Anne's feelings on the matter.

ANNE LAY awake for a long time that night wondering what she really did think of Lord Holland. During their last walk along the lake together in Scotland, he had stopped just short of a declaration of love, but she had been grateful that he had not gone so far. That it was his intention to do so and to ask for her in marriage while he was at Pemberley, she was fairly certain. That he was extremely clever, well read and a brilliant musician she could not deny. In addition, he was remarkably handsome, an agreeable and amusing companion, and had every appearance of a gentle and kind disposition. And how could she forget the courageous and daring way in which he had rescued Elizabeth! A man should certainly be brave, whatever other virtues he might possess. It should be a simple matter to fall in love with Lord Holland, she reflected, except for two things which stood in the way; the first was that she doubted that anyone could be sincerely in love with her, least of all such a paragon of a young man, and the second was her attachment to her cousin.

As if in search of an answer, she got out of bed and went to sit before her mirror. A single candle illuminated her countenance in the glass, and she looked at herself earnestly. Even Anne could see that she had changed a great deal since she had left Rosings only a short time ago. Activity and exercise in the fresh air had given her complexion a fine color and her figure was graceful and elegant. The hours she had spent riding had taught her to carry herself with a natural dignity and assurance and to look at the world with a steady gaze. The most striking transformation, however, was in the expression of her beautiful grey eyes, where timidity and uncertainty had been replaced by animation and a kind of good-humored, lively interest, which lit up her delicate face as the candle lit up the small circle of her dressing table.

Anne, of course, did not fully appreciate how very lovely she had become, but even she could perceive that she was altogether much prettier than she would have thought possible.

"Perhaps it is *possible* that he is in love with me," she mused, a novel idea indeed for the girl who had grown up as the sickly, plain daughter of Lady Catherine. She returned to bed and tried to sleep, but was kept awake by the question of whether she could ever love Lord Holland. She had adored her cousin Fitzwilliam for so long and she could not imagine that this would change, but from what she could tell he did not return her feelings. No, she was only like a younger sister to him, and no doubt he was in love with the perfect Lady Emma, as her mother insisted. Could she transfer her affection to Lord Holland who certainly seemed to be a worthy man? Then she would be out of Lady Catherine's power forever!

CHAPTER 37

The pleasant interlude of the small party at Pemberley lasted only until the following week when a series of grand equipages began to appear at the front portico of the house.

The first carriage belonged to Lady Grinspoon, who had been pressed to be one of the guests at Pemberley that autumn when she had parted from the Darcys in Scotland. When she did arrive the lady was doubly welcome, for she had brought Darcy's young sister with her. Georgiana had been visiting a school friend for several months, since shortly after her brother's marriage, and her return had been eagerly anticipated.

"Lady Grinspoon, you are a good friend indeed to bring us our Georgiana," said Darcy as he embraced his sister. "I was about to leave for Devon when I received your letter with your kind offer. Thank you for your care of my sister."

"Why it was no trouble at all," cried her ladyship, with her usual bright animation, "I pass right by Mr. Hamilton's gates every time I go into Devon to visit our old family place. I have known that young man and his sister all their lives and love them as my own. Their mama was one of my dearest friends. They were all sad to see Georgiana's visit come to an end."

Georgiana echoed her brother's thanks and said that she had never enjoyed a journey so much.

"We have had a fine time together, have we not, my child?" replied Lady Grinspoon, "Why, Miss Darcy has helped me work out the entire plot of my next novel, listening to me rattle on about it with the greatest patience. I shall have to give you credit as co-authoress when the work appears, my dear."

Elizabeth had gone up to Georgiana to place her arm around the girl's slender waist and kiss her. "My dear new sister, now that we have you back at last we shall not be parted again. You belong with us here at Pemberley."

Anne had been curious to see her cousin, whom she had met only twice, and not for some years at that. The young ladies were barely able to exchange the usual expressions of good will before being caught up once more in the flurry of activity requisite to arrival at a country house, but Anne found Georgiana walking in the garden later that day. A stone bench under a large elm provided a setting for conversation, and the first mundane remarks were exchanged as to Miss Darcy's recent travels and the attendant details as to weather and road conditions.

"How happy I am to see this garden," said Georgiana, "I spent so much time here with my mother that it is a sacred place for me."

"You have been away from home for so many months," said Anne, "How very often I have heard your brother and Elizabeth regret the fact and wish that they could hurry your return."

"It seemed best to me that a newly married couple should be allowed an extended period to themselves," replied Georgiana, "and I have been very well contented to remain with my friends in Devonshire. They have shown me every kindness imaginable and were so good as to express great sadness at my departure."

"I'm afraid that any good effect of your consideration for your brother and his bride has been undone by my presence for all this time," said Anne, feeling the unintended sting of her cousin's words.

Georgiana was instantly aware of her own tactlessness and said with some agitation, "Please do not misunderstand what I said, for my brother has written to me several times about the delight that he and Mrs. Darcy have found in your company."

Anne, who perceived that she had at last met with a creature as sensitive and highly strung as herself, hastened to reassure Georgiana that there was no reason to distress herself.

"I actually do believe that they have not at all minded having me about," she continued, "I have come to love them both very much, and they are the first people with whom I have ever felt quite at ease." Then with a smile, she added, "The only other person being Mr. Grey, who has the gift of making anyone his friend in a moment."

"Ah, Mr. Grey, or rather Lord Conarvan as he was called when I last saw him. I do remember him from his visits here years ago. He could always make me laugh with his droll observations."

It took some time for Anne to tell her cousin all that Mr. Grey had done since his arrival at Pemberley, from saving the house from the consequences of a serious leak in the library, to scandalizing the neighborhood by concealing his identity as the son of the infamous Lord Harwith.

"Good heavens! He certainly does make an impression wherever he goes, does he not?" cried Georgiana.

"Indeed, things can never be dull when Mr. Grey is about, but I have not yet told you how he rescued a puppy last week."

Anne told the story in a way that was very much to the young man's credit, but in her further discourse she did not reveal anything of Mr. Grey's evident *tendresse* for Lady Margaret out of a sense of discretion. Georgiana was left to wonder if Anne might herself be in love with the gentleman.

The two young ladies found each other quite *sympatique* and still had not exhausted subjects of mutual interest when Elizabeth and Lady Grinspoon came to find them.

ELIZABETH DARCY HAD NOT BEEN BROUGHT up with any expectation that she would become a great lady and mistress of a splendid country house. Even had her parents imagined such a glorious destiny for their daughter, neither their means nor their tastes would have enabled them to prepare her for such a life. Her father was a gentleman of good family but had long confined himself to scholarly pursuits and took little interest in society. Her mother, a woman of limited understanding and discernment, had not provided Elizabeth with any very useful example; visitors to Longbourn appeared only occasionally and, with the exception of their cousin Mr. Collins, had not stayed long. Mrs. Bennet, although quite particular about her table, did not possess the sort of charm and gift for hospitality that could encourage anyone to linger.

Elizabeth's time of trial had now begun; ensuring the comfort and amusement of a house full of guests was completely new to her, and although she had rehearsed every aspect of her duties in her mind for some months, she was still a bit daunted by her responsibilities. However, by some happy quirk of nature she seemed to be well suited to her new role, for her lively mind and high spirits rejoiced in constant activity and challenge. She and Mrs. Reynolds, the housekeeper, got on very well together, and all the servants were delighted to see Pemberley come back to life after all the years when Mr. Darcy had so often been absent and had rarely entertained friends.

For the moment Mrs. Darcy would be spared the presence of anyone very difficult or formidable, although there was some possibility that Lady Catherine would spend Christmas at Pemberley at the same time as the Bennets and the Gardiners. Elizabeth could not think of her mother and Lady Catherine in the same drawing room without a shudder, but the dreaded event was still many weeks away, and she hoped to think of some clever way to manage things so as to mitigate any serious consequences.

Elizabeth's happiest moment came with the sight of the Bingley carriage turning the last curve of the drive. All morning she had been running to the windows that overlooked the courtyard in front of the house every time she imagined the sound of wheels. Darcy had been observing her childlike excitement with loving amusement. Finally he came to share her vigil, with his arm close around her waist.

"You know, my darling, that we really cannot expect them before afternoon," he said, kissing her gently.

"Oh, of course you are right, dearest," replied his wife, "but I cannot bring myself to think of anything else until Jane is here at last. I suppose that it is absurd to waste the entire morning watching for them."

"If all goes well you will see your sister almost every day and I will enjoy having Bingley's company again."

"Ah, that would be perfect happiness indeed!" cried Elizabeth, "but I must not allow myself to think of it yet."

Mr. and Mrs. Bingley had not yet settled on a permanent home and it happened that a large estate only a few miles distant from Pemberley had recently been put up for sale. Lord Faulconer was attempting to assist the widow of the late Sir Henry Blanchard by finding a purchaser and had mentioned the circumstance to Darcy. Now all should depend on whether Jane and Bingley liked the place and would come to live near Pemberley. Elizabeth had never seen Thrushfold Hall, but had heard that it was by no means perfect, being in poor repair and old fashioned. It might be unacceptable to a young couple who could afford to buy the finest of houses, so Elizabeth had been attempting to not let herself hope. They were all to ride over to see the Hall when Lady Blanchard should next be down from London in two week's time. How difficult it would be to wait so long in suspense!

Finally Elizabeth ran off to inquire for the fourth time that day as to the preparations for her sister's arrival and to drive Mrs. Reynolds to distraction in a way that was quite unusual. If this Mrs. Bingley was a duchess there could hardly be more fuss, thought the housekeeper, following her mistress to examine once more all the arrangements in the pretty guest chamber that overlooked the garden.

At last they arrived and Jane, who had never seen Pemberley, was in suitably unrestrained raptures at the beauty of the place.

"How *lovely* everything is here!" she cried, throwing herself into Elizabeth's arms while Darcy and Bingley shook hands. "Never have I seen any place so exquisite! A blessed spot worthy of my Lizzie! It is so wonderful to be with you at last."

They had not been together since May when the two young couples had been in London, and the separation had been much longer than the sisters had ever known before. The Bingleys had been at Netherfields, a fine old house near Longbourn, and had been considering whether to buy the estate, which was only leased by the year. Although Jane would never have said so, even to Elizabeth, it had become evident that it was possible to live too close to their mother, Mrs. Bennet. Daily visits and lectures on every subject had worn down even Jane's angelic patience and Bingley's good humor. Elizabeth was happy to see that her sister was well and more beautiful than ever, and to observe the perfect harmony between Jane and her husband; surely there could be no more severe test of a new marriage than several months of Mrs. Bennet's company.

After all the necessary greetings had been exchanged with the other residents of the house, the two ladies had a few moments alone in Elizabeth's sitting room.

Several minutes were needed for Jane to comment on all the wonders of Pemberley, on the graciousness of Darcy, and the delight of finding such a pleasant company at the house. To her, the wealth and importance of the establishment meant little except as it contributed to her sister's happiness. Had Elizabeth been wedded to a gentleman of modest means and living in a simple cottage, Jane's delight with everything around her would have been the same.

"All is well at Longbourn, Lizzie," she finally said, "Mama and Papa and Mary are in good health. Kitty was with us at Netherfield all the summer and would have been very much happier to accompany us here, but it seemed best that she spend some time at home. Mama's feelings were a bit hurt that she had been away for so long, especially as you will probably be having her for a long visit beginning with Christmas."

"And Lydia? How did you find her when she visited you last month?" inquired Elizabeth, "I have had a few letters but have not seen her since we were in London last spring."

"Oh, Lizzie, she seems just the same, as gay and thoughtless as ever. And Wickham was with us for some time as well, until even my darling Charles was almost out of temper," and Jane looked distressed, "I know that I am being unkind, but I fear that Wickham does not improve on better acquaintance, and I do not believe that he would be bothered to know us were it not for Charles' generosity in helping them get by."

Elizabeth sighed; she had also been plagued by frequent applications for money from Lydia, and she generally contrived to assist her younger sister in some small way. Darcy, who had paid out huge sums to rescue Wickham from debt and to induce that worthless young man to marry Lydia, would no longer have any dealings with him, although Lydia by herself was permitted to make brief visits in London.

"You are always kind, my love," replied Elizabeth, "Only you and Bingley would be forgiving enough to have Wickham in your house. My husband can hardly bear to hear his name."

Jane knew something of Darcy's deeper reason for detesting his brother-in-law, which was a dark secret to the world. Georgiana had been only fifteen when Wickham had attempted to persuade her to elope with him, his object being her fortune, and he had almost succeeded in his design. Fortunately the young girl had loved her brother too well to deceive him and Darcy had been able to prevent a disastrous alliance.

"Well, I suppose there is a 'Wickham' in every family, and we must ignore him as best we can. But, dearest Jane, I am guessing that you have something else to tell me. You gave me a hint in your last letter. "

Then the joyous tidings burst forth and the two sisters were in each other's arms again crying happy tears.

"Is it not too wonderful, Lizzie?!" cried Jane after a few minutes, "I only wish that we could be in a home of our own before my confinement. I know it sounds ungrateful, but Mama's presence every day would be very difficult at such a time, and I would like to be away from the neighborhood of Longbourn."

"Let us hope that you will like Thrushfold Hall, and if it is acceptable we will do all that is necessary to make it ready quickly. And, dearest, there is an excellent physician in the neighborhood, so all will be well."

"Oh, I could live anywhere to be near you, Lizzie. If only there is a roof and the appropriate number of walls it will do very well," said Jane, "I am afraid that Charles is a little more particular. He admires

Pemberley so much, and I think he dreams of something along the same lines. But of course there is no other house like it and I hope that he will moderate his expectations somewhat."

Elizabeth reflected that gentlemen, even though they be the best of friends, will always be in competition over something: houses, horses, or exploits on the hunting field.

"Well, if the Hall is not large enough Mr. Bingley can knock it down and build something else, and you will stay here with me while he does so. And now my love, I will not be easy unless you rest for a few hours before dinner. We must take very good care of you."

Later that evening the two sisters were again to be found sitting by the fire in Elizabeth's sitting room. The opportunity to share their impressions and thoughts before retiring to bed, as they had done their entire lives before marriage had ended the tradition, was too delightful to resist. Besides, Jane had endless questions and observations about the other occupants of the house.

"Mr. Grey is as amusing and good-natured as you had described him. How he made us laugh with his stories."

"We love having him here with us at Pemberley. Darcy dreads the time when he will take his leave and vanish on some new adventure, who knows where," replied Elizabeth.

"But surely you can persuade him to find some occupation that will keep him in the neighborhood?"

"We are trying to think of something, but Mr. Grey has almost completed his work on the library and he is too proud to stay as our guest much longer." The Darcys knew nothing of their friend's plan to take orders. Elizabeth, who threw caution to the winds when talking with her sister, then told Jane that Mr. Grey was suspected of being in love with Lady Margaret of Castle Faulconer, and that disappointment in that regard might be enough to drive him away.

"She must be an unusual young lady not to return the affection of such a man," said Jane, "Perhaps some misunderstanding has separated them."

This led to a long explanation of Grey's early misrepresentation of himself, and a description of Lady Margaret, who, while a charming and admirable person, did not seem likely to relinquish any prejudice once it had been created.

After some commentary on the sadness of disappointed love, Jane went on to speak of Miss Darcy, whom she had found to be somewhat reserved and almost pensive, not seeming very interested in her companions. "That good Lady Grinspoon succeeded in bringing her out of herself a bit at dinner, but it was clearly a difficult task."

"Yes, I am concerned to see Georgiana even more reticent than before. I hope that it is just fatigue and that we shall soon see her happier. I already love her dearly, and am determined to be her true friend," said Elizabeth, who was really concerned about the young girl.

After a few moment's reflection Jane added, "But you know, Lizzie, my greatest surprise this evening was Miss de Bourgh, who is nothing like what I expected. I was quite amazed to find her not a pitiable, frail, shrinking little thing, but a very pretty girl, who can come out with a bold and witty remark, delivered in a way that is almost dashing. How can this be the pathetic creature you described to me in your letters when you first visited Rosings?"

Elizabeth laughed, and remarked that it was quite remarkable what being relieved from the influence of an oppressive mother could do. She went on to describe the gradual transformation that had begun to take place as soon as Anne was out of the neighborhood of Rosings – and Lady Catherine.

"Although I have begun to appreciate that Lady Catherine does possess some good qualities, I hope that Anne will never again be under her control. I am afraid that she would lose all that she has gained."

"Heaven forbid!" exclaimed Jane, "For she is certainly a very interesting young lady. She listens to everything with such animation, and as well as being quite lovely, her eyes shine with a striking intelligence. How I would like to cut my hair like hers! How very original and chic!"

Jane was then given some information regarding the fascinating Lord Holland, the possibility that he would inherit a great title, and how he was expected to arrive soon and resume his courtship of Anne.

"Goodness!" cried Jane, "Why Miss de Bourgh may someday be a marchioness! That should be good enough even for Lady Catherine."

A sound at the door signaled that Darcy and Bingley had come in search of their wives, and further confidences between the sisters had to be delayed until the next day.

~

THE WEATHER WAS RATHER fine for the time of the year and the ladies were able to enjoy the many pleasant walks to be found at Pemberley. Anne was still able to ride on most days, but hunting was about to begin and Darcy was firm in his determination that his cousin was too inexperienced to go near the field even to follow at a sedate distance.

"Now that I know you better, Anne," he said when the subject arose between them for the third or fourth time, "I have no doubt that as soon as you saw us begin to move out there would be no restraining you from joining in. For all your natural good sense, I perceive a streak of audacity that I have no desire to encourage. I was alarmed to see you jump that hedge when we were out with Grey yesterday, after I had clearly told you to go around by the gate."

"A very trivial hedge indeed, cousin," replied Anne, "Why it would be no barrier to a small pony, much less to Eilis."

"No jumping of any significance until you have been riding for a year," said Darcy in his most decided and unanswerable manner, "After all, I am responsible for your safety." And so matters were left, and Anne was more than a little annoyed that she should be so thwarted. Once the gentlemen were fully engaged with hunting they would only occasionally have time to go out riding with her.

The presence of her friend Lady Grinspoon was a consolation at least, and they spent many hours talking and laughing together. They made every effort to include Georgiana in their conversations and outings but found that she preferred to spend most of her time alone, devoting many hours to practicing the pianoforte in the music room. Jane was a delightful, gentle companion, but at most times seemed to be with Elizabeth, enjoying the renewal of the close bond that had always been so important to them both.

"Let us go for a walk by the river, my dear Miss de Bourgh," Lady Grinspoon would say, "and leave Mrs. Darcy and Mrs. Bingley to themselves, for I think that they have much to talk of." Even if rain threatened or the wind was cold, the two friends would be off for two or three hours at a time, through the woods and over the steep hills, for they were both indefatigable walkers.

Many of Anne's opinions on worldly matters were influenced by her conversations with Lady Grinspoon. The older lady had a rather skeptical outlook on the relations between men and women that was certainly at variance with the romantic novels that had made her a rich woman. She gave Anne a copy of *Cecilia* on first arriving at Pemberley, saying, "My dear, if you find the sinister characters and misdeeds in the book overdrawn, I can assure you that they are not."

Later, after reading the novel, Anne commented with a laugh, that in spite of Mrs. Burney's great skill as a writer, it was the virtuous characters that she had difficulty crediting.

One windy day, Lady Grinspoon and Anne were walking in the garden and were engaged in another of their interesting *tête à têtes* that were so helpful in alleviating Anne's ignorance of various important matters.

They had almost reached the house and Anne was saying, "Dear Lady Grinspoon, you are my undoubted authority in this as in so many things, but surely our Creator in His infinite wisdom has so fashioned things that we are at our most ridiculous in the midst of what should be most sacred."

"Yes, my dear, it all sounds most absurd and rather alarming, I suppose, but only when considered in the objective and dispassionate way in which we have been discussing the subject."

Anne was about to reply when she looked up toward the top of the steps they were ascending and saw Lord Holland. He had apparently just arrived and looked remarkably handsome in his traveling cloak, with heightened color from the crisp air and his dark hair somewhat windblown; a more romantic figure could hardly have been imagined.

He greeted the ladies eagerly and ran partway down the steps to meet them. Anne found herself put completely out of countenance by the unexpected appearance of her admirer. Blushing deeply she stammered out some sort of greeting and made as quick an escape as possible into the house, leaving Lord Holland to look after her with bewilderment.

Lady Grinspoon, who had come to like Lord Holland for so resembling one of the heroes in her novels, was very amused by the scene, and merely said that she supposed that Anne had not felt at her best in her muddy boots with burrs clinging to her skirt, "for we have been walking these last two hours over some very rough ground and through a little wilderness of low thickets."

"Why, I never saw Miss de Bourgh look so lovely," replied the young man in apparent dismay, "How I wish she had not hurried away, for now I fear that she would just as soon I had not come."

Anne flew into the house with the intention of going to her room until she had regained her composure, but as she passed through the hall she heard Elizabeth call to her from the music room.

"Anne, dear, is that you? Why are you in such a tearing hurry? Oh, do come and join me for a moment."

Anne checked her dash towards the stairs and went into the music room with pounding heart and flushed cheeks. Elizabeth was standing by the pianoforte holding some sheet music and looked even more beautiful than usual, with heightened color and shining eyes.

"Look, dearest, Lord Holland has brought such wonderful things, all the most interesting music to be had in London, much of it just printed. What a pleasure it will be to have so many new works to play."

As if to demonstrate, Elizabeth sat down and played a few bars of a sonata, smiling in delight as she did so.

"If only my skill were greater and I could perform with so little effort as Lord Holland does with his violin." She added with a laugh, "But I will not despair. Only another ten or twenty years should make me a proficient."

"Indeed, cousin," said Anne, "although I cannot lay claim to any great knowledge on the subject, I think that you play extremely well."

By now Anne felt more tranquil and her pulse had returned to its usual quiet rhythm. She sat on the bench by Elizabeth and asked in as disinterested a tone as possible, "How is it that Lord Holland is here? I had not heard that he was to be expected today."

"Oh, a letter came by express this morning and the man himself followed hard upon his message," said Elizabeth, looking at Anne attentively. "But you do not seem very pleased at his arrival. He found you and Lady Grinspoon in the garden, I surmise?"

"Yes, his appearance caught me by surprise," replied Anne.

"My dear, as we both know, Lord Holland is here because he admires you very much and undoubtedly means to make an offer for your hand as soon as he can find an opportunity, that is if you give him any encouragement at all," said Elizabeth, taking the girl's hand affectionately. "Of course, I think that your mamma would be delighted at the idea of the match. I need hardly tell you how she would rejoice to see you a marchioness some day."

"Only on condition of the death of that unfortunate young man, Lord Holland's brother. Such calculations seem very cold-hearted to me," said Anne.

Both young women thought for a moment of Lady Catherine and how little they looked forward to her arrival at Pemberley.

"Well, Anne," said Elizabeth, "you will have some time now to decide if you can really be attached to Lord Holland. I must say that I find him a very agreeable, gentlemanly and remarkably talented man. And of course the fact that he saved my life does much to recommend him to my good opinion. But if you find you cannot love him then Darcy and I will help you to dismiss his suit in a courteous manner and defend you in your decision against your mother."

After this speech, Elizabeth could not repress a sigh; how very disagreeable things could become if Anne decided against the young nobleman. Lady Catherine's disappointment would make everyone miserable.

"You are so very good to me, Elizabeth," cried Anne, embracing her with gratitude, "In truth, I do not know what I think of Lord Holland. He is everything that is amiable, I am sure, but it seems difficult to know him. There is an impenetrable reserve about him somehow, but perhaps that will pass away with a better knowledge of his character."

"For now you have nothing to do but try to enjoy yourself and be as lighthearted as you can," said Elizabeth. "I hope that you will help me to amuse all this company, for as inexperienced as I am at playing a great lady, I will need you a good deal."

Anne retreated to her bedchamber and did not see Lord Holland until the company gathered in the drawing room before dinner that evening. He came over to her and bowed with a friendly smile, and if he felt any resentment at her abrupt departure earlier in the day, there was nothing in his manner to suggest it.

"My dear Miss de Bourgh," said the young man with a laugh, "if your reaction to my appearance in the garden was any indication, I might have been the ogre in a fairytale come to devour the unfortunate heroine. Perhaps you felt more secure in your little tower at Lord Munford's castle in Scotland."

"Yes, there was something terrible in your aspect when you were towering above us at the top of the steps, with all the capes of your traveling cloak blowing about you like the wings of a great predatory bird," replied Anne, "I was quite terrified until I gained the safety of the house and realized that it was only the sedate and gentlemanly Lord Holland."

He looked pleased to be the object of such raillery from a young lady who had generally been so reserved for most of their acquaintance. "A giant predatory bird! I don't know when I've been so flattered in my life!"

Lady Grinspoon came to join them and offered the observation that she often amused herself by attempting to determine what variety of birds her acquaintance most resembled. "I must say that I know more wrens and crows than anything else. The seagulls are the worst."

The conversation continued in this whimsical manner, but after a few minutes Anne noticed that Lord Holland was looking about the room as if searching for someone. Then he said, "Ah, there is Mrs. Darcy. I should ask her if she found anything of interest in the sheet music I brought for her today. Perhaps we can persuade her to play something for us after dinner." He bowed and made his way across to Elizabeth who was standing with her sister. Anne watched as she greeted him with a smile and then after a moment laughed and shook her head at something he had said to her.

"Dear Mrs. Darcy," said Lady Grinspoon, "She draws everyone to her with her beauty and high spirits. See how the entire company gravitates to her part of the room. I think I will plan my next novel around a similar young lady."

"Surely it would impossible to write a novel about a married woman," observed Anne after some reflection, watching as Darcy went to stand by his wife, "for after marriage nothing happens to a person ever again."

Lady Grinspoon gave Anne a sidelong glance, the look of tolerant amusement that "experience" always has in readiness for "innocence."

CHAPTER 38

The initial assemblage of guests in a large country house is somewhat similar to the first rehearsal of a symphony; an occasional dissonance is to be expected. So far, at least, the company at Pemberley had gathered together without any false notes disturbing the harmonious composition. Everyone seemed to have a good opinion of everyone else and to be determined to enjoy themselves, although at times Elizabeth noticed in Darcy some return of the reserve that had been such a notable feature of his character when she had first known him.

She spent some part of every day teasing him out of his detached unsociability, seeking him out in the library after she was done with her responsibilities in the breakfast room.

"Is it safe to enter the lair of the beast this morning?" she would ask, looking cautiously around the high bookshelf that partly separated his desk from the rest of the room, "If the lion's tail is whipping about in that threatening manner that I have seen recently, I dare not proceed further."

Some times Darcy would appear so abstracted that her banter would be met with a blank, cold look as if he did not see her. Elizabeth had learned, however, that his darkest moods could not resist her arms about his neck and her cheek against his, and after a moment he would lean back into his chair with a sigh of contentment. Sometimes she would press him to explain the reason for his comparative gloom after so many months of perfect happiness, but could get no answer beyond "the weight of responsibility associated with a large estate."

One day Elizabeth replied "Dearest, you have taught me too much about Pemberley for me to accept that explanation. You have an excellent steward and everything here runs with a truly boring efficiency. If you have lost all your money it might be well to tell me for I will cancel my order at the dressmaker's. If you are involved in some plot to burn down parliament, invent a flying machine, emigrate to the West Indies or take a second wife, it would probably be best to include me in your deliberations."

This would raise a hint of a smile, but Elizabeth could get nothing out of the irritating man, and although she hid her dismay well, she could never quite stop thinking about this change in her husband. In their private relations he was even more affectionate than ever and his passion for his wife seemed only to increase with time, but every day brought some evidence of his mysterious sadness. There was so much for Elizabeth to do, with her guests to be entertained, that she was unable to spend very much time interrogating her husband about this change in humor.

Perhaps, she reflected, he does not tolerate having so many people about, in which case I give up all idea of large house parties in the future. I would much rather have a cheerful husband.

The chief source of joy to Elizabeth during this period was having her sister with her every day. They spent hours in conversation, talking about all that had happened to them during the past year and planning for the happiness of living within easy distance of each other should the purchase of Thrushfold Hall prove practicable.

"Unless it is a perfect wreck, we will surely want to buy it," said Jane more than once, "for it is the only property that is on offer anywhere near Pemberley. Oh, how I do wish that Lady Blanchard would come sooner so that we could go to see the place!"

There was some distraction during this period of anticipation, for hunting was to begin and the gentlemen could talk of nothing else. The ladies had to make some effort to display untiring interest in the prospects for abundant foxes, the possibilities of frost, of ground that was too hard, or too soft with rain, and of course all the complications of equine health and canine temperament. Only Anne did not weary of the subject, and she repeated her request to be allowed to ride at least part of the way with the hunt on the first day out. Darcy, however, was unmovable on this point, and she had to resign herself to being a mere observer.

Lord Holland was as attentive as he had been in Scotland, and they fell into the habit of walking together every morning along the river near the house. Lady Grinspoon would start out with them but soon disappeared in search of some bird or other interesting phenomenon. Anne had to admit to herself that she enjoyed the young man's company. That he was clever, good-natured, well informed and agreeable no one could deny. She was still a bit put off by his remarkably handsome countenance and figure but was beginning to overlook even these flaws, and to think that beauty did not necessarily make a person conceited.

~

ON THE THIRD day after his arrival Lord Holland began to speak of their time at Castle Munford. "I will always be attached to the place for it was there that I first began to know you. I often think of our last walk together along the lake. Do you remember our conversation?"

"How could I forget it, Lord Holland?" said Anne, beginning to walk a bit more quickly, "As I recall I did not allow you to finish expressing your thoughts on that occasion, and it might be better not to bring up the subject again now."

"I would never do anything to displease you, Miss de Bourgh, but you must know what I hope for and that I am here at Pemberley only for you. If I am persistent you must blame your beauty and intelligence that so impressed me in Scotland. I only ask that you will be so kind as to be willing to know me better; until then you may be sure that the fear of a rejection will keep me silent for the present."

Anne stopped and turned to him with a smile, "You are an optimist, Lord Holland. What makes you think that I will ever like you better than I do now?"

"You are very hard on me," said the young man with a laugh, "I trust not to any attraction of my own, but to your kindness which may learn to see my few good qualities. Could not love follow, for I understand that compassion can be the beginning of love in a lady's heart?"

"I know nothing of ladies' hearts," said Anne, proceeding along the path again, "but if you avoid sentimental expressions and flattery we will get along much better and who knows, someday we may be friends. But I beg you, no more talk of my beauty, for of all things I most detest such false praise." Then she added with a laugh, "Of my intelligence I may sometimes be willing to hear more."

After this interview Lord Holland did not again attempt to attempt to express his intentions towards Anne, but he continued to make every effort to win her regard. She looked forward to seeing him every morning and would have been disappointed if they had not had the opportunity to be together. She learned of foreign lands and storms at sea, of great whales and the albatross, of music and painting and natural philosophy; Anne had a susceptibility to information and anyone who could tell her something new of the world was sure to gain her interest.

"So you will be going out with us tomorrow, Holland?" inquired Darcy the next morning at breakfast.

"Yes, you are very good. I would like it of all things, for this is as fine a country as I have seen anywhere, and my horses are quite rested from the journey here. What excellent stables you have! I am grateful for your hospitality, Darcy."

Anne was sitting at the other end of the table next to Mr. Grey and with the familiarity of an old friendship grumbled to him about her exclusion from the next day's sport.

"It seems to me that in the country all that ladies are allowed to do is to stand about and admire the gentlemen while they enjoy their amusements. Do you not think I ride well enough to go at least part of the way with you?"

"Well, you have made remarkable progress in a very short time," replied Grey carefully, "and if we were in some other part of England I would agree with you. But do consider that this is remarkably rough country, very rocky and with an unforgiving steep sort of terrain. Some caution, my dear Miss de Bourgh, if that idea is not too foreign to your reckless nature." Grey found it amusing to represent Anne as always likely to go off on some dangerous adventure.

"No doubt if you had a wife you would not allow her to ride at all. You would be a tyrant, I am sure," said Anne with a laugh, "You are all alike."

"By *all* I suppose you mean sensible, rational men who do not wish to see their wives or sisters come to grief?" Then, looking rather forlorn, Grey added, "But I do not suppose that I will ever have a wife, so your speculation on the subject is rather pointless."

Anne, who realized that she had hit on a sore point, said quickly, "Well, do not despair, Mr. Grey. Perhaps some woman will come along who does not find you completely unbearable. For now, let us go riding today, for after hunting starts I will be immured here while you and the rest of the gentlemen are out and about."

~

THE NEXT MORNING dawned cold and frosty but the ladies at Pemberley were not deterred from riding over to Castle Faulconer in the Darcys' barouche in order to view the hunt as it rode out. The gentlemen had already ridden off with a great deal of noise and high spirits; even Darcy was like an excited boy on the first day of hunting.

"I wish *we* had some excuse for being undignified and wild," said Anne as they made themselves as comfortable as possible in the carriage, in spite of a chill wind that threatened to make their noses red and carry away bonnets and shawls.

"Oh we will have a very pleasant morning all the same, Anne," said Elizabeth who was carefully enveloping Jane in a fur rug. Poor Jane was the object of constant and excessive solicitude on the part of everyone in the house, now that her condition was known, and even with her sweet disposition she was beginning to find it tiresome.

"Have mercy, Lizzie," she cried, "You will suffocate me!"

"There, there, Mrs. Bingley," said Lady Grinspoon consolingly, "You will have to become used to such overzealous attention on the part of your family and may as well make the most of it. I assure you that *next* time no one will bother about you at all."

Even with some degree of bustle and delay, they arrived at the castle soon after Darcy and the other gentlemen, who had taken some detour on the way to examine an important ditch or other obstacle to see if it had been amended in the manner that had been ordered some weeks before.

As the carriage entered the courtyard they were surprised to see Lord Faulconer ride over to greet them on a big chestnut hunter that had enjoyed some repute in years gone past. The old gentleman looked a good deal more active and robust than when Elizabeth had first made his acquaintance.

"Why, Lord Faulconer, are you joining the hunt this morning?" asked Georgiana in surprise, "I thought that you had given it up."

"Well, Miss Darcy, you must blame Mr. Grey, who has made it his policy to insist that I begin riding again. It has been a bit of a revolution for me and for this lazy old nag of mine as well." As if in protest at this unflattering description his horse snorted and danced about in a creditable imitation of a high-strung, mettlesome creature. At the same moment Mr. Grey made his appearance and rode up to the carriage in the quiet, confident manner that always characterized him on horseback.

"Mrs. Darcy, Lady Grinspoon, Mrs. Bingley, Miss Darcy, Miss de Bourgh! I am delighted that you have had the fortitude to come and admire us this morning. Otherwise there would be very little purpose in getting up so early and going to the bother of dragging these poor horses out of their nice warm stalls. But are you not a bit hot and cramped in that carriage? I can barely distinguish you under all the rugs and so forth."

"They are very sensible, Grey," said Lord Faulconer with a smile, "Ladies are not so impervious to the elements as you are, after all your years of wandering about and sleeping under the stars and tramping through the mountains."

As if to contradict the idea of ladies being fragile creatures, Lady Margaret came trotting over to them and pulled her horse up rather short with a little drama of rearing and pirouetting. She looked very lovely in her elegant black habit, with locks of her auburn hair escaping from under a charming little hat.

"Really, my dear," said her father indulgently, "there is no need to make such a fuss. See, you have put old Corncrake quite out of countenance." At the same time he got his irritated horse under control and could not help smiling with pride at his beautiful daughter.

Lady Margaret, who seemed to be in the highest spirits, greeted the ladies with delight, then turned to acknowledge Grey in a formal and rather cool manner. However, after a few minutes of general conversation she turned to him and said, "I must again express my thanks to you, Mr. Grey. I would not be riding Bucephalus today had you not saved his life last summer."

Grey, pleased at this civil speech, could only bow. The number of horseman in the forecourt of the castle had by now increased and had become very noisy, with neighbors greeting each other and hallooing in a way that Anne found quite amusing.

"I don't know when I've witnessed such unselfconscious enjoyment," she said to Georgiana who was seated beside her, "It is almost alarming."

"Oh, they will be very different by late in the day. The gentlemen will come back to Pemberley tired and mud-stained but still willing to spend *hours* telling us every detail of what has occurred. Much patience will be required on our part."

"So, it is our duty to seem interested in the peregrinations of every fox and the description of every bit of ground over which it took flight?" inquired Anne.

"Indeed," relied Georgiana, "and endless discussion of the virtues of every hound and the ill-temper or otherwise of every horse."

"Well, that is something to lock forward to," said Anne who was becoming restless in the confinement of the carriage and would have loved to jump out and commandeer the mount of some startled rider so that she could be more than an observer for once.

Elizabeth was happy to be where she was and to have the opportunity to admire her husband, who was riding about the courtyard greeting his friends. To her there was no doubt that he was the finest and most distinguished man there, and not for the first time she felt a shock of astonishment that he was really her husband and that she possessed his entire love and devotion.

There is no one else like him, she thought, admiring his tall, upright figure and noble bearing. Perhaps it would be best if he does not know quite how much I adore him. A little insecurity, now that we have been wed some months, may ensure that he continues to value me as much as he does now. And Elizabeth, who had unknowingly acquired such a poisonous notion from her mother, resolved to conceal something of her passionate love from her husband.

She saw Lord Holland ride up to Darcy and say something to him. Her husband could be seen to reply in a courteous but somewhat cold manner. For the first time it occurred to Elizabeth that Darcy might not particularly like the young nobleman.

She was speculating as to why this might be so when Squire Redfern joined the party gathered by the barouche. He made his bow in a gentleman-like manner, but it quickly became evident that all his attention was for Lady Margaret. Poor young man, thought Elizabeth, he is obviously mad for her, but she treats him like nothing more than a faithful dog.

The Squire was glad to report that the Master was ready to move out and that he had come to alert them. Darcy, along with Bingley and Lord Holland trotted over to say their farewells.

"You are too popular," said Bingley, "We could not get near you because of the crowd gathered round." Then addressing his wife he added, "My love, you will go into the castle and warm yourself by the fire, will you not?"

"Do not be uneasy, Mr. Bingley," said Lord Faulconer, "All is in readiness for the ladies, and as I plan to ride only a short way with you, I will soon return to see to it that they have everything possible for their comfort."

Darcy had made his way to his wife's side to smile at her, at last taking her hand and bowing over it as gracefully as might the most dashing cavalier to acknowledge the mistress of his heart. Elizabeth felt herself blush and her pulse quicken, but laughed in a light-hearted way and sent him off with a jest about saving the countryside from the depredations of foxes. Lord Holland did not fail to say something gallant and amusing to Anne before turning his horse and following the others out of the gate. Elizabeth commanded her coachman to drive to a high point of ground nearby from which they could watch the riders as they vanished over the far hills at an ever-quickening pace.

JOHN GREY HAD no idea of making any great display of superior horsemanship, or of leading the field as they made their way in a great noisy gallop across the rocky ground and over hedges and stonewalls. But as modest as he was, it was natural to wish to prove himself to be the most daring and boldest man there, with the lady he worshiped only a few yards away. At first he had some care for Lord Faulconer, watching him out of the corner of his eye, for it had been some years since his friend had been out with the hunt. After the first long run, however, Lord Faulconer very sensibly turned back to return home, and there was nothing to deter Grey from making it his business to keep up with Lady Margaret. She took every fence in her usual fear-less manner, while many more sagacious riders went around by convenient gates or lower walls. Occasionally she would glance at him with some annoyance and surprise when she found him still near her after some particularly formidable obstacle. The three other gentlemen from Pemberley seemed equally determined to break their necks and none was willing to hold back.

After an extended gallop across a high meadow and through the ranks of some startled cattle, the hunt found itself almost halted by the obstacle of a six foot wall with only one low spot where it could be traversed. The Master and a few of the huntsmen were through it quickly and off again, but Grey because of consideration to another rider who was struggling with his horse, became delayed by the crowd. He was chaffing with the annoyance of losing his place in the field when he saw Lady Margaret break away from the rest and gallop off along the wall towards some woods.

She must know another way to get through, Grey thought, and as if compelled by an irresistible impulse he followed her as quickly as possible, detaching himself from the milling pack of riders.

Lady Margaret was vanishing into a dense forest at the top of the hill, but Grey was in time to note her general direction, and when he reached the tree line he was able to discern a path that she must have taken. Here he noted that the stonewall had partially fallen down and was a mere three feet high. His horse crossed it easily at the spot where the trail seemed to continue into the woods beyond, and after a few moments he found himself in a large clearing. Lady Margaret was there, having dismounted to adjust her girth; her color was high and she seemed rather agitated. Grey heard her muttering in annoyance at the intransigence of her saddle and the restless movement of her horse.

"Oh, do be still for a moment, Buccie!" she was saying as Grey leapt down and went to her side.

"Here, Lady Margaret," said Grey, "Do let me assist you," and he moved toward her to examine the situation.

The young lady's expression was hardly a welcoming one. She flushed and said, "Mr. Grey, of all people! Thank you, but I do not need your help. I suppose you followed me here." And she pulled down the stirrup leather with a snap of annoyance. "But as long as you are here, perhaps you would be so good as to give me a hand up."

When they were both remounted she made a motion as if to whirl about and gallop out of the clearing, but before she could do so Grey took hold of her horse's bridle. She was clearly outraged at his daring to take such a liberty. "Do let me go, Mr. Grey! This is insupportable."

He obeyed her at once and said, "I am sorry to detain you, Lady Margaret, but I must beg you to explain the excessive dislike you seemed to feel for me. I know I have made some mistakes of judgment since I came into the neighborhood, but surely you can forgive me and we can be friends again."

"How can I ever be friends with a man who has lied to us? My father may overlook your deception but I cannot. You are altogether a different person from what you led us to believe."

"I can only ask your understanding and forgiveness," said Grey, "surely that is something we all should try to grant our fellow creatures."

"Very well, Mr. Grey, you are forgiven. Now please move out of my way!"

"Of course," said the young man sadly, "but you must let me say one thing before I let you go forever. You must know that my heart is completely yours and has been from our first meeting when I encountered you on the hill near Pemberley. How could it be otherwise? Perhaps I have no right to speak to you like this but I love you too much not to tell you now when I have this one opportunity. There will never be anyone else and if you could at least hate me a little less it would be some comfort to me."

Grey half expected her to hit out at him with her crop, but to his astonishment she seemed to sag into her saddle and in a moment began to weep and then leant forward as if to hide her face in her horse's mane. He heard her say, "Oh, you are cruel to say such things to me. You don't know what you are doing!"

He was reaching out to take her hand when there was a sound of hoof beats from the direction from which they had come and Squire Redfern rode through the trees with some amount of bustle and self-importance. Lady Margaret turned her horse away but the gentleman had caught a glimpse of her distress and came trotting up with his face dark as thunder.

"Good God, Lady Margaret! What has happened?" and he looked at Grey as if considering whether to strike him dead on the spot.

"Oh, it is nothing at all," said the lady, composing her face and trying to smile, "1 turned my ankle a little when I dismounted to adjust my girth. Fortunately Mr. Grey came along and helped me."

"How very shocking!" said the squire, looking suspiciously at Grey, "I am most distressed and will insist on escorting you home and then summoning a doctor."

"Indeed, you will do no such thing," said Lady Margaret coldly, "It is a trivial sprain, and I mean to see this day out to the end." Then she galloped off with a fierce kick to her horse and such reckless speed that the two men were startled and alarmed. The squire followed and Grey was left alone in the clearing, for he had no heart to continue. His mind was in turmoil and he had never felt so completely exhausted, even after the most demanding mountain climbing he had ever done in the Swiss Alps. If this is the effect of love, he thought, then it will surely be the death of me.

He rode out of the woods at a gentle pace, went over the stonewall in a sedate manner as if any jarring motion might do further injury to his nervous equilibrium and eventually found himself moving in the direction of Castle Faulconer. It occurred to him that Lady Margaret's father might be anxious for news of her; what the old gentleman must suffer in his anxiety for her when she was out with the hunt must be terrible indeed.

His supposition was correct and he saw Lord Faulconer walking in the terraced gardens above the river. When he saw Grey coming across the bridge the older man waved to him and walked to the fore-court of the castle to greet him.

"Ah, very glad to see you, my dear Grey! Do you know anything of my daughter? I had thought that she might ride back with you."

Grey gave a brief report on what he had seen of Lady Margaret's progress with the hunt and added that he did not suppose that she could be expected to return home for another hour or two. Feeling that he must find some excuse for his having left the field early he explained that his horse had not seemed up to the rest of the day, "I suppose that I have not worked him quite as intelligently as I thought."

"Well, to tell the truth, I am glad of it," replied Lord Faulconer, "the ladies have all returned to Pemberley and it is good to have your company. It is always an anxious time for me until my daughter returns."

Soon the two men were seated by the fire in the library and Grey's host had provided him with brandy to undo any ill-effects of the late afternoon chill. They talked for a while of the ground they had both covered in the morning and then a silence fell in the room. It was beginning to grow dark and both men were thinking of Lady Margaret and hoping that she would return at any moment.

After some hesitation Grey began to relate the story of what had happened in the clearing; how he had attempted to speak to the young lady of his love and how he had been rebuked so severely.

"There must be no secrets between us, Lord Faulconer," said Grey, "I have told you of my hopes regarding your daughter and you have been so kind as to give me some encouragement to address her, in spite of my lack of fortune."

"As to that Grey, how could I object to a young man who is not only a dear friend but also the heir to one of the greatest estates in England. But even were you to be always poor I would still wish of all things for you to be my son-in-law, if only Margaret could see her way to accepting your devotion."

"Far from returning my affection, I am inclined to think that your daughter hates me. It certainly appeared to be the case today. I would not have been surprised if she had struck me with her crop, she was so angry."

Lord Faulconer did not reply for some moments and when he did it was in the manner of one who has undergone a difficult inner struggle.

"On the contrary, my friend, I believe that she cares for you very much indeed. I know her well and have daily evidence that she does not dislike you, but in fact holds you in some regard."

Lord Faulconer looked sad and continued, "How I wish that I could give you some hope. However, my dear Grey, I do not think that your love is likely to prosper; I do not think that my child will ever marry."

Grey was dismayed to receive so much hope and so much discouragement in the space of a few moments.

"But why? Why should she not be happy? As I have told you, I mean to take orders and I will wait however long it takes for her to look upon me with favor. I will find some parish as close to her as possible and perhaps someday she will change her mind."

"Unfortunately, it is more difficult a problem than mere indecision or reticence on my daughter's part. There are reasons why she hates

343

the idea of putting herself into the power of love and I fear that her mind will not change. I had hoped that it would, after seeing some evidence of her affection for you."

"Please, Lord Faulconer, can you not tell me where the difficulty lies? Was there a prior attachment that has led to Lady Margaret's disillusionment? If so, surely my constancy will prove my trustworthiness eventually."

"Oh, no. As far as that is concerned, her heart has been completely untouched." Lord Faulconer rose and poured more brandy. He had the air of one who has said more than he had intended, "It is a family matter, one that I am not at liberty to speak of as much as I do trust you, Grey. Even if I could explain, it would not alter the situation."

Grey, in desperation, would probably have dared to press to hear more of this mystery, had not Lady Margaret come sweeping in to the room, followed by Squire Redfern. She seemed to be high spirits and greeted them gaily.

"Why, Mr. Grey! I did not expect to find you here. Well, you have missed what will no doubt be accounted the best run of the season. What a pity."

Then turning to Lord Faulconer she said. "Father dear, here is Squire Redfern who is perishing from cold, so do give him some of your brandy. He has escorted me home in the best manner of the faithful knight."

When they were all seated Lady Margaret continued to give a detailed narrative of the afternoon's run, and if she felt any confusion at seeing Grey it was not apparent. To Squire Redfern she was kind and complimentary, and the young man was obviously in heaven at this unexpected turn of events. After a few moments Grey could bear no more and after thanking Lord Faulconer for his hospitality he took his leave.

He rode back to Pemberley slowly, trying to imagine with all the ingenuity at his disposal what could be the impediment at which Lord Faulconer had hinted. There was certainly nothing that he could conceive of that could alter his feelings for Lady Margaret. Dark family secrets or scandals were as nothing to him; he had seen too much of the world to care for its opinion when the happiness of one

344

he loved was at issue. It was well past dusk when he reached Pemberley and he took the back way into the house in order to change for dinner and join his friends as quickly as possible. In truth he had little enthusiasm for company, but felt an obligation to Darcy and Elizabeth to present a cheerful countenance and add something to the evening's society. He entered the library where everyone had gathered; it was the warmest room in the house at that season of the year and Elizabeth had abandoned the custom of spending the autumn evenings in the chillier drawing room. She came to meet him with a radiant smile and everyone seemed glad to see him.

"Why, Grey, my dear fellow, we were about to send out a search party," said Darcy joining them, "Did you decide to pursue a fox into the next county?"

"No, indeed not," replied Grey," My horse seemed quite done in and I turned back early, stopping in to see Lord Faulconer for a bit. How did everything turn out?"

Of course he was assured that he had missed the best run ever seen in that country, and half a dozen voices commiserated with him on his bad luck, while adding details of the day's sport that Grey in his present mood would have preferred not to have to hear. Normally he would have been as interested as any man in the room, but tonight all he wished to do was to find a quiet corner and a large brandy.

The reason for Mrs. Darcy's particularly high spirits was soon evident; she had received a letter from her father to the effect that the Bennets would probably wait until after the New Year to arrive at Pemberley.

"It is unfortunate that they will not be here at the same time as Lady Catherine, in order to promote the family relationship," said Lady Grinspoon, "You must be very disappointed."

"Oh, very!" exclaimed Elizabeth with the air of one who had just been granted a stay of execution. "But of course by that time Lady Catherine plans to return to Rosings."

"Well, my dear," said Lady Grinspoon. "No doubt at some future time you will have the pleasure of having them all here together."

"No doubt," said Elizabeth with a shudder. Jane had been standing nearby and added, "Dear Lizzie, by then we will be settled nearby and we will somehow divide our duties as hostesses." In spite of the fact that they had not yet seen the house that was for sale at such an easy distance from Pemberley, it was a settled thing between the two sisters that the place must be found acceptable and purchased, even if it should all have to be torn down and rebuilt. Jane and Elizabeth could not endure the idea of being separated again now that there was a possibility of being neighbors.

Anne had been watching Grey and could perceive that he was very much out of spirits, even though he had managed to seem his usual self to the more casual observers in the room. He had withdrawn to a little alcove and was making some pretense of examining a volume there.

When he became aware of Anne he turned and smiled at her, "Well, Miss de Bourgh, here is one that I have not yet entered into the catalog. How could it have escaped my notice, do you suppose?" Then he began to talk of the hunting and believed he was making a fair effort at hiding his dreary mood when Anne interrupted him.

"You may deceive everyone else in the room, Mr. Grey," she said softly, "but to me you have become perfectly transparent. Why this is so I cannot tell, but it is clear that you have received some kind of serious blow."

Grey tried to laugh off her remark, but at the expression of compassionate understanding and affection in her eyes he found himself speaking to her with a greater frankness than he would have thought possible. They were just far enough from the rest of the company who were gathered by the fire that he felt confident that they would not be overheard. He told her of his encounter with Lady Margaret in the clearing in the woods and of her rejection of his overtures, but said nothing of the hint of a family secret that had been intimated in his conversation with Lord Faulconer; that he felt he had no right to mention.

"And so, Miss de Bourgh, I have been debating what I shall do next. Either I shall go down to Cambridge after Christmas and begin my studies so that I may take orders in the early spring, or I shall leave for the continent and take up my wanderings again. What would you suggest? Surely it is best for me to leave the neighborhood and not return for a very long time, if ever."

Anne looked thoughtful and did not reply for several moments, until Grey wondered if he had said too much. Finally she spoke, "I have known for some time that you love Lady Margaret. One would have to be a great simpleton not to know it, although most people are too involved in their own affairs to take any notice. I saw the way that you looked at her the first day when we went to church, before the journey to Scotland. Mr. Grey's heart is well and truly lost, I thought. So there is no surprise here, except that I would never have thought you likely to give up so easily. A man who has done all that you have in life to be disheartened by what you have related? It would all be very well, except for the fact that I am sure that she loves you in return."

Grey was so startled at this statement that he lost some of his composure and a light of fierce hope appeared in his eyes, "Why do you think that, Miss de Bourgh? Oh, anything you can say to alleviate the despair I feel will put me in your debt forever."

"You must understand, Mr. Grey, that my life up until now has been of a rather peculiar nature. I was rarely permitted to speak as my mother always interrupted me, and because I was considered to be sickly I was always relegated to a corner with my governess. It would have been an intolerably dull existence had I not learned to observe my fellow creatures with a lively interest. I have acquired the ability to see what no one else takes the trouble to; it is a habit of mind by now and I do not think I can break it"

Anne smiled at the eagerness in her friend's countenance and continued, "But I will not torment you with these asides. I am convinced from careful observation that Lady Margaret, in spite of her determination to conceal the fact, is very much in love with you."

She turned as if to make sure that she could not be overheard, then continued, "With your logical mind you will want specifics, not just a general assurance. Well, I have observed that when you are in the room Lady Margaret has eyes for no one else, although she is careful not to be seen watching you. As soon as you turn in her direction she manages to appear completely indifferent to your presence, but I know that from the corner of her eyes she is aware of everything you do. I have surprised expressions of sadness and longing in her face after one of these long glances she has directed towards you. Also you will realize, if you consider it, that her visits here are always timed to find you here with us. A few days ago she arrived when you were unexpectedly out, and while she made a joke about her good fortune in not having to tolerate your presence, she was in fact quite put out, stayed but a few minutes and did not display her usual good nature as a guest."

She had Grey's rapt attention and he remained silent as if expecting more, "I see that you are wishing for something in addition, but surely you are aware that sometimes we simply know something without being able to prove it. I am sure in my heart that Lady Margaret loves you and that it will be very unfortunate if you leave without making a good deal more of an effort to secure your happiness and hers."

Grey seemed to consider for a while and then said, "How fortunate I am to have you as a friend, Miss de Bourgh. You have saved me tonight from some very dark thoughts and a loss of hope. 1 thank you very much and beg that you will continue your observations if you do not think it unreasonable to share them with me."

CHAPTER 39

$\mathcal{F}$inally the day arrived for the visit to Thrushfold Hall. To everyone's disappointment Lord Faulconer was slightly indisposed with a cold and he and Lady Margaret were unable to join their friends for the outing. Lady Blanchard had travelled down from London and was to accompany the party from Pemberley to view the place. So much did she dislike her former home that rather than stay there for her visit to the neighborhood she had elected to honor Lady Templeton with her presence. On the morning of the excursion, a carriage was sent to collect her there and by ten o'clock the entire company set out, the gentlemen on horseback. Anne had very much wanted to ride as well, but Darcy had pointed out that their destination was at least a good twelve miles away and that she would be cold and fatigued by half that distance.

Lady Blanchard was a handsome woman of about forty who had but one topic of conversation, which was the extraordinary importance of her position in the London social milieu. She wearied the ladies with accounts of her triumphs in the fashionable world for the entire journey. Elizabeth, who as a result of her first season in London with Darcy knew most of the people of whom the lady spoke, could only look at her with wonder at such shameless exaggeration. This prolonged narration was followed with a commentary on how intolerable it was to be in the country. "An absolute wasteland! How can you stand to be here for months at a time?" Elizabeth had been told by her husband that Thrushfold Hall, which had been in the family for generations, was being sold to support the extravagant style of living Lady Blanchard had adopted since the death of her husband four years before.

As if her company were not tiresome enough, she had brought along her extremely spoiled six year old son, who made everyone wretched by constantly squirming about and kicking the seat. Elizabeth and Jane exchanged looks that said very clearly how much they hoped that the business with Lady Blanchard could be concluded that day so that they need never see her again.

Anne, Georgiana and Lady Grinspoon had the good fortune to be in the second carriage and knew nothing of Jane and Elizabeth's martyrdom. They spent the time in very good spirits, inventing ridiculous plot twists for Lady Grinspoon's next novel. Anne was delighted to see that Georgiana could laugh and enjoy being a light-hearted girl, as hitherto she had seemed so serious and reserved.

After driving through a small, prosperous village they arrived at the entrance of the park, which was in a state of disrepair with one of the gates hanging off the hinges. A neglected gatehouse completed the picture of a place unloved and rarely visited by its owner. After another mile or two they went around a curve and had a view of the house beyond a lake and sitting on rising ground. "Well, at least it has a lake," joked Bingley, "something in common with Pemberley."

Most of the building dated from the time of Queen Anne, with an ill-conceived addition from about 20 years before. An ancient avenue of elms that wound along the lake gave the place its only bit of distinction. The gentlemen, who had not expected much, were still somewhat dismayed.

"I have not been here for many years," said Darcy, "but I must say I remembered it as a more cheerful place."

They had halted on a little hill that gave them a good prospect, and looked at the house in silence for a few minutes, then Grey spoke, "If you can ignore the ill-proportioned portico and the associated block on the left and see the original building, you will find that there are real possibilities here."

The other three men had learned to respect Grey's opinion, but it was difficult to see much hope for the dreary house before them.

"My dear Grey, if you can help us find a way to make this house into something tolerable I will be eternally grateful, as my wife has set her heart on living near her sister," said Bingley, who was disheartened.

At that moment they heard hoof beats approaching and when they turned their horses they were astonished to see Fitzwilliam cantering towards them.

Darcy and Bingley greeted him with delight. Grey who had known Fitzwilliam from years ago was also pleased to see him, saying, "Excellent! We will have a first-rate opinion on this house for I remember that you are quite knowledgeable about such things." Lord Holland, who had only known the colonel slightly, nodded politely and rode decorously off to one side so as not to impede the happy and animated conversation between the old friends.

Fitzwilliam gave them an account of how he happened to be there.

"I arrived late yesterday and not wanting to put Mrs. Darcy to any inconvenience I stayed at the inn at Lambton. When I arrived at Pemberley this morning they told me where to find you and it sounded like such an important outing that I decided to follow you. Darcy, I hope you do not mind that I borrowed a fresh mount from your stables."

"My dear fellow, this is the best of surprises!" cried Darcy, "But how is your leg? Are you up to such long rides?"

"Oh, I am pretty much healed, thank you," replied Fitzwilliam, "It was only a small break, but my mother would make such a fuss, the doctor summoned from Edinburgh and so forth. But now I have seen my parents back to Yorkshire and here I am, for a week or two anyway."

They rode down the hill to Thrushfold Hall where they could see that the two carriages had stopped before the front portico and the ladies were descending. The exclamations of amazement and joy at Fitzwilliam's appearance took several minutes, for he was a great favorite with them all, and Lady Blanchard began to become impatient with the delay in entering the house. However, when the young man was introduced and she realized that he was the son of Lord Munford she at once became everything agreeable.

Anne was almost overcome with happiness at the arrival of her cousin, especially after she had ascertained that he had suffered no serious consequences from his recent injury and was able to walk up the steps to the house with only a slight limp.

"My dear Anne," Fitzwilliam exclaimed, going over to her with an irrepressible smile of delight on his face, "How very good to see you and to find you enjoying the company of your friends." He could see at once that far from being the shy girl always on the fringes of every group, that there was a freedom of expression and movement about Anne that he had not seen before.

"Oh, cousin, how wonderful it is to see you!" cried Anne, giving him her hand and with a becoming flush of color in her cheeks, "and how do you come to be here so unexpectedly?" Fitzwilliam repeated his explanation to the assembly of ladies who encircled him and he was gratified to feel that nothing in the world could have given everyone greater pleasure than his arrival.

At last they were all through the door and into the entrance hall of the house. It was fine and spacious but felt dank and cold. The building had been extensively altered to fit the questionable taste of Sir Lionel Blanchard two decades before when he had inherited the place. Grey and Fitzwilliam, as the two architectural experts in the company, at once began to confer solemnly about the many crimes that had been committed against the unfortunate mansion and the loss of the fine old woodwork that must have been found there originally. They had to restrain their remarks against such barbarism because of the presence of Lady Blanchard. The rest of the company listened to them as to the most sagacious oracles, Mrs. Bingley and Elizabeth in particular, so eager were they that the house be found acceptable.

"Oh, I do believe that all that old wainscoting and so forth will be found in a lumber room in the attics above," interjected Lady Blanchard, "I do assure you that my husband was never known to throw anything away."

This was good news and they went on into a large reception room with long and very beautiful windows that had fortunately escaped Sir Lionel's alterations. As they were all admiring a lovely view of the lake, Lady Blanchard's steward and housekeeper hurried in, both very concerned not to have been at the door to greet the visitors.

Fitzwilliam and Grey began to ask the steward innumerable questions about the house and the group started to make their way through the principal rooms, all of which were large and well-proportioned although dreary and neglected. Mrs. Bingley clung to her husband's arm with many a sigh, because she could imagine how he was comparing this sad place with Pemberley and she began to despair of ever persuading him that it could be an acceptable habitation. Her Charles, she knew, was determined to acquire a great countryseat to mark the beginning of a distinguished heritage for his son. For herself she cared little for grandeur and everything for being near her dear sister.

Grey and Fitzwilliam had retreated to one corner of the room to compare their impressions without offending Lady Blanchard by the frankness of their remarks, but they need not have worried for the lady was holding forth on her fashionable engagements for Christmas when she would be visiting "some of our most distinguished families."

Lord Holland had moved to Anne's side and had many interesting remarks to offer on the possibilities of Thrushfold Hall, for his taste and knowledge were considerable. He was amusing and so clearly happy in her company that she forgot for a while to observe all that her cousin Fitzwilliam was saying and doing at the other end of the room.

Holland had developed a way of looking intently into her face that attracted Anne as well as making her self-conscious. Sometimes the expression in his dark eyes was so distracting that she had trouble hearing what he was saying and would be embarrassed to have to ask him to repeat himself. On this occasion he broke off his gaze to look over at Fitzwilliam.

"Your cousin is very much an expert on these things, is he not?

And he is a distinguished officer as well, I believe. A man of many talents, and I suppose a great favorite with you?"

"Why, he must be a favorite with anyone who knows him," said Anne, "He combines great gifts of intellect and temperament with kindness and good sense. He has been my friend and advisor for all my life."

"It is certainly to his credit that you think so highly of him," replied Lord Holland, "I will hope for the privilege of knowing him better." Then he added, "I have heard something to the effect that he is soon to be engaged to a young lady of great wealth and accomplishment in Bath. Is it true?"

Anne, who despite having heard so much of this rumor still hoped that it was false information, felt a pain settle about her heart and all happiness fled from her at once.

"It was the word that was going about in Bath when I visited my brother there a brief visit just two weeks ago," continued her interlocutor, "and from my own observation, I saw that your mother, Lady Catherine, was paying a good deal of attention for Lady Emma."

Lady Catherine's last two letters had not mentioned the Lady Emma, giving Anne some hope that the entire thing was one of her mother's unfounded inventions.

At that moment Fitzwilliam looked about the long room to search for Anne and when his eyes fell upon her where she stood in the opposite corner, his face lit up with pleasure. Anne, who had never before felt such a marked sense of his attention towards her, felt her entire being respond with joy, only to be brought back to dismay by Lord Holland's next words.

"Lady Emma's mother was clearly on the best of terms with your mama as well, and they seemed to be in private conference together in the pump room. I very much wanted to take the opportunity to be presented to Lady Catherine but did not wish to intrude on their conversation. But has your cousin said nothing about the matter to his family?"

Anne was looking intently at her cousin as the group proceeded up the staircase to see the upper chambers, and the long delay in her answer to Lord Holland might almost have been considered discourteous. The young man, who was given to marking every change in her expression and mood, could easily follow the direction of her gaze. "He has said nothing to anyone, as far as I know," she replied at last, making an effort to return her attention to her companion, "Certainly, he would have informed us of so serious an intention, so there must be nothing to it. You know that ladies with very little occupation will build castles in the air and invent matches for all their relations."

Lord Holland only smiled, and then added, "You have never happened to meet Lady Emma Foxworth? She is accounted the greatest beauty in Bath and she is a fine musician as well; her performance at the pianoforte must be considered quite remarkable."

"I have never been to Bath and, as you know, have had little experience of society in general," said Anne in a decidedly cold manner, and she walked over to Elizabeth and the other ladies to escape any further conversation on such a distressing subject. But while she tried to attend to her friends' discussion of the possible decoration of the picture gallery through which they were now walking, she could not stop comparing herself to that paragon of young ladies, Lady Emma. Not for the first time she mentally reproached her mother for denying to her the opportunity to become accomplished at *something*.

At that moment Fitzwilliam came over to her and asked her opinion on the coffered ceiling and whether she thought it should be retained or replaced. As it was a subject in which she could hardly have been less informed, it was evident that her cousin had been motivated by a desire to speak to her and draw her into the discussion. He was looking into her face expectantly as if her idea on the subject should determine the entire fate of the project, when he was called over by Grey to examine some rotten windowsills.

Lord Holland was immediately at her side once more. The two of them were standing before a large portrait of a lady, apparently the mother of the recently deceased baronet. To Anne's astonishment Lord Holland reached out and took her left wrist in his hands gently and turned her palm upwards as if he would kiss her hand.

"Why, see, Miss de Bourgh how similar this bracelet you are wearing is to the one in this portrait. What an odd coincidence," and he went on holding her hand in his for several seconds while gazing into her eyes. It was the gesture of an accepted lover who had no doubt as to the reception of his attentions. Anne was so surprised that she was motionless for a moment until he released her hand and smiled at her.

She looked about the room in concern lest anyone should have witnessed this tender exchange and to her dismay saw that the only person looking in their direction was Fitzwilliam, who by some unlucky chance had turned that way. He looked at first surprised and then very grave, his displeasure evident in his usually amiable countenance. Lord Holland, who was still smiling complacently, bowed slightly towards Fitzwilliam, then turned back to Anne. She had the pain of seeing her cousin look coldly at her and then turn away.

As they continued their tour of the house Grey had on several occasions to draw Fitzwilliam's attention back to the matter at hand, for the young man who had been examining everything so attentively now seemed liable to stop before every other window and gaze distractedly out at the neglected park. After a while, however, he seemed to recall himself to his task and was soon examining chimneys and making his way with Grey and Bingley into the attic to look at rafters. The rest of the company was content to remain below and wait, since the dust and dirt of these upper reaches were excessive.

The gentlemen finally ventured out onto the roof that had a magnificent view of the surrounding countryside. Bingley, who had a dislike of heights, stayed safely in one spot as his friends ventured out fearlessly to look at some brickwork. When they returned Fitzwilliam suggested that a London architect be called upon to come on consultation as soon as possible to confirm the opinion that he and Grey had formed.

Below, the rest of the group awaited them impatiently, while wandering about looking at the rooms that had been unused for so long. Anne felt confused and very angry with Lord Holland, blaming him for the look of disapproval from Fitzwilliam that had given her so much pain. She decided to avoid her suitor and stay close to Georgiana and Lady Grinspoon.

Finally they were all back downstairs and Grey and Fitzwilliam were ready to pronounce their verdict. It would have been helpful if

Lady Blanchard had had the discretion to leave during these deliberations but she stayed to hear everything they said and seemed unmoved by any criticism of her old home. The two young men began with the caveat that they were not architects and had only amateur opinions to offer, but that they thought that despite some obvious problems due to several years of poor maintenance, the house was basically sound and had good potential as a fine country residence for a gentleman's family.

"The only thing is," said Grey, "that you will have to completely tear down the addition, including the front portico, and begin again. The original portion of the house is a distinguished building, but has been defaced by the unfortunate nature of the later portion. You can live quite comfortably here while you make the appropriate changes, and the cost will be only a little more than constructing a new house."

Bingley looked a little pale at the idea of such an outlay to make an ancient and run-down dwelling acceptable when he could have built a fine new mansion for the same amount, but the joy in Jane's countenance was enough to convince him that Thrushfold Hall should be theirs, whatever the expense and inconvenience. Besides, the very age of the place had a charm for him, as a man with a large but new fortune acquired by his father in trade, and longing for the distinction of an old estate and county associations. The house was not Pemberley, but in its own way, with sufficient money and time, might be as distinguished.

Lady Blanchard, who had begun to chafe a bit during the prolonged assessment of the Hall, was delighted at this outcome, for Mr. Bingley was not a man to haggle over the price, and she believed that she should soon find herself a rich woman. It was agreed that their attorneys in London should work out the details of the sale and that the new owners should take possession within two weeks. Fitzwilliam was to undertake to engage the architect he had mentioned, and work on the interior would begin almost immediately, as soon as competent workmen could be engaged.

"Oh, it is certainly the most beautiful house I have ever seen," cried Jane, embracing her sister and almost dancing around the hall with her, "excepting, of course, Pemberley, which must always be accounted the finest of all."

On the return journey almost everyone was in excellent spirits. Anne, however, was in a state of considerable agitation of mind and had difficulty in responding to her friends' happy conversation. Lady Grinspoon and Georgiana were delighted with the prospect of so much family happiness as would flow from the Bingleys living at such an easy distance of Pemberley.

"Never was so much felicity better deserved than by dear Mrs. Darcy and Mrs. Bingley," cried Lady Grinspoon, "Why, we should all contrive to live near to those who are dear to us. Why do we tolerate separation from them when life is so short? I believe I shall buy a little cottage nearby just to have the joy of seeing you all every week."

Georgiana, who had come to love Elizabeth as a dear sister, had taken an immediate liking to Jane and echoed Lady Grinspoon's sentiments enthusiastically. Anne murmured something in agreement, but her thoughts were all centered on the scene in the picture gallery and the look of strong disapprobation that she had seen on the face of Fitzwilliam. She was very angry with Lord Holland; he had never taken the slightest liberty before. Why he had chosen that moment to take her hand in the manner of a man who has long possessed the heart of his lady was something she could not imagine, but she was vexed and distressed almost beyond bearing and it was all that she could do to appear in a fairly normal temper before the other occupants of the carriage.

The more she thought about the little scene the more puzzled she became. Why was Fitzwilliam so angry? She had tried to catch his eye as they all prepared to set out for Pemberley, but he seemed not to know that she was there, got on his horse without a glance in her direction and cantered off before the other gentleman were even mounted. Anne knew very well that everyone assumed that her engagement to Lord Holland was something to be expected at any time and that her friends looked at the match with favor. Her mother, in ecstasies at the idea that her daughter would be a marchioness as soon as the inconvenient older brother should consent to die, had written to Darcy to encourage him to forward the match. Darcy, she had observed, had not shown much warmth of manner towards the young man, but everyone knew that Darcy was reserved and that some degree of time and effort were required to secure his friendship. There was certainly every indication that he approved the match or he would never have asked Lord Holland to Pemberley.

Why then, she asked herself, was Fitzwilliam so demonstrably outraged at the tender moment he had witnessed? True, Lord Holland had been rather unfortunate in the timing of his attentions, but a man in love was generally pardoned for such infractions, as long as it was clear that his intentions were honorable. He was everything that a girl might wish for in a suitor; of noble birth, handsome, clever, with an impressive figure and the power to charm his company wherever he might happen to be. Everyone seemed to like him and sometimes she herself thought that she really might come to care for him if she allowed herself to do so. Why, then, in opposition to the good opinion of all should her cousin disapprove?

About halfway through the trip home they stopped at an inn for some refreshment and Anne had to be impressed with the gentle attentions of Lord Holland, who could not be easy until he was sure that she had been provided with everything for her comfort. At the same time she found herself avoided by Fitzwilliam, if only in a way that was solely apparent to her.

When they continued on her way Mr. Grey was obliging enough to take her place in the carriage and give her his gentle mare to ride the rest of the way, as he had thoughtfully had a saddle brought for her and the arrangement was easily accomplished. Anne was touched by his kindness and happy to be out of the carriage, which she had begun to find stifling. Now, at last, she would have an opportunity to talk to her cousin and discover what he was thinking, for it never occurred to her that he would not speak frankly to her.

They rode along at an easy trot for about a mile, during which she stayed close by Fitzwilliam's side as he talked to Bingley about the many changes that would have to be made at Thrushfold Hall and advised him as to how to make the place habitable as soon as possible, for Bingley had a romantic notion of being in his new home by the new year. He was polite enough to include Anne in the conversation, occasionally asking her opinion about what she had thought of the way in which his father had transformed his castle in Scotland into a comfortable dwelling. But he seemed so cool and indifferent, with so little of his usual affectionate manner towards her, that Anne found herself becoming angry with her cousin and a feeling of resentment replaced the chill about her heart.

After a few minutes of hoping that he would once again become the person she knew and loved so well, she could no longer tolerate the presence of this stranger who looked like Fitzwilliam, and she cantered off impulsively. Lord Holland, who seemed to have been waiting for just such an opening was immediately at her side and the two continued at a quick pace until they were somewhat ahead of the others.

Soon Anne slowed her horse to a trot; she felt tired and although she did not wish to enter into a private conversation with Lord Holland, it was clear that she had made it difficult to avoid. Indeed, an impartial observer might have assumed that such had been her design in going ahead of the group in such a dramatic fashion. The young man himself certainly seemed to be in high spirits and rode close by her side with his usual careless grace.

"A great day for your family, Miss de Bourgh! How delightful it will be for two such devoted sisters to be settled at such a convenient distance to one another."

Anne turned and could not help smiling at her companion. It would have been difficult not to, for he seemed full of happiness and enthusiasm on that day. She had never seen him more animated. She was still quite vexed with him for his display of intimacy in the picture gallery but could think of no way to reproach him without seeming a prudish fool. Perhaps his gesture had been nothing out of the ordinary and she was certainly no judge of such things. She thought of asking Lady Grinspoon about the propriety of Lord Holland's behavior when the opportunity should present itself, but it would be so difficult to describe what she had felt, that it would be best to forget the entire matter. Consequently she allowed herself to fall into easy conversation with her companion, now and then breaking into a canter out of sheer exuberance, for the day had become one of those exquisite clear fall afternoons that are so intoxicating for an outing on horseback.

After a half hour Anne was surprised to find that they were out of sight of the rest of the company and although she pulled back to a walk there was no sound of hoof beats or carriage wheels to be heard. She was very conscious of the fact that it must appear to Lord Holland that she had sought to be alone with him and she felt herself flush with confusion. His face was suffused with a bright elation and before she could regain her equanimity he began to speak in the most animated and earnest manner.

"Miss de Bourgh, forgive me if I cannot help but make use of this opportunity to tell you what I am sure you already know, that I love you with all my heart and that my one wish in life is to make you my wife and spend a life of perfect happiness with you." She was afraid that he would try to take her hand, but he only rode close to her side, looking into her face with the intent gaze that had always filled her with a strange agitation that she could not define.

He went on rapidly, "I made an attempt to speak to you of my feelings in Scotland, but did not press the matter as I could see that you were hesitant to hear me, but I can no longer be silent. I beg you, give me some hope that you can return my affection."

Anne felt as if she had been struck dumb and had never felt so completely at a loss. Her heart beat so quickly that she began to be afraid that she might faint from the excessive emotion that she was experiencing. But what kind of emotion was it? She could not tell; she could only feel the force of Lord Holland's will as he tried to fix her eyes with his. When she resisted looking at him, he did lean forward and take possession of her hand and raise it to his lips. She pulled it away as if from a flame and was almost in tears.

Finally she did find her voice, but was humiliated to hear how tremulous it was, "I cannot hear this right now, Lord Holland. I am aware of the compliment you pay me with your addresses, but I beg you will excuse me from making any answer at present."

In fact, Anne was afraid that any further speech on her part would lead her to break into tears and her only desire was to avoid that disaster. No doubt she should answer his proposal in some definite way, but so confused was her mind that she was unable to think of a rational way in which to express herself. Indeed, she could not tell what her answer would have been if it had been possible to summon up more self-control. The man was so overwhelming in his brilliant presence and beauty that for a moment she felt she could not resist him if he spoke another word.

The young man was by no means disheartened by Anne's reaction for he took the degree of her perturbation as encouragement and might have pressed his advantage had not the other horsemen come cantering up behind them. Bingley was in the lead and joined them, talking with the greatest good humor and not seeming to notice Anne's distress. She was able to regain her composure quickly as Bingley gave himself over to soliciting Lord Holland's opinion on every aspect of Thrushfold Hall.

"I have been hearing much of your excellent taste and wish to take advantage of your good judgment if you will be so kind. What can you suggest for a proper music room? What do you think of the park? Would you take down those old elms?"

Lord Holland's gracious efforts to reply to all of Bingley's questions took the rest of the journey back to Pemberley and Anne was able to listen in silence and be left to her own reflections.

Darcy and Fitzwilliam, at a slight distance behind, were left to themselves and had not exchanged many words when Fitzwilliam could not restrain himself from saying, "Well, is there a definite engagement between Anne and Lord Holland? They seem to take a lively interest in each other from what I observed today,"

Darcy was rather surprised and answered, "Why, no. They are not engaged as far as I know and surely there would be no reason for concealment as no one could reasonably object to such an attachment. In fact, I have frequent letters from my aunt urging me to forward the match. It is not a very pleasant aspect of Lady Catherine's character, but she points out that the older brother, whom she sees fairly often in the pump room, looks likely to die at any time, and she is thrilled at the idea that her child will be a peeress."

"But how much do you really know of the fellow?" asked Fitzwilliam irritably, "Have you made all possible inquiries?"

"Absolutely," replied Darcy, "I have asked all the most reliable people of my acquaintance and there is nothing to be said against him. He is rich, clever, and gentlemanlike. To be sure, giving up his commission in the navy was a bit odd, but no one in the service has had an ill word to say about him that I can discover. By all accounts he served his country well and faithfully."

"But really, Darcy," cried Fitzwilliam, "What sort of man gives up his post- captaincy? It makes it look as though he counted on his brother's dying."

Darcy was rather taken aback by his cousin's vehemence and replied. "By everything I have been told such an expectation seems more than justified. And Lord Holland has certainly devoted himself to looking after his ailing brother's interests."

"You mean the interests of the estate which he expects to inherit. I tell you, Darcy, I have a bad feeling about this man and I intend to watch him carefully while I am here. There may be something not quite as it should be about Lord Holland."

Darcy was a little offended at the idea that a questionable young man would have been admitted to Pemberley and allowed to court their cousin Anne, but he said no more and the two rode on in silence for a few minutes until Fitzwilliam spoke again.

"Do you think Anne loves the fellow? I suppose that he is just the type to appeal to an inexperienced girl."

Darcy looked thoughtful and replied, 'I think she certainly likes him. They are much together and she always seems to enjoy his company. However, Anne is cautious by nature and this may be the reason that they are not yet engaged. I suppose Holland has too much sense to urge his suit until he is sure of a favorable reception."

"Good!" exclaimed Fitzwilliam. 'The more time I have to study the fellow, the better I will like it. But as I told you in Scotland, I do not think that he is the man for her."

Darcy was a bit mystified as he could not see any apparent reason for his cousin's dislike of Holland, but there seemed to be nothing further to say on the subject and they were soon talking of other things.

CHAPTER 40

$\mathcal{T}$hose of the party on horseback took a slightly longer route back to Pemberley as Darcy wished to show them an attractive path through the woods; consequently they were about half an hour later than the rest of the company in reaching the house. It was pleasant to find that Lady Blanchard had taken herself off to Lady Templeton's and they would not be further burdened with her company. Darcy entered the drawing room first and found Mrs. Bingley and Lady Grinspoon standing by Elizabeth who was seated in a chair before the fire. They had an air of concerned sympathy and he was afraid for a moment that she might be unwell.

When Elizabeth saw her husband, however, she leapt up and ran to greet him with a somewhat unconvincing air of gaiety.

"Why, my dearest, here is a letter from your aunt that was here when I returned," she cried, "You will be delighted to hear that she has decided to honor us with a visit much sooner than we had hoped; next week in fact."

"Good God!" exclaimed Darcy, very much taken aback and unable to contain an initial reaction of dismay. The rest of the party of riders had just followed him into the room and looked at him curiously.

"Indeed, my love," Elizabeth went on in an animated way, "and

Lady Catherine adds that she plans to bring a friend with her as well; Lady Emma Foxworth about whom we have heard so much."

As she said these words she could not help looking over at Fitzwilliam. In fact everyone else in the room turned in his direction. But if he had any particular reaction to the news of the approach of this young lady to whom he was assumed to have an attachment he did not betray it. He looked very cool and said, "How very inconvenient for you, Mrs. Darcy, who already have a full house to contend with. I am very fond of my aunt, but I fear that this does not show much consideration on her part."

"Oh, not at all," replied Elizabeth bravely. "We shall be delighted to see them. What an unexpected treat it is."

"My dear friend," said Lady Grinspoon, "It is too much, and I think I should take myself out of the way. I should really return to London soon in any case."

"Please, no, Lady Grinspoon," cried Elizabeth, taking her hand affectionately, "It would be so very helpful to have you here. I beg that you will not think of leaving. You must all of you stay, or I will be very unhappy indeed." She suddenly had visions of all her guests fleeing at the approach of Lady Catherine and of being left alone with her.

Lady Grinspoon patted her hand kindly and said, "Well of course, my dear, I will stay if I can be of any use to you at all."

Anne, very much horrified at the news of her mother's imminent arrival, found some excuse to go to her room as quickly as possible.

After a few minutes Darcy was able to persuade Elizabeth to go upstairs to rest for a while and having escorted her there he spent the next hour holding her in his arms and trying to reassure her. At first he proposed writing to his aunt and telling her that changing the date of her visit would be the cause of too much inconvenience, but Elizabeth would not hear of it.

"No, my love! You are very good, but your aunt would be very much offended and since this is the first overture of good will she has made I do not want to do anything that might cause ill feeling. We have plenty of room and can make the east wing ready for her quickly enough."

Darcy was unable to change his wife's mind in spite of saying. "You know that she is only coming because she knows from her sister that Fitzwilliam is here and she is determined to forward a match between him and Lady Emma. My aunt always has some campaign underway which is designed to run other people's lives."

"Is there an understanding between Fitzwilliam and Lady Emma?" asked Elizabeth, drying a few stray tears that she had been unable to repress.

"I wish I knew," replied Darcy, "I asked him something about the situation when we were in Scotland, but you know how reserved he can be, and how off-putting when anyone, even I, asks him anything personal. He merely said that she was an agreeable young lady and that they had some interests in common. I cannot imagine what that means."

The result of this conference between husband and wife was that they would do their best to entertain Lady Catherine and her young friend and hope that Darcy's aunt would be more agreeable than they had reason to expect. "After all," said Elizabeth, "we knew that she was coming anyway. What are a few extra weeks added to her visit?" To this Darcy made no reply, but merely kissed his wife and thought to himself that she was very brave indeed.

To distract herself from her worries Elizabeth went down to the music room to practice the pianoforte for an hour. This was something of a habit with her in the late afternoon when the house was quiet and most of her guests were off entertaining themselves by walking or riding. She was playing a rather sad and meditative piece when Lord Holland appeared in the doorway.

"Oh, I do love Field's nocturnes," he said, "and how well you play that piece. Do you mind if I come in and listen?"

It was not unusual for Lord Holland to join her there at that time of day and they had many interesting conversations about music. She had actually learned a great deal from the young man, for his knowledge was considerably beyond that of most gifted amateurs. Since his arrival they often played together in the evening, much to the delight of their friends at Pemberley.

"Why, I should be very glad of your company," replied Elizabeth,

"Perhaps you could give me your opinion on this passage which is causing me some difficulty."

They looked over the sheet music for a few minutes and then Lord Holland ventured, "So, Mrs. Darcy, it would seem that our ranks are to be swelled by two more guests. I admire your fortitude in undertaking so much."

Elizabeth laughed and said that there was plenty of room and that, after all, Lady Catherine was part of the family and welcome at any time.

Holland looked thoughtful for a moment and then said, "I did meet her ladyship once, although I am sure that she does not remember the occasion. I was riding in the park with my friend Wentworth and we encountered Lady Catherine, who was taking the air in a very grand equipage. It was one of her rare trips to London, I suppose. Wentworth went to greet her, as she and his mother are old friends. He was so good as to make me known to her as well, but unfortunately she was very angry with her coachman for some offense and I do not think she really noticed me. I hope to make a better impression this time; you know of course how important her good opinion is to me."

Lord Holland had on several occasions made very open statements to Elizabeth as to his intentions towards Anne and she had listened sympathetically to his confidences.

"Why, I am sure she will like you very much indeed," she said, "How could it be otherwise?"

At such kind words Lord Holland looked quite pleased and said that he only wished that it might be so. As to Lady Catherine's letters to Darcy indicating her approval of the match he naturally knew nothing. He went on, "I am glad of the opportunity to make her acquaintance under such favorable circumstances, although I feel that I should make my departure from Pemberley fairly soon. I have trespassed on your hospitality long enough and would not wish to intrude on your family gathering as the Christmas season approaches."

Elizabeth had not thought about Lord Holland's departing any time soon and she was dismayed when she thought of it. Surely he must be asked to remain until something should be settled with Anne one way or another. But had she been honest with herself she would have realized that she desperately wished for allies to help her endure Lady Catherine's visit. The young nobleman was an invaluable asset at Pemberley with his gift for conversation and the excellence of his musicianship; even Lady Catherine might be distracted from continual criticism by his presence and the delight of hearing him play every evening.

"Good heavens, you do not mean to leave us!" she exclaimed, "Why we shall be very disappointed if you do not remain through Christmas."

Lord Holland made the usual polite remarks about causing inconvenience to Mr. and Mrs. Darcy by overstaying his time with them and initially asserted that he must soon take his leave of them, but after a few minutes expressed his delight at the prospect of staying longer at Pemberley.

At this moment Darcy happened to enter the room; he stopped rather abruptly when he saw his wife and Lord Holland sitting together, then walked in to join them. Elizabeth jumped up and went to him eagerly, taking his hand affectionately.

"Why, here is some good news, my darling," she cried, "Lord Holland has agreed to stay with us through Christmas; we will not be deprived of his company and his wonderful playing which we enjoy so much every evening."

A sensitive guest would hardly have been reassured by Darcy's cold reception of this information. He stood very still for a moment, looking into his wife's face and then at Holland with no great warmth. But after a few seconds he seemed to recollect himself and managed to smile graciously, "Very glad to hear it, Holland. We would have been sorry to lose you."

After this exchange Elizabeth went off to see to some arrangements for dinner and Lord Holland to walk out in search of Anne. Darcy was left alone and went to the windows and looked moodily out at the lake and the view that he loved so well. It had taken all of his self control to speak politely to Holland and he was disturbed to find just how much he had been looking forward to the young man's departure. It was illogical of course; he had been tacitly promoting a marriage between Holland and his cousin Anne by entertaining him at Pemberley. Now he realized that he had been hoping that something would be resolved on that front quickly, so that Holland would leave for Bath to seek Lady Catherine's permission for the match. At least Holland would have been out of the house for a while in that case. But now, conveniently, his aunt was to join them and it was likely that Anne's suitor would remain for quite a while.

Darcy was annoyed with himself; he knew that his dislike for Lord Holland was unfounded; the man was a good match for his cousin. But he now had to confront the fact that seeing him standing next to Elizabeth had made him almost mad with a rage that he had concealed only with the greatest difficulty

I really must get hold of myself, he thought. This jealousy I feel when anyone comes near Elizabeth is degrading and absurd, especially in this case when I know that Holland is in love with my cousin. Somehow, I must overcome this despicable tendency.

LORD HOLLAND'S good manners were very much in evidence later that evening as the company assembled in the drawing room. Approaching Mrs. Darcy in his usual modest way he ventured to observe that it might be well if he were to be relocated to another bedchamber for the better convenience of Lady Catherine and her friend.

"I hope you will not take it amiss, Mrs. Darcy, if I say that even so magnificent a house as Pemberley cannot possess an unlimited supply of such exquisitely appointed rooms as the one you have given me. I should be happy to move and can make myself comfortable anywhere." Fitzwilliam and Grey had been standing near enough to hear this gracious offer and immediately came over and insisted that they too should give up their present accommodations. Elizabeth was a bit overwhelmed because very soon there seemed to be a competition between the gentlemen as to who would make the greatest sacrifice for their hostess' convenience and she believed that an argument was about to begin as to who would have the honor of sleeping in the barn. Darcy came over and quickly decided the matter; Lord Holland

and Fitzwilliam would remove themselves to rooms over the stable block. These were perfectly comfortable if one did not object to being awakened early by all the commotion in the courtyard. Grey was by no means to change as he had occupied the same room for so many months.

Elizabeth was greatly relieved as she had been at a loss as to how she might find acceptable bedchambers for both Lady Catherine and Lady Emma. Now they would have very pleasant rooms with a view of the lake. The only person who was less than pleased with the outcome of the conversation was Fitzwilliam who did not enjoy the prospect of having Lord Holland as a neighbor as he had formed such a dislike for the young nobleman. Had Elizabeth been aware of all the undercurrents of ill-will among some of the gentlemen in the house she would have been very much dismayed.

For that evening she was happy; the perfect tenderness and affection that Darcy had shown towards her earlier in the day and his solicitude in wishing to spare her the difficulties of Lady Catherine's premature arrival had touched her heart. At dinner her eyes sought his across the long expanse of polished table and when his gaze met hers, she could not look away. Lady Grinspoon had been making some remark, but Elizabeth seemed to lose the entire thread of their conversation and had to apologize to her friend.

"My dear," said the older lady, "as if I could fail to understand. Remember that I spend my time writing romances; it has rarely been my experience to encounter one in real life."

Elizabeth could only blush and laugh, and in few minutes found herself aware once more of her husband's eyes upon her, but this time there was a sadness in his face that seemed inexplicable to her. How she wished she could run to him in that moment and ask him the reason for the melancholy that she had seen in Darcy more frequently of late.

Anne, seated between Darcy and Fitzwilliam, was finding the evening difficult and her spirits were much oppressed. When she spoke to Fitzwilliam on several topics he was all polite interest and kindly attention, but there was a feeling that he had somehow distanced himself from her. The old openness and understanding that had always been theirs was missing in a way that was subtle but deeply depressing to Anne. Her pride would not allow her to show her dismay, and by the end of dinner she was beginning to experience some resentment and even anger towards the person who had always been her greatest object of affection and veneration.

It was something of a relief to encounter Lord Holland's warm admiration and eagerness to converse with her when they all reassembled in the music room later. When he was prevailed upon to play, first with Elizabeth, and then with Georgiana, she had to admit to herself that it would be impossible to find a more accomplished, agreeable man or one with a more strikingly handsome appearance. His playing was so full of fire and emotion that she had to ask herself how it was that she had been able to resist falling in love with him; surely she must be the only young lady in England to be capable of such coldness. Now, she thought, why not allow herself to return his affection? Why not accept a match that was approved by her mother and all of her friends and relations? But there was one person whose approbation was most essential to her and that was Fitzwilliam. Perhaps after a week or two, when her cousin had had more time to know Lord Holland there would be an opportunity to ask his opinion.

The unaccustomed length of her ride that day had fatigued Anne and she was glad when Elizabeth suggested that they all retire somewhat earlier than usual. This plan did not apply to the gentlemen, who all retired to the billiard room that Darcy had recently had installed, but the ladies were happy to go to their rest. Anne found her maid waiting for her and sank down gratefully into an armchair by the fire.

"Celestine, it would seem that we are to expect my mother, Lady Catherine, somewhat earlier that had been anticipated."

Celestine, who had naturally been aware of this fact for several hours, merely raised an eyebrow. Then she looked sympathetically at Anne, for she had become fond of her young mistress, who now submitted to Celestine's tyranny in every aspect of her dress and the arranging of her hair with the meekness of a lamb.

Anne continued wearily, "We may expect my mother to disapprove of the changes that these last few months have made in my appearance. A major crisis in regard to my hair is certainly inevitable."

Celestine muttered something in French that Anne could not quite understand, then said with a shrug, "Well, my lady, there is no way to make your hair grow faster, and as for your old dresses, I have given them all away. Let us hope that her ladyship will not be so discontented as you think."

Anne was amused by the sly smile with which Celestine accompanied this remark. Soon she was lying awake in her bed, trying to sort out the confusing events of the day. A harsh rain was beating against the windows and she wondered what kind of sport the gentlemen would have the next morning and whether Fitzwilliam would join the hunt in spite of his injured leg. Knowing him, she believed that he would not only go out but lead the field and surpass even Lord Holland in boldness. She fell into a reverie in which she compared the two men. Certainly Lord Holland was by far the more handsome; even her partiality for her cousin could not blind her to the fact. Rather than masculine beauty, her cousin possessed distinction and a nobility of bearing. To Anne, in her girlish reflections, he moved with the strength and dignity of a lion and the grace of a falcon in flight. How she adored the light of intelligence and feeling in his countenance. For Anne there was in Fitzwilliam such a perfect mixture of the qualities that she loved, of sound good sense and youthful high spirits, of romantic daring and the most perfect gentleness and kindness.

CHAPTER 41

$\mathcal{T}$he next morning the hunt was to start out from Pemberley. Some of the ladies were still asleep when the friends and neighbors began to assemble at the house.

Elizabeth had been up quite early, making sure that all the preparations were properly attended to. Anne had kept her company, being as useful as possible and greeting new arrivals as they appeared, should Mrs. Darcy have been called away for some reason.

Lord Faulconer and his daughter were among the earliest guests. Anne was glad to see them as she had become fond of the old gentleman and felt genuine admiration for Lady Margaret. A plan had been approved by Darcy whereby Anne would follow the hunt for a short distance under the protection of Lord Faulconer; after a half hour or so, he would escort her back to Pemberley. This was a compromise since Darcy still considered Anne far too inexperienced a horsewoman for anything more demanding. "Perhaps in a year or too," was his inevitable reply to her entreaties. This always led Anne to wonder where she might be in a "year or two" and under whose authority.

Lady Margaret looked exquisitely lovely in her hunting attire and seemed in very high spirits. She greeted everyone cheerfully, but Anne, who observed the lady carefully, saw that she glanced around the room in an impatient way as if searching for someone. In a few minutes Mr. Grey entered, booted and great-coated as if for a journey, and went up to Darcy and Elizabeth.

"How sorry I am to miss today's sport," he was heard to say, "I will be thinking of you all and hoping that you have a good run and everything to your enjoyment."

"My dear fellow," replied Darcy, "we will miss you very much, but will look forward to your return in a week or so."

"I will be back by a week from Wednesday," said Grey, "and will write if I am to be delayed."

Then the young man went around the room to say "hail and farewell" to everyone, all of whom felt a real affection for him, with the exception of Squire Redfern, who was pleased to have him out of the county.

When Grey came to stand before Anne and Lady Margaret, he said with a bow, "I wish you both a very pleasant outing. I only beg, Lady Margaret, that you keep an eye on Miss de Bourgh, who is to be allowed her first foray into the field today. Attempt, I pray, to discourage that tendency to reckless exploits to which her friends know her to be all too prone."

This was said in a very serious manner, but Grey could not keep the expression of amused affection from his eyes.

"Oh, yes, Mr. Grey," said Anne, laughing, "One need only know me for the briefest time to imagine my impulsive nature getting me into all kinds of scrapes. It has been the watchword of my life, as my mother could tell you."

Lady Margaret looked puzzled and not particularly pleased by this exchange, "I will do my best, certainly, Mr. Grey, but Miss de Bourgh is the last person I would have thought to require restraint."

"More's the pity," said Anne, "Well, have a good journey, Mr. Grey. Try not to get lost and find yourself on the wrong continent."

Grey bowed once again to them both and in a moment was out of the house and cantering down the drive.

As he left, Lady Margaret seemed irresistibly drawn to the windows that overlooked the path he had taken and Anne moved in that direction with her.

"You and Mr. Grey seem to be on very easy terms with each other," said the lady, as she looked out at the frost covered park with its bare trees, "He certainly addresses you with a greater freedom than I would have imagined very likely. You have only known each other since the summer, I believe?"

"Why, yes," replied Anne, "but there is something about Mr. Grey that makes one feel that one has known him forever. He is so frank and good-natured."

"You say this of him, but I recall that when he first came among us, he concealed his identity and it was only revealed by the interference of Lady Templeton."

"I think that if you knew more about his history and the nature of his father, Lord Harwith, you would forgive Mr. Grey for what he did," said Anne, "He has used the name 'Grey' for many years, since his break with his father, and with such a parent, who could blame him for wishing to come into the neighborhood 'newly-minted' as it were."

"Perhaps," said Lady Margaret gravely, "My father chooses to over-look it, and I have great confidence in his judgment. But, you must admit, Miss de Bourgh, that there is something rather secretive about Mr. Grey. Why this sudden departure without any explanation as to where he was going?"

Anne was by now very much amused and more than a little grati-fied. Here was more evidence that she had been correct in believing Lady Margaret very much attached to John Grey. The young lady was obviously almost overcome by the need to talk about him, although she was attempting to hide her interest.

"There is no secret about Mr. Grey's journey," said Anne, "He is such a modest person that I am sure that he did not flatter himself that you would have any interest in his plans. He has gone to Cambridge to arrange for his sojourn there after the New Year. You must be aware that he means to take orders."

"Why, yes, so I understand. My father mentioned it just lately" then after hesitating a moment Lady Margaret asked, "but what will he do then? Perhaps he plans to settle somewhere nearby?"

"Well, that is hardly a matter under his own control. He must find a parish, and they are not so easily come by, it would seem. But Mr.

Grey is so fortunate as to have a good friend in Wales with a living in his gift, which may soon be available."

Anne then had the satisfaction of seeing Lady Margaret turn pale and cry, "Good heavens! Wales! But that is so far from Derbyshire." Then recollecting herself she added, "The Darcys will be very disappointed to lose Mr. Grey. It will be a sad thing for them. And, of course, my father is quite fond of him."

Anne could not suppress an unworthy feeling of delight at the lady's distress. She had great affection for Mr. Grey and could not help being out of patience and rather angry with Lady Margaret for causing her friend so much unhappiness. How this young woman could be such a fool as to spurn his love was something Anne could not understand. She would have been unkind enough to twist the knife again if it could have assisted Mr. Grey's interests, but there was a flurry of activity and it was time to go.

LORD FAULCONER WAS DELIGHTED to have been given the pleasure of attending Miss de Bourgh. They were to go a little distance with the hunt and then turn back to Pemberley. Anne was to be allowed to take a few low jumps under his supervision, but he had decided that it would be prudent to stay to the rear and hang back as much as possible. There was not an inch of the country that Lord Faulconer did not know well and Darcy felt perfect confidence in the older man. There had been a short gallop that Anne had found wonderfully exhilarating, but now everyone was at a halt in the cold air while the hounds worked a small woodland. Anne was wild with excitement and caught up in the anticipation of another headlong plunge forward. Lord Holland rode up to her and said something complimentary, but Anne barely heard him, so keenly was she watching the huntsmen and the hounds and waiting for the chance to be off again.

The moment was soon upon them and the field was off at great speed. Anne forgot all about staying behind and returning to Pemberley at a sedate pace. Her character was a strange mixture of timidity and fearlessness; she might dread the very idea of some undertaking, but once engaged upon it she forgot her trepidation and was brave to the point of recklessness. Lord Faulconer, who had expected something of the sort, stayed near her every moment and was at her side when the fox went to earth and they were all brought to an abrupt halt.

"Well, Miss de Bourgh, you did very well indeed," he said, riding up to her, "but now I think 1 must exert my authority as your appointed guardian for the morning and escort you home."

Anne was about to protest, but there was that air of gentle authority about the old gentleman that made it unthinkable to argue with him. She turned her horse to join him, but not before several of her acquaintance had congratulated her on riding so well.

"Upon my word," said Lady Margaret, "It is astonishing to know that you had never been on horseback until a few months ago, Miss de Bourgh. You will outstrip us all very soon, if only Mr. Darcy will find you a faster horse."

"Do not listen to my daughter," said Lord Faulconer, as they trotted off in the direction of Pemberley, "That little mare is perfect for you. It's Mrs. Darcy's horse is it not? I remember when Darcy bought it from us for her. Heaven forbid that you follow my child's example and become dissatisfied with anything less than some fire-eating beast."

Anne said that she was more than happy to be riding Eilis and that she was very grateful to Mrs. Darcy for allowing her to do so.

"That's very good, very sensible," replied her companion. "And if an old man may be allowed to pay a compliment you look extremely well today. You are one of those young ladies who look born to ride. There is a certain style and dash that sets you apart, as though you were fit to do more than sit by the fire and do needlepoint."

Some impulse led Anne to ask, "Did Lady Margaret's mother also ride?"

Lord Faulconer looked at her sharply, as if no one had ever asked him such a question before, then looking straight ahead said softly, "Why, yes. She was a fine horsewoman; my daughter is very much like her, in that as in many other ways."

Anne would have liked to know more, but it did not require great perspicacity to realize that the subject was not a welcome one. Darcy had mentioned that Lady Faulconer had died some ten or twelve years ago, but had not said anything of the circumstances.

They rode along in silence for a few minutes, and then Lord Faulconer said, "Now, Lord Holland is a bold rider. 1 understand that he rescued Mrs. Darcy from a very dangerous runaway in Scotland."

Anne replied that such was the case and gave a brief account of what had occurred.

Lord Faulconer nodded thoughtfully and then said, "I knew his father well, and have met the older brother at my club on several occasions. Holland I had never met before, but I suppose that he went to sea at thirteen or fourteen and so has not been in evidence for some time."

Anne looked at her companion with some degree of curiosity, "Was his father your friend, Lord Faulconer?"

"Yes, he was a fine man, immensely rich, of course, but with a great sense of the responsibilities of his rank; an intelligent, kindly, modest person, and very good company. I visited him once in Scotland. It is a magnificent place with endless acres of moors and lochs, a vast kingdom in itself."

"And the current marquess, what of him? Is he like his father?"

"I would say that he is," replied Lord Faulconer, "It is a sad thing that his health is so precarious. No doubt you've heard the story."

"Indeed, all I know is that he is in delicate health, an affliction of the lungs, I believe, and that he is in Bath in the hope of some amelioration of that condition, but I know few of the details of his situation."

"You surprise me," said Lord Faulconer, shifting in his saddle to look at her more directly, "I would have thought, from Lord Holland's attentive manner to you, that you would know a great deal about his family."

Seeing that she only colored slightly and was silent, he continued, "Well, you must not have heard about how the young man almost drowned?"

"I've not heard the story in any detail," said Anne, and very much interested now, she begged him to continue.

"The marquess had a very reckless habit of swimming in the loch every day in the summer. Can you imagine how bitterly cold the water must be even at that time of year? However, he was always a strong young man and insisted on this unwise regimen, which he thought beneficial. One day a sudden storm came up and he found himself exhausted from battling the waves. He was at the end of his strength and would have gone under for good just a short distance from shore, but by the grace of God, his steward saw him and was able to rescue him."

"Good heavens! What a dreadful story! Was Lord Holland there at the time?"

"Yes, as I understand it he was visiting and appeared on the scene in time to help pull his brother to safety. At first it seemed that the only ill consequence of the adventure would be a lingering fatigue, but unfortunately, an affliction of the lungs developed thereafter and the result is as you have heard. The poor fellow has been many months in Bath and has consulted the best physicians both there and in London, but there has been no improvement. In fact, I hear that his friends expect that he will not survive the winter."

Anne said, "I have heard as much from my mother, who has been resident in Bath for several months."

Lord Faulconer replied, "Yes, I imagine that your mother is well informed on the subject. Now, Holland seems quite a good sort. Plays the violin a bit too well for a gentleman, but I suppose he can't help it." Then Lord Faulconer chuckled at his own small joke.

They talked on of general subjects until they reached Pemberley. Lord Faulconer was to spend the rest of the day there and stay for dinner. Elizabeth had prepared a comfortable spot for him by the fire in the library, with a pile of books that she had thought might interest him. His daughter was to meet him there later and remain for dinner along with several more of the Darcys' friends.

Anne found that she was not at all fatigued and believed that she could have very well stayed out all day with the hunt. How interesting it was that there was every day more evidence that far from being frail and sickly, she was actually blessed with what might be considered a robust constitution. When she had an opportunity for a conversation with Lady Grinspoon later that afternoon she felt compelled to speak of this discovery to her friend, who was by now quite a confidant.

"All my life my mother has insisted on my having one sort of disposition and constitution, and now I find that 1 am something altogether different. Why, I would be happy to spend all day on horseback out in the rain and come back to eat a hearty dinner and sleep soundly afterward. No nervous exhaustion, no fainting spells. My dear Lady Grinspoon, this is alarming indeed! If my mother has made such a serious error in this regard, then I must assume that everything else she has told me may be incorrect"

Lady Grinspoon laughed and replied, "Your mama is typical in this at least; she wishes to mold her daughter into a semblance of some image that is dear to her heart. Why she should want to think you a poor, weak sort of creature I cannot imagine. I do hope that learning that your parent is not infallible is not too disconcerting, my dear. It is something that all children must come to understand sooner or later."

"I never thought that my mother's understanding was perfect," said Anne, "but I did think that she knew something of the world and human nature. Now I am compelled to follow my own judgment, since I find things to be quite different from what she led me to expect."

She was thinking of many instances in which her mother had been proven wrong by recent events. Her uncle, far from being a reckless spendthrift, had turned out to be a responsible father who had managed the family wealth meticulously and who intended to provide a fortune for Fitzwilliam. Lady Catherine had warned of the guests she would meet at her uncle's castle being less than perfectly respectable, but as far as Anne could tell they were all the soul of propriety, as were the people she had encountered at Pemberley. In addition, now when Anne looked into her mirror she had begun to think that perhaps she was not, in fact, so very plain as her mother had told her; there were times, indeed, when she felt herself to be almost pretty.

"Lady Catherine is going to find the change in you quite a shock," said Lady Grinspoon, "I must say, that as a novelist I would like of all things to be there to see her reaction. But no doubt after the initial surprise she will be delighted with how well and strong you look."

"You are not at all well acquainted with my mama, are you, Lady Grinspoon?" replied Anne, "I'm afraid that such a storm is to break over Pemberley as has never been seen here before."

~

ELIZABETH, in the meantime was in the music room, planning for the evening to come; perhaps a little dancing would amuse her friends. She went through the appropriate pile of sheet music and chose what she thought best. It was her intention to ask Georgiana to play, although it was always difficult to overcome the young lady's reticence. Elizabeth had begun to adopt a kind of informality in her manner of entertaining her guests, and her greatest wish was to put everyone at ease, not to make some impression of extraordinary grandeur as Lady Catherine sought to do at Rosings. This seemed to suit Darcy as well, for although there was still something reserved and stately about her husband, he disliked any kind of superficial display and was pleased with the simple elegance of Elizabeth's arrangements. Her taste and discernment had grown in subtlety and refinement very rapidly and fortunately Darcy was capable of appreciating his wife's abilities.

Elizabeth sat down at the piano for a moment, but did not open the instrument. She stayed there some time deep in thought. A thousand details could have occupied her mind; certainly the impending arrival of Lady Catherine might well have filled her with anxiety. However, that concern was very much less important than a recurrent sense of unease in regard to her husband. While Darcy was generally as loving and devoted as she could possibly have wished, she was increasingly aware of his moods of abstraction when he seemed distant and almost cold towards her. This caused Elizabeth the deepest distress, for her husband was everything in the world to her. Perhaps he has begun to tire of me, she would think, and this idea caused her such pain that she could restrain her tears only with the greatest difficulty. The next moment would lead her to wonder if she should show less of her adoration for Darcy. I have bored him by being over-fond and attentive, Elizabeth would reflect, for he fell in love with me when I showed him absolutely no encouragement and now that he is sure of me, I have lost some of my value in his eyes.

This explanation for the change in her husband had gradually gained strength in Elizabeth's mind and she had begun to act almost unconsciously in a way that was slightly less affectionate and warm-hearted. She forbore to look across the room full of guests to catch his eye as she had been in the habit of doing so often. She removed her hand from his an instant sooner than she had been used to do, or occasionally found some reason to disengage herself from his embrace as they watched the sunset from the window-seat. By these little stratagems, feigning a coolness that she did not at all feel, she hoped to regain her power over his heart.

While she was tormenting herself with this idea of her husband's growing indifference, there came the sound of male voices in the hall; her husband had returned with his friends. Normally she would have leapt up and run to greet Darcy, but instantly decided to remain where she was, lest she appear overeager. He appeared in an instant, followed by Fitzwilliam and Bingley and looked around the room quickly as if he expected someone else to be there. Elizabeth wondered at the expression on his face, which could only be described as stern. She was afraid for an instant that there had been some accident in the field, when he said rather curtly, "Holland is not here then? We assumed that he had arrived before us, as he completely vanished after the last run."

"Not very likely," said Bingley with a laugh, "considering the blistering pace you kept us to on the way back here."

Darcy's countenance softened and he went up to his wife saying, "So you are all alone, my love, and I'm afraid you have had a dull afternoon."

"Not at all," replied Elizabeth, rising rather abruptly and moving away from her husband a few paces. She had been hurt and offended by his manner of entering the room; why should Lord Holland's whereabouts be more important than an affectionate word and look for his wife? She contrived to smile unconcernedly and added, "On the contrary, it has been a very pleasant day. We ladies have been able to amuse ourselves perfectly well without you gentlemen."

Bingley said something to the effect that from time to time it must be agreeable not to have the men underfoot, while Fitzwilliam sensing something different in the air looked at Darcy and Elizabeth with a slightly puzzled expression.

"Well, now you have returned and we must make the best of it," said Elizabeth laughing, "But do go into the library, where there is a good fire and everything to revive you after your day in the cold." Then she led them there without so much as a glance at her husband.

Lord Holland met them as they crossed the hall towards the library. He was striding in the direction of the music room with some appearance of eagerness when he saw the others. He looked a bit confused for a moment, then said, "Why, you have all returned. My horse seemed all done in so I came back early. Otherwise I would have been with you at the end."

"We came back a little before time as well," said Bingley, "Darcy became bored with the way things were going and hurried us here." Then he turned to his old friend and said teasingly, "Perhaps you are beginning to feel your age, Darcy and cannot quite last the entire day."

Fitzwilliam, who had been looking thoughtfully at Darcy said, "Nonsense, Bingley. I think that my cousin has a few good years left. With such a delightful house as this, I am surprised he ever leaves, even for a matter of hours." He said this with a smile for Elizabeth, but she seemed inattentive, her eyes on her husband.

Darcy made a gesture of impatience and said, "It will be a sad day when I cannot out-ride *you*, Bingley. Come and let us move to into the library, for I must own that I am perishing from hunger. Some sherry and a biscuit would be most welcome."

"I do think that we can do better than that," said Elizabeth, leading the gentlemen there.

CHAPTER 42

*H*owever much Anne might like and trust Lady Grinspoon, there was one secret that was never shared with her friend, or indeed with anyone, and that was the place that her cousin Fitzwilliam held in her heart. Nothing could have induced Anne to speak of her love for the young man, so hopeless did she believe her situation to be. After all, she thought, he was so infinitely above her in every respect, aside from the advantages that her wealth might offer. And if the conversation she had overheard at Castle Munford were based on fact, then her uncle would remedy even that deficiency soon enough.

Anne was very young in experience if not in years, and she had the idea that she could somehow alter her inmost self and learn to love Lord Holland. She spent some time every day thinking about his talents and virtues and admitting that he possessed every quality to recommend himself to any woman. Anne was a highly rational being who had begun to see that life held possibilities she could not have imagined only months before. She understood that she could either marry or resign herself to her mother's oppressive rule forever. Since Fitzwilliam did not return her feelings, then surely her best course of action was to try to attach herself to another worthy man who did profess a sincere attachment.

No heroine with a true sense of romance would be capable of such calculations, of course. For a *genuine* heroine the only possibility would be a lifetime of regret for her lost love shut up in a remote and gloomy tower somewhere, with a view of the sea, and endless mourning for what might have been. Anne was made of hardier stuff, and even with a heart full of pain thought that she might at least make something interesting out of her life.

She had spent so much time trying to bend her mind and emotions to her will that she was almost sorry when Fitzwilliam came up to her immediately when the gentlemen entered the library that afternoon.

Anne was sitting with Lady Grinspoon and Jane when Elizabeth came in with the four gentlemen who were more cold and fatigued than they would have been willing to admit. The ladies had been sitting around the fire, talking about the wonderful transformation that was to take place in the Bingleys' new house. The architect from London had been there for a week and would be presenting his preliminary plans in a few days time. Anne had been saying that she hoped Mr. Grey would have returned from Cambridge by then so that they might have the benefit of his opinion. As Elizabeth led the gentlemen into the room she seemed in good spirits, but Anne sensed something rather forced in her manner. Darcy, she noted with surprise, did not, as usual, position himself next to his wife, but went to another corner of the room and, with an expression of moody displeasure, spent some time looking over some sketches that had been left there by the architect.

The possibility that there could be some sort of coolness between two people so devoted to each other was very strange, and Anne was wondering at such an inexplicable development, when Fitzwilliam came to stand beside her. This was the first time since his arrival that he had done so, for although he had been civil and even kind in his manner of addressing her, he had shown no inclination for private conversation. Now, sitting down next to her and looking into her face with some of his old bright interest and warmth, he asked her how she had liked the hunt.

Anne had been so unhappy about her cousin's coldness towards her that this sudden friendliness was almost too much for her, and she was afraid that if she looked up at him that she might be unable to restrain her tears.

"Oh, I was delighted with the brief experience I had of it," she replied, "if only dear Lord Faulconer had not been so reliable a protector and taken me away just when things became exciting." Anne tried to smile as she said this, but her emotions were in such turmoil that she maintained her composure only by an effort that made her appear rather cold and abrupt. She was furious with herself for her lack of poise; here finally was an opportunity to talk with Fitzwilliam, and she hardly felt able to talk at all. He asked her a few other questions in a gentle tone, wondering all the while at her distracted manner.

Then it occurred to her that there was a very real danger that Lord Holland would walk over to them and interrupt their conversation, as he was in the habit of staying at Anne's side as much as possible. She looked across the room to find the young man and saw that he was talking with Elizabeth. Unfortunately, Fitzwilliam followed her gaze and comprehended its direction. He believed in that moment that his cousin must be in love with Lord Holland, an idea he had resisted for as long as possible.

Anne at last managed to smile up at him with open affection but the damage was done. Her cousin was no ordinary person and had already decided to try to change his opinion of Lord Holland and to take a more favorable attitude towards the match. If Anne loved the fellow, then Fitzwilliam would do what he could to promote her happiness and not give into his natural dislike for her suitor. While feeling a great and unaccustomed pain in his heart, he remarked, "Lord Holland was certainly one of the best riders there today. I understand that he excels at many things."

"Why, yes, he is considered to be a competent horseman, I believe," replied Anne rather impatiently, as she had no interest in speaking of Lord Holland.

"Certainly, he is an exceptional musician," continued her cousin.

"No one could deny it. We have all enjoyed his playing so much these last few weeks."

"He has, I believe, a very fine estate of his own in Somersetshire," continued Fitzwilliam, "inherited from his mother's side of the family."

"Oh, yes," replied Anne, "but he spends little time there," and then she broke off in confusion. She certainly did not wish to give the impression of having an intimate knowledge of Lord Holland's affairs. "But how do you come to know this, cousin?"

"1 have made it my business to know as much as possible of Lord Holland. It's a simple matter to make inquiries of one's circle of friends. 1 would do this in the case of any gentleman who displayed such evident admiration for you," and then Fitzwilliam paused a moment and continued softly, "and whose attentions you seemed to find agreeable."

Anne felt both dismay and frustration and would have given anything to be able to express her true feelings at that moment; that she liked her suitor well enough and had even been trying to learn to love him, but that her heart would always belong to her cousin. She could not conceal the truth from herself. Seeing both men together as they were now would have removed all doubt had she still entertained any. Lord Holland was standing with Elizabeth and Mrs. Bingley at the other end of the room and certainly no man could have better illustrated in face and figure the ideal of every young girl's romantic fancy. He must have been saying something amusing, as both ladies were laughing.

In contrast, here was Fitzwilliam close beside her, as she had dreamed of seeing him for so many weeks. He would not have been considered handsome, at least as the term is commonly used. His features were too strong for beauty, but distinguished by the look of high intelligence and spirit that lit up his eyes in a way that was irresistible and endlessly fascinating to Anne. His figure was tall and active, rather than graceful in the manner of Lord Holland.

Anne was trying to think of something to say, but did not know how to express herself to her cousin, who was assumed by everyone there to be in love with the young lady who would soon be arriving with Lady Catherine. What a fool she would make of herself by allowing him to guess her feelings, and how unpleasant for her cousin to find himself the object of an affection which he could not return.

While she was struggling miserably with these thoughts, Fitzwilliam said, "Since there is no hunting tomorrow, let us go out riding, just the two of us. There are some things I would like to say to you, Anne."

She had just assented to this proposal, looking into his face and trying to maintain her composure, when Darcy made a very unwelcome appearance and interrupted their conversation.

"Well, Anne. Your mother should be here in a few days. That should certainly enliven our little party here." Darcy seemed to be making a very unsuccessful attempt at joviality. What on earth is the matter with him? thought Anne, for this false gaiety was not at all like Darcy.

"And she brings with her the delightful Lady Emma. Tell me, Fitz, is she as remarkably beautiful as everyone says?" continued Darcy, laying a hand on his cousin's shoulder.

"No one would call her plain, I suppose," replied Fitzwilliam, rather taken aback. If he had not known better he might have thought Darcy a little the worse for drink, but that surely was impossible. He was saved from any further conversation on the subject of Lady Emma by the announcement of dinner.

Anne found herself seated next to Lord Holland, with Lady Grinspoon on his other side. She was obliged to converse with them and could only catch a glimpse of Fitzwilliam now and then at the other end of the table, where he was talking to Mrs. Bingley and Georgiana. Never had her emotions been in such tumult; she was unable to eat more than a few bites and felt weak with the intensity of feelings she could hardly analyze. What could her cousin have to say to her? Perhaps he only wished to inform her of his forthcoming engagement for what else could it be? She chided herself whenever a dream of something infinitely wonderful, a vision of perfect happiness stole into her mind. Don't be such a fool, she told herself.

Lady Grinspoon noticed that her young friend was pale and that her hand seemed to tremble when she took up her wineglass. "Are you quite well, my dear Miss de Bourgh?" inquired the older lady, and Lord Holland was immediately all solicitude as well. Fortunately the plea of a slight headache was enough to protect Anne from further inquiries.

~

COLONEL FITZWILLIAM WAS WALKING across the stable yard to his bedchamber later that night when he stopped to take in the beauty of the starry sky. It was bitterly cold and there was a penetrating wind across the cobblestones, but he was a soldier long inured to such discomforts; in fact he had made it a point of honor to be indifferent to them. He paused and looked up contemplatively. Fitzwilliam was not a man who had known much of indecision or self doubt, but now he found himself very much at a loss. His attachment to his cousin Anne had been growing in strength for some months and he had come to rely on being first in her affection, but now he believed that he had come to an understanding of his own feelings too late. She had seemed much more interested in looking about the room for Lord Holland than in talking to him! How distracted and inattentive she had been and what more certain symptom of love could there be?

He was going over every detail of his few moments with Anne when he felt the presence of someone at his side and turned to see Lord Holland.

"Pray, excuse me, Colonel, but I wonder if I might speak with you for a few minutes?"

Fitzwilliam looked at the other man rather coolly. Holland was not someone with whom he had any interest in conversing at that or any other hour, but he replied courteously, "I will gladly hear anything you wish to say, Holland."

It would have been logical to move indoors at this point, but neither of them was about to admit to a dislike of freezing wind, so they continued to stand in the middle of the stableyard.

"I have not had the pleasure of more than a very limited acquaintance with you, Colonel, although I do have the honor of knowing the other members of your family rather well. On this basis I hope you will not take it amiss if I speak to you frankly."

"I prefer frankness," replied Fitzwilliam, "It saves time."

Then Holland went on to express himself in a manner that did him credit, as even Fitzwilliam was forced to acknowledge. It was imperative, he began, to explain his intentions and situation in life to the colonel, who stood in the position of an elder brother to Miss de Bourgh. He spoke of his great admiration and affection for the young lady, and his hope that she would soon consent to be his wife. His standing in society and his fortune were good and he would be happy to submit to any examination of his circumstances that the colonel might think appropriate.

"I have made inquiries," said Fitzwilliam, "and can find nothing against your character or position in life. Do you believe that my cousin returns your affection?" he added, dreading the reply.

"It is not for me to say, since I have yet to win her consent. Miss de Bourgh is too intelligent and sensible a young lady to give her heart without the most careful thought. She has listened to my sentiments with a most kind, if reserved, attention."

That tells me exactly nothing, said Fitzwilliam to himself, then he looked sharply at Holland and said, "There is nothing dearer to me than my cousin's happiness, and I will do anything in my power to ensure it. Anyone who compromises her perfect felicity and tranquility of mind will have me to deal with. However, if it becomes clear to me that she truly loves you, 1 will not oppose the match." Holland seemed elated at this assurance, and left the colonel with thanks for having listened to him. Then Fitzwilliam was able to reflect on what he had heard.

He paced about the courtyard, oblivious to the cold and argued with himself. If she loves Holland, what right have I to interfere? Why make her wretched and ruin the close friendship we have by telling her of my own feelings? And there were so many difficulties to be overcome. Fitzwilliam walked about restlessly for a few more minutes and then decided that he would insist knowing the truth when they went out riding the next day.

Having chosen his course of action, Fitzwilliam felt more comfortable, but then he remembered another problem. My God, he thought, Lady Emma would be here in two days' time! That could make things very complicated indeed.

CHAPTER 43

*A*nne somewhat alarmed her maid the next morning by the energetic way in which she leapt out of bed and demanded that her riding habit be set out and her boots sent down for a polishing. "And where have you put my crop, Celestine?" demanded the young lady impatiently, "I am going riding with my cousin right after breakfast."

Celestine was appalled at such an unseemly degree of enthusiasm so early in the day. "My lady, breakfast is not for another hour, so perhaps it would be well to sit by the fire and have the coffee I have brought you. And, if you will permit me to say that it is not at all a good thing to expose your complexion to the cold morning air. Just look outside and see the heavy frost."

No particular time for their outing had been named by Fitzwilliam, but Anne knew that he enjoyed riding in the morning and she wanted to be ready to set out whenever they had the opportunity to leave. As it happened, it was afternoon before they were able to do so. There was an endless amount of conversion at the breakfast table, and afterward, Anne was detained by the other ladies, who solicited her opinion on the gowns that they planned to wear the next week. In eight days time something very significant was to happen;

the great Pemberley ball, once the event of the winter in the neighbor-hood, was to be given for the first time in many years. Not since the death of Darcy's mother had the ball taken place, but Elizabeth had wanted to please her husband by reviving the custom. The joy of the county families on receiving their invitations had been extreme, for they saw that the days of splendid hospitality at Pemberley were to come again. Elizabeth had spent hours planning the ball with Mrs. Reynolds. The project was less daunting than might have been expected because the housekeeper and the butler, Jenkins, had not forgotten how to make preparations.

Anne had paid little attention, having already decided with Celestine what she should wear. What else was there for her to do? However, for some reason the other ladies imagined that she must find their ruminations as interesting as they did. The one thing to cause Anne trepidation was the fact that Lady Catherine was to arrive in time for the ball. As Anne saw it, the prospect of her mother's presence was dreadful indeed, but as it was something that had to be faced, she wanted it to be over with as soon as possible.

When Anne finally escaped from the ladies' conference, she found that Fitzwilliam had been drawn into another review of the architect's plans, which lasted for some hours. It seemed almost miraculous to Anne when she found herself leaving the courtyard with Fitzwilliam at two o'clock, unencumbered by any other companions. She had been certain that some unwelcome addition would volunteer to ride out with them. She had most feared that Lord Holland would insist on taking some exercise, but fortunately he was in the library talking to Elizabeth about the musicians for the ball and did not seem to be aware of Anne's quiet departure.

They took the path along the river and rode in silence for some time. Fitzwilliam had a great deal to say, but for once in his life found himself at a loss for words. Anne began to be shy and awkward in the face of such an unaccustomed silence on the part of her usually lively cousin. There was a low meadow to their left and Anne on an impulse went off across it at a fast canter. The sun had come out and what had been frosty ground began to change to mud under the horses' hooves.

In a fit of exuberance the two riders broke into a gallop and were soon making their way up a long hillside. They stopped at the summit, where a splendid view opened up before them. Anne had been liberally splattered with mud and there was a large spot of it on her cheek; she laughed with delight and brought her horse around so that she could face Fitzwilliam. He thought that he had never seen anyone so lovely. It seemed that the moment to speak had arrived and Fitzwilliam began to say, "Anne, there is something I must ask you…"

He hesitated, trying to find the words, and they had looked at each other for several moments in silence, when they were startled by the sound of a carriage on the park road just below them.

"Good God!" exclaimed Fitzwilliam, "It is Lady Catherine!"

"Two days early," said Anne mournfully, "How very like my mother. Why did we not expect it?"

Her impulse was to whirl about and take off at a gallop, but Fitzwilliam, seeming to read her mind, said, "It's too late Anne. They have seen us and there is nothing for it but to ride down to them. Be brave, my dearest."

So dismayed was Anne at this turn of events that she did not hear this last endearment which Fitzwilliam had never before used. With a sense of dread she trotted over to the carriage and greeted her mother who was leaning out of the window.

It took a moment for Lady Catherine to comprehend that the mud- spattered young lady with the becomingly rosy cheeks and bright eyes was in fact her daughter. When the truth dawned on her, she sank back into her seat and exclaimed, "Merciful Heaven!" She leaned forward again as if to make sure that her first perusal had not deceived her, then repeated "Merciful Heaven!" several times more.

How long this might have continued was unclear, but Anne became aware of a cheerful lady greeting her in the most animated way, "Why, it must be Miss de Bourgh! How I have been looking forward to meeting you. Your mama has told me so many lovely things about you all these months. But she did not mention that you were a horsewoman."

Anne was about to reply when the young lady noticed Fitzwilliam.

Her joy at seeing him was unmistakable and she greeted him with evident delight. He bowed and smiled in a way that was certainly more reserved, but there was no doubt that they were well acquainted.

Anne saw with dismay that Lady Emma was as beautiful as had been so widely reported and even this brief exchange suggested that she had rare charm as well. How eagerly she looked at Fitzwilliam; surely this journey had been undertaken for his sake alone.

Lady Catherine had by now recovered some of her composure, and said in her habitual commanding tone, "This has been a dreadful shock, Anne, and I will demand an explanation as soon as we reach Pemberley. For the moment, get down from that horse immediately and join us in the carriage before you are thrown and injured or catch your death of cold. As for you, Fitzwilliam, you are one person I would never have believed could disappoint me so bitterly. We will discuss your part in this as well."

Fitzwilliam made a motion to dismount and assist Anne, but before he could do so he heard her say, "Indeed, Mama, I will not join you. We are only a few mintues from the house and it is easier for me to ride back. I will see you there." And without waiting for a reply, she turned her horse and cantered off. Fitzwilliam followed her and in five minutes they were back in the courtyard. He had expected to see her distraught or in tears of vexation, but she only looked determined and said, "If there is to be a war, I tell you now, Cousin, that I will never give way." Then Anne remembered the affectionate greeting she had witnessed on the part of Lady Emma and felt there could be no mistake as to its meaning. With that thought she was able to restrain her tears only with the greatest difficulty and she walked into the house without another glance at Fitzwilliam.

ANNE INTENDED to run to her bedchamber to change out of her riding habit, but met Elizabeth in the hall. She hastened to relay the dreadful news just as the sound of Lady Catherine's carriage was heard at the front door. To her great credit, the young Mrs. Darcy did not cry out in dismay, but only said, "How kind of your mama to come to us as early as she could, for she is part of our family and welcome at any time. Would you be a dear and tell my husband that she has arrived while I go to greet Lady Catherine. He is in the library with Mr. Bingley." Then Elizabeth, with a very convincing show of serenity, went to the front door to meet the dragon.

Darcy was with Bingley and the architect from London; they were standing over a large table and studying some plans for the renovation of Thrushfold Hall. When Anne had told him the news, Darcy merely shook his head and said with a rueful smile, "Why, that is just like my aunt. She has always enjoyed catching people off guard. I should have expected it."

When Anne returned from her errand with the gentlemen she found that her mother had already been ushered into the library and given a chair by the fire. Lady Emma Anne saw at once, was standing with Fitzwilliam in a far corner of the room and talking to him with great animation. As she did so she occasionally touched his arm in a manner that suggested that they were on terms of some intimacy. Anne felt all the pangs of grief, jealousy and disappointed love, and it was only with difficulty that she could turn her attention to her mother.

She approached Lady Catherine and was offered her cheek to be kissed.

"Sit beside me, my child," said her mother, "it is not my intention to terrify you. Yes, I must own that I am angry and disturbed, but fortunately have had a few minutes in which to compose myself."

Lady Catherine did not, in fact, look very composed; there was a hectic flush and cold fury in her face that belied her restrained tone of voice.

"You are young and inexperienced, Anne, and must have been expected to make some errors of judgment My resentment and indignation must be directed at those who promised to care for and protect you in my absence."

At that moment tea was brought in and Elizabeth suggested that Lady Catherine take some refreshment.

"Certainly not, I will accept nothing in the way of hospitality from this house before we have had a family conference and I hear some sort of explanation. I am half inclined to take my daughter away at once and never return to Pemberley."

"Very well, aunt," said Darcy, who could imagine worse things than Lady Catherine's threat coming true, had it not been for his affection for Anne, "but let us move into the drawing room. Our other guests will soon appear and would enjoy finding some tea and a peaceful spot in which to drink it." He went over to the other new guest and said, "Lady Emma, I am delighted to welcome you to Pemberley and hope that we will be able to make your visit as agreeable as possible."

Elizabeth had sent a servant to find Georgiana so that she might entertain Lady Emma until the dreaded interview with Lady Catherine might be over. When Darcy's sister entered the room, her aunt greeted her affectionately in a manner that was markedly different from what her own child had received.

"Dearest Georgiana," cried Lady Catherine, embracing her, "It is far too long since I have had the joy of beholding you. Why, my love, how pretty you have become. You have always been my idea of a perfect young lady, accomplished, graceful and sweet-tempered."

The introduction to Lady Emma was made, and leaving the two ladies to become better acquainted, the procession towards the drawing room began, Lady Catherine leading the way, as if Pemberley were her house, not Darcy and Elizabeth's. When they reached the door of that room, Lady Catherine turned to Anne and said sternly, "Anne, there is no reason for you to be here. Go and make yourself presentable. It would be well for you to rest and I will come to talk to you later."

To the great surprise of all present, Anne looked at her mother unflinchingly and replied, "Mama, I have no intention of absenting myself from a discussion that concerns me. I am nearly seven and twenty."

Lady Catherine was so taken aback that for once she found no rejoinder, and in a moment they were all seated around the fire in a grim little circle. Fitzwilliam looked across at Anne; he was very impressed with her courage and wanted to give her a smile of encouragement, but she never looked at him.

Having caught her breath for a minute, Lady Catherine was soon able to launch into one of those tirades for which she was so renowned. Her first victim was Fitzwilliam, as it was he, after all, who had suggested the plan of Anne's spending several months with Darcy and Elizabeth. And he had been the source of her greatest shock in allowing Anne to be out on horseback in the dreadful cold air. God knew how often such a mad escapade had occurred. Had he lost his mind? Had he no respect for the precise instructions given by a careful mother to preserve the health of her only child?

By then she was out of breath, having been speaking almost at the top of her voice. Indeed, she could have been heard through a large part of the house had anyone been so indiscreet as to listen.

Fitzwilliam looked at his aunt in respectful silence, much to her annoyance, "Well, have you nothing to say!" she cried.

"I think it would be best if I defend my actions after you have finished, Aunt. No doubt you have accusations of a similar nature to make against Darcy. Perhaps afterward we could present our point of view when you are ready to hear it."

"Not just against Darcy!" exclaimed Lady Catherine, giving way now to a real frenzy of anger, "My greatest disappointment is that his wife, who should have had a woman's natural sense of caution and propriety, has allowed my Anne to be transformed into some kind of wild, unruly creature with no respect for her station in life and her mother's admonitions. Well, what could I have expected, given Elizabeth's connections and lack of understanding of good society?"

Darcy jumped up in a rage and defended his wife in the strongest language; never had he spoken to his aunt in such a manner. Elizabeth had never seen him in such a state and looked on in wonder. There might have been a permanent rift in the family had not Anne interrupted him.

She rose from her seat and stood in front of the fireplace with so much resolve and energy that she hardly seemed recognizable to her mother, who looked at her in amazement.

"It is enough!" Anne cried, "You must allow me to interrupt you, cousin, before you say something that can never be unsaid. In any case, it is for me to defend myself and I demand the right to do so. I am not a child and will no longer be treated like one!"

"Sit down at once!" said Lady Catherine, who felt almost afraid of this stranger who looked like her daughter, "How dare you use such a tone with me. You have no right to demand anything and will do as you are told!"

Anne stood her ground, although her hands shook so that she had to hide them behind her back. Her voice was firm, however, and she spoke with some eloquence in defense of her friends.

"It is one thing for you to abuse me, Mama," she began, "but I will not have you say hard things of those who have been so wonderfully kind to me. No one could have been more careful of my wellbeing and happiness than Darcy and Elizabeth. They have let me live like an intelligent, rational being with a value in the world, instead of a wretched invalid to be pushed into the shadows and ignored. I insisted on learning to ride. I thought it would be good for my health and as anyone can see I was correct."

Here Lady Catherine tried to speak, but Anne looked at her with such blazing eyes and determination that for once she was reduced to silence.

"If you please, Mama, I must be allowed to finish. As for your insulting words to Elizabeth, I will not tolerate them. There is no one more gracious, kind and more completely a gentlewoman than she. It is Elizabeth who has honored our family by becoming part of it, not the other way around."

Here Anne had to pause for a moment, but for once Lady Catherine did not interrupt; she was almost overcome by the unimaginable experience of being defied by her family. Had every natural law been overthrown and the beasts of the field acquired human speech it could have been no more astonishing to her.

"As for Darcy and Fitzwilliam, they have always been my best friends. Although, thanks to your confining me as an invalid all this time, I have not known them as well as I might have, it has always been certain that I could look to them as to affectionate and reliable older brothers." Had Anne been able to observe Fitzwilliam's face at that moment, she would have seen him wince at this last phrase. "You should be thanking my dear friends for all they have done for me. I feel well and strong and have an interest in the world for the first time since I was a child!"

Fitzwilliam came to stand by Anne. He had been very impressed by her bravery and how well she had expressed herself, but could see that she was now exhausted and near tears. 'Aunt," he said, "you and I have always understood each other very well and you know that I have ever been ready to tell you my opinion without dissimulation. You must understand that this change in my cousin is a good thing and that you should feel happiness and pride at what she has accomplished. For years, although with the best intentions, you have kept her from becoming what she was meant to be."

Lady Catherine was, in her own way, an intelligent woman. In the days before her recent illness she had always congratulated herself on her excellent constitution, but over the past few months she had learned that being in delicate health had its own advantages. Now, when she found herself faced with such determined opposition, she decided to employ her most effective weapon; she suddenly fell back into her chair with her hand at her heart, in an apparent swoon.

"Anne! Anne! My child," she said in a weak voice, "You have killed your mother."

Everyone rushed to her side; she was, in fact, quite pale and did look ill. Lady Catherine was unresponsive at first, but after a moment murmured, "My child, all my life I have cared for you. Oh, to end my life with the sound of such bitter, cruel words." Then she sank back and did not open her eyes again.

Darcy went out to send for the physician and Lady Catherine was quickly carried to her bedchamber and put to bed. Everything was done that perfect care and solicitude could suggest. The house was in an uproar and there was much concern on the part of their other guests. With the best will in the world they had been unable to avoid hearing some of the loud voices coming from the drawing room. Lady Emma, who seemed genuinely fond of Lady Catherine, was particularly anxious to be of assistance.

"I would be most grateful if you will sit with her for a while once the physician has come and made his pronouncements," replied Elizabeth who was attending to a thousand details, all the time with tears in her eyes. There was a moment when she met her husband in the hall as they hurried on different errands. They were at once in each other's arms and Darcy was murmuring words of comfort and encouragement to his exhausted wife.

"My darling Elizabeth," said Darcy, smoothing her hair and kissing her, "how can you ever forgive the insult you received today. I know that I shall never forget it, and as soon as my aunt can travel, I will insist that she leave the house. She will not be invited back. The family connection means nothing to me compared to your happiness."

He led Elizabeth to her sitting room where they could be alone for a few moments. She was glad to have an opportunity to collect herself, all the while holding Darcy's hand and looking into his face with all the joy of renewed confidence in his love for her. "Let us see what happens, my love," she said at last, "Your aunt is an unhappy woman who spoke in haste and anger. We should not let ourselves be affected by her first reaction to what must have been a severe shock. When she has had time to think on it, no doubt she will regret her unkind words."

"You are much too forgiving, my angel," replied Darcy, "I cannot imagine how I shall ever be on good terms with Lady Catherine again. There cannot be an apology abject enough to satisfy me."

Elizabeth rested in her husband's arms for a few minutes in perfect contentment, all the worries of past weeks forgotten. Then she turned to give him a smile that held more than a hint of mischief, "Oh, my love, I have one regret. How I would have loved to be present when Lady Catherine first laid eyes on Anne in her mud-stained riding habit and recognized the poor oppressed girl who left Rosings a few months ago. What a scene it must have been!"

The doctor arrived and after spending a half hour with Lady Catherine was happy to be able to report that there was nothing amiss other than fatigue and nervous excitement. Only let her ladyship take a draught that had been prepared for her and pass the night quietly and she would be perfectly recovered by the next day.

This news was a great relief to everyone, and especially to Anne, who had been wretchedly awaiting the doctor's verdict. She had been sitting in the library with Lady Grinspoon at her side. Lord Holland had said words of comfort and reassurance, as had the Bingleys, but they were now standing at a discreet distance as Lady Grinspoon talked to her young friend.

"My dear, your mother will do very well. I do assure you of that," said the older lady taking Anne's hand, "You are correct in saying that I do not know her well, but we have met on a few occasions and that was enough for me to see that she is a woman who cannot bear opposition. This response was to be expected and I am glad it was not any worse."

"But, dear Lady Grinspoon, what am I to do? I cannot return to the life I led with my mother before. It would certainly kill me, from boredom if from no other cause."

"You shall come and live with me!" cried her friend, "How delightful it would be. My daughters have left home and I cannot imagine anything that would give me greater pleasure."

Anne looked at the older lady sadly, "How very kind you are, Lady Grinspoon, but I could not subject you to the angry resentment of my mother."

Lord Holland started towards them from across the room, and Lady Grinspoon said in a low voice, "Ah, here he comes, the answer to a maiden's prayer."

At that moment Fitzwilliam appeared and confirmed an earlier brief report from Darcy; Lady Catherine was in no danger and would soon be completely recovered. The only thing that remained to be done was to write to Dr. Crawford and let him know of the incident and solicit any further suggestions he might have.

"Anne, will you come and help me compose the letter? You express yourself so well and concisely."

"Why, of course, cousin." replied Anne, rising eagerly and in a moment they were seated together at Darcy's desk.

Fitzwilliam found some writing paper and began to mend a pen. He seemed distracted and fatigued, but looked at Anne with such affectionate concern that she felt a surge of joy in the midst of her unhappiness.

They composed a brief letter to Dr. Crawford describing Lady Catherine's collapse and giving the name of the local physician should a further consultation be needed.

"Your writing is very clear, Anne, not like my chicken scratch," said Fitzwilliam, when they had finished. Then he looked at her earnestly and continued, "Try not to distress yourself, although things must seem very unpromising at the moment." He hesitated, and then said, "Those who love you will not suffer you to return to the imprisonment you endured for so many years."

Anne was near tears and unable to speak, so strong were her feelings. Fitzwilliam looked over towards the other occupants of the room as if afraid of being overheard, then said, "The next few days will be difficult. There is something I must arrange that has been in preparation for some time. I want to explain it to you, but there is a problem in that I have..." To Anne's extreme frustration, Darcy entered the library and walked quickly over to them.

"Your mother is awake, Anne, and is asking for you."

When Anne, accompanied by Darcy and Fitzwilliam, entered Lady Catherine's bedchamber they found Elizabeth and Lady Emma seated at her bedside. All seemed to be peaceful and serene and no observer would have imagined all the distress and agitation of the past few hours. Lady Catherine was lying propped up on some pillows with her eyes closed but she fixed her gaze on Anne as soon as she entered the room.

Lady Emma tactfully went out at once. Elizabeth rose and said, "Your mama wished to see you before she takes the sleeping draught that the doctor has prescribed, Anne. Take this chair, my dear, and we will leave you alone."

"That is unnecessary, Elizabeth," said Lady Catherine, "You and Darcy may stay and hear what I have to say to my child. It will only take a moment and then I will rest. It has been a difficult day."

Anne began to say that the conversation might wait until tomorrow, but her mother said abruptly, "Pray, do not interrupt me. I will say what I must and then you shall all leave me."

"I have come to Pemberley for two reasons; first, for the pleasure of visiting my family at this time of year and enjoying with them the Christmas season, and secondly to meet the young man who is, apparently, anxious to marry my daughter."

Lady Catherine paused briefly and once again found herself interrupted.

"Before you say anything more, Aunt, there is something that must be settled at once, or you and I will have nothing further to say to one another," said Darcy, whose face retained much of the anger of a couple of hours earlier during the scene in the drawing room.

Lady Catherine was astonished; was this her quiet, deferential nephew who had until today spoken to her with such respect? The episode in the drawing room seemed like a bad dream to her, but was she now to relive it?

"I must insist that you apologize to my wife immediately. What you said was intolerable, but I will try to forgive you if she will."

Darcy looked so fierce that Elizabeth might have remonstrated with him for being so harsh with a sick woman, but she knew him too well now to do so.

Lady Catherine wondered, from Darcy's expression, if she would be ejected out into the cold and wet and not even allowed to stay the night if she did not comply with his demand.

"I was overcome by the shock I had received, and spoke rashly, Elizabeth. It was an ill-judged remark," she said, sinking wearily back against the pillows.

"Not good enough, Aunt," said Darcy, relentlessly, "You will have to do better than that."

Lady Catherine looked confused for a moment, searching the faces of her companions as if she had not understood Darcy's words. Then she said, "What I said about you was entirely untrue, Elizabeth. You are certainly a gentlewoman in every respect and all that I see of you confirms that you are a credit to our family. I do apologize most sincerely."

"Very well, that will suffice for now," said her nephew, "You are welcome to say whatever else you wish."

"From what I have seen today, I am not sure anyone could have restrained this rebellious girl," said Lady Catherine, with some of her old fire, "but I know my duty as her mother and will bring her to reason and obedience now we are together again. Is that not true, my child?"

Anne felt extraordinarily weary. A headache throbbed in her temples and all she wished to do was be alone, but she replied, "That depends on what you mean by those terms, Mama. I have my own ideas now about what is reasonable."

Her mother found this an outrageous response, "You are impudent, Anne, but I know how to deal with an ungrateful, foolish child. I am here to judge the acceptability of Lord Holland and his pretensions to your hand. When I left Bath, it was clear to all that his older brother was not likely to survive, so that the connection is certainly worth considering. To be, at last, a marchioness is no small thing, and indeed the sort of alliance I think to be only fitting with your fortune and lineage."

Fitzwilliam, who was standing by the windows and observing the scene in silence, hoped that Anne would deny that the match was acceptable to her, but was saddened when she did not interrupt her mother.

"If the match does not seem likely to come off, then you will return with me to Rosings where I will devote all my time to instructing you in the attitude and behavior befitting your situation in life and making sure that you do not endanger your health with any more riding or running wild out-of-doors. Mrs. Jenkinson I will dismiss. You have no need for a governess since I will be devoting myself to you entirely."

Anne began to speak in defense of her old friend, Mrs. Jenkinson; to dismiss her at this stage of her life was unthinkable, but Lady Catherine said, "No, not one more word, I must rest. It will have to wait for later."

It seemed best to leave her to sleep, and Elizabeth said, "Is there anything else that you require, Lady Catherine?"

"Yes, yes, my dear, now that you ask. Would you be so good as to send to the inn at Lambton and ask Sir Wilfred Richardson to wait upon me here tomorrow. He is staying there and expecting to hear from me."

"Sir Wilfred Richardson!" exclaimed Darcy in surprise, "The gentleman who was in Scotland with us, a very good shot and an agreeable companion. He was so kind as to take our letters to you in Bath."

"Yes, that is the gentleman." replied Lady Catherine impatiently, "He insisted on escorting us on our journey here, but stopped at the inn as he did not wish to impose on your hospitality."

"Why, we will send to him at once, and invite him to stay here at Pemberley," said Elizabeth.

"Yes, do so, my dear, only for heavens sake, leave me to sleep now."

They found Lady Emma in the library with the rest of the company, and she looked amused when she heard of Lady Catherine's request. "Dear Sir Wilfred! He is Lady Catherine's faithful knight. He would not hear of us making the journey alone and rode most of the way, scouting the countryside and seeing to our every need like the perfect chevalier."

"How very kind of him," said Elizabeth, in wonder at such devotion.

"But he would not come here," continued Lady Emma, "He left us at the park gates and said that he would wait at the inn in case we had any other commands for him before he returned to Bath. Oh, no, he said, he could not trouble you here at Pemberley, since he had no invitation."

Elizabeth went to her desk at once and wrote a note to the gentleman, begging him to come to Pemberley, and saying only that Lady Catherine was suffering from a slight indisposition. Within an hour Sir Wilfred had arrived, full of apologies for intruding on the party at Pemberley, but equally distressed when he was told of Lady Catherine's illness, which was attributed to fatigue from her journey. It took a good deal of persuasion to induce him to accept the hospitality of Mr. and Mrs. Darcy, but by dinnertime he was installed among the other guests. The entire company was quite subdued that evening, and the presence of her mother oppressed Anne greatly, even at a distance. There was never another opportunity to talk with Fitzwilliam. Indeed, Lady Emma stayed so close by his side that there would have been some difficulty in managing a private word with her cousin. When she finally went to sleep that night, Anne could have hardly felt lower in her mind.

CHAPTER 44

wo days later John Grey was cantering up the last rise on his way back to Pemberley. All his business had been arranged satisfactorily at Cambridge, and in fact almost too much so, since now he had the feeling that the course of his life had taken a new direction that could not easily be altered. He did not doubt his decision to take orders, as the life of a clergyman was something that was likely to be agreeable to him and he had a true desire to do good in the world, but there was nothing else in his situation that could promise future happiness. Instead, his heart was full of an unvarying pain and sadness that he concealed as best he could.

As he reached the top of the hill, he saw a small figure seated on a large flat stone and was surprised to see in a moment that it was Anne. She was staring out across the countryside and seemed to become aware of him only gradually.

"Why, Miss de Bourgh!" he cried, "Out in this cold? And sitting on that particular rock, which is well known to be the remains of a fairy circle? This is not wise." So saying, he leapt off his horse and went up to her. She was clearly glad to see him but her face was not a happy one and he thought he detected the traces of recent tears.

"Do you think the fairies will be angry with me, Mr. Grey?" she asked, smiling at him with what was obviously some degree of effort, "It seemed to me an excellent place to enjoy this lovely view."

"A lovely view, perhaps, but with a bitter wind. Here, take my muffler and wrap it about your head and neck." Then the young man sat down beside her after tethering his horse to a small tree nearby.

"So, tell me all the news of Pemberley. Has anything of note occurred in my absence?"

"Actually, a great deal," replied Anne, "We have three new inmates." Then she proceeded to tell him about her mother's arrival with Lady Emma, and the subsequent addition of Sir Wilfred. So much confidence did she feel in Mr. Grey's friendship, that she told him the story of the family contretemps with Lady Catherine.

"Family disputes are by no means unknown to me, Miss de Bourgh, and I sympathize with all my heart. We can only hope that in time your mother will understand how misguided has been her comprehension of you."

Anne wanted to hear all about Mr. Grey's journey and would not agree to take refuge from the chill by returning to the house, so her companion gave her an account of all he had done in Cambridge and described the place, as she had some curiosity about it. Her interest was genuine, but she found that her mind tended to wander back to her own troubles, as the past two days had been terribly difficult.

On the day after her ladyship's arrival, Anne had seen her mother only briefly and always in company with Elizabeth. To her daughter, Lady Catherine said little, apparently unwilling to renew the dispute of the day before. There had been so much improvement in her ladyship's condition that she was expected to join the rest of the party that evening. Lady Catherine was particularly eager to see Sir Wilfred and expressed her gratitude to Elizabeth for securing his presence.

When Anne finally went down for breakfast, she was pained to learn that Lady Emma and Fitzwilliam had already gone out riding. "They were off quite early," said Georgiana, "and I am concerned that they had very little to eat. But I am sure they will return soon for it is extremely cold today." Lord Holland was there and had clearly been waiting for her. He could not have been more agreeable and thoughtful and he made sure that she had coffee just as she liked it. He was certainly a very observant young man and had made a study of all Anne's preferences and interests. Every day his knowledge and appreciation of her seemed to increase and it was difficult not to be flattered.

Anne had no desire to go riding or walking that day as her spirits were so low, but she hoped that she was managing to conceal her unhappiness. She spent the rest of the morning playing chess with Lord Holland, while Lady Grinspoon sat at a desk nearby and worked on her latest novel, and Georgiana could be heard practicing a sonata in the music room. Mr. and Mrs. Bingley, along with Darcy, had driven over to Thrushfold Hall to review some details with the architect. Anne tried to concentrate on the game, for Lord Holland was a very good player and they were well matched, but she could not help listening with half an ear for Fitzwilliam's return.

Finally she heard Lady Emma's voice in the hall, and in a moment she and Fitzwilliam had entered the room with a rush of frosty air. The young lady greeted them all gaily and went to the hearth to warm her hands while Fitzwilliam followed her and stood at a little distance. Anne felt almost afraid to look at the newcomers. There was a feeling of dread in her heart and she had to force herself to raise her eyes to where they stood.

Lady Emma looked even more beautiful than ever and Anne acknowledged to herself that it was impossible to imagine any man resisting her. But the thing that struck her with despair was the expression on the lady's face; never had Anne seen such joyous exaltation on a human countenance. There could be no doubt that something momentous had occurred, for nothing else could explain Lady Emma's brilliant eyes and almost uncontrollable animation. Anne looked fearfully over at Fitzwilliam who had walked over to answer some remark of Lady Grinspoon's. In contrast, he appeared quite calm and unmoved, but Anne took no comfort in this; perhaps lovemaking affected young men in such a way, and no doubt proposing marriage was a tiring business. She leant back in her chair and met Lord Holland's eyes. He was watching her rather closely and she hoped that he had not guessed how she was affected. She gave her attention back to their game, and tried to ignore everything else.

Fitzwilliam came over to them and made a few general comments about the weather and chess, seeming to find an excuse for approaching Anne. With a great effort, she replied to him with what she hoped was an air of pleasant unconcern, then fastened her eyes to the board in a way that did not encourage further interruption.

Since then Anne had found herself avoiding Fitzwilliam because the grief she felt was too great for her to endure being close to him. On several occasions he had seemed to seek out her company, but she had found some excuse to break away from conversation with her cousin. The two days since the contretemps in the drawing room had gone quietly and even her mother had been fairly agreeable, no doubt garnering her strength for another battle with her daughter. Anne did observe that the presence of Sir Wilfred seemed to work a significant change for the better in Lady Catherine. The gentleman had such a high opinion of her mother that by some alchemy she was forced to behave well. Lady Catherine was especially inclined to be civil to Lord Holland and frequently monopolized his attention. Anne was too wretched to dwell on the significance of this. She only thought about the possibility of Fitzwilliam's engagement to Lady Emma being announced at the ball.

SHE HAD WANDERED up to the fairy rock with the idea of considering everything that had happened and of forming some plan for her future life, a life that seemed to hold no possibility of including her cousin Fitzwilliam. Mr. Grey was someone she was always very glad to see, but it was clear to him that she was attending to his story only with the greatest difficulty.

"Well, that is all that I can really tell you about Cambridge, Miss de Bourgh, and I fear it is a dull place judging from your degree of interest in my narrative," he said smiling at her, "Would you like to tell me your troubles, or do I presume too much?"

Anne found herself telling Mr. Grey about the apparent under-standing between Lady Emma and her cousin, saying only that she hoped that Fitzwilliam would be happy with the lady, but that she wished she could be sure that his choice was a fortunate one.

Grey studied her face in silence for a moment and then said, "You love your cousin. Miss de Bourgh. I admit that I suspected as much from the day we received word of his riding accident; there was no mistaking the distress and concern I saw on your face."

Anne did not attempt to deny her feelings. It did not seem necessary to do so, as she felt perfect trust in Mr. Grey's discretion.

"It does not matter now," she said, "No doubt their engagement will be announced soon, perhaps tomorrow night. You have not seen Lady Emma. Her beauty is remarkable and I can not imagine how my cousin could fail to be in love with her."

Grey looked thoughtful for a moment, and then said, "You should not rely on mere appearances, or despair until something definite is known. In any case, you are very beautiful too, and I cannot imagine that Lady Emma is your superior, or even your equal."

Anne stared at him in disbelief, then gave a small, bitter laugh, "Really, Mr. Grey, here I thought you were a connoisseur and a man of taste. How can you make such a ridiculous remark?"

Grey looked very serious as he turned to face her directly, "Please listen carefully, Miss de Bourgh, because this is a bit of essential information that your mother and the other people around you have somehow forgotten to impart to you. I am speaking as your friend, not as some idle flirt or flatterer. Do you believe me?"

Anne, very much abashed, had to look away to avoid her companion's solemn gaze, "Of course, I believe you, Mr. Grey. I know you would never lie to me."

"Then listen for once to the truth about yourself. You are very beautiful. I have seen your face before. Botticelli painted your countenance many times and I had seen you in his paintings in Italy before I ever met you." Then he smiled and continued, "By the way, were you living in Italy in the fifteenth century by any chance?"

Anne could not help smiling at this absurdity, "Not that I remember, but perhaps my memory is at fault."

She was so taken aback by what Grey had said that she could

hardly think of anything else to say, but then asked, "You have not told me if anything has changed in your own situation?"

"You mean in regard to Lady Margaret? I have not seen her yet, but I have no reason to believe that anything will be different. I am determined not to give up yet. No, I am ready to tolerate being rejected a few more times."

"Do you think it is possible to learn to love someone after marriage, even though you begin with only liking and respect?" Anne asked, thinking of Lord Holland.

Grey replied after a moment's hesitation, "For myself, I could not marry as a sort of compensation for the loss of a greater love. No doubt I shall end an old bachelor. But everyone is different and the only thing for it is to follow the advice inscribed at the temple of the Delphic oracle."

"Which was?" asked Anne

"'Know thyself.' Only think of all the great spiritual truths that could have been chosen for that sacred place, but that was the one that was considered the most important."

"You are very informative, Mr. Grey, if not particularly helpful in resolving my difficulty."

"Ah yes, the difficulty posed by your noble suitor, Lord Holland. You see, Miss de Bourgh, I sympathize with all my heart, but it would be criminal of me to influence you in one direction or another. Know thyself! That is the most valuable thing I can offer."

Then the young man jumped up and said, "I have not given into despair and neither should you, my friend. I have great hopes of this ball. When I was in Spain I learned a wonderful dance called the fandango. At the critical moment I will leap into the center of the ballroom and perform the dance with consummate skill and daring! How will Lady Margaret resist me after that?"

Anne could not help but laugh at his enthusiasm.

"Come, Miss de Bourgh, no more sitting about glumly for us! Give me your hands, and I will teach you the fandango here and now!"

Down in the valley, two woodcutters were walking slowly home and noticed two young people dancing on the hilltop. "I tell you, Ned," said one to the other, "This old world gets stranger all the time."

412

CHAPTER 45

*W*hen Anne and Grey arrived at the house they were greeted by Elizabeth. "It is good that you happened along, Mr. Grey, and insisted that Anne return. Her mother has just been asking for her, and if she suspected that her daughter was out in this weather it would be a very bad thing for us all."

Anne ran upstairs to warm herself by the fire in her bedchamber and let the color in her cheeks subside. She had already thought of an explanation for where she had been: discussing her gown for the next evening with her maid. Celestine had become very loyal and would never betray her. Her friends in the house knew that it was better to plead ignorance of Anne's whereabouts in most instances.

When she went down to the library she found all the residents of the house assembled there. Mr. Grey had just entered, having changed from his traveling attire, and was being introduced to Lady Catherine.

"Perhaps you remember my old friend, John Grey, Aunt," said Darcy, "You met him once when we were boys, but you would have known him as Lord Conarvan."

Lady Catherine stared at Grey through her lorgnette, an irritating habit she had recently acquired, and replied, " Grey? Why Grey? That is very odd, young man. Can you throw off a distinguished family name as if it were a worn-out coat?'

"Why, yes, Lady Catherine, apparently one can," said Grey with a bow.

"It is excessively odd of you, one might almost say eccentric. One should beware of eccentricity, Mr. Grey. It looks like a sort of conceited self-importance."

Darcy intervened to defend his friend, "No one could say that in this case, Aunt. No man was ever more modest."

"Well, we shall see," said Lady Catherine suspiciously, "Come and sit beside me. I knew your mother, a most elegant and superior lady."

Grey spent the next half hour being questioned by Lady Catherine. Her manner of inquiry was devoid of tact or a sense of what was appropriate; she seemed to feel that her position in the world made such things unnecessary, but she did relate a few stories about his mother that Grey had not heard before. He had adored his mother and her death at such an early age had been the worst blow of his life. At the end of their interview, Grey understood that there had been no exaggeration in what he had heard of Anne's imperious mother and he felt the greatest sympathy for his young friend. How has she survived being brought up in such oppressive circumstances? Grey asked himself, Miss de Bourgh must have a tremendously strong character.

After Lady Catherine felt that she had extracted the last bit of interest from her conversation with Mr. Grey, she turned her attention to Elizabeth, who was standing nearby with her sister. Mrs. Bingley had been favored with her ladyship's minute interrogation the day before and had not enjoyed the experience. Before her marriage to Bingley, Mrs. Darcy's sister might have escaped notice, but now Lady Catherine wanted to know everything about the lady and to offer endless suggestions for the renovation of Thrushfold Hall. Bingley, as well, had been the beneficiary of her advice; no detail was too minor for the exercise of her ladyship's wisdom and there had been interminable discussion of drains and roof tiles.

"Elizabeth, my dear," said Lady Catherine," How delighted you must be at the prospect of tomorrow's ball. To renew the great tradition at Pemberley is no small thing. I made a great effort to arrive in time for the event."

Elizabeth replied that, indeed, she was very happy that she and Darcy had been able to plan such an entertainment for their friends and neighbors.

"And the best thing, my dear," continued her ladyship, "is that I am here to assist you. Why, you have not had the opportunity of learning what may be required, and I promise that I will stay at your side all day tomorrow."

Darcy walked over and took his wife's hand, "Aunt, you are too good, but you must not tire yourself. I believe that everything is under good control." He knew that his wife had already suffered through several hours of Lady Catherine's interfering advice.

At this point, Sir Wilfred came over and remarked that the weather was improving and showed some promise of being comparatively mild the next day. There had been, he added, some discussion of showing Lady Emma a little of the countryside. Had Lady Catherine forgotten? Her presence would certainly be required as she was so familiar with this part of Derbyshire and Mr. Darcy would be otherwise engaged.

Lady Catherine replied, "You are correct, Sir Wilfred, perhaps we should keep to that plan for it may be the last acceptable weather we can expect for a while. Well, we will not stay out long and you may rely on me, Elizabeth, to come back and be of assistance to you."

Elizabeth looked gratefully over at Sir Wilfred. He was a dear, thoughtful man and she was infinitely grateful to him for arranging that she might be free of Lady Catherine's presence for even a few hours. He smiled back at her reassuringly. It seemed that he understood Lady Catherine's more unfortunate qualities, but was still devoted to her. It was most remarkable and a great blessing to them all.

The evening passed very quietly and there seemed to be general sentiment that it would be wise to retire early in view of the ball the next evening. Darcy was glad of this, for he wished to see Elizabeth rest as much as possible. The morning would, no doubt, bring all sorts of unexpected complications and difficulties. Certainly the ball promised to be a success, for the Darcys' invitation had been accepted by all those fortunate enough to receive one. A few last minute additions seemed to be likely as well. Fitzwilliam had asked if one of his officers might be allowed to attend. "I have received word that Captain Malvern is staying in the neighborhood and I would be very much obliged, if you do not mind, Mrs. Darcy, if he could be included. He is an agreeable and intelligent young man."

Elizabeth was pleased to add to the number of dancing partners for the young ladies who would be at the ball. Her dream as a hostess was to see everyone dancing, with no unfortunate girl left to sit looking on. Having been without a partner on several occasions and knowing how unpleasant it was to be pitied as one "slighted by the gentlemen," she did not wish such a thing to occur at *her* ball. She was excited and only a little afraid of all the responsibility for such a great event. "I do not think I shall sleep at all, my love," she said to her husband after they had retired for the night, "I will lie awake thinking about a thousand details and wondering if I have forgotten anything." Darcy, as always, was able to lull her into sleep, talking to her softly about the cherished moments they had already spent together in the time since their marriage. "The ball will be splendid, my dearest," said her husband, stroking her hair, " but all that really matters is that we are here with each other and always will be."

Anne had counted on escaping to her bedchamber to read and try to forget, for a while at least, the dreary pain that would not leave her in peace. She had been made wretched by the sight of Lady Emma constantly at Fitzwilliam's side and often appearing to speak to him in a very confidential way. Although she did not expect to be able to sleep, if only she could spend the night in peace perhaps it would be possible to get through the ordeal of the ball with some degree of equanimity. Alas, when she was but a few paces from her door she heard her mother call to her from the other end of the hall.

"Anne, my child, be so good as to join me for a while. I have some things to say to you that cannot be put off."

These were the words that Anne had been dreading. She was surprised that she had not been subjected to a private conversation with Lady Catherine before now and it took all her strength to turn and walk into her mother's bedchamber with the despair of a prisoner on his way to a place of execution.

416

"Come and sit here by the fire with me, Anne, and we will have a nice chat."

Anne began to do as she was bid, but Lady Catherine said abruptly, "No wait a moment. Stand there and let me look at you, child."

Her mother studied Anne briefly and then gave her permission to be seated.

"Your hair is, of course, a disaster, but it will grow back after all."

"I like my hair this way, Mama," said Anne recklessly, "It is very convenient and many people have been kind enough to say that it is most becoming."

Lady Catherine sniffed contemptuously, "People will say anything. No doubt they were just flattering you. At least you have a few gowns that will be appropriate for tomorrow night, the ones you took with you when you left Rosings."

"I am afraid, Mama, that those gowns are in London," replied Anne, not mentioning that Celestine had given them away to the under-housemaids.

This led to something of a minor explosion and a tirade against Celestine, who would have to be dismissed. "She is a very pert, impudent young woman, and I do not approve of French maids in any case."

Then Anne had to listen to a long monologue in which Lady Catherine enumerated all the errors into which her daughter had fallen since leaving her mother's tender care. This was followed by a description of the corrective regimen to which Anne was to be subjected on her return to Rosings. At last there came a small concession; perhaps Anne might be allowed to ride occasionally if some gentle pony could be found.

"I admit that you are looking rather well, and there may be an argument in favor of some limited outdoor activity," said her mother graciously, "but, of course, it will be considered a reward for adhering to my wishes in all things."

Anne was so disheartened by now that she could not repress a sigh. She had no intention of submitting to her mother's tyranny but at the moment she could not see any escape. Her friends Darcy and Elizabeth, as well as Lady Grinspoon, had offered her a home, but she could imagine how miserable Lady Catherine would make them if they attempted to interfere.

"This brings me to another subject," said her mother, "I have spent some time with Lord Holland, and he has made a favorable impression on me, *very* favorable in fact. Before I came here I made careful inquiries about the young man and have found that he is rich in his own right, with an excellent estate in Somerset. In addition, I have narrowly observed his older brother in Bath and have seen that he is a frail, sickly creature, not likely to live long."

Anne was ashamed of her mother's unfeeling attitude towards the unfortunate marquess and was disgusted that Lady Catherine had so little sense of compassion, but she decided to hold her tongue for the time being.

"In this matter alone I must say that you have acted with discretion, for you have waited until I could come and approve of Lord Holland before accepting his proposals. Oh, yes, my child, he has told me frankly that he has made you a proposal of marriage and since he is such a remarkably pleasing young man, I will assume that it is a sense of filial duty that has made you put off giving him a definite answer. For this I commend you."

Anne did not know what to say, as she could not decide in her own mind what to do about Lord Holland. Fitzwilliam, as she now felt certain, was lost to her forever; surely it might be better to be married to a man she liked and found intelligent and amusing than to return to the prison that she would find at Rosings. Since her conversation with Mr. Grey she had spent hours trying to resolve the dilemma without feeling any wiser.

"It would be something to be a marchioness, after all,' continued Lady Catherine, "and it is an old family, not some new-made title, and worthy to be united to the de Bourghs."

Anne murmured something to the effect that the Moncrees seemed to be well thought of and that her uncle had said favorable things of Lord Holland.

"Oh, your uncle," said Lady Catherine dismissively, "Well, I suppose his opinion may be worth something. But the point is, child, that I give you permission to listen with favor to Lord Holland. Of course, it would grieve me to lose you, but no doubt you would visit often. I daresay there could be a marriage in the spring, in which case you would have only a few months at Rosings. Well, we would have to bear the separation as best we could."

Anne reflected silently that if she were married her visits to her mother would be rare indeed. If she were married, she thought, all her mother's power over her would cease and what a great blessing that would be. She must have looked extremely weary, for even Lady Catherine was sensitive enough to notice her fatigue.

"Run along to bed now, Anne. That is enough discussion for tonight. I must say that I am pleasantly surprised that a rich, handsome, intelligent nobleman like Lord Holland would wish to marry you, even with your great fortune. It seems extraordinary, but I suppose that stranger things have happened."

Anne was so grateful to be free to leave that she was almost inclined to ignore her mother's last remark, but at the door she turned and said, "I do not think it so strange, Mama, for I am clever and agreeable and have even become rather pretty recently. I see no reason why Lord Holland should not be in love with me." So saying she left the room, not waiting for a reply from Lady Catherine.

THE NEXT MORNING Elizabeth ran to the windows as soon as she was awake and threw back the curtains. "Oh, my love, it is going to be a fine day!" she cried, hurrying back to seek refuge from the chill under the covers. "It is clear and the sun is coming up so brilliantly. There is just a light frost and it is all so beautiful!" she added, kissing her husband, who was still half-asleep. Darcy murmured something about being very much gratified to hear it, and drifted off again.

Although it was still so early, Elizabeth could not sleep. This ball meant so much to her as a way to restore Pemberley to all its grandeur and reputation for hospitality in the county. When Darcy's mother had died, all such activities had ceased and it had been a great loss to all the local families. Lord Faulconer never gave balls, although Lady Margaret would certainly have been willing to do so had her father been at all amenable to the idea, so there was something of a void in the neighborhood. Surely there had to be a splendid ball at one of the great houses to make the winter complete, and so Elizabeth had begun to plan for it soon after they had come to Pemberley. On their first morning there after the return from London in the summer, Darcy had been naming some of the ancestors who were to be seen in the many portraits in the picture gallery. This was a very fine, large room with two splendid marble fireplaces and a long range of windows overlooking the lake. The collection of paintings was exceptional and reflected the taste and refinement of several generations of Darcys.

"This was where my parents held the Pemberley ball every winter, at the beginning of December," Darcy had said, "It was a wonderful thing to see the house lit up and all our friends here, full of good cheer. It marked the beginning of the Christmas season for everyone here about." Then he had gone on to speak of his memories of the ball with great fondness. Elizabeth, whose enthusiasm sometimes outran her sense of caution, had not been long in proposing that they revive the custom, and now the day had finally arrived to accomplish it.

Fortunately she was well supported in her great project. Darcy had his own long list of responsibilities, for he would not simply rely on his small army of servitors but went over all arrangements himself to make sure that everything was in order. Georgiana spent some hours going over the choice of music with the musicians when they arrived early that morning and Anne was delighted to stay near Elizabeth's side and assist her in any way possible. It pleased her to be useful and avoid her mother at the same time.

HAPPILY THE WEATHER was favorable for an outing, and to Elizabeth's infinite relief she was free of Lady Catherine's presence for much of the day. Lady Grinspoon now saw a way to make herself truly useful to her friends, and attached herself to Lady Catherine, flattering and distracting her with questions about various subjects related to the heritage of the Darcys and the de Bourghs, and lengthening the time spent touring the countryside as much as possible.

The kindly Lady Grinspoon also made a point of praising Anne to her mother, detailing the young lady's excellent qualities and giving Lady Catherine all the credit for having such a remarkable child.

"What a fine education she has received," said Lady Grinspoon, "Why she is so well-informed and expresses herself beautifully, but at the same time so modestly. I can see what great care you have taken with your daughter, Lady Catherine. Such sagacity is rare in a parent."

Lady Catherine never had any difficulty accepting recognition of her superior abilities as her due, but Lady Grinspoon was exceptionally clever in the way in which she offered up little tidbits of flattery to the other lady's inexhaustible appetite for praise.

"And she rides so very well!" continued Lady Grinspoon, "But she must take after you, for I hear that you are a splendid horsewoman. How fortunate for Miss de Bourgh that she has a mother who understands the importance of outdoor exercise. She owes her good health to your well-founded philosophy on the subject, I am sure."

This approach might have been a little too obvious for anyone but Lady Catherine, but she was delighted with Lady Grinspoon, and began to take credit in her own mind for the evident improvement in her daughter. Before long, if subjected to this subtle form of re-education, she might even have convinced herself that she had always encouraged Anne to have an active life and venture out into the world. Sir Wilfred caught the drift of the conversation and echoed Lady Grinspoon's assessment of Miss de Bourgh.

"I am pleased to see that the young lady takes after you in having an excellent constitution, Lady Catherine," he said, "and that she shares your good sense and excellent understanding."

All during the conversation, Lady Emma was silent and inattentive; she looked out at the beautiful landscape with the dreaming expression of a woman in love who can think of nothing but her beloved. If she regretted that Fitzwilliam had remained at Pemberley to go about with Darcy and share his activities for the day she did not show it but seemed perfectly content.

By late afternoon all was in perfect readiness, and Anne decided to take a brief walk in the garden, as she had been indoors all day. She had not gone far when she heard herself hailed by Lord Holland as he came around some shrubbery and into her path.

"Miss de Bourgh! How fortunate this is!" he cried, coming up to her side and smiling down at her, "But I must be candid with you. I ventured out with the hope of finding you here. Will you be so very good as to grant me a few minutes' conversation. It is, to me at least, very important"

In a moment they were seated on a stone bench that gave a pleasant view of the lake. Anne had by now learned to be quite at ease with Lord Holland. Although she had a very good idea of his purpose in seeking her out, she was over the stage of being abashed or shy in his company, even when he came close to speaking of his intentions towards her.

"I have restrained my desire to speak to you again of my feelings for you, Miss de Bourgh, since I understood that you wished to have more time to consider my proposal. I hope you will allow me to mention the subject now, as it is the dearest thing to my heart."

Anne looked at him attentively and nodded. She felt perfectly calm without any of the extreme agitation she had known on the occasion his first two proposals; *Perhaps*, she thought, *these things become quite mundane after a while, and it may be that marriage is something that is very quickly a dull affair.*

"You know of my love for you but I have not had the opportunity to tell you why I esteem you above all other women. You have beauty, of course, but it is the superiority of your understanding and the purity of your character that make me wish to spend the rest of my life adoring you. Beauty is all very well, but in combination with the other qualities you possess I see the woman I had always hoped to find but had never dared to dream existed."

This avowal might have been more effective had not Anne read similar passages in Lady Grinspoon's novels. She had to make an effort not to smile. "You are working against your own interests with such a pretty speech," she said lightly, "It would be cruel of me to marry you and be certain of disillusioning you in short order. I am not the woman you describe, and I very much doubt that she even exists."

Lord Holland laughed, "That is another thing I love about you, Miss de Bourgh! Your good sense and your wit! The only disadvantage is that I am telling the truth and you are too modest to see it" He paused, then reached over to take her hand. Anne immediately withdrew it - but in such a gentle way that he did not seem disheartened, and he continued on.

"We would not only be husband and wife, but best friends as well," he said with animation, "How delightful would be our time together! Think of all the interests we share. Everything would be arranged as you wish: where we live, what we do and how we occupy our time. We could travel anywhere you like, for I know that you have a great interest in the world and a curiosity to see more of it. Whatever you desire, it will be the first business of my life to bring it about. I do not believe in a husband tyrannizing over his wife, and you shall do what you want, be it hunting or traveling abroad or anything that strikes your fancy."

By now his enthusiasm had reached such a pitch, that Anne interrupted him, laughing, "Please, Lord Holland, you paint a very charming picture of married bliss, but remember that I have not yet accepted you!"

The young man's face grew serious, and he said, "Alas, Miss de Bourgh, I am all too aware of that fact. Is there any chance for me? I dread to ask the question, lest the answer crush my spirit, but I must know."

Anne was silent for some minutes, and could not decide what to say. For a time all she could think of was *freedom*! The joy of living as she pleased, without the dread of her mother's interference, was like a wonderful dream to Anne, and this handsome, talented, adoring young man offered her such a life. Why should she not accept it? What else could she expect that would offer her a greater chance of happiness?

She looked into his eager face, and almost felt that she loved him. Did he truly see her as an intelligent and beautiful woman? She had never imagined that anyone could see her thus, but something made her hesitate, and after another few moment's reflection she said, "I am very grateful for your high opinion of me, Lord Holland, and I do not feel justified in withholding an answer any longer."

He leaned towards her with a countenance full of passionate emotion, but she drew back, "I pray that I may be given until tomorrow morning to spend a few more hours in considering your very flattering proposal. I promise that you will have your answer then." And so saying, Anne rose and led the way back to the house.

CHAPTER 46

*E*lizabeth had given much thought as to what she would wear on this important evening, and her gown had been ordered some time before from the atelier of the finest dressmaker in London. She still found it remarkable to possess such clothes and jewels as Darcy had lavished upon his young wife since their marriage. Occasionally, Elizabeth thought of her old dresses, mended or remade season after season and felt astonished to be surrounded by such splendor.

She had dressed and was looking into her jewel box for the necklace she had planned to wear when her husband entered the room. Elizabeth smiled up at him; surely there had never been such a handsome man as Darcy, or one who looked so well in evening dress.

"How exquisite you are, my love," he said, coming over to her and kissing her, "That dress is the color that becomes you best, deep crimson like the wine dark sea."

Elizabeth noticed that Darcy had a leather box half concealed behind his back. He smiled and produced it, saying, "Something I have been keeping for this moment, a little gift almost worthy of your loveliness."

She opened the box and had to catch her breath, for there was a magnificent necklace of rubies and diamonds, and a matching set of earrings. She looked at them in wonderment for a moment, then turned to Darcy, "My love, I never imagined anything so exquisite. Can you comprehend what it means to me that you should give me something so beautiful? You really must think *me* beautiful too, and that makes me more happy than you can know."

She put on the earrings and Darcy fastened the necklace around her neck. "My father brought the rubies back from India, and after we were married I arranged to have them reset, as the original design was too heavy and old fashioned for you. Do you remember the jeweler we visited in London where I bought you an emerald ring?" Elizabeth said that she did indeed remember, and that the ring was one of her favorites.

"Well, the real reason we went there was so that the jeweler could see the lady who was to wear this necklace and design it accordingly," said Darcy laughing, "What a lot of correspondence there has been about this, and the necessity for having it completed by this evening. And who do you think brought these baubles to me? Our good friend Bingley, when he came from London."

Elizabeth looked at herself in the mirror with fascination, trying to believe that she really was the lovely, elegant woman she saw reflected there. She was not vain, although she thought herself well-enough looking, but this was something of a revelation.

Darcy sat down beside her and said, "I dare not touch you, for you seem like an immortal goddess to me," and then he kissed her anyway, "You have given me all the happiness my life has held. Before I knew you, I never dreamt that I could love so deeply and see the world as a place filled with bliss and joy. It is all because of you, my beloved"

After a few minutes Darcy said, "Well, dearest, let us go survey our house and admire everything and have a glass of champagne before our guests arrive."

PEMBERLEY WAS INDEED a splendid sight that evening. There was the brilliance and warmth of a hundred candles and a fire in every hearth. Dozens of fragrant plants had been carefully brought in from the hothouses and there were boughs of holly everywhere. Darcy and Elizabeth walked about, enchanted with what they saw. "It does me good to see the house like this, my darling," said Darcy, "It has been many years, too many years by far."

"Then we shall do this every year, my love," replied Elizabeth, taking his arm as they walked the length of the gallery a second time, "I must say that I have really enjoyed the preparations and it was not so daunting as I expected."

Darcy looked at his wife with adoration; his beloved had done everything for this great event as if she had been used to the responsibilities of a house like Pemberley all her life. Elizabeth had abilities he had not even suspected before their marriage and this discovery was a constant source of delight to him. She did not see the way that he looked at her because Georgiana had appeared at the far end of the gallery and was hurrying towards them.

"Oh, how perfect everything looks!" she cried, "Why, it is as I remember it to have been when I was a child, when Mama was here. Dearest sister, thank you for reviving this most loved tradition." Elizabeth was gratified by Georgiana's words and pleased to see the young lady so animated and happy. It was an unusual occurrence and Georgiana's apparent tendency to melancholy had become a source of some concern to those who loved her.

Soon the Pemberley houseguests began to appear, full of happy anticipation and high spirits. Lady Catherine normally tried to make a grand entrance after everyone else was assembled, but on this occasion she had joined the company promptly, was unusually gracious and did not mention above nine or ten things that she would have done differently.

"But where is Anne?" was the question that soon went round the group of friends, for no one had seen her yet. "I did see her for a moment before I joined you here," offered Georgiana, "She looks very beautiful and I do so admire her gown." In a moment Anne appeared at the end of the room and was somewhat taken aback to find all eyes turned towards her. Elizabeth went over to her and said, "How very lovely you look" and led her over to the group by the fire. There was a flurry of conversation and the only person who did not join in was

Lady Catherine, who was examining her daughter through her lorgnette with an unreadable expression. Anne made a great effort not to meet her mother's gaze and was pleased to have Mr. Grey come to her side.

"Why, Miss de Bourgh," he said, "I had a parrot the color of that gown once, and a very nice bird it was. It flew off through the window one day though. I hope you are not planning any such thing!"

An ordinary compliment might have made Anne self-conscious, but now she was able to laugh, "I hope that it was at least a valuable bird, not something with drab, molting feathers."

"No, indeed," replied her friend more seriously, "It was a beautiful creature, the color of a clear blue pool under the summer sky."

Anne glanced about the room in search of her cousin Fitzwilliam and saw that he was standing with Lady Emma at the far end of the gallery and that they were apparently deep in conversation. She felt a degree of misery that told her very clearly how her heart lay, but she forced herself to smile and look indifferent to everything but the pleasures of the ball. She was glad to have her attention claimed by Lord Holland who had evidently been waiting for her and hastened to remind her of her promise to dance the first two dances with him. "I am not likely to forget," replied Anne affecting a cheerfulness that she was very far from feeling, "for you mentioned it at breakfast and again when I met you in the library not three hours ago."

"I must take care then, Miss de Bourgh, or you will begin to suspect that dancing with you is the most important thing in the world to me."

She was spared the need to reply to this remark by the advent of Lady Catherine, who was annoyed that her daughter had not immediately come to her to make her obsequies. She made her way to Anne's side with her usual grand manner and the company parted as fishing boats might clear the way for a royal barge.

"You will excuse us, Lord Holland," she said, "I must have a few words with my child. Mother and daughter matters, you know, must always take precedence."

Lord Holland moved off obediently and Anne fortified herself for whatever critical remarks her mother might have prepared to cloud her enjoyment of the evening.

"You really look rather well, my dear; that gown is not amiss and I must say that the color suits you."

"Why, thank you, Mama," replied Anne, surprised to hear such kind words from her mother.

"Your hair, of course, is not at all the thing, but I will soon find you a new maid who will arrange it properly. But do try, for once, to look animated, for you have never been able to smile and look pleased with your company. It is a very great drawback at such gatherings. Well, at least you will have some partners and will not be left to sit looking neglected, for I am sure that Elizabeth will not allow you to be ignored."

"Thank you, Mama, for your encouragement and kind remarks. No doubt recalling them during the next few hours will add greatly to my pleasure in the ball."

Anne could not restrain her sarcasm, but Lady Catherine suspected nothing, for she had too high an opinion of her own sagacity to think it possible that her advice could be unwelcome. "As for me, dear Anne," she added, "You must not be surprised when you see your mother dancing, for I have promised Sir Wilfred that I will do so."

This was extraordinary news, for Anne had never known her mother to dance.

"Yes, I have said that I will do so, even though it has been at least twenty years."

At that moment Sir Wilfred came over to them and Anne was amazed to see her mother looking so pleased and youthful when he made his appearance at her side.

The guests had begun to arrive and in a very short time the grand space was full of people eager to talk and dance, the music began and Anne had a very fair hope of not having to speak to her mother again for the entire night.

Darcy and Elizabeth were now greeting their friends, many of whom were new acquaintances for Elizabeth. She was enjoying herself immensely and thought everyone charming.

"Well, Darcy, so Pemberley is reborn, is it?" said Lord Faulconer, shaking hands with his host, "The neighborhood has greatly missed this ball for the last ten years, but everything is different now that Mrs. Darcy is here. You have done well. How pleased your parents would be."

Darcy was full of an almost unalloyed happiness at that moment; he could see Elizabeth moving among their guests with such grace and natural elegance that he felt almost overcome with love for her. He could observe that she remembered to watch over Georgiana and make certain that his shy young sister was not allowed to feel at a loss.

"Mrs. Darcy is so very beautiful," said Lady Margaret with sincere admiration, for she had come to like Elizabeth best of all the women she knew. "And how well those jewels become her. A *petit cadeau* to mark the occasion, I suspect."

Darcy only smiled. It was unusual for his old friend Lady Margaret to notice something as mundane as jewels, although she herself was wearing some fine sapphires that had been in her family for one hundred years. They matched her dress of dark blue silk and enhanced the color of her eyes and auburn hair. Grey had been watching her from across the room since she had arrived, in awe of her and almost afraid to approach. Lord Faulconer called to him, however, and they were soon in conversation about the prospects for heavy frost over the coming few days and the effect it might have on the next week's hunting. At the same time Lady Margaret had to restrain herself from glancing at Grey; she had never seen him looking so well and thought him the handsomest man in the room. She remembered the first time she had seen him walking up the hill towards Pemberley in a mud-covered coat and a hat with a candle in the brim. The memory that she had thought him a vagrant or a house-breaker made her laugh aloud.

Grey looked at her and held her gaze for a moment, "What is so amusing, Lady Margaret?" but she only shook her head and laughed again.

"I very much suspect that your laughter is at my expense, but you will be punished for your unkindness by having to dance with me, for as I recall, you were rash enough to promise me the first two." So saying, Grey led her away to join the dance to the great satisfaction of Lord Faulconer, who watched them with approbation. How well they look together, he thought, still hoping for his daughter's happiness, for he knew that she loved Grey, however much she tried to hide it.

The long gallery was soon filled with all the county families who had been friends of the Darcys of Pemberley for generations. They were universally full of praise for everything they saw. Everyone was enchanted with Mrs. Darcy, and any rumors of less than distinguished family connections were dismissed as absurd. Why, one look at their hostess and the perfect way in which she had greeted them and opened the ball made it clear that she must have some connections among the nobility, for how else could a young bride have such an air and manner? Everyone was in a fine mood and would have been pleased to believe Elizabeth a princess. The only unkind note was sounded by Lady Templeton, who was unable to enjoy the evening unless she found something to criticize.

"Well, I suppose she is handsome enough, although I have it on good authority that her uncle keeps a shop in Meryton," she said to Mrs. Chase, the mayor's wife, "but I do feel that the jewels are a bit overdone. Something more modest would be suitable for a new bride."

Mrs. Chase could only reply that she found Mrs. Darcy's *toute ensemble* exquisite and that if her own husband ever wished to present her with similar adornments, then she would have no objection in the world.

Anne was the object of only slightly less curiosity than was Elizabeth, for it was known that she was the heiress to Rosings and rumor had it that she was to be a marchioness someday. She was pronounced a "beautiful girl" and quite distinguished, if a bit reserved. Everyone knew on the authority of the very best gossip that the present Marquess of Roscree was near death in Bath and that soon Lord Holland would come into the title and estates. The young man's devotion to Miss de Bourgh was evident to all; he seemed unwilling to leave her side for a moment and yielded her over to her other promised partners with a reluctance that stopped just short of ill humor.

The first of these other partners was Mr. Grey, and Anne was delighted to see him and to have a bit of a respite from the intensity of Lord Holland's attentions. "Well, Miss de Bourgh, and how do you find the ball," inquired her friend with mock solemnity, "You must find it exhausting with such a determined suitor at your elbow every moment."

"I begin to think that you do not like Lord Holland," said Anne, "What fault do you find in him?"

"Why nothing really, except that I have been in the same house with him for several weeks and do not feel that I know him at all. He is a very reserved sort of person, is he not?"

"I do not know how to judge such things or what to expect of people in that regard," replied Anne, "Certainly he has told me a great many things about himself in a very open manner." She felt disturbed by Grey's words and looked across the room to see Lord Holland dancing with Elizabeth.

"Be observant, my friend, and you will find that there is a pattern in terms of where you are likely to encounter him during the day. Have you not noticed it? Watch the direction of his gaze and his expression and you may discover something of significance."

"What on earth are you talking about, Mr. Grey," asked Anne, rather annoyed, "It is not like you to be so mysterious."

"It is because I may find that I am quite incorrect about Lord Holland," said Grey with a laugh, "No doubt he is the best fellow in the world. I will observe him further and give you my valuable opinion later in the evening if there is anything to say."

For the first time Anne was quite put out with Mr. Grey. Why would he begin such a subject and then leave her wondering? When they came together again she demanded, "It is unfair to be so enigmatic about something that is so crucial to my happiness."

"You are right, and we will talk of it later this very night. Only let me have a little longer to consider the matter."

Anne was eager to continue their conversation and was vexed by her mother's arrival at her side at the end of the set. Lady Catherine had remarks to make on her daughter's dancing and undertook to correct Anne's faults.

"You must be more aware of your posture, my child, and do try to smile and look more pleased with your company."

"Yes, Mama, of course," replied Anne with some impatience. Her attention was drawn to her cousin Fitzwilliam who was presenting a young officer to Darcy and Elizabeth. He was a fine looking gentleman-like man with a distinguished air and she heard him express his thanks for being invited to Pemberley.

"We are delighted that you are here, Captain Malvern," said Darcy, "We are always happy to meet one of Colonel Fitzwilliam's officers." After Fitzwilliam had completed the necessary introduction of the young man, he walked over to where Anne stood with her mother.

"My dear Fitzwilliam," said Lady Catherine, "This is the first moment we have had for a chat this evening. What do you think of Elizabeth's arrangements? It is not a bad effort for someone so new to her high station as mistress of Pemberley."

Fitzwilliam replied that he believed Mrs. Darcy to possess brilliant gifts in many aspects of life, and in particular, promoting happiness wherever she happened to be. "This ball," he added, "must be considered a triumph."

"High praise indeed," said his aunt, "but it is early yet. However, I am not displeased by what I have seen so far."

With a bow Fitzwilliam reminded Anne that she had promised him the next two dances. Anne, who had thought of little else all evening, gave him her hand, with mingled joy and trepidation. She was afraid that she would hardly be able to talk with her cousin and that he would see her emotion. He also was very quiet at first, but his eyes were full of warmth and interest whenever their glances met.

"You are the loveliest woman in the room," he said, the second time the dance brought them close together, "I always knew that it could be so. Is this really my little cousin who was so shy of company?"

Anne could think of no reply; these words were something of which she had dreamed many times but had never expected to hear. In the next moment, however, she noticed that Fitzwilliam's attention was directed across the room; he was looking at Lady Emma, who was dancing with his young staff officer, Captain Malvern. At that moment Anne felt completely forgotten, so intense was her cousin's gaze, and all her happiness turned to cold despair.

When the dance was over Fitzwilliam led her to a corner of the room that was somewhat less crowded. His eyes were very bright and he seemed to be struggling to find his normal tone of voice and manner.

"Anne, you will hear many things concerning me in the next few hours. Remember all that you know of me and do not let others influence you. How I wish I could tell you everything."

He seemed about to say more, but was interrupted by the appearance of Lady Emma at his side.

"It is very hard when a lady must search out her partner," she said, with her usual light-hearted gaiety, "but is this not our dance, Colonel Fitzwilliam?

Fitzwilliam bowed and acknowledged that such was the case, offering an apology for his inattention.

"You must think me shameless for seeking out your cousin, Miss de Bourgh," laughed Lady Emma, "but I cannot do without the colonel. He is quite essential to my felicity."

I can well understand it, thought Anne sadly as she watched them enter the dance, for heaven knows that he has always been essential to mine.

She was distracted from her reflections by finding Mr. Grey standing beside her. "You promised me this dance, Miss de Bourgh, and I am here to claim that honor."

"You hardly seem in a proper state of mind for dancing, Mr. Grey. I will release you from your obligation if you tell me what has occurred to make you look so gloomy?"

"It is clear that I can never hide my feelings, Miss de Bourgh, especially from you, it seems. I will tell you as you have proven your friendship so often and I am not inclined to conceal anything from you. Lady Margaret and I have quarreled or at least she has decided to quarrel with me."

Anne looked about the ballroom and exclaimed, "Why, where have they gone? Where are Lady Margaret and Lord Faulconer?"

"They have left the ball, on the excuse of Lady Margaret's

headache, she who probably never had a headache in her life. I made the mistake of telling her that I wished to dance with her forever and would not give up the dream of doing so. Poor stuff, of course, but my feelings for her have done away with any wit I once possessed."

"I am surprised that she was so affected by what you said, but I think her reaction is a hopeful one." Anne reflected on the matter for some moments, and then said with some force, "You must go after her, Mr. Grey. Do not wait for tomorrow."

"Pursue her to her father's house at this time of night, Miss de Bourgh? It is hardly a discreet course of action, although that cannot matter to a man in love. But do you not think that it would make things worse?"

"No, it is your best chance," said Anne with a degree of confidence remarkable for one who had never before presumed to give advice to anyone, "Go to her, Mr. Grey, for it is the last thing she would expect, and that is how to win Lady Margaret."

Grey was obviously convinced, for he went at once to find Darcy and request the use of a horse.

"I will not be so absurd as to ask you where you are going, Grey, but perhaps you have not observed that it has become bitterly cold and begun to snow. But such trivial concerns will not alter your determination, I suspect."

"Not in the least, Darcy, and I am grateful to you for not arguing against my intention."

"Very well then, go, and God's speed. At least do not gallop the entire distance, for I am concerned for my horse, if not for your neck, and the road is probably icy by now."

Elizabeth came to her husband's side in time to see their friend Grey go bounding off down the stairs. "I begin to think that our ball is not a success, my love, for people are leaving and we have not yet had supper," she said with an ironic smile.

Darcy took her hand, saying, "I think you can guess what is afoot, my Elizabeth. In the meantime I can only say that there has never been a finer ball at Pemberley and that I wish above all things to dance with my wife."

CHAPTER 47

By the time Grey had reached Castle Faulconer he had begun to doubt the wisdom of his course of action. Surely the occupants of the castle would have all gone to bed by now and his appearance at the door at that hour would make him seem ridiculous. He had almost decided to turn back when he noticed that a faint light could be seen at the window of what he knew to be the library. Perhaps one of the servants was about; Grey thought that he might leave a message that he had wished to ascertain that his friends had reached home safely in the snow. This also sounded ridiculous to him, but at least he would leave quickly without creating a disturbance.

He was surprised to have the door opened by Lady Margaret, still attired for the ball and carrying a large candlestick.

"Good heavens, Mr. Grey!" exclaimed Lady Margaret, equally amazed to see him, "I heard your horse in the courtyard and thought that there must some sort of emergency with one of the tenants. Are you mad to come out in this weather?"

Grey was covered with snow and must have looked very cold, for Lady Margaret added, "Well, now that you are here, you had best put your horse in one of the stalls and come in to warm yourself for a bit." Then she closed the door with some degree of impatience.

Grey returned in a few minutes and made his way into the hall, where he found Lady Margaret waiting for him.

"Everyone has gone to bed, as you see, but there is a fire in the library and I will give you some brandy." She turned and led the way, but suddenly stopped and said, "Whatever rash idea has made you come here tonight had better be abandoned, Mr. Grey. I am in no humor to hear any more and am likely to throw you out into the cold on very little provocation."

Grey could think of nothing to say. The hallway was filled with a silver light from the rapidly falling snow and he was too overcome by her beauty to speak. She fell silent too, but then with increased annoyance in her every movement, led him to a chair by the library fire and brought him a glass of brandy.

"Please, be comfortable, but it is best, no doubt, that we limit our conversation to commenting on the ball or the weather. I hope you will respect my wishes in this."

Grey sat in silence for some time, drinking his brandy and looking into the fire, wondering how to proceed. It was not in his nature to be deterred from speaking his mind, but he feared that anything he said would offend Lady Margaret; trivial remarks on the ball were quite beyond him at that moment. When he looked over in her direction he caught an expression in her face that he had never seen before: a gentle and wistful melancholy. In a second she had adopted her former disdain, but it was too late and before she could protest Grey was at her feet.

"I beg you to let me speak, Lady Margaret, and then I will leave and you need not see me again. I have no wish to offend you, but I cannot bear to go through life without having told you my feelings."

The lady began to rise, but then settling into her chair said ironically, "It seems to me that you have stated your feelings on more than one occasion. The exercise will be equally pointless this time as well, but if you must do this, I will listen… for a moment at least."

"This is different, this is my formal proposal of marriage, the first that I have ever made and certainly the last that I will attempt."

When she began to speak, Grey interrupted her, "Please, before you answer, allow me to state the advantages of at least considering my offer. There is my love for you, which gives me no peace because the thought of life without you is unthinkable. From the moment I saw you on the hillside near Pemberley there has been no possibility of loving anyone else."

"Pretty words, Mr. Grey, but hardly original. I have heard them before."

"Now you hear them from one who alone is able to love you as you deserve, because I understand you. Through all the months during which you have been so sarcastic and dismissive towards me, I have seen beneath it; you are everything that is gentle and loving. That you pretend to be otherwise is the result of some terrible pain you have suffered. I do not know what it is, but I sense it every time I am with you."

"That is absurd, you presume too much. You know nothing of me."

"Only listen, Lady Margaret, for I offer you everything that I have in the world: the prospect of our little cottage in my small parish in Wales, where we will go for long walks in the mist with our dogs and sit by our hearth in the evening, never tiring of looking across at each other. If we are careful we will be able to afford a pair of old nags to go riding when it is not too wet. You will help me with my sermons, for I suspect you would be excellent at composing them. The best thing is that we will always be together, and that is the greatest thing that I can conceive, do you not agree."

He found the courage to look up into her face and was astonished to find that tears ran down her cheeks. He took her hands and said, "You love me, I know it now."

For a moment Grey thought that he had succeeded and he felt an overwhelming happiness. She leaned forward and kissed him and they were very quiet, but suddenly she leapt up and cried, "Oh, I cannot, I cannot! Do leave me, for the love of God."

She ran from the room, leaving Grey in a very bad state of confusion and despair. Just as he was thinking that he must go to find his horse and make his way back to Pemberley, the door opened. He jumped up with a tremendous exaltation, only to find that it was Lord Faulconer.

"You certainly have the ability to discompose my daughter, Mr.

438

Grey. I just met her on the stairs in a very emotional state, but I perceive that you are no more tranquil than she is. I am glad that I decided to come to see what was happening. I heard your horse in the courtyard. Is it not a bit late to be paying visits?"

Grey apologized, but Lord Faulconer said, "Never mind, my dear fellow, it is excusable under the circumstances, and I do believe I understand what has happened. You have proposed marriage to my child and have not received a very favorable reply, alas."

So saying the older man opened the library door and looked out to ascertain that they were alone, then motioned to Grey to be seated.

"Here, have another brandy, for I have a story to tell you that will explain all, a story I would not have thought to reveal to a living soul."

ANNE HAD WATCHED her friend Grey leave the ball with a mixture of approval and something like envy. At least he could do *something*, take action to attempt to order his life as he wished! In a moment she found that Lord Holland had come to stand beside her.

"I see that Mr. Grey is off on a mission," he said, "and one need not be very acute to guess what it might be. An agreeable and highly intelligent, one might even say brilliant young man, but transparent as glass."

"And you, Lord Holland? Certainly no one could call you transparent. One senses very deep water and hidden reefs where you are concerned," said Anne, wondering if it were possible to break through the measured calm of his demeanor, for there was something almost reckless in her mood that night. At the same time she watched for Fitzwilliam with part of her attention, while not allowing her eyes to wander in search of his tall form. Well, no doubt he had taken Lady Emma in to supper; she would insist on it.

"You find me difficult to read, Miss de Bourgh? I am encouraged then, for I have learned that you love a mystery, the more complex the better. Once again, I offer myself up to you as a subject for lifelong study and promise to try to remain enigmatic for as long as possible."

"Perhaps it would be disconcerting to live with an unsolved riddle every day, Lord Holland," replied Anne with a laugh, "You may be harming your cause with that promise."

He became grave and looked down at her with a very serious expression, "I can assure you that I would wish to be understood and known to my very soul by my wife, that is by the wife I hope to have. If there be anything deep in my character, I do assert that love, *your* love, Miss de Bourgh, would find it out and in doing so bless my life."

Anne had not expected such a reply, given in a tone that was full of emotion, and she was confused. Lord Holland had the ability to surprise her as few people did. All evening he had been gay and attentive, but had not spoken of love.

Her hand was resting on the railing at the top of the steps, and he laid his own over it with a perfect gentleness that caught her off guard, and she did not withdraw from his touch.

"I must leave for Bath in a few days time to attend my brother, whose health is even worse with the onset of winter. I have waited, I believe quite patiently, for your answer to my proposal of marriage. May I expect some reply before my departure? Will you indeed let me know your decision tomorrow morning as you promised? I would not press you for the world, but I do hope for some relief from this suspense."

Anne withdrew her hand from his and looked down to the hall below where she could see Darcy and Elizabeth emerge from the supper room. They were accompanied by Jane and Bingley, the latter with a protective arm about his wife's waist as they began their progress up the marble steps. Elizabeth was laughing at something Darcy had said, looking up into his face with eyes shining with happiness. Holland followed Anne's gaze and his expression became grave.

"We could know an equal felicity together, Miss de Bourgh. I beg that you will trust me in this, for I know it to be so. I want only to be with you and devote my life to making you happy."

Then Fitzwilliam appeared with Lady Emma and the two of them followed the party returning to the ballroom. Captain Malvern was in close attendance as if awaiting his colonel's instructions on some matter, for his countenance was expectant and thoughtful. Lady Emma, as usual, was enchantingly graceful and lively.

When Elizabeth saw Anne and Lord Holland she hastened to them and took Anne's hand affectionately. "My dear, you have not eaten! Please do go down and take something. I am sure that Lord Holland will escort you."

"Indeed, Mrs. Darcy, I would be honored to do so," and the young man offered Anne his arm.

As they descended the stairs, they passed Fitzwilliam and Lady Emma who cried, "Why, I have never enjoyed a ball so much, Miss de Bourgh! This evening must now rank as my idea of perfection and I will always remember how happy we all were together. Do you not agree, Colonel?"

Fitzwilliam murmured something in assent and they moved on, with the faithful Captain Malvern close behind. Anne happened to find her eyes caught by her cousin's and she had the impression that he looked at her with an unusual intensity and was unwilling to break his gaze, but then the moment was gone and Anne thought she must have imagined it.

As Lord Holland walked with her into supper, Anne said, "I will have an answer for you tomorrow, in the garden where I walk every day. Is that soon enough?"

GREY HAD ALWAYS SUSPECTED that some mystery was attached to the family at Castle Faulconer: the father, so somber and detached from the world, and the daughter displaying a degree of coldness and cynicism that seemed inexplicable in one so young. He was eager to hear what Lord Faulconer had to tell him and leant forward with perfect attention to what followed.

"For some years I have lived an almost reclusive life, venturing to London and Bath only occasionally to let my child see something of society. Even those small attempts at providing a normal life for my daughter have been unwelcome, as Margaret would never leave the country if it were up to her. She has absolutely refused to spend a season in London and at her insistence I have given up every idea of taking a house there and introducing her to the company of those with whom she would naturally associate as the daughter of a peer. Our life, my dear Grey, was very dull until you came to the neighborhood and I had the pleasure of learning to know you and enjoying the gift of your friendship. You have brought me out of myself and I am very grateful. Until tonight I had not attended a ball for years. You were probably unaware what an extraordinary event it is for me to go to an evening party. Darcy was quite surprised to see me actually appear tonight."

Grey had heard Darcy remark that it was a rare honor to see Lord Faulconer at the ball, and that it was no doubt a compliment to Mrs. Darcy.

"Yes, I did indeed wish to pay tribute to that exquisite and gracious lady," continued Lord Faulconer, "but it was also to ensure that Margaret would be there to give you an opportunity to forward your courtship."

Grey could only murmur his thanks and his wish that the evening had turned out more favorably. He was grateful for Lord Faulconer's remarks, but had a great desire that he would get to the point.

Finally it seemed that the story was to be told.

"Everyone assumes that my spirits have been long depressed because I am in mourning for my wife and that I cannot recover from losing her. This is absolutely true, but the reasons for my sadness are more complicated than that, as you will hear. We married when she was quite young and there were twenty years of difference in our ages. If you wish to know what my wife was like, you have only to look at Margaret, for the resemblance is remarkable and there is also a great similarity in character and disposition, the same impetuosity and sweetness. I was very happy in my marriage for many years, especially after my daughter was born and life seemed almost complete. We had hoped for a son as well, but it was not to be."

Lord Faulconer hesitated for a few moments as if it were difficult to continue. Grey was wise enough to say nothing and stared at his glass of brandy, thinking how fine the color of it was in the firelight.

"When Margaret was twelve years old, my wife developed a weakness of the lungs. She had always been somewhat prone to the condition, but it worsened over the course of an unusually severe winter.

The physician warned that another exacerbation of her illness could prove fatal and advised us to go to Italy for a year to avoid cold weather and allow my wife to recover."

"Would you be so kind, Lord Faulconer, or do I presume too much? What was your wife's Christian name?"

"Isabella," was the reply, made with obvious effort, and Grey surmised that it had been many years since those syllables had been spoken in that room, "My wife's name was Isabella."

"We found an old palazzo in Rome and were quite contented there for several months," continued Lord Faulconer, "Isabella loved to take Margaret on excursions and teach her about art and history, for my wife was an accomplished and well-informed woman. It was there that my child began to acquire her knowledge of architecture and her admiration for Italian gardens. I was so very happy to escort them everywhere and simply listen and admire their enthusiasm."

"In the natural course of events we were invited to become involved with the most elevated society of the city, and were constantly in demand for some fête or other. At one of these gatherings we met a young nobleman, an Italian prince, who was one of the most highly regarded personages in Rome. He was, I suppose, a figure of romance in the tradition of popular novels: a bold rider, a swordsman famous for his duels and an amateur scholar of some note. He was engaged to marry one of the most beautiful heiresses in Italy."

Grey looked up to encourage his friend to go on; he could guess what was coming.

"My beloved wife had the misfortune to fall under the spell of this man, who turned out to be a fiend of selfishness and conceit. I suspected nothing until the day that she left us and disappeared with her seducer. I contrived to keep her disgrace a secret by inventing the fiction that she had gone to the mountains for her health. Obviously there may have been rumors going about in Rome, but the vile man who had taken her from us had covered his tracks well. From Margaret I could conceal nothing; she had seen her mother steal out of the palazzo at dawn and meet her lover. Can you imagine what the child suffered at being deserted by her much loved mother? Can you now understand why her trust is so hard to win and why she is scornful of the very idea of a faithful and sincere attachment?"

Grey could indeed understand and it was with difficulty that he restrained his emotions at the thought of Lady Margaret's grief and disillusionment.

"The final act of the tragedy came quickly. I traveled the country in search of my wife. All I wished was to rescue her from the pit into which she had fallen. I knew her health to be delicate and had a sense of dread as to her fate if she were not recovered soon. I believed her lover to be incapable of honor or true affection. After three months I heard that a beautiful Englishwoman was very ill in Sienna and I hurried there with Margaret, whom I could not bring myself to leave in Rome. It was indeed Isabella; she had been deserted by the Prince and lay dying in a convent there. We found accommodation in an inn nearby and I visited her every day, for she was too weak to be moved. The best doctors in the town and those I brought from Florence assured me that her life could not be saved. Margaret begged me to take her to her mother, but I hesitated. I did not wish her to see the poor, shamed, ravaged woman who now only wished to die."

"How terrible it must have been for you, Lord Faulconer. You wished your daughter to remember her mother as she had been."

"Indeed, that was my idea of what was best, but the decision was taken away from me. Margaret followed me to the convent and made her way to the dying woman's bedside just before she expired. She was there during Isabella's last moments and the terrible grief of seeing that sad death has stayed with her always and blighted her youth."

Grey now understood his Lady Margaret's frequent depression and tendency to retreat from the world. How could anyone recover from such a tragedy?

"My grief was made even more dreadful when I was unable to avenge myself on the monster who had brought about my wife's destruction. I searched over much of Italy for the prince, intending to kill him in a duel. Despite his skill, I believe that my rage and hatred would have made me the victor. However, my agents brought me the intelligence that he had been stabbed to death in Venice by the

444

brothers of another lady he had wronged. Thus I was robbed of my revenge."

The two men sat in silence for several minutes, until Lord Faulconer said, "Now that you know the story of her mother, you may wish to reconsider your intentions toward Margaret."

"Reconsider my intentions!" exclaimed Grey with something close to anger, "You should know me better than that, Lord Faulconer. I love your daughter more than ever after hearing how she has suffered while still a child, and then having to live with such a tragic secret all these years."

"Alas, I fear that there is little you can do to change her resolution to remain alone and a captive of her disillusionment."

"Perhaps you are correct, sir, but I am a stubborn man, and will not give up easily, I can assure you. I must go to Cambridge in a few weeks time to continue my studies there and arrange my ordination, then I am to be in my parish in Wales in March."

"So soon, my dear Grey," asked the older man sadly, "It will be very hard to lose your company. Perhaps you will return from time to time?"

"Indeed I shall, and with as strong a purpose as ever," replied Grey.

"It is a long way and a hard journey," murmured Lord Faulconer, who wondered if his friend would really have the heart to make another attempt to win his child. Once in Wales it seemed likely that he would forget her.

CHAPTER 48

A hostess should feel complimented when guests stay late into the night, and show no inclination to return to their own homes. Elizabeth was pleased that the Pemberley ball seemed to be such a great success, but the time came when she would have been grateful to retire wearily to her bedchamber and sleep the next day away. Darcy saw that his wife was fatigued and would have swept his friends out of the house if possible. Finally the last carriage pulled away from the front portico and Elizabeth was able to lean against her husband with a contented sigh. He held her close and said, "My love, I believe that I shall carry you upstairs, for I think that you are too exhausted to walk there yourself."

Elizabeth laughed and protested that she was very well and not really tired at all, but at the second landing her husband did pick her up, and in minutes she was half asleep, tucked under a warm eiderdown that he had arranged, for it had been chilly seeing people off at the door.

Darcy kissed her and was about to go to confer with the butler and make all secure for what little remained of the night, when Elizabeth called him back.

"Oh, do come back, dearest, and let us talk of the ball for just a few minutes,"

Darcy, happy to oblige her, sat down on the bed and they went over some of the more notable aspects of the evening.

"I do think that everyone seemed in good spirits and to enjoy themselves greatly," said Elizabeth, "I do not believe that I will ever again feel any trepidation about giving a ball."

Her husband smiled and said that he was glad to hear it, as she had such a remarkable gift as a hostess.

"You put everyone at their ease. There was great elegance, but nothing overly formal or stiff, so it was natural to see such a happy company. I'm not surprised that they stayed so late and kept us from our bed until dawn."

"There is one thing, however, that seems odd," replied Elizabeth, "Some members of the group disappeared rather abruptly. I noticed that Mr. Grey vanished after Lady Margaret's departure and has not been seen again."

"Poor Grey," said Darcy, "It is not difficult to imagine where he went. I daresay he was turned away at the door of Castle Faulconer and is riding about forlornly somewhere. No doubt he will be back by breakfast."

"You know I like Lady Margaret very much, but I cannot understand her unkindness to your friend. From my own observation I think that they are perfectly matched."

Then Elizabeth seemed almost asleep when she opened her eyes and continued, "But the other thing is - Fitzwilliam also disappeared a few hours ago. He came up to me and said very kind things about the ball and then I did not see him again."

She half sat up and exclaimed, "Why, here is a coincidence...Lady Emma left early as well...at approximately the same time, after staying as close to Fitzwilliam as possible the entire evening. I thought her behavior a bit unusual, in fact." Looking at Darcy questioningly she continued, "Well, I think I must be very tired to have such fanciful ideas,"

"What are you thinking?" asked Darcy, although by now he was beginning to know his wife's mind almost as well as his own.

"Do you think that they may have eloped?" Then she smiled at the absurd idea and sank back into the bed.

"That would be an odd thing to do since there can be no opposition to the match," said Darcy.

Elizabeth again half asleep turned her face to her pillow and said, "Of course that is correct, but people do such strange things."

Darcy kissed her and left the room. When he went downstairs he found the butler in the front hall awaiting any further orders.

"No, Jenkins, you go and get what rest you can. You and the entire staff did splendidly tonight and Mrs. Darcy and I are very pleased. I am just going out of doors for a few minutes and will lock up the house when I come back in."

It was very cold with a faint lightening of the sky in the east. Darcy walked around the house and across the courtyard towards the stable block where Fitzwilliam's bedchamber was situated. It was perfectly quiet and still, except for the occasional sound of a horse moving about in the stables. He was surprised as he reached the stone steps to the bedchambers to see his head groom appear with a lantern.

"Why, Wilkins," said Darcy, "Why are you still up?"

"I was checking on the chestnut mare, sir" replied Wilkins, "She's been restless and off her feed, but now she seems right enough."

Darcy said he was glad to hear it, and then Wilkins continued, "I am glad to see you, sir, because I was given a letter for you and I did not know if I should wait until morning, although the gentleman said I should."

"What gentleman?"

"Why, it was Colonel Fitzwilliam, sir. He left here in his carriage at about one this morning. He was in a great hurry and his manservants could hardly move fast enough for him. He is usually such a patient sort of gentleman."

Hiding his consternation, Darcy asked, "Has anyone else from the house made a hasty departure this night."

"Well, sir, with all the gentry's horses to attend to it was hard to keep track, but just after the Colonel left a carriage entered the yard here. I saw a lady in a cloak come out of the back door of the house and be assisted into it. I wondered why a lady would use that door. They drove off with some speed."

Darcy took the letter and said absently, "Let us hope that things have settled down for now, Wilkins. I will see you later."

When he entered the house Darcy tore open the letter and read it by the light of the candle that Jenkins had left for him. The contents were startling enough that he read it twice before exclaiming, "Good heavens, what a situation and how I am to explain it in the morning?"

~

LADY CATHERINE MUST HAVE SLEPT VERY little after the ball ended, for she could have been observed hurrying along towards her daughter's bedchamber quite early, not having even bothered to call her maid. She found Anne already awake and dressed and drinking a cup of coffee.

"Is it not a bit draughty in that chair there by the window, my child?" inquired Lady Catherine. After a moment of testing for insidious cold vapors by waving her hand near the sill, she sat down opposite her daughter.

"Will you take coffee, mama?" asked Anne politely, gesturing towards the large silver pot that sat on the table between them.

"Indeed, I shall not!" replied Lady Catherine indignantly, "I do not approve of coffee; it is not a proper drink for a well-brought up girl. Tea, *weak* tea, is the only thing for an Englishwoman to take in the morning. When we return to Rosings I will ban all coffee from the house and the gentlemen will just have to bear it."

Ignoring her mother's threat, Anne rang for Celestine, "Tea then, Mama? Celestine, do please bring some tea for Lady Catherine. Oh, but before you go, would you refill my cup? Merci."

Anne's mother could have continued to press the subject of her child's lamentable taste for coffee, but even Lady Catherine could sense that this would be undignified, and in any case she had more important things to discuss.

"I observed you with Lord Holland all during the ball and it seems that the two of you are on very friendly terms. His attentions could hardly be more marked and you certainly appeared to receive them graciously. I must say that you looked rather well and at times smiled and were almost animated. At the end you were pale and dull, but no doubt you have not the strength for such a long evening."

Anne could find nothing to reply and only looked at her mother expectantly.

"I have not made my way here at this hour to discuss the ball," continued Lady Catherine, "but to hear once for all if you mean to accept Lord Holland. I have been extremely patient, but your indecision is becoming absurd. At this rate he will surely give up and look elsewhere. He can do much better, especially in regard to beauty and wit, although your fortune is, of course, exceptional."

Her mother's capacity for such blunt cruelty was too familiar to surprise Anne, who merely sighed and replied, "As for that, Mama, I will soon have something to tell you, but I beg that you will not press me this morning. I am tired and have much to think of."

"You have much to think of!" exclaimed Lady Catherine resentfully, "I too must make plans. I would like to know if you plan to return to Rosings for good and live out your life there as a spinster. It is unlikely that you will receive another offer of marriage in spite of your inheritance. Your youth is passing away quickly and you never were pretty. Certainly no one like Lord Holland will take notice of you again. To think that you could have every expectation of being a marchioness someday! The older brother is not an obstacle, as I have seen for myself, and not likely to live until spring."

"Poor young man," said Anne softly, "I pray that he may recover."

Her mother only looked at her in disbelief.

"But to continue, Anne, there are other matters on my mind and I do not need the complication of worrying about you any longer."

"Why, what matters are those, Mama?" asked Anne with the first show of interest since her mother had entered the room.

She had then the quite unique experience of seeing her mother look confused and almost blush.

"As it happens, Sir Wilfred is to buy Grantham Park and thus will be a close neighbor. I must return to Kent with him soon to see that everything goes well and that he is not cheated by that old Mr. Crawley."

"Sir Wilfred is to live near Rosings!" cried Anne, "But what of his estates in Wiltshire? How extraordinary, but of course it is due to his devotion to you, Mama."

Then she could not resist asking slyly, "Why, dear Mama, do you mean to marry Sir Wilfred?"

"What an idea, Anne!" replied her mother, somewhat too forcefully, "I have no thought of such a thing at present."

"But Mama, why should you not? A marriage proposal at your age! How romantic, for now I am sure that he has proposed, after observing the two of you at the ball,' continued Anne, who felt that she for once had the upper hand with her mother and was dangerously close to laughter at the absurdity of it "He is a rich baronet of good family and if only three or four family members should have the goodness to die, he will inherit a peerage. *You* might become a marchioness!"

Anne was later ashamed of how she had spoken to her mother. She had been sarcastic and disrespectful, but the years of suppressed rebellion had all come out in a moment. That she was no longer afraid of Lady Catherine came to Anne all at once and with that realization a sense of freedom that was completely new.

Lady Catherine was no fool, and she saw that her dominion over her child had ended. This was not so unwelcome as might have been expected, for it is a matter of unceasing labor to subject another intelligent being to one's will. Her immediate reaction was anger, however.

Rising she said, "There cannot be any need for further discourse between us. You have a choice: either accept a very favorable offer of marriage or return to Rosings with me. You are my child and I will not suffer that you should remain with the Darcys or pay any extended visit to Lady Grinspoon, although she has said repeatedly that she wishes you to do so. What would the world say of a mother who allowed her unmarried daughter to live away from her home? I am quite recovered now and will reestablish order at Rosings. You will live there by my rules: no riding about the countryside, no novels, no evening parties since your health would suffer, for as I observed, you were overtired last night. The odious Celestine will be dismissed!"

Lady Catherine rose to leave and as she reached the door, turned and added contemptuously, "And, of course, there will be *no coffee*!"

BREAKFAST, which had been delayed until ten o'clock, was a rather subdued affair; it seemed that everyone was more inclined to think about last night's ball than to discuss it. Lady Grinspoon did talk amusingly for a few minutes about balls as described in well-known novels and how difficult it was to make scenes of gaiety entertaining.

"Dark moonless nights with danger abroad, stormy seas and threatening reefs, the heroine lost in a trackless forest… these things are easy to write about, but accounts of happy people disporting themselves at a ball are very hard to make interesting."

Anne ate with little appetite. Lord Holland had hurried to her side as soon as she entered the breakfast room and had insisted on carrying her plate and recommending various dishes.

"Indeed, Lord Holland, I do not eat sausage and would be glad of nothing more than toast."

"Perhaps sausages are an acquired taste," he replied, "but if we are ever in Alsace you may change your mind."

Anne did not bother to reply to this idea, but merely shrugged slightly as they sat down next to each other. She had acquired this Gallic mannerism from Celestine and the gesture suited her somehow.

Peace and desultory conversation seemed the order of the day, until Lady Catherine, her voice raised almost to a shout, was to be heard in the hall. Sir Wilfred, who had been reading the paper, jumped up at once and went to investigate.

"Well, go to the stables and find out!" they heard Lady Catherine exclaim, followed by the butler's apologetic response that "Yes, my lady, I will go at once."

Anne was alarmed to have her mother storm into the room with even more self-importance than usual and sink into a chair by Elizabeth. Several voices began with anxious inquiries; what could have occurred to disturb the tranquility of the house to such a degree? Even Grey, who had been gloomily silent, looked up with mild curiosity. Only Darcy seemed unsurprised by his aunt's outburst.

"Oh, do all stop talking at once," cried Lady Catherine, "and I will tell you what has occurred. I already have such a headache!" So saying, she leaned back weakly and took the tea Sir Wilfred had brought as a restorative.

"Lady Emma is gone! Yes, gone! I went to her bedchamber to see if she were awake and how she did. Imagine my shock when I found her room completely empty. All her things! Not a trace of her or her maid." Of course all the questions began to fly through the room again.

"I have no idea what has happened," continued Lady Catherine irritably, "To think that I have been such a friend to the girl and she leaves in the night without a word to me. What will her mother say?"

The butler entered at that moment and with some trepidation made his way past and spoke to Darcy. His tone was low, but everyone managed to hear what he had to say.

At Lady Catherine's order he had gone to inquire after Colonel Fitzwilliam and now could verify that the gentleman was gone as well. He had left on horseback at about one o'clock in the morning, and his servants had immediately followed him with his chaise.

"Eloped! " cried Lady Catherine, "why it is as plain as day! Eloped and they are halfway to Scotland by now!"

"But why would they do such a thing?" asked Jane, who until now had paid very little attention to the possibility of courtships going on around her, "I thought that Lady Emma's mother looked upon the match with considerable favor. There could hardly be any objection to a gentleman like Colonel Fitzwilliam, the son of an earl and so highly regarded by all."

"I think this must be some romantic fancy of Lady Emma's," said Lady Grinspoon, "she is a delightful young lady, but surely none of us would consider her very steady. It is hardly for me to say it, but I think that she has read too many novels. Just yesterday she made the remark that a marriage ceremony in the usual way must be a dull affair and that a truly passionate attachment would be better fulfilled by a daring elopement."

"What nonsense," growled Darcy, "such imprudence and foolishness!" He turned away and looked out of the window.

Several in the group asked if he knew anything of what had occurred. "Nothing that I am at liberty to reveal at present, so please do not ask me again." So saying, Darcy left the room and none but Elizabeth had the courage to follow him, for he had rarely looked more forbidding.

Anne, during this drama, had felt the shock of it almost as a physical blow, and her entire strength was taken up in an effort not to reveal her reaction to the news. An elopement! She had felt that there was no hope, but she had not expected Fitzwilliam to disappear from her life in this way. She had imagined a prolonged suffering of months, starting with the announcement of an engagement, then preparations for his marriage which would absorb all family conversation, followed by the ceremony itself, which she would be expected to attend. To attend it, that is, unless she could find some way to die in the interval, which surely would be preferable to seeing her cousin tie himself forever to someone as frivolous as Lady Emma.

Even as she experienced this death of hope, Anne was interested to observe her mother across the table, being comforted by Sir Wilfred. Lady Catherine's expression of distress, Anne saw now, was slowly changing to an ill-concealed satisfaction, even delight.

"Of course, we must deplore the practice of elopement," said her ladyship, addressing the entire group, "It is such a shock to the family, and now dear Lady Emma's poor mother is deprived of giving her daughter the wedding appropriate to her position in the fashionable world. My kind friend will, I trust, not be too distressed at this turn of events or think that I have neglected my duty towards her child."

Everyone hastened to reassure Lady Catherine that no mother could have taken more tender care of the headstrong Lady Emma. It was not her fault if two young people had been impetuous, and it would all end well since the marriage was of a nature to give satisfaction to both families.

"Well, I must go and write to Lady Pamela at once," cried Lady Catherine, springing up almost gleefully. "Do send word when some letter arrives from those dear children, which must occur soon."

Anne looked after her mother as that lady bustled from the room and thought that this was a denouement that must be very much to

Lady Catherine's taste. It was the match she had been promoting in Bath with Lady Emma's mother and now Fitzwilliam would be married to the rich and beautiful daughter of a good family. No bother now with an elaborate wedding or worries that the match might be broken off; it was a *fait accompli* that must be highly gratifying to Lady Catherine. She had always longed to be a matchmaker but this was her first success.

Anne was suddenly aware of Lord Holland, who seemed to be studying her countenance attentively.

"I suppose we will never know exactly why your cousin and Lady Emma did such an extravagantly romantic thing. I do not condemn them. No, I rather envy them and wish that I could have the adventure of carrying my love off to a simple marriage, then to a castle in the Highlands where we could hide away from the world and learn to adore each other even better than before. Do you think that is where they will go? Does not Colonel Fitzwilliam have a remote and beautiful estate near his father's castle?"

"I do not know what they may do," replied Anne wearily, "but I doubt that my cousin will be away from his regiment for very long. Despite appearances, he is a very responsible person." So saying she rose to leave the room and was instantly accompanied to the door by Lord Holland who asked softly, "Shall I wait for you on the lower terrace in half an hour, Miss de Bourgh?"

CHAPTER 49

*E*lizabeth was alarmed to see her husband so distressed, and for the first time she felt put out with Colonel Fitzwilliam whom she had always regarded as a perfect example of a gentleman, level-headed and reliable and a credit to his family.

She found Darcy standing by the fireplace holding a letter; he looked inclined to throw it into the flames.

"My darling, what has occurred to upset you? This elopement is inconsiderate and absurd, of course, but I think you find it worse than the rest of us do."

"This is a letter from Fitzwilliam containing some very crucial information," Darcy replied, "Unfortunately, I am enjoined not to disclose it to anyone until we have received word of some kind from Lady Emma. It is too ridiculous. Fitzwilliam apologizes more than once for placing me in such a position." Darcy shook his head in disgust, "What an indiscreet young lady. I wish she had never come to Pemberley."

Then he managed to smile and put his arms around his wife, "Come and sit with me, my love, and I will tell you what is happening with our absent friends. I respect my cousin's request for secrecy, but I know he would not object to my confiding in my second self, my own Elizabeth."

Elizabeth's response to what Darcy had to relate was to exclaim, "Good heavens! I pray that Lady Emma will write directly and that we have word from her before the day is out."

~

ANNE MADE her way to her bedchamber with nothing more in her mind than the wish of concealing her emotion from her friends and particularly from her mother. She was surprised to find on reaching her door that no tears had appeared; the blow was too great and what she felt was a pain that overwhelmed all other sensations. Her hope of solitude was disappointed when she found Celestine weeping pathetically in an armchair by the window.

"Why, Celestine, what is the matter," asked Anne, taking a chair as well. "You need not run off. Just sit there and tell me what has happened."

"Oh, my lady, your mama has spoken so unkindly to me this morning. I met her in the corridor and she said that I must be gone by the end of the week. She threatens that she will not even give me a letter or allow you to do so. I will starve in the street!"

This example of her mother's unkindness made Anne feel even more depressed. Her head had begun to ache and she was in danger of joining Celestine in a torrent of weeping.

"Do not distress yourself anymore. My mother has a ridiculous prejudice against the French and takes it out on you, but even she would not dismiss you without a reference."

Celestine stopped crying quite so loudly but looked unconvinced.

"In any case, you do not need to seek another position. I have talked with Lady Grinspoon and she is very happy to take you into her service. Later, perhaps, I will have my own establishment, and you may return to me if you wish."

"Ah, then you are to marry Lord Holland! *Grace à Dieu!*" cried Celestine with delight, "Everything will be perfect, my lady. You will be a *duchess* someday and one of the greatest ladies in the kingdom! Oh, what jewels and carriages you will have." Then she began to rush about the room straightening pillows and rearranging Anne's dressing table and speaking rapidly in French. Anne could never understand her when she spoke so quickly, but it was plain that Lord Holland was *"tout à fait comme il faut"* and that her maid was delighted with the match.

Anne did not bother to say anything more or to point out that Lord Holland had an older brother who might be so inconsiderate as to go on living and that in any case she would be a marchioness rather than a duchess. She went back down the stairs and on her way encountered Mr. Grey, who was ascending them. They paused together on the landing.

"Well met, Miss de Bourgh, I had some idea of seeking you out in a moment."

"You are prescient, Mr. Grey," replied Anne, making a great attempt to look cheerful, "for here I am. Was there anything in particular you wished to say?"

Grey seemed a bit at a loss and did not reply at once. They were facing a large window that gave a view of the lake and the river beyond it.

"I do believe, Miss de Bourgh, that there is someone waiting for you on the terrace. I hope you do not mind my making the observation."

They both looked out to where Lord Holland stood near the partly frozen lake. He was quite still despite the cold and had the attitude of a man meditating on some deep subject.

"I continue to find Lord Holland rather an enigma, although I've been all these weeks in the same house with him. I do not say that as a criticism, but he seems difficult to know."

Anne did not reply for there was no way to deny what her friend had said.

"I have been thinking a good deal lately of the nature of love, Miss de Bourgh," said Grey, turning his gaze from the window and looking at Anne, "but of course, you understand why the subject should occupy my mind."

"Yes, I do know why and I still trust that all your meditations and endeavors will end in happiness."

"At this point that seems extremely unlikely, but at least I have come to some conclusions. For example, I have discovered a method of knowing decisively whether or not one is truly in love."

"Do tell me, Mr. Grey, for I may need to make use of your technique in the very near future."

"Very well, then. It involves imagining the most remote and desolate wind-swept countryside and a small cottage in the most isolated spot of all. You have an excellent imagination, I know, so this will not be difficult for you. You are to think of the person whom you may or may not love with your whole heart. Imagine that you are there in that cottage for the rest of your life, or at least for a few months. There is no one else about, just the two of you with the wind and rain lashing your cottage and a fire on the hearth and only enough for simple comfort. You can see all this clearly in your mind?"

"Yes, I can see it," replied Anne, her eyes fixed on the interior of the stone cottage that her mind had created.

"Now, imagine yourself alone there with the person who has been the subject of your thoughts. Does that cottage seem like the very model of paradise on earth? Do you feel that you could be happy there forever if only that one being were there as well?"

The picture was so vivid to Anne that she felt in danger of weeping. To hide her emotion, she looked away and shrugged slightly, "Can there really be such love in this imperfect world."

"You cannot deceive me, Miss de Bourgh," replied Grey, with a very serious air, "You know very well that it does exist. So beware. If that imagined cottage does not seem like a vision of heaven then it is not a strong enough affection for a feeling and sensitive soul."

"I will remember what you have said, Mr. Grey," said Anne solemnly as she turned to continue down the stairs, "and I thank you for being so good a friend. There are very few like you."

Grey detained her for a moment with a gentle hand on her arm and said, "I do not know what has occurred in regard to your cousin, but I very much believe that appearances may be deceptive. Now go and act in accordance with your *heart*, my friend."

The cold was sharp that morning and Anne had worn the fur cloak that she had found so ridiculous when it had been purchased for her in London. Now she had to admit that its warmth was quite welcome.

She felt chilled and anxious; even at this moment, as Lord Holland came eagerly to her side, she was uncertain what she would say to him.

He was dressed for riding and wore a greatcoat against the frigid wind that came across the lake. Anne wondered if he had intentionally attired himself in a style that made him even more handsome than usual.

There was a boxwood maze to one side of the terrace, rather extensive, but not difficult as far as finding one's way in and out. It had been designed by Darcy's mother in the time when a boxwood maze was all the rage and no country house could be without one.

"Shall we walk here for a bit, Miss de Bourgh," asked Lord Holland with a bow, and indicating the break in the wall of boxwoods, "for we shall be sheltered from the wind."

It seemed strange to Anne that it was necessary for them to seek a few quiet moments together in this winter landscape, but Pemberley was so full of guests that there was no private spot other than the garden. In any case, she walked there every day no matter what the weather.

They walked to the center of the maze and sat together on a bench there. Lord Holland, with great respect and delicacy, repeated his proposal and his affirmations of love. He expressed himself well and the light of real affection and esteem seemed to shine forth from his dark eyes. Then he began once again to describe the felicity they would know once they were married, how they would travel and spend their time doing whatever would add to Anne's happiness.

"I know that you will wish to be near your dear friends," Lord Holland continued enthusiastically, "and I hope you will be glad to hear that I have found a large property to buy within a few miles of Pemberley. Lord Fawn wishes to sell it to settle some debts. There is no proper sort of house, but we shall build one, a splendid house that will be exactly as you would like it to be."

By now the young man was quite animated and seemed to be full of detailed plans for their future together. All the while Anne sat quietly observing him with a cool detachment that would have been

460

discouraging to a suitor paying more close attention than Lord Holland was at the moment.

She found herself going back to what Mr. Grey had said on the landing and she tried to picture living alone in that imagined cottage with the man before her. He was brilliant and accomplished and they shared many interests, but the thought of night coming on with only a lonely hearth on the moors and Lord Holland at her side filled her with more than indifference; she felt a chill of apprehension at the idea that struck her more deeply than the morning frost. She told herself that she was being foolish and that the match promised to be as favorable as anything she could hope for in a life without her cousin. Everything she knew of Lord Holland proclaimed him to be an honorable and virtuous man, but still the cold would not leave her in peace.

He finally paused and looked at her questioningly, "I trust that what I have been saying meets with your approval. Dear Anne, you do not speak. May I interpret this silence as one of assent?" He attempted to take her hand, but she leapt from the bench and stood as far from him as the confines of the little square of grass would allow.

Anne realized that she should have interrupted him some minutes before. It was as though she had been lost in some far away part of her mind and now she had to correct any favorable impression Lord Holland may have formed. However, what came out was not particularly subtle or kindly expressed.

"I am sorry, Lord Holland, but I cannot marry you. No, I cannot! I am very sorry but it is impossible!"

Anne did not realize how passionately she spoke or how her eyes blazed with a sort of defiant indignation, as though her suitor had insulted her. She felt unaccountably angry and knew that she was being unfair to a man who had shown her only respect and admiration. With a great effort she made herself speak more calmly, "I beg you will forgive my manner of expressing myself. I have lived a very sheltered life and am unused to ..."

Anne forced herself to look at Lord Holland who had risen and was pacing about at the other side of the bench. There was hardly enough room for two people who seemed about to be on unfriendly terms with each other. What she saw in his face was not the sadness of disappointed affection or even resentment, but a cold fury and contempt that repelled her. She had read of rejected suitors in Lady Grinspoon's novels and this was not the reaction she had expected.

"I thought you an intelligent young woman. Surely you do not mean to throw away such a chance as this!" This was said in such an uncivil tone that Anne was amazed. Was this the impeccably courteous Lord Holland? She realized that everything she had seen of him had been a mask and that this was the real man before her.

Then he seemed to make some tremendous effort and said in a softer voice, "Pray forgive me. You do not know what I suffer. I beg you to reconsider, for your refusal will kill all possibility of happiness for me." She watched with astonishment and horror as he forced his features to assume an expression of tender love and entreaty.

"I must leave you now, Lord Holland," Anne forced herself to say in a voice that shook with revulsion, "After this there is no force on earth that could persuade me to be your wife."

She attempted to leave by the only opening in the hedge, but he stepped in front of her to bar her way. For an awful moment she believed that he would seize hold of her arm.

He looked down at Anne and said, "You are a fool! When I saw you in London for the first time I almost felt pity for you; you were so small and plain, especially next to Mrs. Darcy. But in Scotland I found that you had improved and had become somewhat interesting. I could have molded you into a woman worthy of being my consort. Yes, I have felt real affection for you and would have been a better husband than you deserve."

"Let me by at once!" cried Anne, "I have never imagined such a brute as you have proven yourself to be."

"One more thing," said Holland, looming over her, "You are even more idiotic in your feelings for your cousin, that blockhead Fitzwilliam. He cares nothing for you, but I have watched you and I know that you love him. Now, he has even eloped with another lady and you still persist in thinking of him and refuse a man ten times his worth."

"I did not know that such a demon as you could exist, Lord

Holland. Allow me to leave or I will scream until the entire household joins us here."

He finally let her pass and she ran through the maze, letting her cloak fall to the ground in her haste. Anne was so distraught that as well as she knew her way she soon found that she had taken several wrong turns. She stopped in a long *allée* to get her bearings and began to walk back in the opposite direction. After a few moments she was appalled to find that she was just on the other side of a wall of boxwood from Lord Holland. Her breathing had slowed and the grass was wet; he did not hear her, but she certainly heard him.

He was cursing with language that she had never heard before and would not have believed possible. Her name was interspersed in the horrid words in the most hateful way. He paused briefly and she heard him cry out softly, "Oh, God! I will have you yet! I will not be thwarted by a stupid fool!" Then he began to thrash the boxwood with his riding crop with a vehemence that was terrifying. Anne had rarely experienced fear in her restricted world at Rosings. She had been frightened when Elizabeth's horse had run away in Scotland, but the rage and violence just a few feet away held her motionless with terror. All kinds of visions of what he might do if he caught her in the maze came to her mind. Of course it was ridiculous; Englishmen did not offer to do harm to women, no matter how angry they might be.

The thrashing of the unoffending boxwood seemed to take a course towards the opening out of the central square. In a few moments he might be in the same part of the maze where she was standing. The thought gave Anne such a burst of energy as she had never experienced and she ran until she reached the safety of the terrace. She was afraid that Lord Holland was immediately behind her, but all was silent. Then she had the unpleasant feeling of being observed and continued her flight until she reached her bedchamber. The house seemed strangely quiet and she was glad to be able to throw the lock on her door.

～

AN HOUR later Anne went in search of Elizabeth, dreading to meet

Lord Holland as she made her way down the stairs. Hearing voices in the library, she opened the heavy doors and went in. Darcy, Elizabeth and Lady Catherine were engaged in some very serious discussion and Anne's mother did not look pleased. It was too late to withdraw. Perhaps her refusal of Lord Holland was the subject of this family conference; that would be very unpleasant indeed.

"Oh, Anne, there you are," cried Lady Catherine, "do come sit with us. What a disaster has befallen us all and particularly your unfortunate mother. It has made me quite ill!"

"Why, what on earth has happened," asked Anne, taking a chair by Elizabeth, "Have you heard from Fitzwilliam?" she inquired, dreading the response.

"Indeed, we have," said Darcy, "and from Lady Emma as well."

"Where have they gone? They are married, I suppose," asked Anne, wishing she could go away without hearing anymore.

"Lady Emma is married," said Darcy, "but not to Fitzwilliam. She has eloped with the young captain who was here at the ball. It had been planned for some time, and flawlessly carried out, I must admit."

Lady Catherine broke out in a tone of angry resentment, "Fitzwilliam knew of it! He, in whom I have ever had the utmost trust and confidence. What am I to tell the wretched girl's mother? I was responsible for her, and will be disgraced when this story is known."

Anne's entire being was suffused with joy and relief. Fitzwilliam was *not* married to the empty-headed Lady Emma! His life would not be ruined by having united himself forever to a fool. She wondered aloud, "It seems very odd that Fitzwilliam would have assisted at this reckless undertaking. It is not at all in his character."

"I will spare you from hearing the silly note from Lady Emma to your mama," said Darcy, "She and her new husband are in Scotland by now and I do not think we will see them again. I will, however, read to you the letter left for me by our cousin on his departure last night."

Darcy,

I regret that I will be partly responsible for giving you a few very uncomfortable hours. Please do not share the contents of this letter until you have received a communication from Lady Emma. I am pledged to secrecy as to her whereabouts until she and Captain Malvern are well away and safely married. No doubt the household will believe that I am the bridegroom in this little romance. I rejoice that it is not so and only regret the part that I have been forced to play in the affair.

Captain Malvern, a very worthy young officer of excellent family, but poor, chanced to meet Lady Emma in Bath two years ago. They formed a strong attachment almost at once, but the lady's family was unalterably opposed to the match. They assumed that their daughter would make a grand alliance of some sort and eventually forbade her even to see Malvern. As his colonel and friend, I heard a great deal about the situation, and recommended that he and Lady Emma continue to try to win approval of the marriage. With enough determination they would succeed. In the meantime, the lady, whom I believe to be one of the most indiscreet women in creation, made it her habit to involve me in a tête à tête at every gathering in Bath, giving rise to the speculation that we were soon to be engaged. All of our conversations, of course, consisted of her begging me for news of Malvern and entreating me to take notes to him. Naturally, I refused to be part of any subterfuge of this kind.

Unfortunately, they began to meet in secret about six months ago. As I was about to depart for Pemberley, Malvern came to me in a state of desperation and presented his case to me with the frankness of an honorable man who has made a serious error in judgment and has no alternative but to ask the help of his friend. I know that I need only say that circumstances now made an elopement an absolute necessity and at the earliest date possible.

You know me well enough to understand how I have detested the role I have been forced to play in this business. Thank God, it is over and the two young people are safe, although they will have little enough to live on and may well be rejected by their families. I hope this will not be the case, and I will continue to assist them if I can.

As for my own movements, I was forced to take myself out of the way, and as it happened I received word only yesterday that my old friend, Mr. Thornton of Hampshire, is quite ill and may not survive. I am hurrying there to be with him, as he has asked for me.

Darcy, share this letter with Anne, Elizabeth and my aunt as soon as you feel you can, given the exigencies of Lady Emma's situation. I will write to

you from Hampshire when I have seen Mr. Thornton. Thank heaven you
now all know the truth and I am no longer in false position.
  Fitzwilliam

Lady Catherine was the first to speak, "I have never imagined such disgraceful behavior by a young lady from a distinguished family. I am sorry that you had to hear the truth of the thing, Anne. Why does Fitzwilliam mention your name first as being one to hear the letter? Surely he should have addressed these ill tidings to me and not Darcy. And you, Darcy, should have come to me at once!"

"You were asleep, Aunt, and my instructions from Fitzwilliam were clear."

Lady Catherine might have gone on for some time berating everyone she could think of, but they were interrupted by the entrance of Jane, Bingley and Georgiana, who had just returned from surveying the repairs going on at Thrushfold Hall.

Jane burst out in delight, "Everything is going so well! The plaster-work is splendid and all the chimneys are repaired. The house may be ready for us by early spring!" Instead of the enthusiastic inquiries they had expected, Jane and Bingley were surprised to be met with only blank and preoccupied faces.

"Whatever has happened?" cried Jane, "Is something amiss?"

"Lord Holland's carriage passed us on the road," said Bingley, "He must have been in quite a hurry, as his horses were already in a lather and he did not wave to us."

Anne meanwhile had slipped behind a large wall of bookcases; she had longed to escape from the room, but her route was blocked by the Bingleys. There had begun a flurry of explanations with everyone speaking at once. Jane, Bingley and Georgiana soon heard of the elopement of Lady Emma and Captain Malvern and of Fitzwilliam's letter. After several minutes of excited conversation on this subject, everyone remembered the interesting fact of Lord Holland's abrupt departure.

"Good heavens, Anne must have refused him!" Lady Catherine exclaimed in her most forceful tone of voice. "Why, of all the most foolish and obstinate things I have ever heard of!"

Her ladyship looked about the library in search of her daughter in order to begin those reproaches that would take some considerable time and thus could not be begun too soon.

"Why where is Anne? She has left us in that sly way she has, always disappearing when I have the most pressing need to speak to her." Then Lady Catherine, forgetting for the moment that she was in a fragile state of health, leapt up with all her old energy and rushed out of the room in search of her child.

CHAPTER 50

The fine wrought iron gates of Thornton Abbey were fully twelve feet high, thickly covered with ivy and had not been closed for several years. The gatekeeper, an elderly man with a wooden leg, had long ago lost interest in his duties. Mr. Thornton never went in or out and no one else seemed very interested in how well the grounds might be guarded. The dilatory Cerberus was delighted to see young Colonel Fitzwilliam come through the gates and greeted him cheerfully.

"Your lordship is most welcome. The master will be so glad that you have arrived."

Fitzwilliam was happy to hear that his old friend was still alive, as he had feared that he would arrive too late to see him again. He urged his tired horse to a trot and continued towards the house, and as he rounded a curve of the drive was startled to see a handsome carriage approaching from the direction of the hall. Fitzwilliam was obliged to stop to allow the equipage to pass and in a moment found himself face to face with its occupants. A window was opened and a young lady leant out to speak to him.

"It must be Colonel Fitzwilliam!" she exclaimed, "How delighted I am that you are here, for we were sorry to leave poor Mr. Thornton. But, thank God, he is better and may very well recover."

Fitzwilliam bowed and expressed his thanks for such welcome news and begged that he might be informed as to whom he was obliged for this good report of his friend.

"Oh, I do apologize!" said the lady, who was young and quite beautiful, "I am Miss Delaford."

Fitzwilliam saw that there were two other occupants of the carriage: a distinguished elderly lady and a pale young man, who nodded politely but seemed reluctant to disturb his position under a heavy fur lap rug.

"We must not keep you here in the cold, Colonel, and it is time for us to make haste, for we are in a most dreadful hurry to travel north as quickly as the horses can carry us, but I am so glad to have seen you." So saying the young lady motioned to the footman and the carriage moved off.

Fitzwilliam continued and after a moment remembered that he had heard of Miss Delaford before. Good heavens! It was the lady to whom Stanley Thornton had been engaged and who had broken with him for some reason only weeks before the young man's death at sea in a fleet action. Stanley had cared nothing for his life after losing her and had thrown himself into battle with reckless courage.

What on earth could she be doing at Thornton Abbey? It seemed very odd and the question would have occupied Fitzwilliam's mind for the next half mile, except that he slipped back into thoughts of Anne. Indeed, he had thought of nothing else for all the long journey, wondering if she had accepted Holland and finding the idea intolerable. In his pocket was the letter he had intended to leave for her, a letter that explained all his feelings for her. When he had seen her with Holland at the top of the stairs and observed the intimate way in which they spoke to each other and that she allowed his rival to hold her hand in the manner of an accepted lover, it had seemed wrong to send his cousin such a communication. It could do no good and would only injure their friendship. I suppose that I may have the rest of my life to realize that I have made a terrible error, thought Fitzwilliam as he pulled up before the door of the hall and turned his horse over to the servant.

Mr. Thornton was to be found in his favorite retreat, his library, which in the present circumstances had been made into a bedchamber for the sick man. A large screen had been positioned to conceal his bedstead and the room looked much as usual. Fitzwilliam's old friend, who had been moved to an armchair by the fire, greeted him with as much surprised delight as his weakened state allowed.

"My dear Colonel, I had not hoped to see you again in this life, for my doctor assured me that I was unlikely to survive. And now I have brought you all this way and apparently I am being so contrary as to show signs of recovery."

Fitzwilliam expressed his delight at finding his friend better than he had dared hope.

"I probably would have made my departure from this world, except for the skill of the London physician who has been attending me these last six days. He came at the behest of Miss Delaford, who has known of him in Bath where he spends part of the year. Oh, he is the best medical man in the country, as I have learned to my benefit. My local doctor is a bit put out, but far too much in awe of Dr. Crawford to complain."

"Dr. Crawford!" cried Fitzwilliam, "Why he is my aunt's physician. I first met him when he came to attend her at Rosings a few months ago."

"It is only to be expected that Lady Catherine de Bourgh would have the most skillful care available," said Mr. Thornton, "I hope that his treatments have been as efficacious in her case - as in my own."

"Yes, indeed. She is quite well now, although, of course, she must be a bit more cautious of her heath than before her illness." Fitzwilliam was rather surprised by the coincidence of finding that Dr. Crawford was to be found spreading his good offices so widely among those who were dear to him. He also wondered at the expense of bringing so distinguished a physician to this remote part of Hampshire. He hoped that it would not strain Mr. Thornton's resources past the breaking point, for the house and grounds looked as poor as ever.

"But you must be terribly fatigued, Colonel, and I am a bad host to keep you here when you must be longing to rest. Shall I ring for tea or would you like to retire to your bedchamber for some repose until dinner?"

"You are very kind, sir. I am really not at all tired and I would enjoy some tea of all things."

As he spoke the library door opened and Dr. Crawford walked in. He came over to Fitzwilliam with his usual energetic and kindly manner and the two men greeted each other with much satisfaction at their reunion.

"I had hoped that you might arrive before I would be obliged to return to London, Colonel. If not, I would have written and sent a messenger to find you wherever you might be between here and Pemberley."

This seemed rather a remarkable way to begin the conversation, and Fitzwilliam was somewhat taken aback.

"Mr. Thornton and I have much to tell you that may be important to those dear to you in Derbyshire. How were they all when you left? Is Lady Catherine well? And Miss de Bourgh?"

"They were well enough, thank you, Doctor," replied Fitzwilliam with some puzzlement, "but I do beg you to explain what you have to tell me."

Dr. Crawford took a seat next to his patient and checked his pulse for a moment.

"Tea, weak tea, for you Mr. Thornton, but I rather think that the colonel would do better to have a brandy in hand for this conversation. But we will begin with recent events here at the Hall."

"As you know, my dear Colonel," began Mr. Thornton, "I have been very ill for some weeks and in fact did not expect to survive. That is why I sent word to you, who have been such a good friend all these years. I am so grateful to you for making such haste to come to Thornton Abbey for I know that you have many other demands on your time." He continued with a gentle smile, "I feel almost guilty for my dramatic improvement in the last two or three days which has made your trip seemingly unnecessary. That is the trouble with sick old people; they are likely to be quite unpredictable in their approach to taking leave of this world. In this case, the blame for my continued existence must fall to our good doctor, for I would surely have died without his ministrations."

Fitzwilliam could only be surprised at the clarity and vigor with which Mr. Thornton expressed himself. This was the return of a friend whom he had not seen for several years, not since before the death at sea of Stanley Thornton. Dr. Crawford's physic must be great indeed to have brought about such a change in mind and body.

"I do not deserve quite as much praise as you are inclined to heap upon me, Mr. Thornton," said Dr. Crawford, settling into his chair with an understandable air of complacency, "All I had to do in this case was to gather up all the potions with which your former physician had been dosing you all this time and throw them away. Immediately you began to improve and I expect to see an even greater transformation as time goes on."

Turning his brandy glass in his hands thoughtfully, Dr. Crawford continued, "It is considered bad form to criticize a fellow practitioner, but I used the word 'physician' ironically when referring to Dr. Brown. He is nothing of the sort and should be banned from the care of patients. I have not yet decided what course of action should be taken against him."

"After Stanley died, as you know, my spirits were most dreadfully depressed," said Mr. Thornton, "Dr. Brown began a course of treatment which was intended to ameliorate my state of mind, but which has in fact had the opposite effect. All this time I have lost interest in everything, neglecting to eat or take exercise and allowing my estate to fall almost into ruin. The last few days I have felt like one who awakens from a most awful dream in which I lacked the strength to do the most simple things and lived in a kind of haze of inertia. And always Dr. Brown was there, urging me to take his medicaments with the utmost regularity."

"The man is not ill-intentioned and I believe he actually thought he was being helpful to his patient," said Dr. Crawford, "He is as incompetent a fool as any I have come across in many years of practice, although I have seen many similar cases. I have often been given credit for being a medical genius merely because I withdrew harmful drugs and waited for the patient to heal himself."

472

" I am convinced that you should be given every kind of praise for genius and the highest kind of medical understanding," said Fitzwilliam, "for I would never have hoped for such a dramatic restoration of my old friend."

"Well, I thank you, Colonel, and will show my appreciation by getting to the point of our narrative, since you will have to leave Thornton Hall at first light tomorrow."

"Will I indeed?" replied Fitzwilliam, who had thought to delay his departure for Pemberley until after breakfast.

"Yes, for you will agree that there is not a moment to be lost. I would suggest that you tell the story, Mr. Thornton."

"I will begin it at any rate," replied the older man, pulling himself up in his chair and looking unusually intent. "As you came up the drive you encountered a young lady in a carriage with two companions?"

"Yes. She was so gracious as to introduce herself, a Miss Delaford, I believe she said."

"She was with her fiancé and his aunt. Had she not visited me and brought Dr. Crawford I might not be alive tonight."

"Then she has my eternal gratitude," said Fitzwilliam, "but I have heard her name before, have I not?"

"It is Miss Delaford who was engaged to my son Stanley. She wrote to me three weeks ago to the effect that she was to be married soon but could not be happy in her forthcoming nuptials until she had seen me and given me some explanation as to why she had broken with my son. I had heard from her before; she had written a most kind letter after Stanley's death, in which I sensed a grief almost as profound as my own. In this case I replied that I would be most happy to welcome her here, but that she must expect to find me a feeble invalid as my medical man had not been able to bring about any improvement in a rapidly worsening illness. Indeed, I told her that she should come as soon as possible if she wished to see me before I died."

"I had a reason for being one of the party, as I have been attending Miss Delaford's fiancé for the last six weeks," explained Dr. Crawford. "Once I met Mr. Thornton and talked with him for a while I was almost certain that I could be of assistance to him. Fortunately he was of the same opinion and asked me to act as his physician. Since I could see that it was a question of saving his life I had few scruples about ousting Dr. Brown from his sinecure."

This was all very fine, thought Fitzwilliam, but he certainly felt no wiser as to the point of the conversation or how it could affect the time of his departure in the morning. He must have looked slightly impatient, for Dr. Crawford took over the story of Miss Delaford and related the facts in his usual succinct fashion.

"Miss Delaford belongs to a distinguished Devonshire family with connections to the nobility. Her father had been rich and respectable with a fine estate near Dawlish. Unfortunately, he had taken up gambling and lost almost all his property, ending as a wretched suicide. His wife and daughter had moved to Bath where they lived on a small income supplemented by the kindness of a wealthy aunt who bought a house for them and visited frequently. The generous lady also saw to it that Miss Delaford received an excellent education and the opportunity of a place in the best society of Bath. When Stanley Thornton was introduced to Miss Delaford, their mutual esteem and affection developed rapidly and they were soon engaged. It was in every way an eligible match and to the satisfaction of all concerned. Understandably enough, Miss Delaford had a horror of gambling and asked her fiancé to promise that he would never enter an establishment where that vice was practiced. If ever he did so, she declared, the engagement must be at an end. Lieutenant Thornton had absolutely no interest in the activity and was happy to give the young lady all the assurances she could wish. Plans for the wedding were soon under way and there could have been no happier couple anywhere in England."

"Now the story takes a tragic turn,' said Dr. Crawford, "Another naval officer had conceived a passion for Miss Delaford and was determined to alienate her from Lieutenant Stanley and willing to use any means to do so. At the same time, he represented himself as a kindly friend to both of the young people. You may as well know his name at once: Lord Holland, or Captain Holland as he was known at that time."

Fitzwilliam, who was very tired and had been exerting himself to stay awake for the last few minutes, was instantly alert and exclaimed, "What! That Lord Holland who is at Pemberley, the brother of the Marquess of Roscree!"

"Indeed, as far as I know there is only one Lord Holland," replied Dr. Crawford, "and I regret to tell you that he is a skulking villain."

"I was sure of it! I never could stand the fellow since I first had the misfortune to encounter him at my father's a few years ago. Please tell me quickly what you know of him, for I must return to Pemberley with this intelligence at once."

"He destroyed my son's happiness by slowly poisoning Miss Delaford's mind against Stanley, who had served on Holland's most recent command as first lieutenant," explained Mr. Thornton, "She is an intelligent young lady, but his methods were subtle and he played on her greatest fear by insinuating that my son was a gambler. Holland claimed to have seen Stanley leaving a gambling den in Port Mahon. This was true, but my son had only entered the place long enough to try to save a friend who was ruining himself there; he never gambled. When Stanley answered her as an honest man would, that he had been there, Miss Delaford would not hear his explanation, but banished him at once, refusing thereafter to speak to him or communicate with him in any way. After ten days or so she relented, but it was too late. Stanley had already taken ship and died in battle before her letters could reach him."

"But how did she learn of Holland's duplicity, after thinking him an honorable man?" asked Fitzwilliam.

"After Stanley's death and on Holland's return to England, he made his intentions toward Miss Delaford very clear, at first in a respectful way, then, after she rejected him, in a manner to leave no doubt in her mind that he was a complete liar and scoundrel. She even began to fear for her safety and sought refuge with relations in Ireland for a time to escape the man."

Fitzwilliam sat in silence, at a loss for a few minutes. The thought that he had been right about Holland was no great comfort. How had so many people been taken in by such a man?

"Miss Delaford has suffered greatly," said Mr. Thornton, "She can never recover completely from the loss of my son, but it is to be hoped that she will be happy in her marriage to the Marquess of Roscree.

"What! Is she marrying Lord Holland's brother?" cried Fitzwilliam.

"Yes, they met in Bath. When you passed their carriage in the drive, you would have seen the marquess and his aunt, Lady Orme, accompanying Miss Delaford."

"It seems rather remarkable that the young lady should happen to marry the brother of the man who has been her tormenter."

"Not really," said Dr. Crawford, "The marquess was engaged in attempting to learn the truth about his younger brother's character. He had heard something of Miss Delaford's troubles and applied to her for the facts of the matter. They fell in love and there you have it."

Fitzwilliam had become increasingly restless in his chair and now rose and stated that he intended to leave at once for Pemberley.

"My cousin must hear the truth about this vile man as soon as may be. There is not a moment to be lost."

His friends pointed out that it was by now quite late on a very dark night and that he should at least sleep for a few hours before his departure.

"I will leave just after daybreak. That will give me all the sleep I need."

"Let me caution you as a last word on the subject," said Dr. Crawford as they went upstairs, "Be very careful about Holland. I have reason to think that he may be even worse that you might suspect."

At first light Fitzwilliam was in the courtyard of Thornton Hall, urging the servants to hurry their preparations for departure with an impatience that they had rarely experienced from him. As he stood waiting, a respectable looking man approached him hesitantly and introduced himself as the steward, Mr. Mason.

Fitzwilliam regarded him with no very friendly eye. It was impossible to think well of the steward of a place in such run-down condition as Mr. Thornton's house and grounds.

"Oh, I know that you must have a poor opinion of me, my lord," said Mr. Mason, who seemed distressed and almost near weeping, "but I do assure you that I do know my business. I have always been held in high esteem and there's nothing much that I don't know about managing an estate such as this."

Not giving Fitzwilliam a chance to speak, the agitated steward went on, "It's just that for these last years Mr. Thornton has not allowed me to do anything! I have had to watch all go to ruin. 'Mason, let it all fall down, the house, all the buildings, and let the pastures go to hawthorn and briers, for it means nothing to me now.' That's what he would tell me every time I would beg to be doing something."

"I'm sorry to hear it," replied Fitzwilliam coldly, "but why in heaven's name are you telling me all this?"

"Why? My lord, since you are the heir, I had to take the opportunity to tell you that I am not incompetent. I have great hope now that you will have some influence here."

"Heir! Heir to what? Explain yourself, for I have no idea to what you refer."

"Heir to Thornton, sir, and thousands of acres of the best farmland in England. But did you not know? Everyone at Thornton has known since the attorney was here four months ago and I and Mr. Alford, the butler, stood witness to the old gentleman's will."

Fitzwilliam felt only bewilderment at the steward's revelation; never would such a thing have occurred to him. He looked about with dismay at the neglected house and grounds and the stable block with its attic roof full of holes and drainpipes hanging askew.

"I know it all looks very bad, sir, but it can be put right very quickly. Just yesterday, Mr. Thornton said that it was to be a new day for the Hall. He does seem so very much improved."

With what money could these miracles be accomplished? This was Fitzwilliam's first thought. He hoped that Mr. Mason was laboring under some kind of strange misapprehension as to the identity of the heir to Thornton.

The steward seemed to read his thoughts, for he continued, "It will be nothing to bring it all about, sir. You may be assured, for how could there be any difficulty for one of the richest gentlemen in this part of England to make all as fine as it ever was! You will see when you next pay a visit."

The servants had everything in readiness and in a moment

Fitzwilliam had leapt into his saddle and given his last instructions as to how they were to follow him with his carriage to Pemberley.

"Mr. Mason, as you can see I am pressed for time. Clearly, I can make no comment as to the condition of Thornton Hall and must refer you to Mr. Thornton." And with a curt nod Fitzwilliam cantered off down the drive, leaving the steward looking sadly after him.

CHAPTER 51

The first two days after Fitzwilliam's departure found Pemberley more peaceful than might have been expected after the events that had taken place on the night of the ball. Lord Holland had sent word that he had been obliged to make an urgent trip to London on business of his brother's and that he would return soon and send word as to when he might be expected. By then everyone in the house knew that Anne had rejected his suit and it seemed surprising that he planned to make another appearance.

"You have crushed his spirit or broken his heart, I know not which," said Lady Grinspoon, as they sat together in the library, "It is difficult to say with such a controlled sort of man."

"I have done neither," replied Anne, "and I doubt very much that he has a heart." Then she told her friend something of the way in which Lord Holland had responded to her refusal.

"Good heavens! He is worse than some of the villains in my novels," cried Lady Grinspoon, "I was taken in by him, I must admit, and I do regret having ever encouraged you to think of him. Have you told your mother about his behavior?"

"No, nor do I intend to. She would not believe it, so little does she think of my understanding. I've said nothing to anyone but you, Lady

Grinspoon, for I have some hope that Lord Holland will not show his face here again in spite of his stated intention to do so."

"Yes, let us trust that he will send for his things and not trouble us again. The only good thing to come out of this is that he will provide the model for a very convincing scoundrel in my next book."

Lady Catherine received a letter from Lady Emma's mother that was surprisingly forgiving.

"We have always feared something like this, for she was a willful, difficult child and did not improve. She has great charm and accomplishments and no sense whatever. At least the young man is from a good family."

This certainly exhibited the capacity for philosophical resignation on the part of Lady Emma's mama.

Lady Catherine did not miss an opportunity of reproaching her daughter with having lost a splendid matrimonial prospect. She came to Anne's bedchamber morning and evening to bemoan her child's wrong headedness.

"You will never marry now, I suppose, for such a chance does not come about more than once. Well, I suppose that you will live with me at Rosings as you always have, for I have no thought of returning to Bath anytime soon."

To all her mother's speeches Anne would reply with a few set phrases, such as "I suppose we shall see, Mama," or "I am sorry that you hold such an opinion, Mama, for I cannot agree." Against her daughter's refusal to be intimidated or provoked, Lady Catherine began to lose much of her pleasure in her old pastime of subjugating Anne to her will.

At breakfast on the second morning after the ball, Mr. Grey announced that he would be leaving Pemberley immediately after Christmas in order to begin his time at Cambridge. The library, he explained, was catalogued, and he could think of nothing else to do there, as much as he enjoyed taking his ease in such pleasant company.

"I do assure you however, Darcy, that when I do leave it will be in a decorous and civilized manner, not in the way of the last few guests who have taken their departure. I will even depart in broad daylight and bid everyone farewell at the door."

"You will return for a visit before you leave for Wales, will you not, Grey?" asked Darcy, who was very sorry to lose his friend's company.

"Oh, I will try to do so if you are so kind as to want me, just a sort of flying visit as my parishioners will no doubt be awaiting my arrival with painful suspense."

"Indeed, Mr. Grey, we are so very sad to think of Pemberley without you," said Elizabeth, "and we will hope to see you here again often."

Grey managed to thank her with a fairly cheerful countenance, but inwardly he reflected that it might be a long time before he would see his friends again. It would be too painful to be in the neighborhood of Castle Faulconer. Since the ball he had fallen into a state of despondency which was quite unprecedented for him and which he took care to conceal from everyone.

"Surely, you have not given yourself over to despair, Mr. Grey," said Anne when she found him in the library later that day, "I cannot believe that you would allow a few setbacks to induce you to give up hope."

"A few setbacks, Miss de Bourgh?" he replied, "Perhaps one must know when to give up the field and turn one's attention to other things. For myself, I am looking forward to my time at Cambridge. I've not spent more than a few days there for some years. Why do you not come to see the place with Darcy and Mrs. Darcy while I am there? What a fine tour we could give you, Darcy and I."

"I'm certain that you and my cousin Darcy were a formidable pair when you were students together."

"Indeed we were. And Bingley, you know, was there as well, but a couple of years behind us. We had to look after him and protect him from the usual snares of university life. All in all, we had an excellent time and even occasional leisure enough to study. It would have been perfect had not that fellow Wickham been there as well."

"Oh, yes, the infamous Wickham. Do you know that I have never met him, although I suppose he is some sort of relation now, by way of being married to Elizabeth's sister."

"That is a great misfortune," said Grey, "He was always a dreadful trial to Darcy, who constantly had to help him out of various scrapes and money difficulties. The worst thing was that Wickham never lost an opportunity to attempt to come between Darcy and his father in the most cunning and underhanded ways."

"I had no idea of this, Mr. Grey," said Anne, "How Darcy must have suffered."

"He did indeed. Association with someone like Wickham must forever change one's view of the world. Darcy adored his father and to see the old gentleman be taken in by the wiles of such a person was very hard." After a pause Grey continued, "I can only rejoice that my friend has found a wife who has healed all his old sadness. She is the only woman who could have done so."

They were silent for a moment, then Anne said, "But you have cleverly gotten us off the subject. What about you, Mr. Grey? Surely you will not forsake your love and disappear into Wales, never to be heard from again?"

"Sometimes, Miss De Bourgh, the best decision is to refrain from making any decision at all. No, I will never give up, but for now my only plan is to go exploring caverns with Dr. Gilmore-Jones as much as possible for the next weeks. It is a wonderful pastime. A few hours of wandering about in mud and freezing water takes one's mind off other things to a remarkable degree."

Anne was in a most pensive state of mind. She had the comfort of knowing that her cousin Fitzwilliam would not live out his days married to a foolish woman who would eventually drive him to weariness and despair. Anne knew that he was at heart a serious man and could not live without intelligent companionship. Twenty times a day she found herself lost in dreams of a future in which Fitzwilliam would love her as much as she had always loved him, and twenty times a day she told herself that she was a fool to indulge in such ideas. Then she would review every moment in which they had been together over the past few months and found that she could not completely give up hope. If only she could know what he had intended to say to her at the ball.

DARCY WENT UP to Elizabeth's sitting room that evening where he knew that she would be waiting for him. It had become their habit to sit before the fire for a time, talking about the day's events, before retiring for the night. Gradually in this way they had come to share their feelings, opinions, hopes and ideas. It was the best time of the day for them both.

"Well, my darling," said Darcy settling in beside her on the sofa and putting an arm around her shoulders, "As I mentioned before dinner, I have had a note from Holland in which he announces that he will favor us with another visit in three day's time. Just to bid us farewell and thank us for our hospitality, as he puts it. How unpleasant that will be for Anne."

Elizabeth moved more closely into her husband's arms and felt the most blissful contentment. To her he was very nearly perfect and she loved him more than she would have thought possible. Except for his occasional inexplicable dark moods her happiness would have been complete.

After a moment she said, "Perhaps he is returning to show that he has no ill feelings or resentment at being rejected. It could be that he desires to part with Anne on terms of civility."

Darcy moved away slightly and replied, "You think well of him, I suppose. After all, he has been a pleasant enough guest and certainly you and he play very well together."

Elizabeth looked up into his face and saw that he was staring at the fire and did not return her gaze.

"He is well enough, I suppose, but he has not that open temperament that I admire."

Darcy smiled at last and said, "And do you find that I have an open temperament?"

"To me, at least, you do, but perhaps not to others. I believe that I am always aware of your feelings, although their origin may be obscure. Of course it would save a great deal of trouble if you were simply to explain yourself to me."

"Then you would know everything and become bored with me, or,

483

even worse, you might find me a less worthy man than you believe me to be."

"That is impossible," said Elizabeth, sitting up and, taking her husband's hands, she kissed them, "You are all that is good and loving and steadfast!"

"Beloved, may you always think thus." replied Darcy fervently, "And now to bed, for it is late."

"Oh, I am not in the least fatigued," replied Elizabeth.

THE NEXT MORNING the gentlemen were to ride over to Thrushfold Hall to inspect the most recent repairs to the Bingleys' future residence. It was to be a most exciting matter of looking at tiles, wainscoting and plaster work and the plan was to set off immediately after breakfast. Much to Darcy's dismay, Lady Catherine had expressed a determination to go as well. When the subject had arisen at dinner on the day before, she had announced that her advice would be invaluable at this stage of the renovation.

"You know that I am an expert in these matters, nephew, and even though it is over an hour's journey to Thrushfold Hall I am happy to undertake it for the sake of Mr. and Mrs. Bingley. As you will recall, I was of great assistance to Lord Dumbello in the matter of planning his hot houses and designing the proper drains. 'Ah, Lady Catherine,' he has often said, 'every time I enjoy an orange I inwardly thank you for your sagacity and am glad that I consulted you instead of the London engineer who had been recommended to me.'" Then she nodded graciously towards Jane and continued, "My dear, I have taken a great liking to you and tomorrow it will be my pleasure to ascertain that all is being done properly. After all, we must make sure that you are protected from drafts and damp before you move to your new home. Alas, it has been my sad experience that not one mason in a thousand can truly point up a chimney with something approaching mastery."

Later in the music room Lady Grinspoon came up to Darcy and offered to be one of the company on the excursion to Thrushfold Hall.

"We will all go, and with some effort Anne, Georgiana and I may distract Lady Catherine's attention while you attend to the matters at hand. Then, perhaps, she will not insist on climbing up on the roof with you and the other gentlemen."

In the morning Jane felt a bit fatigued and Bingley insisted that she stay at Pemberley. He was even ready to stay behind himself and would have had the physician summoned, but he was reassured at last and set off with the group. Jane stayed in bed and Elizabeth spent most of the day sitting with her; there was the all important subject of the baby's name to occupy them. By two o'clock Jane had fallen asleep and it seemed a good time to attend to some of the household business. The house seemed very quiet to Elizabeth as she descended the stairs. Usually it was full of activity and she could not remember being so without company at Pemberley. She went into the library and sat down at her desk with the intention of writing a letter to her mother, but instead spent a while looking out of the window towards the approach to the house. It had become much colder and she thought it might snow by nightfall, but Darcy would no doubt have everyone home well before dusk.

She began her letter without any great enthusiasm, as her mother's last missive had been so full of questions about the ball and what Lady Catherine had worn, that it would be exhausting to reply in detail. The Bennets had now decided to arrive before Christmas, so Mrs. Bennett would be there soon enough in any case, and would be able to see for herself all the grandeur of Lady Catherine.

Elizabeth was describing the wonderful necklace that Darcy had given her on the night of the ball when she heard the door of the library open very softly. She assumed it was one of the footmen bringing in firewood, but looked up when she noticed footsteps approaching her desk. She was astonished to see Lord Holland standing before her, flushed from the cold air and wearing a greatcoat.

"Good heavens, Lord Holland! What a surprise you have given me. We did not expect you until day after tomorrow."

"Yes, I am a bit before my time and I hope you do not mind. May I remove my coat? What a good fire you have and most welcome, for it has become rather bitterly cold out."

"I will ring for the butler to assist you," cried Elizabeth, rising quickly and moving across the room. "I am very angry that no one was at the door to greet you."

"Oh, do not blame him," said Holland, flinging his coat onto a chair in a careless way and going to stand by the fire. "You see I did not wish to disturb anyone so I came by the side door. I know it well, having stayed above the stable block next door to Colonel Fitzwilliam."

Elizabeth was puzzled as to how anyone could enter the house without being seen, but she supposed that the servants were at dinner, as they dined early and there were no visitors expected.

"Please do not trouble yourself, Mrs. Darcy, as I will only stay for a few minutes. I seem to have missed everyone, however, judging from the empty stable yard. Are they all gone on some excursion?"

"Yes, to Thrushfold Hall to inspect the progress on the house," replied Elizabeth, "but I expect them back very soon." She felt uneasy without being quite sure why. This, after all, was the courteous Lord Holland who had saved her life in Scotland and always behaved with the greatest *politesse*. Telling herself that she was being absurd, she sat by the fire and motioned him to a chair.

"My husband will be sorry to have missed you. It is a shame we did not know that you were coming." She began to feel uncomfortable under his intense scrutiny as he sat across from her. If only Jane were to join them!

"No doubt Miss de Bourgh will be disappointed," he replied with a faint note of sarcasm, "I suppose it is possible she might be ready to reconsider her rejection of me."

After a moment's silence he continued, "I had become almost fond of Miss de Bourgh and it was unpleasant to realize that I had misjudged her. I thought her quite intelligent and now I know that she is a fool."

Elizabeth looked at him in astonishment, "You are ill-mannered, sir, to speak so of my cousin, no matter how terrible your disappointment."

"I am most unhappy with the total destruction of my most cherished plans, Mrs. Darcy, and I am here because only you can save me."

"I – what have I to do with it?"

"You know very well, and it is cruel of you to pretend ignorance when you know that I am suffering." Holland leaned forward, his face transformed from its usual mask of polite *sang froid* into a visage charged with strong emotion.

"When you know that I have suffered all these months since I first saw you in London. You must know, how else could you have played the way you have with me every evening, letting your passion speak through music. Why is that women seek to inspire love and then make a pretense of not knowing what they have done."

Elizabeth had only been truly afraid once before, when her horse had bolted and this very man had saved her from destruction. This was even more terrifying. He looked like her idea of someone who could commit a crime and it was not difficult to imagine his hands around her throat even as he continued to speak of his love for her.

"You certainly comprehended at once that I sought to marry Miss de Bourgh in order to be near you. Why else? She is rich of course and did not displease me, but there are many others I could have had."

He leapt up and began to pace about the room; unfortunately he stayed between Elizabeth and the door and she did not dare to attempt to escape. She listened for any sound that might indicate the presence of one of the servants, but at the same time was afraid that Jane might come in and be shocked by this madman.

"I saw the way you looked at me even in the beginning, the glances that you gave me, so full of desire. the very mirror of what I was feeling myself. You are so bored with the tiresome, arrogant Mr. Darcy. What a mediocrity he is, I thought, and how could he have captured this exquisite, brilliant woman?"

Elizabeth almost spoke the words that came to her mind. "You are mad," but some beneficent influence prevented her from doing so.

"But it does not matter now, my beloved, for we will be together in spite of the caprice of Miss de Bourgh. I have arranged everything and you will come away with me." So saying he placed himself before her and stood there his face alight with eager determination.

"As I said, I came in through the side door, having left my coach at the gate near the southern edge of the park. I have spies in the neighborhood and in this very house, so was able to hear last night about the proposed outing of most of the company. Your servants are all gone from here thanks to a report of a fire in the village. Oh, yes, there is indeed a fire – that was easily arranged."

Now Elizabeth remembered to have heard some activity in the stable yard and the sound of a departing farm wagon but she'd not thought much about it.

"As for the servants who stayed behind to attend you," continued Holland, "my minions have arranged for them to enjoy a little rest in the pantry, so we will not be disturbed. Everything is in readiness and we will send for your things later."

Elizabeth had been examining every possible means of escape from her captor, feeling that she would go mad herself if she had to remain in the same room with him much longer. If he came any closer she would have to scream and hope that one of the servants could come to her aid. But what effect would it have on Jane to be awakened by some violent scene. What if she were to rush downstairs and fall!

Lord Holland knelt down in front of Elizabeth's chair and leaned towards her, "I feel as though I have waited forever to kiss you and I cannot endure it any longer."

With all her strength Elizabeth put her hands against his shoulders and pushed him away. He was so surprised that he fell backwards in a most undignified manner. This was her only chance and she ran to the door and almost succeeded in getting it open when she felt his hand close over hers.

"Why are trying to leave me, Elizabeth? I know that you love me, so this must just be some little game you are playing to torture me a bit longer."

She felt herself pinned against the door and found that she was screaming without realizing how she had begun to do so. There was no one to hear, and Jane, one floor and a corridor away, remained sound asleep. Holland pulled her further into the library and forced her face close to his own. She had never imagined anything so terrible as the expression in his eyes and fought to release herself with all her strength.

Elizabeth tried to scream again, but found that her tormenter's hand over her mouth prevented her from doing do. She felt that she would suffocate if he were to persist for a moment longer and wondered why she had not tried to flee as soon as he had entered the room. How stupid she had been!

A moment later she felt herself released from the dreadful pressure of his arms and she almost fell to the floor. Darcy had entered the room and thrown Lord Holland halfway across it with tremendous force. The two men would have been well matched had not Holland been taken by surprise. When he tried to rise from the floor, Darcy picked him up and flung him against the fireplace fender and had there not been the grace of two inches might have committed murder.

"Oh, stop in God's name!" cried Elizabeth, "before you kill him."

The shades of Pemberley might have been polluted by a most unseemly fracas had not Grey and Bingley come rushing into the library.

"Good God! What is happening here?" cried Bingley, shocked at the sight of the usually dignified Darcy who was almost unrecognizable in his rage.

Grey, who was very much more acute, knew at once what had occurred and stepping over to Lord Holland said, "It is time for you to leave, Holland. Bingley and I will escort you out of the house."

Holland was no less furious than Darcy and looked as if he were about to fly at him and return his assault with equal violence. However, the presence of two very determined allies seemed to make him think better of it.

"You will hear from me before tomorrow morning is over, Mr. Darcy. As soon as I have found my seconds they will call upon you to arrange the matter."

"The sooner, the better," replied Darcy, who still appeared beside himself with anger. His friends carefully escorted Holland out, avoiding as best they could any proximity between the two men.

After the door had closed Elizabeth rushed into her husband's arms, but she found little comfort there. He was shaking with fury even then and in a moment pulled away from her and began to pace about the room, evidently attempting to bring his emotions under better control.

After a pause he burst out with, "My God Elizabeth, how did that fellow happen to be here! What could have given him the idea that he could insult you in this manner?"

Elizabeth was so surprised that she could find no reply.

"By God, why must you make every man who ventures into our orbit in love with you? Is not my devotion enough? Yet you seem determined to fascinate all the world. You let your beauty and vivacity shine so brightly that you draw all towards you wherever you go."

Elizabeth began to feel an anger even greater than any that had been evinced in that room so far.

"Mr. Darcy," she said with deadly coldness, "I hope that I misunderstand you. You seem to be implying that I am somehow responsible for what has just occurred."

Darcy, looking at his wife and seeing her expression and posture, realized that his outburst had been an error of the worst kind and he hastened to add, "I do not accuse you of anything wrong, nor could I ever doubt your purity, your innocence, but surely you are sometimes prone to be carried away with your power instead of tempering your ability to enchant those around you."

Elizabeth did not speak for a moment for it was difficult to find words to express how deeply she had been offended. Finally, she looked at him with an expression of complete disdain and said, "How very generous of you not to doubt my purity. I must certainly be grateful for such a mark of confidence. It would seem that my crime has been that I am simply myself, unguardedly and uncalculatedly myself. I am fond of company and laughter and enjoy seeing our friends happy as well. I never thought that I was doing anything wrong in being lively and animated. In fact, I believed that was one of the things that you have always loved about me. Clearly, I was wrong."

Darcy now began to be horrified at what he had said and only wished he could take it back; never had his Elizabeth seemed cold and removed from him since their marriage.

"I expressed myself badly," he said, "I was beside myself with the shock of finding that wretch here with you and the thought of the danger you were in has driven me mad."

"Sometimes what is said in anger reveals a truth that would otherwise never come to light. I thought that our souls were as one and I would never have imagined you capable of harboring such opinions."

By now Darcy was ready to fall on knees to ask her forgiveness, so alarmed was he to see her so distant and full of contempt. He tried to take her into his arms, but she avoided him and put out a hand to ward him off.

"I would like to go to my bedchamber now and be left to myself, if you will allow me to do so. It has been a most horrible day: first to be assaulted by a vicious madman and then to find that my husband, the being in whom I have entrusted all my life and my honor, thinks so meanly of me. I do not know, Mr. Darcy, if I will ever be able to forgive you and resume our marriage as we have known it."

He tried to take her hand and began, "Oh do forgive me my love. I am such a fool. Please stay with me and I will try to explain." But his wife repeated that she must insist on being left alone and quitted the room, leaving Darcy in the most miserable state of mind he had ever known.

CHAPTER 52

*A*bout mid-morning on the following day, Colonel Fitzwilliam rode into the courtyard of Pemberley. He had had an exhausting journey from Hampshire, pausing only as long as darkness and icy roads had made it necessary. In his impatience on this day he had left his servants with his carriage and had come ahead with the fastest horse available. His first intention was to find Anne and discover whether or not she had engaged herself to Lord Holland. In either case, it would be his duty to reveal the truth about the man and kick him out of the house if need be.

As he jumped down from his horse and handed the reins over to a footman, he was surprised to see Mrs. Darcy run down the steps in a sort of desperate haste.

"Oh, thank God you have returned, Colonel!" she cried grasping his hand and looking up into his face. "I had given up hope that anyone could help me."

"Good heavens, what has happened to distress you so, Mrs. Darcy? Let me take you into the house, where you can calm yourself and rest."

"No, oh no! There is not a moment to be lost. You must find them before it is too late."

"I will do so, I assure you," replied the colonel, unable to imagine what could have occurred, "but please let us go into the house for five minutes so you can explain what has happened. It is too cold for you to be out of doors."

Fitzwilliam led Elizabeth into the hall and was able to persuade her to sit down by the library fire.

"Here is a little brandy, Mrs. Darcy, and you are to drink it at once."

After Elizabeth had taken a few sips, the colonel inquired, "Where has everyone gone? Why are you all alone?"

"Sir Wilfred has taken all the ladies to Thrushfold Hall. Ah, that he were here! Colonel, my husband has gone to fight a duel and I know that he will be killed unless you can find him and stop it. Mr. Bingley and Mr. Grey are gone as well; they must be serving as his seconds."

"A duel!" exclaimed Fitzwilliam, "How can this be? No one despises dueling more than Darcy. Only barbarians settle their disputes in such a manner as he has always averred."

It took a few minutes more for the story to be told. Elizabeth in her wretched state of fear did not hesitate to recount the entire story of what had occurred, including the quarrel with Darcy.

"You see, I refused to forgive him for what he had said to me, and now he has gone away, I know not where, and I may never see him again. I have been so stupid, Colonel. There were two gentlemen here after dinner and they spent some time in the gunroom closeted with my husband and Mr. Grey and Mr. Bingley. I only learned this after they had all gone away this morning and the butler told me of it, for last night I kept to my room and did not see anyone." Elizabeth could not control her tears at this point, although the brandy had seemed to calm her somewhat, "Then I knew what must be afoot, but by then I was here all alone. You cannot imagine what I felt when I saw you riding up the drive."

"Even had I been here it would probably have been impossible to dissuade Darcy from his purpose. I am sure that Bingley and Grey made the attempt." Fitzwilliam knew Holland's reputation as a duelist and could not doubt that his cousin might well be killed in the encounter.

"I cannot deny that the situation is grave, Mrs. Darcy, but I think that I know where they will meet. I will go there and try to intervene.

You must try to hope that all will be well. And now I will leave you, but will send word as soon as may be."

Fitzwilliam ordered that the fastest horse in Darcy's stable might be brought round and set off at a gallop with one of the grooms in attendance. There was no doubt that the servants were already well aware of what was in progress, and the man might be needed to bring some message back to Pemberley.

The colonel was a soldier who had early learned to conquer fear; his profession required it and his temperament was naturally intrepid. When the life of his dearest friend was in danger, however, it was difficult for him to banish a terrible sense of dread. Darcy was skilled with sword and pistol, but Holland was known for his superior mastery of both methods of destruction.

There was a secluded inn at the edge of a woods about five miles from Pemberley; it was known as a favorite rendezvous for resolving affairs of honor and Fitzwilliam could remember hearing Darcy deplore the foolishness of those who met there to settle their disagreements. "This is after all, the nineteenth century, not the middle ages, and one would hope for a more civilized resolution of personal conflicts," he would say with a scornful expression, when there was news of some injury or death that had taken place in the clearing near the hostelry.

Clearly Fitzwilliam's surmise had been correct, as he recognized all three of the horses tethered in front of the door to the inn. If there were any others they must have been put into the stable behind. On entering he found Bingley, Grey and Darcy sitting before the fire in a disconsolate manner. The first two gentlemen leapt up and were obviously glad to see him, but Darcy merely glanced in his direction without rising, apparently without surprise or interest at his cousin's arrival.

Fitzwilliam went to take a seat by Darcy's side and said quietly that they must have a conversation in some more private setting.

"Surely there is nothing that Bingley or Grey cannot hear," replied Darcy indifferently, "They know all that has passed."

"Even so, let us go outside for a few moments."

"It's damnably cold and I would like to keep my hands warm for as long as possible. I've chosen pistols and you know that it is hard to shoot well with frozen fingers."

When Fitzwilliam did not reply and only looked more determined to have his way, Darcy sighed and rose to go, "Very well, let us go check on the horses."

Fitzwilliam began by urging Darcy to give up the duel as an absurd and murderous practice which Darcy himself had often decried.

"Of course, you are correct, but I can assure you that if ever you have a wife and someone dared to insult her, you would do just the same. Can you deny it?"

"No, it is impossible to deny that that would be my first inclination. But think of Mrs. Darcy; she is overcome with anxiety and begged me to come and stop you."

For the first time Darcy became animated, "Then she does care? Do you think she may in time forgive me? You know, I presume, in what a despicable manner I have behaved? I have offended the most beloved and perfect being in existence."

"Don't be a fool, Darcy," replied Fitzwilliam roughly. "Of course she forgives you. No woman ever loved her husband better than she loves you. If you could know what she is suffering, you would leave here at once and rush to her side. Forget this idiotic business and come back to Pemberley."

Darcy looked for a moment as if he would jump onto his horse and do just that, but then he became grave and said, "Thank you for letting me know that she still feels affection for me, although I must admit that it makes it more difficult to face death. You know that I have no choice in the matter."

Fitzwilliam could perceive that further argument would be fruitless and the two of them went back into the inn. All four gentlemen sat silently for the next half hour until Bingley remarked, "The fellow is now an hour late and I believe that he may not be coming at all."

This was a welcome thought to all present, even Darcy, but he said, "We must wait another hour at least. Surely he will send word if he is unavoidably detained."

They continued there, each with his own thoughts. Bingley hated being away from Jane's side and worried about her even as he dreaded what might happen to his friend in the duel. Grey pondered his coming departure for Wales, which might sever him from Lady Margaret forever. He had used every argument in his power to deter Darcy from this meeting, but had had no more influence than Fitzwilliam. Fitzwilliam's thoughts were all of how he might save his cousin, but it appeared to be hopeless. If this disaster had not occurred, he might even now be with Anne. He wished urgently to know how she bore the revelation of Holland's true character.

Darcy, of course, thought only of Elizabeth. He was grateful that they had had a few months of such great happiness. Only the strongest sense of honor prevented him from galloping home to her without delay. He thought with deep shame of the way in which he had spoken to her. During all the time spent at Thrushfold Hall the previous day he had experienced an awful sense of dread, until finally he had rushed everyone back to Pemberley before the inspection of the house had been concluded. At least he had been able to save his Elizabeth from the loathsome Holland.

The next hour seemed endless, but then the sound of a carriage was heard in the forecourt. They all rose to see in what state Holland might have arrived with his seconds. Perhaps he had brought a surgeon; in his depressed spirits Darcy had refused to do so that morning. He did not know that Grey had arranged for a medical attendant to wait in another part of the inn in case he should be needed.

The surprise was very great when they looked out of the large bay window and saw a very grand equipage with armorial fittings, attended by several footmen and out-riders. A tall, slender gentleman leaning on a cane descended and proceeded to enter the room.

He was a man of about five and thirty with a pale but engaging countenance and Fitzwilliam recognized him at once as the gentleman he had seen driving away from Mr. Thornton's house in the company of two ladies. There was a polite exchange of bows and Fitzwilliam stepped forward and said, "You are the Marquess of Roscree, I believe. I am Colonel Fitzwilliam. Please allow me to name the rest of the party."

"Oh, I believe I have met Mr. Darcy in London on one or two

occasions, although it has been some years ago," said the marquess in a pleasant and friendly way, " I am delighted to make your acquaintance, Mr. Grey, Mr. Bingley."

This interview would have been very charming for all concerned had not the four gentlemen from Pemberley been wild with curiosity to know what was afoot. With any luck, thought Grey, this nobleman had come to inform them that Lord Holland had been kicked to death by his horse that morning.

"Well gentleman, I hope that you will not be too disappointed to learn that my brother will be unable to keep his appointment with you today. In fact, for I must not keep you in suspense, you will not be seeing him again."

"Not ever?" asked Bingley.

"Not in this life" was the reply, "and almost certainly not in the next."

There was an astonished and gratified silence for a moment, then Grey called out, "Innkeeper! Bring us several bottles of your best claret."

Fitzwilliam added, "And tell the servant to attend us at once. We have an urgent message to send to Pemberley."

"You see," continued the marquess after the wine had been handed round, "my brother, Lord Holland, is now on his way to take ship for Virginia on a vessel I happen to own. I do assure you that he will not lose his way between Derbyshire and Portsmouth, for he is accompanied by a formidable and vigilant escort. In a week's time he will be well at sea and we may hope that he will spend his remaining years repenting the actions that have led to his removal from his native land."

"Good heavens!" cried Bingley, "Why have you arranged for your brother's exile? Of course we are more than delighted to hear that he is gone, but I am surprised that his elder brother should share in our complaisance."

"I will tell you the entire unfortunate story, gentlemen, for I know that you will respect my confidence. In any case, I doubt that the facts of the matter will long escape public knowledge."

The marquess settled into his armchair in a manner that suggested that his tale might take some time. Darcy was almost overcome with eagerness to return to Pemberley and Elizabeth, but he forced himself to listen attentively to the nobleman's narration. The man had probably saved his life that day and it was only right to show him every courtesy.

"My brother is certainly capable of charming any company into which he is introduced and his intelligence and talents should have secured him a better fate. Unfortunately, I must aver that he is and always has been completely lacking in character and conscience. For many years I tried to deny the truth, for it is hateful to realize that one's nearest relation is a villain. This became evident most forcefully when he was required to give up his commission. The world believes that he did so in order to assist his ailing brother with the family estates, but the circumstances were quite otherwise. While at Toulon two years ago he was guilty of an outrage against a young lady of good family. I will spare you the details, but this despicable crime could have led to his imprisonment or worse. It was only because of my influence and the fact that his admiral had been my father's closest friend that my brother was allowed merely to leave the service. There was further recompense in the form of a large settlement on the lady, as you can imagine."

"But why was the wretch not publicly disgraced? How has he been allowed to continue to go about among respectable people?" exclaimed Darcy in disgust.

"I must bear the responsibility. My brother was so convincing that the fault had not been all his and that there was guilt on both sides. I am ashamed to admit that I believed him and wished to think that he could reform. Now I realize that he has been culpable on many other occasions in similar circumstances, but has been clever enough to cover his tracks. To sum up, gentlemen, he is a blackguard of the worst description."

"Why take action now?" asked Grey, "What has precipitated his enforced departure for Virginia?"

"I have been contemplating this measure for some time. There is someone very dear to me who also came into some danger at the hands of Lord Holland. Fortunately she escaped any personal harm, but hearing of his actions made me begin to consider how he might best be disposed of, so to speak. A few weeks ago my valet, who has been in my employ for two years, disappeared taking a good deal of silver and other valuables. At about this time I engaged a new physician whom you know, Dr. Crawford. After one examination this wise and brilliant man told me that I had been poisoned and that this was the reason for my prolonged and almost fatal illness. By good fortune, some of my trusted servants were able to find the valet and he quickly confessed that my brother had paid him to introduce a lethal substance into my food over many months."

The marquess paused for a moment, visibly shaken by the recollection, then said, "Think of it. For over a year I thought that I was dying. My doctors despaired of my life and I would have died had not a benevolent fate intervened. This plot against my life began even before the attempt to poison me. I recently learned that my brother made no effort to save me when I was drowning in a loch in Scotland. He was seen to stand by watching me struggle and only intervened when my steward happened to see me and came to my aid. This information was given me by a servant who was afraid to speak out until now."

"It has taken me three weeks to make all my arrangements and to ascertain where my dear brother had gone, for he was never very communicative about such things. Thank God for Dr. Crawford who was able to inform me that Holland had insinuated himself into your circle at Pemberley and was attempting to persuade Miss de Bourgh to marry him."

Nodding to Fitzwilliam he continued, "When I encountered you in the drive at Thornton Abbey, I was setting out in all haste to come here and prevent my brother from bringing misfortune on your family. I did not feel that I could entrust such an important mission to anyone else and I arrived at Lambton yesterday. My agents seized him as he was preparing to make his way here early this morning. With a bit of persuasion he was good enough to inform me of your meeting place. How happy I am to have prevented this duel; Holland would have killed you, Mr. Darcy, without the slightest hesitation or remorse. We may all be thankful that he is gone. Let us hope that he enjoys the climate and society in Virginia. He will spend the rest of his days there managing my cousin's plantations. If he attempts to return to England my agents will make sure that he regrets it."

Grey reflected that it might be well to warn the unfortunate inhabitants of Virginia of this wolf in their fold.

There were still many questions to be asked about Lord Holland's infamous career and the Marquess of Roscree answered them all patiently. Finally he rose and said that it was necessary for him to depart in order to make some progress back in the direction of Bath. Darcy urged him to spend the night at Pemberley before undertaking such an exhausting journey.

"I thank you with all my heart," was the answer, " but my health is so improved that I do not mind it. Besides, I have much to do. I am to be married in three weeks time!" The countenance that had been so grave until now became bright with happiness.

Fitzwilliam thought of the beautiful young lady he had seen in the carriage at Mr. Thornton's, Miss Delaford, who had been Stanley's's fiancé. Thank God she was safe from Lord Holland.

When Darcy and his friends returned to Pemberley they found the house in something of an uproar. Lady Catherine had been told about the duel on her return from Thrushfold Hall and had spent the intervening time tormenting everyone around her. Elizabeth was her chief victim, for she had to endure being blamed for allowing Darcy to go off to the appointment with Lord Holland.

"I did not know of his intention, Lady Catherine, and if I had it would still have been impossible to prevent him."

By this point all the ladies had assembled in the library to await any news. Elizabeth and Georgiana were in a dreadful state of mind and Anne, Jane and Lady Grinspoon tried to comfort them as best they could. Surely Darcy's good sense would prevail, they ventured, or, if not, everyone knew him to be perfectly capable of defending himself. This was well meant if not entirely convincing. All the while Lady Catherine paced the room like an angry lioness, exclaiming at regular intervals that she would never have allowed the present crisis to occur, if only she had been consulted.

"After all," she said at last, "before his marriage Darcy consulted me about everything. "

At this Elizabeth's patience was exhausted, "Lady Catherine, you have said quite enough. I would have thought it impossible that anyone could make this terrible day even more horrible for me, but you have succeeded. If you cannot contain yourself I must ask you to leave this room and remain in your own chamber until we have tidings of my husband."

Lady Catherine was speechless for several moments; no one had ever before ordered her from a room. She finally took a seat in an armchair and was thinking how she might answer such an intolerable affront, when she met Elizabeth's eyes. There was such grief and agony of spirit there that even Lady Catherine was touched. There was as well a strength and determination about Elizabeth's bearing that made the older woman decide to be silent.

Another hour went by. Jane sat on a sofa between Elizabeth and Georgiana with an arm about each of them. Her simple faith that all would be well was the only source of comfort for Darcy's wife and sister. Suddenly the butler came in with a radiant smile and presented a note to Mrs. Darcy. Of course he could surmise what it contained, as could the entire household within moments of the messenger galloping into the courtyard with a joyful greeting. All the servants at Pemberley loved their master and had been full of fear for him that day.

Elizabeth tore the note open; it was brief, but in her husband's usual clear hand and stated,

My beloved, all is resolved and I am well. There has been no duel. I will return to you as quickly as may be.

"He is safe! He is safe!" she cried, jumping up and almost dancing with relief. Then Georgiana was in her arms and weeping with joy.

"What, has he killed that worthless young man? I do congratulate my nephew on his skill at arms," exclaimed Lady Catherine entering into the spirit of the moment.

IT WAS ALMOST another two hours until the gentlemen returned. Elizabeth was unable to leave her position at the windows that gave a prospect of the drive and was beside herself with impatience to see her husband. Finally, when it was almost dusk, she saw the four horsemen cantering up to the house and in a moment she had run into Darcy's arms. As to whether this were a breach of decorum Elizabeth could not have been more indifferent. There was, however, no escaping a general assembly in the library of all of the occupants of the house and Darcy was soon besieged with questions.

"For goodness sake," cried Elizabeth, "Do let them have a moment to warm themselves by the fire," and so saying she rang for the servant to bring wine and refreshments.

Fitzwilliam's first concern was to find a spot near Anne; he was afraid that she would be distressed by the new revelations about Lord Holland. He pulled up a chair beside hers and spoke to her in a low voice, "Are you well, Anne? I have been so anxious to speak to you, but as soon as I arrived I had to leave in search of Darcy."

He looked into her face with some apprehension, but was relieved and delighted to find an expression, not of sorrow, but of quiet happiness.

"You must know that I never cared at all for Lord Holland," she said so softly that only he could hear, " Never, no, never. He has not injured me. I am only so glad that my cousin is safe, and that you," Anne hesitated, "that you have returned."

At that point Darcy began to give a narration of what had occurred at the inn. It seemed useless to try to keep anything from the ladies, as they seemed to know so much already. He was frequently interrupted by cries of horror and indignation, which allowed him an opportunity to sip his wine and to make sure that the other gentlemen were well supplied.

"Lord Holland must be one of the most vile creatures in the world, "said Lady Catherine, "It is well for you Anne, that I always advised you to be cautious in how you received his addresses."

"Yes, Mama," replied Anne, with a meaningful glance towards

Fitzwilliam, "You certainly have displayed your usual wisdom throughout this entire affair," a bit of irony which was understood by everyone but Lady Catherine.

"I like the idea of his being exiled to the wilderness of Virginia. It will be a useful device in the plot of my next novel," remarked Lady Grinspoon.

All the company enjoyed a late dinner that had something of a celebratory quality about it, and then everyone showed an inclination to retire early. Fitzwilliam somehow contrived to have a moment's private conversation with Anne before she was called away by her mother.

"If the weather is better tomorrow, if it is not as cold, and if the ice has melted, then perhaps you would go out walking with me. I will show you where I used to fish for trout as a boy."

"I will walk with you, cousin," she replied, looking up at him with the same beautiful expression he had seen in the library, "and it will take more than cold and ice to prevent me."

ALL EVENING DARCY had thought of nothing but the moment when he could be alone with his wife. At last they were together in her sitting room as they had been but two nights before, but how different everything was now. During that forty-eight hours, they had quarreled for the first time since their marriage and all that they were to each other could have been destroyed. Darcy had the sense of having suffered a near fatal blow, even though no duel had taken place, and that he must have the courage to probe the wound to see how severe the damage might be.

"My Elizabeth, you are all that is generous and good, but do you really believe that you can love me as you did before? Tell me the truth; can you forgive me, not just for what I said, but for the defects of character which I wished could be forever hidden from you?"

She took his hands and replied, "You must hear me now, for there will never be a moment of greater importance to us than this. I love you more than ever and nothing can ever change that for me. All the hours I waited for you today were full of the worst suffering I have ever known, but I have learned to understand us both in a way that I never would have otherwise."

"You must tell me everything, my beloved."

"I was so very angry with you, but I came to reflect that your words had their source in an old wound that had nothing to do with me. I know you too well to think that you could really doubt my love or my loyalty."

"To my shame I have been possessed by jealousy all the time I have loved you," replied Darcy, "The first time I saw you speaking to Wickham I began to burn with this terrible and unworthy emotion. Since we have been married I have never wanted to share you with anyone and if we could have stayed here at Pemberley never seeing another soul I would have been content. Now you know the worst of me."

"This explains many of your dark moods when you seemed to draw away from me," said Elizabeth, "I never knew why and drew back from *you*, as I feared that you were becoming tired of our marriage. You cannot imagine the pain that idea has given me."

Darcy took her in his arms and said. "Forgive me for not confiding in you. I wanted you to think me better than I am."

"I also am imperfect in so many ways," said Elizabeth, "I see that there is some truth in what you said and that I am too unguarded sometimes. I am so caught up in the simple enjoyment of life, its pleasures and absurdities, and I expect everyone to understand me. I can see now that a man like Holland might well misinterpret my character. I have tried to teach you to be more lively but I need to learn something of reserve and caution from you."

"No, do not change, my Elizabeth, for you are perfect in my eyes," replied Darcy, "The fault is all mine and I can only promise that from this time forward I will tell you my every thought and feeling so that nothing can ever come between us again."

What wife can resist for long being told that she is perfect? It seemed miraculous that a day that had begun with so much potential for tragedy should end with the most complete happiness and mutual confidence they had ever known.

CHAPTER 53

$\mathcal{P}$emberley was peaceful at last; everyone had gone to rest except for Anne who came back downstairs with a candle to light her way. She had put on heavy shoes and her fur cloak and in a few minutes had unlatched the hall door and was outside on the terrace. She had never known such an overwhelming emotion as she felt this night and she could not be still. She had seen something in Fitzwilliam's countenance that gave her hope that he might indeed love her. No matter how often she told herself that she was wrong, she could not forget what she had sensed when they had stood together in the library.

She walked very quietly up and down the length of the terrace, not wishing to start the dogs barking and alarm the household. She was beginning to feel cold when she heard Fitzwilliam say very softly, "Not a good night for stargazing, dearest Anne, not with this full moon."

"I could not sleep either," he said coming close to her, "All I could think of was you." They were silent for a few minutes then Fitzwilliam said in a passionate rush of words, "All I wanted to do was tell you what I feel for you, my Anne, what I have always felt, although it has taken me so long to understand it; I love you and only you. Tell me that there is hope for me, if you can."

Once again Anne could not speak, but she found the courage to raise her eyes to his and her expression spoke for her. In that moment there was a perfect understanding between them and Fitzwilliam drew her into his arms and kissed her lips, very softly at first and then many more times, as they held each other close, everything else forgotten, there in the cold moonlight. After a while they sat on a stone bench, as it was unthinkable to separate to seek the warmth of the house. Anne, who would have stayed there all night, was shivering slightly and Fitzwilliam said, "It has become colder, my love; do you think that you might share some of that very capacious cloak? I think that it will keep us both warm."

After another interval that left her breathless, Anne at last found her voice, "I have read in Lady Grinspoon's novels that it is quite to be expected that a young lady may accept a kiss from the gentleman she intends to marry, but are you certain that so *many* kisses are allowed?"

"In this matter, my dearest one, I think we may make our own rules."

They remained there for another hour, during which there was very little conversation, but simply the joy of being together and discovering a new universe of passion and bliss.

WHEN ANNE AWOKE the next morning she had to assure herself that what had happened on the moonlit terrace had not been a dream. Surely, there had never been such happiness before! She saw that a heavy rain was falling but resolved that nothing would prevent her walking with Fitzwilliam. Not even if the flood of the millennium should submerge Pemberley, she thought. By the time she went down to breakfast, however, the weather had taken on a more favorable aspect. As usual she was the first to enter the dining room except for Elizabeth, another early riser.

"My dear Anne, have you slept well? Is it not a beautiful morning?" Elizabeth looked quite overflowing with happiness and Anne was delighted at the transformation from the distress of the day before.

"Here is your coffee, my dear. Colonel Fitzwilliam has already breakfasted and has taken such an interest in the weather that he has gone out to inspect conditions for himself. Mr. Grey was up and about before any of us and has gone to explore some cavern with Dr. Gilmore-Jones. So, for once you and I are not the earliest creatures about the house."

Anne enjoyed her morning conversations with Elizabeth. She had learned that Darcy's beautiful wife was a more serious person than might have been expected from a superficial acquaintance. Anne was impressed with how well Elizabeth had borne up under the anxiety of waiting for some word of her husband's fate on the day before and how firmly she had put Lady Catherine in her place.

"You were very brave yesterday, Elizabeth," said Anne, "and I admire how well you deal with my mother. I wish I could learn to do so."

"I have never been through such a terrible ordeal and if I seemed brave it was only assumed. My father is something of a stoic philosopher, at least in theory, and he has influenced me, I suppose. As for Lady Catherine, you know that one is never able to deal with one's *own* mother. My mama is quite able to reduce me to incoherent frustration in a few minutes conversation."

At last everyone began to appear and take a place at the breakfast table. Anne could see that her mother was about to issue some command or criticism for her daughter's benefit, but fortunately Lady Grinspoon diverted her attention.

"I understand, Lady Catherine, that you are an expert on china. I intend to purchase a new dinner service and in view of the difficulty of acquiring Limoges these days, I would be grateful if you could suggest an alternative."

Inwardly blessing Lady Grinspoon, Anne slipped out and made her way to the music room. Celestine had left her fur cloak on the piano bench so that Anne might be off in a moment when the opportunity to escape from her mother should arise. French doors opened from the music room onto the terrace, from which it was a simple matter to gain the path that encompassed the lake.

Anne found Fitzwilliam waiting for her by a sculpture of Artemis with her bow that stood at the bottom of a great stone staircase. The goddess, who seemed to be taking aim at some object on the other side of the lake, had been agreed upon as their meeting place. A fine, cold rain had begun to fall but they paid little attention to it.

"A wonderfully private spot, is it not?" said Fitzwilliam, "Just the sort of place where one of Lady Grinspoon's heroes would venture to kiss his beloved."

After a few minutes he observed, "I am becoming rather fond of that cloak."

Anne laughed and replied, "Have you ever seen such an absurdity? This ridiculous thing was purchased at my mother's insistence, but today I am glad enough for it."

They walked towards a folly at the other side of the lake as the rain had become rather more penetrating and it had at last occurred to them to seek shelter. This was a Greek temple that had been constructed by Darcy's father and it offered a fine view of Pemberley, and the valley and river in the other direction as well.

"I think that Brunefenn needs a folly," said Fitzwilliam, "Shall it be a temple or perhaps a Druid stone circle?"

"So am I to decide the matter?" said Anne smiling up at him.

"Of course! As I told you that day in the chapel, the châtelaine must decide everything. Did you not know that I meant you?"

"I never dreamt of such a thing. How could I when everyone was talking of your engagement to Lady Emma?"

"If only we had been left alone there for a few minutes longer, I might have found the courage to speak."

They walked on for a while, and then Fitzwilliam began, "Anne, you told me yesterday that you had not been injured by the duplicity of Lord Holland. All this time I was afraid that he had every quality likely to gain your affection."

"I tried to bring myself to love him and at times thought I might someday succeed, but in the end could not convince myself. In spite of all that he did to try to win my approbation there was always something that made me distrust him. I do not understand it, but can only be grateful that I never felt more for him. My indifference to his fate, my relief at his banishment makes me realize that I never really cared for him in the least."

508

They had come to the temple and sat on a marble bench together. "You will never know, my Anne, how I detested the role that I had to play in Lady Emma's intrigue with Captain Malvern. Did you despise me when it seemed that I had eloped with her?"

"Oh, no! I could never do that. I was only miserable at the idea of your marrying someone unworthy of you."

They were surprised after a while to find that what had seemed to be a brief time had in fact been an hour. The rain, that had fallen heavily while they sat in the folly, had almost ceased. "We had better start back or we will be missed," said Anne reluctantly, "but first I have something I must return to you."

"Return to me?" said Fitzwilliam, "What on earth is it, my darling?"

"Only this," replied Anne, drawing an object from a pocket of her cloak and presenting it to her beloved. "Do you recognize it?"

Fitzwilliam was a loss for a moment and then said, "Why it's an old glove of mine, or at least I think it is. How did you come by it?"

Anne explained, "You dropped it in the library at Castle Munford. It has been my treasure and my comfort all these months. How many times have I taken up this glove and kissed it, with your dear face so clearly in my mind's eye." So saying, Anne took Fitzwilliam's hand and held it to her cheek. "So now you know what a romantic I am – or perhaps how foolish."

"So you truly have loved me for so long, even when I thought you were forming an attachment to Holland?" asked Fitzwilliam.

"Yes, my dearest," said Anne, "I've loved you forever, even before I understood it myself."

At last they walked reluctantly towards the house. "I will speak to my aunt as soon as I can find her, Anne," said Fitzwilliam touching her cheek, "I do not know what sort of reception I can expect, but it is a matter of courtesy."

"Oh, let us wait a day or two," cried Anne, "I am so happy and would like to have some time together before my mother knows what has happened."

"Whatever you wish, my dear love, but do not be afraid of Lady Catherine. She will never come between us." Fitzwilliam saw that Anne was not convinced and after a moment he added, "Come, let us walk in the garden a bit longer, for there is something else I must say to you."

"You remember that when we were children we loved each other dearly. You were always my favorite although you were four years younger. I could not imagine that you would not be my best friend forever. You were such an intelligent and adventurous child. Do you recall that I included you in all our rambles about the countryside, even when Darcy objected."

"I remember everything we ever did, probably much better than you do," replied Anne, "all the exploring, and looking for turtles and climbing of trees."

"Then your father died and the next time I visited Rosings your mother had decided that you were an invalid, subject to the same complaint that had deprived her of her husband and her son. My darling Anne, my little friend, had disappeared and become a pale, sickly child who was not allowed to run and play, who was confined to her room or made to sit quietly in a corner with her governess. Just one time more I dared to carry you for a ride on my horse. Do you recall?"

"It is one of my best memories, that canter up the hill and the view of the sea in the distance. My mother was so angry that I was afraid that you would never return to Rosings."

"I gradually lost you after that day, Anne, and I slowly forgot how much you had meant to me, until I saw you in Scotland and knew that you had finally returned, with all your true spirit and eagerness for life. I do not understand how this miracle occurred, but I can only be grateful and vow that I will never lose you again."

Any thought of returning to the house was forgotten as they walked through the bare winter garden.

"Are you sure that you are not cold, my Anne?" asked Fitzwilliam after a while.

"Oh no, not at all," Anne replied, "I have so many things to ask you. Did you not think me changed when you came to Rosings in June and found me sitting in the tree?"

"Yes, what a surprise it was to find you out of doors in an old oak tree, reading Reverend White's work with such interest that you did not even hear me approach. It was quite wonderful to me and caused me to begin thinking of you again as a person, not an invalid. But then, that evening when you were so silent and did not defend yourself against your mother's tyranny, I wondered if you could ever defy her. Nothing has ever been more important to me than the plan we devised with Dr. Crawford to remove you from my aunt's influence."

They talked about the days that had followed and the time spent on the riverbank fishing. "I already loved you," admitted Anne, "but could not imagine that you could ever care for me. To me you have always been my ideal, my angel of light." This precipitated such a tender avowal of Fitzwilliam's love for her that Anne could imagine no more perfect happiness.

"It was in Scotland that I at last understood what my feelings were for you, Anne," he continued, "When I entered the drawing room and saw you standing there, so changed but so familiar, it was the *lightning bolt* that made everything clear to me. And now we will never be parted and I will be able to hold you like this forever."

◇

THEY WERE AMAZED to realize that another hour had passed and returned to the house as quickly as possible, slipping in quietly through the music room.

"Another commotion at Pemberley?" said Fitzwilliam as they reached the front hall, for there was the sound of several people speaking at once, of which Darcy's voice, recommending calm, was the most prominent.

All the occupants of the house were standing about, their attention fixed on Dr. Gilmore-Jones, who stood there in a muddy coat, waiting for an opportunity to speak.

"Please be silent," commanded Darcy, "so that we can comprehend what has happened. Dr. Gilmore-Jones, do I understand that Mr. Grey is lost in the cavern that you and he have been exploring?"

"I do not know that he is lost, Mr. Darcy, but he is most certainly trapped," replied Dr. Gilmore-Jones, who was shaking with cold in his wet clothing.

"Let us get you to the fireside before you perish from pneumonia," said Elizabeth, leading the way into the library. In a moment Dr. Gilmore-Jones was seated by the fire, brandy in hand and wrapped in a blanket.

"We were on our way out of the cavern when Grey saw a side passage he wished to investigate. In the few minutes he was gone there was a tremendous flood of water in the main route we had been following, a consequence of the heavy rain of last night and this morning. So you see, I was on one side of the torrent and could not get back to him."

"Did you call out to him?" asked Bingley, "Could you communicate at all?"

"Oh it is impossible to hear anything over the sound of an underground river," said Dr. Gilmore-Jones, "It all happened so quickly. I had been attempting for an hour to persuade Grey to abandon our plans for the day's sport, but he was very set on going a certain distance. You know how he can be when his mind is set on a course of action."

Everyone nodded; this was a well-known facet of Grey's character.

"You do believe he is alive, do you not" asked Anne, "and that there is every hope that he will survive?"

Dr. Gilmore-Jones seemed to be weighing his answer carefully, and then finally said, "That would depend on whether he was caught by the sudden rush of water. He may have had the opportunity to retreat to higher ground, but there is no way of knowing. And certainly we must trust that he still has some source of light, some dry tinder. If he is without light, then it is a very dire situation indeed."

It took all of Anne's self control not to cry out in anguish at the idea of her friend in such a horrible predicament. There was a general outcry and Lady Catherine demanded indignantly, "Why in the world would supposedly intelligent men expose themselves to such dangers? I have never heard of anything so absurd."

"What can we do to assist Grey, Dr. Gilmore-Jones?" asked Darcy, "Surely there is something, for we shall run mad, all of us, if we cannot take some kind of action on his behalf."

"If he is alive he will wait for the waters to subside and then attempt to find his way back. We also must wait, unfortunately. Once the passage can be negotiated I will lead a party to search for him. It would be well to stand watch by the entrance to the cave, for if by some chance he does emerge, he will certainly be cold and exhausted to the point of death if not given immediate succor."

Elizabeth at once rang for the butler and gave orders for everything that might be required, while Darcy went to give instructions for assembling a rescue party. There was a great clamor as everyone announced his intention of being part of the vigil. Dr. Gilmore-Jones was pressed to take a hot meal and change of clothes as his own health might be in danger.

"Yes, very well," he replied, pale with exhaustion and worry, "but I beg you will send a messenger to my wife to let her know that I am safe. As soon as possible I wish to return to the cavern."

Within an hour there was an assemblage of carriages and farm carts around the entrance of the Gaping Pillbox. Not just the company from Pemberley was to be found there, but also neighbors from every direction had come to see if they could be of assistance. Very soon, Lady Margaret Faulconer came galloping into the clearing and leaping down from her horse came running up to Darcy. Her face was stained with tears as she took his hands impulsively and cried, "What is being done to recover him? Oh, tell me is there any hope? What can I do?"

Darcy explained the situation to her as calmly as he could and Lady Margaret could be seen to make a tremendous effort to regain self-control. At that moment Lord Faulconer's carriage appeared and the old gentleman came over to Darcy with an alacrity no one would have expected from him. Once it was understood that nothing could be done until the water receded Lord Faulconer tried to persuade his daughter to return home.

"I will never leave this place until we have rescued him," she replied, pushing her loosened hair back from a face swollen with crying, "Do not bother to attempt to change my mind."

"Lady Margaret and I will wait together," said Anne, who had come up to join them, "We will be fine sitting in the carriage so do not concern yourselves about us." The other ladies had been persuaded to return to Pemberley as dusk was coming on and it was increasingly cold with a hint of snow in the air.

Darcy knew that argument was vain, so he had a makeshift shelter thrown together hastily and a brazier fetched to warm the two young ladies.

Fitzwilliam came to see that they were installed with as much comfort as was possible and informed them that he, Darcy and Dr. Gilmore-Jones were about to enter the cavern to ascertain whether the water level had changed.

Anne walked with him long enough to say, "I will be anxious every moment until you return. You must be careful for you are everything in life to me."

In the half darkness Fitzwilliam took her hand and kissed it, "Do not worry about me, beloved. I will never leave you."

Lady Margaret and Anne sat silently in the small hut trying to stay warm; occasionally Anne heard a stifled moan from her companion and saw her lean forward with her head in her hands in an attitude of despair. This went on for a while until Anne finally exclaimed, "I know that I have little knowledge of the world, but really, Lady Margaret, you are the greatest fool I ever expect to encounter."

"I beg your pardon, what did you say?" inquired the other lady in surprise.

"I believe that you heard me. I said that you are the most consummate fool I have ever met."

"You have chosen a good time to insult me, Miss de Bourgh, for I have absolutely no interest at this juncture in asking you to explain yourself."

"I will explain myself anyway, Lady Margaret, for it is time someone spoke to you frankly. It is obvious that you love Mr. Grey, that he has your heart completely and it is equally certain that he returns your feelings. Yet all these months you have made him wretched by your foolish and stubborn behavior. To know that my friend is in such danger and to see your misery after all your pretended indifference is really most vexing. I am altogether out of patience with you."

Lady Margaret looked as if she were about to come out with some cutting retort, but then Anne saw her collapse into helpless sobs.

"You are right. It is all true and if he dies it will be my fault and I will never be able to tell him how I feel."

Anne now felt real pity for the young lady and putting her arms about her shoulders did her best to comfort her.

"You will see him again, I am sure. Mr. Grey has been in much worse scrapes than this, and a miserable cavern in Derbyshire will not be a match for him."

When the gentlemen returned from their reconnaissance the news was not very encouraging. The underground river was still an impassable obstacle and they had turned back very disheartened. Grey had now been in the cavern for more than ten hours and it seemed unlikely that he could survive the night if he were sitting wet and cold somewhere beyond reach.

They all stood around a large bonfire that had been constructed to warm those who had come out to help with the rescue. Anne and Lady Margaret had joined the group, as they could no longer endure sitting in the hut awaiting further tidings. There was no conversation as everyone was beginning to feel that all hope was past.

Darcy saw a figure emerge from the gathering darkness and assumed it must be a new addition to the rescue party, as the man was coming from a direction opposite to the opening of the cavern. In a moment he heard a familiar voice inquire cheerfully. "What's afoot, my good old Darcy? Why are you all standing about in the dark at this time of evening?"

Grey joined the circle by the fire with no more éclat than if he had been for a little stroll after dinner.

"I hope you are not out here making all this fuss because I am a trifle late. I was most inconvenienced by the necessity of finding another way out of the labyrinth. It's a good thing I had plenty of tinder." Then he chuckled agreeably as if his appearance were the most ordinary thing in the world.

His composure was thoroughly demolished by Lady Margaret who ran to him and threw herself into his arms as she wept with joy and relief.

"That, Darcy, is something I had never hoped to see," said Lord Faulconer with satisfaction, "Come my dear friends, let us leave them alone for a while. My carriage will bring them back to Pemberley. Perhaps in an hour or so they will notice that we have gone."

"If I had known that I could win you by becoming lost in a cavern, I would have done so months ago," said Grey, "Will I have to do this as a regular thing or have you really decided that you love me?"

"Oh, do hush" she cried, "Oh, hush my love – and kiss me." Lady Margaret's assurances took some considerable time and it was late when they arrived at Pemberley to find everyone famished from hunger, but waiting to go into dinner. While Grey went to change into dry clothes, Lord Faulconer took the opportunity to speak to his daughter.

"Is it really decided, my dear child? Are you betrothed to Mr. Grey? That certainly is my impression judging from the way in which you greeted him tonight."

"It is true, Papa," replied Lady Margaret, who seemed inclined to either laugh or cry from joy, had she been able to decide between the two reactions.

"And you will not change your mind? May I be assured that tomorrow morning you will not find some reason to continue to be wretched and send the poor fellow away after all?"

"You may be sure that I will never be separated from Mr. Grey again. It is really very simple; I find that I cannot live without him."

There had never been a happier company at Pemberley than those assembled that evening. Even Lady Catherine could find no ground for criticism or complaint and for once she seemed delighted with everyone. Lord Faulconer arose to announce the engagement of his daughter to Mr. Grey and was met with cries of delight and congratulation.

"You have made a good choice, my dear," said Lady Catherine to Lady Margaret in her confidential tone of voice, which could be heard by everyone at the table, "I have found him to be an excellent young man, if a bit unorthodox, but that will keep you from becoming bored with him. I can see that you are a little unconventional yourself. And of course someday he will be immensely rich and inherit a great title, which should be most gratifying to all concerned."

Before the Faulconers departed, Lady Margaret spoke to Anne for a moment, "You were absolutely correct, Miss de Bourgh. I have been the worst sort of fool and you were justified in what you said. I hope that we may be friends, for Mr. Grey thinks so highly of you."

Anne said that such a friendship would gratify her fondest wishes and would have liked to tell Lady Margaret of her own betrothal, but it did not seem right to do so until Lady Catherine had been informed. It was difficult, as Anne's heart was so full of joy that she feared that it would overflow and become evident to all. Fitzwilliam caught her eye from across the room and there was perfect understanding and love in his expression. His countenance, to her the most beautiful of all human visages, filled her mind as she fell asleep that night.

CHAPTER 54

Fitzwilliam was eager to speak with his aunt and persuaded Anne to let him do so on the following afternoon. "There is nothing to be gained by delay, my darling," he said, "and I am so happy that I hate to conceal what has happened from our friends. How delighted Darcy and Elizabeth will be, for they are so very fond of you."

Anne agreed, but could not quite throw off the old dread of her mother's ability to poison any good thing that came into her daughter's way.

"You know that she may be very unpleasant and heap you with reproaches."

"Yes, I know," replied Fitzwilliam, "but I am not afraid of my aunt. I am used to cannon fire and can hardly be impressed by any ammunition at Lady Catherine's disposal."

When he was finally closeted with his aunt and had said all that was necessary, her reaction was not at all what he had expected. Lady Catherine rose and came to sit next to him. She patted his hand affectionately and far from being agitated, was perfectly composed.

"My dear William. What a dear, kind young man you are. I am very touched."

"It has nothing to do with being kind, Aunt."

"I know your heart, nephew, - always trying to assist others, never thinking of yourself. Now you have such compassion for my poor Anne, such pity for her disappointment in regard to the odious Lord Holland, that you would sacrifice all your own inclinations to comfort and support her."

"Aunt, you are quite mistaken, for I love Anne with my entire heart. I wish to be with her above all things."

Lady Catherine merely smiled incredulously at this assertion.

"She is a dear girl and of course her breeding as a descendant of some of the oldest and most distinguished families in England is impeccable, but let us be frank; it is hardly credible that you should be in love with Anne."

It took an extended interview for Fitzwilliam to persuade his aunt that he was, in fact, very much in love with his cousin.

"But she was intended for Darcy," said Lady Catherine," and now that he is married and this other prospective husband has turned out to be such a villain, I can see very little reason for her to marry. You know that I love you dearly nephew, but after all, you are a younger son and not rich. What is the point?"

"Only this, Aunt; that we may be happy."

Lady Catherine looked at Fitzwilliam quizzically for a moment, and then she shrugged and said, "Oh well, as for that, happiness is very much over-rated. It hardly ever amounts to anything in the long run."

After a bit of reflection she added, "Well, I will think on it and let you now my decision tomorrow. It is all very odd and I cannot comprehend why you should wish to marry a sad, dull girl like Anne. I am sure that it is not for her money, because you have had plenty of other chances to acquire an heiress. I know you well, nephew, and have observed that you have used your relative poverty as an excuse not to wed."

By now Fitzwilliam was only too glad to escape and did not bother to argue any further with his aunt. As he left her, he said, "Dear Aunt, I hope that someday you will realize that Anne is a remarkable and lovely person." Lady Catherine seemed to be afflicted with some kind of incurable blindness as to Anne's true nature and it seemed improbable that her perception would ever change.

Later that day Fitzwilliam and Anne went into the library and found Lady Catherine in earnest conversation with Sir Wilfred.

"Ah, Colonel, Miss de Bourgh, I do wish you joy," cried Sir Wilfred, leaping up and offering Fitzwilliam his hand, "This is wonderful news!"

"Sir Wilfred thinks that I should approve the match," added Lady Catherine rather sulkily, "and I have so much faith in his good judgment that I have decided to give you my blessing."

"Dear Mama," cried Anne, "You have made us very happy indeed!"

"Yes, yes, of course," replied Lady Catherine, submitting to Anne's embrace, "but I have a few things to say to you both which you may as well hear now."

Fitzwilliam and Anne seated themselves and were all polite attention. Sir Wilfred made as if to leave them alone, but Lady Catherine called him back.

"Please do remain, Sir Wilfred, for you have so much good sense that you may be able to add something to my remarks." Sir Wilfred obediently returned and took his place.

"First, understand that you will be poor," began Lady Catherine in a gloomy tone of voice, "and you have never known what it is to live upon a narrow income, Anne."

"Six hundred a year, while not wealth, is surely not poverty, Aunt," protested Fitzwilliam.

"It *is* poverty, when all the claims upon the purse of a colonel of a regiment are considered. The expense of keeping up an appearance consistent with one's rank, the entertainments expected of a senior officer."

Here Lady Catherine paused and shook her head, "How you will manage I do not know. While you are a great heiress, Anne, the terms of your father's will do not require that I give you anything during my lifetime and as you are aware the cost of maintaining Rosings has been particularly severe of late."

Anne and Fitzwilliam had never expected any help from Lady

Catherine and were therefore not at all dismayed. They knew her too well to expect any other reaction to their engagement.

"However, a larger problem is your health, Anne. How do you know that you will not become a burden on this dear, good man. I know that you have shown signs of improvement these last few months, but will it last? My beloved husband often did well for short periods, only to lapse into illness again. It was the same with my little son during his short life."

"There is nothing at all wrong with me, Mama," said Anne, unable to be silent any longer, "and I do not believe there ever was anything amiss. I am more than equal to anything that will be required of me as Fitzwilliam's wife. As for poverty, who regards that when one is with the person one loves above all else in the world?"

"Ah, romantic ideas, my child. Do not forget that it is very likely that Fitzwilliam may be killed in some battle or other. We do not live in peaceful times and his is a dangerous profession. You will be left a poor widow on my hands, no doubt."

"My dear Lady Catherine, enough of these gloomy reflections!" interjected Sir Wilfred, "You have nothing to do now but rejoice! Your daughter is to be married to an honorable and distinguished gentleman who is as dear to you as if he were your own son. Your child is restored to health and her future life promises perfect felicity. I enjoin you to throw off all these somber ideas and let us be as happy as this event requires. Please announce these joyous tidings to our friends at once. I will accompany you to find Mr. and Mrs. Darcy."

Sir Wilfred had so much influence with Lady Catherine that it was the work of a moment to shepherd her out of the room and leave Anne and Fitzwilliam alone.

"I have never thought before about your being killed," said Anne, very near tears.

"Oh, do not worry about such things, my love," replied Fitzwilliam, putting an arm about her waist and drawing her close, "I am very good at dodging bullets."

"Do you love the army very much? Is being an officer essential to your happiness?"

"Why not at all, Anne. I try to excel at my profession, but it is not particularly to my taste. A younger son, you know, must do something and I was grateful to my father for purchasing my commission. The life of a country gentleman has always been my ideal, were it only possible."

"Do promise me something then, my beloved," said Anne looking up into his face very seriously, "If ever we are able to afford to do so, you will resign your commission and we will live a quiet life in the country. A small farm would suit me very well and we could always be together."

Fitzwilliam was glad to give his very solemn promise that he would do so whenever the best interests of his country should allow him to do so with honor, and Anne was the happiest she had ever been. Their solitude was interrupted a moment later by all the company of Pemberley bursting into the room to wish them joy. Toasts were made and the stately library had never been the scene of so much gaiety.

"I think that a double wedding would be the thing to do, said Grey, shaking hands with Fitzwilliam, "Lady Margaret and I plan to be married as soon as possible in the New Year. No doubt such an arrangement would suit you and Miss de Bourgh very well also."

"I would like that of all things," cried Fitzwilliam, "do you not agree Anne?"

Anne was about to add her eager assent, but Lady Catherine had heard Grey's suggestion and hurried over to express her disapproval.

"The son of an earl and a young lady of my daughter's distinction to be married so quickly! It will never do! It will take months to arrange the ceremony, which must take place at Rosings."

Shortly after this exchange Sir Wilfred found an opportunity to take Anne aside for a private conversation.

"Your mother means no harm, Miss de Bourgh, although I know that at times she has made your life very difficult. She may never see you as you really are, but I assure you that her love for you is sincere, if misguided."

"You are so very kind, Sir Wilfred. I am aware that her consent to my marriage is largely due to your influence."

"I am devoted to Lady Catherine and seek what is best for her as well as for you. You see, I have loved her for many years, since I first saw her riding in the park in London, and that sort of attachment does not die. I know that your mother has some faults, but her life has been difficult in many ways."

"How fortunate my mother is to have the affection of someone like yourself, Sir Wilfred."

"I am the one who is fortunate, Miss de Bourgh. I must tell you that on several occasions I have asked Lady Catherine to marry me. Whether she will ever consent I cannot say."

"Oh, I pray that she will!" cried Anne, "What a happy event that would be."

"In any case, now that I plan to purchase Grantham Park I will be living only two miles from Rosings. I have other news as well."

"What news, Sir Wilfred?"

"I will be taking your mother away from Pemberley in three days time. I have just persuaded her, and we are to leave for London, and thence to Kent after spending Christmas in town."

"But Christmas is only ten days from now! The roads may be very bad and it is such a journey! Is this wise?"

"We shall do very well as we are in no great hurry to be in London. We may decide to stop on the way at the houses of some of my relations. But in any event, Miss de Bourgh, I wish you to know that my departure with Lady Catherine is a gift to you, an engagement present if you will. I want you to have this time to be with Colonel Fitzwilliam and your friends in complete enjoyment of the season. Your mama might always have something to say that could spoil some of that pleasure for you. Let this be the best and happiest time you have ever known!"

~

THREE DAYS later Lady Catherine said farewell to Anne, generously imparting some last words of wise council.

"You know, Anne, you must not show too much affection towards Fitzwilliam. Gentlemen soon tire of young ladies who are so fond as you obviously are. Some reserve, my dear!"

Anne nodded, having not the slightest intention of paying heed to any of her mother's advice.

"I hate to leave, my child, but Sir Wilfred has business in London which cannot wait. You know there is no one better, but he does need looking after in some ways and I think that his solicitor may not be quite the thing. How poor Sir Wilfred has managed all these years without me, I cannot imagine."

How different the house seemed without Lady Catherine! What a strange and delightful tranquility descended on Pemberley. Every day was full of happy and confident discourse between the friends gathered there and there was daily visiting between Pemberley and Castle Faulconer. One week before Christmas Mr. and Mrs. Gardiner arrived from London and Elizabeth's happiness was complete. Mr. and Mrs. Bennet and Kitty and Mary had traveled with them and Elizabeth had the joy of being with her father after some months of separation.

Mr. Bennet had a few moments private conversation with his daughter soon after his arrival. "My dear Lizzie, I can see that you have made an excellent choice of a husband. His welcome could not have been more gracious. As for his wealth, I do not at all hold it against him and plan to take full enjoyment in his magnificent library for many years to come."

Mrs. Bennet was so awed by the splendor of her surroundings that she was much less talkative than anyone had ever known her to be. She looked in vain for imperfections in the beauty and comfort of Pemberley and she was more agreeable than Elizabeth could have hoped. For Kitty and Mary every day was a revelation and they seemed to change for the better in such a rational and pleasant ambience.

Surely this was the finest Christmas season anyone could remember and Pemberley had never been so full of merriment and good cheer. It snowed a great deal that winter and the sleighs were brought out for excursions that delighted everyone.

On Christmas morning Fitzwilliam found a moment alone with Anne and gave her a small box wrapped in silk. "This is something my father sent by special courier; did you observe the rider who appeared yesterday?"

"Yes, there was the wonderful letter from your parents. How much I appreciated all the kind things they said about our engagement."

"There was also this little package. Do open it, my darling."

It was an ancient and beautiful ring that had been in Fitzwilliam's family for generations. "It is just the right size. I was afraid it might be too large for such a small hand as yours, Anne."

"It shall never leave my hand as long as I live," said Anne.

"Well, you must make room on that finger for another in only a few weeks time."

"Only a few weeks? Can it be so soon?"

Fitzwilliam drew her close and replied, "I have been closeted with Mr. Devereaux, Mr. Grey and Lord Faulconer this morning."

"How very clever you gentlemen are, planning everything," said Anne playfully, "Should not Lady Margaret and I have been there?"

"Of course we are only here to serve at the pleasure of our ladies, like good knights" replied Fitzwilliam with a smile, " If you do not like February 14, why it can be changed."

"Less than two months!" Anne could not believe that her happiness would be complete in so short a time.

"And then we shall never again be apart, my love."

CHAPTER 55

*L*ady Catherine did attend her daughter's wedding. In truth, nothing would have kept her away, although Sir Wilfred spent the many hours of the journey to Pemberley listening patiently to her lamentations.

"My own daughter not to be married from Rosings! It is the most outrageous thing I have ever heard. How will I explain it to my friends?"

"They will understand it to have been the romantic fancy of four young people and not give it another thought, my dear Lady Catherine."

This was not convincing to her ladyship who believed that her own activities and those of her family must be of consuming interest to the entire world.

"And why must they have insisted on a double wedding? And why such haste at this dreadful time of year?" Lady Catherine looked with disgust at the passing hills on which a fine snow had begun to fall.

Sir Wilfred patiently explained once more that the date had been determined by Mr. Grey's obligation to leave for his parish in Wales within the month.

"Ridiculous!" cried his companion, "Wales! A man with his family connections to accept a parish in that most desolate corner of the kingdom! It is very odd."

And so the conversation went for the long journey to Pemberley. When they finally arrived Lady Catherine found that Lord and Lady Munford were already at the house. Indeed, they were the first to greet her as she entered the hall. There had been no meeting for several years, ever since Lady Catherine had decided to quarrel with her brother for some trivial reason that no one could even remember. There was some resentment on the lady's side that Lord Munford had become wealthier than ever through some very wise investments, when Lady Catherine had always been pleased to consider him a foolish spendthrift. For anyone to act in a manner contrary to her prejudices was always an unforgivable affront to her ladyship's sensibilities.

As it happened, the rest of the party at Pemberley had driven over to Thrushfold Hall as the Bingleys had moved to their new home the week before and were eager for a first visit from their friends.

Lady Catherine was not particularly pleased to find herself having tea with her relations but made the best of the situation by taking the opportunity to complain of the injudicious match that would be consecrated in just three days' time.

"I am sure that I cannot imagine how they will live on such a narrow income, for I will not be able to help them. My expenses at Rosings are very heavy."

Her brother and sister-in-law looked concerned and Lord Munford said, "Why, my dear sister, I had no idea. You know that I always stand ready to assist any of my family who are in need."

Lady Catherine flushed in vexation, "Of course, it is nothing like that! However, I cannot reward such youthful impetuosity. To marry on such a narrow income."

"Perhaps the rents from Brunefenn will be useful," replied Lord Munford.

"Why, yes. Anne told me that you had bestowed that estate in Scotland on Fitzwilliam. But I cannot imagine that a few thousand acres of gorse and bog will yield much of an income."

Lord Munford was as amiable and generous a man as could be

found anywhere, but at this point he could not suppress a smile of triumphant gratification.

"Well then, perhaps the four thousand a year that I will be settling on my son will alleviate their poverty somewhat."

Ladies do not fall out of their chairs in astonishment, but Lady Catherine came very close to doing so. For a moment she was speechless; the idea that her brother-in-law was a poor manager and a spendthrift had long been one of her favorite, although completely unfounded, *idées fixes*.

"I am surprised," she admitted at last, "and certainly I am pleased that they will have enough to keep the wolf from the door. But has Fitzwilliam the good judgment to be put in possession of such an income, for I have noticed that he has expensive tastes?"

It was only with great difficulty that her companions suppressed their amusement. This was so typical of Lady Catherine as to seem comical or tragic, according to the general mood.

"Why has he never mentioned this to me?" she continued, "I am most provoked that Fitzwilliam has kept such an important matter from his affectionate and devoted aunt."

"For the very good reason that he knows nothing about his expectations, nor will he until the morning of his wedding" replied Lord Munford, "I have raised my younger son to be a man of independence and self- reliance. He would always do very well, with or without a fortune."

We may almost pity Lady Catherine at this juncture. Her tastes and temperament, if not her intellect, seemed to have formed her for the role of a benevolent despot. A vast empire full of obedient serfs would have suited her well. Now she had lost her daughter, who had been most completely under Lady Catherine's rule all these years. How she had looked forward to occasionally dispensing little gifts of pocket money to her impoverished child and demanding in return the most slavish gratitude for such condescension! Alas, now her only slave was Sir Wilfred, but even he was beginning to show an alarming tendency to assert his own will.

❧

THE DOUBLE WEDDING in Lambton was certainly the most thrilling event to occur in Derbyshire for many a year. Not just one but two earl's sons! The brides also descended from noble stock and heiresses as well! The streets of the village were full of those who wished the young couples well as they left the church on a day that showed as blue a sky and mild an air as any rational person could expect in February. There had been a hope for a small, quiet wedding on the part of the principals in the ceremony, but very soon it had become clear that all the gentry of the county must be invited or take offense forever.

Anne would have been reluctant to be the focus of so much public attention had she not been too in love to see anyone but Fitzwilliam. Even her mother's last admonitions as to the conduct of married life had passed over her with no effect whatsoever. How handsome Fitzwilliam was in his regimental uniform and how superior to every man on earth!

It would be impossible to experience greater felicity, thought Anne looking up into Fitzwilliam's face as they said their vows. After a few moments she glanced over at Grey and Lady Margaret and had to admit to herself that perhaps there were a *few* fortunate souls whose happiness came close to theirs that day.

The celebration at Pemberley was never to be forgotten, so beautifully had Elizabeth arranged all things and so splendid were the food and wine, the tables set in exquisite fashion with all the flowers the hot houses of the estate could provide. Even Lady Catherine was impressed and in her inmost heart admitted that she could have done no better. From this time on her ladyship began to boast to her friends of her lovely and gifted niece, to the surprise of all those who had been subjected to Lady Catherine's rants at the time of Darcy's marriage. With Elizabeth herself, of course, her ladyship was careful to avoid anything that might be considered praise.

By three o'clock Mr. Grey and Lady Margaret were obliged to set off on their long journey to Wales. Lord Faulconer hid as best he could his dejection at losing the company of his daughter. The joy he felt at her marriage to Grey almost prevailed over the sadness of parting.

"I hope that you will come to us very soon, sir," said Grey as the two men shook hands, "It is a small parsonage, of course, but we will make you comfortable there."

"Oh, yes. Papa," cried Lady Margaret, embracing her father with tears in her eyes, "do promise to visit us when the weather improves and the journey will not be too hard for you."

"No journey can be too hard that ends at your hearth," replied her father, "I will come in a few months after you are settled."

"I will miss Grey," said Darcy as the carriage disappeared around the first curve in the drive, "May they be happy forever and come back to us someday."

"We will go visit them, my love, "said Elizabeth embracing her husband, "I would like to see those wild mountains of all things."

"What a romantic you are, dearest," replied Darcy, kissing her, "and how glad I am that you are exactly as you are. Do not change, ever."

∿

ANNE AND FITZWILLIAM had a very different journey to make that afternoon, to an old house in a remote and beautiful part of the estate. Only Darcy and Elizabeth knew where they were to go. They slipped away so quietly, as the guests were enjoying all the delights of the feast, that even Lady Catherine's vigilance did not witness their departure.

"Where have they gone, Darcy?" she asked indignantly, "I had important words to say to them and you know I must return south in two days."

"Dear Aunt, I would certainly tell you but I am bound in honor to keep their destination a secret."

"Really, Nephew. What a way for Anne to treat her mother. I am most seriously displeased!"

∿

THE HOUSE STOOD on a hilltop with a view of endless green hills and no other habitation for miles. Servants had been there for some days putting all to rights and preparing for the arrival of the newly married couple. The light was beginning to fade as Anne and Fitzwilliam stood enchanted by the great expanse of earth and sky before them.

"Although Darcy seems to be a very serious person, he knows what it is to be in love," said Fitzwilliam. "He and Elizabeth have made everything perfect for us."

"Let us enter this dream and never leave it," said Anne, "This is where we will always dwell in our hearts wherever we may be."

CHAPTER 56

*L*ady Margaret stood at the window of the parsonage in Wales that had been her home for two years. She was often to be found at this spot in the early evening, waiting for her husband to return from his rounds in the parish. When she saw him walking up the path from the village below she ran to the door and out into the chill air to greet him.

"Come and warm yourself, dearest," she cried, "You are cold from walking about all afternoon."

"Not at all, love," replied Grey, embracing her, "I've been obliged to take tea and biscuits in three different houses and my kind parishioners are always so eager to make me comfortable that I am half scorched from sitting too near their fires."

"They have all come to love and revere you, as well they should," said Lady Margaret when they were seated together in their sitting room. The house was a simple one but the mistress of the parsonage had made it a warm and cheerful place.

"Two letters came today which I believe will interest you," said Grey, handing them to his wife, "I will give you a few moments to read them for yourself."

"One from Darcy and one from Mr. Devereaux. Why, it is a good day for letters! No bad news I hope," asked the lady, looking up at her husband.

"Read on, my love," replied Grey, pouring himself a glass of sherry, "Start with Darcy's."

After a few moments of silent perusal of the letters, Lady Margaret burst out, "Mr. Devereaux to become bishop! And Darcy offers you his living!"

"The old bishop died six weeks ago as you recall," said Gray, sitting down beside his wife, "I suspected at the time that Mr. Devereaux would be chosen. He will certainly grace that high office."

Lady Margaret looked about the well-loved house where they had shared so many months of perfect happiness, "And so we are to leave this dear place? You know that I have come to love it here. It is just as you promised me it would be, that night of the ball at Pemberley."

"The cold winter wind rattling at the windows while we huddle by the hearth," said Gray, "The long rides on our old nags and rambles with the dogs. Ah, I knew that this simple life would suit you."

"I will be sad, in a way, to go, but when I think of seeing my dear father and knowing that he will never be alone again! What a very happy event for everyone."

"And Darcy and Elizabeth are truly delighted at the thought of having us so near them. I have missed our friends."

After a moment Lady Margaret asked, "You know that papa will want us to live at the castle for some of the time. Do you think you would mind it?"

"I like and esteem your father so very much that I can imagine nothing better. Some part of each week we will spend with him. And in general I have never objected to a castle as a dwelling," replied Grey laughing and holding her close.

∼

In Hampshire at about the same time, Anne and Fitzwilliam were walking about the grounds of Thornton Abbey. It was a fine day and much warmer than the bracing air of Wales ever allowed.

"How much it has changed here since I first saw this place," said

Anne, "The garden will be beautiful this spring and the hall is again a noble building."

They had been there most of the winter visiting Mr. Thornton, although by now they could not really be called "visitors" for Fitzwilliam was the acknowledged heir to the estate and had assumed responsibility for restoring it to its former grandeur as one of the finest in Hampshire.

"Do you think that Mr. Thornton will be strong enough to accompany us to Scotland in August?" asked Anne drawing close to her husband who put his arm about her.

"I believe that he will. He told me that he would even like to join us on our shooting parties, a pastime he used to enjoy very much years ago."

"How dear he is, and how he treats you as another son. I am much happier with Thornton Hall as my home than I ever was at Rosings. Had you not lectured me that day and almost driven me to leave with Darcy and Elizabeth, I would still be the forgotten little shadow of a person living at my mother's beck and call and terrified of the world."

"I spoke so roughly to you that day. Do you forgive me, my love?"

"Forgive you? You saved my life and now it belongs to you."

Fitzwilliam had resigned his commission two months before and done so without anything like regret. He had been a fine officer but it had been a matter of duty to serve, and a necessity as a younger son. The life of a country gentleman was perfectly to his taste and now he and Anne could be always together.

"And we shall stay with Darcy and Elizabeth on our way north!" cried Anne, "How delightful it will be to see them! And Mr. Grey and Lady Margaret!"

By early August Fitzwilliam and Anne were en route to Pemberley. Mr. Thornton did accompany them, so improved was his health. The first visit that they made was the one that gave Anne some moments of dread. It was necessary to spend three or four days at Rosings, something that duty demanded every few months.

Sir Wilfred now lived just two miles from Rosings and was with Lady Catherine almost daily, listening patiently to her concerns and admiring her understanding of a wide range of topics. Anne was constantly astonished at the devotion of the kindly, philosophic man. His affection must be genuine, she thought, for he was rich and could live anywhere, but he seemed to have no other ambition than to remain at Lady Catherine's side. Increasingly, however, he had learned with a few gentle words, to check some of Lady Catherine's tendency to tyrannize. Mrs. Collins thought very highly of the baronet and visits to Rosings were much more pleasant for her, thanks to his interventions.

Mr. Thornton was made very welcome, especially as Lady Catherine had investigated and learned of the extent of his lands and fortune. She took Fitzwilliam aside at one point to make a few observations.

"You have certainly done very well for yourself, nephew, to be heir to one of the finest estates in Hampshire! With Anne's fortune one day, you will be as rich as anyone – even Darcy!"

The interlude at Rosings certainly gave Anne no pleasure, except for the time she spent with Mrs. Collins. That lady had made her home a charming place and even Mr. Collins seemed to have improved and become more of a rational being. Their little son was so fortunate as to resemble his mother in appearance and intellect.

ON A FINE, warm afternoon they reached Pemberley. How beautiful it was with the avenue of oaks and the lake shining in the golden August light!

As the coach reached the house they found their friends waiting for them and they were directly caught up in whirl of eager greetings, embraced and welcomed with exclamations of joy.

How well everyone looked! It had been far, far too long since they had all been together! An hour later the entire party were all settled on the terrace overlooking the lake and had begun to satisfy all the mutual questions that must be asked on such occasions.

A very important personage who was for some time the center of attention was the Bingleys' little daughter, who was just now beginning to talk and who loved to crawl about under the tea table.

"We drove over this morning," said Jane, who was lovelier than ever, "as we could not miss this wonderful reunion."

Mr. Grey and Lady Margaret had come to Pemberley with Lord Faulconer. Anne was happy to find that Grey had not become overly grave and dignified in his role as a clergyman. It was Lady Margaret who was different. It was difficult to believe that this person, so easy and full of happiness and laughter, had once been prone to coldness and reserve.

Grey found a moment to speak to Anne as they leant against the balustrade and watched Bingley playing with his child on the lawn. "Well, my dear friend, we have come through some difficult times together, have we not?"

"And how well it has all turned out," Anne replied, "Did you ever expect to find such joy in this world?"

"Yes, I think I did. I was always an optimistic fellow. But you helped me more than you will ever know, with just a few words at the right moment."

"You did the same for me, Mr. Grey. We shall be friends for life, shall we not?"

"Of that there can be no doubt."

Elizabeth and Darcy had left their guests for a few moments and when they reappeared it was with some éclat.

"Well, Fitzwilliam," said Darcy who was carrying a small child in his arms, "What do you think of my son?"

Fitzwilliam looked carefully at the little being, just eight months old, and replied solemnly, "Why Darcy, that is the finest boy I ever beheld. What an extraordinary look of intelligence there is about him."

"You are right, cousin," said Darcy, laughing, "the finest boy and the best wife in England. And I am the happiest man in the kingdom!"

"No doubt, old friend, that you are *one* of the happiest," said Grey who had joined them, "but there are a few others here ready to contend with you for the title."

IT WAS LATE that night before all the most essential words had been spoken and news exchanged by the party of friends, but finally everyone retired for the night, all that is except Darcy and Elizabeth.

They sat in the moonlight on their favorite seat by the lake.

"How delightful it was for us all to be together this evening," said Elizabeth, "It is like a dream to have them all here."

"And to know that we are all going to Scotland together. It is kind of Lord Munford to make room for so many of us. Of course, to stay at Brunefenn with Fitzwilliam and Anne will be splendid. What an extraordinary gathering it will be! Just promise me that you will not go riding unless I have approved the horse."

"I promise that I will never again go riding without you," replied Elizabeth.

"Or anywhere else, my darling?"

Elizabeth's most loving reassurance on this point was all that Darcy could desire and soon they returned to the house.

ABOUT THE AUTHOR

Lee Elliott is a writer and artist who lives in the western mountains of Virginia with her husband, an environmental scientist, their four dogs and innumerable chickens.

When not at work at the computer or on the farm, her favorite activities are hiking, fly fishing, sea kayaking and ordering too many books on Amazon.